THE
KINGDOM
OF
NORTHUMBRIA

The Complete Series

JAYNE CASTEL

WINTER MIST
PRESS

Historical Romances by Jayne Castel

DARK AGES BRITAIN

The Kingdom of the East Angles series
Night Shadows (prequel novella)
Dark Under the Cover of Night (Book One)
Nightfall till Daybreak (Book Two)
The Deepening Night (Book Three)
The Kingdom of the East Angles: The Complete Series

The Kingdom of Mercia series
The Breaking Dawn (Book One)
Darkest before Dawn (Book Two)
Dawn of Wolves (Book Three)

The Kingdom of Northumbria series
The Whispering Wind (Book One)
Wind Song (Book Two)
Lord of the North Wind (Book Three)
The Kingdom of Northumbria: The Complete Series

DARK AGES SCOTLAND

The Warrior Brothers of Skye series
Blood Feud (Book One)
Barbarian Slave (Book Two)
Battle Eagle (Book Three)
The Warrior Brothers of Skye: The Complete Series

Epic Fantasy Romances by Jayne Castel

Light and Darkness series
Ruled by Shadows (Book One)
The Lost Swallow (Book Two)

Visit Jayne's website and blog: www.jaynecastel.com

Follow Jayne on Twitter: @JayneCastel

***

To my darling Tim.

***

Contents

THE WHISPERING WIND 7

WIND SONG 251

LORD OF THE NORTH WIND...463

ABOUT THE AUTHOR 663

THE WHISPERING WIND

BOOK ONE
THE KINGDOM
OF NORTHUMBRIA

JAYNE CASTEL

Maps

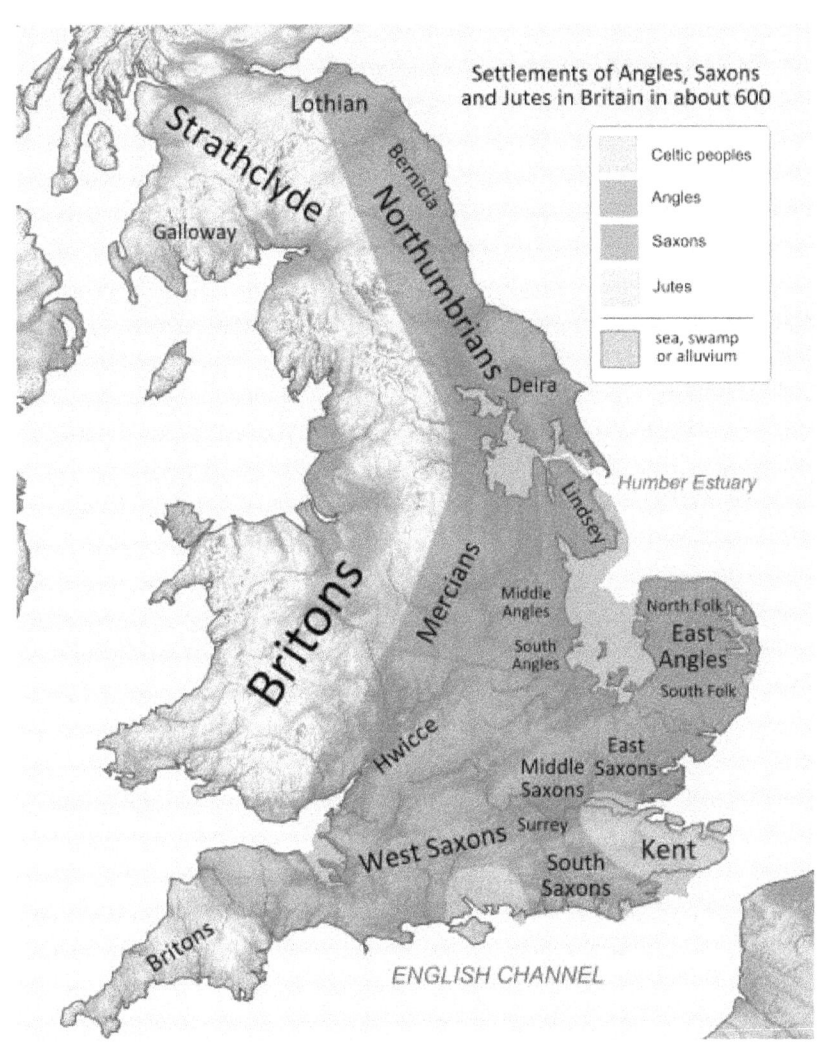

Settlements of Angles, Saxons and Jutes in Britain in about 600

Celtic peoples
Angles
Saxons
Jutes

sea, swamp or alluvium

Lothian

Strathclyde

Galloway

Bernicia

Northumbrians

Deira

Humber Estuary

Lindsey

Mercians

Middle Angles

South Angles

North Folk

East Angles

South Folk

Britons

Hwicce

East Saxons

Middle Saxons

Surrey

West Saxons

South Saxons

Kent

Britons

ENGLISH CHANNEL

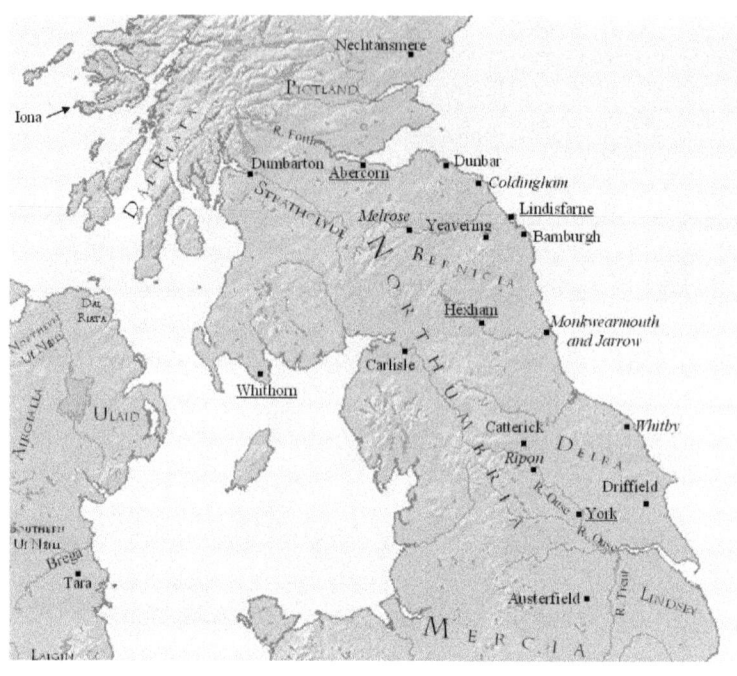

The past cannot be changed.
The future is yet in your power.
—*Unknown*

Prologue

Harsh Words

Eoforwic, Kingdom of Northumbria, Britannia

Summer, 670 AD

LEOFRIC FOLLOWED HIS father into the ealdorman's hall. They crossed the floor, their boots crunching on rushes. The rank odor of dog's piss and rotting food wafted up, and Leofric screwed up his nose. He glanced at the servants gossiping together as they stood around a gently bubbling cauldron of what smelled like boar stew—clearly they were an idle bunch.

"Remind me again why we're here, fæder?" Leofric drawled.

Wibert of Driffield glanced back at him and frowned. "Because Godwine has summoned us."

"Yes, but why?"

His father did not answer. Instead he led the way to the end of the hall, before stepping up onto the platform that ran around its perimeter. "This way," he grunted. Wibert reached for the heavy tapestry that shielded Godwine's alcove from the rest of the hall. "The ealdorman wishes to speak to us in private."

Leofric followed his father through the curtain and stepped into a small yet richly furnished space. Plush hangings covered the timber walls and thick furs lay underfoot.

Godwine of Eoforwic was waiting for them, standing before a glowing hearth. To his left stood his two blond and strapping sons: Berhtulf and Wybert. To Godwine's right stood Halwend—his most trusted warrior. Tall and broad-shouldered, his bare arms covered in silver and bronze armrings, Halwend was an intimidating sight. Leofric knew the warrior well; he had drunk with him in the meadhall on many occasions. The two men exchanged nods as Leofric entered.

Leofric stopped next to his father, his gaze settling upon the ealdorman. Twenty years his elder and built like an ox, Godwine was as feared as he was respected. Leofric knew his father idolized the man.

"You called for us, Godwine?" Wibert greeted the ealdorman heartily, as an old friend. He stepped forward, and lord and thegn embraced. Godwine slapped Wibert heartily on the back before his gaze flicked to Leofric.

"Aye," he boomed, "although it is your son I wish to speak to."

"Lord Godwine." Leofric dipped his head.

Godwine looked him up and down, taking his measure. "How old are you, Leofric?"

"Twenty-one winters."

"And still not handfasted?"

Leofric shrugged. "I'm in no hurry to be wed, milord."

Godwine laughed, a deep rumble in his chest. "Marriage is good for a man—it grounds him."

Leofric glanced from the ealdorman to his father. He did not like the sly look on his old man's face. *What are they up to?*

"I've called you here to make you an offer," the ealdorman continued, "a very generous one." He held Leofric's gaze a moment before smiling. "I offer you the hand of my only daughter, Hrothwyn."

Leofric stared at Godwine for a few moments before shock gave way to incredulity. Then he laughed. "Is this some kind of jest?"

The words fell like a woodman's axe in the small space, and a deathly hush followed. Beyond, Leofric could hear the rise and fall of voices and clang of iron pots as the ealdorman's lazy servants made a pretense of working.

He met the ealdorman's gaze once more and saw shock in his eyes. Both his sons had gone red in the face. Next to Leofric, his father appeared to have swallowed his tongue.

Eventually, the ealdorman spoke, his voice a low rumble. "Are you refusing Hrothwyn?"

Leofric held his gaze. "I am."

"Leofric!" Wibert found his tongue at last. "Shut up, you dolt!"

Godwine held up a meaty hand, forestalling his friend. "Let the lad speak. I am curious to hear how he can better the offer of an ealdorman's daughter—perhaps he is he aiming for the daughter of a king instead?"

Leofric ignored the look of warning Halwend was giving him and fought back a sneer. "I care not for status. Even if your daughter was a princess of Northumbria I would refuse her."

Godwine scratched at his dense brown beard, his dark eyes narrowing into glittering slits. "Aye, and why is that?"

Leofric gave another careless shrug. "She looks like a sow."

Another silence fell in the alcove, only this one felt charged—as if a storm had rolled in overhead.

"Idiot," Leofric's father growled. His pale, lightly freckled face had turned the color of liver; his hazel eyes were murderous. "Do you know who you're speaking to?"

Leofric turned on his father, his own temper rising. "Is this all I'm worth? You never sold any of my brothers into slavery?"

His father gave him a look of pure scorn. "Slavery? Your brothers have all done me proud. You don't even have the wits to be grateful."

"She's fat and ugly, fæder," Leofric snarled back. "I'd rather spend the rest of my days a monk than wed such a woman."

Wibert of Driffield spat out a curse and lunged. His fist slammed into his son's mouth. Leofric staggered back and only just managed to keep his feet. Eyes smarting from pain, he glowered at his father, wiped blood away from his injured mouth and clenched his fists by his sides. If the old bastard struck him again, he would hit back.

A few feet away, the ealdorman of Eoforwic had gone very still. Despite the warm day, he wore a wolf's pelt about his broad shoulders, making him look even more threatening. His expression was stony as he raised a hand and clicked his fingers. "Hrothwyn—come here."

The hanging behind the ealdorman parted and a short, heavyset young woman appeared. She was dressed in a fine, blue woolen gown, with a heavy leather belt studded with amber around her thick waist. Her frizzy brown hair was pulled back in an elaborate tangle of braids. Despite that today was not a feast day, she was dressed for a celebration. However, her round face told a different story. A deep flush mottled her cheeks and her eyes—the same shade of brown as her father's—gleamed with unshed tears.

Leofric went cold. She had heard every word.

"You were to be betrothed today," Godwine said, his voice cold and flat. "Hrothwyn was waiting to come forward to take your hand."

Leofric stared at her. He saw the hurt—feral and raw—in her eyes and knew he was to blame. He could make no excuses. There were no words to undo it—so he held his tongue.

The ealdorman broke the weighty silence. "If it is a life dedicated to Christianity you prefer, then that is what you shall have."

Leofric tore his gaze away from Hrothwyn, who was now staring down at her feet, tears streaming down her florid face, and focused on the ealdorman.

Godwine gave him a cruel smile. "You said you'd rather spend your days as a monk. There is a famed man of god, a monk named Cuthbert, who now lives upon Lindisfarena. He has sent word for the devout to join him in contemplation upon the isle. He will welcome you, I am sure."

Panic exploded in Leofric's chest. "Just wait a moment, milord," he gasped, all arrogance gone. He would have rather been buried alive upon a bed of hot coals than spend the rest of his days on some wind-swept rock bent in prayer. He had only tossed those words at the ealdorman in defiance earlier—he had not really meant them. He still had no wish to wed the ealdorman's unattractive daughter but suddenly he regretted his hotheaded response. "Let's not be hasty."

The ealdorman ignored him. Instead he twisted his head to the right, the cords of his neck straining as he sought to restrain his anger. "Halwend."

"Yes, milord," the warrior replied—his voice flat, devoid of emotion.

Godwine gestured to Leofric. "Take this cur and escort him to Lindisfarena today. My sons will go with you."

Halwend nodded, stepping forward. He, Berhtulf, and Wybert formed a semi-circle around Leofric, cutting off any chance of escape. Satisfied, the ealdorman turned his attention back to the young man before him.

The look on Godwine's face chilled Leofric's blood, as did his final words.

"You could have been my son by marriage, but you have insulted my family this day," he said coldly. "If I ever discover you've abandoned the monastery, I'll kill you."

One month later …

Chapter One

A Warm Welcome

Bebbanburg, Kingdom of Northumbria, Britannia

AELFWYN GAZED AT the wooden ramparts silhouetted against the northern horizon. Her stomach fluttered.

Bebbanburg.

"We're here at last." She glanced right, at where her mistress, Aethelhild, rode. As usual, the princess's face, framed by a headrail, was a picture of serenity. If she was anxious or worried, Aethelhild hid it well.

Feeling Aelfwyn's gaze upon her, Aethelhild glanced her way, her sharp blue eyes spearing her handmaid. "It's impressive, is it not?"

Aelfwyn nodded, a grin stretching her face. Even at this distance, the great fort put the 'Golden Hall' of Rendlaesham, seat of the King of the East Angles, to shame. Bebbanburg perched high upon a rocky outcrop, commanding a view for many furlongs distant. "Aye," she replied. "I can hardly wait to see inside."

Aethelhild smiled back, although the expression did not reach her eyes. "You will, soon enough."

Aelfwyn watched Aethelhild turn her attention back to the road ahead. She knew the princess did not wish to be wed again. She had been handfasted at sixteen, to an ealdorman twenty years her senior. Their fifteen-year union had been childless and when her husband choked to death on a piece of mutton, Aethelhild had wanted to take her vows and become a nun. However, her father—Ealdwulf, King of the East Angles—had other plans for his daughter.

She was too valuable to be allowed to spend the rest of her days in an abbey.

Turning her own gaze north, Aelfwyn looked once more upon the outline of Bebbanburg, to where the late afternoon sun turned the wooden ramparts gold. Although her mistress bore her duty stoically, this new life presented an opportunity for Aelfwyn. For months, she had dreamed of this moment, of the day she would arrive at the northern stronghold.

This was a new beginning, for she had chafed under the restrictions of her old life in Rendlaesham. She was the youngest of six daughters. Her father had been desperate to find a use for her—one that did not include providing a dowry. Paying for Aelfwyn's five elder sisters had bled him dry.

Few options were open to her. It was either become a nun or serve a highborn lady. Since, unlike her mistress, a life in the service of god had never appealed to Aelfwyn, she had chosen the latter.

Aelfwyn turned her face up to the sky, enjoying the sun on her face. It had been a long, tiring journey from Rendlaesham. It was high summer, but they'd had days of misty rain. The sun had rarely shown its face, lost behind a curtain of grey. Aelfwyn was tired of riding—and tired of eating hard cheese and stale bread. It would be a luxury to have a roof over her head again and sleep near a fire pit.

The women rode in the midst of a company of warriors: East Angle spearmen whom the king had charged with protecting the princess and her handmaid. The rumble of men's voices around them mingled with the crash of surf. They rode close to the sea now. Aelfwyn breathed in the salt-laced air and felt nervous anticipation tug at her breast. Her new life was about to begin.

The fortress of Bebbanburg inched slowly closer, until the rocky mount on which it stood become the heavens. The outcrop of red rock towered at least ninety feet above the patchwork of farmland below it.

Aelfwyn craned her neck as they trotted up the last incline toward the low gate. The Northumbrian flag—eight yellow rectangles on a blood-red field—fluttered in the sea breeze from one of the guard towers above her.

Ahead the gates drew open to admit them. Excitement fluttered once more in the pit of her belly, and Aelfwyn urged her pony on.

They rode up the main thoroughfare of Bebbanburg; a dirt street flanked either side by byres, stables, and the workshops of armorers, weaponsmiths and carpenters. Folk ventured out to greet them; a sea of curious faces stared up at the Lady of the East Angles and her escort. Aelfwyn could see no hostility on their faces, yet she felt slightly uncomfortable all the same.

I wonder what they think of us.

On the western edge of the outcrop, the Great Tower of Bebbanburg rose high above the carpet of thatched roofs below. It was grander than Aelfwyn had expected. The tower was much sturdier than the 'Golden Hall' of the East Angles, which was a huge timbered structure with a gleaming straw-thatch roof.

They entered the inner palisade through the high gate, into a wide yard. A sprawling stable complex spread out to their right, whereas an orchard of apples and pears took up the left hand-side of the space. The Great Tower intersected these two areas.

Aelfwyn grinned—she had entered a green and peaceful world crowned by a wide sky. It felt like a hawk's eyrie up here. Still smiling, she dismounted from her pony and hurried across to help her mistress.

"Do you think it's more beautiful than the Golden Hall?" she asked Aethelhild as she brushed horsehair off her mistress's robes to ensure she looked presentable to the king.

Aethelhild nodded. "Much more so." However, her gaze had turned inward, and she refused to meet her maid's eye. Aelfwyn realized that despite her aura of calm, the princess of the East Angles was dreading what lay ahead.

They entered the Great Tower. Two East Angle warriors led the way, followed by the princess and her handmaid. A knot of four more warriors brought up the rear. The interior of the tower was a great red-hued cavern. Torches hung from braces on the walls, and four massive fire pits burned bright, illuminating the faces of the ogling crowd. Men and women—the king's retainers and their wives and children—gawked at the East Angle princess and whispered amongst themselves.

Aethelhild strode, stiff-backed, through their midst, looking neither left nor right. Aelfwyn hurried after her, impressed by the princess's poise.

The king awaited his betrothed, seated upon the heah-setl.

He was not what Aelfwyn had been expecting.

Unlike King Ealdwulf of the East Angles—who was of middling years, with a mane of grizzled blond hair and an expanding waistline—Ecgfrith of Northumbria was young. No more than five and twenty winters, he was slim with short sandy hair. He was dressed simply in a linen tunic with a gold trim and doeskin leggings. A grey squirrel cloak hung from his shoulders, fastened with gold-plated clasps. Aelfwyn noted that he had a long, sharp-featured face and a watchful gaze that did not leave his betrothed as she made her way across the hall toward him.

A small group of highborn—members of the royal family—stood behind the king. Among them was an older woman with a plump face and greying dark hair coiled in a tight braid around her crown. Aelfwyn guessed this was the King's mother, Eanflaed, widow of King Oswiu.

Watching the Queen Mother, Aelfwyn wondered what she thought of this match. The princess, at thirty winters, was much older than her betrothed. There was also the fact she had never produced any children during her previous marriage. Back in Rendlaesham folk gossiped that the princess was barren.

Even so this marriage represented a strong political alliance between the Kingdoms of Northumbria and the East Angles—a chance to forge lasting peace.

Ecgfrith rose to his feet, his face still serious. "Welcome to Bebbanburgh, Aethelhild, daughter of Ealdwulf."

The two warriors leading the way stepped aside to allow the princess to come forward. Aethelhild curtsied and dipped her head. "I thank you for your welcome, sire."

Ecgfrith smiled, an expression that softened his solemn face. He stepped down from the high seat. "Was your journey pleasant?"

"Comfortable enough, despite the rain."

The king's gaze shifted over the escort amassed behind his betrothed, before settling upon Aelfwyn. She dropped her eyes to the rush-strewn floor but could still feel the weight of his stare pressing her down.

"I see you have brought a servant," he murmured.

"Aye, Aelfwyn is my handmaid."

"There are plenty of girls here who would serve you just as well—you can send her back to East Anglia with your father's men."

Aelfwyn stifled a gasp, dismay flooding through her. *Don't send me away.* She glanced up to see her mistress meet the king's eye.

"Aelfwyn is my loyal servant. I wish for no other handmaid," Aethelhild informed him. "The warriors who have accompanied me north are my father's gift to you. They and Aelfwyn should remain here."

Their gazes held, and Aelfwyn glimpsed the unspoken challenge between them. A muscle feathered in the young king's jaw before he smiled once more—but there was no warmth in his hazel eyes. "Very well," he said finally. "If it means that much to you, they all may stay."

Ecgfrith and Aethelhild were to be handfasted upon the first evening of the princess's arrival at Bebbanburg. There was just enough time for Aethelhild to bathe and dress for the ceremony, while the king's household prepared the interior of the Great Hall.

Hidden from view inside an alcove by a thick fur hanging, Aelfwyn unpacked the gown her mistress had brought for the occasion and hung it up on the wall to air while Aethelhild bathed. The dress was lovely—pale yellow with embroidered gold hems. Aelfwyn and Aethelhild had made it themselves, a job that had taken them nearly all of last winter.

The chatter of voices reached them from beyond the alcove, as did the scent of baking honey-seed cakes and the aroma of roasting venison; there would be a great feast this eve after the handfasting.

Aelfwyn did not speak to her mistress as she helped her prepare for the wedding. Aethelhild was not fond of prattle, and the stern look on her face as she sat in the iron tub, scrubbing at her arms as if she wished to remove a layer of skin, warned Aelfwyn from showing any excitement about the coming ceremony.

After Aethelhild had bathed, Aelfwyn combed out her long dark hair, which was drying in heavy curls down her back. After years of being married and then recently widowed, Aethelhild usually covered her hair with a headrail. It was a pity, in Aelfwyn's opinion, for her mistress had beautiful hair. It was so different to Aelfwyn's own mane, which was pale blonde and as fine as thistle blossom; Aethelhild's braids were twice the thickness of her handmaid's. Tonight the princess would wear her hair loose for the last time in public. After that only her husband would see her hair unbound.

Aelfwyn helped Aethelhild into her gown and laced up the back. Her mistress was tall and slim, although with enough curves to fill out her gown beautifully. Aelfwyn wished she was tall like Aethelhild—tall enough to look men in the eye. Although well proportioned, she was tiny in stature; something her sisters had teased her mercilessly over.

When Aelfwyn stepped back to check everything was in order, her resolve to hold her tongue slipped. "You look like an angel, milady."

Aethelhild looked up from where she had been smoothing her full skirts, her mouth twisting. "Do I? I feel like a martyr."

Aelfwyn attempted a smile. "Surely, there are worse husbands?"

Aethelhild shook her head. "I wish for no husband—I want only to be left alone."

Aelfwyn stared back at her, taken aback at her mistress's vehemence. For once, Aethelhild's shield of ice had splintered, and Aelfwyn glimpsed the desperation that bubbled underneath.

"I tire of having no say in my fate," Aethelhild concluded, brushing past her maid to retrieve the heavy amber necklace her father had gifted her for this occasion. "I feel like a fattened sow at market."

Chapter Two

Refusal

AELFWYN STIRRED IN the furs, slowly awaking to the sound of industry in the hall beyond her alcove. She slept in a tiny space, to the left of the king and queen's quarters. It may have been cramped—just big enough for her to cram in her meagre belongings and bedding—but it was a luxury after having to share an alcove with her older sisters, two of whom snored. This was her own, private, space.

Stretching, Aelfwyn inhaled the scent of fresh griddle bread. However, she was not hungry this morning, not after last night's magnificent feast. She had also consumed more wine than she was used to, and had a dry mouth and slight headache as a result. Still, she had enjoyed the celebration. She adored handfastings.

Aelfwyn quickly plaited her hair in two braids and pulled on a woolen dress over the sleeveless linen tunic she had slept in. She did not usually sleep this late. The feasting, drinking, and dancing had gone on until early morning. She hoped the queen would not scold her for it.

She emerged from her alcove to find the Great Hall of Bebbanburg a hive of activity. Slaves were carrying out rushes soiled by food and drink—and worse—and replacing them with fresh ones. Women stood at long work benches pummeling dough into flat wheels before cooking them on an iron griddle that hung over the fire pits. Children played on the floor, getting in the way of the work of the slaves who were doing their best to clean up last night's mess. Men sat at long tables, breaking their fast with bread and broth, while the royal family sat upon the high seat.

Aelfwyn paused, surveying the table upon the heah seatl. It looked a somber, tense meal. The king sat accompanied by his mother and the bishop. Ecgfrith did not look in a good mood. The Queen Mother murmured something to her son and he snapped a response back at her, clearly irritated.

Bishop Wilfrid, who had conducted the handfasting ceremony the night before, was a tall, spare man with a long, angular face, penetrating dark eyes and a mouth that wore a permanently downturned expression, making him look disapproving. He had a thick head of grey hair, shaved into a tonsure at the crown, and a neatly trimmed beard and moustache. The bishop was the only one at the table with any appetite. He bent low over his bowl of gruel, slurping loudly.

Aelfwyn looked around the busy hall once more, watching as two lads battled with wooden swords near one of the fire pits. One of them, a good-looking boy with a head of dark wavy hair was shouting insults at his opponent. "Cur! Taste my blade!"

The other lad, a heavy-set boy with pale, freckled skin and a shock of red hair, had gone the color of a freshly chopped beet. "No—taste mine, Pictish dog!"

A plump woman with a harassed expression and thick brown hair tied back in a messy braid, descended upon the boys brandishing a wooden spoon. "Bridei, Heolstor—stop it this instant or I'll tan your arses red."

The boys ran off, still hooting insults at each other.

Aelfwyn's gaze continued its journey around the interior of the Great Hall. She frowned.

Where is Aethelhild?

She dared not approach the high seat and ask the king. Ecgfrith sat slumped in his great oaken chair, his expression mulish.

Have the newlyweds quarreled already?

Aelfwyn ducked behind the tapestry that shielded the king and queen's living quarters from view. She stepped into a lofty space, warmed by a single fire pit in its center. A pile of furs sat in one corner, and leather trunks sat next to them. Fine tapestries, depicting hunting scenes and the bristling outline of Bebbanburg itself, hung from the damp stone walls. A single window, its wooden shutter open this morning, let in a stream of golden sunlight.

Aethelhild sat under it, upon a wooden stool, calmly winding wool upon her distaff. Aelfwyn halted and let the tapestry fall behind her. Her mistress looked completely different to the bride dressed in shimmering gold who had knelt before the high seat at the young king's side the night before. A crisp white veil hid her luxurious dark hair and she wore a plain dun-colored woolen tunic that covered her shape. With the sun pouring over her, she looked like a nun at work blessed by the light of the lord, her face beatific in contemplation.

Aelfwyn took a tentative step forward. "Milady?"

Aethelhild looked up, her piercing blue gaze settling upon her handmaid. "Good morning, Aelfwyn. Did you sleep well?"

Aelfwyn nodded. "And you, milady?"

Aethelhild smiled. "Like a babe. Come, join me—I need someone to tease out this wool." She motioned to the basket at her feet.

Aelfwyn did as bid, pulling up a stool next to the queen and picking up a handful of wool. It was springy and oily in her hands, and smelled of lanolin. She teased out a length of it and began feeding it to Aethelhild, who wound it onto her wooden spindle.

"Aethelhild, is something amiss?" she asked eventually.

The queen glanced up. "No, why do you ask that?"

"The king is seated at the high table alone, with a face like thunder, while you sit in here at your distaff."

The queen sighed, her mask of serenity slipping. "I am tired, Aelfwyn. I wish for some peace."

Aelfwyn frowned. Her mistress suddenly seemed drained. She wondered how their wedding night had gone, although she was too shy to ask such questions. They worked in companionable silence for a short while before Aethelhild spoke.

"There are so many things I have no choice in," she began, her voice barely above a whisper, "but my body is still my own."

Aelfwyn looked up, confused.

Aethelhild met her eye. "I refused to lie with Ecgfrith last night—and I will continue to do so."

Aelfwyn gasped. "But you are his wife."

"And if he wants to bed me, it will be by force." Aethelhild's face hardened. "I had many years of misery, wedded to a brute who used me like a hōre. I will not willingly submit to a man's touch again—ever."

Aelfwyn stared at her mistress with a mixture of awe and fear. The idea of refusing one's husband was unthinkable. Despite Aelfwyn's shock at the queen's audacity, Aethelhild impressed her.

"How did he react?" she asked, keeping her voice low lest someone overheard them.

"As you'd expect. He pleaded, threatened, whined—and then sulked." The derision in Aethelhild's voice made Aelfwyn wince. She had never realized how much her mistress resented men. "He'll try again, I'm sure—but the answer will still be the same."

"Would you like some wine, milord?"

The strains of a lyre floated through the Great Hall, rising above the rumble of conversation, as Aelfwyn stood at the king's elbow with a jug of sloe wine.

Ecgfrith looked up, watching her a moment before he smiled. "Aye."

Aelfwyn squirmed under the intensity of his stare before she filled his bronze cup. Then she moved on to Aethelhild.

Ecgfrith leaned back in his chair, took a sip from his cup, and shifted his gaze to the dark-haired lad at the far end of the table. The two boys Aelfwyn had seen play fighting together had joined the royal family for the noon meal. "Bridei," he called out. "A message arrived from Dún Duirn at dawn, from your father."

The boy, whose mouth was currently full of bread, looked up. He swallowed his mouthful, his dark-blue gaze shining. "Does he want me to go home?"

Ecgfrith gave the lad a cold smile. "No—he sent word that your mother is ill. The healers believe she will die within the next few days."

Bridei blanched and gripped the edge of the table for support. The freckled lad next to him cast Bridei a worried look but said nothing.

Once Bridei had recovered sufficiently, he met the king's gaze once more. "I should go to her today, milord."

Ecgfrith shook his head. "Your father wants you to continue to foster here until you come of age. He does not want you to come home."

The lad stared at Ecgfrith, his eyes blazing. "He said that?"

Ecgfrith nodded.

"I don't believe you."

"Bridei!" the Queen Mother snapped. "Mind your manners—you address your king."

"I care not." Bridei scrambled to his feet, his lean frame shaking from the force of the emotions he was trying to keep in check. "He lies."

Aelfwyn watched Bridei leap down from the high seat and dash across the hall. He dodged a slave bearing a steaming cauldron of broth, leaped over a sleeping dog, and disappeared outside. Pity stirred in her breast. He was a Pictish fosterling, far from his kin, who had just learned his mother was dying. Could Ecgfrith not treat him better?

"Impudent pup." Ecgfrith raised his cup and took a deep draft. "I'll whip his backside myself next time he speaks to me thus."

A heavy silence fell upon the table then. Aethelhild eventually broke it by attempting to make conversation with the Queen Mother.

"Have you had any news from your daughters of late, Eanflaed?"

The Queen Mother looked up from pulling meat off a rabbit carcass, her face creasing in a frown. "Osthryth is as well as can be expected," she sniffed. "Wedded to that Mercian savage, Aethelred. But Elflaeda is very happy at Streonshalh Abbey."

Aethelhild smiled. "You must be proud. I hear the Abbess Hilda is a great healer."

Eanflaed nodded, her expression softening as she thought of her youngest daughter. "The abbess has sent word that Elflaeda is highly skilled in surgery. The lord has gifted her with healing hands."

Ecgfrith snorted at this, and his mother cast him a quelling look. "You should be proud, milord. Your sister will be Abbess of Streonshalh one day, mark my words."

"Pious women grate on my nerves," he muttered under his breath.

Aelfwyn saw her mistress tense at this insult, while the Queen Mother visibly blanched. A strained silence descended upon the heah seatl.

Grateful she had been born a thegn's daughter and not a highborn lady, Aelfwyn quickly moved off down the table and finished pouring the wine. Her initial excitement to be in Bebbanburg had left her. Suddenly she missed her father's hall, even her sisters' bickering. She longed for her parents' easy conversation and the laughter she had grown up with—this place was an adder's nest in comparison.

It was a relief to step down off the high seat and join the folk at her table below.

Chapter Three

The Flower-Seller

THE FIRST FEW days of Aelfwyn's new life at Bebbanburg passed swiftly. It was a cool summer this year, with many days of leaden skies and chill winds, but even so Aelfwyn ventured outdoors whenever she could.

She helped the other servants in the garden behind the Great Tower and picked sour plums off the trees in the orchards. She worked alongside the cooks as they baked bread in the clay ovens outside.

Once her chores were done, Aelfwyn often ventured beyond the high gate into the town proper. She always looked forward to exploring this lofty fort. Bebbanburg fascinated her. High wooden ramparts surrounded the fort, with wooden towers at each corner so that Ecgfrith's men could spy visitors from any direction. There were two principal ways through the town. The first, the King's Way, led between the low and high gates. The second road was named the Dragon's Back, which stretched from south to north along the ridge. Small lanes branched off the Dragon's Back, leading to the wattle and daub homes of ceorls, the free folk living within the town.

One morning, Aelfwyn decided to visit the market in the square just inside the low gate. The gate was open, letting in a steady flow of cottars and merchants who had come to sell and barter.

A cool wind blew in from the sea, and Aelfwyn wished she had brought a shawl with her. The grey woolen dress she wore was sleeveless, and her bare arms prickled with cold. The weather was definitely bleaker here compared to Rendlaesham, especially since the fort was exposed to the elements. It was the downside of having such a commanding view of the surrounding land. Aelfwyn spied dark clouds out to sea, warning of approaching bad weather.

Trying to ignore the wind, Aelfwyn wandered through the market, breathing in its sights and smells. An elderly woman was selling medicinal herbs, while next to her a farmer was trying to sell a gaggle of noisy, honking geese. Although penned inside a rickety enclosure, the birds were aggressive, hissing and flapping at any prospective buyers who wandered too near.

Aelfwyn gave the geese a wide berth and wandered past a row of stalls selling bread, rabbit pies, and plum cakes. The aroma of baking pies made her mouth water. She had a purse containing a handful of thrymsas, which her mother had given her should she ever need them. As tempting as the pies were, Aelfwyn knew her gold coins were too precious to waste on them.

"Violets and primroses for the pretty lass!" A woman with wild auburn hair, carrying a basket of blue and purple posies, stopped before her. The woman's daughter clung to her leg; a little girl of around five with an impish face and the same untamed hair as her mother.

Aelfwyn was sorely tempted, even more so than by the pies. She adored flowers. "How much?"

The woman smiled back. "Half a thrymsa for four posies."

Aelfwyn gave in to temptation. She would keep a posy for herself and decorate her mistress's bower with the rest. She dug into the purse on her belt and extracted a coin, which she snapped in half.

The woman took the gold, observing her with a shrewd eye. "You're new here, aren't you?"

"Aye, I'm from Rendlaesham."

"An East Angle." The woman's eyebrows lifted. "You're a long way from home."

"I'm handmaid to the queen," Aelfwyn explained, accepting the posies of violets and primroses.

The woman's smile faded. "Is it true what they say about her?"

Aelfwyn tensed. "I don't know ... what do they say?"

"That she is barren and cold. The king's men often visit the meadhall in town—their tongues flap when they're in their cups. There's talk she won't let Ecgfrith near her."

"Aethelhild is a gentle, god-fearing woman," Aelfwyn replied, stiffening. She hated that folk were gossiping about her mistress. "She endured a brutal marriage before coming here—the king just needs to be patient with her."

The woman gave her a speculative look. "Ecgfrith is not a patient man—and he's used to getting his own way."

The woman reached down and caressed her daughter's unruly mop of auburn hair as she spoke. Aelfwyn watched the pair of them, suspicion dawning. Something in this woman's tone suggested that she spoke from personal experience. She knew the king well.

Is this child his bastard?

Aelfwyn's stomach churned. It was not uncommon for kings to father children from local women. Ecgfrith was young and until eight days ago had been unwed. As if sensing her suspicions, the woman stepped back, her gaze shuttering.

"Enjoy the flowers," she said lightly, before taking her daughter's hand. "Come, Hea."

Aelfwyn nodded and clutched the posies to her breast as the flower-seller moved off. Her encounter with this strange woman had left her uneasy, as if a cloud had just passed over the sun. There was something fey about the flower-seller. She reminded Aelfwyn of the seer who lived in Rendlaesham—a frightening old woman who could look into your soul.

Suppressing a shudder, Aelfwyn turned and made her way out of the market, and up the King's Way toward the Great Tower.

It's just the cold, she told herself.

Despite her unsettling encounter, Aelfwyn did not hurry back to the Great Tower. Over the last few days she had done her best to escape its somber atmosphere—and the tension between the king and queen.

Although Aethelhild had not spoken of her husband again, Aelfwyn did not need to be a seer to divine that things were strained between them. At meal times, the couple sat in stony silence, barely acknowledging each other's presence.

Oddly, Aethelhild appeared more serene and reserved than ever. She had taken to wearing a wooden crucifix upon her breast, and she accompanied the Queen Mother to church every morning. Meanwhile, the king's mood worsened with each passing day. He grew surly and spent increasing amounts of time out hawking or hunting with his men.

Aelfwyn crossed into the inner palisade through the high gate. She thought on the flower-seller's warning and felt a tickle of foreboding. *Ecgfrith is not a patient man—and he's used to getting his own way.*

She worried for her mistress. Aethelhild had a strong will, but there would come a day when the king would not take no for an answer.

"Is anything amiss?"

Aelfwyn looked up from her embroidery to find Aethelhild watching her steadily. They sat at their usual place near the open window inside the royal alcove. Outside, the late afternoon had turned greyer still, and the gusting wind now had drops of rain in it. The fire pit behind them guttered in the hearth, but the queen refused to close the shutters. She had spent most of the day within her chamber and liked to work with the natural light filtering in.

"No," she replied quickly. "Why do you ask?"

"You're a little pale and distracted."

"I visited the market without a shawl this morning." Aelfwyn blurted the first excuse that came to mind. "I think I might have caught a slight chill."

The queen's gaze shifted to the clay pot filled with violets and primroses on the table next to them. "The flowers are lovely, but you needn't have gone on my account."

Aelfwyn smiled. She was pleased the flowers brightened up her mistress's day. "I enjoyed the outing—it was no bother."

She looked back down at her work—the hem of one of the queen's dresses she was embroidering with gold thread—and did a few neat stitches. However, she was aware that Aethelhild was still watching her. Eventually, unable to bear the scrutiny any longer, Aelfwyn met her gaze.

"Are you enjoying your new life in Bebbanburg?" Aethelhild asked.

"I am," Aelfwyn responded hesitantly, "although it's different to what I expected. Folk don't seem as friendly here as in Rendlaesham."

Aethelhild smiled. "That's only because they don't know you, Aelfwyn. With your kindness and sunny smile, you will soon make friends here."

Aelfwyn blushed. She was not used to compliments, least of all from Aethelhild. "Have things gotten easier for you, milady?" she asked. "Has the king respected your wishes?"

The queen nodded, although her expression tightened. "Aye, he has— although not without making his opinion of me clear. I fear that I have made an enemy out of him. I am fortunate though, for some husbands would merely force their wife to submit to them. Ecgfrith is not such a man."

Aelfwyn tensed, wondering if she should share what the flower-seller had told her. She decided against it. Aethelhild was not a woman to appreciate idle gossip. "I'm sorry this is not the life you wanted, milady," she said finally. "It seems unfair."

Her mistress smiled then, although her eyes held no brightness. "One thing I came to understand years ago, dearest Aelfwyn, is that few things in life are fair."

Aelfwyn watched the queen a moment, not knowing what to respond. For a woman with such strong faith, it was a fatalistic comment; the words of a woman who had lost all hope for the future.

As if realizing the impact her declaration had on her young handmaid, Aethelhild reached across and placed a hand over hers. "Don't look so concerned. Your happiness is a beacon of light in my life. Although you may not realize so now, your bright disposition will smooth many paths ahead for you. Whatever happens—don't ever let that light go out."

Aelfwyn's brow furrowed. She found her mistress's words cryptic, and the note of warning in them made her even more worried than before. She opened her mouth to query Aethelhild, but the clang of iron behind them forestalled her. The time of the evening meal was upon them.

The queen put aside her work and rose to her feet, her skirts rustling, and cast her handmaid an apologetic smile. "Come, Ecgfrith awaits."

Chapter Four

Upon the Lonely Isle

SHEETS OF RAIN blew across the windswept island of Lindisfarena, bringing with them a chill from colder lands to the north.

Leofric bowed his head against the gale, drew his homespun robes close against him, and hurried up the path toward the monastery. The leather bag stuffed with driftwood thudded against his spine with each step.

If this is summer, I can't wait till the bitter months, Leofric thought with a grimace. This far north the wind seemed to drive into a man's bones. His damp robes chaffed his skin, providing little protection from the weather, and he longed for the thick fur mantle they had stripped him of upon his arrival here.

Ahead, a collection of low, wooden buildings sprawled before him. Hemmed in by the headland on three sides, it was the most sheltered spot on the island. The roof of the priory rose higher than all the others, peeking up from the center of the complex.

Despite his desire to get out of the rain, Leofric felt no relief that his destination lay a short distance ahead. He wished he could turn around and run from it—the driving rain and high tides be damned.

One long month had passed since Halwend and Godwine's sons had hauled Leofric here and dumped him at the feet of Cuthbert. The moon had been waxing when they rowed Leofric across from the coast, with the fires of Bebbanburg lighting the southern sky. He had tried to escape twice on the journey from Eoforwic, so he went before the prior with a bruised eye, split lip, and trussed up like a Yuletide goose.

The moon was now waxing once more—two more nights and it would be full.

Leofric quickened his step, squinting at the pitch torches guttering at the entrance to the monastery. He was late for Night Prayers—again.

This time it was not his fault. After the usual silent evening meal of coarse bread and pottage, he had gone off to collect driftwood for the feeble hearth that burned in the hut he shared with three others. Bad weather had closed in, and despite that it was still summer, Leofric had not wanted to spend the night shivering under his one coarse woolen blanket. Dusk fell swiftly with the bad weather, and his wandering had taken him to the northern edge of the island, to Snook Point, where he had lost track of time.

Leofric passed under a wooden arch, his feet splashing through puddles as he made his way across the central yard toward the church. He passed low timber buildings, their windows all dark as everyone was at prayers.

Reaching the church, Leofric dumped his bag of wood, stepped into the stone entranceway, and pushed back his sodden cowl. Underneath, his auburn hair had been cropped off close to the scalp. He had not yet shaved off the hair at the crown of his head into a tonsure though, for he was still a postulant—the prior had not yet accepted him into the order.

The thought of taking the vows of poverty, chastity and obedience and becoming a novice here soured Leofric's stomach. He could not bear the idea of spending the rest of his life here rotting away on this rock—yet that fate was inching ever closer.

Dripping water, Leofric squelched his way into the church, where a group of twenty men knelt in prayer upon the roughly paved floor. He inhaled the acrid smell of burning pitch, which filled the iron cressets lining the walls. The flames guttered and flickered in the drafts as the storm outside tried to force its way in through the cracks in the walls and shutters.

Cuthbert stood upon a raised wooden platform. Dressed in a dyed blue habit, his head dipped, he cut a solemn figure. Torchlight gleamed off his shaved crown, his hands clasped before him in prayer.

Leofric's sandals scraped on the stone as he approached. The sound caused the prior to glance up. His brown eyes flashed in annoyance, his lips thinning, before he cast his gaze downward once more. Knowing that would not be the last of it, Leofric took his place at the end of the row of kneeling monks. A slender youth with close-cropped blond hair looked Leofric's way as he knelt down. Deorwine gave him a pained look, but Leofric merely grinned back.

A cottar's son who had grown up near Bebbanburgh, Deorwine had proved to be a much-needed friend during the month Leofric had lived on Lindisfarena. Unlike some of the monks who lived here, Deorwine still acted as if there was a world beyond the monastery and this lonely isle.

The stone pavers were cold and hard beneath Leofric's knees as he knelt. He closed his eyes. Instead of praying, he listened to the drum of rain on the roof and the sound of it lashing against the walls of the church. Low-lying with no woodland to protect it, Lindisfarena sat very exposed to the elements. It was a godforsaken spot, but perhaps that was why the monks had chosen it.

The wet wool of his habit started to itch his skin, making it feel as if an army of ants marched up and down his back. By the time Cuthbert straightened up and lowered his hands, Leofric was clenching his jaw in discomfort.

Silently the monks filed out of the church, heading toward the low-slung dwellings outside where they slept. Leofric made to follow them, at Deorwine's heels, when Cuthbert's voice—low but commanding—halted him.

"Brother Leofric—stay."

Letting out the breath he had been holding, for he had hoped that this time he might be excused his lateness, Leofric halted. He turned to face the prior, as behind him the church emptied. Cuthbert approached him; his gait unhurried, his manner as serene as ever.

The prior was over two decades older than Leofric, although he wore his years well. He had a lean, gentle face with earnest eyes the color of rich earth. His hair and beard were thick and ash-brown, although his long, slightly hooked nose gave him a hawkish appearance.

However, his mouth revealed the most about the prior. Cuthbert's lips were small and pursed, hinting at a character that enjoyed self-denial and austerity. Such a mouth had never reveled in sensuality of any kind, whether it was for food, mead, women—or men.

"Brother Leofric," the prior greeted him with a shake of the head. "Late again ... may I ask why?"

"I was collecting driftwood for the hearth, Father," Leofric answered, dipping his head. "The bad weather caught me by surprise, and I lost track of the time. I'm sorry, it won't happen again."

Cuthbert let out a soft sigh. "You said the same thing two days ago, and a day before that. Please only apologize to me if you actually mean it."

Leofric glanced up, surprised at the prior's shrewdness; that was the closest Cuthbert had ever come to telling him off outright. Their gazes met and held for a heartbeat.

"Piety, diligence, and obedience," Cuthbert began quietly. "These are the values all the monks here live by—only *you* do not share our beliefs."

Leofric opened his mouth to excuse himself but the prior intercepted him. "I know Godwine of Eoforwic forced you to come here. I understood from your first night here that you are not made to be a monk."

"Then send me away, Father," Leofric said, hope rising in his chest. Maybe Cuthbert had finally come to his senses. "You speak the truth—this is not my place."

Cuthbert's pursed mouth compressed slightly. "I do not give you leave to go—it would only bring death upon you. The ealdorman made it clear there will be a price on your head, if you ever leave Lindisfarena. Whether or not you wish it, he has condemned you to this life."

Bitterness rose within Leofric. The walls of the small stone church closed in on him, and he struggled to breathe. He hated this life: the meanness, dullness, and endless routine of it. The youngest of five sons of a wealthy thegn—for his father was Godwine's most favored retainer—he had lived a free, charmed life until the day he insulted Godwine of Eoforwic's daughter.

Unlike his two elder sisters, who worked hard from dawn to dusk alongside his mother to run his father's hall, Leofric's days had been spent riding, hawking, hunting—and whoring. As soon as he was old enough, he had enjoyed many nights in Eoforwic's meadhall, in the company of lewd women who drank alongside the men there. It might have been shallow, but he had loved that life and would have given anything to return to it.

Leofric's feelings must have shown plainly on his face, for Cuthbert watched him steadily, sympathy in his dark eyes.

"Is such a fate so terrible?" he asked.

Leofric dropped his gaze, his cheeks warming under the prior's scrutiny. Cuthbert had an uncanny ability to make him feel unworthy; something no one had ever had the ability to do. His father and brothers had taunted him growing up—the fate of the youngest son—but their insults had flowed off him like water off an oilskin cloak. Cuthbert was different. He never stooped to insults, or even raised his voice. Yet with just a quietly spoken observation he made Leofric feel like a spoiled, callow youth.

"You may not realize it now," Cuthbert continued, when it became clear that Leofric had nothing to say, "but everything happens for a reason. God wanted you to come here, to learn humility and obedience."

Leofric gritted his teeth but held his tongue. *Hang your sniveling god.* He had grown up believing in Woden, Thunor, and Freya, and it had felt right to him. Then his father—to find favor with Godwine—had forced his entire family to be baptized. He had destroyed the stone idols of the gods that had once decorated their home and beaten his children if he caught them favoring their old beliefs.

Perhaps seeing he was getting nowhere, the prior inhaled deeply and stepped back from the younger man. "Go to your pallet now and think on what I have said. As punishment for your lateness you will spend tomorrow morning here in church, praying with me to atone for your lack of diligence."

Leofric tensed and glanced up, scowling at the prior. He would have preferred a beating to a morning of prayer—it bored him witless. "But I've got chores to do."

"Your brothers will take care of them for tomorrow," Cuthbert replied.

The prior then turned away, signaling that their conversation had ended.

Leofric left the church and retrieved his bag of damp driftwood, before returning to the squat timber dwelling that he shared with Deorwine and two other postulant monks. He was in a foul mood. The thought of spending the morning on his knees chanting made him want to run out of the monastery and throw himself in the churning sea.

Worse still, Cuthbert had made his situation clear. The prior was not responsible for keeping Leofric here—Godwine of Eoforwic was. Both of them knew the truth.

It was as black as pitch inside the dwelling, and he could already hear two of his companions snoring. Life was physically grueling upon Lindisfarena; they must have fallen asleep the moment they stretched out on their sleeping pallets.

Leofric left the bag of wood near the door before moving carefully in the dark, around the edge of the one-room hut. His pallet lay under the tiny window on the far side of the dwelling, next to Deorwine's.

Reaching his destination, he stubbed his toe on the edge of the pallet and muttered a curse under his breath. Then he stripped off his damp habit and climbed under the coarse, itchy blanket. Outside, the wind and rain buffeted the wooden frame of the hut, probing through the cracks like seeking, cold fingers.

"Leo ..." Deorwine whispered, his voice barely audible above the roar of the storm. "Are you in trouble again with the prior?"

Leofric snorted. "Of course."

"I don't understand why you were late again. You know—"

"Enough," Leofric growled. "I don't need you preaching to me as well."

Deorwine obeyed and fell silent. After a few moments, Leofric started to feel like a cur for snapping at him. "How do you bear it, Deorwine?" he asked finally, despair pressing down like a boulder upon his chest.

"What?" Deorwine mumbled, half asleep.

"The thought of spending the rest of your life here. Never having a woman again. Never being able to hunt, drink, and fight like other men."

In the darkness, he could almost sense his friend's smile. They were around the same age, but they came from vastly different worlds. Leofric knew his approach to life often amused as much as it bemused his friend.

"My village is poor," Deorwine replied. "Life is mean and hard. Every winter brings fear of starvation or dying from the cold. My father looked like an old man at thirty winters and my mother died birthing her eighth child. Before coming here, all I had to look forward to was back-breaking toil in the fields."

"But you'd have a woman at least."

Deorwine gave a low laugh. "I wouldn't want to put a wife through such a life. To get her with child and then fear she'd die birthing it, to watch her youth and fairness wither years before they should."

Taken aback, Leofric considered his friend's words. "Surely you're exaggerating. The life of a cottar isn't so bad."

"Says the son of a rich man," Deorwine countered, although there was no bitterness in his words.

Chapter Five

Cat and Mouse

"WHAT DID YOU say your name was, girl?"

Aelfwyn poured milk into the king's cup and tried to quell the nervousness that fluttered in the pit of her belly. She wished Ecgfrith would ignore her. Mealtimes had turned into a game of 'cat and mouse'. Yesterday evening she had caught the king staring at her while she helped serve the evening meal. Ecgfrith's gaze now lazily traveled the length of her as she served him. He did not seem to care that his wife, kin, and retainers all looked on.

"Aelfwyn, milord," she replied, deliberately averting her gaze.

"And who is your father, Aelfwyn? Does he serve the King of the East Angles or one of his ealdormen?"

"He's thegn to King Ealdwulf, milord."

She could feel Ecgfrith's gaze on her face and sensed her mistress tense beside him. Kings did not indulge in chatter with their servants; his sudden interest in her background only made Aelfwyn more nervous. However, Ecgfrith had not finished his interrogation.

"Surely he could have found a better fate for you than this, fair Aelfwyn?"

Surprised, she glanced up. Instantly his gaze seized hers. Ecgfrith's eyes were unusual, light hazel with grey around the pupils. They held her fast.

"What do you mean, milord?" she asked, heat rising up her neck.

"A handmaid?" His eyebrow lifted. "A girl of such beauty should be a lady of a vast hall, with servants waiting upon her."

Aelfwyn's blush rose further. She finished her task of filling his cup and accidently splashed some milk over the rim in her haste to be gone from his side.

"Sorry, milord," she gasped, backing off. The king merely watched her, unsmiling, his unnervingly intense stare scorching her.

"You're frightening the maid, Lord Ecgfrith." Bishop Wilfrid spoke up, wiping broth off his neatly trimmed grey moustache. He had glanced up from his meal long enough to notice Aelfwyn backing away from the king. His tone was censorious, although the king did not heed him, his gaze never leaving Aelfwyn.

"Am I?" he replied. "I was merely exchanging pleasantries."

"My handmaid is the youngest of many sisters and had few choices open to her." Aethelhild spoke then, her voice colder than Aelfwyn had ever heard it. "Aelfwyn's service to me is an honor indeed—for me as much as her. The bishop is right, you are plainly frightening her."

Ecgfrith cast his wife a cool look. "I don't remember asking your opinion, wife. If I wish to address your handmaid, I will."

With that, he downed his cup of milk in a couple of gulps and slammed it down on the table in front of him.

"Aelfwyn," he called out. "My cup is empty."

Inhaling deeply, Aelfwyn turned from where she had been about the fill Lady Eanflaed's cup and reluctantly retraced her steps back to the king. Out of the corner of her eye, she saw the Queen Mother stiffen. Lady Eanflaed's mouth pursed in disapproval, and she cast a stern look at her son—one which the king ignored.

He was punishing Aethelhild by humiliating her loyal servant.

"So," he said, as she leaned over him to refill his cup, his voice low and intimate. "The youngest of many sisters. Are they all as fair as you?"

Aelfwyn stiffened. "Much fairer, milord." It was true, her sisters were all beauties; her family had always considered her the runt of the litter.

Ecgfrith laughed softly. "So fair yet so modest—I like that in a woman."

Aelfwyn glanced over at Aethelhild and saw that her mistress sat rigid in her chair, her face pale and pinched. As he had hoped, Ecgfrith was wounding her. Anger at his rudeness bubbled up within Aelfwyn. He was like a spoiled child, misbehaving because he had not gotten his own way.

Deftly, she finished pouring milk into his cup, before she moved down the table to Lady Eanflaed.

The king's gaze followed her.

Aelfwyn avoided the king and queen for the rest of the morning.

After her humiliation, she felt embarrassed to face Aethelhild, worrying that her mistress would somehow think it was her fault—that she had encouraged him in some way.

To distract herself from the anxiety that now gnawed at the pit of her belly, she threw herself into her chores. There was always plenty to keep her busy in the Great Hall of Bebbanburg. The cooks were preparing apple pies for the noon meal, and Aelfwyn worked alongside them, peeling and coring the apples before making pastry for the pies.

Around her, the Great Hall bustled with activity. The air smelled of damp leather and wool, mingled with the smoke from the four hearths that burned inside the tower. A storm had howled for most of the previous night, battering the stone walls. Aelfwyn had lain awake in her alcove listening to its fury. She had liked the feeling of being snug and warm among her furs while the rain and wind raged outside.

Aethelhild disappeared into her quarters after breaking her fast and only emerged briefly to eat at noon. Aelfwyn served them again, her stomach churning as she circuited the table with a jug of wine. Mercifully, the king ignored her this time, although this only increased Aelfwyn's sense of unease. He was toying with her and Aethelhild, waiting until the pair of them relaxed before pouncing once more.

After the noon meal, Aelfwyn went out to the kitchen gardens behind the tower, where she helped other servants weed the beds of cabbages, carrots, kale, and onions growing there. Hemmed in on three sides by the inner palisade and the tower on the other, the gardens were sheltered from the prevailing winds.

It was a cool, gusty afternoon and feathery clouds chased each other across the sky as Aelfwyn worked. She listened to the gossiping of the servants around her and slowly relaxed.

She had been so excited to travel north to Bebbanburg. Unlike Aethelhild, she had seen her new life as an opportunity—a chance for some freedom. But things were not working out quite as she had planned. She had not realized her mistress intended to refuse her new husband or that Ecgfrith would unnerve her so. She had always thought of Ealdwulf, King of the East Angles, as a coarse, rough man—but she realized now that Ealdwulf was straightforward and good-hearted in comparison to Ecgfrith. She had never seen him take pleasure in humiliating his women-folk like the King of Northumbria did.

Once the weeding was done, Aelfwyn reluctantly returned indoors, where she passed the afternoon sewing and spinning at her mistress's side. Aethelhild was withdrawn today, and the two women barely spoke as they worked.

The anxiety that had subsided slightly while Aelfwyn worked indoors returned, causing her stomach to cramp.

Does she blame me?

She longed to confront Aethelhild about it but lacked the courage. The look of anger on her mistress's face that morning warned her of bringing up the subject of the king's behavior.

A rosy dusk settled over Bebbanburg, promising better weather for the following day. The evenings were longer here in the north, the twilight stretching out for an eternity before darkness settled over the land.

Aelfwyn usually enjoyed the long evenings, but today she longed to retire to the privacy of her alcove, where she could be alone with her thoughts.

After a light supper of braised onions, cheese, and bread, Ecgfrith settled down to a game of Cyningtaefl—King's Table—with the bishop. Engrossed in moving the carved stone pieces across the wooden board, the king barely acknowledged the queen as she rose from his side. Aethelhild bid them all good night and made her way back to her quarters without a glance in Aelfwyn's direction. Often after supper, once Aelfwyn had finished helping the slaves and servants clean up, the two women would sit together by the firepit for a while with a cup of warm milk. Tonight it appeared the queen did not wish for company.

Blinking back tears, Aelfwyn stared down at the tabletop she was wiping down.

Tomorrow I will speak with Aethelhild, she promised herself. She could not bear to let Ecgfrith destroy their friendship.

The rain had rolled off to the south but it was a windy night. Aelfwyn retired to her alcove early, listening to the wind roaring and gusting around the tower, pummeling its walls with mighty fists. She loved this time of day, especially if the weather was bad outside. A faint glow from the fires filtered through the hanging that divided her alcove from the rest of the hall, illuminating her small, private space.

Although the alcove was cramped with a low ceiling that made it impossible to stand up without bashing one's head, it was a cozy, warm spot. She had placed her furs against the far wall, with her clothing neatly folded opposite. She also had a tiny wooden trestle table where she had put a jug of water and a cup; and a dish of drying lavender, which scented the air.

Aelfwyn lay awake for a while, mulling over the day's events and over what she would say to her mistress the following day. Evenings were the only time she had the luxury of losing herself in her own thoughts.

Beyond her alcove, the hearths slowly burned down to embers, and slaves extinguished all but a couple of cressets near the doors leading out to the privies. The rumble of conversation died away as the residents of the hall retired to their alcoves or stretched out on their cloaks upon the rush-strewn floor.

Aelfwyn eventually dozed off. She was dreaming of home—of the sun gleaming off the golden thatched roof of Rendlaesham's Great Hall as she wandered home from market—when a hand clamped over her mouth.

The dream disintegrated, scattering like a pile of autumn leaves. Aelfwyn's eyes snapped open, and she found herself staring up into the king's face.

Ecgfrith smiled down at her, his hazel eyes dark with desire. He lowered his body against hers, pressing Aelfwyn into the furs.

Then he raised his free hand and placed a finger to his lips, warning her to keep silent. "It's just you and me now, fair Aelfwyn," he whispered.

Chapter Six

Innocence Lost

ECGFRITH LEFT AELFWYN'S alcove shortly before dawn.

She lay still as he slipped from the furs. He fastened his breeches and crawled out of the alcove, the hanging falling softly behind him. Scarcely breathing, Aelfwyn listened to the padding of his bare feet as he returned to his quarters next door. Around them, the Great Hall slumbered—oblivious to what had transpired just feet away overnight.

Not that any of them could have done anything to prevent it—even if they had cared. Ecgfrith was the king, and his word was law.

When Aelfwyn was sure the king had indeed returned to his quarters, she finally stirred. She gingerly sat up, wincing at the burning between her thighs, and reached for her clothing. She had worn a light shift to bed, as she usually did in case she had to venture outdoors to use the privy, but Ecgfrith had ripped it off her.

Shivering, Aelfwyn fumbled in the darkness before locating a linen under-tunic and a woolen over-dress. She pulled them on; her breathing coming in short, ragged bursts. Then she pulled on her rabbit-skin boots and the fur cloak her father had gifted her.

Finally dressed, Aelfwyn crawled to the edge of her alcove. She slipped out onto the narrow platform that ran around the edge of the hall. A carpet of slumbering bodies stretched across the floor—it was still early, dawn had not yet broken.

Aelfwyn skirted the perimeter of the space, past the guttering cressets at the entrance, and into the entranceway with corridors leading off it to the storerooms. She did not tarry here either; instead she made her way outside into the stable yard beyond.

Every step was agony. It hurt to move, to breathe—to think. She felt as if she was somehow outside her body, looking down on the small, hunched, cloaked figure that hobbled across the shadowed yard.

The sky was beginning to lighten in the east. A warm wind tore at her cloak, and she pulled up her hood to shield herself from it. The high gate was closed, but one of the warriors guarding let her through when she mumbled an excuse about needing to visit a healer.

Only she no such intention.

Free of the inner palisade, she walked, wincing with every step, down the King's Way toward the low gate. She knew the gate would not open before dawn but she wanted to be there when it did. The wind pushed against her, whipping tendrils of hair in her face. Her braids had come loose during the night, and her hair was in disarray underneath her hood.

Before the gates a crowd of folk had gathered: merchants and farmers keen to be off at first light. Aelfwyn joined them, standing on the edge of the group. A few curious looks flicked her way but she ignored them; instead keeping her gaze fixed upon the roughly cobbled ground beneath her feet. Let them stare—she cared not.

Eventually the gates creaked open. The jostling crowd poured through. Aelfwyn followed them down the pebbly causeway to the road below. At the bottom, instead of following the others, she veered east onto the reed-covered dunes. The sun was rising over the sea, a glowing coal that turned the indigo sky deep blue.

Aelfwyn slid and stumbled down the dunes, whimpering under her breath as she moved, to the stretch of sandy beach at the bottom. The tide was high, and the wind had whipped the North Sea into a fury.

Huge waves crashed upon the shore, creating a briny spindrift that misted over the beach. Crying softly, Aelfwyn stumbled toward the churning surf. She wished she could erase the previous night from her memory, obliterate it forever.

Ecgfrith had used her repeatedly. He had taken her maidenhead without a shred of gentleness, his hands squeezing and pummeling her body as he ground into her. All the while, he had kept a hand clamped hard over Aelfwyn's mouth, almost suffocating her.

She had thought she was going to die.

Aelfwyn had fought him initially but then terror and pain had taken over, paralyzing her. After that she had lain prone and unmoving—corpse-like—as he had done what he wanted with her for the rest of the night.

Now all she wanted was to remove any trace of him from her body. To wash herself clean, to erase the bruises his rough hands had left. To scrub away the blood that was drying on her thighs and the seed he had spilled inside her.

Aelfwyn choked back a sob. He had broken her from the inside out, shattered her happiness and soiled her innocence. Nothing mattered anymore.

The instinct that had driven her from her bed and out of Bebbanburg ebbed. The numbness seeped away leaving agony in its place. She bent double as it hit her like a punch in the belly.

Regaining control, Aelfwyn eventually straightened up, tears streaming down her face. She unfastened her fur cloak, letting it fall onto the wet sand, and kicked off her boots. Then she stumbled forward into the foaming sea.

Gulls wheeled overhead, their cries mocking her. Her mistress had been right; there was nothing fair about the world of men. She had been a fool to believe so.

The waves crashed against her, nearly knocking Aelfwyn off her feet. Somehow, she managed to stay upright and plow on. The chill of the water made her gasp but did it not lessen her resolve. She had to get free of Ecgfrith, to cleanse herself of him.

The sea would embrace her.

Chapter Seven

The Girl on the Shore

DEORWINE STRUGGLED TO keep pace with his friend's long stride, his cheeks pink from the wind that buffeted the island. "We should go back, Leo. We'll be late for None."

Leofric cast him an irritated look. "We're not far away from the monastery. We'll hear the bell ring for prayers."

"But if you're late again—"

"For the love of Christ, Deorwine will you stop nagging."

Deorwine's face hardened. "If the prior hears you speaking like that, he'll wash your mouth out with lye."

The two young men walked along the southern edge of the island, past Pilgrims' Way—the tidal pathway that linked it with the mainland. It was mid-afternoon, and the tide was rising fast. Leofric looked out across the swirling water and marveled at how just how quickly the tide came in here. When they had emerged from the monastery a short while earlier, there had been nothing but an expanse of glittering sand and mud.

When Leofric made his escape from this place, he would have to time it carefully.

Even the threat of death at the hands of Godwine of Eoforwic was not enough to keep him on Lindisfarena. Leofric would leave here and travel far away to a place the ealdorman would never find him. If he got desperate, he could always venture up into the wilds of Pictland or to the Kingdom of the Franks across the sea, south of Britannia.

Wherever he ultimately went, one thing was certain: his days upon this foul rock were numbered.

Leofric planned to take a walk along this path often, at different times of day, so that he could track the ebb and flow of the tides. It appeared the mornings and evenings were the safest times to cross to the mainland, although he needed to watch the tides for another couple of days to be sure.

Of course he had not shared his plans with Deorwine—and nor would he. They had become as close as brothers of late, but he knew his friend would try to stop him, or would go to the prior.

Leofric took in his surroundings: the rough track, worn smooth by monks' feet; and the windswept hill studded with a few stunted trees that rose to his right, blocking his view of the sea to the north. Then his gaze shifted south out across the water to the outline of the great rock of Bebbanburg in the distance. He could see the palisades outlined against the pale sky, smoke drifting up from the roof of the Great Tower rising above it. The fortress fascinated Leofric; he wondered what it was like up close.

Deorwine suddenly stopped, catching hold of Leofric's sleeve. "There's something up ahead—look!"

Leofric reluctantly turned away from Bebbanburg and looked north, up the shore to where Deorwine was pointing. His friend was right, it was still some way off and at first looked like a rumpled pile of sacking laying upon the smooth sand. However, as he stared at it, Leofric realized that it was not sacking at all.

It looks like ... a body.

Without uttering a word, he set off at a run down the narrow track with Deorwine close at his heels. The nearer he got, the surer he became that a corpse had washed up on the beach. He saw a glimmer of pale blonde hair. The figure was small and laying face down on the sand. At first he thought it was a child, but as he drew closer he changed his mind. The figure, although small, had too many curves to be that of a child.

Behind him, he heard Deorwine mutter a prayer, for he too had realized what had washed up on the shore: a young woman.

Leofric reached the prone figure and knelt at her side. The girl lay above the rising water, and Leofric wondered if she had been all morning, since the last high tide. She wore a sodden woolen dress, which had tangled around her slim legs, and her feet were bare. Her hair, the color of sea-foam, was plastered against her skull.

Deorwine crouched next to Leofric, his sensitive face creased in concern. "Is she dead?"

"I don't know—help me roll her over."

Together, they shifted the girl over onto her back. Her eyes were closed, and her skin chalk-white. For a moment Leofric feared the worst. Then he leaned over her, placing his cheek just above her nose and slightly parted lips—and felt her breath feather against his skin.

"She's alive!"

Deorwine gasped. "She is?"

"Aye," Leofric murmured, "although she won't keep breathing for much longer if we don't get her inside and warm. Help me carry her."

Deorwine rose to his feet, his expression perturbed. "Shouldn't we go and get help instead. We shouldn't really touch a woman ... we're monks."

"Not yet, we're not," Leofric reminded him, "and the prior won't think highly of a postulant who lets a woman die on the shore because he was loath to touch her."

That settled it. Deorwine lived in fear of disappointing Father Cuthbert. Reluctantly Deorwine stepped forward and took hold of the girl by the calves, while Leofric lifted her by her shoulders. Together, they turned and started back along the path toward the monastery.

Although she was small, the girl was a dead weight in their arms, and both men were out of breath by the time they reached the final incline to the complex. As they struggled up the hill, the bell for None—afternoon prayers—sounded; a hollow clanging that echoed across the island.

"We'll be late!" Deorwine sounded panicked and for a moment, Leofric thought his friend was going to drop the girl and flee; such was his terror of tardiness. However, Deorwine merely hurried his pace, jogging up the last stretch to the first of the buildings.

"Where should we put the girl?" Deorwine panted. "Should we take her straight to Cuthbert?"

"Not yet," Leofric replied. "One of the store huts isn't being used at the moment—we'll put her in there."

"But—"

"Don't argue with me, you'll only make us later."

They carried the girl into the store hut, a small, ramshackle building on the edge of the complex. The air smelled of barley and onions, the last things to be stored in here. Leofric laid the girl down on some sacking. There was no time for anything else at present. Still, he hesitated—Leofric did not like to leave her here alone when she was clearly in need of help.

Despite his concern, Leofric found himself silently admiring her. The girl was lovely. She had a sweet, heart-shaped face; full and beautifully molded lips—and although he could not see her eyes, her dark blonde eyelashes lay against her smooth skin like butterfly wings. His gaze traveled down her body then, appreciating the lush swell of her breasts, the dip of her waist, and curve of her hips—made evident due to the wet wool of her clothing that clung to her like a second skin.

Nothing the direction of Leofric's gaze, Deorwine scowled at him. He shoved Leofric toward the door. "Enough. We'd better get to prayers."

They hurried across the deserted yard toward the church; all the other monks were already inside and the low chant of male voices reached them as they neared the entrance. They were just about to go in when Leofric pulled Deorwine up short.

"Don't say anything to Cuthbert for now," Leofric warned his friend.

Deorwine's eyes grew huge. "We can't hide this from him!"

Leofric set his jaw stubbornly and pinned Deorwine with a hard stare. "Yes we can. Best not to bother the prior. Don't worry—I'll take full responsibility for it."

Deorwine stared at him a moment before reluctantly nodding. "I'll do what you say for now—but I think you're being a fool."

Leofric grinned at him. "That's never stopped me before."

"Late again?" The disappointment in the prior's voice made Leofric cringe inside.

He and Deorwine stood before Cuthbert in the empty church. The None prayers had ended and the other monks had returned to their chores.

Cuthbert's gaze shifted to Deorwine and his pursed mouth puckered further. "Only this time you are not alone."

"It's not Brother Deorwine's fault," Leofric interjected. "I insisted we take a walk along the shore after our chores. He didn't want to go far but I told him we could easily get back to the church for prayers ... I was wrong."

Cuthbert's gaze shifted to Leofric, his expression hardening. "At least you no longer bother with insincere apologies."

Next to Leofric, Deorwine blanched at the prior's censure. "I ... I am sorry—"

"Quiet." The force of Cuthbert's command choked off whatever Deorwine was about to say next. "You are too easily led, Brother Deorwine. You must not let Leofric tempt you from the path of piety, diligence, and obedience."

Deorwine bowed his head in wordless apology while Leofric silently bristled at these words. *Christ, the prior can be a sanctimonious prick.*

As if reading his mind, Cuthbert's gaze snapped back to him, his face suddenly hawkish.

"Tomorrow, you will both spend all morning and all afternoon in silent prayer at my side."

Leofric nodded although he was silently fuming at the command. "Yes, Father."

Outside, Leofric stalked across the yard, ignoring the stare of one of the monks who was scattering grains for fowl. The frequency with which Leofric got into trouble provided the only excitement to the monastery's endless routine. He had begun to realize that many of the younger monks were in awe of him—something Leofric found disconcerting. He had never attracted so much attention in his life.

"We should have told the prior about the girl," Deorwine hissed in Leofric's ear as they made their way toward the store huts. "He'll banish us both if he finds out."

"Of course he won't," Leofric replied, gently elbowing his friend. "You worry too much."

Deorwine's answering frown spoke volumes. Sometimes it was hard to reconcile that they were both the same age—Deorwine often acted like a boring older brother. "And you don't worry nearly enough."

They were now out of earshot of the monks who worked in the monastery's central yard. However, they still needed to be careful for there would be flapping ears—Cuthbert's spies—everywhere.

Leofric stopped and turned to Deorwine, lowering his voice further. "Go to the kitchens and get yourself a cup of broth and piece of bread while I see if I can find some blankets and a dry robe for the girl."

Deorwine blanched. "But it's not yet supper; the brothers on kitchen duty won't give me any food."

Leofric's gaze narrowed. "Tell them the prior asked for it, tell them whatever you must to get the food. She'll die without it."

Not waiting for his friend to make another feeble excuse, Leofric turned on his heel and stalked off to find some blankets.

Chapter Eight

Alive

AELFWYN AWOKE TO the feel of coarse cloth against her skin and the musty smell of grain and onions filling her nostrils. A heartbeat later, she realized that she ached all over and that her temples pounded cruelly.

She groaned, wondering if she was awaking from a fever. For a merciful moment, she did not remember anything—but then it all rushed back.

Ecgfrith on top of her, hurting her, smothering her.

The numbness.

The agony.

Running into the churning sea to escape it.

Her eyes snapped open, and she found herself staring at two young men, roughly her own age. They crouched in front of her, watching her intently. Fear spiraled up from Aelfwyn's gut. Her recent ordeal made being alone with two men feel as if she had awoken into some living nightmare.

She was just about to let out an unearthly scream when she noticed that the men wore brown home-spun robes. Both men were handsome, with close-cropped hair—not a style that most men favored—one blond, the other red-haired. Aelfwyn realized they must be monks.

Her terror subsided; surely monks would not harm her?

Aelfwyn's gaze shifted to her surroundings. She lay propped up against a pile of sacking in a dimly lit building that smelled like a store house. A small earthen cresset burned on one of the empty wooden shelves lining the cramped space, casting the store in pale, flickering gold.

The redhead, the most striking of the two monks, favored her with a slightly lopsided smile that made a dimple form on his left cheek. "Good to see you're awake. We were beginning to worry." He handed her a wooden cup. "Here—it's just broth but it will do you good."

Aelfwyn nodded mutely, taking the cup with trembling hands. Her throat was raw from swallowing salt water, and her tongue felt swollen and dry. She sipped gratefully, nearly whimpering in relief as the hot liquid, tasting of onions, carrots and mutton bones, slid down her burning throat.

Wordlessly, the blond monk, his blue eyes wide with what appeared to be a blend of fascination and fear, passed her a hunk of coarse bread upon an oilskin cloth.

"It's not much, I know," commented the redhead with a trace of irony in his voice, "but meals are simple upon Lindisfarena."

Lindisfarena.

The sea had not swallowed her, as she had hoped. Instead it had carried her a short distance and dumped her upon the holy isle just a few leagues north from Bebbanburg.

Fear cramped Aelfwyn's belly, making it difficult to keep down the broth; she was not safe here. Tears pricked her eyelids, making them burn brutally. Despite her best efforts, she was alive—and if she was still alive then Ecgfrith could find her and hurt her again.

"Don't look so worried," the red-haired monk said, his voice soothing as if he was quietening a panicked horse. "You'll come to no harm here."

Aelfwyn nodded and forced back the tears. She glanced down and saw that she wore nothing but a scratchy monk's habit.

Anguish resurfaced. They had undressed her, had seen her naked body.

"My clothes," she gasped.

"They're drying behind you," the blond monk told her, his own voice quivering with nervousness. "We had to get you into dry clothes."

She nodded once more although mortification still burned through her. After what she had just endured, knowing that two more men had looked upon her nakedness when she had not been able to give permission, was too much.

Hot tears slid down her face. She looked down at the rapidly cooling cup of broth she clasped, trying to regain control.

She did not want these two men—two strangers—to see her terror, her grief. She had to keep a rein on it until she was alone.

Leofric watched the girl weep. Her glittering blue-grey eyes were filled with so much pain it was difficult not to reach out and comfort her. Yet he knew she would shrink away from his touch.

When he and Deorwine had peeled those wet clothes off her, he had seen the livid bruises on her body—covering her arms, breasts, and upper-thighs. The look of terror on her face when she had first awoken only confirmed his suspicions.

Leofric exchanged a glance with Deorwine. His friend's mouth had thinned in anger; he too knew. Deorwine was a gentle soul but his blue eyes glittered with fury at what someone had done to this girl.

Leofric glanced back at her. He was no stranger to women; he had bedded his first at thirteen and was currently enduring his longest stretch ever without female company. Yet he had never—and would never—force himself on a woman.

The young woman hunched before him—desperately trying to stem the tears that flowed down her pale cheeks—bore wounds that were far worse than bruises; wounds no one would ever see.

"We need to go," Deorwine reminded him quietly. "There will be trouble if we neglect our chores."

Leofric nodded and reluctantly rose to his feet. Deorwine was right—he had already angered Cuthbert enough for one day.

"You need to stay inside this store room," he told the girl gently. "No one knows you're here, and it's safer for all of us if it stays that way. One of us will be back later, with more food and water."

The young woman looked up, her watery gaze meeting his. "I should go—I don't want to cause trouble." Her voice was husky and trembled slightly.

"You're not," Leofric replied firmly, "and as soon as you're strong enough, we'll find a way to get you off the island and back to the mainland." He smiled down at her and saw the fear and mistrust in her eyes. "I'm Leofric, by the way—and this is Deorwine. What's your name?"

The girl stared back at him, hesitating before she answered him. "Aelfwyn."

"What monster did that to her?"

Leofric glanced across at Deorwine as they made their way to the monastery gardens, a short distance from the store huts. His friend's vehemence surprised him.

"A man who likes to hurt women," he replied.

"But how did she end up here—did he try drowning her? Was raping her not enough?"

Leofric shook his head. "Either that or she threw herself into the sea afterward." The haunted look on the girl's face told him that this was more likely the case.

Deorwine did not reply to that although Leofric could see he was seething. Leofric did not blame him. He too would have liked to geld the man responsible—yet rape was more common than perhaps Deorwine realized. His friend had grown up in a tiny village before coming to live on an island inhabited by peaceful monks. In Eoforwic, Leofric had seen another side to life. Many of the men who frequented the town's meadhall used the whores who plied their trade there badly. He had seen a number of the girls with blackened eyes and split lips—and worse.

Deorwine wished for a world where innocence was protected, where brutality and cruelty did not exist—sadly no such world existed. Leofric was not sure it ever would.

They reached the gardens—a walled area where the monks grew most of their food—and got to work alongside the other brothers who weeded, harvested, and sowed. The wind, which had howled for days, had died down and a breathless calm settled over the world. The smoke, rising from the building where monks prepared supper, drifted straight up into the sky. Around them, the shadows were lengthening as the long twilight began.

Leofric unsheathed the knife he carried at his belt and began cutting out the cabbages, some of which were on the verge of going to seed. All this cabbage would mean days of stinking pottage but like the other monks, Leofric knew that even overcooked cabbage stew was better than an empty stomach. Lindisfarena brought in very little from the mainland as Cuthbert wished for the monastery to be as self-sufficient as possible.

A short time later, the bell rang for supper. Leofric resheathed his knife and hoisted the basket of cabbages under his arm. He then followed the stream of hungry monks into the long, low-slung feasting hall attached to the kitchens, where they would eat their final meal of the day. Only the supper was not likely to be a feast—but a watery gruel, hard cheese, and even harder bread.

This evening though Leofric did not dwell on the unappetizing fare he endured daily. Instead he was thinking about how to smuggle more food back to Aelfwyn once supper was over.

Chapter Nine

In Search of Aelfwyn

SUNLIGHT FILTERED INTO the store hut through a crack in the wooden door—alerting Aelfwyn that she had indeed slept through the entire night and most of the morning too. Stretching on her makeshift bed, she glanced over at the wooden crate next to the pile of sacking and saw that one of the monks had left her a cup of milk and a large wedge of griddle bread and cheese.

Her mouth watered at the sight of it—she was ravenous.

She sat up, rubbed sleep out of her eyes, and started on her meal, not pausing until only crumbs remained on the wooden plate. Outside, she heard the scrape and rustle of monks moving around, going about their daily tasks. Although she would heed her saviors' counsel to stay hidden, she longed to venture out into the sunlight and stretch her cramped limbs.

Instead she stood up, wincing at the aches and pains in her body, and peered through a gap in the door planks. It was a calm and sunny day outside. Two monks—although not the two who had saved her—were busy stocking the shelves of the hut opposite: huge wheels of white cheese from the milk of sheep and goats that Aelfwyn guessed must also live on the island.

They finished their task, bolted the door shut, and moved back toward the center of the complex. Aelfwyn watched them go, relieved they had ignored her hiding place. However, she would not be able to remain here much longer; Leofric and Deorwine had been kind but they risked much by hiding her.

At the next low tide I will go.

Aelfwyn left the door and sat back down on her pile of sacking. Leofric had visited her once more last night, to make sure she was well, before leaving her. Although she appreciated his concern, she had been relieved to see him go. Only then did she unleash the grief—the pain—she had been bottling up ever since she had first awoken.

She had curled up on the sacking, stuffed a fist in her mouth in an attempt to stifle the noise, and sobbed until exhaustion swallowed her. She felt drained this morning—and although letting herself go last night had taken the rawness off her grief, it was still there, shadowing every moment.

Reaching behind her, Aelfwyn checked the state of her linen under-tunic and the woolen dress she had worn over it; they were both dry, although a little stiff from the salty seawater.

She shucked off the monk's habit she wore and quickly dressed in her own clothes. Then, for warmth, she pulled the habit over the top of her dress. She had left her fur mantle and boots on the beach; the monks robe would have to take its place, and could offer her some disguise once she reached the mainland.

What then?

Ecgfrith had torn Aelfwyn's old life away from her. She would never return to Bebbanburg, not while he ruled it. Nor could she return home to Rendlaesham. Her parents would be ashamed of her—if they believed her story at all—and were likely to send her right back to Northumbria.

I'll never see Aethelhild again.

Tears smarted Aelfwyn's already red-rimmed and swollen eyes. Ecgfrith had destroyed everything. She loathed him for it but was powerless to take vengeance to make him pay for what he had done.

Once she left Lindisfarena the only option open to her was the one she had once shunned in favor of service to Aethelhild: to take her vows and become a nun. Nunneries and abbeys were not just places where women could worship God in peace, but islands of safety in a brutal world.

The abbey of Streonshalh lay some distance to the south. They had passed it on the journey from Rendlaesham; Aelfwyn reckoned it was at least ten days' journey on foot. She was not sure she was capable of traveling that far—especially on her own. If the king's men did not catch her she would likely die of thirst or hunger first.

Aethelhild had told her that Hilda was a big-hearted woman who protected the nuns in her charge like a she-wolf. Aelfwyn did not dwell on what would happen to her if Hilda did not welcome her at Streonshalh. She felt broken—a husk. Part of her did not care what the future held.

Her only hope was that she would never again set eyes on the King of Northumbria.

Leofric was the first of the order to spot the men crossing to the island from the mainland. They rode on sturdy ponies, two abreast, having waited for the tide to ebb so they could make the journey across the Pilgrims' Way.

He had just finished his silent vigil at the prior's side, and was trying to ease the cramps in his limbs. The bell for the noon meal was just moments from ringing, but to stretch his stiff legs, Leofric had left the monastery and walked down the slope toward the shore.

As soon as he saw the men, Leofric turned and jogged back up the incline to warn his brothers. These were the first visitors to the isle since his arrival here, and even at a distance he could see they were warriors, for their spears bristled like porcupine quills against the sky.

Prior Cuthbert went forth to greet the newcomers, with his flock of monks gathered close behind him. As a postulant, Leofric brought up the rear, next to Deorwine.

"Who are they?" one of the other postulants whispered, peering over the shoulder of the monk in front of him.

"One of them carries a Northumbrian standard," Deorwine whispered back. "They're the king's men."

Leofric watched the newcomers closely. The men reminded him of the swaggering warriors who filled Godwine of Eoforwic's hall: renowned fighters, their arms gleaming with béagas—armrings—and clad in leather, mail and iron. The sort of men he had planned to join the ranks of, before he ruined everything for himself.

Jealousy curdled his stomach at the sight of them. Godwine had ensured that Leofric could never serve one of the lords of the north. Once he left here, he would have to travel far to avoid the ealdorman's wrath.

The band of men rode up the path toward the monastery, leather creaking and bits jangling. They halted a few yards from where Cuthbert stood. One of the warriors, a big man clad in a mail vest, swung down from his horse and crossed to the prior. He then knelt before him and kissed his hand.

"Father, forgive the intrusion on your solitude," he rumbled, his rough voice and appearance at odds with the gentleness of his actions. Leofric raised his eyebrows; this man might have looked like a fierce pagan warrior, but he clearly followed Cuthbert's god.

"There's nothing to be forgiven, Boden," the prior replied with a gentle smile. "Tell me, what brings Ecgfrith's men across the perilous sands?"

The warrior rose to his feet. "We search for a girl—the queen's handmaid. She disappeared from the Great Tower yesterday morning and has not been seen since." The warrior's gaze left Cuthbert's face, traveling over the monks assembled behind him. "She is small and fair with pale blonde hair. Her name is Aelfwyn. Have any of you seen her?"

Leofric's pulse quickened at the warrior's words. He felt Deorwine shift nervously beside him. Although Leofric did not look his way, he bit down on the urge to kick his friend in the shin. He could sense Deorwine's struggle not to answer the king's man.

Keep your mouth shut.

Mercifully, Deorwine did just that. The crowd jostled in front them as the other monks cast looks at each other and shrugged their shoulders. A chorus of 'no' drifted back to the waiting warriors.

"It appears none of us have seen this young woman," Cuthbert said eventually. "Why do you believe she would come here?"

"We found her cloak and boots washed up on the shore in front of Bebbanburg," Boden replied, "and thought she may have tried to cross to the isle."

The prior shook his head, genuine concern darkening his gaze. "If she attempted such a journey on a rising tide she would have been swept out to sea."

"That is also my thought."

Silence stretched between them, before Boden turned and crossed back to his horse.

"If you see the girl—bring her back to Bebbanburg," he said. His voice hardened, as did his gaze. "She might not be of right mind. The king wants her returned safely."

Cuthbert nodded. "You have our word."

Aelfwyn stared up at Leofric and Deorwine, fear coiling hard knots in her belly.

"I knew they'd come," she whispered. "I knew they'd start looking for me."

Leofric knelt down so his gaze was level with hers. His eyes—hazel-green and fringed by auburn lashes—fixed her coolly.

"They said you are handmaid to the queen. Is that so?"

Aelfwyn nodded, her pulse fluttering at the base of her throat.

"They also said you were 'not of your right mind'—what did they mean?"

Terror rose up within Aelfwyn; she felt like a cornered hare with nowhere left to run, nowhere left to hide. "I don't want to talk about it," she gasped. "Don't make me ... I just can't."

"Be gentle, Leofric," Deorwine said, his sensitive face creased with concern. He hunkered down next to Aelfwyn and reached out a hand to comfort her. His gaze widened in alarm when she shrank back from his touch. "I'm sorry," he said quickly, withdrawing his hand. "It's just that we can see you've been through a lot, and we just want to help."

Aelfwyn nodded. She wanted to believe him, but after what Ecgfrith had done, she did not think she would ever trust another man again. "I must go," she finally managed. "I have to leave here ... now."

"Not so hasty," Leofric spoke up, his tone firm. "It's the middle of the day, and the tide is high. You wouldn't get five yards before someone spotted you, and after that you'd have nowhere to run."

Tears blurred Aelfwyn's vision. She scrambled to her feet, heart pounding. "I can't go back there ... I can't."

"Aelfwyn," Leofric's voice, calm and sure, drew her out of her panic. "Look at me."

She did. He was standing close to her and was a lot taller than she was. Aelfwyn had to crane her neck up to meet his eye. He smelled nice, the faintest whiff of lye soap mixed with a spicy masculine smell. It was a comforting scent, and her pulse slowed slightly.

"Don't worry," he said, his mouth curving into that cocky half-smile she had seen the day before. "We'll help you get off this isle. The tide recedes at dusk. Wait till then, and I'll escort you back to the mainland myself."

Chapter Ten

Cuthbert's Orders

"ARE YOU TRYING to play the hero—or are you really this stupid."

Leofric turned, surprised by Deorwine's vehemence. "Neither. I'm just helping her."

"No—you're acting like a fool. How are you going to get Aelfwyn safely to the mainland in darkness, let alone return here without anyone noticing you're gone?"

"Hengist and Eomer sleep like the dead—they won't notice I'm gone," Leofric replied with a grin. "There's a full-moon tonight so we'll be able to see to make the crossing. You can keep a look out and if—"

"There you go again, telling me what to do. You just assume I'm helping you."

They were carrying sacks of turnips toward one of the store houses. The two men spoke in hushed tones, although Deorwine's voice was growing more strident with each passing moment.

Leofric stopped, his grin fading. "You are—we're both in too deep now. You saw how terrified Aelfwyn is of going back. We have to help her."

"But what then? Have you even stopped to think about what happens after you leave her on the shore? She has no food—no one to protect her. How long do you think she'll last before the king's men track her down?"

Leofric frowned. Deorwine had no idea that he was planning to make his escape from the island tonight. Aelfwyn would have protection because he would lead her south. He would leave her at the abbey at Streonshalh before disappearing into the wild. However, if Deorwine got a whiff of his true plans he could ruin everything. "At least she'll have a chance," he replied, setting his jaw. "If we hand her over to Cuthbert, she has none at all."

Deorwine glared at him. Leofric could see that although his friend was still furious with him, Deorwine was going to cooperate.

"I rue the day I met you," Deorwine muttered.

Leofric laughed and slung an arm over Deorwine's shoulder, playfully shoving him forward so he nearly dropped his sack of turnips. "Admit it—life was dull before I arrived."

Deorwine cast him a jaundiced look. "No, it was peaceful."

A glowing, breathless dusk settled over Lindisfarena. It was a sultry evening and cloudless—the perfect weather for what Leofric had planned. He sat in Night Prayer, listening to the steady chanting of the monks around him, and counted the heartbeats until it was over.

He did not care that he was taking a huge risk—the potential rewards more than compensated for it. Actually, he could not believe his stroke of good fortune. Wyrd—fate—was definitely with him today. Escorting Aelfwyn to safety was exactly the excuse he had needed. Deorwine would never have helped him otherwise. Unlike the other two they shared lodgings with, Deorwine was a light sleeper; there was no chance of Leofric sneaking off unnoticed. This way, he had his friend's help; even if Deorwine did not know Leofric would not be returning.

Eventually Night Prayers ended, and Leofric followed the others out into the balmy evening. The sun was just sliding behind the headland to the west, leaving a trail of flame in its wake. Leofric grinned at the sight of it, his belly tightening with excitement.

Good weather tomorrow. Perfect for a journey.

The monks all retired early; life was hard here and none of them stayed up after nightfall, as they would all arise from their pallets at the first blush of dawn. Leofric followed Deorwine, Hengist, and Eomer into their hut. Inside, he stripped off his habit and climbed onto his hard straw pallet. Unlike other evenings, he and Deorwine did not chat in low voices— something they often did until one of the others complained. Instead they lay in silence, waiting for the appointed time.

Leofric lay on his back, listening to the breathing of the men around him. Deorwine's breathing was quiet, measured and watchful—he was still very much awake—but the other two soon fell into a deep slumber. Leofric waited a while longer, scarcely breathing, until Hengist and Eomer were snoring like old dogs.

Only then did he slowly ease himself out of his pallet. Deftly, he wriggled into his habit, before picking up his sandals and creeping from the hut. Outside, the moon was rising, casting a silver veil over the complex and making the thatched roofs appear frosted.

Leofric had just finished lacing his sandals when Deorwine emerged from the hut and carefully pulled the wattle doorway closed. Once he too had put on his sandals, the two made their way toward the outskirts of the monastery.

Both young men were light-footed, moving from shadow to shadow like wraiths. Although Leofric was pleased that the weather was good and that a full moon would light his way, the night's stillness bothered him a little. It was so quiet that even his breathing seemed far too loud in the silence. He kept his mouth shut and breathed through his nose, but he was still aware that every sound he made, every scrape of his sandals against dry earth, seemed magnified.

They reached the store hut where Aelfwyn hid. Deorwine kept watch, while Leofric opened the door and poked his head inside. He could see nothing in the darkness, but he could hear her breathing. "Aelfwyn—it's Leofric. Are you ready?"

"Yes," she whispered.

"Come on." He reached into the darkness. "Take my hand so I don't lose you."

There was a moment's hesitation. Leofric had seen her reaction to Deorwine earlier; he knew that she was loath to touch a man. Still, he did not want to leave her behind as they raced for the shore. Then he felt cool, slender fingers fold around his hand. The sensation of her skin touching his caused a frisson of warmth to slide up his arm. Her touch was gentle yet firm, and he felt a surge of protectiveness. Pushing the sensation aside, for distraction was the last thing he needed at that moment, he led her from the hut.

Deorwine led the way out of the monastery complex, weaving in and out of the scattered buildings, until they reached the slope leading down to the shore. They would leave Deorwine here. Leofric and Aelfwyn would make a break for the silver-hued sand-flats that lay between them and Bebbanburg.

Leofric's pulse started to race. Freedom was so close he could almost taste it—yet this escape was proving almost too easy. The fine hair on the back of his arms prickled in warning. Something was not right, but he had no time to dwell on what exactly disturbed him about the night.

Perhaps the unnatural silence after days of howling wind was getting to him.

Deorwine stopped, allowing them to pass silently by. There would be no time to thank his friend, or properly say goodbye—and for an instant, Leofric was sorry. They had become close, and Deorwine deserved better. Still his friend thought he was coming back so it was best not to make him suspicious.

Adrenalin surged through Leofric, masking his earlier uneasiness. He needed to focus on escaping. He squeezed Aelfwyn's hand gently and tensed, ready to break into a sprint.

"Stop them!"

Cuthbert's voice cut through the still night like a loosed arrow.

Leofric's heart leaped against his breastbone and he nearly stumbled. Any thought of bidding his friend goodbye vanished. He started running, dragging the girl after him.

Dark figures appeared from the edge of the complex, hurtling toward them. Aelfwyn whimpered but managed to keep up with him, her breathing coming in ragged gasps.

Behind them, Deorwine cried out. Leofric's stride faltered once more before he forced himself to focus on the gleaming expanse of wet sand that stretched before them. A few more strides and they would reach it— perhaps then their pursuers would fall back. It was a desperate hope but it was all he had to cling to.

A heartbeat later, someone tackled him from behind.

Aelfwyn screamed, the sound shattering the night's eerie quiet.

Leofric pitched forward onto the hard, stony ground, the air rushing out of his lungs. Aelfwyn's hand ripped from his, and she screamed again.

"Let me go!"

Leofric tried to rise, to help her. Yet there was a man sitting on his back, pinning him to the ground. Rage filled him and he twisted like a serpent, his fist slamming up into his assailant's face. The monk gave a muffled cry and fell off him—but two more took his place. They threw themselves on top of him, pinning him to the ground despite the fact that he bucked and writhed under their grip. He kneed another one in the cods; the monk gave a strangled yell and collapsed onto the ground next to him.

Three more monks piled on top of Leofric, determined to subdue him.

"Brother Leofric—cease this madness!"

Still struggling, Leofric looked up and saw a man's outline looming over him. He recognized the prior's tall, lean silhouette. Despair choked him. Freedom had been so close he had almost tasted it—only to be ripped from his grasp.

The mood inside the church was ominous, the air heavy with repressed anger.

Aelfwyn knelt on the paved floor, in between Leofric and Deorwine, and stared down at her trembling hands. Tears ran silently down her cheeks, but she paid them no mind.

It was over—she was going back to King Ecgfrith.

To her right, Deorwine sported a bloodied lip, his expression panicked. To her left, Leofric glared at the prior, his hazel-green eyes blazing with defiance.

She was grateful that they had tried to help her, but neither of them could do anything more. They had taken a risk on her behalf, and now she had gotten them both in trouble.

Eventually, Prior Cuthbert spoke. "Words cannot express my disappointment in you both."

Aelfwyn heard Deorwine's breathing quicken, whereas Leofric had gone still.

"I did not want to believe it, when one of your brothers came to me this afternoon with news he'd overheard you plotting to spirit away the girl you were hiding under the cover of night." The prior paused here, as if considering his next words carefully. "If the king thinks I lied to his men—that we've been hiding the girl here—he will punish us all."

"Just tell him the truth," Leofric ground out. "Tell him you had nothing to do with it."

Cuthbert glared at Leofric, a muscle ticking in his cheek. "You will learn penitence for your grievous disobedience—in the meantime this young woman cannot stay here."

Aelfwyn looked up, for the first time meeting Prior Cuthbert of Lindisfarena's gaze. He did not have hard face, or unkind eyes. Perhaps, she could convince him to help her.

"Please, Father," she said, her voice trembling. "I didn't mean to trouble you—or your monks. I washed up on the shore and they took care of me. Can I not stay here and serve you?"

The question brought gasps from the group of monks amassed behind them. Some of them started muttering under their breaths, but Cuthbert stilled them with a gesture.

"You cannot stay here, Aelfwyn. I will not risk the king's wrath."

"Then send me to Streonshalh, and I will devote the rest of my life to god."

Cuthbert regarded her, concern in his dark eyes. "You have a gentle soul. A nun's life would indeed suit you—but unfortunately that decision is not mine to make. You are part of the king's house-hold and he wants you back."

"Don't send me back there," Aelfwyn replied, swallowing the sobs that rose up within her. "I can't return to Bebbanburg."

The prior frowned, concern flowering into naked worry. "Why are so you so afraid, child?"

"I don't ..." Aelfwyn began. "I can't ..."

She was desperate to tell the prior the truth, but the words lodged like dry bread in her throat. If she told them the sordid tale, she would shatter into pieces—and what then? Would a room full of men believe the words of a hysterical young woman over those of a king?

Instead she buried her face in her hands and started to cry in earnest.

"Father Cuthbert," Leofric said, his voice edged with anger. "The girl's body is covered with bruises. I'd say she was attacked and raped before she tried to take her life by running into the sea."

Aelfwyn's sobs choked off. Her head snapped up, and she stared at Leofric, shocked that he knew what happened to her. She had no idea her body was livid with bruises. However, when her gaze shifted to the prior, she realized the young monk had committed a grave error.

Cuthbert now looked angry. His finely shaped brows had knitted together, making his long aquiline nose look even beakier. His pursed mouth thinned into a hard line. Around him the other monks had gone silent. Aelfwyn saw the shock and censure on some of their faces.

"You and Deorwine looked upon this girl's naked body?" he asked, his voice flat.

"She was wet and cold, Father." Leofric's tone was unrepentant.

Cuthbert's gaze swung round to Deorwine. "Is this true?"

Deorwine made a choking sound. "We were only trying to help her, Father. We didn't touch her."

"Enough," Cuthbert snapped. "Not another word. Neither of you understand what you're meddling with. This monastery and others like it in this kingdom only exist because the king permits it. This girl is Ecgfrith's property. Your behavior threatens us all."

Aelfwyn saw Deorwine blanch. His slender frame started to tremble, and he bowed his head.

Silence stretched out inside the church. Aelfwyn held her breath, awaiting the axe to fall. Eventually, the prior spoke once more, his voice regaining its gentleness as if he had fought and mastered the anger that had risked consuming him.

"Leofric and Deorwine—you will both escort Aelfwyn to King Ecgfrith at first light. You will go alone, for I want none of your brothers to suffer for your crime. When you go before the king, you will tell him the truth—that you found her, hid her, and lied to his men about her whereabouts." The prior's gaze fixed upon Leofric as he spoke his final words. "Once Ecgfrith has exacted his punishment upon you, return here and receive god's penance."

Chapter Eleven

Deorwine's Ruse

AELFWYN WATCHED THE sky lighten to the east and knew her doom had come.

She stood in the yard at the heart of the monastery while around her monks moved about, their hoods pulled up as if they were all trying to avoid looking at her; faceless ghosts amongst the shadows.

Although it was not cold, Aelfwyn was shivering. Grateful she still wore the monk's robe on top of her woolen dress, she drew it close about her. Nearby, a goat bleated as someone led it out of its enclosure for milking. Aelfwyn inhaled deeply in an attempt to steady her nerves, breathing in the scent of wood-smoke from a nearby hearth. Life went on as usual upon the Isle of Lindisfarena this morning. It was as if last night had never happened.

Yet it was not so for her.

Last night had dashed her hopes, leaving only despair in its place.

Leofric and Deorwine emerged from the church, where the prior had spoken to them in private. Deorwine was ashen and looked close to tears, whereas Leofric's usually sanguine face was serious, his jaw tight.

Despite her fear for her own fate at the hands of Ecgfrith, she was sorry that she would also bring his wrath down upon these two men. They had only tried to help her. She hoped the king would show them mercy.

Aelfwyn shuddered, shoving aside thoughts of Ecgfrith.

The two monks approached her. "Come, Aelfwyn," Leofric said, his voice gruff. "We must go now."

Wordlessly, she followed them out of the complex and down to the shore. It was an irony that they walked the same route they had attempted to flee down in darkness. This time no one tried to stop them, for this time they were not running away but doing the prior's bidding.

They walked in single-file across the sands, with Leofric leading, Aelfwyn behind him, and Deorwine bringing up the rear. The Pilgrim's Way—the route all travelers used to cross from the mainland to Lindisfarena—was the only safe place to cross. Otherwise you risked stepping into soft sand or mud that had sucked many unwary travelers to their deaths.

They had gone a short distance across the wet sand when Aelfwyn spoke. The manner of their departure from the monastery bothered her. "Why has Cuthbert not sent an escort of monks with us?" she asked quietly. "Does he not fear we'll try and flee again?"

Ahead, Leofric gave a bitter laugh. She watched his shoulders tense. "Worry not, he has already dealt with that possibility," he replied. "If Deorwine and I are not back before None, he will send an emissary to the king with the next low tide, with his permission to hunt Deorwine and me down and kill us."

Horrified, Aelfwyn glanced over her shoulder at Deorwine. The young man's gaze was bleak, telling her that his friend was not lying. "But the prior is a man of god," she gasped. "He abhors violence."

Deorwine shook his head, avoiding her eye. "It appears we've stretched his patience too far this time."

"This time?" Leofric gave another humorless chuckle. "Aye, poor Deorwine. His friendship with me has cost him dearly. I have a habit of getting myself into trouble—only I managed to drag him into it this time."

Aelfwyn did not reply, although the situation now made more sense to her. She realized that both young men were still postulants—they were undergoing a trial period before taking their vows. Neither had tonsures, and they wore fawn-colored homespun robes, unlike the other monks whose robes were a deep walnut brown.

"I'm sorry," she said eventually, keeping her gaze upon Leofric's broad shoulders so she would not stare at the bulk of Bebbanburg to the south as they crossed the sand flats. "I've brought trouble upon you."

Deorwine snorted at this. "When Leofric's around, trouble finds you. You're not to blame."

Leofric glanced back then, hurt flashing across his handsome features. He opened his mouth to say something but then thought better of it and turned away once more. Watching him, Aelfwyn wondered at Leofric's decision to become a monk; unlike Deorwine, he seemed wholly unsuited.

They walked the rest of the distance in silence. It was a still, mild morning, and the air was humid and briny. Try as she might, Aelfwyn could not remain focused on Leofric's back. Soon Bebbanburg towered over the surrounding lands like a red stone king of giants, the fort resembling his jagged wooden crown.

The closer they got to the beach, the sicker Aelfwyn felt. Now that she had stopped conversing with the monks, there was nothing to distract her from what lay ahead. She could not bear to meet Aethelhild's eye again, not after what the king had done. She could not stomach the idea of standing before Ecgfrith and pretending as if nothing was wrong, as if he had not taken everything from her.

Nausea rose within Aelfwyn, bile stinging the back of her throat. Her legs started to feel weak and her stomach churned. Images from two nights earlier resurfaced.

His hot breath on her cheek.

His hand pressing down on her mouth, suffocating her.

They reached the edge of the wide stretch of sandy beach. The fortress lay to the south, at least three leagues distant, separated from them by a jutting spit of land edged in silver sand. It was still a way off, but the sight of Bebbanburg brought back every terror Aelfwyn had felt while Ecgfrith trapped her beneath him.

Her stomach convulsed, and she dropped to her knees on the wet sand, throwing up the broth and stale bread she had consumed before departing Lindisfarena. She was aware of the monks stopping nearby, their gazes riveted upon her—but she was past caring. Sending her back to Bebbanburg would be the end of her—they had to know the truth before they delivered her to the Ecgfrith.

"I can't ..." she gasped. "I can't go back there. Not to him."

She was aware of her companions approaching and hunkering down next to her.

"Who, Aelfwyn? Who are you so afraid of?"

She looked up into Leofric's concerned eyes. She had to tell him; she had to let this out before it was too late.

"You were right," she choked the words out. "Someone raped me ..." She paused to gather her courage. "It was Ecgfrith."

Silence met her words. For a few horrible moments, Aelfwyn thought her fears were about to be realized—that despite their earlier kindness these two monks would turn on her, blame her, or call her a liar.

Yet Leofric's face did not show any such disdain. He stared at her, a muscle in his jaw feathering.

"The *king* raped you?" he finally ground out.

She nodded. "Queen Aethelhild would not lie with him. He was angry." The words came out in breathless gasps. "She and I are close—I think he wanted to punish her."

Behind her, Deorwine muttered an oath under his breath.

Aelfwyn's belly contracted once more but this time she managed not to be sick. "It was just one night," she told them as she got to her feet, wretched and trembling. "But it was only the beginning. If you take me back to him, it will never stop."

Leofric continued to watch her, his lean frame rigid. He glanced toward the towering bulk of Bebbanburg, before he glanced over Aelfwyn's head at Deorwine.

"I know what you're thinking," Deorwine replied, "and you're right—we cannot deliver Aelfwyn to him."

Aelfwyn straightened up, shocked. She glanced at Deorwine's serious, determined face and then looked at Leofric's angry one.

"They'll track us down and kill us," Leofric reminded him. "I might deserve that, but you don't. I've ruined things as it is for you."

Deorwine smiled, his face suffusing with warmth. "You haven't—for I'm not going with you."

Leofric's gaze narrowed. "But Cuthbert will punish you for letting us go."

"Not if he thinks you didn't give me a say in the matter." Deorwine's smile faded. "Take Aelfwyn south—to Streonshalh. The nuns will take good care of her there."

Aelfwyn noticed that Leofric still did not look convinced. Meanwhile, her heart was starting to pound against her ribs. Fate had snatched freedom from her grasp—was it now handing it back to her?

"Cuthbert won't believe you," Leofric pointed out. "He'll know you let us go."

"Then we need to find a way of convincing him." Deorwine walked up to Leofric so they stood only a couple of feet apart. "Roughen me up a bit; blacken my eye and give me a split lip. Make it look like we both put up a good fight."

Leofric stared at him a moment before he threw back his head and laughed. "I'm going to miss you."

Deorwine grinned back. "And I'll be pleased to be rid of you—spoiled, selfish turd. Now give me a beating!"

Leofric snorted. "You'll have to insult me better than that, if you want me to lash out in anger."

Aelfwyn stepped toward them, alarmed. "Is this really necessary?"

Leofric nodded, his gaze still on the blond monk before him. "He's right. If the prior suspects Deorwine let us go, he'll cast him out of the order."

Aelfwyn pulled her robes close about her and backed off, her earlier nausea resurfacing. She hated violence. It was selfish to involve these two brave men in her dilemma, especially after all they had done for her.

I should go now while they're distracted.

Aelfwyn took another few steps backward and stopped.

Go where?

Aelfwyn's shoulders slumped as the truth hit her. She needed Leofric's help, or she would not get far. She would not survive a day on her own.

"Come on then," Leofric said with a sigh. "You'll make this easier though, if you throw the first punch."

Deorwine blanched. "I can't hit you."

"Holy Mary's tits, Deorwine. Stop being such a maid!"

Deorwine's mouth compressed. "Don't blaspheme—you know I hate it."

Leofric gave him a wolfish smile. "By Christ's cods."

"Stop it!"

"By Saint Joseph's stinking arsehole."

Deorwine lashed out with his left fist, landing a punch in Leofric's stomach, before striking him in the mouth with his right.

Leofric staggered back, blood gushing from his lip. He glared at Deorwine, the look of shock on his face almost comical. Aelfwyn slammed a hand over her mouth to stop herself from breaking into hysterical laughter; the world had gone mad. It was like watching a show put on by mummers for her benefit.

Leofric gave a roar and charged at Deorwine.

Aelfwyn turned away. She wanted no part in the ridiculous game these two were playing. She cringed at the sound of fists pounding against flesh and covered her ears with her hands to block it out.

When she turned back, Leofric was climbing off Deorwine. His friend spat out a gob of blood on the sand and took the helping hand Leofric offered him. Deorwine got to his feet, clutching his left eye. Both men had split lips and Deorwine's nose was bleeding.

"Good," he mumbled, before attempting a smile and wincing. "I should have a black eye by the time I get back to the isle."

Aelfwyn approached him, horrified at the sight of his bloodied swollen face. She cast Leofric an angry look before focusing once more on Deorwine. "Are you hurt?"

He gave her a bloody half-smile. "Nothing that time won't fix, Aelfwyn." He then turned back to Leofric. "The tide's coming in now, so I won't go back to Lindisfarena until it ebbs. That will give you time to gain a head start on the king's men. They won't be able to start hunting you until this afternoon."

Leofric nodded. "We'll make sure we're as far south as possible by then." He stepped forward and clasped Deorwine against him in a bear hug. "I'll never forget this. You're a true friend."

Deorwine's eyes were shining as he pulled away. "And you're a boil on my arse—but I'll miss you all the same."

Chapter Twelve

Fleeing South

THEY DID AS Deorwine bid, leaving him on the wide swath of sand before cutting west through the rush-clad dunes. Aelfwyn glanced once more back at him, at the brave young monk who was taking a terrible risk on her behalf. Her heart leaped in her throat as she saw him standing there, watching them flee.

He saw her look back and raised a hand in a silent farewell, his battered face solemn.

Then the dunes swallowed Leofric and Aelfwyn, and Deorwine was lost from sight.

She and her companion did not speak for a while. They were both lost in their own thoughts, both focused on getting as far as possible from Bebbanburg before news of their escape had Ecgfrith sending men after them.

It was a clear, bright morning with a light breeze trailing in from the sea. A landscape of tilled fields and meadows where sheep and goats grazed stretched out around them. It was unnervingly open terrain, for they had not yet reached the woodlands that hugged the coastline further south. Aelfwyn felt exposed as she hurried after Leofric, struggling to keep up with his long stride. Initially, he had set off at a brisk walk, but now he jogged.

Aelfwyn ran close behind him. She had pulled up the hood of her robe to hide her identity, concerned that one of the cottars working the fields around them might spot her. After a while she started to sweat copiously under it, for she wore two layers of clothing beneath the coarse habit. On her feet, she wore rope sandals, which Cuthbert had gifted to her before her journey across the tidal flats. The rope rubbed her feet, and she knew they would be raw by nightfall. Nevertheless, it was preferable to running barefoot.

The sun rose high into the sky, beating down on their backs. Leofric's pale, lightly freckled skin shone with sweat but he breathed easily, making much lighter work of the journey than Aelfwyn.

Shortly after midday, she could go no farther. Her legs felt as if they were filled with rocks, her feet were burning from where the sandals cut into them, and her breathing came in ragged gasps.

Crumpling to the grassy ground, she called out to Leofric. "Please ... I need to rest. I can't go on."

Leofric turned to her, his face glowing from exertion. He nodded, drawing his forearm across his brow, and approached her. He lowered himself to the ground next to Aelfwyn, his gaze meeting hers. "We can't stay here for long. Bebbanburg is still too close. We need to make sure we're well into the woods before dark."

Aelfwyn nodded back. She was exhausted but knew her journey had just begun. She was not as strong or as fit as Leofric, and could not run as far, yet she did not want to slow him down. He and Deorwine had given her back her freedom; she would not waste this chance. Not when every footstep took her farther from Ecgfrith.

Leofric shared some water from a leather skin attached to his belt but, true to his word, he allowed them only a short rest before he rose to his feet. He favored her with one of his charming smiles; a grin she wagered had won over many a maid. "Come—no time for dozing in the sun."

He reached down and helped Aelfwyn up. The hand that clasped hers was warm and strong, as it had been when he had led her down the shore in darkness the night before. Initially she had been loath to touch him, to touch any man, but Leofric had won her trust. She instinctively knew he would not harm her. Unlike Deorwine, he came across as irreverent and cocky—yet she sensed the goodness beneath the brash shield he presented to the world. Now, as then, his touch gave her strength.

They set off once more, Leofric jogging ahead, his gaze scanning the surrounding fields as he went, with Aelfwyn panting a few yards behind. Ripe barley grew here, the golden stalks waving in the gentle breeze. There were no folk about; all had retired indoors for their noon meal. Although it was the hottest time of day—on what felt like the hottest day this summer— it was a good time to travel.

On and on they ran, following a curved path, west and then south, giving Bebbanburg a wide berth. Yet the fortress was always there, even when it was reduced to a red speck on the horizon. Only when the shadows started to lengthen and they entered the woodland at last did they finally lose sight of it.

Inside the woods they slowed to a walk. Cool air feathered against Aelfwyn's heated skin and the rich smell of damp earth and lush foliage filled her nostrils. She was so hot she felt like a pulsing, glowing coal—as if she could have lit a hearth with her cheek. The blood roared in her ears; her heart thundered against her ribs as if it was trying to break free from her chest.

She trailed behind Leofric, noting that finally he too looked exhausted. Sweat had soaked through his habit, plastering it to his back, and darkened his short hair to auburn. His breathing now came deep and even.

"Can we … stop now?" Aelfwyn finally asked. She had not spoken in a long while, not since they had stopped for a brief rest mid-afternoon and Leofric had refilled his water bladder from a brook. However, she was not sure how much longer she could go on. She felt close to collapse.

Leofric turned toward her, his gaze apologetic. "Not yet. They'll be hunting us now. We will take a short break at dusk, and then we'll have to press on."

Aelfwyn stared at him, stricken. The news almost brought tears of despair to her eyes. Seeing her expression, he gave her an exhausted smile. "When we're far from here, you can rest for days—but until then it's foolish to linger. The king wants you back … he will send everything he has after us."

Cold fear crept through Aelfwyn, making her forget about her rubbed-raw feet, aching limbs, and burning lungs.

Unwittingly Leofric had reminded her of the things Ecgfrith had said to her during that long night. He had told Aelfwyn of the plans he had for her. Whispering endearments in her ear as he had hurt her, Ecgfrith had said she was wasted as a handmaid—that Aethelhild did not deserve her. She belonged to him.

"Aelfwyn … are you well?" Leofric had noticed her distress. He stepped toward her, brow furrowed. "What is it?"

She sank to her knees, her breathing coming in short, painful gulps. "Don't let them take me back to him," she whispered. "Please kill me before that happens."

He knelt before her and hooked a finger under her chin, lifting her face so that their gazes met. They were so close that Aelfwyn could see the flecks of green and hazel in his irises.

"You're not going back there," he promised her. "Not while I draw breath. We're going to outrun them. We're going to leave all of this behind—but to do that we need to keep moving. Find your courage, Aelfwyn because you're going to need it. Find your strength—because that's the only way out of this." He paused here, his mouth quirking slightly. "Can you do that?"

Wordlessly, she nodded.

A moment later she was on her feet, her hand clutched tightly in his, and they were running.

Aelfwyn was sleeping deeply when Leofric knelt next to her. He looked down at her face and paused. He was loath to touch her as she looked so serene; her rosebud lips slightly parted, her long lashes resting against her milky skin. She was lovely … fascinating.

He had never met a woman like Aelfwyn; even wounded and scared she had a rare courage, a pureness of spirit. Her goodness made him feel seriously lacking in comparison. Deorwine was truly her savior; his friend had a stout heart and a good character. Yet she trusted Leofric, had thrown herself at his mercy and looked to him to protect her. If Aelfwyn knew who he truly was, of the life he had wasted thus far, she would surely despise him.

The opinion of others had always mattered little to Leofric—but the thought that Aelfwyn might judge him rankled. He was surprised to realize he wanted Aelfwyn to respect him. He could not let her down.

The baying hounds in the distance jerked him back to the present. They were still a way off but nearing fast. Their howling had awoken him from a fitful doze just moments earlier and had brought him to Aelfwyn's side.

Gently, he shook her awake. "Come, Aelfwyn," he whispered. "We must go now."

Her eyelids fluttered. She opened her eyes, her blue-grey gaze focusing on him. She gave him a slow, sleepy smile—one which caused an unexpected blade of lust to arrow through him—and stretched. "Is it morning already?"

He shook his head, trying to ignore the hardening of his cock. There was something unconsciously sensual about that smile, but this was the last thing he needed.

Not now.

"Get up," he said, his tone sharper than he had intended. "Dogs hunt us."

Her eyes widened, the smile faded, and she scrambled up, brushing leaves and undergrowth off her disheveled robes.

There would be no more resting.

Leofric led the way south through the trees. A full moon lit their way, casting a hoary light over the woodland. Behind them, the barking and yelping grew louder.

Panic surged through Leofric. Now he realized how the deer and boar he had spent his life hunting felt. The terror of knowing men and hounds were out for your blood was enough to make a man lose his wits.

He glanced over his shoulder at Aelfwyn. She was struggling to keep up with him, her face ashen. He slowed his pace and reached out for her hand, trapping it inside his.

"Run, Aelfwyn," he commanded. "Run like the wind."

They sprinted through the woods, the trees passing in a blur, the night air cool on their faces. Behind them, the sounds of pursuit grew ever louder: the howling of the dogs, the tattoo of hooves on the forest floor, and the shouts of men excited now their dogs were hot on the scent of their prey.

Leofric crashed through the forest, ignoring the bramble and blackthorn that tore at his clothing and skin. Ahead the trees drew back, and he spied the glitter of moonlight on water.

A river.

Hope soared in his breast. Had it merely been a trickling stream, the waterway would have done them no good, but a river—and what looked to be a swiftly flowing one—was a different matter entirely.

He hoped Aelfwyn could swim.

There was no time to speak, no time to tell her what he was planning to do. Behind them, he heard the crash of horses and dogs tearing through the undergrowth. If they continued running, their pursuers would soon overtake them.

It was their only escape route.

Leofric grasped Aelfwyn's hand tighter still. He knew he was probably hurting her, but he could not afford to lose her now. Together, they hurtled down the mossy bank and into the swirling current. He heard Aelfwyn gasp at the chill but she uttered no complaint, even when he hauled her after him into deeper water.

A moment later the current lifted them off their feet and carried them away. Aelfwyn tensed and began to flounder in the water. "I can't swim!"

"Relax," Leofric soothed her. "Just keep hold of me."

The baying of dogs and shouts of warriors echoed across the river, and Leofric caught sight of a flurry of movement in the woods behind them as the first of their pursuers broke through the undergrowth.

Their fate was in the hands of the river now.

Leofric lay on his back, pulling Aelfwyn tight against him, and let the swift current carry them away into the night.

Chapter Thirteen

The Warrior in the Woods

AELFWYN STARED UP at the star-sprinkled night sky and at the silver disc of the moon. She tried to ignore the chill of the water, to relax against Leofric's body as he had ordered, but it was nearly impossible.

Her heart still thrummed in her chest, terror constricted her throat. Her lungs burned from exertion, and she felt weak with shock at how close they had come to capture—how close they *still* were to being caught.

The angry shouts of their pursuers and the excited caterwauling of the hounds were fading into the distance. The river had narrowed slightly since they had thrown themselves at its mercy, and was now flowing even swifter than before. Its current tossed them around like logs. Aelfwyn prayed there were not any rocks hidden beneath the water, which would slice them to ribbons.

Terrified, she clung to Leofric—the only thing between her and drowning. She would sink like a sack of peat if he let go of her.

"Relax," he called to her over the roar of the river. "You'll float easier if you don't fight the water."

Aelfwyn made a choking sound and tried to obey him. He made it sound simple but it was near to impossible to relax her body when terror pumped through her. Instead she concentrated on her breathing which was coming in short, panicked puffs. She tried to slow and deepen it.

She kept her gaze fixed upon the dark curtain of night stretching above her, at the moon's friendly face. Leofric appeared to have handed his fate over to the river; she tried to do the same.

For a while the current carried them southeast, toward the coast. Eventually the river flowed into a wider, tidal watercourse—one that appeared to flow out into an estuary. The moon was sinking low in the sky when Leofric carried them to shore. He swam on his back, propelling himself toward the muddy, reed-covered bank on the southern shore with lazy strokes of his right arm, while with his left he kept Aelfwyn pinned against his chest.

Aelfwyn crawled up onto the bank, collapsing at the top. Her limbs felt boneless and weak, and she was shivering. She heard an odd rattling noise and realized that it was her teeth chattering.

Leofric helped Aelfwyn to her feet, his eyes glowing in the moonlight. "Come on," he panted. "We've got a lead on them for now, we don't want to waste it."

Aelfwyn nodded, trying to wring water out of her sodden robes. She had not thought it was possible to feel so miserable, so uncomfortable—so utterly exhausted. There was no point in complaining though. She knew what had to be done, even if she was starting to doubt she would last the rest of the night.

Leofric took hold of her hand and led the way south, away from the river. She stumbled after him. Her body felt as if it no longer belonged to her; she kept going out of sheer force of will alone.

Her companion spoke little during their flight south. Like her, Leofric fought exhaustion; his breathing gradually grew more ragged, his expression ever more grim.

By the time the first glow of dawn spilled across the sky to the east, both of them were stumbling as if drunk. They reached a copse of trees—ash and oaks—carpeting a shallow valley, where Leofric finally stopped. Under the sheltering boughs of an old oak, he let go of Aelfwyn's hand and sank to the ground. The moment he let go of her, Aelfwyn's remaining strength left her; it was as if he had been keeping her going, and now he had severed the physical connection exhaustion barreled into her like a charging boar.

Aelfwyn's legs gave way under her, and she crumpled. Lying on her back, she watched dawn stretch its rosy fingers across the sky, which was turning from a deep indigo to a rich blue. Her pulse thudded in her chest, her blood roared in her ears, and she felt sick from exhaustion.

Eventually, she was able to glance right at where Leofric lay, spread-eagled like her, staring up at the lightening sky. His chest was heaving, his habit clinging to his lean, muscular frame. She could feel the heat emanating off him.

Feeling Aelfwyn's gaze upon him, Leofric glanced across at her. He gave her an exhausted smile. "You did well," he panted.

"I'm not sure how I managed it," she admitted, her own voice coming in short gasps, "although I'm not certain I can get up again."

"You will," Leofric replied before pushing himself upright with a groan. "We have to keep moving."

Aelfwyn rolled onto her belly, breathing in the scent of damp earth and crushed grass as she did so. "I'm sorry, Leofric," she murmured. "You're a hunted man because of me."

Her companion gave a soft laugh, although the edge of bitterness to it made Aelfwyn glance up in surprise. Leofric was looking away from her; she saw tension in his shoulders.

Aelfwyn struggled upright, feeling wretched. "Are you angry with me?"

He glanced her way, his gaze widening. "No—of course not." He paused then, breaking eye contact with her once more. "Don't blame yourself for this. I knew what I was doing when I chose to help you escape. The price on my head now has nothing to do with you."

Aelfwyn frowned, confused. "I don't understand."

Leofric shook his head. "It's a tale for another time." He got to his feet and dusted himself off. "I'll tell it to you when we don't have the king's men breathing down our necks; when we're dry, warm and safe."

He reached down and pulled her up, smiling at her. Despite Aelfwyn's exhaustion, despite the trauma of the past few days, his nearness affected her. He had a melting smile. The glint in his eyes—a blend of boyish mischief and purely masculine confidence—made the base of her belly flutter.

Discomfort swiftly followed. Aelfwyn gently extracted her hand from his and averted her gaze. Her reaction to him reminded her of how it was between men and women. The world was full of men like Ecgfrith who took what they wanted without asking, without caring of the consequences. If Leofric thought she was encouraging him, he might become such a man.

Aelfwyn stepped back from him and pulled her damp robes tightly around her. "You're right," she replied, her voice subdued. "We must press on."

They walked south through the woodland, following what appeared to be a goat-track through the clusters of trees. Aelfwyn had no idea where they were, or how far they had traveled. She cast her mind back to her journey north with Aethelhild, to the towns they had passed.

"Where are we?" she eventually asked Leofric, who now walked at her side.

He glanced her way, blinking as he emerged from the fog of his own thoughts. "I'd guess that the tidal river we emerged from was the Tinanmuðe. If we continue due south, we'll soon cross the Wear. After that, it's a straight run down to Streonshalh."

Aelfwyn nodded. She recalled crossing the Tinanmuðe on the way north, and the magnificent stone bridge that the Romans had left behind spanning the glittering water. They were farther south than she had realized.

"Do you think they know we're traveling to Streonshalh?" she asked.

He shrugged. "It's possible—but it's still your safest choice."

"And what about you?"

Leofric's gaze held hers, the corner of his mouth quirking. "I'll make sure I disappear."

Something about the way he said that made Aelfwyn uneasy. "Where will you go?"

He shook his head and broke eye contact. "It's safer for you not to know."

Aelfwyn was mulling over his response, and wondering why he was being so secretive, when the snap of twigs up ahead caused her to halt mid-stride. Beside her, Leofric had done the same, his body tensing.

A moment later, a man riding a stocky bay horse emerged from the trees.

He was young—of a similar age to her and Leofric—dressed in a sleeveless leather vest and breeches, his feet clad in fur boots. Owing to the balmy weather he wore no cloak, and his brown hair was loose, curling over broad shoulders. Over one shoulder, the man carried a quiver of fletched arrows and a longbow.

Aelfwyn stopped breathing. At first, she had thought he was one of the king's men, but he was coming from the wrong direction and was alone. Then she realized that he was probably the son of a local ealdorman or thegn out hunting.

Upon seeing the two of them on the path ahead, the man drew his horse to a halt. He had a heavy-featured face and a square jaw.

"Wes hāl!" Leofric called out, although Aelfwyn could hear the forced friendliness of his tone. Like her, this warrior's presence alarmed him.

"Wes hāl," the man responded in kind, his gaze sweeping over them. "What is this ... a monk and a maid on the road together?" He urged his horse forward a few steps and drew up alongside them. "I've yet to see a stranger sight."

Up close Aelfwyn saw that the man carried a seax—a long bladed knife— at his waist. Muscle corded his bare arms. He studied Aelfwyn first, and she grew rigid under his hot stare. Then his gaze shifted to Leofric, and he frowned.

"I know you ..."

Leofric raised an auburn eyebrow. "Do you? I don't recall your face."

The warrior continued to stare at him. "Aye, I do. You're one of Wibert of Driffield's sons."

Leofric inclined his head. "Well met, although I still cannot say I know you."

"Thunred," the young man replied. "My father serves the ealdorman of Eoforwic. I remember seeing you drinking in the meadhall."

Leofric did not reply right away, and watching him, Aelfwyn noted his face grew pale. "You're a long way from home," Leofric replied eventually.

"As are you," Thunred answered. "I heard the Wibert's youngest whelp got himself sent to Lindisfarena after he insulted the ealdorman." Leofric did not reply to this jibe, and Thunred sneered. "You're some way from the isle. And who's this pretty thing? Monks are supposed to shun the company of women are they not?"

"I've not yet taken my vows," Leofric replied through gritted teeth, "and I'm not forbidden to accompany women on journeys. I'm escorting this maid to Streonshalh Abbey, upon the orders of Prior Cuthbert."

Thunred gave a rude snort, his gaze raking Aelfwyn from head to toe. "Too winsome for a nun. I bet you'll give her a good plowing before you hand her over to the abbess—if you haven't already."

Aelfwyn started to feel ill at these words. Leofric gave Thunred a hard look. "I'm charged with Brunhild's protection."

"Brunhild?" Thunred's gaze remained upon Aelfwyn, and he licked his lips. "How about you share her with me too before you go on your way?"

"Are your ears filled with mashed turnip?" Leofric snapped. "I told you—she's under my protection."

Thunred's mouth curled. "Don't be selfish. A monk won't know how to service a woman properly. She needs a real man between her thighs." Thunred unsheathed his seax and kicked his feet from the stirrups. "Stand back and learn, monk. This shouldn't take long."

Aelfwyn backed off, terror rising within her. "Get away from me," she hissed.

Thunred laughed and swung down from the saddle. "Feisty, isn't she?"

Leofric stepped in front of Aelfwyn, between her and Thunred. "The maid doesn't sound keen," he said, his voice quiet and cold. "I think it's best you leave her be."

Aelfwyn continued to back away, noting as she did so that Leofric had drawn a knife from the sheath he wore at his waist. It was a thin-bladed knife, one used for boning fish or whittling wood. It looked pitiful next to the gleaming seax-blade the warrior before him wielded.

"Out of the way." Thunred made to shoulder Leofric aside.

Leofric slashed out with his knife, catching the warrior on the forearm, just above the leather bracer he wore. Thunred jumped aside, cursing foully. Blood flowed down his arm but the warrior paid it no mind. Instead he turned on Leofric, Aelfwyn forgotten.

"Maggot-spawn," he growled. "I'll gut you for that."

Aelfwyn screamed as Thunred lunged at Leofric. The seax-blade flashed and Leofric ducked just in time to avoid being stabbed in the neck. Aelfwyn watched in horror as Leofric dodged another swipe.

Her companion was quick and strong but surely no match for the leather-clad warrior attacking him. She backed off further, torn between wanting to flee for her life and not wanting to abandon the man who had been her savior until now.

Despair crushed her ribs, making it difficult to breathe. They had come so far only to meet their doom now.

Chapter Fourteen

Truths

THE FIGHT ENDED as swiftly as it had begun.

One moment, Leofric had been dodging seax thrusts—one of which nicked his right shoulder—the next he leaped under his opponent's guard and buried his boning knife to the hilt under his ribs. Thunred roared, toppling backward with Leofric on top of him.

Aelfwyn watched in horror as they struggled together for control of Thunred's seax in a deathly embrace. Maddened by rage and pain, the warrior stabbed his weapon up at Leofric's neck. Leofric had released his grip on the knife still embedded in his opponent's torso and had taken hold of Thunred's right wrist. Leofric's face was hard, his expression savage; like his opponent, he was fighting to kill.

The seax blade inched closer to Leofric's exposed throat. Aelfwyn covered her mouth with her hands as another scream rose within her. Thunred was fearsomely strong, even though Leofric was pushing his whole weight against him.

Then she watched Leofric reach down and twist the hilt of the knife embedded under Thunred's ribs. The warrior yelled in agony, his grip slackening just for an instant.

That was all Leofric needed—he yanked his boning knife free before slamming it down into the base of Thunred's neck.

Blood spurted, and the warrior's body kicked and twitched under Leofric as Thunred died.

Aelfwyn had never seen a man die before. She had heard of folk stoning thieves to death in Rendlaesham, or the king taking a man's head for treachery, but she had never actually seen a man take another's life. It was far worse than she had ever imagined—far bloodier, far more brutal.

She sank to her knees and vomited, throwing up water and bile—the only contents in her stomach.

When the retching subsided, she looked up to see Leofric climbing off Thunred's corpse. Leofric's face was ashen and blood-splattered. He looked fey, dangerous; for the first time Aelfwyn was afraid of him.

"You killed him," she whispered.

Leofric looked her way. His eyes had deepened to a brooding forest-green as his gaze met hers. "It was kill or be killed. He was going to slay me and then rape you."

His words made Aelfwyn flinch. "But ... how did you learn to fight like that? You're ... a monk."

Leofric's mouth twisted. "I had a life before Lindisfarena, Aelfwyn—and I didn't end up on that isle by choice. All the men in my family are warriors. I'm the youngest of five sons. I had to learn how to defend myself as soon as I could walk or my brothers would have beaten me to a pulp."

Aelfwyn grabbed fistfuls of her habit and clenched tightly to stop her hands from shaking. "So you've killed before?"

Leofric shook his head, before glancing down at where Thunred had stopped twitching. "He was my first."

Silence stretched between them.

After a few moments, Leofric started to untie the girdle around his waist. Aelfwyn tensed as she watched him. "What are you doing?

He glanced up. "I'm going to swap my clothes for his. He has weapons and a horse—we need them both."

Aelfwyn stared at him, horrified. "You're going to wear the clothes of the man you've just killed?"

"Aye, and you and I are going to ride his horse."

"But that's ..." Aelfwyn spluttered, struggling to find the words to describe just how vile this situation was.

Leofric met her eye, his own gaze hard. He was clearly losing patience with her. "This is life," he snapped. "It's not sweet and it's not pretty—but before you look at me with scorn remember I've just saved both our lives."

Aelfwyn held his gaze—both resenting him and fighting the truth of his words. Leofric said nothing more. He simply stood there watching her. After a few moments, Aelfwyn folded her arms across her chest and frowned. "What?"

His mouth curved. "I'm about to undress. If the sight of a naked man offends you then I suggest you look away."

Aelfwyn's face flamed. He was mocking her, and she hated him for it. Clenching her jaw to prevent herself from spitting at him, she turned her back while he undressed.

She waited while he shucked off his habit, pulled the dead man's clothes from him, and donned them as his own. To distract herself, Aelfwyn listened to the sounds of the morning: the rise and fall of the dawn chorus, the whisper of the wind through the trees, and the rustle of Thunred's horse cropping at grass nearby.

"You can turn around now."

Aelfwyn swiveled to find Leofric standing behind her, buckling Thunred's belt around his waist. The corpse at his feet now wore a monk's habit. Dressed as a warrior, in blood-stained leather, Leofric looked like a different man entirely—taller, broader, and older. His close-cropped dark red hair gave him a lean, dangerous look. He noticed Aelfwyn's stare and raised an eyebrow.

She scowled at him in response, daring him to mock her once more.

Aelfwyn helped Leofric drag Thunred into the bushes and cover him with branches. It was customary to burn a corpse, but a pyre would likely call their pursuers directly to them. There would be no burial for Thunred of Eoforwic.

Leofric threw the quiver of arrows and longbow over his shoulder and mounted the horse. Then he reached down and pulled Aelfwyn up so that she perched in front of him. The odor of leather, horse, and blood filled Aelfwyn's nostrils. The feel of Leofric's body against her back unnerved her. She sat rigid, clenching her jaw, as Leofric urged the horse forward.

This morning had changed how she saw Leofric.

Until their encounter with Thunred she had trusted him implicitly. He had been her savior and it had been easy enough not see that there was a man beneath the monk's habit. Now it was as if she was traveling with a stranger. Dressed in leather with a seax strapped to his waist and a longbow on his back, he looked as he really was; a wild young man who had somehow been forced into a life that had not been his choosing.

Leofric turned the horse south and urged it on to a brisk canter. He rode well, and the horse responded to him in kind, lengthening its stride so that its gait was as smooth as possible for its riders. Aelfwyn's back started to ache with the effort it was taking to sit rigid and not lean against him for support, but still she persisted.

Thunred had been a brutal reminder of what men were like, and how they were capable of behaving. She could not wait to reach Streonshalh and be free of them. For the first time, she understood Aethelhild's desire for a life of seclusion away from the violence and cruelty of men.

How have I lived to twenty winters and not realized?

She had grown up in a prosperous household, in a thriving town, and had never known a day of strife in her life before going to live at Bebbanburg. Reality had been a cruel blow—one that Aelfwyn was not sure she would ever recover from.

They rode south for a while longer before the trees drew back and they traveled through open, windswept country. At noon they took a brief rest by a stream, where they refilled their water skins, let the horse drink, and ate bread and cheese from the saddlebag Thunred had carried with him.

They spoke little during their rest, each dealing with the events at dawn in their own manner. Leofric appeared in a brooding mood. His gaze was far off, his expression pensive, as he skimmed stones across the stream and waited for Aelfwyn to finish her bread and cheese.

For her part, Aelfwyn felt tense and unsettled. Until now, she had focused on her immediate survival; on escaping the men and hounds at her heels. Streonshalh still lay a few days' ride away on horseback. Although they were now far ahead of their pursuers, she worried about what the next days would bring.

She was not foolish enough to assume they had outrun the hounds—Ecgfrith's men would still be tracking them south. They had to ensure they widened the distance between them and their pursuers over the next few days.

They resumed their journey, cutting east toward the coast this time. A brisk breeze, laced with brine, blew in from the sea. It stung Aelfwyn's face and whipped her hair from its braid so that it flew around her face as they rode. She now leaned back against the wall of Leofric's chest; her back had been agony after a while and it had been impossible to sit without touching him, so she had been forced to give in. Even so, it was a relief not to be on foot. Her feet were aching and sore from where the rope sandals had cut into her, and her thigh and calf muscles were tight and cramped.

Their mount was swift, even with two passengers, and carried them quickly south along the wild Bernician coast. Gulls swooped, their lonely cries echoing, and out to sea storm clouds rolled in.

By the time dusk approached, the wind had spots of rain in it.

They camped for the night on a hillside studded with rocks and brambles. Halfway down the hill loomed a large boulder with a ledge that provided some shelter underneath. Leofric unsaddled the horse, rubbed it down with a twist of grass, and hobbled it next to the boulder. The horse, an apparently unflappable beast, began cropping at grass; ignoring the rain that was now starting to fall in large, wet splashes.

Aelfwyn wriggled under the lip of the boulder and watched the sky darken overhead. Leofric squeezed in next to her as the rain began in earnest, pattering down on the dry earth.

There was little space in their makeshift shelter, especially with saddlery and Thunred's bag of hunting provisions keeping them company.

"No fire tonight," Leofric announced, peering out at the rain. "The rain would just put it out anyway, and besides, I don't want to draw any more attention to us."

Aelfwyn nodded. He would not get any complaints from her. Despite the rain, it was not cold this evening, especially here out of the wind. However, her stomach was rumbling. It seemed like an age since her noon meal of bread and cheese. She dug around in the saddlebag and retrieved an apple each and a large piece of cheese wrapped in oiled cloth.

"That's it," she said, passing Leofric his share of their meagre dinner. "The end of our food."

"We'll buy some food in the next village we pass tomorrow," Leofric promised, patting the small purse he now carried at his waist. "We've a few thrymsas, plus I can hunt so we won't starve."

They lapsed into silence then, each intent on devouring their supper. The apple was sweet and the cheese quite salty but good. Afterward, Aelfwyn took a sip from the water skin before passing it to Leofric. The rain drummed down on the boulder above their heads and ran in streams off the edge. Moments later, Aelfwyn heard the rumble of thunder in the distance.

"Is the horse alright?" she asked Leofric finally. "Won't the storm frighten him?"

"Nerves of iron that one." Leofric grinned at her, his face shadowed in the gathering dark. "Don't worry about him."

Aelfwyn pulled her knees up against her chest and rested her chin on them. She was exhausted and longed to stretch out upon a soft straw pallet and pull dry, warm furs over her head. Instead she would have to sleep upright tonight or risk getting soaked.

She glanced back at Leofric. He was staring out at the rain, his face pensive. She was still wary of him but the shock of this morning's fight had dimmed somewhat, and she felt embarrassed at her behavior after he had killed Thunred.

"You probably think me ungrateful," she began hesitantly. "It's just that I've never seen a man killed in front of me before … but I am glad you saved me from him."

Leofric glanced at her, and she saw a flash of white as he grinned. "I saved us both—he wasn't going to let me live."

"Did he really know you?"

"Aye." Leofric's voice changed, the tone turning guarded.

Undaunted, Aelfwyn pressed on. It had been bothering her all day; she had to know the truth about Leofric's past, about who he really was. "He said the ealdorman had sent you to Lindisfarena for insulting him—was that also true?"

She saw Leofric's barely perceptible nod.

"What happened? Why did you insult him?"

Leofric gave a soft laugh. "I was waiting for this."

"For what?"

"All the questions."

Aelfwyn stiffened, her cheeks growing hot. She was glad it was too dark for him to see her embarrassment. "If you'd rather not talk about it …" she began.

"No, it's fine," he replied with a sigh of resignation. "My past isn't something I'm that proud of, that's all."

Aelfwyn let a few moments of uncomfortable silence pass before she spoke once more. "Why?"

Leofric raked a hand through his short hair. "Where to begin? Let's just say I come from a family of hot-headed men who do as they please. My father brought me up that way—only he wasn't so happy about my arrogance the day I refused to wed the ealdorman of Eoforwic's daughter."

Aelfwyn did not reply, waiting instead for Leofric to continue. After a few moments he did, albeit reluctantly. "I told him I wouldn't marry her ... I insulted her—only I didn't realize she was standing behind the arras, listening to every word." Leofric paused here, considering his words before he continued. "Godwine of Eoforwic is not a man lightly crossed I discovered. Since I said I'd rather spend the rest of my days as a monk than marry a woman who looks like a sow, he decided to send me to Lindisfarena. He made it clear that, if I ever ran away, he would hunt me down and kill me."

Aelfwyn digested these words. There was a lot to take in—none of it good.

Leofric had already proved not to be the gentle monk she had thought he was; watching him fight and kill a man had shattered her illusions there. Yet the thought of him insulting and humiliating a young woman made her ire rise.

He was a spoiled brat.

She had thought him noble in helping her escape south, but he had probably been planning to flee Lindisfarena anyway. She just made it easier for him.

She was tired of living in a man's world. She was sick to the teeth of men deciding women's fates—of judging a woman by her fairness and little else. Leofric and all men like him sickened her.

"So both the king's men and the ealdorman's men will be after your blood now?" she asked finally, when she had managed to leash her temper.

"Aye," he replied heavily.

Aelfwyn pulled her robes tight around her and turned her back on him. "Good."

Chapter Fifteen

Uneasy Companions

GOOD.

AELFWYN'S LAST word to him before retiring for the night was a hard slap across the face. He had just poured out his guts to her—told her the bald truth without fancy words or lies—and she had turned her back on him.

It should not have bothered him, but it did.

He stared at her back, willing her to turn and face him—to look at him with softness in her eyes as she had until this morning. Instead she ignored him, her breathing deepening as she fell asleep against the rock.

What did you expect?

Leofric looked away from Aelfwyn, his gaze shifting to the wall of darkness beyond their shelter, to where the rain hammered down. She was a sensitive, gentle soul who clearly shunned violence. He had not wanted her to see him kill the warrior, but the fight had spiraled out of control.

Thunred had been a bully, and Leofric had wounded his pride. Leofric found himself fighting for survival. In the end, he had taken Thunred's life in order to save his own.

Aelfwyn had not understood, and he had sensed her tension for the rest of the day. It was as if a chill wind had blown in between them, when before they had traveled in easy camaraderie, her trust in him absolute.

Leofric had not realized how much he liked being Aelfwyn's protector until she looked at him with horror in her eyes.

But her reaction earlier paled to the scorn in that one word before she turned her back on him.

Good.

She was right of course. It just hurt coming from her.

Fatigue settled over him in a heavy mantle, weighing down his limbs. He wanted to stay awake, to keep watch in case anyone crept up on them during the night. However, the drumming of the rain—accompanied by the deep, rich scent of wet earth—was too difficult to resist. Now that he was no longer running for his life, he felt his tension slowly release.

Leofric slid into sleep's waiting arms.

He awoke to find himself on his back, water dripping on his face.

Blinking, he pushed himself up, out of the way of the steady trickle of water that ran off the edge of the overhang. He glanced behind him, at where he had left Aelfwyn the night before and found only the leather pack and saddlery sitting there.

Leofric tensed.

Where is she?

He crawled out from under the lip of the rock and stretched. *Jesu*, he felt like an old man after sleeping on the hard, damp earth. The horse stood nearby, watching him with a docile gaze. It gave a low whicker in greeting.

"Morning," Leofric replied. "Have you seen our mistress?"

The horse merely gazed at him. Leofric stepped close and ran a hand over the bay's noble face. "I don't know what Thunred called you, but if we're going to become traveling companions, you need a name."

The gelding nudged him gently and rubbed his head against him.

"How about Windræs?" Leofric murmured. "You are certainly fast enough."

"Storm of Wind ... it's a fine name for him."

Aelfwyn's voice made Leofric turn. She stood a few feet away. Her expression was friendly enough although her gaze was guarded. Her fine blonde hair had long come free of its braids and framed her face, as pale and soft as thistle down. With the light behind her, she looked like one of the angels Cuthbert had droned on about.

Leofric's breathing tightened, and he suddenly felt lightheaded. "There you are," he drawled, in an attempt to cover up his lack of composure. "I thought you'd run off."

Her full lips pursed. "Run where? You know I'll never reach Streonshalh Abbey without your help."

There it was—another slap to the face—the only reason she would suffer his company.

"Aye." Leofric turned back to Windræs and ruffled the horse's forelock. "You've got some sense at least."

"There's a stream at the bottom of the hill," she continued, her voice clipped now. "I've filled our water bladders."

"Good." Leofric kept his gaze from her and ducked under the ledge to retrieve Windræs's saddle and bridle. "Let's get going then."

They rode south in silence.

The woodland grew deeper; ancient groves of oaks that seemed to spread out forever around them. Numerous paths, hunting tracks mostly, wove their wave through the forest, although they met no one that morning.

After a night's rest, Windræs was full of energy and eager for a run. He tossed his head, fighting the bit slightly as Leofric forced him to set a slow canter through the trees. There were tree roots and potholes on the path—making it dangerous to let the horse have his head—and a long ride ahead. Streonshalh lay another two days' ride to the south, and Leofric did not want to tire Windræs out.

Aelfwyn sat in front of him, as stiff as a plank of wood. Eventually exhaustion would force her to lean into him, as it had the day before, but for now she fought to keep herself upright. Leofric could feel the tension emanating from her.

They reached a village just before noon. The hamlet was tiny, hardly more than a scattering of wattle and daub huts with sod roofs around a central clearing. The folk here had cut the woodland back, giving themselves enough space to plant out fields of vegetables and create pens for fowl and goats.

Children played in the dirt as Aelfwyn and Leofric rode in. The youngsters' faces came alive with curiosity when they spotted the strangers.

Leofric leaned forward, so that his mouth was near Aelfwyn's ear. Her hair tickled his face, and he found himself inhaling the sweet scent of her skin. "We're man and wife," Leofric whispered, "if anyone asks."

He felt her body go rigid. "Is that necessary?"

"It's the only excuse they'll likely believe. Let me do the talking."

She said nothing to that although he sensed her outrage. Leofric swallowed a smile—he preferred anger to revulsion.

They did not linger long in the village. Leofric used one of Thunred's thrymsas to buy food from a local woman: a loaf of freshly baked bread, butter, some boiled eggs still in their shells, and half a dozen crisp apples. Then they continued on their way for a short distance, until the village lay behind them, before stopping to eat.

They sat on the banks of a meandering stream with the sun on their faces, with Windræs grazing behind them. After last night's storm the air was heavy with moisture, making it feel even hotter. Leofric's skin was starting to itch under his dirty leather vest and breeches. He didn't like wearing another man's clothing, and worse still Thunred's dried blood still covered him. As soon as he had eaten, he would wash the grime off himself. For the moment, he had his empty belly to contend with.

Leofric's mouth watered as he opened the bag of food. He was starving. He tore off a hunk of bread and passed it to Aelfwyn with a pat of butter, and one of the eggs. She gave him a nod of thanks and balanced the food on her knees. He noted her hands shook from hunger as she peeled her egg. Neither of them had eaten properly since fleeing Lindisfarena, and it was starting to wear on them.

The fare was simple and fresh—food had never tasted so good. Leofric sighed with pleasure as he swallowed his last mouthful. Aelfwyn bit into an apple, her gaze focused on the gentle babbling waters of the stream.

Leofric stood up and started unbuckling the leather armor that covered his chest.

Aelfwyn glanced up, her grey-blue eyes widening in alarm. "What are you doing?"

"I smell worse than a rutting goat," he muttered. "I need to wash."

"What, right here?"

Leofric could not help himself. Her shocked face goaded him into teasing her. "You don't have to look," he said with a grin. "Unless you want to ..."

Aelfwyn's mouth thinned and her shoulders stiffened. Not dignifying his comment with a response, she swiveled round so that her back faced the river and took another bite of her apple.

Leofric's grin faded. His pleasure in tormenting her was always short-lived. He just felt like a cur afterward.

He cast aside his leather vest and pulled the woolen tunic underneath over his head. As he did so, he noted the angry red slash on his left shoulder, where Thunred had cut him. It looked like it needed cleansing, but a bath in the stream was the best he could do for now. He stripped off the rest of his clothing and brought his undershirt with him into the water to clean.

Wearing a damp tunic would mean he would smell like wet sheep for the rest of the day—but that was preferable to the reek of stale sweat, and worse.

Aelfwyn finished her apple, even devouring the core, before throwing away the stalk. She was hungry for another but prevented herself from reaching for one. There were two reasons why she did not: the first was that she knew they should ration their food, and the second was that the bag of food sat behind her.

She would have to turn around to retrieve it—and risk glancing at the naked man in the stream.

Behind her, she heard the splash of Leofric washing.

He seemed to be taking his time, whistling cheerfully as he bathed. Aelfwyn gritted her teeth. She did not mind him bathing—for he definitely needed to wash—it was the arrogance, the unspoken challenge in his gaze she did not like. His lazy sensuality when he teased her made her feel flustered, hot and cold all at once.

Aelfwyn sighed. He was taking his time. At this rate, the king's men would catch up with them.

Then the splashing halted and Aelfwyn tensed. A few moments passed, and she heard no further sound from the river.

Has he finished?

Bristling with impatience, Aelfwyn cast a glance over her shoulder—and froze.

Leofric was swimming in the water hole about ten yards away.

He glided through the water like an otter. Sunlight dappled his skin through the clear water. Entranced, Aelfwyn watched him surface. He had his back to her; water streaming down his broad shoulders, the lean column of his back, and over his tight buttocks.

Aelfwyn's mouth went dry. His body was beautiful: lean and muscular.

What are you doing?

Heart pounding, she turned away.

A moment later, she heard the splash of Leofric wading to the riverbank. She stared down at her lap, face burning, and tried to regain control of herself. If he saw her face, he would know she had been watching him.

"It's safe now," he said from close behind her. "I'm clothed."

Clenching her jaw at the amusement in his voice, she turned to face him. She only hoped her face had stopped flaming. However, she found him only partially clad. Naked to the waist, he sat on the grassy bank and pulled on his boots.

"It's a relief to get that stinking armor off me," he admitted. "I really don't want to put it on again." He motioned to his left, where he had wrung out his woolen tunic and laid it out on a flat rock.

"We really shouldn't linger," she said stiffly.

"We'll move on in a short while," he promised her. "I just need my tunic to dry a little."

Aelfwyn nodded before her gaze fixed upon the wound on his left shoulder. She frowned. "Did Thunred do that?"

He nodded, glancing down at the cut. "Luckily, I got him worse."

Aelfwyn snorted and came closer to inspect the cut. Up close, it was swollen and an angry red. "A lot of comfort that will give you when it poisons your blood."

She looked up, her gaze meeting his. His hazel-green eyes held her fast, and she felt the blush returning to her cheeks. She wished he would not look at her like that—it made her insides melt like tallow. "If the wound sours," she said sharply, to mask her discomfort at his closeness, "Thunred will get his wish."

Chapter Sixteen

Arrival at Streonshalh

LEOFRIC STIFFENED, HIS shoulder throbbing dully as Aelfwyn pressed a handful of dark green pulp into his wound. "God's bones, what's that?"

She glanced up from her work, their gazes meeting. They were so close that he could see the blue flecks in her grey eyes. Her cheeks were slightly flushed.

"It's Woundwort," she said quietly. "My mother swears by it."

"For what?" Leofric's nose wrinkled at the pungent odor the herb emitted. "To keep evil spirits away from the hearth."

Aelfwyn gave him an exasperated look. "To keep wounds from souring."

After inspecting the livid cut on his shoulder, Aelfwyn had gone off into the trees, reappearing a short while later with a handful of herbs. Intrigued, Leofric had watched her mash them to a pulp on one of the large flat rocks by the river. She had worked deftly, her pale brow furrowed in concentration.

"I need to bind the wound," she said, stepping back and inspecting her handiwork. "To keep the Woundwort inside."

"I don't think Thunred packed any clean linens," Leofric replied with a shrug, "but you can tear some material off my tunic if that serves."

She shook her head. "Wool won't do." With that, she leaned down and pulled up the hem of the woolen dress she wore. Underneath, Leofric spied a fawn-colored linen undertunic.

Deftly, she tore a wide strip off the hem. Looking on, Leofric caught a glimpse of the shapely calves and fine ankles underneath. "You're a resourceful wench," he admitted, grinning at her.

Aelfwyn approached him once more, and although her face was serious Leofric could have sworn he saw her eyes twinkle. His charm was starting to wear away at her; slowly eroding the wall of ice she had built between them.

"My mother always stressed the importance of a woman having skills," she said quietly as she bound his shoulder. "My father provides well for my family, but we are not high-born. Women have to be more than wives and mothers."

Leofric nodded. "It's the same in my family. My two older sisters have never been idle a day in their life."

Aelfwyn's gaze met his. "Unlike their younger brother?"

He quirked an eyebrow. Was she teasing him, or criticizing? "It's a man's world, Aelfwyn," he replied quietly. "I'm not to blame for that."

She huffed and finished tying the bandage. "No, but you take full advantage of it."

Leofric shrugged, favoring her with a slow smile. She was challenging him, and it surprised him. When they had first met he had thought her a gentle, timid soul but he was beginning to realize she was far tougher than he realized. Her ordeal at Bebbanburg had stripped away her illusions about life, but in doing so it had forged her anew. He noted the iron resolve in her and decided he liked it.

He rose to his feet and reluctantly reached for his damp tunic. He could have sat here all day, with the sun on his skin, having Aelfwyn fuss over him, but she had spoken true earlier. They lingered at their peril. Windræs was swift and had carried them far ahead of their pursuers—however, that did not mean they were safe.

A chill settled over Leofric then, like a shadow passing over the sun, when he realized that it did not matter how far he ran, he would always be a hunted man.

Thanks to Godwine of Eoforwic, he would never be safe.

Aelfwyn stretched, slowly awakening to the sound of chirping birds. A cool breeze kissed her face and she opened her eyes. A few feet away, Leofric kicked dirt over the embers of last night's fire.

It had been the first fire they had dared light since fleeing south. They were now far enough ahead of their pursuers that Leofric had decided to risk it. They had roasted two conies and sat in companionable silence afterward as they consumed their meal.

Aelfwyn yawned and sat up. "Morning."

Leofric glanced up. "Good morning. Did you sleep well?"

She nodded, rising to her feet and brushing leaves and twigs out of her hair. "I think I'm finally getting used to sleeping on the ground."

Leofric smiled. "You won't have to for much longer. If we ride hard today, we should reach Streonshalh just before dusk."

Aelfwyn tensed—warring with an odd blend of relief and anxiety. She longed to be safe within the abbey's walls, but she also knew that a very different life awaited her, one that she would never have chosen willingly.

"I thought you'd look happier at the news," Leofric said, watching her intently.

Aelfwyn frowned at him. Leofric was far too sharp; he never missed a thing.

Over the past two days, since she had dressed his wound, she had thawed toward him; it was hard to stay angry at a man who wielded charm like a weapon. She was also grateful to him for keeping her safe, and for hunting and providing for her.

"I am happy," she replied. "I just wonder what the future has in store. What if the abbess doesn't admit me? What if she gives me back to the king?"

Leofric considered her questions, his face unusually serious. "Aye, those are both valid concerns." He paused here, his gaze trapping hers. "You don't have to go to Streonshalh, Aelfwyn. Travel south with me instead and start a new life."

Aelfwyn stared at him. His suggestion caused her belly to tighten in a blend of excitement and terror—a reaction which shocked her. "Start a new life ... with you?"

Leofric's gaze had turned shuttered. He had seen her reaction. "Is that such a repellant idea?"

"No ... yes ..." Aelfwyn stuttered. She felt flustered, hot. "I can't do that, Leofric."

He shrugged, and she knew he was feigning indifference—that her reaction had hurt him. "Very well," he said, turning away. "Then you will just have to take your chances with the abbess."

It was not a good start to the day. They resumed their journey south, riding along the windswept coastline, but they did so in silence.

Windræs flew, his feathery hooves eating up the furlongs. The wind, coming in from the southeast, churned up the sea. Gulls and herons swooped low over the surf, their cries mingling with the boom of the crashing waves. Aelfwyn was glad they were riding along the coast again; the sea calmed her pitching stomach, soothed her jangled nerves.

She had not meant to offend Leofric, to insult him.

But surely he realized she could not go away with him. At the moment, their journey together had a purpose. He was her protector—nothing more. If she continued to travel with him though, their relationship would change. She had already seen the naked interest in his eyes at unguarded moments; noted the way he watched her sometimes. She did not fear him, but ever since Leofric's fight with Thunred she did not trust him either.

He was a man, after all. He would try to stake his claim on her sooner or later. She could not bear the thought of being forced again. Her body was her own, and she would keep it that way.

The farther south they traveled, the firmer Aelfwyn's resolve grew. The arrival at Streonshalh had arrived just in time. The past few days together had forged a bond between her and Leofric; one she did not want.

One she had to sever.

True to Leofric's prediction, they reached Streonshalh close to dusk. Long shadows blanketed the cliffs, and the sun was close to sliding behind the grassy hills to the east.

Aelfwyn spied the abbey, many furlongs before they reached it: a solid building of wood and stone, surrounded by a high wooden fence. It commanded over the surrounding land.

As they rode along the headland north of Streonshalh, Aelfwyn glanced down to the scheduled harbor below. Tidy, timbered fishing huts with thatched roofs and squat tanning sheds clustered together, blanketing the bottom of the hillside. A few rowboats bobbed against a wooden jetty, reminding Aelfwyn that folk here made a living out of the herrings they caught in the cool waters at the mouth of the River Usk.

Smoke rose from the roofs of the houses, and she caught a whiff of roasting mutton on the wind. Her stomach growled; it felt a long while had passed since she had last eaten at noon.

They forded the River Usk and rode up the steep path toward the abbey. Then, instead of approaching Streonshalh, Leofric turned Windræs southwest across the upper pastures and circled around two furlongs south of the abbey's main gate. There he drew the gelding to a halt.

"I shall leave you here." Leofric swung down from the saddle before reaching up to help her dismount. "It's best the nuns don't see us arrive together."

Aelfwyn nodded and slid to the ground. He was right; she would have a hard enough task in explaining who she was and why she had come. Seeing her arrive with a leather-clad warrior would not help matters.

Aelfwyn shucked off the voluminous monk's habit she wore over her long tunic and stuffed it into Leofric's saddlebag. She did not wish to explain that either. Then she then turned to Leofric, raising her chin to meet his eye.

The wind buffeted them, whipping her hair into her eyes. Blinking, she pushed it aside. The solemn look on Leofric's face, the steadiness of his gaze, made her breathing quicken. He would not make saying goodbye easy.

"Thank you, Leofric," she began softly, "for everything."

His mouth twisted. "You don't have to thank me."

She reached forward, her fingers closing over his hand. "I do—you saved me. I'll never forget it."

He placed a hand over hers, trapping her fingers between both his hands. The warmth and strength of him seeped into her, warming her to the core. "You don't still revile me then?" he asked softly.

"Revile you? Of course not."

"I'm sorry I'm not the man you thought I was."

So was Aelfwyn. She wished she had never learned of his past, but there was no undoing it. Still, she did not want any bitterness between them now, not when these would be the last words they would ever speak.

"I have no right to judge you," she replied with a tremulous smile. "Not when I am far from perfect myself."

He squeezed her hand gently. "You are perfect ... and without you my days will feel sunless."

Aelfwyn stared up at him, surprised by his admission. She stared into his face, looking for a trace of mockery but there was none. He had meant those words.

"I do not like leaving you here," he continued, his gaze never leaving hers, "Not when I don't know how the Abbess Hilda will receive you."

Aelfwyn shook her head. "But you must."

He watched her for a heartbeat longer, his eyes deepening from hazel to green with intensity. "I will wait here," he told her before he jerked his chin south. "Just beyond the line of those hills—every day at sunset for the next five days."

Aelfwyn tried to extract her hand from between his, but he held her fast. "You don't need to do that."

"I do," he replied firmly. "I can't ride away not knowing whether you will be safe here or not."

"But, it's not for you to—"

Before she could finish her sentence, Leofric drew her to him and covered her mouth with his. It was a gentle, sensual kiss. For an instant, Aelfwyn melted into him, lost in the feel of his lips—smooth, soft and warm—on hers. Heat flowered in the pit of her belly at his touch.

Then reality doused her like an icy bucket of water. She turned rigid in Leofric's arms.

Leofric pulled away, his hands releasing her as he did so. His mouth quirked when he met her eye once more. "I know I should apologize for that—but I won't." He stepped back, creating a gulf between them. "Five days, Aelfwyn. After that I'll ride away and leave you to the life you have chosen."

Chapter Seventeen

Hilda and Elflaeda

AELFWYN WATCHED LEOFRIC mount Windræs. She pulled her flapping robes around her, remaining where she was as he reined the horse south.

He did not look back.

When he disappeared over the brow of the windswept hill, she turned and faced her destination: Streonshalh Abbey. The setting sun had burnished its wooden fence bronze. Smoke rose somewhere inside the perimeter, where presumably the nuns would be preparing the evening meal.

Aelfwyn breathed in slowly and deeply. Leofric's kiss had unbalanced her; even now she could still feel the lingering touch of his lips on hers. She could not bring herself to be angry at him. The kiss had been chaste, although her body's initial reaction to it had not—until memories of the night Ecgfrith had used her had rushed in and extinguished the warmth of his touch. The wound the king had inflicted on her, a wound no one could see, had barely scabbed. One kiss had ripped it open.

Aelfwyn blinked back tears. *Be strong*, she berated herself. *You can't crumble, not now.*

She wished Leofric had not made that promise. It was foolish and risky on his part; King Ecgfrith's men still hunted them both. He needed to get himself as far as possible from Streonshalh—and fast.

I should have refused him. I should have told him to leave tonight.

But she had not.

Slowly, she began walking toward the abbey. Inside, she heard the bell clanging, hailing the nuns to prayers. Soon that bell would mark her days. Leofric had just escaped from such a life. Yet she and Leofric were not alike. He was wild and free—keeping him locked up in a monastery would be like trying to harness the North Wind. Instead she sought solitude and peace. Rather than a life of religious contemplation, she sought a haven from the world of men, and the abbey would provide it.

Aelfwyn lengthened her stride and headed toward the gate, toward a fresh start.

Abbess Hilda of Streonshalh Abbey fixed Aelfwyn in a clear, gentle gaze. "You have traveled far, child. You must be exhausted."

Aelfwyn nodded. After recounting her tale to the abbess she felt exhausted, drained.

Hilda, a handsome woman who looked well into her fifth decade, had listened to her tale in silence. She had not even flinched when Aelfwyn spoke of the rape, although Aelfwyn had seen the tension in her shoulders, the flash of outrage in her eyes.

Dressed in a flowing white habit, a blue veil covering her hair, the abbess was a sobering sight. She had a face that would have been beautiful in her youth: high cheekbones, bright blue eyes, and a sculpted mouth. But it was her manner that put Aelfwyn at ease: gentle and softly spoken with an air of quiet strength.

Aelfwyn wondered what the abbess thought of her slanderous allegations. The abbey was under the protection of the King of Northumbria. In her relations with Ecgfrith, the abbess had to tread carefully.

They sat alone together in the library—a cool, peaceful space—at a small table. A shelf with a handful of leather bound volumes sat along one wall. The greasy smell of tallow hung in the air from the many candles burning along the walls.

"Do you believe me, Mother Abbess?" Aelfwyn ventured.

Hilda met her gaze and nodded. "There is no lie in your eyes, child."

"You will not turn me over to the king?" Aelfwyn did not want to ask the question, but it burned within her. She had to know if she could trust Hilda.

The abbess's expression grew stern, her mouth thinning. "Ecgfrith is not the man his father was. He is my lord, but that does not mean I condone what he has done."

Aelfwyn watched her, silently impressed by Hilda's open defiance of her king. She felt a pang of guilt for bringing such trouble to the abbess's door. To risk so much for a complete stranger was generous indeed. Yet desperation made Aelfwyn seek assurance. "So I can remain here?"

The abbess smiled, her face softening. "A nun's life is not for everyone. Of course, we will welcome you among us, if that is what you truly want, but you may stay here as an aspirant first. Once a few days have passed we will discuss whether you are ready to become a postulant, or whether a different life would suit you."

Anxiety twisted Aelfwyn's belly. "But there's nowhere else for me to go. I can't go back to Bebbanburg or Rendlaesham."

Concern clouded Hilda's deep-blue eyes. "Do not worry so," she said, reaching forward and placing a cool hand over Aelfwyn's. "No one is casting you out."

Hilda rose to her feet with a rustling of crisp robes. "Come. It grows late, and you have not eaten. I will take you take you to the refectory. There will be food left over from supper."

Aelfwyn nodded, grateful for the abbess's kindness. She was indescribably weary and her temples throbbed.

Hilda sat her down at a freshly scrubbed oaken table while she fetched a wooden platter of bread, cheese, and apples from the adjoining kitchen. A large hearth dominated the far end of the refectory. Embers glowed dully in the fire pit, casting a soft glow over the shadowed walls.

Aelfwyn ate quickly, although with the abbess watching her she tried to mind her manners. Hilda observed her with unnerving intensity, as if considering something.

"It's a long way from Bebbanburg," Hilda said finally, "and although you are weary and hungry, I find you in a remarkably fit state. Did you receive help on the journey?"

A chill slithered over Aelfwyn's skin. She had not wanted to lie to Hilda about how she had managed to reach Streonshalh. Instinctively, Aelfwyn knew it was best to leave Leofric out of her tale. "Aye, Mother Abbess," she replied huskily. "A family traveling south on the road out of Bebbanburg gave me passage for a spell, and the folk of the villages I passed showed me great generosity by giving me food and drink."

Hilda gave a gentle smile. "The Lord was certainly looking over you, to bring you safely to our door."

Aelfwyn forced herself to return the smile although her meal now sat queasily in her belly. God would surely strike her down for her lies.

Sister Elflaeda was lying on her sleeping pallet, drifting between wakefulness and sleep, when the creak of the door opening roused her. Bleary-eyed, she pushed her curtain of dark hair from her eyes and propped herself up onto her elbows.

"Who goes there?"

A young woman stood in the doorway. Pretty, blonde and dressed in a travel stained blue woolen over dress and tattered linen tunic, the girl carried a guttering clay cresset. The two other nuns that shared the dwelling stirred, peering up from the edges of their blankets at the newcomer like sleepy owls. The girl ignored them, her gaze fixing upon the nun who had addressed her.

"Are you Elflaeda," she whispered.

"*Sister* Elflaeda," the nun corrected her with an imperious tilt of her head. "Who are you?"

"My name is Aelfwyn. The abbess has told me that I should sleep here." Elflaeda heard the nervousness in the young woman's voice. "She also asked that you go to her; she wishes to speak with you."

Elflaeda rose from her pallet and reached for her habit. She dressed quickly before realizing that the girl—Aelfwyn—was still standing there watching her. Elflaeda made an impatient noise and motioned to the empty pallet beside the door. Until three weeks ago it had belonged to Sister Hereswith—until a fever claimed her life.

"You can sleep there."

Elflaeda made her way across the starlit yard between the squat, thatch-roofed dwellings where her sisters slept. A chill breeze caught at her veil and whipped her habit against her legs, but she paid it no mind.

She frowned as she approached the annex attached to the back of the church: Abbess Hilda's house. Life at Streonshalh Abbey was one of rigid routine—early to bed, early to rise. The abbess never summoned her this late.

Elflaeda halted before the door to the house and knocked gently.

"Enter."

She obeyed and found the abbess sitting on a stool by her sleeping pallet, a leather bound book of prayers in her hands. Although larger and better built than Elflaeda's own dwelling, the abbess's home contained few possessions. Fresh straw covered the ground, and apart from a wooden cross above the abbess's sleeping pallet, nothing else adorned the walls.

"Sister Elflaeda," the abbess greeted her with a smile. "I apologize for the lateness of my summons—please come in and shut the door."

Elflaeda did as bid although the tension in the abbess's shoulders concerned her. "Is something amiss, Mother Abbess?"

Hilda motioned to the low stool opposite her. "Please take a seat, Sister."

Elflaeda perched on the stool although her nervousness was growing by the moment. Why was the abbess behaving so strangely?

"You have shown Aelfwyn to her sleeping pallet?" Hilda asked.

Elflaeda nodded, her curiosity piqued.

The abbess's gaze met hers. "Aelfwyn traveled here from Bebbanburg to seek our protection."

The younger woman frowned. "Our protection?"

"Yes, she has endured much." Hilda's mouth tightened as she said these words. "She was handmaid to King Ecgfrith's new queen, Aethelhild."

Elflaeda knew about her brother's recent marriage, although she did not see what it had to do with the girl.

"The king forced her," Hilda continued. "He raped her."

The nun stared at the abbess, shocked by her stark words, as much as the admission itself. "Who? The handmaid?"

Hilda nodded. "Aelfwyn fled from Bebbanburg at dawn the next morning, and has been running ever since."

Elflaeda blinked. She felt slightly numb, as if they were not talking about her brother, the King of Northumbria. Eventually, she found her voice. "You believe her?"

"I do."

Anger curled in the base of Elflaeda's stomach. She had never been close to her elder brother, but she would not have a lowborn girl spread slander about him.

She respected the abbess deeply, looked up to her as a beacon of goodness and piety, but she was shocked Hilda would take the word of a servant girl over that of her own king. Still, she was careful not to let her feelings show on her face.

"I know this is difficult, Sister Elflaeda." Hilda's voice gentled. "No one likes to hear ill of their kin."

"My brother would not rape a woman," Elflaeda replied stiffly. "I cannot believe it."

Hilda held her gaze, understanding in her eyes. "The truth is sometimes ugly. Aelfwyn is terrified of the king. She believes he will send men after her to bring her back to Bebbanburg."

Elflaeda choked back scorn. Who did this wench think she was? To think herself worthy of a king's attention—to make up vicious lies about Ecgfrith. Elflaeda clenched her fists, although taking care to keep them hidden in the folds of her robes. She had a good mind to storm back to that lying slut and rake her fingernails down her face. With great self-control, Elflaeda managed to rein in her anger and keep her expression neutral.

"What will you do with her, Mother Abbess?" She kept her voice low, respectful even if she was seething inside.

"I have agreed to let her stay here as an aspirant. If she takes to life at Streonshalh, she can take her vows."

The nun could still her tongue no longer. "You will take her word over the king's, Mother Abbess?"

Hilda fixed the younger woman in a cool, penetrating stare; one she had seen her use with other nuns but never her. Elflaeda had always been a favorite. "I called you here as a courtesy so that you would hear it first from me," she said, her voice iron cloaked in silk. "I hope you won't cause me to regret doing so."

"Of course not, Mother Abbess," Elflaeda replied hurriedly, swallowing her indignation and casting her gaze downward, feigning contrition. "I only wished to be sure of the girl's words—after all she is a stranger to us."

Chapter Eighteen

The Outsider

THE FIRST RAYS of dawn peeked through the cracks in the doorway and shutters, casting a pale light over the interior of the hut. Aelfwyn stirred on her straw pallet, relishing the luxury of a proper bed for the first time in days. Her gaze shifted over to where the three nuns she shared quarters with were rising.

The nuns were all reasonably young, none of them more than five and twenty winters, although they looked older once they donned their habits and veils. Their habits made them appear the same—sisters indeed.

None of them paid her any mind as they dressed. The one called Elflaeda did not glance her way once. Watching them, Aelfwyn felt an outsider, an imposter. She rose from her sleeping pallet, shook out her blanket, and quickly rebraided her hair. Then she followed the nuns out into the dim morning.

A fog had drifted in from the sea overnight, wreathing the abbey complex in milky white. The nuns crossed the courtyard toward the church, their cloaked forms like wraiths in the misty dawn. Having nowhere else to go, Aelfwyn trailed after them.

They filed into the church, silent save for the rustling of their skirts, the soft whisper of their sandals on the paved floor.

Around twenty nuns gathered in the silent space. Aelfwyn lingered at the back of the group, watching as they knelt in rows. The abbess arrived, bringing with her a faint scent of lye and dried lavender. She cast Aelfwyn a quick but reassuring smile and swept up to the altar.

Aelfwyn hurriedly knelt, although she kept well back from the nuns. She bowed her head and listened as Abbess Hilda began to recite the first prayer of the morning. Her voice, low and gentle, broke the heavy silence. Aelfwyn listened to the prayer, her hands clasped in front of her as her mistress, Aethelhild, had once taught her. However, her mind kept wandering. She found herself noting how cold the stone was she knelt upon; how empty her stomach felt; how her throat was dry and she kept having to swallow to prevent herself from coughing.

She thought of Leofric. Would he really wait every evening? Where was he right now?

The rise and fall of the abbess's voice jerked her back to the present. *Stop it. Concentrate.*

Yet her thoughts returned to their last moments together before he had turned and ridden away. Traitorously, her mind fixed upon the feel of his lips on hers, the warmth and strength of his arms around her.

Aelfwyn squeezed her eyes shut and forced herself to think of something else. *Enough*—such thoughts would do her no good. Had her recent experiences taught her nothing about men? This was her new life now, and she needed to embrace it or the abbess would never let her stay.

After prayers, the nuns broke their fast with fresh bread and broth in the refectory. It was a silent meal and a solemn one. Aelfwyn could not help but compare it to the mornings in Bebbanburg's Great Hall. Raucous, chaotic and full of life; with slaves and servants dashing about, and children and dogs getting underfoot. It was also different to her parents' home—she and her sisters bickering as they helped their mother bake wheels of griddle bread on the hearth.

Aelfwyn found the silence disconcerting. It made her own thoughts feel too loud. There was little to distract her from her own worries; the inner chatter that the business of everyday life usually drowned out.

She ate her bread slowly and savored the hot broth made with mutton bones, and took note of the nuns seated around her. They all looked so serious, their gazes inward.

Is this what a life of contemplation does to you?

Her gaze reached Elflaeda, who sat further down the table, and lingered.

There was something familiar about the young woman. She had a round, pretty face and dark eyes framed with long lashes. Last night, Aelfwyn had noticed she had long hair, as dark as a raven's wing. However, it was the pugnacious set to the girl's jaw and her haughty manner that reminded Aelfwyn of someone.

Elflaeda. That name was also familiar. Had she seen the girl before?

Frowning as she tried to remember, Aelfwyn glanced down at the bowl of hot broth before her.

Then it struck her.

At Bebbanburg she had heard King Ecgfrith's mother Eanflaed speak of her daughters. One had married a Mercian prince, the other had taken her vows at Streonshalh. Aelfwyn remembered the Queen mother's proud face as spoke of that daughter to Aethelhild.

Aelfwyn's stomach clenched. She looked up to find Elflaeda staring at her. The look of dislike on her face was impossible to ignore, as was the accusation in her dark eyes.

She knows.

The bread and broth churned in Aelfwyn's belly. The abbess must have told Elflaeda the night before. Aelfwyn tore her gaze away, her heart slamming against her breastbone.

She had only been here one night and already she had made an enemy—one who could destroy her hopes for a new life.

The mist had burned away when Elflaeda made her way out of the abbey. The sun was warm on her face and, after spending the morning weeding the vegetable beds, she was sweating slightly.

She left her sisters bent over the beds of onions and carrots and made her way out of the garden, past the tangle of rosemary, thyme and sage, before cutting right. The quickest route out of the abbey was through the side gate, next to the vegetable plots, but she did not want the other nuns to see her leave.

Instead, she hurried across the inner courtyard, her sandals scuffing on hard-packed earth, past the Great Hall and guest house to the top gate.

Eflaeda slipped out, leaving the gate ajar so she would not have to draw attention to herself when she returned. Outside, the tang of molten iron reached her, carried on a gentle sea breeze that cooled her heated cheeks. The ironsmith's hearth burned below, the clang of a hammer on hot iron echoing up the cliff face.

She had to hurry. Soon the bell would ring for noon prayers—but before it did, she had a task to complete. She had chosen her moment carefully, telling her sisters that the abbess had asked her to run an errand before the morning's end.

In her hand she carried a scrap of rolled vellum. She had brought a few pieces of the precious writing material from Bebbanburg and used it to write letters back to her mother. She was loath to waste any of it, but the message she had inscribed was clear and concise.

Elflaeda made her way down the steep cliff path toward the village of Streonshalh. Below, she spied the boat builders' huts, huddled together near the wooden quay. She knew that merchants often stopped here on their way north. With any luck, there would be one willing—for a thrymsa or two—to deliver a missive to King Ecgfrith.

Ecgfrith would learn of Aelfwyn's lies. Perhaps this would help mend the rift between brother and sister. Ecgfrith had little time for her piety, but after this he might look upon Elflaeda more kindly. It might make his rare visits to the abbey bearable.

Elflaeda slid on loose pebbles, and nearly fell, but managed to catch herself in time. The path down the cliff was steep in places, and one misplaced step could send her tumbling to her death.

Heart pounding, she glanced up at where the sun beat down. Noon was nearly upon them; she had to hurry. Pursing her lips in determination, the nun pressed on.

Aelfwyn completed a line of stitches and looked up. The abbess sat opposite her, winding wool onto a distaff. The abbess had requested she join her in the weaving shed. The two of them sat on a raised platform, opposite a group of nuns who worked at large looms on the other side of the room.

The scene—the two of them hard at work by the open window—reminded her of the afternoons she had spent with Aethelhild, weaving, sewing, or embroidering.

A wave of homesickness crashed over her—not for Rendlaesham and certainly not for Bebbanburg, but for Aethelhild. Ecgfrith had stolen so much more than her innocence that night. He had taken her closest friend.

The abbess, sensing Aelfwyn's stillness, glanced up. "You look worried, Aelfwyn. Is something amiss?"

Aelfwyn lowered her gaze. The abbess was a clever woman and very observant; she would have to be more careful to conceal her emotions around her. "I was just wondering about my mistress, Aethelhild," she admitted finally, before meeting Hilda's eye once more. "She never wanted to remarry, but the King of the East Angles would not let her take her vows. After her handfasting, Aethelhild decided that she would remain chaste. The king was furious."

The abbess's gaze widened. "She is strong indeed to defy her husband. Many women would not have the courage."

Aelfwyn looked away. "I'm sure he will make her pay for it, Mother Abbess—if he has not already."

"You think he used you to punish her?" Outrage laced Hilda's soft voice.

Aelfwyn nodded. "In part." She paused, remembering the look of venom on Elflaeda's face that morning. "Mother Abbess—what if he comes here looking for me?"

Aelfwyn glanced up, and saw the abbess stiffen. She stopped winding wool onto her distaff and set it aside. "Then I would do my best to hide you. I would never betray your trust, child."

Relief washed over Aelfwyn, swiftly followed by guilt. "But if he discovers you lied to him, he could—"

Hilda reached out and placed a reassuring hand on Aelfwyn's forearm, cutting her off. Her touch was cool and firm, her gaze resolute. "He won't."

Dusk settled gently over the land, bringing another late summer's day to a close. Although it had been a warm afternoon, the air had a nip to it; a reminder that the fires of autumn were not far off.

Leofric waited on the brow of the hill astride Windræs, looking northeast toward Streonshalh Abbey. The gelding shifted impatiently and tossed his head, his bit rattling. Leofric leaned forward and stroked the horse's neck. "Just a while longer," he soothed.

Glancing up, Leofric's gaze returned to the high wooden fence that snaked around the perimeter of the abbey complex. He stared at the gates, awaiting the moment they would open, and Aelfwyn would step outside.

116

He waited as the sun slid behind the hills at his back—but she did not emerge.

What am I doing here?

Leofric had asked himself that numerous times ever since leaving Aelfwyn the day before. What madness had possessed him? He was a hunted man; he could not waste precious days lingering near Streonshalh, waiting for Aelfwyn to change her mind.

What did he care anyway?

She was a comely young woman and good company, but he owed her nothing. He had done what he had promised: brought her safely south and kept her from falling into the king's lecherous hands. Surely that was enough?

And yet the thought of riding away, of leaving her alone at Streonshalh, had bothered him—it still did. Aelfwyn was gentle and sweet, but she was no more made for a life of religious worship than he was. He had to give her a chance to change her mind.

The sun set and darkness settled over the hills.

She's not coming. Disappointment soured Leofric's mouth, and he grew angry with himself for it. *Get ahold of yourself.*

He reined Windræs around and headed for the woodland that carpeted the valley behind him. It was time to make camp for the night. This was only the end of Aelfwyn's first full day at Streonshalh; she still had four more nights to make up her mind. He would wait and be here should she decide to join him.

Yet a part of him wondered if he waited in vain.

JAYNE CASTEL

Chapter Nineteen

Confrontation

AELFWYN REACHED UP and plucked an apple, before depositing it into her basket. She had climbed this tree to reach the fruit on the highest branches and found herself enjoying her task.

For the first time since her arrival at Streonshalh, she felt at peace. *Perhaps life here will suit me after all.*

Aelfwyn hummed to herself as she continued to pick apples. She carried a wicker basket slung around her neck to leave her hands free for climbing and picking. It was harvest time. Back in Rendlaesham, the orchards carpeting the hills outside the town would be brimming with ripe fruit.

Sighing at the memory of how she and her sisters had played in the orchards—or hidden there when they risked a beating from their parents—Aelfwyn let her gaze travel across the jumble of thatched roofs. The orchard, filled with apple, pear, and sour plum trees, also functioned as a graveyard. Unlike common folk, who still burned their dead upon pyres in the manner of old, nuns and monks buried theirs. These graves were not like the barrows of kings—great hills that rose against the skyline—but small, neat mounds, marked by carved stones.

On the way inside, Aelfwyn had spotted a handful of gravestones, the newest of which had belonged to a nun named Hereswith. She had the uneasy feeling that she had taken Hereswith's sleeping pallet. No one had said as much, but her suspicions had more to do with what they did not say; the way the nuns sharing her hut averted their gazes every time they entered or left their dwelling.

Aelfwyn's gaze shifted to the roof of the church next to that of the great hall, rising high above the others.

Unlike Lindisfarena, Streonshalh felt like a real community. Perhaps its proximity to the village, to the rest of the world, instead of sitting upon a lonely isle, made it feel so. Monks also resided here. A community of brown robed brothers, they attended evening prayers in the church with the nuns and worked alongside them at many tasks.

Aelfwyn glanced down at her basket. Almost full, it was starting to grow heavy, pulling at the back of her neck. Time to empty it, for she should fill another before afternoon prayers.

She climbed down from the tree, careful not to let any of her apples tumble. The tangy scent made her stomach growl, and she was tempted to help herself to an apple. The noon meal had been lean and supper was not for some time yet.

She may have done just that, if someone was not waiting for her.

A small figure swathed in an undyed homespun habit stood a few feet away. Aelfwyn's gaze went to the nun's face, and her brief lightness of mood dissipated.

Elflaeda.

The nun stood silently watching her with all the friendliness of a hawk circling a dormouse. Aelfwyn had hoped that the young woman's coolness toward her would eventually thaw, but if anything her attitude had worsened. Aelfwyn had caught her glaring at her during mealtimes. Eflaeda watched her now, and the look on her face was venomous.

"Wes þū hāl, Sister Elflaeda," Aelfwyn greeted her with a hesitant smile. "How goes your afternoon."

Elflaeda's pretty face twisted into a sneer. They were alone in the orchard, and the young woman clearly saw little point in keeping up pretenses.

"It would improve greatly," she began through gritted teeth. "If I did not have to share breathing space with a hōre."

Despite that she had not expected a friendly response, Aelfwyn flinched. Elflaeda's foul language was at odds with her sweet, comely face and demure manner. Not knowing what to do, Aelfwyn clutched her basket to her breast. "Elflaeda," she murmured. "I don't know what you—"

"Are you going to weave more lies, like you did with the abbess?" the nun cut in.

Aelfwyn inhaled sharply. "I told Abbess Hilda the truth."

"Is that the best you can do?" Elflaeda's mouth twisted. "You bleat like a witless sheep."

Aelfwyn stared at her. The girl had a sharp tongue. "Think what you want," she replied, "but you were not at Bebbanburg. You do not know what happened, what your brother did."

"He is your king." Elflaeda stepped forward, eyes blazing. "Name him as such."

Aelfwyn swallowed bile but held Elflaeda's gaze. "King Ecgfrith raped me," she said haltingly. "He waited until late, until his hall slumbered, and then he crept into my alcove. He took me by force and—"

"Stop it," Elflaeda hissed, her face turning pink. "I'll not listen to your filth."

"You came here—you cornered me," Aelfwyn countered. Her face had grown hot and tears stung her eyelids. This girl was a bully—and she was barring the way out of the orchard.

"To get the truth from you," Elflaeda countered, taking a threatening step toward her. "Not to listen to more falsehoods."

"I've told the truth."

Elflaeda drew herself up, and for a moment Aelfwyn thought the nun would lash out at her. "You're a *nithing*," she snarled. "A lowborn handmaid who thinks herself better than a king. Don't think I'm a fool. I see what happened. You lured him into the furs and then wanted more than to be his lover. You demanded to be his queen, and when he refused, you ran away. Now, you're determined to spread poison about him."

Aelfwyn grew still. The nun's accusations wounded, but they were so far from the truth they were bordering on ludicrous.

As if sensing a change in Aelfwyn, Elflaeda stepped back, her gaze narrowing. "So you won't deny it?"

Aelfwyn took in every detail of Elflaeda's face. She did not look at all like her elder brother. Clutching her basket of apples to her breast like a shield she started to sidle past Elflaeda. "You know what he's like," she whispered. "Why do you defend him?"

Elflaeda's gaze narrowed. "Hwæt?"

It was time to go. Aelfwyn's stomach cramped, and her heart now thudded against her ribs. She hated confrontation at the best of times, but the young woman's vicious words flayed her like boning knives.

"I see it in your eyes," Aelfwyn gasped the words before her courage deserted her. "You're afraid of him."

Elflaeda flinched as if Aelfwyn had just slapped her. Her face was white, her eyes blazing, but she stepped back to let Aelfwyn pass. The nun did not say a word as she left.

Over the next three days, Aelfwyn threw herself into life at Streonshalh. Her confrontation with Elflaeda had left her unsettled and upset. She lost her appetite and did not regain it till the following evening.

The whole incident had left a bitter taste in her mouth.

Slowly Aelfwyn's upset ebbed away. She tried her best to fit in with Streonshalh's routines; rising with the first light of dawn in the morning and retiring to her pallet as soon as dusk settled over the clifftops. The clanging of the bell for prayers was a constant throughout the day, with meals and chores squeezed in-between. It was not so different from her life as a servant in a Great Hall; only here there was no king to fear.

The sixth day of her new life arrived, and Aelfwyn awoke feeling melancholy.

The evening before had been the last that Leofric would wait for her. It had come and gone and she was still here. He would wait no longer.

Perhaps he had given up waiting days before.

The thought made her feel strangely tearful.

Dawn prayers seemed insufferably long that morning. It was a chill morning, almost cold enough for a frost to settle and a reminder that a long, dark winter lay ahead. What would life be like at Streonshalh during the bitter months? Would she regret coming here then?

After prayers the nuns gathered with their brothers in the refectory and consumed a silent meal of coarse bread and broth. What Aelfwyn would have given for some freshly churned butter and a boiled egg. Since arriving here her stomach growled constantly. Little wonder the nuns—Hilda included—were all lean without a spare inch of flesh. There was no risk of running to fat on such fare as this.

After breaking her fast, Aelfwyn went out to help two of the monks with milking. A heard of goats grazed the pastures above Streonshalh. Hardy beasts with sleek brown and black coats, curved horns, and intelligent golden eyes, the goats were pleasant company.

She sat milking one of them, her forehead pressed into its warm belly that smelled of meadow flowers and dry grass. As she worked, once again, her thoughts wandered to Leofric.

Where was he now? She hoped he had managed to elude the king's men. Her blood chilled at the reminder of Ecgfrith.

She had not spoken to the abbess again of her fears. Hilda had made it clear that the king would never know she lived with them—that she would lie to him if necessary. Yet Aelfwyn did not feel safe. The Queen Mother was likely to make a trip to the abbey soon to see her daughter. Aelfwyn was putting Hilda in danger by remaining here.

What if Elflaeda told her mother? Worse still, what if the king accompanied her?

Aelfwyn squeezed her eyes closed and concentrated on milking the goat. She focused on the rhythmic squeezing of its two teats as frothing milk filled the wooden pail before her.

She had to stop worrying about the future. It was time she started living in the moment, or she would surely drive herself mad with fear.

Chapter Twenty

Elflaeda's Penitence

AELFWYN EMERGED FROM the weaving shed, after an afternoon of spinning wool, and glanced up at the sky. It was the color of iron with low cloud blocking out the sun. Once noon had passed the day grew cold.

A chill seeking wind blew in from the sea, buffeting the walls of Streonshalh. It whistled through the complex, sending up dust in Aelfwyn's face. She bowed her head against it, drew close the homespun habit she had taken to wearing, and hurried across the courtyard.

The wind whipped at her hair, which she had plaited into two braids, and freed a few strands. Aelfwyn pushed it out of her eyes, reminding herself that soon a veil would cover her head and shroud her hair from the world.

She should enjoy the feel of the wind in her hair while it lasted.

Supper was approaching, and the abbess had sent her to the kitchen to help the sisters working there. The savory aroma of stewing rabbit, onions, and turnip greeted her as she stepped inside the wooden annex attached to the back of the refectory. Aelfwyn's mouth watered at the smell.

Finally something other than overcooked pottage.

Six nuns, their sleeves rolled back, their faces flushed, worked inside the smoky space. Some bent over worktables pummeling dough or chopping vegetables, while others worked over the large fire pit in the heart of the space, tending the cauldron of stew that bubbled there.

One of them, a tall thin woman named Berta, looked up from kneading bread dough. "Good afternoon, Aelfwyn. What brings you to here?"

Aelfwyn smiled at her; she liked Berta. The woman had around forty winters, and possessed a long, angular face and brown eyes full of warm humor. "The abbess sent me here to help."

"Not much left to do," the nun replied, before glancing around her, "although we need some herbs gathered. The stew needs some flavoring."

Aelfwyn nodded. "Which ones?"

"Thyme and sage."

Aelfwyn left the kitchen and made her way to the herb garden; a small plot edged with stone that sat to one side of the vegetable enclosure. The light was growing dim, the shadows lengthening—another sign that the evenings were drawing in.

Aelfwyn looked up at the sky and felt a pang. Leofric was out there somewhere—she hoped he was well.

The scent of woody herbs greeted her as she knelt by a growth of sage. She had just picked a handful and was reaching for a few sprigs of thyme when she heard the scuff of a sandal on dirt behind her.

She glanced over her shoulder and saw Elflaeda standing behind her.

Aelfwyn tensed, her pulse quickening. She did not want to be cornered again but she could not let Elflaeda to continue to bully her.

"What do you want?" she asked coldly. However, upon looking closer, she saw that Elflaeda wore a different expression to when she had faced her in the orchard. The look of belligerence was gone. The girl's face was guarded, her gaze nervous.

"I would speak with you a moment," Elflaeda said, her voice trembling slightly.

Aelfwyn plucked the sprigs of thyme and rose to her feet, facing Elflaeda. Something in the nun's manner uneased her far more than the scorn of their last meeting. "What's wrong?"

Elflaeda brought her fine-boned hands together, as if in prayer, but instead wringing them together. "You were right," she said finally, haltingly, as if each word pained her. "About my brother."

Aelfwyn watched her intently, waiting for Elflaeda to continue.

"I am afraid of him. He wears a mask in public, one that few get to see beneath," Elflaeda said softly, her gaze dipping earthward. "Only, as his younger sister, he did not bother to hide who he really was. I'm nothing to him."

Aelfwyn's breathing stilled. She had sensed something in Elflaeda that day in the orchard, a brittleness that had lain just beneath her spite.

"He didn't use his fists to wound but his tongue," Elflaeda pressed on, her gaze still downcast. "In front of our parents he was the dutiful son, but whenever we were alone, Ecgfrith would torment me. He told me I was fat, ugly and witless—repeatedly—wearing me down over many years. Part of the reason why I was so eager to come to Streonshalh was to escape him."

Aelfwyn loosed the breath she had been holding. "You know what he's like, but you were prepared to think the worst of me all the same."

Elflaeda's head snapped up, her dark eyes flashing. "He's my brother." Her eyes glittered, and she glanced around her as if afraid someone might overhear them. Then she stepped closer to Aelfwyn. "He's coming—you must leave here."

Aelfwyn's blood turned to ice. "Hwæt?"

Elflaeda's gaze met hers, and she saw the panic there, the regret. "When you first arrived here and I learned of your tale, I acted rashly. I sent a message with one of the fishermen from the village to Bebbanburg. The king will be on his way by royal barge now."

Aelfwyn stepped back from her, her fists clenching at her sides, crushing the herbs against her palms. Elflaeda stared back, stricken. "It was a mistake, I see that now—but at the time I thought he would think upon me more kindly if I helped him. May the lord strike me down for my foolishness."

Aelfwyn could barely hear her above the thundering of her own heart, the rasp of her panicked breathing. He was coming for her.

"The king will be here by the morning," Elflaeda concluded, her voice barely above a whisper. "You need to go now if you have any chance of escaping him."

Aelfwyn supposed she should feel grateful to Elflaeda for warning her. However, any words of thanks lodged in her throat. Did Elflaeda fully comprehend what she had done?

"You have brought the king's wrath down upon the abbess," Aelfwyn struggled to get the words out. She was suddenly breathless with panic.

Elflaeda shook her head. "Worry not, I will tell him that Hilda had no idea who you were." She reached out a hand, her face pleading. "Give me those herbs and go now, before they lock the southern gate for the night. Please, Aelfwyn. You must run."

Blinking, Aelfwyn reached out and placed the crushed herbs into Elflaeda's outstretched palms. Then she nodded.

"I will tell the others you have a headache and have gone to your pallet early," Elflaeda assured her. "No one will know till you're well gone."

Aelfwyn nodded. "Thank you," she whispered hoarsely. Then she picked up her skirts and without a backward glance hurried away, heading toward the southern gate.

The wind was gusting, bringing spots of rain. It howled across the exposed hills above Streonshalh. It was a bleak evening; purple clouds rolled in overhead promising a night of rain, and the churning sea behind the abbey's bristling outline was the color of pitch.

Spots of rain spattered across Aelfwyn's face as she slipped through the gap in the southern gate. There had been no time to collect any belongings. She was running out into the gloaming, into a gathering storm, with not even a cloak to cover her homespun tunic.

Despair rose in her throat, threatening to choke her.

Why couldn't have Elflaeda told me this yesterday?

The day before Leofric had still been here. He had given her five days— and she had wasted them. Now it was too late.

Aelfwyn ran up the hill, her gaze focused on the southern horizon. The day before Leofric would have been waiting there, outlined against the stormy sky. This evening there was only a sea of waving grass.

Something twisted deep in her chest. Regret, sadness—and self-recrimination.

Idiot. Coward.

She should have seen this coming. Of course Elflaeda would betray her.

Aelfwyn was out of breath by the time she crested the hill, but she pushed herself on. She knew it was futile, but she would not throw away her one last chance at freedom. The light was fading and thunder rumbled in the distance. She needed to find shelter before the storm exploded overhead.

Stumbling in haste, Aelfwyn ran down the hill toward a scattered copse of oaks. She sprinted toward the trees, panic giving her feet wings. It was difficult to see in the fading daylight. She had gone only a few paces into the copse when she tripped on a tree root.

Aelfwyn sprawled across the ground. She let out a string of curses, a sob catching in her throat. This was hopeless. She was barely a furlong from the abbey, and she had already come to grief.

"Not giving up yet, are you?"

The man's voice made Aelfwyn catch her breath. She pushed her hair out of her eyes and gazed up to see Leofric astride Windræs just a few yards away. His gaze met hers.

Joy flooded through her, unexpected in its intensity.

"You're still here," she gasped, feeling like a fool the moment the words had left her mouth. "I thought you left yesterday."

Thunder rumbled directly overhead. The gelding threw up his head, snorting, and danced sideways. Leofric leaned forward and stroked the horse's neck. Yet he did not look away from Aelfwyn. "I thought I'd give you one more day ... just in case you needed more time."

Aelfwyn climbed to her feet and brushed moss and dirt off her skirts. Relief had made her feel weak and shaky.

"I had planned to stay, despite the danger I was putting the abbess in," she admitted quietly, "but one of the nuns has betrayed me. Ecgfrith knows I'm here."

Leofric glanced back in the direction of the abbey, his gaze narrowing. He then urged Windræs forward so he drew level with her. He reached down for her hand. "If the king's on his way then we must make haste," he said, his fingers curling around hers. "Come on."

Chapter Twenty-one

The Crossing

THE STORM RAGED for an entire night and for most of the following day. Icy needles of rain lashed against the travelers, and even Windræs lost some of his zest for the journey. The gelding held his head low, his ears flattened back against the elements.

Leofric and Aelfwyn spoke little.

Aelfwyn huddled against Leofric's chest. He could feel her shivering but could not risk stopping, could not risk lighting a fire to warm them both. He knew the king would have arrived in Streonshalh by now and his men would soon be tracking them south.

He remembered the last time they had ridden together; how she had sat perched stiffly in front of him, barely suffering his company. He had to remind himself that she did not travel with him now out of choice either. If the king's sister had not betrayed her at the abbey, she would be there still.

That she had not willingly chosen to leave Streonshalh should not have bothered Leofric, but it did.

Beyond the copse of oak that had sheltered Leofric for a few days while he waited for Aelfwyn, the land around Streonshalh was bare and windswept, offering no protection from the biting wind and the stinging rain that drove in from the north.

The farther south they rode, the more nervous Leofric became. The bad weather eventually cleared and the sun warmed their wet clothing—but Leofric knew they were riding into danger, not just away from it. They neared Eoforwic now and his home village of Driffield, a short distance from the town.

Godwine of Eoforwic's lands.

Although it would have been quicker to cut across country, Leofric turned Windræs along the coast, giving Eoforwic a wide berth as they approached the mighty Humbre.

They reached the estuary on a bright, windy morning, three days after leaving Streonshalh. Dark waters sparkling in the sun, the Humbre estuary formed a natural border between Northumbria and the kingdoms of southern Britannia—Mercia to the south and west, and the smaller kingdom of Lindesege to the east. Once they crossed the Humbre, they would no longer be under the sway of King Ecgfrith, and hopefully out of reach of the likes of Godwine of Eoforwic.

Of course Leofric reminded himself that neither of them were safe while they remained in Britannia. Still, outside Northumbria they would be harder to find—and catch.

The Humbre was a dark, wide expanse that was impossible to cross on foot, even at low tide, for you risked becoming stuck in the mud halfway. As such, they rode west along its banks. Further inland the waterway narrowed, eventually becoming the River Ouse—the river that flowed west to Eoforwic.

Leofric knew this land well. Many folk lived upon the banks of the Ouse, the villages growing more numerous as they neared Eoforwic. The ealdorman's men patrolled this area; they would have to take care.

It was the early afternoon when he reined in Windræs on the banks of the Ouse. The river had narrowed here, although it was still at least twenty yards across. Aelfwyn dozed against his chest. Sensing something amiss she stirred, blinking sleepily.

"Why have we stopped?"

Leofric grinned down at her. "Time for a swim."

She stiffened. Leofric knew he should not tease her. She had not enjoyed their last river journey and could not swim.

"Don't worry," he assured her. "Windræs will do all the work this time."

Aelfwyn sat up properly, her gaze traveling across the gently flowing Ouse. "But it's so wide ..."

"Aye, but he'll manage it."

She looked unconvinced, but Leofric did not give her time to fret further. Instead he urged Windræs forward, down the gently sloping bank and into the river.

"Lean forward and take hold of his mane," Leofric instructed her. "We're both likely to get a bit wet so ready yourself. Sit tight."

He felt her tension, her fear, but he was pleased when she did as bid without complaint, keeping her worries to herself.

Windræs hesitated on the water's edge and Leofric urged him forward. "Come on lad, take the plunge."

A moment later, the gelding did just that. With a snort, Windræs leaped forward into the water and struck out toward the far bank. Leofric leaned forward as well, loosening the reins so that the horse could find his own way across the river.

Chill water soaked through Leofric's breeches, splashing up as far as his waist. Beneath him, he felt Windræs's powerful body flex and expand as the horse swam. The gelding kept his head just above the water, his nostrils flaring.

"Good lad," Leofric soothed him. "Just a bit farther."

Windræs reached the far bank and lurched out of the water, nearly unseating both his riders in the process. He bounded up the steep back and stopped at the top, his sides heaving from the effort. Leofric and Aelfwyn slid off him and stood back while the horse shook himself dry like a dog. Then Leofric removed his saddle so that Windræs could roll on the grass.

"See," Leofric said, glancing over at Aelfwyn, who stood a few feet away. "I told you not to worry."

She gave him a weak smile in response but said nothing. Leofric frowned, concern shadowing his mood. "You've been so quiet since Streonshalh," he noted quietly. "What's wrong?"

Her cool, blue-grey gaze met his. Her eyes were the color of the North Sea.

"Nothing really," she replied. "I just wonder about the future. Wherever we go they will hunt us."

"They'll give up eventually," Leofric said, with more confidence than he actually felt. "The bitter months are coming—once we get away from the north we should be safe for the winter. Once spring arrives we will see about traveling farther afield."

He saw alarm flare in her eyes. "But where will we go?"

Leofric shrugged. He had not thought that far ahead, not when their immediate survival was at stake. "I don't know," he admitted, before he grinned. "Let's cross one river at a time."

Aelfwyn pulled her woolen cloak around her and stared out at the softly undulating landscape below her. It unfolded like a rumpled mantle, the trees nestling between soft green hills.

It was a cold morning, and her breath clouded the crisp air. She was glad of the cloak, which Leofric had bought for her at a village two days earlier. He had paid for it with a bronze arm-ring, one of Thunred's. They now had only a couple of thrymsas left—after that they would be penniless.

At least they would not starve; she had seen that her companion was a skillful hunter. Leofric had managed to provide fresh meat most evenings now that they were far enough south to risk a fire. He took care of them both—and she was grateful—only it did not ease her worries about the future.

"Beautiful land, is it not?"

Leofric had padded up behind her so quietly she had not heard him; a hunter's gait. Aelfwyn started slightly before smiling at him. He looked well. His pale skin had tanned a light gold, and his hair was starting to grow. When they had met it had been a dark red fuzz against his scalp, but now it was thickening and showing strands of gold and dark brown against the red. Now that she had gotten used to seeing him dressed as a warrior she had to admit that leather suited him far more than a homespun monk's habit ever had.

"It is," she agreed. "Where are we now?"

"In the Kingdom of the Lindesege, we crossed the border yesterday."

Aelfwyn's gaze widened. "I thought we were remaining in Mercia?"

Leofric grinned back. "I changed my mind. I decided Lincylene might be a good place to spend the winter."

Aelfwyn had heard little of Lincylene, the capital of this tiny kingdom. The Kingdom of Lindesege lay between the mighty Humbre to the north and a stretch of water bordering East Anglia named The Wash to the south. Its capital had once been a Roman stronghold, but Aelfwyn knew nothing else about the town. Perhaps that was why Leofric had chosen it—a quiet place for them to lay low for a while.

"How far away from Lincylene are we?" she asked.

"Less than a day's ride."

Aelfwyn turned away from the view. They stood atop a low hill surrounded by woodland of ash and beech. Nearby Windræs cropped at grass. Aelfwyn watched him fondly. The horse had saved their lives—they would never have been able to outrun the king's men without him.

She sensed Leofric's gaze upon her then and glanced up, to find him watching her, a slight smile on his lips.

Not for the first time, Aelfwyn noted how handsome he was—when he smiled the effect was devastating. There was a melting intensity to his hazel-green eyes; he looked at her in a way that made her feel hot and cold at the same time. She had caught him watching her the day before. Like then, she was both flustered and flattered by the attention. However, it warned her that the time for them to talk about the nature of their relationship had arrived.

"Leo," she began huskily, calling him by the shortened form of his name she had taken to using. "You know I'm grateful to you, don't you?"

His smiled widened. "Of course I do."

"I never properly thanked you ... for waiting for me at Streonshalh. I'm still not sure why you did it."

He stepped closer, his smile fading. "Don't you?"

Heat flowered in Aelfwyn's breast, and she forced down a blush. How many women had he wilted with that gaze? "No," she murmured, feigning ignorance, "I don't."

He reached out, his hand gently stroking her cheek. Aelfwyn's breathing grew shallow; her body swayed toward him, betraying her. She clamped down on the melting sensation coursing through her veins and focused on his face.

"Leo ... we need to talk about us, about what we tell people."

He cocked his head. "What do you want to tell folk about us?"

"Do you think they'd believe we're brother and sister?"

He chuckled. "No. One look and you can see we don't come from the same family—they'd know that was a lie."

"So you think we should pretend to be man and wife?"

Again that slow smile that caused her lower belly to tighten and catch fire. "Is that want you want?"

Aelfwyn straightened her spine, raising her chin to look him squarely in the eye. "It would be in name only. I can't give you anything else ... you know that."

He held her gaze for a moment, disappointment flitting briefly across his features—so quickly that she almost missed it—before he nodded. "If that is what you want?"

She nodded.

He smiled once more, although this time his gaze was hooded. Then he turned toward Windræs. "Come, wife—we have a long day's journey ahead of us, if we want to reach Lincylene by nightfall."

Chapter Twenty-two

Lincylene

AELFWYN'S FIRST GLIMPSE of Lincylene was of a stone wall and a cluster of thatch and turf roofs rising into the pale sky. The town perched atop a hill and commanded a view of the surrounding fields and woodland for many furlongs distant. A crumbling dun-colored stone wall encircled it, built centuries earlier.

"My grandfather told me the Romans called it Lindum colonia," Leofric told Aelfwyn as they rode by a small lake and up to the town gates. "They built a legionary fortress at the crown of the hill."

Aelfwyn craned her neck to the top of the town. She could see a high thatched roof, possibly that of a great church, but no sign of the conquerors who had occupied Britannia for many centuries before returning to their homeland.

It was a golden evening, that rare quality of autumn light when every detail stood out in sharp relief. The setting sun stained the town walls the color of rich honey, and the scent of wood smoke laced the cool air.

They rode into Lincylene through a magnificent stone archway and into a roughly cobbled street that led up to the top of the hill. Folk thronged the streets at this time of day. An old man roasted chestnuts on a brazier and sold them to passersby. Children chased each other through the crowd, their cries echoing above the chatter of women who gossiped together on their way home after working in the fields outside the town.

Aelfwyn breathed in the life, the vitality of this place and instantly loved it. She was glad Leofric had brought them here.

They turned off the main thoroughfare and onto a narrower, unpaved street, dominated by a long, windowless building. Leofric brought the horse to a halt in front of it.

Leofric swung down from Windræs, leaving Aelfwyn still seated upon his back. He met her eye. "If anyone asks our names are now Lenred and Aeaba."

Aelfwyn nodded, appreciating caution.

Leofric winked at her. "I'll ask about lodgings at the meadhall—won't be long."

Aelfwyn watched him disappear inside the meadhall. The ripe smell of fermented honey drifted out onto the street from the open doorway, as did the sound of drunken male voices and singing. It was the domain of men; Aelfwyn had never set foot in one. She remembered her father returning from Rendlaesham's meadhall many an evening, his breath reeking of ale as he sang songs of brotherhood, valor, and reckoning—warriors' songs.

Aelfwyn glanced about her, at the men who came and went from the hall. Some of them cast curious or appraising glances in her direction but none approached her. Before entering the town, she had brushed her hair out of its two braids, a look that marked her as a maid. Instead she had twisted it up and pinned it high on her crown: a married woman's hairstyle.

Leofric did not linger inside long. "They have stables out the back where we can house Windræs," he announced with a grin. "There's an annex at the rear of the hall where we can spend the night."

He led Windræs through to a yard behind the meadhall. A row of stalls faced the yard, and after Aelfwyn had dismounted, Leofric stabled the gelding there. Their lodgings for the night were little better than Windræs's—a flimsy lean-to with a dirt floor that had been hastily attached to the back of the meadhall. However, after sleeping rough for so long, Aelfwyn nearly wept at the sight of a dusty straw pallet up against one wall.

"Cynn who runs the hall says we can stay here for free tonight," Leofric told her. "He seemed like a man who might be able to help us. I'm going to go back in, get us some food and drink, and bend his ear."

Aelfwyn turned away, rolling her eyes and hiding a rueful smile. That was the poorest excuse she had ever heard. It was obvious Leofric was angling for a cup of mead. "Off you go then," she said lightly. "I think I'll lie down for a bit."

She glanced over her shoulder, but he had already disappeared outside. Aelfwyn's smile widened. With a jolt she realized it was the first time she had smiled properly in a while ... since before Ecgfrith.

Her smile faded, and she sank down onto the straw pallet with a sigh.

She tried to think of the king as little as possible these days, and the thought of him did not make her heart pound with terror as it had initially. Time and distance were gentle healers.

Aelfwyn lay on her back and gazed up at the roof. It had been shoddily thatched; she could see large gaps of sky through it. Dusk was settling over Lincylene. Smudges of pink and gold shaded the darkening sky.

Yawning, Aelfwyn closed her eyes. She was bone-weary after the day's long ride. There was time for a nap, before Leofric returned with supper.

Aelfwyn's rumbling stomach awoke her. She opened her eyes to find herself shrouded in darkness, and looked up to see the star-sprinkled night sky twinkling back at her through the gaps in the roof.

She sat up, rubbing sleep out of her eyes. Where was Leofric?

A moment later, she heard footfalls outside the lean-to. Her first instinct was fear. After everything she had suffered recently, she trusted no one. Drunken men filled the hall next door; all it would take was one of them to stumble in here in the darkness. Since taking Thunred's weapons for himself, Leofric had gifted her his boning knife. Heart hammering, Aelfwyn reached down and slid the blade free of its sheath at her waist.

The wattle door crashed open and a tall, broad-shouldered figure, his shape illuminated by starlight, lurched inside.

Aelfwyn shrieked and scrambled backwards. She crouched on the straw pallet, brandishing her knife, teeth bared. "Get out!"

"Aelfwyn—it's me, Leo." Leofric answered, his voice sheepish.

"You nearly frightened me half to death."

"Sorry, I should have knocked first." There was a pause as he set something down on the floor. "I've brought us some supper, only I forgot we don't have a cresset burning in here—wait while I fetch one."

Aelfwyn resheathed the knife and sat down shakily on the edge of the pallet. Her nerves were still a mess.

Leofric reappeared a few moments later bearing a small clay cresset filled with oil that burned brightly. He cast her a contrite grin and sat down, cross-legged on the floor next to the wooden platter he had brought earlier. "Dig in."

Aelfwyn's mouth watered when she saw a loaf of fresh bread, salted pork, and a chunk of cheese sitting next to two cups of what smelled like ale. She pushed herself off the pallet and sat down on the floor next to Leofric.

"My new friend Cynn can talk," Leofric said, tearing off a chunk of bread and passing it to her. "This cost me our last thrymsa but it was worth it."

Aelfwyn stuffed the bread into her mouth, followed by a chunk of cheese. She had never tasted food so good—still they now had no coin left.

"What will we do?" she asked when she had swallowed her mouthful. "How will we survive?"

Leofric gave her the roguish grin that she had come to know well; one that usually meant he had news for her. "Cynn tells me that there is a hut in the woods not far from town. It sits near the banks of the river and until a year ago belonged to a woodcutter. The man lost his wife and children to fever and turned strange afterward. One day he left home and never returned. The meadhall keeper says the hut is in need of repair but it is livable. He insists that no one has claimed the dwelling and that Lincylene is in need of a new woodcutter."

Aelfwyn held his gaze, realization dawning. "You mean we can live there?"

"Aye, for the bitter months at least, while we decide what to do next."

Relief flooded through Aelfwyn, making her feel weak. She had not realized how much tension she had been carrying until this moment.

Leofric held her gaze, his expression expectant. "What do you think?"

Aelfwyn grinned back at him and raised her cup of ale in a toast. "I think that's the best news I've had in a long while."

A crisp morning dawned over Lincylene as Leofric and Aelfwyn rode out of town. The smoke from cook fires stained the sky; the aroma of baking bread wafted through the narrow streets.

Leofric nodded to a merchant who led a goat-drawn cart full of turnips into town. No doubt, the man was heading for the market. The meadhall owner had told him that there was a busy market evening morning at the top of the hill, in between the church and the King of Lindesege's Great Hall. Leofric would have liked to have stopped at the market this morning, but with their purses now empty there was little point.

Aelfwyn sat before him. Her pale hair was piled high on her head, revealing her long, slender neck. It was a different style for her, now that she was pretending to be a wife, and one that made her look older. Leofric focused on the nape of her neck, resisting the urge to lean forward and kiss her gently there.

How would she react?

Badly, most likely.

Traveling with her had become exquisite torture. He was not teasing the day before when she had asked him why he had stayed on at Streonshalh. He had not wanted to admit it to himself, but the longer they journeyed together the harder it became for him to deny his true feelings.

He wanted her.

Sitting this close to Aelfwyn, he could smell the sweetness of her skin and feel her warmth and softness pressed against him. It caused his insides to knot in a wanting so strong it took all his self-control not to pull her against him and bury his face in her neck.

She was lovely—so poised, warm, and gentle. He longed to put a smile on her face, to make her forget her past. He wanted to lie with her and teach her how it should be between a man and woman. He yearned to worship her naked body, to—

Stop it.

Leofric shook his head and gave himself a mental slap. His groin now ached and he inched himself backward slightly, so that Aelfwyn would not feel his rock-hard cock.

He tried to think about things that would deflate his erection—of a rotting sheep's carcass or of Prior Cuthbert sitting on the privy—anything to distract himself from the young woman sitting in front of him.

Leofric had never known frustration like this before. Before his exile to Lindisfarena, women had been easy to come by. Not one had ever denied him.

Only Aelfwyn. She had built an invisible wall between them that he was finding near impossible to breach. He knew why, and he understood her reticence. He just hoped that with time she might trust him, might let down her guard.

For the first time in his life, he was willing to wait.

Chapter Twenty-three

The Woodcutter's Hut

THE WOODCUTTER'S HUT lay around ten furlongs from Lincylene, near the banks of the River Witham. Towering beeches protected the cottage from the east winds, and a gnarled, wild cherry tree grew in the unkempt yard outside the hut.

The small wattle and daub structure was in a worse state than Leofric had anticipated. It was incredible how quickly buildings deteriorated once no one lived in them. Homes needed owners or they went back to nature. The wattle door hung off the hinges, and the shutters of its single window were missing, no doubt taken by locals for their own homes.

Leofric swung down from Windræs and helped Aelfwyn dismount. He then tied the horse to the broken fence before leading the way inside.

It was little more than an empty shell. Looters had stripped what few possessions the woodcutter had left behind, leaving little more than shards of shattered pottery, a broken work table, and a scattered collection of cooking utensils—most of them warped or broken.

Leofric cast a glance at Aelfwyn. She was used to the likes of the Great Tower of Bebbanburg; this hut must look pitiful in comparison. "I'm sorry," he said, pulling a face. "I know it's not much."

She surprised him by smiling. "It's a roof over our heads and with a bit of work it'll be a home."

"Really, you're not disappointed?"

She laughed, and he realized it was the first time she had done so in his presence. "Of course not. I'm not some pampered lady who is only happy in a Great Hall. A home this size suits me just as well, if not better."

He raised his eyebrows.

Her mouth quirked. "Why the surprise?"

"Because you're not like any woman I've ever met."

She snorted. "Then you've not met many women—not all of us care for finery and gold." With that she took off her cloak and hung it behind the door. "By the time I've finished with this hut you won't recognize it."

Aelfwyn climbed up the riverbank carrying an armload of rushes. Behind her, the gentle waters of the River Witham flowed by. It was starting to rain; dark clouds gathered overhead and a brisk wind blew in from the northeast.

Humming gently to herself, she crossed the grassy expanse between the river and the edge of the woodland. A few more paces took her inside the hut. A spartan but clean and welcoming interior greeted her.

In the ten days she and Leofric had lived here, they had both worked from dawn till dusk to make the hut comfortable. Winter was drawing closer; they needed to ensure their dwelling was watertight and warm before then. The air smelled of lavender, wood smoke—and rabbit stew.

Aelfwyn had scattered lavender amongst the fresh rushes on the floor, to give the interior a welcoming scent. The smoke came from the fire pit in the center of the one-room dwelling. Leofric had fixed the roof, leaving a slit in the top for smoke to escape. Even so, the interior did get a little smoky. A dented iron pot—one of the few items she had managed to salvage—filled with simmering stew hung above the embers.

Aelfwyn crossed to the far side of the hut, her feet crunching on the rushes. There, she laid out her fresh rushes on a pile she had been adding to over the past couple of days. They made a good, if slightly prickly, sleeping pallet. With the addition of a few furs, it would soon be very comfortable to sleep upon.

Rain started thudding on the sod roof and Aelfwyn glanced up. It was the first rain since Leofric had patched it—they would soon see if there were any leaks. The rain grew heavier, thundering down upon the roof. She went to the tiny window and glanced out. The deluge was lashing across the land in great sheets, stippling the surface of the river like hundreds of bone needles.

Leofric was out in that weather—she hoped he had found shelter.

Reluctantly, she closed the shutters, shutting out the rich smell of the rain and casting the interior of the dwelling in shadow. Then she lit the collection of cressets that Leofric had fastened to the walls, and went to tend the stew. She was just adding some dried herbs to it when the door to the hut flew open, and Leofric stepped inside. He brought a gust of wind with him that caused the cressets to gutter and the coals in the hearth to glow red.

"God's bones, it's foul out there."

Aelfwyn turned to find him dripping from head to foot, his hair plastered darkly across his scalp, his face gleaming with rain. In his right hand he held up a dead hare by its back feet.

"Well done, Leo." She beamed at him and rushed forward to retrieve the hare. It was magnificent. The meat would last them for days, and she could use the hare's soft pelt to add to the fur wall hanging she was making.

"At your service, M'lady." He smiled back, closing the door firmly behind him. He then sniffed the air. "Something smells good."

"It's almost ready. But get yourself dry first—you're dripping water everywhere."

Aelfwyn turned her back on him to give Leofric some privacy and went to retrieve a drying cloth; a coarse strip of homespun from the monk's robe she had once worn.

She retrieved the cloth, turned around—and stopped short.

Leofric had stripped off his sodden leather vest and linen undershirt. He was now in the process of unfastening his breeches.

"Wait," Aelfwyn squeaked.

He glanced up, his gaze meeting hers. "What?" he replied innocently. Too innocently—he knew exactly what he was doing.

"Take this first." Aelfwyn hurried across to him and thrust the drying cloth into his hands. She then turned her back on him and went to the work table, busying herself with tidying it up, even though the scrubbed surface was already spotless.

She could feel Leofric's gaze burning into her back, and she silently cursed him. He knew the effect he had on her and enjoyed seeing her squirm. Time after time, her body betrayed her.

Aelfwyn blamed Leofric.

Most of the time he was excellent company. Leofric took each day with a matter-of-fact practicality and good humor that made him easy to live with. But then he would ruin the camaraderie between them with one heated look.

A look that set her blood on fire, that made her loins melt. A look that made her want to throw herself into his arms and devour him.

Aelfwyn fought that sensation now. The sight of him half-naked, his wet skin gleaming in the flickering light from the fire pit and cressets, made her ache with desire.

This was what happened when a man and woman spent too long in each other's company. Her gratitude had deepened into something else— something that both feared and excited her.

Something she could not control.

When she had composed herself, Aelfwyn turned around once more to find him sitting by the fire pit. His clothing hung, steaming nearby. Leofric wore little more than a loincloth of homespun around his waist. However, now that she had mastered her emotions, Aelfwyn managed to keep her expression neutral.

She dished them both up stew, into wooden bowls that Leofric had whittled shortly after their arrival here.

Leofric ate hungrily. "The stew's good," he complimented her, holding out the bowl for another ladleful.

Aelfwyn smiled. He was being kind—they both knew she was not a brilliant cook, although the fact they had little in the way of vegetables or seasonings to make her stews more interesting did not help.

"I sold my first load of wood this afternoon in town," he announced as he dug into his second bowl of stew. "We now have two thrymsas in our purse."

Aelfwyn smiled. "Really?"

"Aye, I harnessed Windræs up and managed to drag a log of beech into the market square. I'd only just recovered my breath when a man offered to buy it from me. He's building a hall for his family and has put in an order for five more logs over the coming days."

Aelfwyn clapped her hands together and gave a squeal of joy. Finally things were going right. She liked Lincylene. The town's folk had proved friendly, accepting the young woodcutter and his wife into their midst without question.

For the first time in her life, Aelfwyn felt as if she truly belonged.

"It's good to see you happy, Aelfwyn."

She glanced across the hearth to see Leofric watching her. He wore that enigmatic half-smile she had come to know well. Of its own accord, her gaze dipped to his naked chest, taking in the smooth lightly tanned skin and broad shoulders. Her mouth went dry, and she glanced down at her half-eaten bowl of stew.

"I appreciate everything you're doing for us," she said quietly, her exuberance dimming. "You work hard."

"As do you."

She did not reply, her body going hot under the intensity of his gaze. It suddenly felt too stuffy inside the hut, too cramped for the pair of them. Panic fluttered up inside Aelfwyn. If it were not for the pouring rain, she would have fled outside.

She heard the scrape of his stool and the sound of him padding barefoot across the rush-strewn floor toward her. Panic flowered into fear.

Aelfwyn leaped to her feet. "I'd better wash up."

Suddenly he was there, towering above her—too close, too male, too attractive by half. "Aelfwyn—"

"Leo, please ... I—"

He did not reply but instead gathered her close against him, his hands cupping the back of her head as his mouth slanted across hers.

Aelfwyn's breathing stopped.

The feel of his hard body against hers, the musk of his warm skin, and the softness of his lips on hers caused time to stand still. He parted her lips with his tongue and a hunger unlike anything she had ever known exploded deep within her. She gasped. Leofric groaned in response, his mouth devouring hers, and he pulled her hard against him so that the length of their bodies pressed together.

Then Aelfwyn felt the hard column of his arousal pressed against her belly.

In an instant the melting torpor of desire dissolved.

He was a man. He would hurt her—humiliate her.

With a cry, Aelfwyn twisted free of Leofric. She staggered back, knocking over the stool she had been sitting on, nearly sending it flying into the fire.

"Aelfwyn ..." Leofric's eyes were wide, and she saw alarm in their hazel-green depths. He reached out for her.

"No." She backed away from him. "I can't ... I just can't."

"But I would never hurt you."

Tears blurred her vision, and she shook her head. "It doesn't matter what you say. I'm scarred—deep inside where no one can see. Ecgfrith stripped everything away."

His gaze darkened. "You give that bastard too much power."

Aelfwyn turned away from him, crying freely now. "You don't understand," she gasped.

Moments passed as she struggled to contain her sobs. When Leofric spoke again, she realized he was right behind her.

"Aelfwyn, I'm sorry." His voice was low, husky with regret. "The last thing I want is to frighten you. I let my instincts get the better of me."

Aelfwyn nodded, her breathing now coming in ragged gulps. She was close to unravelling completely, something she had not done since she had thrown herself into the waves near Bebbanburg.

"Come—I'm sorry," he repeated softly, before gently taking hold of her shoulders and turning her toward him. She glanced up at his face and saw his stricken expression. "It breaks me in-two to see you so upset and know I'm the cause."

"It's not your fault," Aelfwyn hiccoughed. "It's me, I'm broken."

"Hush." He pulled her gently against his chest, cradling against her as if she were made of fragile eggshell. "You're still healing, and I'm a blundering oaf. Please forgive me."

Aelfwyn leaned into the hard wall of his chest, enfolded by the strength and warmth of his arms, and felt the last of her restraint unravel. The tide she had been holding back for too long broke free, and she wept.

Chapter Twenty-four

Autumn Fires

AUTUMN SLOWLY SETTLED over Britannia. The trees' cloaks of green changed to red and gold, before the leaves started to fall. The days grew shorter, the nights drew in, and the air grew crisp with the promise of winter.

Winterfylleth arrived. The folk of Lincylene lit bonfires outside the town walls to celebrate the night of the dead; the night their ancestors walked abroad once more. They left candles burning on their windowsills and plates of cakes near the hearth. It was an old practice—to ward off evil spirits and welcome the friendly ones—and a tradition Leofric had grown up with.

He brought Aelfwyn with him to the festivities. They ate apple cake drenched in honey and drank hot elderberry wine, watching folk dance around the fire.

Leofric's gaze traveled over the crowd of revelers, their faces ruddy with cold, and he felt a sense of belonging wash over him when he recognized many of them. He was starting to get to know folk. His friend Waric, whom he often saw in Cynn's meadhall, waved as he walked past. Waric, a man the same age as Leofric with short brown hair and keen grey eyes, had his arm around his young wife's shoulders. Catching Waric's eye, Leofric grinned and waved back.

Leofric spotted the King of Lindesege on the edge of the revelers. Seated upon a wooden dais with his pretty red-haired wife beside him, King Eatta nursed a cup of mead while he surveyed his subjects. Still in the prime of life—no older than thirty winters—the king was tall and broad-shouldered with a mane of thick blond hair and a neatly trimmed beard. Leofric watched Eatta laugh at something one of his retainers had said, and noticed that despite the mirth on his handsome face, no humor reached his sharp gaze.

Beside Leofric, Aelfwyn was wrapped in a new fur mantle she had bought at market the day before. Her cheeks were flushed with cold and wine, her eyes bright as she admired the dancing flames.

"Are you enjoying the festivities?" he asked, raising his voice to be heard over the roaring, crackling fire.

"Aye." She favored him with a warm smile. "I love this time of year. Every Winterfylleth my mother bakes honey and walnut tarts. I'm sure my parents will be enjoying one tonight." Her gaze dimmed slightly as she finished this sentence.

"You miss them," Leofric observed.

She looked up, her gaze meeting his. "Don't you miss your family?"

Leofric shrugged. "Not really," he admitted. "I always felt as if I was getting under their feet—the youngest son is more of a nuisance than anything else in a family as large as mine."

She raised an eyebrow, as if she did not believe him but Leofric merely smiled back at her. A month had passed since the night he kissed her, and he had done his best to mend things between them.

He no longer teased her—provoked her—like before. He had ceased giving her melting looks or brushing his hand against hers whenever she passed him something. It had been a game before—one he had enjoyed playing. He had treated his wooing of her like a hunt without taking into account just how badly the king had damaged her.

For the first time, Leofric wished Ecgfrith of Northumbria was standing before him. He wanted to stab his sword into that whoreson's belly and listen to his screams as he died, for what he had done to Aelfwyn.

She had cried in his arms a long while that night, and he had been able to do nothing but comfort her. He had hoped the tears—the release—would do her good, and it seemed it had. The next day she had been a little subdued but calm. In the days that followed she gradually relaxed in his presence again.

Leofric still ached for her, but now he kept his lust to himself. At night he lay on the rushes near the fire pit, wrapped in his cloak, and listened to the gentle sound of her breathing a few feet away. Occasionally he would torture himself by imagining her naked and pliant beneath him as he kissed and licked his way down her body—however, such thoughts soon became too difficult to bear so he ceased his fantasies.

These days, he tried to think of other things while he waited for sleep to claim him. There was little point in such imaginings. Not when his touch repelled Aelfwyn so.

"Would you like another cup?" He had noticed she had nearly finished her hot elderberry wine.

Aelfwyn nodded and smiled, her lips stained red. "Yes, thank you."

He took her cup, careful to avoiding touching her. "I'll return soon then."

Aelfwyn watched Leofric leave her side and wander a few yards away, to where the owner of the meadhall, Cynn, filled folk's cups with wine from a great steaming cauldron. She watched Cynn and Leofric chat together— they had become fast friends since she and Leofric had come to live at Lincylene.

Cynn was a broad, balding man of around thirty winters, who had a feisty wife and a brood of four daughters to contend with at home. Leofric often joked about how Cynn liked to escape to the meadhall at every opportunity to escape his female-dominated household. His wife, Gytha, was by his side tonight. She was a stout woman with a fair face, startling green eyes and wiry auburn hair. She said something to Leofric and then laughed when he responded, her eyes twinkling with mirth.

Leofric certainly knew how to charm women, Aelfwyn reflected. She was not blind to the fact that wherever they went, maids, wives, and crones all made eyes at him. She watched now as Leofric bid Cynn and Gytha good eve and made his way back toward her, taking care not to spill the steaming cups of wine he carried.

Two young women passed by him. One of them—a beauty with a tumbling mane of dark golden hair—stopped to greet him. The girl tossed her hair and pushed out her plump bosom as she talked to Leofric. She blushed when he flashed her a grin, bid her good eve, and continued on his way.

A white-hot blade of jealousy cut through Aelfwyn's gut, catching her off guard. The desire to leap at the girl and rake her fingernails down her face shocked Aelfwyn to the core.

Where had that come from?

She had no right to be jealous, not when Leofric was not hers. Not when she had shunned his advances.

That girl had done nothing to her. Aelfwyn and Leofric only played at being man and wife for the benefit of the townsfolk. If he wished to seek out female company elsewhere, it was nothing to do with her. Yet the thought made her belly tie itself in knots.

"What ails you?" Leofric asked when he reached her, holding out a cup of wine. "You're flushed."

"I'm just standing too close to the fire," Aelfwyn answered. "Let's move back a bit."

He nodded, and they took a few steps back. On the other side of the fire, near the king's seat, a lad started to play a jaunty tune upon a bone whistle. The maids who had flirted with Leofric earlier started dancing; their unbound hair gleaming in the firelight.

Jealousy coiled in the pit of Aelfwyn's stomach once more, but she did her best to ignore it. This was a new side to her character; one she did not like much.

"Cynn had some news." Leofric bent close, his voice low.

Aelfwyn turned, tensing when she saw the serious look on his face. "What is it?"

"He was at Torksey market yesterday—there were men there, Northumbrians, asking questions."

Despite the warmth of the nearby fire, Aelfwyn went cold. "Ecgfrith's men?" she whispered, dreading the answer.

Leofric nodded, his face now grim. "They were asking folk if they'd seen a young woman named Aelfwyn with pale blonde hair—possibly traveling on her own, or with a monk." Leofric's mouth thinned as he finished this sentence.

Not for the first time Aelfwyn was relieved they both went by different names in Lincylene.

"Are we safe here?" Aelfwyn's fingers clenched around the cup of wine. She did not want to leave Lincylene, not when she was just starting to feel at home. She did not want to start running again.

"I don't know," Leofric replied. "I didn't expect them to track us this far. I thought they'd travel into Mercia instead." He paused then, his gaze shifting to the dancing flames, his expression turning pensive. "Maybe we should leave—go further south."

Aelfwyn's stomach cramped. "Does Cynn suspect it's us they're looking for?"

Leofric shook his head. "He was sharing gossip with me, nothing else. We aren't using our real names. I arrived here dressed as a warrior, not a monk. There are other women with the same hair color as you; I don't think he made the connection."

Relief made Aelfwyn's knees sag beneath her. "Did anyone help the men searching for us?"

"He says not," Leofric admitted, "but I don't want to risk them catching up with us—not now. We should go, before the first snows."

Aelfwyn reached out, her hand fastening around his forearm. Leofric glanced up, surprised, for they had not touched in a month ... not since that night he had kissed her. His skin was warm under her palm but she ignored it—ignored how still he had suddenly gone.

"Please, Leo," she began, her fingers digging into his flesh. "Don't make me leave here, not yet. The snows will arrive soon enough. Ecgfrith's men will stop looking for us. Let's wait till spring."

"What if they come to Lincylene asking the same questions?" he asked, raising an eyebrow. "Do you think no one will tell them that there's a woman who matches that description living in the woods nearby—a newcomer to the town."

"You said it yourself, there are plenty of women matching my description," she countered, "and no one has seen a monk."

His gaze hooded, and he regarded her silently for a few moments. "Are you willing to take that risk?" he asked.

She held his gaze and nodded.

Leofric exhaled sharply. She could see he was wrestling with his better judgement. "I don't like it," he admitted, "but I can see you're going to fight me on this."

She relaxed her death-grip on his arm. "Does this mean we can stay?"

"Aye—but both of us must be wary from now on. I'll not stop looking over my shoulder until we're far from Ecgfrith's reach."

Leofric was pensive during the walk back home. Away from the roaring Winterfylleth fire, the night was cold. A hunter's moon rode high in the pitch sky, and a frost was starting to settle; his boots crunched over it as he walked.

Aelfwyn also said little. He glanced across at her once or twice, but she had pulled up her fur-lined hood, and he could not see her face.

He was not sure he had done the right thing in giving in to her. His instincts—his gut—told him to run, to get as far away from here as possible. But Aelfwyn's pleading gaze, the way she had so desperately gripped his arm, had swayed him. Maybe she was right; they were safe enough here for the time being.

He hoped so.

Yet Cynn's tale worried him. Ecgfrith's men should not still be searching for them. They should have given up by now and returned to Bebbanburg with their tails between their legs. The king was being more persistent than Leofric had anticipated, and this worried him.

Ecgfrith had not taken well to losing his wife's comely handmaid—and he was determined to find her.

Chapter Twenty-five

Eatta's Price

AELFWYN BENT AND collected an armload of twigs before carrying them over to the large woolsack she had brought with her. She stood in a woodland glade, surrounded by towering beech trees. It was a grey, chill day with spots of rain in the air, but she had returned to the woods with Leofric after their noon meal to bring back kindling.

Aelfwyn glanced up at the darkening sky and frowned. The days grew so short this time of year. The air had the dank smell of coming snow.

A few yards away Leofric worked on the latest tree he had felled. Shirtless, his bare torso gleaming with sweat, he prepared the trunk by sawing off branches. Despite herself, Aelfwyn paused a moment to admire him. Leofric had been well-built before their arrival here, but the hard physical work had broadened his shoulders even further and toned his arms and back into hard muscle. Her gaze lingered on the planes of his smooth chest before she turned away, heart pounding.

Stop it. One of these days he'll catch you.

Good to his word, Leofric had done as she had pleaded and now treated her more like a sister. Initially she had been relieved, for she had not been able to cope with his raw male interest. It was now nearly two moon cycles later; Yule and Mother Night—the shortest night of the year—was approaching.

These days Aelfwyn felt differently. There was a restlessness in her; an odd sensation she could not name. Leofric had given her what she wanted. Why then did she feel a hollowness in her gut whenever she looked at him? Why did she stare at him when he was not looking?

Women are as fickle as we are foolish, she thought disparagingly. *Even when we're given what we asked for we're never happy.*

Aelfwyn gathered up another armful of sticks and marched back across to the jute woolsack before dumping them inside. The sack was nearly full; two more armloads should do it and then she would drag it home.

She was just returning to the piles of branches, leaves and twigs littering the clearing, when a group of leatherclad men emerged from the trees.

Aelfwyn froze.

Her first thought was that King Ecgfrith's men had finally found her. Then she realized that she recognized some of the men's faces; she had seen them on her trips to Lincylene. They were the King of Lindesege's men. She recognized Waric—Leofric's friend—at the head of the group.

"Lenred," she called out, only just remembering not to use Leofric's real name. "We have visitors."

Leofric straightened up, wiping sweat off his brow as he did so. Upon seeing the approaching warriors he lowered his saw, although Aelfwyn noted that he kept tight hold of it.

"Wes hāl!" he hailed the men, his tone cheerful.

Aelfwyn remained still, not daring to move. She watched Leofric step away from the felled tree and walk towards the newcomers.

"Waric," he greeted his friend, a grin lighting his face. "I never see you away from the meadhall—what brings you into the woods?"

Waric's gaze was serious when it met Leofric's, and he did not smile. "The king wants to see you."

Leofric's grin faded. "Why's that?"

"That's his business," another warrior replied. He was a short and broad man with a badly pockmarked face.

Leofric raised an eyebrow. "Well as you can see I'm in the middle of something. Tell the king I'll visit his hall once I've finished work for the day."

"This isn't a request," the warrior continued. "The king demands you come with us now."

Leofric's gaze met the man's and held. Aelfwyn saw the tension in his shoulders and wondered if he was considering denying them. It would be foolish to do so. There were ten armed warriors—too many to fight off with a handsaw.

"Come, Lenred." Waric spoke up, stepping forward. "The sooner you do this the sooner you can get back to work."

"Aye." The pox-scarred warrior grinned before glancing across at where Aelfwyn stood. "Your lady wife is coming too—the king wants to see you both."

Aelfwyn and Leofric walked up Steep Hill toward Lincylene's Great Hall. The building loomed before them, its steeply gabled roof a dark outline against the dull sky.

A few folk thronged the street, shopping or going about their business while there was still daylight. They cast curious glances toward the couple flanked by ten of the king's men, who walked past.

Aelfwyn glanced across at Leofric, hoping to catch his gaze, but he was staring straight ahead, his face unreadable. She wanted to speak to him—to have his assurance everything would be all right—yet with the king's men right behind them it would be unwise to say anything.

Her mind whirled, concocting possible scenarios in her head about why King Eatta had summoned them—each more terrifying than the last. All she could think of was that the king had discovered who they were and was about to send them both north to Ecgfrith.

Her knees almost buckled with terror at this thought.

At the top of the hill, they reached Market Square. The wide space was empty at this time of day. Only a stray dog sat gnawing a bone in the shadow of the magnificent church that flanked one side of the open space. Built of local stone and timber with a strawthatch roof, the church made Eatta's hall opposite appear an oversized barn in comparison.

Aelfwyn and Leofric climbed the steps to the Great Hall of Lincylene, following Waric and the pox-scarred warrior. They passed the two spearmen guarding the entrance and went inside.

The interior of King Eatta's hall reminded Aelfwyn of Rendlaesham's famed 'Golden Hall', although this one was a lot smaller, and far less finely decorated. Even so it was like stepping inside the ribcage of a great serpent. Huge oak beams, blackened by countless fires, stretched across the high ceiling. Two long fire pits, circled in stone, dominated the interior, and a wooden high seat rose at the far end. The hall was busy at this time of day: servants chopped turnips and rolled out piecrust on long tables, women worked at distaffs or sewed tunics, men sat drinking and playing knucklebones near the firepit, and children wrestled on the rushes.

The warriors cut a path through them all and led Aelfwyn and Leofric straight up to the foot of the high seat.

King Eatta—blond and handsome but with a hard stare—sat upon an ornate wooden chair. Aelfwyn had seen Ealdwulf of the East Angles and Ecgfrith of Northumbria sit upon similar seats, although neither of those chairs had armrests of intricately carved serpent heads as this one did. The serpent mouths gaped open, revealing needle-sharp teeth.

Eatta's wife sat silently at his side. She was a tall, striking woman with thick red hair and heavily lidded green eyes. Two young daughters clung to her skirts. Her pretty face was a mask of boredom as she surveyed the two individuals her husband had summoned. Retainers—men and women finely dressed in embroidered tunics with squirrel-fur trims and wearing amber and bronze jewelry—hovered nearby, their faces eager.

Aelfwyn and Leofric stopped before the high seat. Aelfwyn quickly dropped her eyes to the rush-strewn floor and hoped Leofric was doing the same.

"You summoned me, milord." Leofric greeted Eatta.

"Aye, Lenred Woodcutter," the king replied. He had a deep, powerful voice; that of a man who was used to being obeyed. "I hear that you've taken up residence in the abandoned hut near the River Witham—that you've been felling my trees."

The knots in Aelfwyn's stomach tightened. At last—here was the reason King Eatta had called them to him.

Although part of her was relieved that his summons had nothing to do with King Ecgfrith, the rest of her filled with dread. They had felt so welcome here—only things were about to change.

"I have been felling trees," Leofric admitted cautiously, "however, I did not realize I had to ask permission, sire."

Eatta watched him steadily. The king had midnight blue eyes and they were unnervingly keen and sharp.

"This is my kingdom," he said finally. "*My* land. You should have come to me upon making your home here. You should have gained my consent."

Leofric did not reply immediately. A tense silence stretched out between the two men—and it was Aelfwyn who broke it. She rushed forward and fell to her knees before the high seat.

"Milord, please forgive us. My husband didn't know he had to ask permission, but we shall ask it now."

"Aeaba," Leofric hissed. "Get up!"

Aelfwyn ignored him. Instead she looked up, her gaze meeting Eatta's. "Milord, we only wish to make an honest living in our new home. It was never our intention to steal from you."

The king held her gaze for a moment longer before he looked once more at Leofric. "Your pretty young wife has a lot to say for herself," he said before giving Leofric a wolfish grin. "How about I give her to my men, and we find another use for that sweet mouth?"

A stunned silence fell in the hall. A moment later some of Eatta's retainers started to snigger. Face burning, Aelfwyn struggled up off her knees and rejoined Leofric. One glance at his face told her he was livid. He held the king's gaze, his own hard.

"Leave my wife out of this," he said, his voice low and controlled. "She was merely asking for your consent—there was no need to humiliate her."

Eatta raised an eyebrow, an amused look upon his face. "What kind of man lets his wife speak on his behalf. If you want permission ask for it yourself."

Leofric inhaled slowly. "Do we have your consent?"

"I'm your king," Eatta drawled. "Address me as such."

"Do we have your consent, sire?"

Long moments passed before Eatta replied. "Yes you do ... but there is a price for my clemency."

Leofric did not speak, silently awaiting the king's judgement. Aelfwyn stared down at her feet, blinking back tears. She just wanted to be away from this unfriendly hall and its cruel, rock-hewn king.

"Give me your money purse," Eatta ordered softly.

Leofric undid the leather purse he carried on his belt and handed it to Waric. The warrior stepped up onto the high seat and gave the pouch to the king. Eatta poured the bag's contents out onto his broad palm.

"There's a goodly amount of thrymsas here," he mused, weighing the gold in his palm. "The folk of Lincylene have been generous with you."

Aelfwyn felt sick as she watched the king put only one thrymsa back in the pouch and return it to Waric. The remaining coins he handed to one of his retainers. That was the only shillings they had, and Leofric had worked hard for every piece of it. Anger flickered in the pit of her belly, and at that moment she hated King Eatta of Lindesege.

"Be grateful I have left you with one thrymsa to your name," Eatta told Leofric, "for it's more than you deserve."

Leofric said nothing, although Aelfwyn saw a nerve flicker in his jaw. He was hanging on to his temper by a thred.

"I see anger in your eyes, Woodcutter," the king said finally. "My price is clearly not high enough."

"It's more than enough," Leofric finally managed between gritted teeth, "and I thank you for the lesson, sire."

Eatta gave a soft laugh. "You're not thankful at all ... and for that I will have to make an example of you."

Aelfwyn went cold. She looked up and saw the king's dark blue eyes dancing with pleasure. He was giving Leofric a challenging look, as if daring him to lose his temper and sign his own death writ.

"If we didn't need a woodcutter locally, I'd take your hand as punishment. Instead I condemn you to a public flogging tomorrow at dawn." Eatta smiled then, although there was no warmth in the expression. "I will wield the rod myself."

Chapter Twenty-six

The Flogging

"PLEASE, MILORD!" AELFWYN rushed forward, only to be hauled back by one of the king's men. "I beg you not to punish him. He's done nothing to earn it!"

"Keep a leash on your wife, Woodcutter," Eatta drawled, dismissing Aelfwyn with a wave of his hand, "or I really will give her to my men."

This caused a rumble of coarse masculine laughter to erupt around them. Heart pounding, Aelfwyn shrugged herself free of the warrior's bruising grasp.

"Don't touch me," she hissed. With a lecherous grin, the man held up his hands and backed off.

Aelfwyn glanced over at Leofric and saw that he had gone pale. However, he looked even angrier than earlier; the king's harsh sentence had not cowed him.

As if remembering that Aelfwyn stood next to him, Leofric shifted his gaze from Eatta then and looked at her. His gaze softened for a moment and the corner of his mouth quirked—as he tried to smile and failed. He opened his mouth to say something to her, but the king cut him off.

"Chain the woodcutter to the wall in here overnight," Eatta ordered his men. "Let's see if that doesn't humble him."

The men dragged Leofric over to the eastern wall of the Great Hall. Aelfwyn followed close behind. They hauled Leofric up onto the platform that ran around the edge of the hall and shackled his wrists to heavy iron chains that hung there. The men laughed at him as he struggled in the iron manacles.

"Wriggle all you want," one of them jeered, "but you won't be getting free until dawn."

Leofric spat at the warrior in response, but this only increased the group's mirth.

"You won't be so cocky in the morning," the pox-scarred warrior told him. "Not after the king flogs your back to ribbons."

They left them then, returning to their cups of mead and the warmth of the firepit. Only Waric lingered, his gaze lingering on Leofric for a moment, his face conflicted.

"Go on then," Leofric hissed at him. "There's no point in looking sorry now."

Waric held his gaze for a moment before dipping his head and walking away.

Aelfwyn stood next to Leofric, her fur cloak pulled tight about her. She waited until they were alone, until the folk inside the hall turned their attention elsewhere, before she spoke.

"I'm so sorry," she whispered. "I thought I was helping—but I just made things worse."

Leofric's gaze met hers. "It wasn't your fault," he replied wearily. "The king wanted an excuse to humiliate me. I shouldn't have lost my temper—I played right into his hands."

Anguish filled Aelfwyn. She had no idea how the king would treat Leofric at dawn. Would he give him a few cracks across the back with a rod, merely for show in front of the townsfolk, or would he inflict as much suffering as possible? Sick with dread, she met Leofric's gaze once more.

"You shouldn't be here," he said softly. "This hall is a den of wolves. You won't be safe if you remain overnight."

Aelfwyn shook her head. "I'm not leaving you."

Leofric's gaze turned hard. "You must. Go to Cynn and Gytha for the night—they will take care of you."

Aelfwyn fought back tears. She did not want to abandon Leofric here, but she knew he spoke the truth. The king's words had frightened her; she believed he would let his men have her if either she or Leofric provoked him once more.

With a sigh of defeat she bowed her head. "Very well. I will see you at dawn."

Aelfwyn left him, making her way across the rush-strewn floor, chin up and shoulders back. Heckling voices and catcalls followed her but she ignored them.

Outside, a grey dusk was settling over the town. The snow that had been threatening all day was now falling; large fat snowflakes floated down silently from a colorless sky. Alone in the square with snowflakes fluttering down like delicate white rose petals, Aelfwyn hurriedly wiped away the tears that blurred her vision and made her way across the square in the direction of Lincylene's meadhall.

Dawn crept over the town, revealing a world blanketed in pristine white. The snow was still falling although it had diminished to a mere flutter.

Aelfwyn stood next to Cynn and Gytha in the middle of Market Square. Her stomach was in knots as she watched a crowd gather around them.

"Carrion crows," she muttered, angry they had come to watch a man suffer. "Haven't they got better things to do?"

"It seems not," Gytha replied. The older woman linked her arm through Aelfwyn's, and she gave her a gentle squeeze. "It's the way of folk to enjoy watching someone else's humiliation rather than their own."

"But I thought people liked us here."

"They do, and in a few days time they'll forget this even happened."

"I won't," Aelfwyn replied between clenched teeth, her gaze sweeping over their eager faces.

Gytha did not answer. She only gave Aelfwyn's arm another squeeze, reassuring her that she was not alone and that she herself was not here to watch Leofric flogged. Aelfwyn leaned against her, grateful for Gytha's presence. She was barely ten winters older than Aelfwyn, but with four exuberant daughters to contend with, Gytha was used to providing comfort and strength.

King Eatta emerged from his hall just as the eastern sky glowed gold. Resplendent in a leather tunic and breaches, a wolfpelt cloak hanging from his broad shoulders, the king navigated the slippery wooden steps outside his hall and strode across the snow toward the waiting crowd.

A cluster of cloaked figures—his wife and daughters among them—trailed after Eatta. The king's warriors, bringing Leofric with them, brought up the rear.

Aelfwyn's throat closed as the king approached. He carried a long ash rod in his right hand, which he trailed lazily after him, its tip slicing a line through the crisp snow. The indolence of his movements scared Aelfwyn. Her heart began thudding against her ribs, and she covered it with her hand, trying to calm herself.

She could not bear to see Leofric beaten, yet she would not leave him to face it alone. Still, she felt sick and weak-kneed at the mere thought of what was to come.

"Courage, Aeaba," Gytha whispered as if she sensed her terror. "It'll all be over soon enough."

They dragged Leofric to where a tall oaken pole cast a shadow over the white square. Then they stripped off the linen tunic and leather jerkin he wore, baring his naked torso to the morning's chill. Finally they tied Leofric up, so he was hugging the pole, with his wrists bound together.

Aelfwyn watched the king saunter across to Leofric, his fur-lined boots crunching in the snow.

"There were twenty thyrmsas in this man's purse," he announced to the expectant crowd. "Twenty pieces of gold for the trees he cut down without my leave. For that he will receive twenty strokes."

An excited hush fell across the square. Bile rose in Aelfwyn's throat. Leofric did not speak after the king's declaration. Aelfwyn was relieved, for it was clear Eatta would need little excuse to increase his punishment.

The King of Lindesege took up his position a couple of feet back from Leofric and brought his arm back.

The crowd held its breath and Aelfwyn started to feel light-headed.

The rod whistled as it cut through the air. The crack as it connected with Leofric's bare back shattered the silence.

Chapter Twenty-seven

Honesty

"VICIOUS, VINDICTIVE BASTARD," Aelfwyn muttered as she sponged Leofric's bloodied back. "He didn't need to hurt you this badly."

Leofric gave a soft moan in reply.

He sat before the hearth in Cynn and Gytha's hall, bent double in agony while Aelfwyn tended to his back.

"Here." Gytha bustled up to them, a clay vile clutched in her hand. "The local herbwife swears by oil of lavender for wounds."

Aelfwyn nodded, her lips set in a thin, hard line. Behind them, Cynn nursed a cup of ale at the table. Either side of Cynn, his four daughters—Ealhgyth, Hilla, Sifleda and Merwyn—looked on with eyes as big as moons. The two elder girls, Ealhgyth and Hilla, were auburn-haired and green eyed like their mother, while the Sifleda and Merwyn—four and six winters respectively—had blonde hair and their father's blue eyes.

Aelfwyn saw the worry on the girls' faces and attempted to soften her features. She did not want to scare them. Still, her hands shook from anger as she took the vial from Gytha. Fury twisted her innards up in knots.

Her gaze returned to Leofric's back, and she studied the bruises and lacerations that criss-crossed it. Eatta had been red-faced and sweating by the time he had finished the flogging. He had put all his force into each stroke of the rod.

Leofric had not cried out once during the punishment, although he ended up sagging against the pole in the end, and collapsed once the king's men unshackled him. His back had glistened scarlet, and when he fell onto the ground his blood soaked into the pristine snow.

The king stood over Leofric's prone body for a few moments. Then, satisfied he had dealt with the woodcutter, he turned his back on him and strode back indoors. His retainers had followed him and slowly the gathered crowd dispersed.

Watching the king stride away, Aelfwyn had wished she were a man. She would have given anything to be able to come after Eatta with a spear and gore him like the pig he was.

Aelfwyn put aside her simmering outrage and used a soft cloth to gently apply the lavender oil to the wounds. Leofric hissed in pain, his body going rigid as she worked.

"I'm sorry this is hurting you," she murmured, "but the oil should soothe the pain soon."

"Thank you, Aelfwyn," he finally managed, his voice strangled. "I'm well enough; it could have been worse."

"Worse?" Aelfwyn drew herself up. "You're lucky you can't see the mess he's made of your back!"

Leofric gave a soft laugh, and then groaned as the movement hurt him.

"Lenred's right," Cynn piped up from behind them. "It could have been much worse. Lucky for you both that the town needs a woodcutter. The king held back this morning."

Incensed, Aelfwyn turned on him. "He'll bear scars for the rest of his life!"

"Aye, but they'll be faint." Cynn held her gaze. "Last year Eatta caught a man groping his wife. He flogged him so viciously that the warrior died three days later from loss of blood."

Aelfwyn stared back at him, a chill passing through her. Seeing her look of horror, Cynn gave an apologetic shrug. "The king's not a man lightly crossed," he warned. "He is also greedy and territorial—for the past three years he has demanded a 'gild' from me for the meadhall."

That caught Leofric's attention. He glanced over his shoulder, his gaze narrowing as it met Cynn's. "He's taxing you?"

"Aye—and every year the price goes up." Cynn's usually good-tempered face creased in anger. "This year he's demanding twenty shillings. If I don't pay, he'll turf us out."

Aelfwyn listened to Cynn's words and glanced over at where Gytha stood silently by the hearth. Her friend looked unusually subdued, and she did not blame her. Eatta risked the ruin of them all.

How quickly things could change. Her life at Bebbanburg had appeared a pleasant one until the night Ecgfrith visited her alcove. Now, once again, a king had cast a shadow over her life and threatened her fragile happiness.

She wished she had listened to Leofric at Winterfylleth. He had tried to convince her to leave here, but she had refused. Aelfwyn had thought only King Ecgfrith posed a danger to them, that Lincylene would provide a safe haven.

Too late she now realized there was no such thing.

"It's still snowing."

Leofric looked up from where he whittled a piece of wood in front of the hearth. "Aye, folk are saying this is the bitterest winter in years.

Aelfwyn closed the window, shutting out the swirling blizzard, and huffed in frustration. "We'll never get away from here at this rate."

"As soon as the spring thaw arrives we will," Leofric assured her. "Don't fret—Ecgfrith won't be able to reach us in this weather."

"It's not him that worries me," Aelfwyn admitted, sitting down opposite Leofric and taking up the tunic she had been mending. "Eatta is a madman. I won't be able to rest until we are out from under his shadow."

Leofric smiled. He regarded Aelfwyn under slightly lowered lids. "He made his point. You heard Cynn—the town needs a woodcutter. It's not in Eatta's interest to kill me."

Aelfwyn met his gaze, noting how handsome he looked in the firelight. His auburn hair was starting to curl at the nape. Seven days had passed since the flogging, and Leofric's back was healing quickly. However, the memory of watching him being beaten had left a scar upon Aelfwyn. She could not let her guard down. "What if you offend him again?"

Leofric gave a soft laugh. "I'll do my best not to."

Aelfwyn glared at him. "Now you're making fun."

Leofric's smile faded. He put aside the wood he was whittling and came to her. He hunkered down next to Aelfwyn so their gazes were level and reached out for her hand. The warmth and strength of his fingers closing around hers made Aelfwyn's heart start to race. They hardly ever touched; their only physical contact was when she dressed his back. His closeness made it difficult to breathe.

"Making fun is the last thing I'd do," he told her gently. "Pride has ever been my downfall, Aelfwyn. It's the reason Ealdorman Godwine banished me to Lindisfarena. I've never suffered being told what to do—not by my father, overlord, or king. If I'd asked Eatta's permission before cutting down any of his trees, I could have avoided that flogging."

She stared back at him, drowning in the hazel-green depths of his eyes. "Can't we just leave here and put all of this behind us?" she asked.

He reached out and brushed away a lock of hair from her face that had come free of its braid. His knuckles lightly grazed her cheek as he did so and she trembled. "We can and will—as soon as spring comes."

She nodded, her mouth going dry. He was looking at her so intently that she felt stripped naked. This look was different to any other he had given her; it was not the melting, seductive gaze of old. Nor was it one full of teasing humor, as was common between them. This look was so fierce that it took her breath away.

"I'll protect you, Aelfwyn," he finished softly, "with my body—and my life."

Later that day, Leofric carried an iron pail of warm mash out to Windræs. The snow was still falling; thick flurries that obscured the surrounding landscape and narrowed Leofric's world to the home he shared with Aelfwyn.

After their intense conversation earlier, it was a relief to go outdoors for a spell. At least she had not flinched away from his touch. She had not recoiled from his intensity, although she had not responded to it either. He had caught her stealing glances at him afterward, her grey-blue gaze questioning.

No doubt she wondered what had come over him.

Truthfully he wondered that himself.

The humiliation of that morning in Market Square remained with him. The feel of cold wood against his naked chest, the sniggering and whispers of the watching crowd—and then the whistling of the rod before it hit him—still haunted his dreams.

The pain had been worse than he had anticipated. He had nearly bitten through his lip as he forced himself not to cry out. He did not want Aelfwyn to see him howl and beg for mercy like a coward. It was bad enough he had seen her look of horror as she helped him off the bloodied snow. Her face had been ashen and wet with tears, but her eyes were what still haunted him—the same bleakness he had seen on Lindisfarena when she had awoken.

Aelfwyn had already been through too much—and he had selfishly inflicted more suffering upon her.

Windræs greeted him with a soft whicker. He had stabled the gelding in a lean-to attached to the back of the hut. Knee-deep in straw the horse looked comfortable enough, although Leofric knew he missed being outdoors.

He sat the metal pail down and watched Windræs take huge mouthfuls of mash. Aelfwyn had added slices of carrot and apple to it as a special treat.

Leofric leaned against the gelding's warm flank, feeling the scabs on his back pull slightly as he did so.

"It'll be Yule soon, Windræs," he said. The horse's furry ears flicked back toward him, but he did not pause eating. "This time last year I was living under my father's roof—without a care in the world."

Windræs snorted into his bucket, and Leofric smiled. "Aye, it was a shallow existence I'll admit—hunting, whoring, and drinking with my friends—but I was happy enough."

The horse threw up his head, scattering mash, and stomped his left back leg, narrowly missing Leofric's foot.

"Alright then ... I wasn't that happy," Leofric admitted, shifting away from Windræs's heavy hoof, "although I didn't know it at the time."

That was the truth of it.

The last few months had been the hardest of his life, the most humiliating. He had been stripped of everything—his family, his rank, his pride—but the gods had given him a gift in return: Aelfwyn.

Chapter Twenty-eight

Yuletide Feast

MOTHER NIGHT ARRIVED with another heavy snowfall. Aelfwyn and Leofric trudged through three feet of snow on their way into town. Fat flakes fluttered down, frosting the surrounding trees and the roofs and walls of Lincylene before them. Smoke from cook fires rose into a washed-out sky. The aroma of roasting meat—boar, mutton, and fowl—reached them.

"I tire of this snow," Aelfwyn grumbled as she struggled through a deep drift. Her legs were far shorter than Leofric's, and she was having difficulty keeping up with him. "I want to see the earth again, and the grass."

Leofric turned and smiled at her indignance. Then he reached back for her hand. "Come on—not much farther."

Aelfwyn clutched his hand tightly, enjoying the warmth of his skin against hers, and attempted to quicken her stride. The heavy snow had rendered them housebound over the past few days. However, Cynn and Gytha had invited them to their home for the Yuletide feast, an occasion neither she nor Leofric wanted to miss.

They reached the town walls and passed into Lincylene under the Roman gate. The streets were deserted this morning, for all folk huddled around their firepits while they sipped mulled wine and waited for their noon feast to finish cooking. The aromas that Aelfwyn had smelled outside the town walls grew thicker within. She inhaled the scent of baking honey shortbread and apple and plum pudding, and her belly rumbled.

Boughs of holly and fir hung over the threshold of Cynn and Gytha's hall. The mouthwatering aroma of roasting fowl greeted them as they ducked inside. Cynn and his family gathered around a long table. The girls sat, their round faces pink with excitement, helping their mother prepare the feast. The two eldest, Ealhgyth and Hilla, rolled out pastry and prepared the filling for an apple pie, while the younger girls chopped vegetables under Gytha's watchful eye.

"Merry Yuletide!" Gytha bustled over to them with two steaming cups of mulled wine. "Come warm yourselves by the fire."

A huge oaken yule log burned in the center of the fire pit, throwing out a considerable amount of heat. Aelfwyn shucked off her fur mantle and handed it to Gytha, who hung it up with Leofric's near the door. Sighing in relief to be out of the biting cold, Aelfwyn wrapped her chilled fingers around the warm cup.

For the first time since Leofric's flogging, Aelfwyn felt welcome in Lincylene once more.

Of course Cynn and Gytha had been good to them, as had a few other townsfolk Aelfwyn and Leofric had befriended since their arrival here. However, she tired of the sniggers and stares whenever she and Leofric ventured into town to shop at the market. Leofric assured her it would stop soon enough, but their gawping galled her nonetheless.

"Your decorations are beautiful, Gytha," she said, gazing around the cozy interior of the hall. Gytha and her daughters had decked the walls and heavy beams overhead with boughs of mistletoe, ivy, and witch hazel.

"Thank you," Gytha replied with a proud smile. "The girls spent all of yesterday decorating."

Cynn sat at the head of the table, his cheeks ruddy from warmth and wine. He beamed at them, and Aelfwyn smiled back. She shared Leofric's opinion of Cynn, and had liked the meadhall keeper from the moment she met him. Cynn was a big-hearted man who had welcomed them into his home like kin.

"Sit down!" he called out to them. "The girls are baking shortbread. It should be ready soon."

They sat down at the long table, upon a low bench. Seated side-by-side, Aelfwyn was aware of Leofric's closeness. His arm lightly brushed hers as he reached out to steal a sliver of apple from Hilla's pie filling. The heat of his leg next to hers made her breathing quicken slightly; a frisson of excitement igniting in the pit of her belly.

It was becoming unbearable—day after day cooped up inside the tiny hut, just the two of them. Leofric appeared unflustered by it, but the enforced closeness was starting to become slow torture for Aelfwyn. The hunger that knotted in her belly now had nothing to with the coming Yule feast.

She did her best to ignore the yearning but when Leofric sat this close to her, it was impossible to ignore.

"Here." She smiled at Hilla and picked up an apple from the bowl in the center of the table. "Pass me a knife and I'll help you get that pie ready for the oven."

The girl beamed and nodded. "Thanks, Aeaba. I could do with some help."

"She'd have the pie done by now, if she wasn't so busy gossiping with Ealhgyth," Cynn complained.

"Oh stop your grumbling," his wife replied before giving Hilla a fond smile. "Let the girls be—it's Yuletide."

Gytha's Yuletide feast was one that Aelfwyn would never forget.

She was a splendid cook, better even than Aelfwyn's mother, who was the yardstick by which Aelfwyn judged good cooking. The table groaned under the weight of the magnificent roast fowl and a platter of roasted and braised vegetables, cheeses, pies, and sweet treats. They ate and drank slowly, enjoying the celebration of being able to eat such rich, delicious food. Now that they had little gold to see them through the winter, Aelfwyn and Leofric ate plainly. One cauldron of pottage would need to last three days, and there was very little meat in their meals.

After the feast, they joined the family on comfortable furs piled around the fire pit. Aelfwyn sat curled up against Leofric. Their friends believed them to be a wedded couple and perhaps wondered why they did not show much affection between them. The warmth and hardness of Leofric's chest against Aelfwyn's back was distracting to say the least, but her belly was full of good food, and the wine had made her drowsy. She dozed against Leofric's chest, and was aware of him gently stroking her hair as he chatted to Cynn and Gytha.

She could have sat like that all night but, eventually, the time came for them to take their leave.

Aelfwyn climbed to her feet and stretched sleepily. Yawning, she turned to Gytha and hugged her. "Thank you so much. I have never felt so welcome in someone's home."

Gytha hugged her back. "And you always will be."

Aelfwyn crossed to where Leofric was holding out her cloak. With a smile, she turned, letting him place it over her shoulders.

"Look!" Ealhgyth squealed. "They're standing under the misteltān!"

Aelfwyn started slightly at the girl's outburst before craning her neck up. Indeed there was a sprig of mistletoe hanging overhead.

"Now they'll have to kiss!" Cynn's eldest daughter clapped her hands together with glee before she and her sisters burst out into tittering laughter.

Smirking, Cynn gently cuffed Ealhgyth around the ear. "They've been waiting all afternoon for you two to stand under it."

Aelfwyn felt her cheeks warm. She glanced over at Leofric who merely raised an eyebrow, his eyes twinkling mischievously. "Come on then," he said softly. "We don't want to disappoint them."

He stepped close to her, before reaching down and cupping her face gently. Then he stooped, his lips brushing hers. He drew back slowly, meeting Aelfwyn's gaze as he did so.

"Give her a decent kiss, man," Cynn goaded him. "Or do you want Gytha and me to show you how it's done."

Leofric cast him a sour look, causing Cynn to bellow with laughter. "I don't need any lessons from you on how to kiss my wife."

With that, he drew Aelfwyn into his arms and kissed her deeply.

Aelfwyn melted into him, her arms coming up to encircle his neck. For a moment she forgot where she was. His kiss set her on fire. When they broke apart, both gasping for breath, the hall had fallen silent. The girls were all blushing, although Cynn and Gytha both wore smug grins.

"That's better, Lenred," Gytha congratulated him with a wink. "That's how a woman likes to be kissed."

Outside in the empty, snow-carpeted street, Leofric was glad the darkness hid his embarrassment.

He could not believe it. His friends thought him some cold fish—a husband who was embarrassed to show affection for his wife in public. Cynn and Gytha had no idea the self-restraint he had exercised over the past few months when it came to Aelfwyn. Her very presence set his veins alight. He ached for her.

The snow had stopped falling, and a waxing moon lit their path home.

They walked side-by-side, but Leofric did not take her hand, as he had on the way here. He could feel the tension between them, stretched tight like a bowstring, and wondered if the kiss had upset her. Although it was over two moons ago now, the memory of her recoiling from his embrace still stung like a fresh wound.

They passed out of Lincylene and took the snow-covered path through the woods toward home. The night was still, the air sharp with cold. An owl hooted in the distance, the sound carrying through the quiet night.

They were halfway home when Aelfwyn suddenly halted in her tracks. She turned to Leofric and reached out, catching him by the arm.

Leofric tensed, his senses on alert. Had she seen something lurking in the trees? He reached for the seax he carried at his waist. "What's wrong?"

"Nothing's wrong, Leo," she said quietly. "I just want to ask you something."

He released the hilt of his seax and focused on her face. The moonlight bathed it in soft silver, outlining her delicate features. She was so lovely it hurt to look at her.

"What is it?" he rasped. Did she have any idea of how much he wanted her?

"That kiss you gave me …" she began hesitantly, "…back there. I—"

"Do you want me to apologize?" Leofric's gut twisted as he said the words. He was not sure how long he could keep up this pretense. It was eating him up inside.

"No—" she replied softly. "I'd like another one."

Chapter Twenty-nine

Giving In

LEOFRIC STARED AT her, lost for words.

"You want me to *kiss* you?" he finally asked, certain he had misheard her.

"Aye," her voice trembled slightly, betraying her nervousness. "If you want to, that is ..."

He gave a soft, incredulous laugh. "You do realize what you're asking?"

"I do."

Leofric gazed at her before reaching out and stroking her cheek. "I don't want to scare you."

"You won't." Her voice was sure, although he felt her tremble under his touch.

With a sigh he leaned down, his mouth covering hers. The kiss started gently, as it had back inside Cynn's hall, but with no one looking at them it quickly deepened.

Aelfwyn's lips parted under his, the tip of her tongue teasing his. Leofric groaned and pulled her hard against him, savoring her mouth like the finest feast. His hands reached up to her hair, unfastening the wifely braids and letting her soft blonde locks tumble down. His fingers tangled in it.

She groaned against his mouth, the soft sound releasing something within him. He gently bit her lower lip, enjoying her whimper of pleasure. Their bodies were pressed against each other now. Leofric was rock hard, and he knew she would be able to feel his arousal pressed against her belly.

But this time it did not frighten her. She reached up, her fingers gently tracing his face as she kissed him back with abandon.

When they finally ended the kiss, Leofric was shaking. This woman was his undoing. It took all his self-control not to throw her down in the snow and take her right there.

"Do you have any idea what you do to me?" he whispered, struggling to regain his composure.

She shook her head. "I'm sorry for making things so difficult," she murmured, "after Ecgfrith I was so hurt and confused."

He reached forward and cupped her face with his hands. "Don't ever apologize to me for that. I'd gut that bastard for what he did. You do realize I'd never harm you—don't you?"

She nodded. "I trust you." She paused then, her gaze holding his. "I want you."

A heartbeat passed, and then Leofric pulled her back into his arms. Their kisses were ravenous now as the floodgates opened, and they released the need they had both spent the past few months denying.

Leofric knew he would not be able to hold back. He wanted their first time together to be slow and tender. He wanted to explore every inch of her body upon the furs, and see her naked skin bathed in firelight.

That was not going to happen.

Her hands moved feverishly over his chest, digging in as she tried to get past the layers of clothing to his skin beneath. When her hands dipped to his groin, and she stroked his straining shaft, he let out a long groan in response. She gasped against his mouth and fumbled at his breeches, eager to release him, to touch him.

Cold air caressed his skin as she freed him, although the feel of her cold silken fingers, gently caressing his inflamed cock, unraveled the last of his self-control.

Leofric gathered her up in his arms and carried her across to the nearest tree—a tall beech that loomed over the path through the woods.

He pushed her up against it, his mouth covering hers once more. His hands slid down her body, cupping her lush breasts. Her nipples were hard pebbles through the linen undertunic and woolen over-dress she wore. He longed to rip those clothes off her and bury his face in her breasts, but there was no time for that—not now.

His hands delved deeper, hiking up her skirts so that he could touch naked skin beneath. He parted her trembling thighs, caressing the silken skin, before he touched the wet heat between them.

"Aelfwyn," he groaned her name. "I want to go slow but I—"

"Leo, please," she panted, widening her thighs and pressing herself against his fingers. "Take me … now!"

Leofric needed no further invitation. He entered her in one smooth motion, sheathing himself to the hilt inside her satin heat. The sensation nearly tipped him over the edge, and he cried out.

In answer, she wrapped her legs around his hips and pulled him hard against her.

Leofric took Aelfwyn there, against the tree trunk, grinding into her until she shuddered and cried his name. Then he plowed her in long, deep strokes, cupping her buttocks as he thrust.

By the time he emptied his seed within her, he was shouting her name—his cries echoing high into the treetops.

In the aftermath, Aelfwyn stirred first, lifting her head off his shoulder and reached up to stroke his face.

"Leo?" she queried softly. "Are you well?"

He gave a soft laugh. "Never better." He leaned forward and nuzzled her neck before groaning. "You taste better than the finest ale."

Aelfwyn smiled at the comparison. "I should hope so. I have no wish to remind you of a meadhall."

He nipped her neck gently in response and she shivered with pleasure. Her body still felt weak in the aftermath of their encounter. He was still buried inside her, and she had locked her legs around his hips to keep him there—however, the night's chill was invading upon their private world, and her thigh muscles were starting to cramp.

She ran her hands lightly up his back, to avoid disturbing the scabs there, and threaded her fingers through his hair. It was still much shorter than most men's, but she could see it would grow into a thick auburn mane.

He pulled back slightly from her then, his face all sharp angles in the dappled moonlight. "I hope I wasn't too rough? I ... forgot myself."

"No, you weren't," she assured him. In truth, the way he'd scooped her up, carried her across to the beech tree, and then taken her there had excited her beyond words. She wanted him to do it again—only next time she wanted them both to be naked with sunlight on their skin.

To think her first experience with a man had nearly ruined things for her. She had never imagined it could be like this. Her coupling with Leofric had been natural, wild, and consensual. Never again would she hold back her instincts with this man. Never again would she let Ecgfrith cast a shadow over her happiness.

"Come, let's get home." Gently Leofric set her down on the ground. Aelfwyn felt a pang of loss as he slid out of her. She let her skirts fall over her naked legs and drew her cloak back around her, while Leofric laced up his breeches.

He then placed an arm around her shoulders and steered her back to the path. Aelfwyn leaned against Leofric, breathing in the scent of him, and they walked back to the hut in companionable silence.

Aelfwyn stirred in the furs, stretching languorously as she slowly awoke.

Faint shafts of pale light filtered into the hut through the cracks in the doorway and shutters, alerting her that it was well after dawn. They had slept in much later than usual.

A smile spread across Aelfwyn's face. She had slept little but had never felt better in her life. She glanced over at the slumbering man beside her, and the smile widened. She and Leofric had spent Mother Night pleasuring each other. Her body felt weak in the aftermath with a pleasant ache between her thighs. No longer would she spend each night alone in the furs, yearning for the man who lay sleeping just a few feet away.

Leofric slept deeply, as if he had just spent days felling trees without rest.

Loath to wake him, Aelfwyn propped herself up on one elbow and let her gaze travel over his naked body. He was delicious to look upon: tall and broad shouldered but with a long-legged grace that many men lacked. Long auburn eyelashes lay against the pale skin of his cheeks. He had a proud face with high cheekbones and a slightly aquiline nose. Aelfwyn's lower belly tightened. She would never tire of looking at him.

As if sensing her stare, Leofric stirred. His eyelids fluttered, and he gave a soft moan before stretching his long body like a cat. He then opened his eyes and looked up into her face.

A cocky smile tugged at the corner of his mouth. "Morning, princess."

"Morning? I think we've slept it away—I'd say it's coming up to noon."

"See what you've done," he grinned. "You've worn me out."

"Oaf." She went to give his chest a playful slap but he caught her wrist and pulled her down on top of him. Aelfwyn squealed and pushed against his chest, but he held her tight. "Have I really worn you out?" she asked, raising a taunting eyebrow. "I'd hoped to spend the day naked in the furs."

"Had you?" He raised an eyebrow. "And there was me thinking you the shy, blushing type."

Aelfwyn stilled, her playfulness fading. "Would you prefer I was?"

Leofric reached up and stroked her cheek before his finger traced her bottom lip, bee-stung from all his kisses. "I want you as you are," he murmured. "I wouldn't change a thing about you."

Aelfwyn smiled down at him, her throat constricting. She had never thought it was possible to feel as if your heart might stop from joy—but this moment, this man, and those words made her believe in happy endings.

Two months later ...

Chapter Thirty

Changes

AELFWYN WALKED DOWN Steep Hill, a basket under her arm. She was on her way back from market. Over the long, bitter months she had ventured rarely into town—almost never without Leofric at her side—but today she had made an exception.

The last of the winter snows had melted away. For the first time in months there was a little warmth in the sun. Aelfwyn also felt in need of company. As much as she loved her life with Leofric, she sometimes felt isolated. Now that the weather had started to improve, he spent his days out felling trees and preparing the logs for market while she ran their home.

Occasionally Gytha visited, and would bring loaves of bread or other baking with her—but it was not enough to stave off the loneliness.

Aelfwyn had just been to the miller, and carried a cloth bag of coarse flour in her basket. She would make a wheel of griddle bread this afternoon to accompany the rabbit stew they would have for supper.

Halfway down Steep Hill, Aelfwyn passed three women who stood gossiping. They were all a few years older than she was—the wives of the baker, the tanner, and the smith—women she had seen at the front of the crowd on the morning of Leofric's flogging. Upon spying her, the women ceased their chatter, and Aelfwyn felt their hard stares fix upon her. A moment later, their spiteful voices reached her.

"Thinks she's too good for the likes of us," the baker's wife said.

"Aye, although I can't imagine why," the smith's wife sniped. "She who dresses in rags and lives in a hovel fit for pigs."

Their laughter followed her down the street.

Aelfwyn glanced down at the homespun tunic that she had girded around the waist with a length of rope. It was plain but not shabby. Around her shoulders she wore a new woolen shawl that she had just finished knitting. It was pale blue, and she was proud of it.

This town had seemed so friendly when they arrived here, but ever since Leofric had fallen foul of the king, folk treated them differently. Gytha had assured Aelfwyn that people would soon forget, but it seemed her friend was wrong.

Aelfwyn squared her shoulders and ignored the taunting laughter that still echoed after her. She had endured worse and would not stoop to their level by responding. Even so, she found herself clenching her jaw and lengthening her stride.

A little farther down the hill she stopped off to see Gytha. Her friend was up to her elbows in flour as she kneaded bread dough. Her daughters worked industriously around her, chopping vegetables for pottage and rolling out pastry for the pies Cynn served in the meadhall in the afternoons.

Gytha glanced up as Aelfwyn entered, her expression clouding when she saw her face. "What's wrong? You look like you've just supped on sour milk."

"You would too if you'd just been attacked by a spiteful gaggle of geese," Aelfwyn replied.

"Clothild, Bruina, and Aethelflaed?"

"Aye."

Gytha snorted and returned to pummeling her dough. "Don't mind them."

"That's easy for you to say, Gytha—they leave you alone."

Gytha smiled. "I have little time for any of them and they know it."

Aelfwyn sighed and took a seat at the end of the table. She always enjoyed visiting Gytha, but her encounter with the fishwives had put her out of sorts. It was a reminder of their impermanence here. She considered Gytha a good friend, but the woman did not even know her real name.

Gytha started to flatten the dough into a large disc. Behind her, a large iron griddle hung over the hearth, where she would bake the dough.

"Things aren't going to improve," Aelfwyn murmured. "We're both treated like outcasts now."

Gytha cast her a look of sympathy. "I've heard the king still bears Lenred ill-will. It appears the flogging wasn't enough to appease him. His men have poisoned many against you."

Aelfwyn sighed and leaned her elbows on the scarred oaken work surface. It had been a mistake to come into town this morning. However, that was not the only reason for her ill-temper.

Since Yuletide—ever since she and Leofric had become lovers—life had changed. Her nights were magical; she lived for the moment they crawled into the furs together. However, her days were not as happy as she would have liked. The isolation was slowly wearing her down. She often found herself missing Rendlaesham. Her parents' home was in the center of town, close to the market; she had grown up surrounded by folk and was not used to spending days alone.

Her relationship with Leofric also unnerved her. Although they had taken a huge step in becoming lovers, she sometimes felt as if she shared her life with a man she barely knew. During mealtimes he kept their conversations light. He did not speak of his feelings for her or of their future together. The closest he had come to opening his heart to her was on Mother Night—and although he made her feel loved in the furs, he had never actually said the words.

"Aeaba—you're not still brooding, are you?" Gytha intruded upon her introspection.

Aelfwyn glanced up and shook her head. "Sorry—I'm not good company today."

Gytha bustled over to her and enfolded Aelfwyn in a motherly hug. "Be patient—things will improve in time."

Aelfwyn blinked back unexpected tears. Gytha's warmth made her feel emotional. "I hope so."

"I'm surprised you don't walk around with a smug smile on your face," Gytha added with a wink. "Few women have a man as handsome as yours."

Her daughters all started tittering, but Gytha ignored them.

"Don't get me wrong, I thank the gods for giving me Cynn, but if I had a man like yours I'd never get any work done. I'd be forever lifting my skirts and dragging him into the furs."

"Gytha!" Aelfwyn's cheeks flamed at the older woman's directness.

Gytha merely laughed and went back to her bread. "Don't pretend to be coy. I've seen the way you look at him. Now off you go—some of us have work to do."

Aelfwyn found herself smiling as she walked home. Gytha never failed to remind her of what was important. However, an undercurrent of uneasiness still tugged at her, for she knew that the time was approaching for her and Leofric to leave Lincylene—she would sorely miss Gytha.

Back home Aelfwyn got to work on making the griddle bread for supper and by the time Leofric walked in the door the aroma of baking bread wafted out to greet him.

"Evening." He leaned down to kiss her and Aelfwyn raised her face to him. The kiss was soft and lingering, promising more. "Did you have a good afternoon?"

"Aye, I went into town for supplies and visited Gytha."

Aelfwyn did not mention her run in with the women; Leofric would only worry over her.

"How are she and the girls?" Leofric dipped his head further and trailed kisses down the column of her neck.

"They're all well—busy as usual," Aelfwyn replied distractedly. It was difficult to concentrate when Leofric did that. Her knees went weak, and she sagged against him, supper forgotten.

"I've yet to see a harder working family." Leofric gently bit her earlobe before sucking it gently.

Aelfwyn gasped, whatever response she had planned flying out of her mind. She turned to him and linked her arms about his neck, kissing him. When they finally broke apart Leofric gave a soft laugh. "Missed me today, have you?"

Aelfwyn smiled. "Clearly."

Leofric glanced behind her at the simmering pot of rabbit stew. "Will supper keep for a bit?"

Aelfwyn nodded.

"Good." With that Leofric scooped her up into his arms. He carried her away from the hearth to the waiting pile of soft furs in the corner.

Aelfwyn rested against Leofric's bare chest, listening to the steady thump of his heart. She felt weak and boneless after their coupling, and so relaxed she could have easily fallen asleep.

Leofric stroked her unbound hair. They lay in companionable silence, listening to the gentle popping of embers in the hearth.

Aelfwyn sighed, running her hands over the smooth, muscular planes of his chest. She would never tire of this; she wanted to stay in Leofric's arms forever. As usual their lovemaking had been heated, edged in wildness. In the aftermath the air was charged with much that was unsaid.

Propping herself up on one elbow, Aelfwyn gazed down into Leofric's eyes. His gaze had turned from its usual hazel to a moss green—a shade she would always associate with passion. He gave her a sleepy smile, reaching up to stroke her cheek. Although Leofric chatted easily most of the time, after they lay together he would often lapse into silence.

"You're lost in your own thoughts again," she chided with an answering smile.

"Aye." He smiled. "You wear me out."

Aelfwyn gave a soft laugh. "I think not." She reached down and traced his lower lip with her fingertip. He bit it gently, his gaze deepening to emerald in the firelight.

"I'm so happy you came into my life," she said, her chest constricting as she said the words. "I had no idea it could be like this between a man and a woman. I can't imagine a world without you."

He inclined his head slightly, another smile tugging at his mouth. "You don't have to—I'm not going anywhere."

"I've never met anyone like you," she continued, determined to have an honest conversation with him, one where he would know what was in her heart. "So full of contradiction—yet you're a better man than most."

He shook his head. "Then you have met few men, sweet Aelfwyn."

She stiffened. "I've met enough to know who I can and cannot trust."

"You know I'm far from perfect," he admonished her, his gaze turning serious. "There isn't much in my life I'm proud of ..."

Aelfwyn pushed herself off him and reached for her tunic. "Why do you always do that?"

He frowned. "Do what?"

"Negate every good thing I say about you."

"I don't ... it's just that as flattering as your good opinion is, I'm not the saint you think I am."

Anger flared within Aelfwyn. She was tired of being made to feel like a fool every time she tried to tell Leofric how she felt. She wanted to tell him that she loved him—but he ruined things every time.

Despite the days and nights they spent in each other's company, she knew little of Leofric's inner thoughts and worries. Sometimes in the midst of passion, she caught glimpses of the man beneath the shield, but the rest of the time Leofric kept the world at bay with brash self-confidence and a wicked sense of humor. She enjoyed his company but wondered at the things he hid from her, at the worries and hurts that he shared with no one.

"I don't think you're a saint," she replied. "Far from it."

He laughed and sat up. "That's better. I was beginning to worry about you."

"Why?" she turned on him, incensed now. "Because I dare talk seriously to you—because I dare show you what's in my heart."

She jumped off the furs and yanked her tunic down over her head. Glancing back, she saw he was no longer smiling. In fact he almost looked annoyed.

"Aelfwyn," he began, "I don't—"

"Stop it," she snapped, trying to ignore her constricting throat. She would not cry in front of him. In his current mood he would likely mock her for it. "Let's eat supper before it's ruined."

Chapter Thirty-one

Troubled

"THE SNOWDROPS ARE coming up!"

Aelfwyn rushed indoors, her cheeks flushed with cold, her gaze shining. "Spring is here!"

Leofric straightened up from stacking an armload of wood against the wall, and brushed bark off his leather jerkin. "Isn't it a bit early to be celebrating? Eōstre is a while away."

"That doesn't matter." Aelfwyn placed the basket of kale she had just picked from their vegetable patch. "Once the snowdrops and bluebells arrive, the bitter season departs."

Leofric smiled at her, and the expression made Aelfwyn's breathing still. Despite their argument two days earlier, she could not find it within herself to keep angry at him for long.

Their gazes held for a moment before Leofric's smile faded. "If winter is behind us then we need to think about moving on."

Aelfwyn nodded. She did not want to leave this home they had made for each other—but after King Eatta's treatment of Leofric, she no longer felt as comfortable in Lincylene. She would miss Cynn and Gytha—they both would—but Leofric spoke true: it was time to think about the future.

"Where shall we go?" she asked.

"I was thinking we could go to the south coast of Britannia," he replied, coming close and reaching for her. "The Kingdom of the Kentish is reputed to be a green and peaceful land. We should be safe from King Ecgfrith there."

"What about the price on your head?" Aelfwyn wrapped her arms around his waist and stared up at his face. "Aren't you worried the Ealdorman of Eoforwic is still searching for you?"

Leofric's mouth quirked into a grin. "He probably gave up with the onset of winter. Godwine's got better things to do than hunt me down."

Aelfwyn held his gaze. "Are you sure?"

"No," Leofric replied with a shrug, "but if we travel south, he'll cease to be a concern."

"You once told me you'd have to leave Britannia to escape him."

"Aye, but time changes a man's perspective. Britannia is probably big enough to lose myself in."

Aelfwyn frowned. "But you'll never get to see your family again."

Leofric's grin twisted. "I'm dead to them, Aelfwyn. When Godwine banished me to Lindisfarena, my father called me a 'nithing'—a man forfeit of name and honor."

Aelfwyn stared at him, wondering that Leofric had not told her of this before.

"I'm so sorry he said that to you," she said quietly. Elflaeda had called her that back in Streonshalh and the name had stung—but to call a member of your family a 'nithing' was the ultimate insult. Leofric's father had disowned him.

Leofric shook his head and released her. "It matters not—the old man and I never saw eye to eye anyway. I'm sure he was relieved to see the back of me."

"Of course it matters," Aelfwyn replied. "Even if he wanted you punished, there was no need to do that."

"It's over with now." Leofric turned away, his tone dismissive. "I don't worry about it, so nor should you."

She watched him retrieve his fur cloak from a hook behind the door, and saw from the tense set of his shoulders that she would continue on the present subject at her peril. Aelfwyn let the matter drop, although it was an effort to do so.

Once again Leofric rebuffed her the moment she tried to get closer to him. Did he not trust her?

"I'm going into town to see if the smith has finished my new axe-blade," Leofric announced, slinging the cloak about his shoulders. "Do you want anything from the market while I'm there?"

"Do you think there will be any berries yet?"

Leofric turned back to her, the good humor returning to his face. "Now you're really being overly optimistic."

Aelfwyn sighed and looked down at the basket of kale. "I'm dying for some fruit—it seems an age since we finished the last of our apples."

"I'll check for you," Leofric promised, leaning down for a kiss, "but don't get your hopes up."

Aelfwyn followed Leofric outside and watched him stride across the grass to the path that led alongside the riverbank. She stood in front of the hut, gazing after him until his tall figure disappeared from sight. Then with a sigh she turned and went back inside.

She carried the kale over to her worktable and started chopping it for the pottage for their noon meal. A slight frown marred Aelfwyn's forehead as she worked; her conversation with Leofric had left her out of sorts. It had not been right between them since their argument—they were beginning to struggle under the weight of too many things left unsaid.

Irritated that her thoughts had turned in this direction—yet again—Aelfwyn scooped up the chopped kale and dumped it in the iron pot hanging above the fire pit. She grew tired of her own insecurity. Leofric treated her like his queen. He worshipped her body as if she was a goddess—what did a few mere words matter?

Aelfwyn's eyes filled with tears. She hated herself for it, but they did.

Leofric left the smith's forge empty-handed. His axe-blade was still not ready although Alric the Smith promised him he would have it the following day.

Whistling to himself, Leofric exited the narrow alley and glanced up Steep Hill. The market would be there for a while yet—there was enough time to drop in to see Cynn first.

His friend was washing cups when Leofric entered the meadhall. His sleeves rolled up, Cynn was frowning as he scrubbed away. It was too early in the day for drinkers, and the long, windowless structure was empty. A low fire crackled in the hearth in the center of the hall, flanked either side by two long tables. At noon and after dusk men, drinking elbow to elbow, would pack those tables.

"Morning," Leofric greeted him cheerfully.

Cynn glanced up. "It's a bit early in the day, isn't it?"

Leofric grinned. "It's never too early for a cup of your finest, but I'm on my way to market and thought I'd see how you were."

Cynn shrugged. "Well enough. I haven't seen you round here often in the evenings of late."

"Eatta emptied my purse," Leofric replied, leaning against the doorframe and folding his arms across his chest. "Not much spare gold for mead these days."

He gave Cynn a long look then. "You don't seem yourself this morning, is something wrong?"

His friend shrugged and gave a tired smile. "Just the look of a weary man. My wife and daughters keep me awake with their prattle."

Leofric laughed. "You have a fine family and you know it."

"Aye—but a man with so many daughters and no sons carries a heavy burden."

Leofric studied Cynn and wondered if he was struggling to gather enough gold to pay the king's outrageous 'gild'. He hesitated to ask about it though for he knew Cynn was proud. He might see a friend's concern as meddling.

"I shall leave you to your work then." Leofric pushed himself off the doorframe. "Shall I come by later for a long overdue game of knucklebones?"

Cynn smiled. "Still think you can beat me?"

Leofric grinned back. "I will—one of these days."

Inside the meadhall, Cynn picked up a cup and dunked it in the pail of dirty water.

A tall, red haired man with hazel eyes.

Three men from Eoforwic had arrived in town yesterday. They had come to the meadhall asking about an outlaw whom the ealdorman was hunting. The man they sought was named Leofric.

Cynn placed the washed cup upside down on the table and reached for another.

What if the man Cynn had welcomed into his home was a liar? He thought back to that incident in the autumn in Torksey, when the King of Northumbria's men were asking folk if they had seen a girl with pale blonde hair and grey-blue eyes. Ecgfrith of Northumbria had been looking for her. The pieces of the puzzle now starting to fit together; Cynn realized that both Lenred and Aeaba were hunted.

Lenred and Aeaba—both false names.

Cynn looked down at the empty cup he held. *Is that a good enough reason to betray them?*

The northerners had spoken of a 'gild'—a great sum of gold—that the ealdorman would pay for the outlaw. It was thirty shillings, more than enough to pay the tax he owed Eatta—plenty to ensure the well-being of his family for the coming year.

Gytha will never forgive me.

But his wife did not understand the pressure he was under. He had barely saved ten thrymsas over the last year, only half of the payment Eatta demanded. He was due to go before the king at Eōstre with the gold. If he did not, Eatta would take everything he had worked so hard for away.

I can't let that happen to my family.

Cynn put down the cup, dried off his hands, and reached for his cloak. The men had told him they were guests of King Eatta, and that they would be staying in his hall for another two days. There was still time to catch them.

Leofric wandered amongst the stalls in Market Square searching for berries.

He knew his evasive attitude upset Aelfwyn at times. He was sorry he had upset her two evenings earlier. He was not sure exactly what he had done wrong—he only knew that the moment she said anything good about his character he felt the need to put her right. He had seen the hurt and anger in her eyes and was keen to appease her.

There was a surprising array of fresh greens this morning, as well as some crisp spring cabbages—but no berries. The small, tart strawberries folk enjoyed with cream, and the raspberries and blackcurrants, would not come till later.

However, he did come across an old man selling apples. They were the last of the winter store, a little shriveled but definitely edible.

"They'll be good in cakes and pies," the vendor told him with a gap-toothed smile. "Sweet and tart with firm flesh."

"You make them sound like a woman," Leofric replied with a grin. "I'll take a bag."

"Less trouble than women," the old man replied, filling the cloth bag that Leofric passed him.

Leofric laughed, and the vendor gave him an assessing look. "Are you the new woodcutter who lives on the banks of the Whitham?"

Leofric's smile faded. Ever since his run in with the king, he had grown wary of folk here. "Aye."

"I need timber."

Leofric raised an eyebrow. "And?"

"My son and his wife have come to live with me. My own wife died two winters' ago, but the dwelling is too small for the three of us—especially since my new daughter is with child. I need wood to build onto the back of my home."

Leofric relaxed, and he smiled. "I felled a beech two days ago," he replied, "and there's also some coppicing oak I can bring you."

"Can you take me to see the wood this afternoon?" the vendor asked. "My son can help you bring it to my home."

Leofric nodded and started to discuss the old man's requirements. The winter had seemed endless, and the snows had taken an age to melt. Aelfwyn was right—spring was in the air. This was a chance for him to earn them some valuable thrymsas before they left Lincylene.

Intent on his discussion, Leofric did not notice Cynn cross the Market Square behind him. The meadhall owner cast Leofric an intent look. His gaze shifted between the woodcutter and the merchant who stood chatting together. Then Cynn quickened his pace across the paved expanse toward the Great Hall.

Chapter Thirty-two

Betrayal

KING EATTA SURVEYED the meadhall owner, his gaze so intense that Cynn started to squirm.

A heavy silence had fallen in the hall, broken only by the sound of an infant whimpering in one of the alcoves. His movements unhurried, Eatta turned his attention to the three men who lounged at the table upon the high seat. Cynn had interrupted a game of Cyningtaefl—King's Table.

"What do you think, Halwend?" Eatta drawled. "Does this sound like the man you're looking for?"

One of them, a heavy-featured warrior with untamed brown hair, put down his chess piece and gave a slow nod. His gaze pinned Cynn to the spot. "What did you say this man's name is?"

"Lenred."

The warrior flicked a cursory glance in the direction of his blond companions. They were both younger men, who clearly looked to him as their leader. "It makes sense he would change his name."

"Aye," one of them replied. "Leofric is no fool—he'll know we're hunting him."

Halwend looked back at Cynn. "When did he arrive in Lincylene?"

"Late summer," the meadhall owner replied.

"That would be about right," the warrior mused. "It was just after midsummer when he fled south."

King Eatta leaned back in his carved chair and slung one leg over the serpent armrest. "So you say this Leofric fell foul of the ealdorman?"

Halwend nodded. "Aye—insulted Godwine's daughter, so the ealdorman banished him to Lindisfarena."

"Only he didn't like being a monk so he ran off the first chance he got," one of the blond warriors added before smirking.

"This man Cynn speaks of turned up here and started cutting down my trees without asking my permission," Eatta told them. "I flogged his back bloody for it."

"Sounds like Leofric," the elder of the three warriors replied. His gaze then met the king's. "If this is the man we seek, do I have your permission to take him, sire?"

Eatta gave a slow smile. "Yes—you do."

"Where can I find this woodcutter?"

"He lives in a cottage by the River Witham, just east of here."

Cynn stepped forward then. This conversation was starting to get away from him. He was keen to receive his gold and did not want the king to take credit for leading these men to the outlaw.

He boldly met Halwend of Eoforwic's steel-blue gaze. "Fate is with you this morning." Cynn gestured behind him. "I saw Lenred on my way in here. He's at the market."

Leofric bid the apple-seller good morning and sauntered off with a bag of apples under his arm. It had been a productive conversation. Cerd, the old man, had promised to visit him this afternoon. A handful of thyrmsas would fill his purse nicely. He would need to buy supplies for their journey south.

Leofric was also pleased that he would not return home to Aelfwyn empty-handed. He had seen the look of disappointment, of hurt, in her eyes earlier.

Leofric had seen the expression increasingly often of late.

Aelfwyn sought to get closer to him. She wanted to learn about the man who shared her home and her life—but the thought of baring his soul to her terrified him. Leofric had spent his life avoiding emotional conversations. The youngest of a brood of rough boys, he had learned early on that showing his feelings led to a bloodied nose or black eye. His brothers had been like a pack of wild dogs, circling him, taunting him. One whiff of fear and they would have torn him to pieces.

Aelfwyn was gentle, sweet, and loving—but the words he longed to tell her stuck in his throat every time a tender moment arose between them.

He showed her with his body every time they lay together. The depths of their passion for each other had surprised him—it still did two months later. He had delighted in showing Aelfwyn what it could be like between a man and a woman; and was relieved to see that she had left Ecgfrith behind. Truthfully he had never been with such a passionate woman. Aelfwyn may have appeared sweet and demure but in the furs she was a wildcat.

Leofric could not believe how wyrd had shone on him. Did he deserve such a goddess in his life?

I'll tell her how I feel soon, he promised himself as he trekked down Steep Hill toward the town gates, *once we're far from here.*

Leofric left Lincylene and crossed the wooden bridge beyond, before turning onto the path through the woods.

Deep in thought, he did not hear the footfalls behind him until they were almost upon him.

The crunch of a twig underfoot made him swing around. Three men approached. They were dressed in boiled leather and heavy fur cloaks, swords at their sides.

Leofric's heart skipped a beat when he recognized their faces. Godwine of Eoforwic's right hand, Halwend stood before him. Two younger warriors with dark blond hair flanked him: Berhtulf and Wybert. The ealdorman's sons were the same age as Leofric—he had grown up with them, hunted and drunk with them.

Today though there was no sign of friendship on their faces.

Halwend stopped a few feet away. He had not drawn a weapon although his stance was alert, his powerful body coiled and ready to spring.

"You led us on a merry dance, Leo."

"Aye." Wybert grinned. "Didn't life on Lindisfarena please you?"

Leofric raised an eyebrow, feigning calm even if his heart had started to pound like a battle drum. "What do you think?"

"Godwine's sour over this," Halwend said, his gaze hard. "He wants his reckoning."

"You insulted our sister," Berhtulf added. "We *all* want vengeance."

Leofric stared back at them, considering his next move. The 'old him' would have taunted them. A year ago he would have told them that their sister did indeed resemble a sow and that the pair of them had faces like horses' arses.

But a year ago he had been a different man—reckless, arrogant, and foolish.

"I'm sorry for insulting Hrothwyn," he said finally. "She didn't deserve it."

Berhtulf screwed his face up and spat on the ground. "Too late for apologies now."

However, Halwend watched Leofric, his expression thoughtful. "You're changed," he noted. "What happened to the mouthy lad I used to beat at knucklebones."

Leofric's mouth twisted. Those evenings in the meadhall with Halwend and the other warriors seemed a lifetime ago. "He grew up."

"That's touching," Wybert sneered and took a menacing step forward, his meaty hands clenching at his sides. "But it changes nothing. You're coming with us."

Leofric tossed the apples into the bushes and drew his seax. "Not without a fight."

Halwend grinned. "That's more like the Leofric I remember. Still got fire in your belly I see."

They advanced on him slowly, all three of them drawing the seaxes at their waists. Leofric backed slowly away and weighed up his options. Things were looking bad for him. Three against one was not a fair fight.

They had him cornered. He could not run, and he would not give himself to them. Still, despair lodged in his throat as Wybert rushed at him.

Wybert's broad face was ruddy, and he struck out in anger, the tip of his blade ripping through Leofric's fur mantle. Leofric struck back, his knife scoring the front of Wybert's leather breastplate. Wybert roared in rage and charged him.

"Careful!" Halwend bellowed. "Your father wants him alive."

A quick and violent scuffle ensued. Leofric put up the best fight he could but, despite his slashing seax-blade, the three of them eventually overpowered him.

Face down on the leaf-strewn path, Leofric struggled as Halwend knelt on the small of his back and bound his wrists behind him.

Leofric had managed to draw blood before they wrestled him to the ground. Both of the ealdorman's sons bore cuts to their arms—only Halwend was unscathed. Godwine had sent the warrior looking for him on purpose. Halwend had nerves of iron, and his valor in battle was living legend in Eoforwic.

"Such a pity your mouth's quicker than your brain," the older man laughed, hauling him to his feet. "You were always good in a fight."

Berhtulf stood, clutching his bleeding arm and glaring at Leofric. "You'll pay for that."

A couple of feet away, Wybert grimaced as he wrapped a strip of linen around his damaged wrist. Blood had already seeped through the material, staining it crimson. The ealdorman's youngest son glanced over at his brother. "Don't worry—he will."

Wybert then turned to Leofric and spat on the ground. "I'll make sure fæder makes you cry for your mother before he cuts off your head."

"Enough talk." Halwend shoved Leofric between the shoulders, pushing him along the path in the direction they had come. "We've got a long ride ahead. Let's ready the horses."

Chapter Thirty-three

The Whispering Wind

AELFWYN WAS HANGING out the washing when she spied a man approaching the hut. Even at a distance she could see it was not Leofric. Although he was of a similar age, this man was not quite as tall, with brown hair.

Waric.

Leofric had once considered the warrior a friend, but after the flogging things had changed. Aelfwyn had seen the conflict, the indecision in Waric's face when he had come to collect Leofric that day in the woods. He followed the king's orders, but it had not sat well with him. Even so, Leofric had considered it a betrayal. The two of them no longer shared stories and drank together in Cynn's meadhall, and Aelfwyn was sorry for it. She wondered, since the warrior was alone, if Waric had come to apologize.

Aelfwyn finished hanging up the last tunic and walked out to meet Waric.

"Lenred's not here," she greeted him with a smile. "He went into town— I'm surprised you didn't see him."

Her smile faded when she saw the stern look on Waric's face. His grey eyes were solemn.

"I know he's not here," he replied. "I also know his real name is Leofric."

Aelfwyn went cold. She hugged the empty wicker basket she carried against her side and tried to master herself. Losing her nerve would not help Leofric—or her.

"Where is he?" she finally managed, her voice barely above a whisper.

"Taken," Waric replied, his gaze dropping to the ground between them. "Three men from Eoforwic have captured him. Cynn has turned him in to the king."

Aelfwyn's stomach twisted. *Cynn has betrayed us?*

"Why?" she breathed.

Waric's mouth twisted. "The gild Godwine of Eoforwic offered was too tempting for him to resist."

Aelfwyn's mind churned. *How could he? Does Gytha know about this?*

"How long ago?" she forced out the words as her pulse began to race.

"Just before noon. Leofric was on his way back here when they took him."

Aelfwyn's mind raced. It was just after midday now. The pottage was simmering over the fire pit, and she had expected Leofric back at any moment.

Without thinking, she rushed forward and clutched at Waric's arm. "There's still time to catch up with him. Gather a group of men and ride after them!"

Waric gently pried her fingers off his arm and stepped back from her. His expression was resolute although she could see the regret in his eyes.

"I'm sorry—but I cannot go against the king's wishes. Eatta gave Ealdorman Godwine's men permission to take Leofric away. It would mean death to any of us who went after him."

Aelfwyn took a deep, steadying breath and tried to quell the panic that was clawing its way up her throat. "Then why have you come?"

"Someone had to warn you." Waric held her gaze as he spoke. "News will spread soon that the woodcutter has gone, and that his pretty young wife is alone in the woods. You've not gone unnoticed these past months; there are plenty of men in the king's hall who would claim you for their own."

Aelfwyn flinched at this. Her time with Leofric had done much to heal the scars of the past, but Waric's words reminded her of how she had felt at Bebbanburg—a lamb amongst wolves.

"You can't stay here," Waric continued, his gaze flicking to the hut behind her. "Gather what you can and come to my home—my wife, Bertha, and I will look after you."

Aelfwyn stared at him. "I don't understand ... why are you warning me?"

Waric's face twisted and Aelfwyn saw his conflict, his pain. "I'm bonded to the king—I have no choice but to serve him. It cost me my friendship with Leofric, and I will not have his wife's ruin on my conscience as well." He took a few swift strides backward then. "Come—before it's too late. Our house is the third on the left along Well Lane. We'll be waiting for you."

Aelfwyn watched the warrior turn and stride away along the path—the same path that Leofric had taken just a short while earlier.

Only he was not coming back.

She turned and stumbled inside, where she sat down next to the fire pit and stared into the flames.

Leofric was everything to her. She could not believe she would never see him again. It seemed incomprehensible. There were signs of him everywhere around her, as if he would walk back into her life at any moment. The piece of rosewood he had been whittling sat on a small shelf against one wall, next to the sword he had taken from Thunred.

A sob rose up within her, but she choked it back. No—she could not accept this was true. Leofric had assured her the ealdorman of Eoforwic would never find him. All this time she had been worried about King Ecgfrith. She had underestimated the man who had exiled Leofric to a monk's life—they both had.

Aelfwyn buried her face in her hands and squeezed her eyes shut. Nevertheless the tears began to flow. They forced their way out from beneath her eyelids and scalded her cheeks.

"No ..." she gasped, barely able to get the words out. "God, no!"

Her life had just shattered.

Aelfwyn was not sure how long she sat there, hunched by the glowing embers as the pottage bubbled away beside her. Even the smell of the vegetable stew burning, as it caught on the bottom of the pot, did not rouse her.

Shock had made her turn inward. Her body was a husk; her mind had detached and traveled far away. Leofric had protected her till now. He had kept her safe during the journey south from Bebbanburg and had looked after her in Lincylene—without him she would not survive long.

Waric was right. She needed to leave this hut before crows started to circle.

Woodenly she rose to her feet and went to fetch a leather satchel. She started filling it with the few possessions she would take away with her. With each item that she stuffed inside, Aelfwyn grew increasingly wretched.

She hated feeling so scared, so lost—so weak. If the positions had been reversed Leofric would have been riding after her by now. Yet here she was whimpering like a frightened child.

Scrubbing at the tears that had started to flow anew, Aelfwyn went outside. A wind had sprung up. It breathed through the trees and ruffled the fresh growth of spring grass. The delicate white heads of the snowdrops she had spotted this morning waved gently.

The wind whispered to her, soothed her. She stood there and turned her face up to it, letting the cool air dry her heated cheeks. The fog of panic, grief and fear slowly cleared, and for the first time since Waric had delivered his devastating news, she was able to think clearly.

There was still much she did not know about the man she had shared her life with for the past few months. Leofric could be an enigma, and he did not trust easily. However, she was certain of one thing—he would never have given up on her. She remembered his promise back in Streonshalh, when they had both been barely more than strangers to each other. He had waited six days, and put his own safety at risk, just to give her a second chance at freedom.

She would not repay him by letting despair take over.

Aelfwyn hugged her arms around her chest and closed her eyes. The wind caressed her face like a lover's touch, giving her strength.

Waric had made a kind and generous offer, but she would not accept it.

After Cynn's betrayal, Lincylene was no longer her home. There was only one choice she could take, only one that would allow her to live with herself: she would go after Leofric.

She would find a way to free him.

Aelfwyn opened her eyes and looked up at the sky. Clouds danced across its pale blue surface. There were still a few hours of daylight left—she would not waste them. She spun on her heel and raced inside, resuming her packing with renewed vigor. She took all the food they had: a loaf of bread, some cheese, and a collection of worse for wear vegetables. It would be at least a five or six day journey to Eoforwic from here, and she had no gold to buy supplies on the way.

Once she had packed, Aelfwyn changed her clothing. Long skirts would hamper her and make her vulnerable. Instead, she pulled on a pair of Leofric's woolen leggings. He wore them under his breeches in cold weather. However, they had just been washed and had shrunk so she was able to fit them. She pulled on a long-sleeved woolen tunic that reached her mid-thigh and a leather jerkin over that. On her feet, she wore leather ankle boots which Leofric had bought her at the beginning of the winter. Then she slung her heavy fur mantle over her shoulders.

Unpinning her hair, she tied it in a tight braid at her nape. If she traveled through towns and villages with her hood up, folk might think her a young man at a distance.

After one last look around the cramped space where she and Leofric had shared the past few months, she then took Leofric's sword down off the wall and buckled it around her waist. She did not know how to use a sword, but she felt safer knowing she carried a weapon.

Aelfwyn went outside, lugging two bulging saddlebags with her, and saddled Windræs. The gelding stood placidly while she fiddled with his bridle and attempted to saddle him. It seemed to take an age, and she was sweating by the time the girth was tight enough. Once again, she was reminded how much she had let Leofric take care of during their time together.

Eventually, satisfied that the saddle was not going to slip round when she tried to mount, and that the bags were secure, she led Windræs out of the enclosure. It took her three attempts to mount—another thing that Leofric had always helped her with—but the gelding waited patiently until she was perched on top.

Windræs was a man's horse, so strong and tall that she felt a child on top of him. However, she knew he had a stout heart and an even temper. Aelfwyn leaned forward and stroked his neck. "Be gentle with me," she whispered to him. "Get me safely to Eoforwic."

Windræs snorted and jangled his bit in response.

Aelfwyn reined him around, glancing back at the hut. Her heart wrenched at the sight of it. Smoke was still drifting from the slit in the roof. She had removed the burned pottage from the hearth, but the embers still glowed. The golden afternoon sun bathed its thatched roof and the lush kitchen garden that Aelfwyn had so carefully tended. The dwelling looked clean, tidy, and well loved—very different to the ruin they had encountered in late summer.

She hated to think she would never return here, but that was the truth of it. Her life at Lincylene had ended. It was time to go.

Aelfwyn turned away from the dwelling and urged Windræs down the grassy path alongside the River Whitham. The wind brought the scent of grass and the pungent smell of river mud.

She urged the gelding into a brisk canter, much to Windræs's chagrin. The gelding tugged at the bit, keen to stretch his legs.

"Easy, boy." Aelfwyn murmured. "We've got a long road ahead—we'd better pace ourselves." Windræs had a long stride, which made him a comfortable ride although her arms were already beginning to ache from holding him back. Even so it was exhilarating to ride him on her own; it chased away her nerves and fear.

They thundered through the woodland. Instead of taking the southern fork, Aelfwyn turned Windræs away from the town and rode north away from Lincylene without a backward glance.

Chapter Thirty-four

The Road to Eoforwic

NIGHT HAD FALLEN when Halwend finally called them to a halt for the day. They had ridden hard since leaving Lincylene—with Leofric bound and thrown over the back of the fourth horse they had brought with them.

The party stopped under a stand of spreading oaks, where the ealdorman's sons yanked Leofric off the back of his horse and dumped him against the trunk of one of the oaks. They then bound him tightly to it.

"You're not getting away again," Berhtulf promised him.

"Not unless you want my axe in your back," Wybert added as he finished tying the rope.

"Enough of that," Halwend spoke up from a few feet away. The older warrior was busy starting a fire. "See to the horses."

Berhtulf and Wybert did as bid, although not before casting warning glances in their captive's direction.

Leofric leaned against the tree trunk and wriggled his feet and hands, in an effort to get some feeling back into them. His ribs ached from being slung over the back of a horse all day—and the back of his head was sore from the punches Wybert had used to subdue him outside Lincylene.

He watched Halwend bend low over the smoking fire and blow gently on the tender flame he had just coaxed to life. He then added dry twigs to it, and a few moments later the camp fire roared to life.

Sitting back on his haunches, Halwend glanced in Leofric's direction. "You've been quiet," he observed. "That's not like you."

Leofric shrugged. He had not spoken to any of them since this journey had begun. There was little point. He was not going to change any of their minds about taking him back to Eoforwic—and the ealdorman's sons needed little excuse to gut him before they reached their destination. "I've nothing to say," he said finally.

Halwend gave him a hard look. "No excuses, no insults? What happened to you, lad?"

Leofric managed a bitter smile but did not reply.

Halwend chuckled before rising to the packs he had unstrapped from the horses. Nearby Berhtulf and Wybert were rubbing the animals down. It was a crisp evening, and the moon was rising above the treetops.

Halwend retrieved some bread and cheese before crossing to Leofric. He then hunkered down and broke off a chunk of bread, before placing a sliver of cheese on top. Then he held it out to his captive. "Here—it's better I do this. The lads are likely to try and choke you."

Leofric took a bite before chewing slowly. "Thank you."

Halwend gave a non-committal grunt in response. Leofric finished the rest of the meagre meal. He was hungry and the bread and cheese were both good. Afterward, Halwend held a skin of water up to his mouth so he could take a couple of gulps.

Then he sat back on his heels and regarded Leofric, his expression inscrutable. "I'd forgotten how much you look like your mother," he said finally. "It's uncanny."

Leofric started slightly—that was the last thing he had expected Halwend to say. He had forgotten that the warrior was the same age as his parents, and that he too had grown up in Driffield.

"Better that than to take after my father," he replied.

Halwend laughed, earning a look of rebuke from Wybert who was now hobbling the horses nearby.

"How is she?" Leofric asked, feeling a pang of guilt as he asked the question. His mother, Cynhild, was a good woman, but in a household of rowdy, dominant men she had become a faded, exhausted figure. Leofric had inherited her features and auburn hair, although he and his brothers all had his father's hazel eyes.

"Well enough," Halwend said with a grimace, "although she was upset over you."

Leofric did not reply. His mother deserved better than the life she had been given. His father was a callous, rough man who had never shown her any tenderness. He remembered her being pretty as a younger woman, but a hard life had worn her looks away to dust.

Halwend moved away, taking a seat near the fire. Presently, the ealdormen's sons joined him, and they shared a meal of bread, cheese, onions and ale together. Ignored, and relieved to be so, Leofric leaned against the tree trunk. He gazed up at the sky through the gaps in the branches above his head.

The stars were coming out, twinkling to life one by one. Back in Lincylene, Aelfwyn would be sitting alone in their hut, waiting for him to come home—and worrying.

Leofric's gut twisted. He did not care what happened to him, but the thought of her alone without him to protect her tore him up inside. She would not be safe there now he was gone. Had someone warned her? Would the king take her into his hall, or give her as a whore to his men?

Stop it.

Leofric squeezed his eyes shut and tried to quell the panic that clawed at his throat. If Eatta touched one hair on Aelfwyn's head he would take him apart piece by piece—either in this life, or the next.

Aelfwyn awoke to the gentle caress of wind on her face. She opened her eyes and saw that dawn was just breaking. It was an ominous sunrise, a bloodred stain to the east promising bad weather to come.

She got to her feet and brushed leaves and dirt off her clothing. The remnants of last night's embers still glowed in the small fire she had lit after making camp for the night. Windræs cropped grass nearby, his front legs hobbled to prevent him from wandering off in the night.

Stretching the knots and aches out of her back, the result of a night sleeping rough, Aelfwyn tried to calculate how far she had ridden the day before. True to his name, Windræs had eaten up the furlongs. A little after leaving Lincylene she had let him have his head—she was sure they were not far behind Leofric and his abductors now.

She crossed to her saddlebags and pulled out some bread to break her fast. Chewing slowly she massaged a stiff muscle in her shoulder and tried to come up with a plan.

She did not regret her decision to go after Leofric. But what did she plan to do once she found him? The sword she carried around her waist felt heavy and cumbersome. It was a man's weapon. She would not be able to wield it without using both hands, and even then she would be as clumsy as a child.

Her mind churned over what lay ahead. What would she do if she caught up with Leofric on the road? The best plan was to wait until after dark before trying to free him. However, if she failed to reach them before Eoforwic she had no idea how she would free him from the ealdorman's clutches.

Aelfwyn's bowels cramped when she remembered Leofric's words about Godwine of Eoforwic. Leofric had offended him deeply. The punishment for crossing him again would be death.

The morning suddenly felt airless. Aelfwyn struggled to breathe as she crossed to Windræs and set about saddling him. The thought she might never set eyes on Leofric again—might never hear the timbre of his voice, see the mischievous twinkle in his eyes or his teasing smile—made her feel as if the sky was pressing down on her.

Life without him would be grey, joyless, and empty. He had brought her back from a dark place and had taught her to trust again. She could not bear the thought of losing him.

Aelfwyn rode through the day, only briefly taking a break to relieve her bladder and water Windræs. They passed settlements along the way, including the bustling village of Torksey, which perched on the banks of a wide canal.

Keeping her hood up, so that folk would not know she was a young woman, Aelfwyn rode through the village. She passed through the market square, through a milling sea of folk who browsed, haggled and bought. The aroma of fresh bread caused her belly to rumble, reminding her that she had little food left. She wished she could have bought some supplies her, but she did not carry any thrymsas. Leofric had been wearing their purse containing the few gold shillings they possessed.

The folk of Torksey paid her little attention as she rode through. This was a busy road, the main route between Lincylene and Eoforwic, and they were used to travelers. Even so Aelfwyn was relieved when she had left the village behind and was riding northwest across gentle folds of heathland, interspersed with hazel thickets. Mid-afternoon, a thick fog rolled in, obliterating the friendly sun. Windræs journeyed tirelessly, his heavy hooves thundering beneath her as they ate up the furlongs.

Still they did not catch Leofric and his captors up. Eventually a grey dusk settled over the land, bringing with it a veil of misty rain. Cold, stiff, and sore, Aelfwyn took a few bites of her dwindling loaf of bread and ate two carrots. After seeing to Windræs, she wrapped her cloak tightly about her and sat down under a spreading birch. She would not light a fire tonight. It was too damp, and she did not have the energy to go foraging for dry wood.

They ride as if the devil were after them.

Staring out at the gently falling rain, she wondered how Leofric was. She hoped they had not harmed him.

What am I doing?

The further she rode the more doubt settled in. With no one to talk to her thoughts turned inward and worry started to gnaw at her. What could she—a lone woman—do against three seasoned warriors?

Leofric would be furious if he knew she was coming after him. He probably thought she was safe with Cynn and Gytha. Little did he know that his friend had betrayed them.

Say she did manage to catch them before Eoforwic—what then? Did she really think she could sneak into their camp under the cover of darkness and steal Leofric away?

Tears stung her eyelids. She squeezed them shut, resting her brow upon her raised knees. She knew it was hopeless, that her behavior was rash and foolhardy, but she could not—would not—turn back now.

Chapter Thirty-five

Reckoning

THREE DAYS LATER Aelfwyn rode into Eoforwic.

Nestled at the confluence of two rivers, the Ouse and the Foss, the town sat upon a gently sloping hill surrounded by high wooden ramparts. It was a still, damp morning, and the sky was the color of smoke. Wooden barges floated on the calm waters of the Ouse, and fishermen's huts lined its reed-covered banks. The air smelled of burning peat and drying fish.

Aelfwyn pulled Windræs up and gazed across the sea of thatched roofs before her. She had never visited the town before—her journey north to Bebbanburg from Rendlaesham had taken her along the coast rather than inland—and she was surprised how large the town was. Within the ramparts she spied two thatched roofs, higher than all the others: Eoforwic's church and the Great Hall that sat next to it.

Inhaling deeply, collecting what was left of her courage, Aelfwyn gathered the reins and urged Windræs on. She would find Leofric there. Despite that Windræs had raced like the wind to catch them up, she had failed. Now he would be in the ealdorman's hands—and his execution imminent.

It had been an exhausting journey. Her back ached from sleeping rough, and her thigh muscles burned with agony at the end of each day's ride. Through it all she had been terrified that outlaws might ambush her.

Yet here she was in Eoforwic. She had no plan now. She had come too far to give up, or turn back. Instead she would go before the ealdorman and beg for Leofric's life. Even if Godwine softened the penalty to exile, at least she would have saved the man she loved.

Windræs clip-clopped across the bridge and through the low gate into Eoforwic. The air within smelled fetid; the stench of excrement mingling with the aroma of roasting mutton and the odor of pigs, fowl, and sheep. Aelfwyn wrinkled her nose and urged Windræs on, up the unpaved road leading to the high gate. Ahead she glanced up at the wooden guard towers. Warriors wearing helmets and chainmail vests stood atop the towers, their spears silhouetted against the pale sky. She spied the Northumbrian flag hanging limply above the high gate, and her belly clenched.

She had not seen that flag since Bebbanburg. It was a chilling reminder that she had returned to Ecgfrith's domain. The sight of so many spearman guarding the high gate also unnerved her. As she drew near, she saw that their shields bore the Northumbrian colors: yellow and red.

Aelfwyn's heart skipped a beat. The ealdorman was powerful and feared—but these were not his warriors.

She had seen the same armor, the same shields in Bebbanburg. These men served the King of Northumbria.

Ecgfrith was here.

Leofric knelt on the rushes before the high seat, his head bowed low.

He felt the gazes of all present stabbing into him but ignored them. Instead his attention was focused upon the man who stood next to the king upon the heah-setl.

Godwine of Eoforwic.

Leofric glanced up, his gaze meeting the ealdorman's. Godwine was as physically intimidating as Leofric remembered: a huge man with grizzled brown hair, a thick beard, and penetrating dark eyes.

It appeared his arrival had coincided with a visit from Ecgfrith of Northumbria. This was not unusual—just very poor timing. Traditionally, the king treated the halls of his ealdorman as his own and would often spend weeks enjoying their hospitality. Leofric remembered Ecgfrith's father, Oswiu, making frequent trips to Eoforwic in the past.

Next to Godwine, Ecgfrith appeared boyish and weedy. This was the first time Leofric had set eyes on the new king. He was young—barely older than Leofric—with a long face and a sharp hazel gaze. Next to him stood a beautiful raven-haired woman. Leofric guessed this was Aethelhild, the woman Aelfwyn had served. A few steps behind the queen stood a priest—a tall, spare man with a long, angular face, penetrating dark eyes, and thick grey hair shaved into a tonsure.

Behind the ealdorman and the king sat two women; the ealdorman's wife and his daughter, Hrothwyn. Mother and daughter looked startlingly alike; both heavyset with round, florid faces and frizzy brown hair. The sight of Hrothwyn made Leofric's chest constrict. He felt as if he was reliving that scene all those months ago—only this time things were far worse for him. Leofric tried to catch her eye, but she stared down at her feet, refusing to look in his direction.

"So they finally found you." Godwine broke the heavy silence. His gaze shifted to Berhtulf and Wybert, who stood to Leofric's left. "Well done, my sons." He then glanced to where Halwend flanked Leofric's right. "I knew you wouldn't fail me."

The brown-haired warrior inclined his head and smiled. "He wasn't easy to find."

Godwine's gaze returned to Leofric. "Do you remember my last words to you?"

Leofric nodded. Since entering the hall he had not spoken. He intended to say as little as possible. His rash tongue had gotten him into this mess, it was best he kept a leash on it now.

"What excuse do you have to make for yourself, Leofric?"

Leofric cleared his throat. "Excuse, milord?" He had the sinking feeling that Godwine was toying with him.

"Surely there was a reason you ran from Lindisfarena?"

Leofric began to sweat. His gaze flicked to the king and queen as he considered his response. He would not mention Aelfwyn, not with Ecgfrith present.

"There was no reason, milord," he began quietly, "other than I didn't wish to remain there."

Godwine snorted. "Once you left the island you should have kept running, boy. I warned you what would happen if you defied me."

Leofric held his gaze. "You did."

The ealdorman glanced over at Halwend. "His parents need to be here for this—go and fetch them before I say anything more."

Leofric dropped his gaze to the rushes, heart pounding. He wondered, since his father had proclaimed him a *nithing*, if they would even come. He did not want to see their faces, or their anger, humiliation, and disappointment in him. However, Godwine knew what he was doing—he would make sure Leofric's punishment had an audience.

He remained on his knees, with the ealdorman's sons standing guard over him, while Halwend went to do Godwine's bidding. Meanwhile conversation resumed in the hall around him. Women went back to their weaving, servants returned to preparing the nón-mete—noon meal—and the king, queen, and ealdorman took their places upon the high seat.

Leofric listened to the rumble of voices, the rise and fall of female conversation amidst the low timbre of men's speech. Somewhere at the back of the hall a newborn wailed before it was immediately hushed.

Leofric heard Ecgfrith speak to Godwine.

"Around the time this man escaped Lindisfarena, my wife's handmaid went missing," he said, his voice a soft drawl.

Leofric stared down at the dirty rushes and felt himself go cold.

When the ealdorman made no comment to this, the king continued. "We discovered that she had thrown herself into the sea and washed up on the isle, where some of the monks took her in. Once the prior discovered her, he sent her back to Bebbanburg with an escort of two monks—however she never reached her destination."

A heartbeat passed, and Leofric could feel the king's gaze boring into his skull, daring him to look up and meet his eye. Pulse racing, Leofric kept his gaze downcast.

"Cuthbert sent word that one of the monks knocked his companion unconscious before escaping south with the girl. It appears an odd coincidence, for this monk's name was Leofric."

A heavy silence fell, but eventually Godwine broke it. "That is a coincidence indeed, milord ... Leofric, what say you of this tale?"

Leofric remained where he was, unmoving, scarcely breathing.

"Leofric." Godwine's tone sharpened. "Look me in the eye and speak the truth."

Reluctantly Leofric raised his chin. The king sat in the center of the high seat, flanked to one side by his wife, the other by the ealdorman. Their expressions were all different. Godwine's face had flushed. The king's features had sharpened—his eyes keen. However, the queen, who until now had worn a detached mask, had gone ashen. Her blue eyes were wide as she stared down at Leofric.

"I did help her escape," he finally admitted. "Aelfwyn was frightened. She didn't want to go back to Bebbanburg."

"Why was she frightened?" Aethelhild spoke up. She had leaned forward in her chair, her gaze locking with Leofric's.

"Silence, wife." Ecgfrith brought up a slim hand and clicked his fingers. His face had gone taut, his hazel eyes dangerous. "I did not give you leave to speak."

Aethelhild's face pinkened. "But I need to know why—"

"You need to know nothing. Still your tongue."

The queen sat back in her chair, obeying her husband this time. However, Leofric saw the way her pulse fluttered in the hollow at the base of her neck, the way her blue eyes slitted with rage. Aethelhild loathed Ecgfrith—that much was plain to see.

Dismissing her, the king turned his wintry gaze upon Leofric. "Where is the girl now?"

Leofric shrugged. "I know not. I accompanied her as far as Streonshalh before I continued south. As far as I know she's still at the abbey."

A nerve flickered in Ecgfrith's cheek. "She's no longer at Streonshalh."

Leofric held his gaze. "Then I have no idea where she is."

Two heartbeats passed before Ecgfrith's mouth twisted into a sneer. "Liar."

Halwend returned a short time later, bringing Leofric's kin with him. Driffield was a short ride from Eoforwic; it had not taken Halwend long to fetch them.

To Leofric's horror he saw they had all come: his father, mother, brothers and sisters. Leofric took one glance at their faces and looked away—he could not bear to see their disappointment.

Wibert of Driffield led his family into the hall. Leather creaking, a squirrel cloak rippling behind him, he strode across the rushes toward his son. Leofric saw Wibert bearing down upon him and rose to his feet to face his father.

Wibert's freckled face had gone the color of raw meat, his usually hazel eyes a vivid, angry green. He reached his son and struck him hard across the face, hitting him with such force that Leofric fell backward and landed on his rump.

"Cloth-headed turd!"

Leofric spat out a gob of blood and attempted a smile. "At least that's better than calling me a *nithing*."

"You're lower than a *nithing*!" his father raged, taking a menacing step toward him.

"Enough, Wibert," the ealdorman rumbled. "It's not for you to deal out justice here—Leofric is mine now."

Wibert straightened up, his gaze flicking to Godwine. A muscle worked in his jaw, for it was clear he wanted to launch himself at Leofric and pummel him into the ground. However, he did as bid and stepped back from his son. His wife, Cynhild, came up to her husband's side. Her grey eyes were pleading as she attempted to take hold of his arm and steer him back to where the rest of the family waited. "Come, Wibert."

"Get off me, woman," Wibert snarled, shoving her aside.

Leofric looked up and met his mother's gaze. Halwend was right, she did not look happy. Grey now threaded her once vibrant red hair, her beautiful features faded by disappointment and grief. A lump formed in Leofric's throat when he saw the pain in her eyes. He did not want his mother to witness this; he wanted to spare her seeing her youngest son executed. But this humiliation was exactly what Godwine wanted.

"Now you're all here, I'll start," the ealdorman rumbled. Godwine sat forward in his chair, his big body tense as he snared Leofric's gaze with his.

"You disobeyed me once more, Leofric of Driffield—and the penalty for that is death."

Behind him Leofric heard a woman, possibly his mother or one of his sisters, start to sob.

"I will wield the axe myself," Godwine continued, "but before you die I want you to feel the humiliation, the suffering, you inflicted upon my daughter when you refused her." The ealdorman gave a cruel smile and leaned back in his chair. "You will be placed in the stocks for three days in the square in front of my hall, so that folk can punish you. On the dawn of the fourth, I shall take your head."

Chapter Thirty-six

Unmasked

LEOFRIC FELT NOTHING as he listened to his sentence.

It was no worse than he had expected. Death would be a relief after being at the mercy of Eoforwic's folk for three days.

Leofric dipped his head, silently acknowledging the sentence. Nothing could change it now, and he would not debase himself further by begging for mercy. Not in front of his family. However, he knew that whatever the outcome, an apology was necessary.

After a few moments he looked up, meeting the ealdorman's hard stare. "I am sorry for insulting your daughter and dishonoring you." His gaze flicked to Hrothwyn. The young woman still stared at her feet. She had not raised her eyes once since he had entered the hall; she could not bear to look upon him. "I know I can't undo what has been done, but I wanted Hrothwyn to hear my words."

A weighty silence settled over the hall. When Godwine answered, his face was stony, his voice harsh. "Your words come too late. They are the desperate plea of a doomed man. You could have come straight back here after leaving Lindisfarena but instead you fled. You're only sorry because my sons caught you."

"I'm not asking you to release me," Leofric shot back, his anger rising. "I was only apologizing."

Godwine's mouth twisted. "So you can meet my axe with a clear conscience?"

Leofric opened his mouth to answer but a woman's plea cut him off.

"I beg you—spare his life!"

Leofric's chest twisted. *Lord, have mercy—no.* He would know that voice anywhere.

He raised his head and looked over his shoulder to see Aelfwyn shoulder her way through the crowd of gawking retainers. His breathing caught in his throat. Dressed as a boy in woolen leggings, a long tunic, and fur cloak, she looked so young, so vulnerable. Her pale blonde hair had come loose of its braids and flowed softly over her shoulders. She wore his sword—the blade he had taken from Thunred—at her side.

Aelfwyn broke free from the edge of the crowd; but two of the ealdorman's men caught her before she could reach Leofric. She struggled in their iron grip, her gaze meeting his across the narrow space separating them. Her cheeks were flushed, and her eyes glittered with tears.

Aelfwyn saw the disbelief flicker across Leofric's face, followed by dismay.

"God's bones, Aelfwyn—what are you doing here?" he breathed.

She had expected a warmer welcome, although she had not planned on barging into the ealdorman's hall.

Aelfwyn had entered the high gate without difficulty, telling the guards there she bore a message from the King of Lindesege. After leaving Windræs in the stables, she had found the yard in front of the Great Hall deserted. Everyone was indoors—and she knew why. Without thinking on the consequences, only knowing that she had to do this, Aelfwyn had mounted the steps to the hall. No spearman guarded the entrance—they had all gone inside to witness the sentencing.

"A bit late to take the lord's name." Godwine broke the deathly hush that followed. "Seeing as you rejected a monk's life." He inclined his head toward the king, a cold smile spreading across his face. "Is this the woman you were seeking, sire?"

Aelfwyn met Ecgfrith's gaze, and her stomach clenched. He was staring at her with a hungry, possessive look. Beside him Aethelhild was pale. She watched Aelfwyn as if a ghost stood before her.

"You're alive," Aethelhild whispered. Her voice broke as she said these words and tears began trickling down her cheeks. Meeting the queen's gaze, Aelfwyn felt as if a giant hand had reached inside her chest and was twisting. Aethelhild had grieved her loss. She must have worried about what had befallen her.

Aelfwyn's vision blurred with her own tears, although she blinked them back. This was not the time for weeping. She gave Aethelhild a brave smile. "Aye—Leofric has been looking after me."

"So I see," the king drawled, his gaze raking her from head to toe. "He has made you his hōre."

Aelfwyn flinched at the insult. She glanced back over at Leofric and saw his face was now ashen. His eyes had deepened to a murderous green, narrowing into angry slits as he stared at the king.

Ecgfrith gave a soft laugh before casting the ealdorman a wry look. "This is quite a development, Godwine. I am pleased I took the trouble to visit you. I came for a spring hunt but have already caught a most valuable prey."

The ealdorman nodded. "Pleased to be of service, milord."

Watching them, seeing the way the two men discussed her as if she was not even present, made fury surge through Aelfwyn's body. She met Ecgfrith's gaze.

"That's all I've ever been to you, isn't it? Prey."

The king stiffened, the smirk fading from his face. His eyes narrowed. Aelfwyn held his gaze boldly. She knew she would pay for this later but right now she wanted everyone here to know who Ecgfrith really was.

Her gaze flicked to Aethelhild.

"He raped me." The words lashed across the hall. "He waited until you had retired for the night, and then he came to my alcove."

The queen held her gaze, and Aelfwyn saw the sorrow in her friend's eyes. Aethelhild was no fool, she had imagined as much. Aelfwyn then shifted her gaze to the ealdorman. She met Godwine's eye, hoping that he might come to her aid. He had sought reckoning for his daughter's honor—perhaps he was a protector of women.

It was a vain hope, but the only one she had left.

"He humiliated me, hurt me," she continued, her voice trembling from the effort to rein in her outrage. "The next morning I ran from Bebbanburg and tried to end my life in the sea—but the waves washed me up on Lindisfarena, where Leofric saved my life. He didn't run from the isle to save himself but to protect me. He knew what the king is, and what would happen to me if I returned to Bebbanburg."

Aelfwyn finished speaking and held the ealdorman's gaze. The reality of her and Leofric's flight from Bebbanburg was not quite as noble as she had painted—but this was not the time for the truth.

Tension crackled through the air, as if a thunderstorm approached. Nausea rose within her when she saw Godwine's mouth twist. The ealdorman looked over at Ecgfrith, his grin widening.

"Clever wench, looking to me for sympathy. She's got a lot to say for herself, this one."

The king did not smile back. His hazel eyes had hooded, his long face was all planes and angles as he fought to contain his anger. Aelfwyn began to sweat; Ecgfrith would make her pay for unmasking him before his wife and retainers.

"She wasn't this mouthy at Bebbanburg," Ecgfrith said finally, his voice frighteningly calm. "Her time with the outlaw has ruined her." The king then cast a cold glance in his wife's direction. "Your sweet-faced little maid has turned into a bold-tongued slut."

"I'm not!" Aelfwyn shouted at him, her voice ringing high into the rafters. The force of her anger astounded her. "Leofric never made me his hōre—you did!"

"Silence!" Ecgfrith hissed, leaning forward in his chair. "One more word, and I will have you flogged to death right here."

Aelfwyn held his gaze. She did not doubt him not for a moment.

"Lower your eyes, girl," the ealdorman rumbled. "You stand before your king."

With great difficulty Aelfwyn obeyed him—although her heart hammered like a spear beating against a shield wall before battle. She did not care what Ecgfrith did to her now. She wanted the world to know who the king really was.

She sensed the mood in the Great Hall had changed. Folk murmured amongst themselves; a ripple spreading out from her, like a stone dropped into the middle of a still lake.

Aelfwyn glanced over at Leofric. He was watching her, a look of awe on his face. However, she saw the anguish in his eyes. Like her, he knew Ecgfrith would make her suffer for humiliating him.

Aelfwyn looked down at the rushes beneath her feet and waited for the axe to fall.

Ecgfrith eventually broke the tense silence. "A shrewish woman is vexing, do you not think, Godwine?"

"Aye," the ealdorman replied.

"A good woman knows her place, but it seems I have been cursed with shrews," the king continued. "I wed a cold bitch who refused to spread her legs for me—so what's a man to do?"

"A woman should obey her husband," Godwine agreed.

"My wife refused me so I took my pleasure with her maid," Ecgfrith concluded. "This is all your doing, Aethelhild."

Aelfwyn looked up to see the queen's face crumpled in anguish. Tears streamed down her cheeks, and her shoulders trembled. Behind her, Bishop Wilfrid stepped close and placed a reassuring hand on her arm. His long, angular face was taut with outrage, and he cast a look of censure in the king's direction.

"Stand back, Wilfrid," Ecgfrith snarled. "I tire of you whispering into my wife's ear like Satan's serpent."

The bishop flinched. Reluctantly he removed his hand from the queen's arm and took a few steps back on the high seat.

Ecgfrith then turned his attention back to Aelfwyn. His cold smile and pitiless eyes warned her that she would not like his next words.

"You could have remained at Bebbanburg and served me," he said gently, his gaze snaring hers. "But you thought yourself too good for it. Since you have so willingly given yourself to this outlaw, you can die at his side."

Ecgfrith straightened up, his gaze meeting the ealdorman's. "When you strike off his head in three days' time, you can do the same with hers."

Leofric lunged forward, his face contorted in rage. "You bastard!"

The hall dissolved into chaos. The screams of Leofric's mother and sisters echoed amongst the rafters as the ealdorman's sons leaped upon Leofric and pummeled him to the ground with their fists.

Aelfwyn cried his name and tried to wrench herself free of the two men holding her, but they had a grip of iron. A roar went up around her, and the world tilted. Tearing her gaze from where Leofric struggled against the two men who had pinned him to the ground, she looked up, catching the king's eye.

Ecgfrith was smiling.

Chapter Thirty-seven

Courage

AELFWYN SQUEEZED HER eyes shut and winced as something foul splattered across her face. Around her the folk of Eoforwic hooted and jeered, encouraging the group of lads bearing slop buckets, who circled the two prisoners.

The wooden jaws of the stocks held her fast. She was unable to move, unable to flee. Misery swamped her—how would she endure three days of this?

"Keep your eyes closed, Aelfwyn," Leofric muttered from beside her.

She was just about to reply when an egg hit her between the eyes. Aelfwyn cried out, gagging at the sulfuric stench of rotten egg as it slid down her face.

"How long will they do this?" she gasped.

"As long as it takes for them to get bored."

Aelfwyn went against his advice then and glanced across at Leofric. Rotten food and excrement splattered his face, although his gaze was defiant; a murderous green that told her he was far from beaten.

They knelt in the heart of a wide square before the high gate. It was a slightly sloping, unpaved square flanked by the fortified wooden gate on one side, with the church and the Great Hall at its back. The gate was open this morning to allow townsfolk in to see the prisoners.

The afternoon was cool with spots of rain in the air. Above them the sky was the color of slate—threatening rain. Despite that she and Leofric would get soaked, Aelfwyn welcomed the rain. It would wash the filth off them and hopefully drive away their tormenters.

"Slut!" One of the lads scooped up a handful of oxen dung and hurled it at Aelfwyn. It splattered over her, and she closed her eyes once more, blocking out the world.

"Cowards," Leofric growled next to her.

"Why?" The word came out in a sob. "We've never wronged any of these people."

"That doesn't matter to them," Leofric replied, his voice flat with anger. "When there's a chance to bring others down, most folk leap to be part of it—remember what happened in Lincylene?"

Aelfwyn did, and she knew she should not be surprised, but the viciousness of this crowd shocked her all the same.

Aethelhild Queen of Bernicia sat at her husband's side upon the high seat and picked listlessly at her supper. Around her the men discussed the upcoming hunt.

"We can wait till after the execution if you wish, sire," Godwine said.

Ecgfrith shook his head before spearing a piece of mutton with his knife. "No need. We'll only be away two days at most and back in plenty of time. All I ask is that we leave the prisoners well guarded while we're gone."

Godwine nodded, glancing across at where his two sons sat opposite. His gaze then shifted to the big man with shaggy brown hair and piercing blue eyes who sat at the opposite end of the table. "Halwend—you, Berhtulf and Wybert will guard the prisoners in our absence."

Wybert, the youngest of the ealdorman's sons, grimaced. "I was looking forward to the hunt." He cast a jaundiced look at where his mother and sister sat further down the table. "I don't want to stay at home with the women."

"You'll be of greater use to me here," Godwine replied, his tone brooking no argument. "I need to know Leofric and that wench are being watched."

"I will see it done," the older warrior named Halwend replied.

Aethelhild stared down at the congealing mutton stew in her trencher. She clenched her jaw and attempted to calm her breathing, to still her hammering heart. Next to her she was aware of Bishop Wilfrid's steady presence. He had said little since taking his place upon the high seat, but she sensed his disapproval, his indignation.

Like her, he had suspected that Ecgfrith had played a role in Aelfwyn's disappearance. Only now their worst suspicions had been confirmed.

Aethelhild raised her gaze and observed the king. She had loathed her first husband—a hulking bully who was free with his fists—but her hatred for Ecgfrith went far deeper. To look at him, you would not have thought he was cruel and sly. Slim and well mannered with bland good looks, he fooled most folk for a while before they saw the man beneath.

Godwine met the king's eye and grinned. "Worry not, milord—Halwend and my sons will ensure our prisoners stay put. Let's go hunting."

"Excellent." Ecgfrith raised a cup of mead to his lips and drank deeply. "We depart at dawn."

Later, when night shrouded Eoforwic, Aethelhild sat by the window in the large alcove she shared with Ecgfrith and awaited her husband's arrival. Usually she would retire much earlier than him and feign sleep when he joined her.

Tonight she waited up for Ecgfrith—for there were things she needed to say.

Putting aside her distaff, Aethelhild rose to her feet and crossed to the small shuttered window on the far wall. She opened it and gazed outside.

The Great Hall stood high upon sturdy oaken foundations and commanded a view for many furlongs distant. A moon was riding high in the cloudy sky. There was a shimmery halo around it, warning of coming bad weather. The thatched roofs of Eoforwic tumbled down the hillside to the ramparts, the fires upon the watchtowers reflecting off the glittering waters of the River Ouse beyond.

Aethelhild sighed. Suddenly she felt indescribably weary. She knew marriages such as hers were the lot of a highborn woman. She had no right to expect more of life—but even so life as Ecgfrith's wife had taken its toll upon her. Even her strong faith brought her little solace these days.

Today had made certain things impossible to ignore.

Ecgfrith eventually joined her. She heard him bid the ealdorman and his men goodnight and caught his light tread across the rushes before he stepped up onto the platform that ran around the perimeter of the hall. A moment later, he pulled the heavy tapestry aside and stepped inside the alcove.

"Still awake?" he greeted her, raising a sandy eyebrow.

"Aye," she replied. "I was waiting for you."

He gave a soft, humorless laugh and began to undress—unbuckling the leather vest he wore over a long-sleeved tunic. "That's a surprise." Ecgfrith then met her gaze, and she saw the challenge in his hazel eyes. "Apologies, wife, but I no longer desire you—in case you hadn't noticed. I take my pleasure elsewhere these days."

Aethelhild took a deep breath and ignored the jibe. "I need to talk to you, Ecgfrith."

"Can't it wait till morning?"

"At dawn you ride out with the ealdorman, there will be no time." Aethelhild rose to her feet. She was a tall woman, and her gaze was level with her husband's. "I must ask two things of you."

Ecgfrith's mouth twisted into a sneer. He shucked off his shirt and started unlacing his breeches. "A wife demands nothing of her husband."

Aethelhild ignored him. "I've asked you before—please let me leave Bebbanburg and take up residence at Streonshalh. You've said it yourself many times before: I am a poor wife. Cast me aside and find another woman who would suit you better."

Ecgfrith stopped undressing, his gaze holding hers. "I would let you go, if I thought doing so would make you miserable. However, you yearn to take your vows and live as a nun for the rest of your life. Why would I do anything to make you happy?"

Aethelhild's chest constricted at these words. He was so unnecessarily cruel. He had made a mistake in wedding her but would not set her free so that both of them could make new lives for themselves.

He shrugged then, an impatient gesture. "What's the second thing you wanted?"

Aethelhild pushed aside her own misery—the sensation of being buried alive—and forced herself to focus on the situation at hand. "Aelfwyn."

Ecgfrith smiled coldly. "I thought you might bring her up."

"Please spare her life," Aethelhild went to him and, reaching out, grasped his arm. Ecgfrith's gaze widened, for she had never willingly touched him in private before. Aethelhild ignored his reaction and pressed on. "She does not deserve such a death. Don't leave her out there at the mercy of the rabble."

Ecgfrith watched her steadily for a few moments, before he reached down and pried her fingers off his arm.

"You refused me." His voice was low and cold. "And Aelfwyn was your punishment. If I spare her life, her fate would be far worse—for I would give her to my men to enjoy before making you watch me take her. You should be thanking me for this clean death."

Bile rose in Aethelhild's throat. There was no talking to Ecgfrith, he would twist every word against her and find other ways to punish Aelfwyn before her execution. Without thinking, Aethelhild lashed out at him. The crack of her palm striking his cheek was obscenely loud in the slumbering hall.

Ecgfrith staggered, caught off guard by her violence, before he struck her back. His fist slammed into her left eye, knocking her clean off her feet. With a strangled cry, Aethelhild fell back onto the rushes.

She sat up, clutching her injured eye, to find her husband looming over her.

"One more word, Aethelhild," he warned her, fists clenched, "and I will beat you bloody."

She stared up at him, despair crashing over her. In his eyes she saw no hope, no mercy—no future.

Aelfwyn shivered as a cold wind buffeted across the exposed square. Even with her traveling cloak wrapped around her shoulders, the chill bit into her. Her legs had gone numb, her shoulders throbbed, and the skin of her face and hands felt tight from the layers of encrusted filth that folk had thrown at her.

The expected rain had not yet arrived, even though the air was heavy with moisture. Mercifully the tormenters had eventually tired of throwing rotten food at them and of hurling insults. As dusk settled over Eoforwic they had eventually slipped away, back to their warm hearths and waiting suppers.

Now that darkness blanketed the town, the square was deserted. The ealdorman had posted guards around the perimeter of the square and by the high gate. Aelfwyn caught two of them standing around ten yards in front of her, their silhouettes outlined against the indigo sky.

"Aelfwyn." Leofric spoke up, his voice husky with fatigue. "Are you well?"

She gave a soft laugh, wincing as the stocks pinched the skin on her neck. "Well enough considering the circumstances."

Silence stretched between them for a few moments before Leofric spoke once more. "This is all my doing—I'm so sorry."

Aelfwyn had never heard him like this—defeated, broken. It tore her up inside.

"This is not your fault," she began huskily. "You were betrayed. Cynn turned you in to Godwine's men."

Leofric went still. When he finally answered, his voice was rough with anger. "Cynn betrayed me?"

"It appears the price of your head was of more value to him than your friendship." Bitterness choked Aelfwyn as she spoke. She still had difficulty accepting what Cynn had done.

"Did Gytha know?"

"I'm not sure."

Neither of them spoke for a while, each lost in their own thoughts. Aelfwyn knew that Leofric would find Cynn's betrayal hard to accept. She had not wanted to tell him, but he deserved to know the truth.

"I don't care what happens to me," Leofric said eventually, his voice subdued, "but I can't bear the thought of you coming to harm."

Aelfwyn considered his words. She twisted her neck so she could glance at him. Yet it was too dark for her to make out his features. "You think I shouldn't have come after you?"

Leofric sighed. "I wish you hadn't."

Tears stung Aelfwyn's eyelids. "I didn't have a choice in the matter, Leo. Staying behind would have killed me."

"Following me will do the same." She heard the bitterness in his voice.

"They tore you away from me," she replied, grief twisting inside her, "without even letting me say goodbye. This way I have the chance to see you, to speak to you again ... before the end."

Aelfwyn heard Leofric inhale. The sound was ragged, and she realized that he was struggling to control his emotions. "I don't deserve you." He spoke the words so softly that she barely caught them. "I did nothing of worth till the day I helped you escape—and even then I did it for me. I never spent a moment of my time thinking about anyone but myself ..."

Leofric broke off then. A few moments passed before he continued. "You changed everything. I love you, Aelfwyn—I only wish I'd had the courage to tell you earlier. Now it's too late."

Tears streamed down Aelfwyn's face as she listened. Her soul ached at hearing the words. She longed to go to him, to wrap her arms about him, place her head against his breast, and listen to his heartbeat. She loved him so much, she felt as if her chest would explode from the force of it.

"It's not too late," she whispered back. "You're telling me now and that's all that matters."

Chapter Thirty-eight

Meetings

IT WAS A cold, blustery morning as Hrothwyn, daughter of Godwine, made her way down the steps of the Great Hall. Pulling her fur cloak about her and blinking at the stinging wind, the young woman's gaze swept across the wide space before her.

On the east side of the square, farmers and merchants had set up their stalls for the morning's market. Women carrying wicker baskets wove their way through the busy stalls, picking up their provisions for the noon meal. Just a few yards away, in the center of the square, Hrothwyn spied two crouched figures, their heads and wrists trapped in a heavy wooden stockade.

Some folk had not come to the square to buy food. A group of lads were out already, circling the lovers like starving dogs. Their taunts and curses reached her, and Hrothwyn clenched her jaw at the vile words.

Enough.

"Lady Hrothwyn," one of her father's spearmen greeted her at the bottom of the steps. "Where are you going?"

"I wish to speak with the prisoners," she informed him, quietly but firmly.

"I don't think your father would be pleased by that."

"My father has given me permission," she lied. Fortunately, Godwine had just departed Eoforwic with the king and a company of warriors for their spring hunt. This spearman would not be able to check with her father until his return.

The man appeared to hesitate, indecision on his face. "Very well," he muttered. "Just don't get too close to either of them."

Hrothwyn gave him a jaundiced look. "They're in the stocks," she reminded him coolly, "and hardly a danger to me."

Not awaiting his response, the young woman squared her shoulders, gathered her courage, and strode out across the square.

Leofric was dozing, lost in a fog of discomfort and exhaustion, when a shadow fell over him. He blinked and looked up to see a short, plump young woman with a round freckled face and wiry brown hair gazing down at him.

"Hrothwyn," he croaked, surprised to see her. He imagined she had come to spit on him, to vilify him like the rest of the folk here. Despite that he knew it was her right—far more than the scavengers that were now trailing into the market square—his heart sank. He did not want Aelfwyn to see this.

"I have not come to insult you," she told him eventually, as if reading his mind.

Leofric cringed inside at these words. They were a stark reminder of how he had wounded her months earlier.

"Look, Hrothwyn, I truly am sorry for what I said," he croaked. His throat was parched, and it hurt to speak, but he had to make her understand.

"You've already apologized," she reminded him, "and I believe that you are truly remorseful."

He looked up into her earnest, solemn face and felt something twist in his chest. Now he was really starting to feel like a turd. "Then why are you here?"

"Because I wanted you to know that I bear you no ill-will—that I wish there was a way I could help you and Aelfwyn." Hrothwyn's gaze flicked to where Aelfwyn silently listened to their conversation, and Hrothwyn gave her a sad smile. "Neither of you deserve this fate."

She then glanced back at Leofric, her smile fading. "I know I'm not comely, my father has told me often enough. Your words didn't come as a shock—I was more afraid that my father would punish me for being unmarriageable."

Leofric held her gaze. "Did he?"

She nodded. "He has found me a husband, a man three times my age who has already buried three wives. He wants a woman to breed him sons—he doesn't care how fair my face is."

Leofric almost flinched at the baldness of her words. There was no self-pity, only cold fact. Hrothwyn accepted her fate, even if it was a cruel one.

Hrothwyn favored him with a sad, self-effacing smile, reached up and placed her hand over the wooden crucifix she wore about her neck. "I will pray for you both."

Aethelhild stood back from the stockade, observing as Godwine's daughter spoke quietly to Leofric. Aelfwyn, her pretty face splattered with dried filth, listened to their conversation, her eyes gleaming with unshed tears.

Aethelhild did not want to interrupt Hrothwyn—for she could see it had taken a lot for the young woman to come outdoors to speak to Leofric. A few lads, buckets full of fresh slops, hovered nearby. Recognizing the ealdorman's daughter, and then the queen, they kept their distance for the moment. Yet Aethelhild knew that the moment she and Hrothwyn departed, they would resume their campaign.

Hrothwyn finished speaking to Leofric and stepped away from him. Aethelhild watched her turn away, before Hrothwyn then made her way back across the square toward the Great Hall.

The boys hovering at the edge of the square made to close in. Aethelhild threw them a venomous look, causing them to shrink back once more, and strode over to the stocks. Aelfwyn saw her coming, her grey-blue eyes widening in surprise.

"Milady," Aelfwyn greeted her huskily, her gaze fixing upon the queen's bruised left eye. Aethelhild knew she was not a pretty sight this morning. Her eye had swollen shut and ached steadily.

"Morning, Aelfwyn." Aethelhild glanced over at Leofric who was also watching her, his handsome face taut with fatigue and despair.

"The king will not want you speaking to me." Aelfwyn's quietly spoken words brought Aethelhild's attention back to her.

The queen smiled. "I care not what the king wants—besides, he's not here to stop me."

Aethelhild then casually glanced around her. There were a number of spearmen guarding the square, but they were all out of earshot.

Good.

The queen took a step closer, trying to ignore the stench of the excrement and rotting food that covered both the prisoners and the stocks. It was strong enough to make her eyes water.

"This is a crime against everything I believe in," Aethelhild began, her voice low and steady, "and I'll not sit by and let those men take your lives."

Aelfwyn stared at her, momentarily struck speechless. When she finally found her tongue, the young woman's voice was hushed. "There's nothing you can do, milady. Please don't put your own safety at risk for us—it's too dangerous."

Aethelhild smiled. "I've decided that some things are worth risking. I'm not just doing this for you, but for myself. I cannot stay with Ecgfrith."

"He did that to you," Leofric observed, his gaze upon her blackened eye, "didn't he?"

Aethelhild nodded. "And he will do worse for I can no longer keep quiet."

"But how can you possibly—" Aelfwyn began, her gaze wide and panicked.

"Let me worry about that," Aethelhild cut her off. She knew it must seem hopeless; she was one woman with only the bishop as her ally. How could she free Aelfwyn and Leofric, and escape Eoforwic?

Aethelhild looked toward the busy market, just yards away. There, her gaze rested upon a red-haired woman wearing a woolen cloak. Aethelhild had spied the woman earlier, while Hrothwyn was speaking to Leofric. She had come to the square bearing a basket. Yet her gaze was not on the piles of spring greens, turnips and onions, but on Leofric.

Cynhild of Driffield had come here to see her son. Aethelhild saw the anguish on the older woman's face, the fury in her gaze, and knew she had found an ally.

She glanced back at where Leofric and Aelfwyn watched her steadily.

"Leave the details to me," she said quietly. "Just be ready when the time comes."

Cynhild walked through the narrow streets of Eoforwic, her heart pounding. It was starting to rain; large wet drops hit her face, but she barely noticed them.

Before setting out on the hunt with the ealdorman and king, her husband had expressly forbidden her from going to the stocks, from seeing their son. Usually she obeyed him in all things—Wibert had taken his fists to her more than once when she had defied him—yet this time she had not done his bidding.

The sight of Leofric, trapped and splattered in filth, had nearly broken her heart.

My boy.

She had never gotten the chance to say goodbye all those months ago. One moment Leofric had been part of their lives, the next he was gone, and Wibert forbade any of the family from mentioning his name.

Although she had always promised herself that she would never single out any of her children for special treatment, Leofric had been her favorite. Perhaps it was because he was the youngest of her brood or maybe it was his sunny, cheeky nature as a child. His older brothers had taken after their father—rough, hard men with bad tempers—whereas Leofric had a kind soul.

Growing up he had been forced to develop a tough skin in order to survive in their family, and inch by inch she had lost her boy to a cocky, selfish young man who lived only to satisfy his own wants. Still, she had sometimes caught glimpses of the man underneath, the man he could be.

She had watched him stand before the ealdorman and the king, listened to him speak to them, and her heart had swollen with pride. Then when his lover had burst in and pleaded for his life, her heart had broken.

She did not know what had befallen him over the past year, but she could see he had changed.

Earlier, Cynhild had watched Queen Aethelhild approach Leofric and Aelfwyn and speak to them quietly. It was a curious sight, to see such a beautiful lady clothed in flowing blue, glide across the filthy square to the stocks. Watching them, Cynhild could see they were speaking of something important—she wished she was closer so she could overhear them.

Then the queen had glanced up, her penetrating gaze snaring Cynhild's.

Frozen to the spot Cynhild had watched Lady Aethelhild bid the lovers good day before she strode toward her.

"Milady." Cynhild had hurriedly curtsied as the queen approached, mortified that she had been caught staring.

"You are Cynhild, wife of Wibert, are you not?" Aethelhild had asked.

"Aye."

Aethelhild had smiled then, an expression that lit up the world. "Will you walk with me a while, Cynhild? There is something I must talk to you about."

A short time later—Cynhild knew what she must do.

The rain started in earnest as she entered a narrow lane. Folk hurried by, dashing indoors to escape the downpour. Cynhild blinked droplets out of her eyes and hurried on. The home she sought lay three from the end—although she had never visited it, she had always known where it was ... just in case things got so bad with Wibert that she needed to seek refuge. There had been moments when she had almost fled here, but she had lacked the courage.

This was different—with her son's life at stake she was finally brave.

She stopped in front of a well-made timber dwelling with a neatly thatched straw roof. Wiping her sweating hands on her skirts and attempting to calm her breathing, Cynhild thought back to Aethelhild's words.

"I will not have Aelfwyn and Leofric's deaths on my conscience. Will you help me free them?"

Cynhild's first reaction had been fear; what the queen was asking would condemn them both to death. However, she had listened to Aethelhild all the same, hope burgeoning in her breast when the queen finally turned to her, fixing her with that penetrating gaze of hers.

They had been walking down the wide thoroughfare that led toward the town's low gate—a good choice for it was a busy, noisy street, and made it difficult for others to overhear them. Goats bleated as they trotted past, the bells around their necks jingling, and a gaggle of geese honked raucously from a nearby pen.

"I have some warriors that came with me from Rendlaesham," Aethelhild told her quietly. "They are loyal to me and will help to free your son and Aelfwyn. Yet our success depends on having help from inside. Do you know any of the ealdorman's warriors? Would any aid us?"

Cynhild's breathing had stopped then.

Indeed, she knew the warrior the ealdorman had left in charge of the prisoners: Halwend.

Here she was standing in front of his door.

Sick with nerves, Cynhild knocked on the sturdy oaken frame. Moments later the door opened and Halwend filled the doorway. He was a big man, broader and taller than her husband, but the years had been kinder to him than to Wibert. Only a few strands of grey laced his thick brown hair, and his blue eyes were as sharp as they had always been. He wore light breeches and a sleeveless linen tunic, revealing the muscular brawn of his shoulders and arms.

"Cynhild." He breathed her name, his eyes widening. "God's bones, what are you doing here?"

"I need to speak to you," she replied shakily. "Can I come in?"

He nodded and stepped aside so that she could enter. Pushing her wet hair from her face, Cynhild walked into a clean, sparsely furnished space, lit only by a glowing fire pit. Something deep within her chest twisted as she stood there. This could have been her home—if only she had been brave enough to follow her heart.

She turned to him, heart hammering, disconcerted to find Halwend standing right behind her.

"I'm sorry about Leo," he rumbled. "He doesn't deserve this end."

His words brought hope to her heart. She looked up at his strong face, a face that bore the scars of a warrior's life. His nose had been broken more than once and had set with a bump in it, and he bore a thin silver scar on his right cheek, visible through his short beard. It was a fearsome face, but she saw only softness in his eyes as he stared down at her.

"I always wondered what your home was like," she said quietly.

He smiled. "And is it how you imagined?"

She nodded before looking away. He had never married, and she knew why. The weight of her guilt made it hard to breathe.

"I'm sorry," she whispered.

Halwend reached out and hooked a finger under her chin, gently raising her face so that their eyes met once more. "What for?"

"For not being braver—stronger. I've spent years regretting the past."

The warrior stared down at her, his expression inscrutable. "There's little point in such regrets," he said gently. "Why would you worry over what you cannot change?"

Tears stung Cynhild's eyes, but she smiled. "You always were more practical than me." She paused a moment, gathering her courage. Then she reached out and placed her hand on his chest. To her surprise, she found his pulse was racing. "I know I shouldn't be here, but you are my only hope," she whispered.

He placed a large hand over hers, trapping her palm against his chest.

"I can't save Leo now," he replied, regret in his voice. "Surely you realize that."

Cynhild inhaled deeply, steeling herself. "Alone you can't—but what if you had the queen's help, and the aid of her men?"

Halwend inclined his head slightly, his gaze narrowing. "Go on ..."

Cynhild told him everything Aethelhild had confided in her—the entire plan the queen had laid out for them. It was a huge risk—Halwend could kill her for treachery—but this time she would not let her fears hold her back.

When she finished Halwend did not reply immediately. He watched her under slightly lowered lids, considering her words, and Cynhild grew nervous. What if she had miscalculated? What if she had imagined the depth of his feelings for her? It was also possible he secretly resented her for choosing Wibert over him all those years ago—a decision she had bitterly regretted ever since.

"Halwend ..." she said finally, dread rising within her. "What say you?"

He stared down at her for a moment, his gaze deadly serious, before he reached out and gently stroked her cheek.

"I will do it," he murmured, "but on one condition."

Suddenly the dwelling felt hot and airless. He was standing so close that Cynhild could hardly breathe. "What's that?" she eventually whispered.

His mouth quirked into a half-smile. "That when we leave here—you come with us."

Chapter Thirty-nine
Night Falls over Eoforwic

AETHELHILD FELT SICK with nerves by the time dusk settled over rainy Eoforwic.

Likewise, Bishop Wilfrid appeared pale and drawn. His tall, rawboned frame quivered with impatience as he paced the rush-strewn floor in the king and queen's alcove. Watching him made Aethelhild feel even more on edge, although she knew he was trying to steady himself for what was to come.

"Are you sure everything is in order?" he asked.

Aethelhild nodded. It was like playing a game of Cyningtaefl: all the pieces were set upon the board—all that remained was to start moving them. "Cynhild and Halwend both know the part they must play," she replied quietly, keeping her voice low. They were alone in the alcove, but she didn't want to risk being overheard, not when she was this close to freedom. "My men are readying the horses as we speak."

Wilfrid stopped pacing and faced her. His face was stern, but his eyes were gentle. After Aelfwyn's disappearance she had increasingly relied on the bishop for companionship. Wilfrid was a good listener, and his gruff manner hid a kind heart. He had made life at Bebbanburg bearable.

"Can you trust those two?" he asked. "What if they betray us?"

Aethelhild held his gaze. "We have to believe they won't. They both stand to gain something from aiding us."

The bishop watched her for a few moments before his mouth curved into a rare smile. "You were wasted as a woman, Aethelhild—you would have made a great man, a leader of armies."

Aethelhild gave a soft laugh before shaking her head. She knew he meant it as a compliment, but the comment stung. "I know a woman's lot isn't an easy one—but I'm glad I wasn't born a man." She met his gaze squarely then. "I intend to make up for lost time once we leave here—to make my life a worthy one."

Aelfwyn sagged against the wooden stockade, barely conscious.

Night was falling—the grey of a rainy day merging into a shadowy twilight. The square inside the high gate had emptied out now, their tormentors having grown tired of sloshing around in the mud while the rain pelted down. The smell of cook fires, the roasting of mutton, and the aroma of baking pies caused her belly to ache with hunger.

Time had lost any meaning for Aelfwyn. The days she had spent trapped inside these wooden jaws had blurred into one long nightmare. She and Leofric had long since stopped talking, each of them retreating into caves inside their minds, a place of refuge where the misery had not yet touched.

Soon the end would come. Aelfwyn tried not to dwell on what awaited them. An axe blade to the neck would be a clean death at least—provided the ealdorman sharpened the blade first.

Tears of despair stung Aelfwyn's closed eyelids. The past few months had taught her so much—but she had only just begun to live. Leofric had brought such joy into her life and soon Godwine of Eoforwic would take him from her before ending her own life.

Aelfwyn swallowed. Her throat was dry.

The warrior, Halwend, had visited them earlier. He had scooped ladles of water out of a pail and held it up for them to drink before feeding them both pottage and bread in turn. Aelfwyn had been surprised the warrior had taken this task on; surely this was a role for one of the women. She had been too hungry and thirsty to question him.

Leofric had also said little as he ate and drank, and Halwend was likewise taciturn. It was only when the warrior rose to leave, picking up the empty wooden platter and pail as he did so, that he spoke.

"I'll be back at dusk with some hot broth—you both need to keep up your strength."

Strength. Aelfwyn felt as weak as newborn lamb. Aethelhild's mysterious visit had made her believe that help was coming, but with the passing of time that fragile hope ebbed away.

The splash of heavy footfalls behind them now alerted Aelfwyn to someone's arrival. A moment later, as he had promised, Halwend appeared with an iron pot of steaming broth in one hand and a smoking pitch torch in the other.

He hunkered down in front of Leofric, meeting his eye. "Bearing up?"

Leofric snorted. "Aye—just enjoying the rain."

Halwend grinned. "At least you smell better for it."

He filled a ladle with broth and lifted it to Leofric's lips. "Drink up, lad."

Leofric did as bid, although his gaze remained upon the warrior. "Why all the concern," he asked finally. "You're fussing over me like a nursemaid."

Halwend's grin widened. "Your mother made me promise to look after you." He fed Leofric another two ladles of broth before shifting across to Aelfwyn. As she sipped at the rich rabbit gruel, Aelfwyn noticed that Halwend's gaze was shifting around the empty square. He was taking careful note of his surroundings. Her stomach twisted; the ealdorman had done well leaving Halwend in charge of them in his absence. The warrior missed nothing.

Aethelhild will never be able to free us with this man watching over us.

Halwend finished feeding her and rose to his feet. He stared down at them, his expression turning serious. "Ready yourselves," he said quietly. "The time is coming."

Without another word he left them, his heavy tread squelching across the mud back to the hall. Once Halwend was out of earshot, Leofric gave a low chuckle.

"I don't believe it—the old dog has turned on its master."

Renewed hope flickered in Aelfwyn's breast. "He'll help us?"

The gleam of Leofric's grin was white in the gathering dark. "It looks that way."

Aelfwyn tentatively tried to shift her weight. She had been kneeling in the mud for so long she felt welded to the earth. The pain in her limbs when she tried to move them nearly made her cry out. Hissing between her teeth, she persisted, stretching out one leg behind her and then the other.

Next to her she heard Leofric stifle a groan as he did the same. "Devil's turds," he muttered. "I'm a cripple."

Aelfwyn gritted her teeth and tried rotating her ankles, one at a time. The numbness was fading, only to be replaced with agonizing pins and needles. "I don't think I can walk," she gasped.

The pain was just beginning to fade when she heard the first signs of something happening on the perimeters of the square.

The rain was hammering down now. The storm hung directly overhead. Thunder boomed and then moments later lightning flashed, illuminating the night in eerie silver. Aelfwyn raised her head, blinking water out of her eyes, and caught a glimpse of two men wrestling against the high gate. A seax blade flashed, and one of the figures crumpled into the mud.

Lightning lit up the square once more, and she saw cloaked figures moving around the edge of the inner palisade. Then darkness blanketed the square once more, and through the hiss of rain she caught the dull thud of fists against flesh and the scrape of iron against wet leather.

"It's starting," Leofric said quietly. "Are you ready, min heorte?"

Min heorte—my heart. The endearment made Aelfwyn's throat constrict. Would she have the chance to touch him, to hold him once more? Hope hung by a thread, a fragile flame flickering in the darkness. One cold breath, and it would go out.

An instant later, she heard the splashes of running feet crossing the square behind them. Cloaked figures appeared either side of the stocks. Aelfwyn heard the grating of iron as the locks sheared off, and the creak of hinges when the top half of the stocks came away.

Aelfwyn almost wept with relief—she was free.

"Come." A woman's voice sounded in Aelfwyn's ear. "We need to move—now."

Aethelhild.

It took two of them to help Aelfwyn to her feet, and she cried out in pain when she tried to straighten her legs and bear weight upon them.

"You can manage it." A man spoke gruffly next to her. Aelfwyn recognized his voice—Bishop Wilfrid.

Next to her two warriors had lifted Leofric out of the stocks. He looped his arms over their shoulders, letting them support him as they headed across the square.

"We must follow." Aethelhild's voice was hard with urgency. "There's no time to waste."

Aelfwyn stumbled her way out of the market square, grateful that Aethelhild and Wilfrid were there to help her. A sheet of lightning illuminated the sky above them, and she caught a glimpse of her friend and the bishop. They were both wearing thick, hooded traveling cloaks.

They followed Leofric and the two warriors under the high gate and down the hill to where a group of cloaked figures on horseback stood waiting. A cluster of riderless horses, all saddled and ready to go, stood on the edge of the group.

The rain was coming down in great sheets, causing a roar as it gushed down the street in rivers, turning the dirt to a sea of mud. Although visibility was poor, the foul weather proved to be their ally this evening. The folk of Eoforwic huddled inside around their firepits, and the streets were deserted. There would be no one, save the guards at the low gate, to witness their escape.

"Mount up," a man commanded. Aelfwyn recognized Halwend's voice.

With Aethelhild and Wilfrid's help she scrambled up onto the back of a stocky bay pony with a large white star across its forehead. Next to her, Leofric managed to mount a large bay gelding unassisted—Aelfwyn's heart leaped when she realized it was Windræs.

Moments later, all the company—around twenty of them—were mounted. Halwend led the way down the hill to the low gate. He rode a massive dun stallion, and was the only one of the company who had not pulled up his hood. The drumming rain plastered his hair to his scalp; his strong-featured face was set in harsh, determined lines.

Aelfwyn followed the others down to the gate. Her mind was a jumble—how had Aethelhild managed to organize this? Halwend was the ealdorman's most trusted warrior. Who were these other men who joined them?

At the low gate, Halwend and four others swung down from their horses and drew their swords. They met the cluster of spearmen who formed a line against the heavy oak and iron gate that barred the way out of town. The grunt of men fighting, followed by the clang of iron against iron and the meaty thud of blades slicing through flesh, rose above the hiss of the rain.

Surely someone will hear us.

Aelfwyn cast a glimpse over her shoulder at the street beyond, half-expecting to see a horde of enraged warriors thundering toward them. Yet the road was deserted.

Halwend cut down the last hapless spearman to face him before ordering some of his companions to drag the bodies out of the way. Then he and another of his companions unbarred the gate.

They rode out of Eoforwic into a squall of driving rain.

Blinded, Aelfwyn guided her pony across the bridge, over the turbid River Ouse. Many of the riders carried smoking pitch torches aloft, the only means they had of lighting the way. However, the rain was doing its best to extinguish them.

Grasping the slippery reins for dear life, her thighs aching already from gripping on, Aelfwyn found herself in the middle of the company.

Fear she might fall off and be trampled underfoot gave way to the thrill of freedom. Her heart pounded in time with the pony's hoof beats. Aelfwyn leaned forward and gave herself up to the moment. The company thundered on, sweeping her away into the night.

Chapter Forty

Outlaws

THEY STOPPED FOR a short while just after dawn, under a stand of spreading oaks, and broke their fast with bread and cheese. A wet, grey dawn spread over a landscape of crumpled hills with clumps of woodland nestled in-between.

The rain had not ceased all that night—but the company paid it little heed as they continued their flight south. They had to make the most of their advantage, for Ecgfrith and Godwine were due back later in the day. Halwend pointed out that owing to the bad weather they were likely to return earlier from the hunt.

Standing under the trees, with fat droplets of water dripping on her head, Aelfwyn was able to take proper note of her traveling companions for the first time since leaving Eoforwic. Aethelhild stood next to Bishop Wilfrid—the two of them looked as bedraggled as Aelfwyn felt.

"Where are we headed?" Aelfwyn asked Aethelhild.

Her friend looked up and their gazes met. "Ely," she replied. "My cousin runs an abbey there."

Aelfwyn found herself smiling—Aethelhild was taking them home, back to the Kingdom of the East Angles. Ely—the Isle of Eels—was an isolated town in the middle of the fens, surrounded by perilous marshes. It was as good a place as any for Aethelhild to make a new life for herself.

A few yards away, Halwend offered a piece of bread to the cloaked figure next to him. A slender, pale hand took the bread before another pushed back the deep cowl concealing the individual's face.

Next to her, Aelfwyn heard Leofric's sharp intake of breath. "Mōder!"

Just four strides took him across the clearing to where Cynhild stood. The woman wept as she threw herself into her son's arms. Beside them Halwend remained silent, a gentle smile softening the severe lines of his face. Aelfwyn watched mother and son reunited, letting them have a few moments alone before she hesitantly approached.

Eyes gleaming, Leofric stepped back from Cynhild and cupped her face with his hands. "I can't believe you were behind this."

Cynhild laughed softly. "I only had a part in freeing you." She glanced across at Halwend, her eyes shining. "Halwend and Aethelhild did the rest."

Leofric shook his head. "How did you get past Berhtulf and Wybert?"

Halwend grinned. "Aethelhild laced their supper with ground Bruisewort root—they were puking and shitting their guts out in the privy when we left the hall."

A few yards away Aethelhild was smiling faintly, clearly pleased with herself.

"With Berhtulf and Wybert out of the way, we just had the guards in the square, and at the high and low gates to deal with," Halwend concluded.

Leofric stepped back from them, putting an arm around Aelfwyn's shoulders. She wrinkled her nose; he smelled as ripe as she most likely did—both of them needed to bathe and change their clothing. Leofric did not notice her smell for his gaze was still riveted upon his mother.

"So you've left him?" he asked finally.

Cynhild nodded, her face growing serious. "Are you angry?"

Leofric shook his head. "He disowned me and then went hunting with the man who condemned me to death. Fæder deserves to lose you—you've always been too good for him."

His gaze flicked from his mother to Halwend. Aelfwyn sensed the closeness between Cynhild and the warrior, the way Leofric's mother's face shone when she looked at Halwend—Leofric had clearly not missed this either.

Seeing the confusion on her son's face, Cynhild gave a soft smile, tinged with melancholy.

"My father promised me to Wibert when I was barely twelve winters old—he was the son of a renowned warrior and a good match. But by the time I wedded your father, just before my sixteenth winter, I'd already given my heart to Halwend." Cynhild paused here, her gaze clouding with sadness, before she continued. "Wibert never knew that I loved another, and I doubt he would have cared anyway." She glanced over at Halwend who was watching her intently. "Halwend came to me on the eve before my handfasting and begged me to run away with him—but I was shackled to my father's will and could not bear the thought of defying him. Not a day has gone by since that I do not regret that."

Halwend reached out and took her hand, gently enfolding it with his. "I waited for you," he murmured. "I told you I would."

Cynhild smiled back. "All my children are grown, there was no longer any reason for me to stay with Wibert—a man who has ever treated me like his theow. It was time to go."

Watching them Leofric had gone still. "I had no idea either of you felt this way," he said softly.

Cynhild stepped forward, reached up, and stroked her son's face. "You weren't meant to."

Two days out from Eoforwic, they heard the first signs of pursuit. The company rode on higher ground, toward the crest of a windswept hill, when the far off baying of hounds reached them.

Aelfwyn's heart sank at this sound—it brought back memories of her flight from Bebbanburg with Leofric. The king's men had been so close to catching them that day, if the river had not carried them away.

She glanced over at where Leofric rode beside her, their gazes meeting.

At the front of the column, Halwend reined in his stallion and turned back to face the way they had come. His keen gaze surveyed the folds of hills to the north before his expression turned grim.

"Godwine's sent many after us," the warrior told them. "One hundred warriors at least."

Leofric gave a low, humorless laugh. "It won't just be the ealdorman out for our blood—my father and the king will have sent men to hunt us down."

Aethelhild spoke up then. "My husband loathes me, but that doesn't mean he'll let me go easily. His pride will be wounded."

"And mine will happily throttle me with his bare hands if he ever finds me," Cynhild added.

Halwend glanced over at Cynhild, his face darkening. "He'll have to kill me first."

Aelfwyn looked to the north. The rain had ceased for a spell, although the sky was still heavy with moisture and there were dark clouds to the east, threatening more bad weather. She easily spotted the army Halwend had seen—such a large group of men was hard to miss. They were still some way back; a bristling carpet of bobbing heads and spears, the yaps and howls of their hounds still faint. However, they were traveling fast.

She turned back to Halwend. "Can we outrun them?"

"For the time being," he replied.

"We'd better hope so." Leofric spoke up. "Twenty against one hundred will not end in our favor."

They rode through the day with no further breaks, traveling at a swift canter southeast. They crossed the River Trente at a village called Winthorpe—a pretty hamlet sitting amongst a patchwork of well-tended fields. The old wooden bridge creaked in protest as they rode across it in pairs. The Trente surged beneath, swollen from the heavy rains.

By the time dusk fell the weather had closed in again. They camped near a tributary of the Trente, making sure to pitch their tents upon higher ground. The warriors saw to the horses and lit fires inside the hide tents. Soon the aroma of roasting rabbit drifted into the air. Despite the pursuers on their tail, Halwend had deemed it safe enough to lights fires tonight. A thick, porridge-like mist had closed in, making it near to impossible for the king's men to find them in the darkness.

The rain pounded down from leaden skies as Aelfwyn and Leofric made their way down to the river's edge to bathe.

They had chosen a bend in the river, far from the swiftly moving current, where it looked safe to enter the water without being swept away. The glow from their camp's fires receded behind them although Leofric carried a pitch torch to light their way. He staked the torch into the soft ground, under the sheltering boughs of an old willow, to prevent the torch from going out. The draping willow branches surrounded them like a living bower while, just beyond, rain stippled the dark surface of the river.

Aelfwyn shucked off her filthy clothes. It felt odd to undress under the rain, but she liked the feel of it on her skin.

Leofric yanked off his tunic and screwed his face up. "I stink like a sty."

Aelfwyn gave him an arch look. "I didn't like to say ..."

He raised an eyebrow in response. "You don't exactly smell like roses either, sweeting."

Aelfwyn stuck out her tongue at him and stepped naked into the cold, swirling water. She felt Leofric's gaze upon her, branding her skin, but she pretended not to notice. As much as she wanted to touch him, her need to bathe dominated all else.

Using a rough cake of lye that Aethelhild and given her, she began to soap her filthy dirt-encrusted skin. She heard a splash a few feet away. Leofric had joined her in their willow-framed bathtub. She caught his sigh of pleasure before he dove under the water. He resurfaced next to her. His gaze slid up her glistening body, taking in her bobbing, pink-tipped breasts, before it rested on her face. His own face was serious; his eyes had deepened to forest-green.

"I've missed you," he murmured, reaching for her. "More than you can imagine."

Aelfwyn sighed, her belly fluttering at his touch, before she reached out and began soaping his chest. "I thought we were both doomed."

"We might still be."

She glanced up, frowning. "Don't say that."

His gaze snared hers. "We need to be honest, Aelfwyn. An army now hunts us."

"We'll outrun them, we'll lose them—just like we did last summer."

His mouth quirked. "I hope you're right."

She continued soaping his chest before moving down to the firm lines of his belly. Then when she reached under the water, she found his shaft hard in her hands. Aelfwyn gasped, need arrowing through her and igniting a fire deep within her core. She started to tremble.

Leofric gently took the cake of lye from her and tossed it onto the mossy riverbank. He then turned to her, smiling wickedly. "We can finish bathing later."

Aelfwyn opened her mouth to protest, but he yanked her hard against him, his lips slanting across hers. The instant his mouth claimed her own she was lost. A groan rose from deep within her, and she parted her lips to allow his questing tongue entrance. His body, strong and hard, entwined with hers, their slick skin sliding as they twisted together.

Leofric sank to his knees in the water, dipping his head to her breasts. Aelfwyn tangled her fingers in his wet hair, reveling in how thick and soft it was now, before the heat of his mouth on her engorged nipple drove all thought from her mind. She clutched him against her, moaning softly as he suckled each breast in turn.

She was panting when he rose once more to his feet. He pulled her against him again, his hands sliding down the length of her back and cupping her bottom. Then in one smooth movement he lifted her high against him and settled his shaft at the entrance to her womb.

Aelfwyn linked her arms around his neck and looked at him, holding his gaze in hers before she sank down upon him.

Leofric threw back his head and groaned. "Aelfwyn."

She answered his groan with one of her own, clasped her thighs around his hips, and drew him even deeper inside her.

Her gaze caught his. "You are mine," she told him fiercely, "and I'll never give you up—not ever."

She kissed him then, wildly, and let her fire consume them both.

Chapter Forty-one
The Rising of the Tide

THE SHOUTS OF the army tracking them—the cry of their dogs—grew louder, echoing across the marshy fenland they now crossed. Great sheets of rain, bringing with it the scent of the sea, slashed in from the east; a reminder that they traveled close to the entrance of The Wash, the square-mouthed estuary to the northeast.

Over the next few days they traveled southeast, inching ever closer to their destination. Yet with every furlong they journeyed, Ecgfrith and Godwine's men drew nearer.

It was heavy going across the fens. The ground was boggy and treacherous in places, and the narrow road—a trackway built by the Romans—was crumbling and badly potholed.

They rode two abreast upon the causeway, forced to slow to a brisk trot on the uneven ground. All the while, the fens grew wetter as the heavy rains started to flood the marshes.

Leofric looked out across the seemingly endless fens, and at the curtains of rain that continued to fall, and felt a pang of misgiving. The sight of the rising water was unnerving.

Perhaps it had been a mistake to head for Ely. The fenland was usually safe to travel during the warmer months, but this spring rain was unusually heavy. They risked being cut off from their destination by the rising water.

As he rode, Leofric's thoughts turned to the events of the past few days. He was still trying to come to terms with all that had happened. However, the hardest thing to swallow was that Cynn—a man he had considered a good friend—had turned him in to Godwine. A pouch of gold coins—that was all their friendship had meant to Cynn in the end. He remembered the last time they had spoken in the meadhall. Cynn had been in a strange mood, off-hand. Leofric's stomach tightened when he realized Cynn must have betrayed him shortly afterward. He would have liked to return to Lincylene, to confront Cynn, but vengeance was not worth the trouble it would bring down upon him and Aelfwyn.

Leofric glanced across at where Aelfwyn rode next to him. Despite the rain, she had pushed her hood back. Her hair, the color of sea-foam, was plastered against her skull. Her eyes were bright and clear, her beautiful face set in determination.

God, how he loved her.

He might have saved her from Ecgfrith all those months ago, but she had saved him from a shallow, pointless life. She had shown him what it was to truly care for another—the power of courage and strength. To think he had thought her fragile when they had first met.

He had never been so wrong.

Her courage had spurred Aethelhild to come to her aid—Aelfwyn had saved them all.

Leofric and Aelfwyn's time alone together since leaving Eoforwic had been stolen. Since making love in the river, they had not had gotten the chance to lie together again. He treasured the memory of that coupling, the wild passion and hunger she had unleashed upon him. No luckier man had ever lived.

"What are you thinking about?"

Leofric came out of his reverie to find Aelfwyn watching him. He flashed her a grin, trying to ignore the caterwauling of the wolfhounds on the horizon behind them. The beasts were out for blood. "Wicked thoughts."

Her eyes twinkled at that, and she laughed. "You will have to share them with me later."

He held her gaze, his grin fading. "I intend to."

The company took a short break around noon, upon a hillock of reeds that afforded them a clear view of the surrounding fens.

"The water is rising fast." Halwend confirmed Leofric's own fears as he passed him a piece of stale bread. "Much faster than I've ever seen."

"It's the spring tide." Aethelhild stepped up next to them with Bishop Wilfrid at her side. Exhaustion lined her face, but her blue eyes were as sharp as ever. Next to her the bishop was pale with fatigue.

"It flows in from The Wash at this time of year and can affect the fens," Aethelhild told them. "But with this heavy rain ..." Her voice trailed away as she considered the consequences of the torrential deluge that had followed them from Eoforwic.

Halwend's expression grew stern upon listening to Aethelhild, and his gaze shifted to where they hunters bristled against the northwestern horizon. "Hounds of hell," he muttered, "they're going to catch us."

"How far till Ely?" Leofric asked Aethelhild.

"I've never traveled to the isle from this direction," she admitted, her smooth brow furrowing, but I'd say we should reach it by the day's end."

Leofric nodded, glancing back at Halwend. The warrior was sucking his teeth, his gaze fixed upon their pursuers. "That's too long," Halwend said. "We'll never make it."

The company set off once more, riding as fast as they dared along the boggy causeway. Windræs made easy work of the journey, demonstrating once again his enormous endurance and strength. However, Aelfwyn's sturdy pony was starting to flag. The mare carried her head low, her ears flattened back as she tried her best to keep up with Windræs's long stride.

They had traveled a short distance from the hillock when Leofric heard one of the men behind him shout out. "They're closing in!"

He twisted in the saddle and peered behind them. Sure enough, Ecgfrith and Godwine's army were little more than four furlongs behind now. The hounds raced out front; their cries chilled Leofric's blood.

"Ride!" he shouted. "Ride—now!"

Halwend and the others answered his call, leaning forward in the saddle and urging their horses forward into a wild gallop along the causeway. It was dangerous to travel so fast on such uneven footing, but the alternative was capture.

The thunder of hooves echoed across the marshes.

Aelfwyn's pony was wheezing, its mouth foaming as it galloped. The poor creature would not last much longer at this rate.

"God save us!" Aethelhild's terrified voice cut through the din. "Look to the north!"

Leofric twisted his head left, as bid, his heart leaping in his chest when he saw what had caused Aethelhild's panic.

The last time he had looked in that direction, toward The Wash, there had been nothing but an expanse of water and reeds blending into rolling mist. Now a hill of water rose from the flooded fens, like a creature of the deep—and it was rushing straight toward them.

Leofric considered himself brave. He had fought and killed and had faced his own death with courage. Yet the sight of that glistening wall of water rushing across the marshes, filled him with such terror that he almost forgot himself.

The world was ending—a great flood that would drown them all.

There was no time to do anything but ride. Sensing the terror that swept through the column of riders, the horses raced as if Nithhogg—the beast of the underworld—was on their tails; even Aelfwyn's pony found one last reserve of strength.

Before them the land rose. Leofric spied rushes waving in the wind and hope rose within him.

They needed to get to higher ground if they had any chance of survival.

The company thundered up the road, the first riders reaching the top of the hill. Leofric twisted his head left once more as he rode, and wished he had not. He and Aelfwyn galloped toward the end of the column, and the glistening wave was barely half a furlong distant.

Beside him Aelfwyn bent low over her pony's neck. Her face was chalk-white and terrified, but she wisely kept her gaze upon her destination—the grassy knoll before them.

They galloped up the incline, just as the water surged in.

Leofric heard the screams of horses and realized that some of the riders behind them had not made it. There were still number of them riding behind Leofric and Aelfwyn, but there was nothing anyone could do to save them.

Leofric and Aelfwyn reached the crest of the hill, where the others had stopped. Then Leofric reined Windræs around.

Only the two men riding directly behind him and Aelfwyn were safe, the rest disappeared under the swirling water—shrieking, kicking, and flailing as the tide swept them under.

Their pursuers were less than a furlong behind them. Leofric's gaze moved to the army of at least one hundred men who had been so close to catching their quarry. He watched the rising tide take them—swallow them whole.

Men, horses, and dogs all went under. The tide swept across the causeway and plucked them off the road like children's toys. Their screams of terror rent the air, and Leofric resisted the urge to cover his ears. He stared at the devastation, hardly daring to believe his eyes.

Cuthbert had spoken of the end of the world, a great flood that would drown them all. Had the prior been right?

Next to him Aelfwyn sat rigid in the saddle, her face stricken. He brought Windræs in close to her and, reaching out, placed a hand on her thigh squeezing gently. He had no words of consolation; no explanations that would make sense of what had just happened. He was struggling to accept it himself.

Glancing around him, he saw they now stood upon a tiny island. An angry sea of briny water bubbled and surged around them. The hill was barely high enough to save them—just a few more yards and the tide would have claimed them too. The rain continued to fall, peppering their skin and lashing across their faces; but Leofric barely noticed.

"Christ on the cross," Halwend blasphemed. "What caused that?"

Next to him Aethelhild shook her head and gazed up at the thick cloud cover above, as if seeking the answers. "I have no idea," she said quietly.

Beside her, Bishop Wilfrid crossed himself.

"There are some spring tides when the moon rides larger than usual in the night sky." One of the warriors nearby spoke up. He was a stocky, red-haired young man with a florid face. "My grandmother told me of them. If you get such a moon, a spring tide, and torrential rains—a great flood will follow."

Halwend let out a muttered string of curses and looked around him. His stallion danced nervously, and he leaned forward, stroking its neck to calm it. "We're trapped here."

"For the moment," the red-haired warrior replied. "But the tide will recede soon enough."

Leofric's shoulders sagged at this news. They had lost six of their group, and watched an entire army swept to their deaths—but they were alive. Their pursuers were gone, and they would soon be able to continue to Ely.

He turned to Aelfwyn, his gaze meeting hers. She managed a tremulous smile. Leofric took her hand, it was ice-cold, but her grip was firm.

"Is it over?" she whispered.

Leofric smiled back, hardly daring to hope, not after being hunted for so long. "Aye," he replied gently. "It is."

Epilogue

Different Paths

Six days later ...

THE ISLE OF Ely sat in the midst of the fens. A town perched upon it, the high roof of its abbey rising over a flat, featureless landscape. High wooden ramparts encircled the settlement, with watchtowers at each corner. Ely's isolation had been both a blessing and a curse over the years—and its inhabitants had learned to protect it well.

Inside the town, in the wide yard before the gates, four travelers prepared to depart. A crowd of well-wishers gathered to see them off.

Aelfwyn glanced up at the sky and smiled. It was a still, sunlit morning. The smoke from the thatched roofs of Ely rose vertically into a bright blue sky. The marshes were alive with the sound of chattering insects.

It was a good day to set off on a journey.

"Are you sure you will not stay longer?" Aethelhild interrupted Aelfwyn's reverie. She stood a few yards away, regal despite the plain homespun robes that now clad her and the veil that covered her glossy raven hair. Next to Aethelhild stood Bishop Wilfrid and her cousin, Aethelthryth of Ely. A smaller, feistier version of Aethelhild—and a few years older—Abbess Aethelthryth had welcomed them into her home with open-arms. Aelfwyn would be forever grateful.

She smiled at Aethelhild and went to her, enfolding the older woman in a hug. "We should go," she told her, "before the king rallies more men to come after us."

"I don't think he will," Aethelhild replied. "It will take him a long while to recover from his losses on the marshes ... nonetheless I understand your urge to leave. You have your own path to follow." Aethelhild broke off here, her gaze shifting to where Leofric, Halwend, and Cynhild stood quietly behind Aelfwyn. "You all do."

Aelfwyn pulled away from Aethelhild blinking back tears. "I'll never forget you, or what you did for us."

Aethelhild laughed. "I'm not completely unselfish, Aelfwyn—you know I also did it for myself."

Aelfwyn smiled. "I'm glad you did." It was true. Although the life Aethelhild had chosen—one dedicated to God—was not one she wanted for herself, she understood that it was the right choice for her friend. Aethelhild looked radiant this morning, her eyes glowing in the morning sun.

She had found peace, and Aelfwyn was glad for it.

The four travelers rode out of Ely into the glittering marshes, two abreast upon the causeway. Nearby, wading birds dug for food, and a cloud of midges hovered over the reed-beds. Aelfwyn and Leofric rode out front with Halwend and Cynhild bringing up the rear. It was such a still, silent morning that the clip-clop of their horses' hooves seemed to echo across the marshes.

Aelfwyn was relieved the weather had cleared. The past few days had been sunny and warm with the promise of the coming summer. After that journey from Eoforwic, she never wanted to see rain again. Even now the memory of that terrible surge of water, the screams of the men it swept away, haunted her in still moments. It would take a long time for the images to fade.

Around ten furlongs south of Ely, the travelers reached a crossroads. Here, the causeway led in four directions: north back to the isle, south toward the lands of the East Saxons, east toward Rendlaesham, or west toward the border of Mercia.

Aelfwyn and Leofric reined in their mounts and waited for Halwend and Cynhild to catch up with them. Leofric patted Windræs's sleek neck and glanced across at Aelfwyn and her mount, before he gave a teasing grin.

"You had a stable full of horses to choose from—why did you choose this one?"

Aelfwyn reached forward and pretended to cup her pony's furry ears. "Don't listen to him, Morgensteorra." She had named her plucky mare Morningstar, for the large white star on its forehead. "He doesn't mean to sound ungrateful." She then gave Leofric a stern look. "This pony kept me safe on the journey here—I'm not leaving her behind."

A smile spread across Leofric's face. "Your soft heart is just one of the many reasons I love you."

Aelfwyn smiled back, warmth spreading through her body at his words. She would never tire of hearing him say that.

"Ready to go our separate ways?" Halwend reined up next to them. His dun stallion tossed its head, clearly impatient to be off. Beside him, Cynhild rode an elegant grey mare.

Aelfwyn nodded, although she saw the hesitation on Leofric's face. She knew he had not been looking forward to bidding his mother goodbye. Aelfwyn and Leofric were heading into East Saxon territory, whereas Halwend and Cynhild were traveling west, hoping to start a new life in Mercia.

"Are you sure you wouldn't rather travel south with us?" Leofric asked.

Cynhild favored her son with a soft smile before she rode up next to him. Reaching out, she stroked Leofric's cheek.

He caught her hand and squeezed it, his eyes glistening. "I'm glad you've finally found happiness, mōder," he said huskily. "It just that goodbye sounds so final."

"Don't say it then," Cynhild replied, her own gaze misted with tears. "Live well son, that's all I ask of you."

Leofric nodded before he glanced over at Halwend. He grinned at the older man. "You look after her, or I'll hunt you down like a dog."

"Insolent pup," Halwend growled, feigning annoyance.

Cynhild drew back from Leofric, her gaze meeting Aelfwyn's. "My son was blessed the day he met you—I wish you both all the happiness in the world."

Aelfwyn smiled. "And I you."

Cynhild glanced over at Halwend, her expression turning mischievous. The years had slid away from her since leaving Eoforwic. This morning she looked young and carefree, her long red hair tumbling down her back in soft waves.

"The abbess gifted me the fastest horse in her stables," she said with a grin. "Are you sure you can keep up?"

Not giving Halwend a chance to respond, she wheeled her horse around and took off west along the causeway. A look of surprise flitted across the warrior's face before he dug his heels into his stallion's flanks and thundered off after her.

Aelfwyn and Leofric watched them go. Windræs and Morgensteorra now sidestepped and tossed their heads, eager to be off as well. The couple watched Cynhild and Halwend until they were specks on the western horizon before Aelfwyn turned her gaze back to Leofric.

"You're not going to challenge me to a race, are you?" Leofric teased.

Aelfwyn reined her pony around, and fell in next to Windræs as they took the southern road. "Not likely." She glanced back at him and raised an eyebrow. "You haven't even told me what our destination is yet."

Leofric winked at her. "That's because I don't have one."

"Hwæt?"

"I'm serious," he replied, grinning widely. "I grew up in the north—I know little of the rest of Britannia."

"So what should we do?"

"Travel until we find our new home. I'm still keen to visit the Kingdom of the Kentish." Leofric's grin faded, and he reached across, sliding his hand down Aelfwyn's arm to cover her hand. "Our destination is unimportant—we'll know the place for us when we reach it. What matters is that we're together. I'm yours, and you are mine."

Aelfwyn squeezed his hand back. He was right. Now they were free to choose their own path together, anything was possible.

"Your mother said you were blessed the day you met me," she murmured, holding his gaze fast in hers, "but I too am blessed. You put me back together again and made life worth living. You're my savior, Leo."

He smiled at her, his gaze shining. "And you are my salvation."

The End

Author's Note

Welcome to the first novel in my 'Northumbria' series. The Kingdom of Northumbria rose to dominance during the latter part of the 7th Century. My series follows the reign of two kings: Ecgfrith and Aldfrith (Flann Fína)—both the sons of King Oswiu, the king who brought Northumbria to its greatest height during this century.

We already meet King Oswiu of Northumbria in my Kingdom of Mercia series—he famously defeats King Penda at the Battle of Winwaed—but this series focuses on his legacy.

THE WHISPERING WIND features many actual historical figures: Ecgfrith, Bishop Wilfrid, Prior Cuthbert, Abbess Hilda and Sister Elflaeda. It also gives you a peek at the hero and heroine of the second book in the series: Bridei and Hea (they both appear briefly in the first few chapters of the book). However this novel's hero and heroine are entirely fictional—Leofric and Aelfwyn might well have existed but history only recorded highborn or religious folk back in those days.

I enjoyed incorporating a few famous religious figures of the day into the tale. The isle of Lindisfarena (Lindisfarne) and Streonshalh (Whitby) Abbey were fascinating to research and bring to life. Both Prior Cuthbert and Abbess Hilda have much legend and folklore attached to them. However, I wanted to depict them both as real people—plus to make an effort to recreate the settings as accurately as possible. Anglo-Saxon monasteries were nothing like the medieval ones we associate with the past—life was not quite as structured in those times; men and women often shared monasteries and the buildings were made largely out of wood, rather than stone.

Of course in the interests of telling a good story, an author sometimes has to blur historical fact a little. Ecgfrith did marry a woman who refused to consummate their marriage—however her name was Aethelthryth. Unfortunately, I could not use this character as the real Aethelthryth had actually appeared in my previous novel, DAWN OF WOLVES. I realized that to use her in this story would make her too old! Instead (in my version) her cousin, Aethelhild, travels north to wed King Ecgfrith.

The 'rising of the tide' incident toward the end of the book is actually based on a legend surrounding Aethelthryth (or in this case, Aethelhild). She did run away from her husband to become a nun. Pursued by her husband's men after fleeing south with Bishop Wilfrid, the queen is said to have caused a miraculous 'rising of the tide', which prevented his men from capturing her. No one knows if this really happened—but I have put my own twist on the event in this novel.

Historical background for *The Whispering Wind*

In the seventh century, England was not as we know it today. The Anglo-Saxon period lasted from the departure of the Romans, from around 430 AD, to the Norman invasion, in 1066 AD. My novels focus on the period in between the departure of the Romans, and the first Viking invasion in 793 AD—a 300-year period in which Anglo-Saxon culture flourished. The British Isles were named Britannia (a legacy of the Roman colonization) and split into rival kingdoms. For the purposes of this novel, we focus on three of them: Northumbria, Mercia and East Anglia. The small kingdom of Lindesege also features in this novel.

Many locations in Northumbria and northern Britannia appear in this novel, although their names are somewhat different to modern-day England. Bebbanburg was the old name for Bamburgh, the seat of Northumbrian Kings for many centuries. At the time of our story, the castle would not have been built, however, there would have been a wooden fort at the top of the rocky outcrop, and, possibly, a Great Tower made of local stone. The nearby island of Lindisfarena is none other than Lindisfarne, also known today as Holy Island. Farther south, Eoforwic (also spelled Eoferwic) is the Anglo-Saxon name for the town renamed Jorvik after settlement by the Danes—today, we know it as York. Our characters make a stop at Streonshalh (Whitby) Abbey and spend the winter in Lincylene—today known as Lincoln. Lincylene was the capital of the Kingdom of Lindesege.

Glossary of Old English (in alphabetical order)

béagas: arm rings
Cyningtaefl: "King's Table", an Anglo-Saxon form of chess
ealdorman: earl
Ēōstre: Easter
fæder: father
handfasted: married
heah-setl: high seat (later called a "dais") for the king and queen
hōre: whore
Hwæt?: What?
Humbre: Humber River
Lindisfarena: Lindisfarne Island (Holy Island)
mōder: mother
Nithhogg: a fire-breathing dragon that lived in the underworld
nón-mete: midday meal (literally "noon-meat")
Streonshalh: Whitby
thegn: a king's retainer

theow: slave
thrymsas: Anglo-Saxon gold shillings
Tinanmuðe (pronounced: tienanmootha): The River Tyne (Newcastle)
"Wes hāl": "Greetings" in Old English
Winterfylleth: Anglo-Saxon Halloween
wyrd: fate

Cast of characters (in alphabetical order)

Aelfwyn: handmaid to Lady Aethelhild—the youngest daughter of a thegn in Rendlaesham
Aethelhild: betrothed and then queen to King Ecgfrith of Northrumbria (daughter of Ealdwulf, King of the East Angles)
Aethelthryth: Aethelhild's cousin—Abbess of Ely
Berhtulf and **Wybert**: Godwine of Eoforwic's sons
Bridei: a Pictish prince fostering at the Northumbrian court
Cuthbert: Prior of the Lindisfarena (Lindisfarne) monastery
Cynhild: Leofric's mother
Cynn: meadhall owner in Lincylene
Deorwine: Leofric's friend on Lindisfarena and fellow monk
Eanflaed: Ecgfrith's mother
Eatta: King of Lindesege
Ecgfrith: King of Northumbria
Eflaeda: Ecgfrith's sister (now a nun at Streonshalh Abbey)
Godwine: Ealdorman of Eoforwic
Gytha: Cynn of Lincylene's wife (they have four daughters: Ealhgyth, Hilla, Sifleda, and Merwyn)
Halwend: Godwine of Eoforwic's most trusted warrior
Hea: daughter of the flower-seller in Bebbanburg
Hilda: Abbess of Streonshalh Abbey
Hrothwyn: Godwine of Eoforwic's daughter
Leofric: the youngest son of a wealthy thegn—comes from Driffield just outside Eoforwic
Oswiu: Ecgfrith's father (deceased)
Thunred: a young warrior from Eoforwic
Waric: one of the King of Lindesege's men
Wibert: Leofric's father
Wilfrid: Bishop at Bebbanburg, Lady Aethelhild's advisor
Windræs: Thunred's horse—name means 'Storm of Wind'

Wind Song

Book One
The Kingdom
of Northumbria

Jayne Castel

Maps

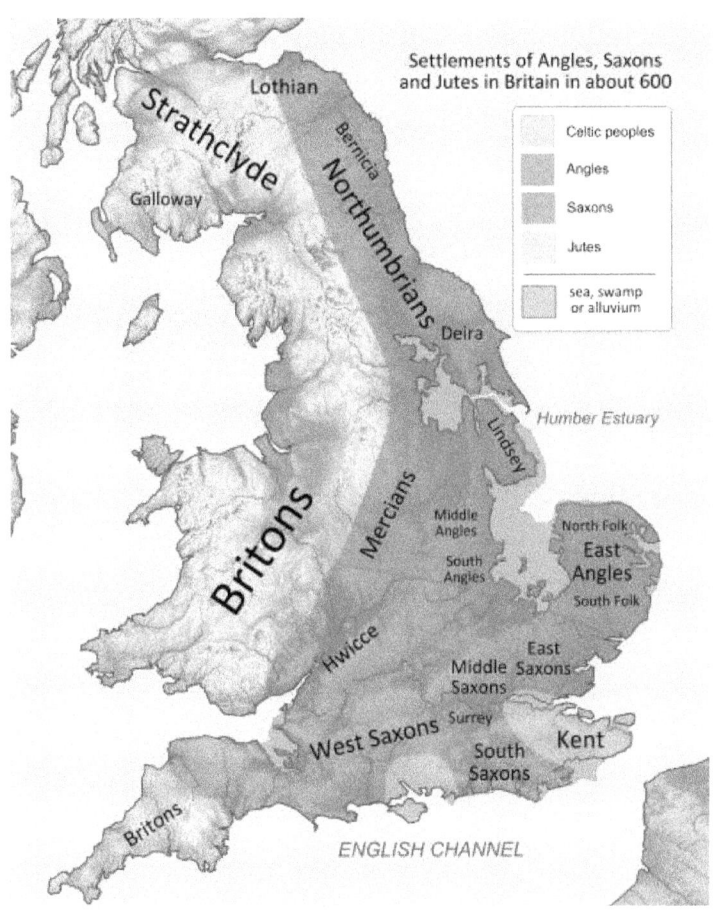

Settlements of Angles, Saxons
and Jutes in Britain in about 600

Celtic peoples

Angles

Saxons

Jutes

sea, swamp
or alluvium

Lothian

Strathclyde

Bernicia

Galloway

Northumbrians

Deira

Humber Estuary

Lindsey

Britons

Mercians

Middle
Angles

North Folk

East
Angles

South
Angles

South Folk

Hwicce

East
Middle Saxons

Saxons

West Saxons

Surrey

South
Saxons

Kent

Britons

ENGLISH CHANNEL

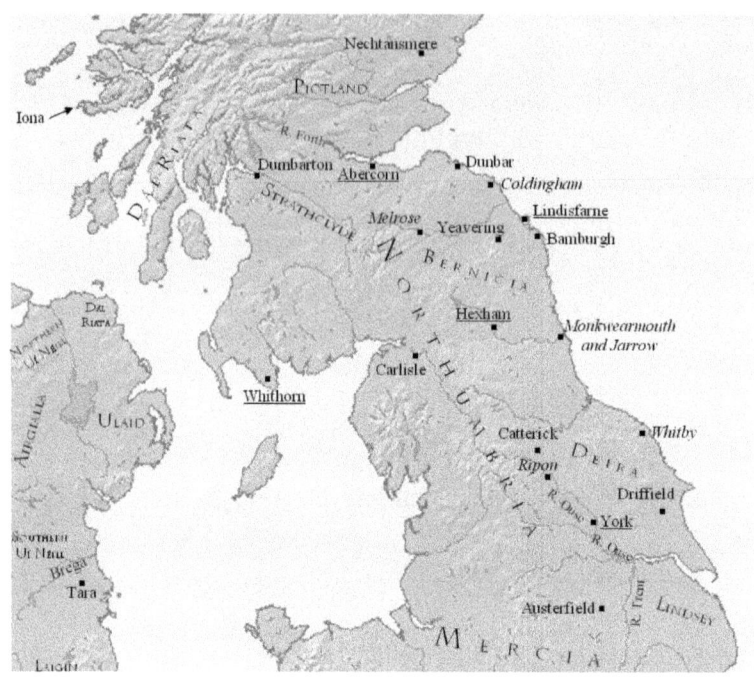

"I have you fast in my fortress,
And will not let you depart,
But put you down into the dungeon,
In the round-tower of my heart,
And there will I keep you forever,
Yes, forever and a day,
Till the walls shall crumble to ruin,
And moulder in the dust away!"
— Henry Wadsworth Longfellow

Chapter One

Hea's Hero

Spring, 676 AD

"PICT TURD—TASTE my blade!"

The wooden sword whistled through the air toward Bridei's face. Rinan, the lad who wielded it, was nearly twice Bridei's size and swung that blade with the full force of his resentment behind it.

Bridei dodged the blow and cut his own practice sword sideways, catching Rinan on the flank. The bigger lad, with straw-colored hair and a scowling face, stumbled. Grinning viciously, Bridei leaped forward and slammed the flat of his blade across the back of Rinan's shoulders, sending him sprawling.

"No, taste mine."

Rinan's curses rang out across the practice yard. He fell to his knees and then scrambled for his sword. The other young warriors, who had gathered to watch the sparring, fell silent. Previously, they had been hooting, and heckling the pair. Rinan's face had turned bright red.

A few feet away, Bridei's friend Heolstor—his only friend among the group—laughed. "You showed him, Bridei."

"Yes, he did." A deep voice boomed across the yard. A tall, broad figure shoved his way through the milling crowd and strode across to where Rinan had just picked himself up off the ground.

Aart, a warrior of around thirty winters with a short beard and wavy brown hair that curled around his shoulders, stopped before Rinan and Bridei. His blue eyes narrowed before he focused his attention upon Rinan. "You overreached, boy. You made it easy for him."

Bridei tensed. Aart had a way of making you feel small, even if you won at swordplay. However, the warrior was not finished. "You can't stand him," he rumbled, "and you let your feelings override a warrior's instinct. That makes you easy to kill."

Rinan nodded, his gaze falling to his feet. His face glowed like an ember.

"He's an upstart Pictling," Aart continued, his tone mild, "and you don't want him here ... I understand that. But if you let your feelings get in the way, he'll beat you every time."

Aart swung around and punched Bridei hard in the stomach.

There was no warning—one moment the warrior had been speaking to Rinan—the next he struck like Thunor's hammer. The blow knocked the wind clean out of Bridei. Gasping, he fell to his knees and clutched his belly.

"You keep your emotions on the inside," Aart concluded, his voice still chillingly calm, "and you channel them. Your enemy should never see you coming."

Bridei sucked in a painful breath. Eyes tearing with pain, he glanced up to see Rinan watching him, unable to hide the smirk on his face. Fury washed over Bridei in a hot tide, and he dropped his gaze to the dirt, listening to the muffled laughter of the other lads as they walked off.

When at last he could breathe, Bridei looked up to find all the others gone—including Rinan and Aart. Only Heolstor remained. The tall, broad-shouldered lad with carrot-red hair gave him a lopsided smile and spread his hands in a helpless gesture. "That was low. Aart is a shit."

"Aye," Bridei wheezed, climbing to his feet, "but I should have realized he'd do that—he's been wanting to put me in my place for months."

Heolstor gave him a sympathetic look. "You've been here a decade. You grew up with us all. How long before they accept you?"

Bridei brushed the dirt off his hands. "Never. Every time they look at me they see a northern savage. They'll never view me any different."

Heolstor frowned and cast a sour look in the direction that Aart had departed, toward the barracks. Then he turned back to Bridei, his expression brightening. "Come on—let's go and get a pie from the market."

Bridei gave a wry smile. Heolstor's next meal was never far from his thoughts. Still, after a hard morning in the yard, Bridei was also hungry.

"Very well," he replied. "Although we'd better hurry or they'll all be gone."

The pair of them walked from the training yard, past the orchard full of pink and white apple blossom, and out of the high gate into the outer perimeter of the fort. Bebbanburg—named after the wife of the man who had built this place—was a compact stronghold, built upon a rocky outcrop that looked out to sea. It had two main thoroughfares: the King's Way, which led from the low to the high gate; and the Dragon's Back, a street that ran the south to north length of the fort.

Bridei and Heolstor walked down the King's Way, toward the market square. It was late morning, and the sounds of industry echoed over the fort: the call of vendors at market, the bleat of goats in a nearby byre, the chatter of women as they shopped, and the clang of iron from the smith's forge—where Rinan's father, Broga, worked.

Ahead, a crowd of men, women and children thronged the wide space before the low gate. It was the only area in the fort large enough for folk to congregate. Farmers, merchants and artisans hawked their wares there most days.

The pie stall sat in the south-east corner, and Bridei and Heolstor headed straight for it. Even from a distance, Bridei could see there were only a handful of pies left. He dug into the pouch at his belt and pulled out a half-thrymsa. It was his turn to pay.

He was half-way across the square, weaving in and out of clusters of women bearing wicker baskets, when he spotted a flash of yellow on the northern edge of the crowd.

Rinan had also come to the market after practice.

Yet he did not appear to be here for the pies. Instead, he was staring at a small, thin girl with frizzy, red hair who had just crossed in front of him. Bridei knew the girl—she was Hea, the daughter of a comely flower-seller. She appeared to be struggling under the weight of two heavy sacks of vegetables. Hea was a sweet, if clingy, creature who often followed Bridei and Heolstor around the fort like a lost puppy.

Rinan watched her with a look of concentration that made Bridei stop, mid-stride. Heolstor barreled into him, nearly knocking Bridei into a wagonload of cabbages.

His friend gave a grunt of frustration. "What is it?"

"Look over there," Bridei replied, his rumbling stomach forgotten, and pointed across at Rinan. Heolstor's gaze followed his, just in time to see Hea disappear into the crowd. A moment later, Rinan set off after her.

Bridei frowned. "What's he up to?"

Hea was halfway home from market when she realized she was being followed.

Her arms were aching, for she carried two heavy, coarse hessian sacks: one full of turnips and carrots, the other full of onions. She regretted not bringing the little wooden cart her mother often used for market. However, she found herself ignoring the burning muscles in her shoulders and arms—instead casting nervous glances behind her as she walked.

A young man followed her along the Dragon's Back.

Hea looked back once more, her pulse racing when she saw he had lengthened his stride and was now no more than ten paces behind her. She knew him—and that was why she feared him.

Broad and strong for his age with a mop of blond hair, Rinan was the son of the fort's iron-smith. Her pursuer glanced up, his pale blue eyes gleaming, and seeing that she had noticed him, he grinned.

Hea's home lay at the opposite end of the fort, not far from the northern guard's tower. To reach it she had to walk along the length of the Dragon's Back and then down a tangle of dirt alleys. Low timber, and wattle and daub houses marched by and the wooden outer palisade cast a deep shadow over the fort. Nonetheless, it had been a bright morning and the dirt street beneath Hea's bare feet was warm from the sun. The sulfurous odor of simmering pottage and the scent of wood smoke hung in the still noon air, reminding Hea that her mother would be preparing their usual meal of barley and vegetable pottage—a thick stew they ate with hard cheese and slabs of griddle bread.

Hea had been looking forward to her noon meal, but now her appetite vanished.

She started to run. It was difficult weighed down by her two bags. At thirteen winters she was small and thin, with only a head of unruly red hair to distinguish her from the crowd of wild girls she usually prowled Bebbanburg's streets with.

She heard a low snigger behind her, and the sound of Rinan's heavy tread quickening. He was enjoying this game. He knew that when she turned right into the tangle of lanes that led down to Hea's home, there would be few folk about.

What does he want?

She should have returned to the market square, but it was too late now. She would have to try and outrun him. Once she reached home she would be safe.

Sprinting, her bare feet flying across hard-packed dirt, Hea veered right and fled down a narrow alley. Washing festooned this lane, but she was so small that she did not need to duck to avoid it. She hoped the linen tunics and woolen hose that dangled overhead would slow Rinan down.

They did not.

She was near the end of the alley when a hand, strong from working alongside his father at the forge, fastened around her upper arm and yanked her backward.

Hea squealed and dropped her precious bags of produce. Turnips, onions, and carrots rolled across the ground. She flailed at Rinan with small, angry fists, pummeling at his broad chest. "Let me go, let me go!"

"Not before I get what I want."

Rinan pushed her up against the wooden framed wall lining the lane. Hea gave a shrill scream of terror, but the lad silenced her with a clumsy, wet kiss.

Tea struggled wildly. His hot breath and rough hands terrified her. This could not be happening—how had she let him catch her so easily? She tried to knee him in the cods, but he twisted away and her knee struck the hard muscle of his thigh instead.

"What are you doing?"

A low voice sounded behind them.

Rinan froze. Keeping his prey pinned against the wall, the smith's son turned his head.

Heart fluttering like a moth trapped in a spider's web, Hea peered around his bulk and saw two young men standing a few feet behind them. Her breath hitched in wordless relief when she recognized the lads: Bridei and Heolstor would save her.

Bridei—the one who had spoken—was tall and lean with a mop of dark hair and brown eyes. At sixteen winters, Bridei already turned women's heads. Heolstor stood next to him: a heavy-set boy with pale, freckled skin and a shock of red hair that was even brighter than Hea's.

Rinan grinned at them. "What does it look like?"

"Help," Hea gasped, squirming under Rinan's bruising grip.

Bridei shifted his gaze from Rinan a moment, to Hea's face. His expression had been neutral before, but now his gaze narrowed. "Hea doesn't want your tongue down her throat—leave her alone."

Rinan snorted. "We're having some fun. You'll get your turn—you can just wait."

"She doesn't look like she's enjoying herself to me," Heolstor growled.

Rinan swiveled around further, so that he was half-facing the two lads, and spat on the ground. "Piss off."

Hea struggled against Rinan's iron grip, but he held her fast, pinned against the rough, wooden wall. All the while, he kept his gaze upon the two lads who were spoiling his amusement. Neither of them moved.

"Let her go," Bridei ordered.

"Upstart Pictling, go roll with the dogs!"

Bridei lunged. The meaty thud of his fist connecting with the young man's nose caused Hea to cringe back. She heard the crunch of bone and sinew give way.

Rinan let go of Hea and staggered away, clutching his nose. Blood trickled through his fingers. Rinan cursed, pain muffling his voice. "You broke my nose!"

"Aye, and I'll break your jaw too if you touch her again."

The blond smith's son stared back at him, his eyes glassy. "You want the little hōre, you can have her."

Hea watched Rinan stagger off, still clutching his flattened nose. She hugged her thin arms around her torso, trembling from the ordeal.

Bridei watched until Rinan had disappeared, before he turned back to Hea, his expression cool. "Did he hurt you?"

"N ... no," she stuttered, suddenly feeling shaky and weepy. Hea blinked back tears and swallowed. She would not weep in front of Bridei mac Beli—the Pictish fosterling who lived in the Great Tower of Bebbanburg as King Ecgfrith's ward. She wanted him to think her strong and brave—worthy of respect.

Behind Bridei, Heolstor huffed out a breath. "Rinan's father will see you whipped for that."

Bridei shrugged, grinning. "He deserved it."

"Aye, but his father has Ecgfrith's ear. You've just given the king a reason to lash out at you."

Hea's chest constricted at this news. She could not bear to see Bridei punished because of her.

Bridei must have witnessed the alarm on her face, for he cast his friend a censorious look and put a brotherly arm around Hea's trembling shoulders.

"Come on. Let's get you home."

Chapter Two

Fair Punishment

HEA RETRIEVED HER scattered vegetables, and the three of them walked the last distance to her hovel.

The wattle and daub dwelling sat under the shadow of the northern guard tower in the corner of the fort, at the end of a row of houses. It was a squat, shabby structure—with a thatched roof that leaked in places—but it was the only home Hea had ever known, and she loved it. Unlike the surrounding hovels, hers had a little garden out the back, where her mother grew herbs and flowers. The garden, surrounded by a high paling fence, was crucial to their survival. Mother and daughter lived by selling posies of flowers and herbal remedies—yet Hea's mother Lewren was also a seer, and some folk in Bebbanburg paid her for advice.

The aroma of vegetable stew and fresh griddle bread greeted them as Hea pushed open the door and led the way inside.

Lewren was standing at the fire pit in the center of the dark space, stirring a cauldron of pottage. She looked up as Hea and her companions entered, her expression sharpening when she saw her daughter's flushed face and glistening eyes.

"Heahburh—what have you been up to?"

Hea winced—her mother only ever used her full-name when she had done something wrong. Lewren's jade gaze hardened as it flicked from Hea to the two young men behind her.

"Rinan followed me home and grabbed me," Hea spoke up before Bridei or Heolstor could answer on her behalf. "He scared me, but Bridei broke his nose."

Hea watched her mother go still, before she drew herself up, her eyes narrowing into glittering slits.

Hea knew she was biased, but she thought her mother beautiful. Lewren was not a tall woman, yet she had presence: a proud stance, curvaceous build and thick, curly red hair that Hea envied. Her own mane was a garish, wild bush. Hea saw the way men's eyes tracked her mother when they walked through the fort together. Yet, for all that Lewren had never taken a lover, or wedded. Any man who dared woo her was swiftly, and coldly, rebuffed.

Lewren never spoke of Hea's father. Only once, years earlier, she had mentioned him—a warrior who went off to battle and never returned. Hea liked to think that her mother still loved him, and that was why she had never wanted another man.

"Don't worry," Bridei spoke up, chest swelling in pride. "He won't bother Hea again."

Lewren nodded curtly, her green eyes still burning. "And I thank you for that."

Hea glanced behind her at her companions. Bridei was gazing at Lewren like a mooncalf, and Heolstor's cheeks had gone pink. Envy stabbed her in the guts.

Why don't they look at me like that?

She knew why—Bridei and Heolstor merely saw her as a child ... for in reality that was what she was.

Lewren's gaze shifted to Hea, her expression softening slightly. "You must keep your wits about you, daughter. Not all males are like these two." She glanced back at the two lads, who were both grinning foolishly at the compliment Lewren had bestowed upon them.

They were not the first males Hea had seen act like fools around her mother. Lewren had an odd status in Bebbanburg; both revered and feared. She was furtive about her abilities, for now that Christianity had come to the north, her skills were seen by some as remnants of the old ways. Yet many folk here still believed in the old gods, and the king appeared content to allow a seer to reside inside his fort—as long as she did not make a nuisance of herself.

Even so, Hea had heard some folk refer to her mother as a 'wicce', an enchantress who practiced magic. She saw fear and hostility in their eyes when they named her thus, but Hea dismissed their mutterings. Her mother was simply gifted; she could see things others could not.

Lewren regarded the two lads in the doorway for a moment before she smiled. "Stay for the noon meal—there's plenty of pottage, even for you two. I swear the pair of you are taller each time I see you. What are they feeding you in the Great Hall?"

Bridei smiled, an expression that made Hea's stomach somersault. He had only recently entered manhood, but already he knew how to charm women. "Plenty of meat—the king says it makes his warriors strong."

Lewren snorted and turned away to fetch wooden bowls for their meal. "Well, you'll get no such fare here. Simple folk can only afford pottage."

"You're too free with your fists, lad."

Ecgfrith, King of Northumbria gazed down at Bridei. The king's hazel eyes were hard in the light of the cressets that burned behind the heah-setl—the high seat—a raised platform at the northern end of the hall within the Great Tower of Bebbanburg. His long, sharp-featured face was grim.

Standing at the foot of the high seat, Bridei shrugged. He knew the gesture was insolent, but he did not care. "Rinan deserved it."

"And why's that?"

"He was frightening a lass so I stopped him."

The king snorted. "You're my ward—not warden of this fort. I dish out punishment here."

Bridei stared back at him, refusing to be cowed. He never enjoyed facing Ecgfrith in this hall, for it was the king's domain. Built of pitted, red stone, the interior of the tower was a warm, airless space. Torches hung from braces on the walls, and four large fire pits burned day and night. There were few windows, just a few slits high up to let out smoke. Alcoves lined the circular chamber, their entrances shielded with richly detailed tapestries and plush fur hangings.

Ecgfrith let out a long sigh and leaned back in his carven throne, his long legs stretched before him. In his thirty-second year, Ecgfrith still had a youthful countenance despite that his short, sandy hair had started to recede at the temples of late. He dressed simply in a long, woolen tunic and leather breeches. He was tall and lean, although strong. His bare arms were finely muscled, and he gave off an aura of contained power. Bridei had seen the king at sword practice with his warriors; he knew Ecgfrith could fight, and fight aggressively.

When the king spoke once more, his voice was soft. "You disappoint me, Bridei … again."

Bridei screwed his face up. What did he care? This man was not his king, or his father—although Ecgfrith acted like he was both.

"I took you in, at your father's request," Ecgfrith went on, as if he had not noticed Bridei's expression. "I let you sleep in my hall, eat at my table—and now you train with my men. Yet I get no gratitude. Instead you cause trouble."

"I didn't," Bridei spat back. "I told you, Rinan—"

"Enough." Ecgfrith's voice lashed across the Great Hall. "Hold your insolent tongue."

A collective gasp sounded in the cavernous space, issued from the clusters of retainers—the men, women, and children who formed the king's household—that formed a semi-circle around the high seat.

Next to Ecgfrith, Queen Irmenburgh shifted uncomfortably upon her smaller chair, and cast a pained look at her husband. She was a pale, thin woman with brown hair pulled back into a braid wrapped severely around the crown of her head. Like her husband, she dressed simply, although her woolen tunic was finely made. A wooden crucifix rested upon her flat chest.

Bridei had always liked Irmenburgh. She was Ecgfrith's second wife—his first had refused to consummate their marriage before fleeing south to run a convent little more than a year later. Bridei had been young at the time, but he remembered Aethelhild of the East Angles; a proud, raven-haired beauty who had defied Ecgfrith at every turn. Irmenburgh was different. She was sweet and gentle—a born peace-weaver. Bridei could see she was trying to meet her husband's eye now, in an attempt to soothe the situation.

Ignoring her, the king's cool gaze flicked to Bridei's right, to where Rinan stood next to his father—a hulking smith with coarse straw-colored hair and a high-colored face, the result of too many nights at the meadhall.

Rinan now boasted two black-eyes, as well as a nose that looked like a boiled, smashed turnip. However, Bridei noted that Rinan also sported a swollen lip and a bruise on his lower jaw ... he had not given him those. Bridei's gaze flicked to Rinan's father, Broga. He would not have wanted that man as his father—all of Bebbanburg knew that Broga was a bully.

Ecgfrith smiled at the smith's son. "How do you wish to see Bridei punished?"

Bridei's guts twisted at this, although he kept his expression neutral. A few yards away, to Bridei's left, stood Heolstor. His friend's usually good-natured face was strained, his blue eyes wide with worry. Catching Heolstor's eye, Bridei suddenly wished he had not interfered with Rinan's fun. Only that the sight of young Hea so terrified had made him act without thinking.

"A flogging," Broga boomed, just as his son was opening his mouth to reply. "A public one, sire."

Bridei's breath rushed out of him. "I don't deserve that," he burst out. "I told you, he had it coming."

Ecgfrith raised a hand to silence him, his gaze still upon Rinan. "A flogging sounds fair punishment. But we'll make it outside the Great Tower, not in the market square. No need to bother common folk with this."

A silence fell over the hall, and Bridei felt the gazes of all settle upon him.

When Ecgfrith spoke once more he was smiling. "Ten lashes ... and Rinan can wield the whip himself, if he so choses." The expression Bridei saw on Ecgfrith's face then made him go cold. "Your punishment will take place now."

Bridei stood in the center of the stableyard and waited for the flogging to begin.

Shirtless, his arms wrapped around a large pole where men usually hitched their horses, his wrists bound, he felt trussed up like a Yuletide goose ready to be spit-roasted. Worse still, all those he had grown upon among had gathered to watch. He spotted Aart a few yards away, grinning at him.

Bridei gritted his teeth. He would make these people pay for this ... one day.

Hearing footfalls behind him, Bridei swiveled his head to see the king, Broga, and Rinan approach. The smith carried a large braided whip, of the type farmers used with oxen.

Bridei's stomach twisted once more. He had been beaten before—many times in fact in the years since coming to foster at Bebbanburg—but Ecgfrith had never used the whip on him.

Ecgfrith gave him a thin smile. "Ready for your punishment?"

Bridei merely glared back at him.

The king gave a shrug and glanced over at Broga. "Give your son the whip and let us begin."

The smith nodded and shoved the leather whip into Rinan's hands. Oddly, the young man looked nervous. Sweat beaded his pale skin, and his swollen face made him look ill. Broga gave Rinan a feral look. "Flay his hide, boy."

Rinan nodded, throat bobbing. He then unfurled the whip and stepped up behind Bridei.

Bridei turned back to the pole and schooled his face into a cold mask. He would not let them see him suffer. He would give none of them the satisfaction. He knew Heolstor was amongst the crowd but deliberately avoided looking his way. His friend would hate to see him flogged, and Bridei did not want to see pity in his eyes.

The first lash, when it came, burned a line of fire across his shoulders.

Bridei clenched his jaw and steeled himself for the next blow.

"Put some force into it," Broga snarled. "I've seen a maid with a stronger arm."

This drew some sniggers from the watching crowd. A moment passed, and Bridei could almost taste Rinan's humiliation, before the whip lashed across his shoulders once more.

It really hurt this time, but Bridei swallowed his cry of pain, letting out a grunt instead.

"Is that it?" Broga's rough voice reached him. "That's the best you can manage?"

"I hit him as hard as I could, fæder," Rinan mumbled. "I can't—"

"Pathetic—step aside and let me show you how it's done."

Fear curled up from the pit of Bridei's bowels. Broga was the strongest man in the fort. He would cut his back to ribbons.

When it was over, Bridei sagged against the pole, his breathing coming in labored gasps. He had done it—not uttered a word as that whip lashed across his back another eight times—only now his back felt as if it had been flayed open. Pain pulsed across his shoulders like a brand.

Aart stepped forward and cut the ties on Bridei's wrists. Legs shaking under him, Bridei leaned against the pole and closed his eyes a moment. It took a monumental effort to remain upright, not to crumple into the dirt. Yet with the crowd of retainers still looking on, he would not give in.

After a few long moments, the waves of dizziness that crashed over him drew back, and Bridei opened his eyes. He pushed himself off the pole and turned to find Ecgfrith waiting for him.

Rinan and Broga stood a few yards behind him, looking silently on while their king had the last word.

"A little less cocky now?" Ecgfrith asked with a smile that did not reach his eyes. "Ready to humble yourself?"

Bridei stared at him, realizing that the flogging had merely been a ruse—an excuse—for Ecgfrith. Just like Aart, he had been looking for a way to put Bridei in his place. Bridei mac Beli was becoming a threat to them all.

As understanding dawned, he gave Ecgfrith the most arrogant smile he could muster. "Before you ... never."

Chapter Three

Exile

ECGFRITH'S EYES WIDENED, and he drew back as if struck.

"I am your king," he replied, the slight rasp in his voice betraying his anger. "You will humble yourself before me—without question."

Bridei drew himself up, ignoring the throbbing in his back as he held the king's gaze. He knew he was playing with fire, but after the humiliation of the flogging he did not care. Years of resentment finally boiled to the surface. He'd had enough of pretending.

"You're not my king," he replied, "and you never will be. I am a Pict, and I swear allegiance to my father. No one else."

The silence that settled over the yard was deathly—and when Ecgfrith broke it, his voice shook with rage. "Ungrateful dog. I have treated you like a son, and this how you repay me."

Bridei's lip curled. "Why would I be grateful to you? I never asked to come here—and you've never, for one moment, made me feel welcome."

Ecgfrith's gaze narrowed into slits, his skin pulling tight over his cheekbones. A thrill of fear went through Bridei then. He was sure he had taken it too far—sure that Ecgfrith would have him executed for his insolence.

"I would slay you, here and now," Ecgfrith ground out, "if I didn't want to start a war with your father. However, my agreement with him is at an end. You are no longer welcome at Bebbanburg. Go home to him in disgrace like the whipped savage you are."

Joy leaped like a hare in Bridei's chest.

Ecgfrith was giving him the one thing he desired. He was no Angle, he would always be an outsider here. He had left his father's fortress, Dundurn, when he was barely five winters old, and had not seen it since. A few years after Bridei's arrival here, his mother had sickened, but Ecgfrith had forbidden his young fosterling to return to Dundurn to say goodbye.

Bridei had never forgiven the king for that—from that moment forward, hate had grown like a canker in his breast. And he had fed it, waiting for the day he would be free of his Northumbrian oppressors.

Now, Ecgfrith was handing it to him. Yet the Northumbrian king was so angry, he did not see the joy in his ward's eyes, the disbelief on his face.

"Pack your bags and keep out of my sight for the rest of the day," he snarled. "I want you gone from this fort by the time I rise tomorrow morning."

"Sit still—this will only take longer if you fidget."

Bridei nodded, although he responded through gritted teeth. "It hurts."

Lewren made a clucking sound with her tongue. "Aye—I'm not surprised. Broga did a thorough job."

Inhaling deeply, Bridei closed his eyes. He sat upon a stool in front of the fire pit in the healer's smoky dwelling, while Lewren applied a paste of fresh woundwort to his back.

"It'll hurt while I apply this," she said after a few moments, her tone softening, "although the herb will numb the pain soon."

Bridei sucked his breath in, forcing himself not to shift on the stool as needles of stinging pain lanced across his shoulders. "Are the cuts deep?"

"One or two are. You'll bear a couple of faint scars—you're lucky it was only ten lashes."

Bridei snorted and immediately regretted the action. The cuts on his back pulsed in time with his heartbeat. "I thought he'd grab the whip and give me a few more after Broga was done."

"After you insulted him?" Lewren added, disapproval in her voice. They were alone in the hovel; Hea was out collecting herbs in the meadows beyond Bebbanburg. "You're lucky he didn't take your head off."

Bridei did not disagree with her. He knew just how fortunate he was, and was still reeling at how fate had just twisted in his favor. Had he not been complaining to Heolstor that morning how he would never be accepted here?

Instead, Ecgfrith had given him his freedom.

Lewren worked for a few moments more, her fingers moving gently over his back. There had been nights when Bridei had lain awake in his alcove in the Great Tower and imagined the fair Lewren's hands on him—just not like this. He was in too much pain to be gauche or embarrassed by her proximity.

Lewren might have been nearly old enough to be his own mother, but Bridei—like most of the lusty young men in the fort—had secretly fantasized about plowing her. A woman of such sensual beauty could surely teach a young man a thing or two in the furs. However, fantasy was as far as Bridei had ever gotten; Lewren was as untouchable as the cold bright stars in the night sky.

"There," Lewren said finally. "As long as you keep them clean and dry, the cuts should heal quickly."

Bridei rose to his feet, retrieved his linen tunic and gingerly put it on. Each movement was agony, and he hoped the numbing effect of the woundwort would start to work soon.

He turned to the healer, favoring her with a lopsided smile. "Thank you, Lewren. You and Hea have always been kind to me."

Lewren held his gaze, her expression clouding. "Does Hea know you're leaving?"

Bridei shook his head. "Can you tell her when she gets back?"

"She'll be upset."

Bridei gave an apologetic shrug, wincing as he did so. "I know she will … but none of us can fight fate."

Lewren's mouth thinned, and Bridei saw a shadow flit across those jade eyes. "Aye," she murmured, "but it's always women who pay the price."

Dusk was settling over the fort of Bebbanburg, a pink-hued sky that stretched out to where the eastern horizon merged with the dark sea, when Bridei stepped out upon the Dragon's Back. Despite his sore shoulders, a grin spread across his face.

This time tomorrow, I'll be free—and far from here.

He was halfway along the dirt street when he spotted a small, thin figure with an unruly mop of bright, red hair hurrying toward him. Hea was barefoot, as always, and carried a basket full of greenery under one arm. She wore a worn, brown wealca—a long, tubular dress with clasps at the shoulders. Her moss-green eyes were wide as she approached him. "Bridei! I've just heard. Is it true you're to be banished?"

Bridei stifled a groan. He had hoped to avoid this awkward encounter.

"Wes hāl, Hea," he greeted her, forcing himself to look glum about the situation. "Aye—I'm to leave at first light tomorrow."

"Folk are saying you were whipped."

"I was, but your mother has taken care of that. Don't worry—I'll mend."

Hea stopped before him, craning her neck up to met his eye. She was an odd-looking wee thing, with a mouth too big for her face, and huge eyes, slightly too far apart. She was also thin and under-developed for her age—not yet showing signs of womanliness—although that had not deterred Rinan. Maybe she would grow into her looks, but she was not a beauty like her mother.

Hea stared at him, her eyes filling with tears. "Woden, no," she whispered, invoking the name of the father of the old gods—one still worshipped by a few in Bebbanburg. "I don't want you to leave." She wrung her hands together, her thin frame quivering from the force of emotion that coursed through her. Bridei watched her, something odd twisting deep within his chest at the pitiful sight.

She was such a sweet creature, a force of nature.

For years now, Hea had shadowed him and Heolstor. Initially, they had been annoyed by the clingy, red-haired imp, but of late he had found himself less and less bothered by her presence.

With a jolt, he realized he would miss Hea, almost as much as he would Heolstor.

"But Bebbanburg is your home," she whispered. "Do you even remember where you're from?"

Bridei smiled. Memories of Dundurn were still etched upon his mind. "Aye, I remember my father's fort, as if I just departed yesterday."

Her eyes widened. "Is it very different to here?"

He nodded before continuing on his way up the Dragon's Back. Hea fell into step beside him. "Bebbanburg is made of wood and sits upon a great rock, whereas Dundurn is stone; a fort built atop a tall, green hill." He paused here and cast his mind back to those early years, when he had run free and wild, and his mother had still been alive. "The wind is different there too," he said after a moment, a wistful smile spreading across his face. "Here, on the edge of the sea, the wind shouts and roars like an angry god. Dundurn sits inland, surrounded by forests, lochs, and burns, and there the wind whistles and sighs. I used to lie awake at night in my father's broch and listen to its song."

Hea glanced sideways at him, her face a picture. "It sounds magical," she breathed.

Bridei's smile widened. "It is."

Bridei left Hea outside the high gate and entered the inner palisade. He had muttered an awkward goodbye and sloped off, although he could feel her gaze boring into his back as he walked.

Bridei did not look back—it was easier that way.

He walked past the guards clad in boiled leather and iron helmets, spears at the ready, and into the wide yard beyond. The sight of the pole in its center, where he had been whipped earlier, made him tense, as did the Great Tower and the oppressive shadow it cast.

Gritting his teeth, he veered right toward where a complex of low slung stables, barracks and store houses crouched. He would not go back into that tower; instead he would gather what he could from the stores and sleep in the stables tonight.

Chapter Four

Farewell

DAWN ROSE OVER Bebbanburg—a grey, foggy sunrise. Mist curled around the base of the Great Tower as Bridei stood next to the trough and splashed icy water over his face. The air smelt rich with the brine-scent of the sea and the aroma of damp earth.

Excitement fluttered up under Bridei's ribs as he breathed in the crisp, salty air.

Finally … I'm leaving.

The wounds on his back still hurt, although after Lewren's healing the pain had subsided to a dull throb. Bridei was alone; no one had risen early to see him off. Ecgfrith had made it clear that when he rose from his alcove he expected to see his ward gone—and for once, Bridei was happy to obey him.

Still, after all these years, it felt odd—and more than a little hollow—to leave so quietly. He had lived longer here than he ever had at Dundurn. He had not spoken the tongue of his people in years. The language of Pictland was far different to the guttural tongue of the Angles and the Saxons: Englisc. He would be rusty, but not only that, he had gotten used to the Angle ways. Even though he gritted his teeth through prayers before supper each night—a ritual which as a member of the highborn he could not escape—it was now part of his life. It had taken him a long while to grow accustomed to Bebbanburg, but he realized his return to Dundurn would be just as strange.

Deep in thought, Bridei re-entered the stables and walked to the stall where his stocky, grey mare Léoma—Ray of Light—stood waiting. Léoma had been a gift upon his thirteenth spring, from the king himself to celebrate Bridei's passing into manhood. The other young warriors received stallions, or at the very least geldings, but Ecgfrith had made a point out of gifting Bridei a filly. The other warriors had teased him mercilessly over it, but Bridei had paid them no mind. Three years on, and Léoma and he were a partnership. The horse was one of the few close friends he had here.

"There you are."

A young male voice, rough with sleep, greeted Bridei. He turned to see Heolstor stride into the low-slung building. His red hair tousled, and his face pinched and tired, Heolstor was dressed in leather breeches, a long woolen tunic, and a traveling cloak—and he carried a leather pack under one arm.

Bridei frowned. "What are you doing here?"

"I'm coming with you."

Bridei snorted, although he was touched by his friend's loyalty. "You can't—Ecgfrith won't like it."

"He hasn't forbidden anyone from joining you."

Bridei raised an eyebrow. "And your mother's going to let you?"

Heolstor strode over to where his gelding awaited in the stall opposite. He picked up the saddle from its rack and slung it over his horse's back. "She doesn't know. Anyway, I'm old enough to choose my own path."

Bridei watched his friend, incredulous. He had known Heolstor a long while and had always believed his friend, although loyal, to be the sort who would never go against his parents, or his king's will.

Still, he felt he had to make Heolstor see sense. He could be loyal to a fault. "You'll make an enemy of Ecgfrith for life, if you join me."

Heolstor met Bridei's gaze over his horse's withers. His expression belonged to someone much older, as if he had spent most of the night pondering his decision. Bridei could see the tension in his face. "That's a risk I'm willing to take."

"But you don't know what Pictland is like, you might hate it ..."

Heolstor shrugged, turning his attention back to the girth he was tightening. "I'm sure folk won't be that different to here."

"Many folk will never have seen someone who looks like you before," Bridei replied. He had to be sure Heolstor knew what he was getting himself into. "They'll stare like you've got three heads."

Heolstor merely laughed. "And you'll tell them to mind their manners."

Their gazes met once more, and Bridei grinned. Heolstor was the only one he trusted enough in this fort to let his guard down with. For the first time, he let his excitement at Ecgfrith's decision show on his face.

Heolstor grinned back. "Come on—let's get moving."

Bridei stepped into Léoma's stall, greeting her by sliding a hand down her neck. She was undergoing her spring molt, and fine, grey hairs came away in a great handful, causing Bridei to cough. There was not time to groom her properly this morning though. Bridei needed to be well away from the fort by the time the king rose from his furs.

As he tightened the girth to Léoma's saddle, Bridei cast another glance at his friend.

Heolstor had finished saddling his gelding and was leading it out of the stall. He carried a light, iron sword at his side and a seax—a long fighting dagger—sheathed across his stomach, Angle and Saxon style.

Heolstor tied the pack he had brought behind the saddle. "I've packed us some food," he announced. "It's not much—just bread, cheese, and some salted pork—but we can hunt on the way."

Bridei nodded. He too had packed some food, and had also brought his longbow and a quiver of arrows with him.

The young men led their horses out of the stables and mounted. Then they rode across the yard to the high gate. The guards flanking it, faceless behind iron helmets, watched wordlessly as the pair passed through the gate and clip-clopped away down the sleeping King's Way toward the low gate.

Bridei inhaled the faint scent of wood-smoke and baking bread. It was still early. The sun was rising over the sea to the east, a glow through the encircling mist—promising good weather for the first day of their journey north.

Halfway down the King's Way, Bridei glanced back at Heolstor. The young man was staring ahead, his face more serious than Bridei had ever seen it. Although he was attempting to be brave, Bridei knew Heolstor was struggling with the consequences of his decision.

"There's still time, you know," Bridei said, keeping his voice low in the dawn hush. "You can change your mind."

Heolstor looked at him, his blue eyes hardening. "You're not leaving me behind."

"But this is your place, these are your people."

Heolstor's jaw clenched before he glanced away. "My loyalty is to you."

Bridei stared at him, momentarily lost for words. His throat constricted, and he turned his attention back to where the King's Way widened out into the market square ahead. Heolstor was the closest thing he had to family in the fort. He and his mother Geisla were the only folk who had welcomed him into the king's hall. Life here would have been cold and lonely without them.

Bridei cleared his throat. "It's a long, hard ride north—are you ready for it?"

Heolstor's answering smile lit up the misty morning like a Yuletide blaze. "I can't wait."

Bridei turned his attention back to the empty road ahead. "What shall we tell the guards at the gate, if they ask? They'll be expecting me to ride out alone."

"Just say Ecgfrith has decided to rid himself of me too," Heolstor replied. "A friend of an upstart Pictling is no friend of his."

A small, cloaked figure awaited them in the market square.

Hea stood, clasping a threadbare, woolen cloak about her, watching the horsemen approach. Around her, the first farmers and merchants were setting up stalls for the morning's trade. The low rumble of conversation drifted across the square toward the riders.

Heolstor let out a low groan upon spying Hea. "What's *she* doing here?"

Bridei sighed. Likewise, he did not want to see Hea this morning. He hoped she would not make a fuss, or start weeping. He just wanted to leave quietly—and quickly.

He drew up Léoma next to Hea and looked down at her pale face. Her eyes gleamed in the dawn light.

"You shouldn't be here," he said gently. "It just makes this harder."

Her eyes glittered with tears and her chin trembled, but she did not start to weep. "I had to say goodbye," she whispered. Her gaze flicked to Heolstor, who had drawn his gelding up next Bridei and was now shifting impatiently in the saddle. "To both of you."

"Goodbye then." Bridei smiled down at her. "Live well."

She made a soft, choking sound, as if swallowing a sob, and nodded.

"Goodbye, imp," Heolstor added with a half-smile, using the name he had bestowed upon her years earlier when he had found her a nuisance. "Look after yourself."

With that, the two young men urged their horses forward and rode toward the low gate. Unlike the high gate above, which had been opened in preparation for Bridei's departure, the heavy oaken and iron gates—the only entrance through the outer palisade—were still closed.

The guards here watched Bridei approach. With a curt nod, one of them gestured to his companions to unbar and open the gates. They observed Bridei curiously, their gazes flicking to Heolstor. Bridei saw the interest on their faces, yet none of them moved to stop his companion, perhaps thinking the king had given permission for the Pictish lordling to travel with an escort.

"Good riddance," one of them muttered as Bridei and Heolstor rode out of Bebbanburg and down the steep causeway beyond.

Hea stood in the midst of the market square, oblivious to the stall-holders setting up for the day around her. Instead, she stared after the two young men on horseback as they rode through the low gate: one tall and lean, with hair the color of a raven's wing; the other stocky with pale skin and a shock of red hair.

She could not believe Bridei and Heolstor were leaving—that they would never come back.

Hea remained there for a while, staring after them, even once they had disappeared onto the causeway that led down to the farmland below. A man carrying a sack of barley jostled her as he passed by, jolting Hea from her reverie. Barely noting the grunt of apology he gave her, she turned and woodenly walked from the square.

The Dragon's Back was quiet at this time of morning; just a few early-risers hurrying off to get choice items from market, before the rest of the fort descended upon it.

Hea paid none of them any mind.

This is all my fault.

Bridei would still have been here, if he had not broken Rinan's nose. An ache took up residence in Hea's chest, and by the time she reached her mother's hovel, tears were streaming down her face.

Bridei had been the only boy she had ever taken an interest in, and her misery now was so great that she felt as if he would surely be the last. She felt as if a great mailed fist was squeezing her heart.

Hea burst in through the wattle door, rushed past where her mother was kneading bread on a table to the right of the fire pit, and threw herself onto the pile of furs at the back of the space.

"It's not fair," she wailed.

Then, she began to sob as if her heart would break.

Lewren had not spoken at the sight of her daughter's abrupt, tearful entrance. However, she knew the reason for it.

With a sigh, she dusted off her floury hands and crossed the space to where Hea lay face-down in the furs. Her daughter's shoulders shook violently, and although her sobs were muffled, Lewren heard the raw pain.

Pity twisted in her breast, and she lay a hand on Hea's back, gently stroking her. For a while she just let her weep, for there was little she could say to change things. She had known that Hea had developed an infatuation for the handsome, young Pict, and had also noted that he did not return the sentiment.

It's for the best, she thought. *There's little point pining after someone who does not want you in return.*

Bridei mac Beli was the son of a Pictish king, and his destiny lay far from here. It was better that the bond between him and Hea was severed now. Her daughter was young enough to recover, to forget about him in time.

Lewren tensed as fragments of her own life intruded; if only she could forget her own past. She knew how such loss felt—the aching, the longing, for a man who would never love you. The rage, the bitterness that filled you afterward. A cruel companion over the years.

Lewren exhaled slowly, forcing back memories best kept buried. Instead, she continued to stroke her daughter's heaving back.

"Hush, Hea," she murmured finally. "Bridei never belonged at Bebbanburg. You must let him go."

Her daughter continued to sob, giving no sign that she had even heard her.

Eight and a half years later …

Chapter Five

The Seer of Bebbanburg

Bebbanburg, Kingdom of Northumbria, Britannia

Autumn, 684 AD

THE YOUNG WOMAN with wild, red hair walked down to the water's edge and cast a posy of violets into the churning sea. It was a chill, overcast morning and the great North Sea was the color of weather-beaten iron. The wind buffeted the solitary figure upon the sandy shore, tugging at her woolen cloak and whipping her curls into her eyes.

Hea paid it no mind; her gaze was upon the bright posy that now lay adrift upon the waves.

Violets had been her mother's favorite flower—they would forever remind Hea of her.

Hea's eyes filled with tears, blurring her vision.

A year had passed since her mother's death, but the ache of loss in her heart did not ease. Lewren had been ill for many moons before the sickness that made her waste away to a skeleton finally took her. Hea and Lewren had tried everything to heal her, every herb and potion in their healer's lore, but none of it had helped.

Even now, Lewren's last words on her deathbed still echoed in Hea's ears. Her mother had been so weak it was an effort to speak. She had lain back on the nest of furs that Hea propped under her shoulders, her once vibrant mane dull in the flickering light of the cresset on the wall above her.

Her hand, fragile and ice-cold, had gripped Hea's with surprising strength.

"Daughter," she rasped. "Don't follow my path. It will only bring you pain."

Hea had gazed down at Lewren, confused by her words. "Mōder? What do you mean?" she whispered, her chest aching at the sight of her mother so weak, so ill. The rail-thin ghost before her bore no resemblance to the woman who had always been her protector, her teacher.

"I've always been prideful," Lewren gasped the words, each one a terrible effort. "Too much so." She paused there, gathering her waning strength before continuing. "I loved your father, but he dismissed me for I was beneath him. I hated him for it, and the bitterness grew within me with each passing year. Now that hate is killing me."

"No, mōder," Hea had whispered, tears leaking from her burning eyes. "You'll get better—you just need to fight it."

"It's too late for me now, but you must heed my words." Her mother squeezed her hand so tightly that Hea's finger bones creaked. It hurt, but she did not pull her hand free. "Don't be a fool like your mother. Find yourself a good man, and make a family together. Sell flowers, heal folk, but cast aside your gift of sight. The old ways are disappearing; if you practice them, folk will turn against you. They'll call you a wicce, and shun you."

Hea had stared down at her mother. This was a shock. Lewren had always encouraged her to use her gift, to nurture it. Now she was telling her to cast it aside. Hea had not understood.

A year later, she still did not.

Turning away from the foaming waves, which had now dragged the posy of violets under, Hea walked across the broad strand of silver sand, climbed the reed-covered dunes, and walked toward the causeway.

Bebbanburg rose above her, a bristling silhouette of wooden and iron ramparts with tall guard towers at each corner. The fort spread across the length and breadth of the massive outcrop of stone that rose above the surrounding farmland and looked out to sea.

Hea climbed the causeway, passing through the low gate. She felt the appraising gazes of the guards as she did so—their hot, lustful looks. Yet they did not utter a word. None of them dared.

In a year, much had changed for Heahburh, daughter of Lewren.

For a while after her mother's death she had lived quietly, doing as Lewren had bid: selling flowers and using her skills as healer. However, contrary to her mother's advice, she had shunned male attention. She did not want any of the warriors who leered at her, or the farmers who flirted with her at market. They were rough, rude and charmless, and she would not give herself to any of them.

Her mother had told her to find a good man, and she would wait until she did.

Then, six moons after Lewren's passing, in the midst of a chill spring, King Ecgfrith had sent for her.

For the first time, she had set foot inside the Great Tower of Bebbanburg, and knelt before the high seat—before the hazel-eyed king and his pale queen.

"I hear you bear a gift," Ecgfrith had said, his gaze intense as he studied her. "The gift of foresight."

Hea had met his gaze, her heart fluttering in her breast. Was this a trap? She knew the king was pious, although not as much as his wife, or his late mother. Was he looking to root out and get rid of those following the old ways?"

She had inhaled deeply and prepared to lie.

"I have need of a seer," the king said quietly. "Can you help me?"

Hea swallowed and tried not to look shocked. Her gaze flicked to Queen Irmenburgh seated beside Ecgfrith. She had seen the queen often over the years, and always thought she had looked kind. Yet that morning her pretty face was stony, her blue eyes narrowed; her thin frame taut with displeasure.

Clearly, the king had not discussed this with his wife—or if he had, she had not given her approval.

"My mother had great talent as a seer," Hea had replied, dropping her gaze to the rushes at her feet. "I'm not sure I'm her equal."

She had glanced up to see the king was smiling. "A gift is a gift," he said. "If you have it, you are of use to me."

And that was that—overnight, Hea's life at Bebbanburg changed. Gone were the leering looks and straying hands of men in the fort; gone were her fears that she would go hungry over the winter.

The king paid her a small leather purse of gold thrymsas once a moon, a small fortune to Hea.

In return, Hea sought answers for Ecgfrith; although sometimes the spirit world gave her confusing and worrying messages. The king was greedy for answers, and the shadowlands did not like the living interfering with them; Hea had to tread carefully.

Hea crossed the market square.

As she walked, she noted how some of the women here gave her wary looks. One or two even whispered together as they watched her, their expressions guarded. Her mother was right—even with the king's protection, a seer was part of the old, dying, ways.

Halfway across the square, Hea heard her name called. She glanced up to see Fritha, the baker's wife who sold fresh bread, cakes, and pies at market every morning.

"You look pale this morn, lass," Fritha greeted Hea with a motherly smile as she approached her stall. "Does something ail you?"

Hea shook her head. "Mōder died a year ago today. The memory makes me melancholy, that's all."

Fritha's kindly face grew serious. The baker's wife had grown up with Lewren, and had been one of her closest friends. "Woden strike me down, I'd forgotten. Is it a year already?"

Hea attempted a smile and failed, she felt oddly tearful and empty today. "I know," she replied huskily. "It feels like only yesterday to me."

Fritha emerged from behind a mountain of bread and cakes and put an arm around Hea's shoulders. "I know it doesn't seem so now, but you will feel better with time."

Hea nodded, letting out a long shuddering breath. Fritha had known loss too; both her daughters had died in infancy, leaving Fritha and her husband childless.

"Here." Fritha ducked back behind her stall and retrieved a loaf of bread. "Get yourself home and have something warm to eat."

Hea's mouth quirked. Fritha, a portly woman with florid cheeks, thought a good meal healed most ills. However, Hea had already broken her fast before going down to the shore and was not hungry. Even so, she took the bread gratefully; Fritha's baking was the best in the fort.

She was just about to bid her friend good day and continue on her way across the market square toward the Dragon's Back, when a clamor behind her made Hea turn.

The pounding of hooves up the causeway beyond the low gate.

As the women watched, a company of horsemen rode into Bebbanburg.

Hea instantly realized they were not the king's men, nor were they Angles or Saxons. Instead, these men wore breeches of plaid. Some were bare-chested, while others wore leather vests, leaving their muscular arms, painted in swirling blue designs, bare. Their hair, mostly long and dark, flowed down their backs. They carried iron swords and square shields covered in leather and painted in tribal designs. Around their shoulders many of the warriors wore plaid cloaks, rather than fur mantles.

Hea's belly contracted. *Picts.*

This was the first time she had seen a company of warriors visit Bebbanburg from the wild lands to the north—lands that Ecgfrith of Northumbria ruled.

She had not seen a Pict in a long while, not since her beloved Bridei departed. Here in Bebbanburg, he had stood out amongst the blond, brown and red-haired men. Yet this was a company of tall, lean warriors with raven-black hair and sharp-features. It brought back memories of the longing that Hea had long buried.

Then she saw him.

He rode at the head of a company of around thirty warriors, back ramrod straight, shoulders thrown back in supreme male confidence. Years had passed, but Hea would have known him anywhere.

She stopped breathing.

At sixteen winters, Bridei mac Beli had been striking. At nearly twenty-four, he was devastating. He was still lean, but his frame had filled out with muscle and his shoulders had broadened. He wore his hair shorter than some of the others, so that it curled around the top of his shoulders. His expression was cool, arrogant. More than that, he carried himself like a man; gone was any gaucheness of youth.

Heolstor rode at his side. Like Bridei, the red-haired lad Hea remembered had transformed into a broad, fire-haired warrior. Swirling blue designs decorated the right side of Heolstor's face, adding to his forbidding presence.

Neither man saw her.

The Picts thundered through the square, sending townsfolk, dogs, and fowl scattering, and entered the King's Way. Hea watched them go, her heart pounding.

"What are Picts doing here?"

Hea heard the fear in Fritha's voice, and tore her gaze away from the horsemen, who were heading toward the high gate. "Worry not," she said with a soothing smile. "Ecgfrith still rules southern Pictland, does he not?"

Fritha grunted, her gaze still on where the last of the Pict warriors disappeared up the King's Way. "Aye, but why should any of them need to come here?"

"Perhaps to pay tribute?"

Fritha looked unconvinced. "More likely to cause trouble, I'd wager."

Chapter Six

At the King's Table

BRIDEI MAC BELI, King of the Picts, strode into the Great Tower of Bebbanburg, looking neither left nor right. Instead his gaze remained fixed upon the man who stood waiting for him upon the high seat.

Ecgfrith of Northumbria had not changed much over the years.

His hairline had receded, and his body was leaner, but he still had that long, watchful face and the pitiless eyes Bridei remembered.

Ecgfrith's was a face Bridei had grown up hating; a face he had longed to see again on the field of battle. How many nights had he imagined looking into those calculating eyes right before he dug his sword into Ecgfrith's guts? Too many to count—yet here he was in Bebbanburg to give the Northumbrian king one chance for peace.

Just one chance was all Ecgfrith would get.

"Lord Bridei son of Beli." Ecgfrith greeted him as he approached. "This is an unexpected pleasure."

Beside the king, Irmenburgh had also risen to her feet, her thin face creased in a smile of welcome. The warmth in her eyes told Bridei she was pleased to see him, yet despite his cordial greeting, Ecgfrith's eyes told a different tale.

The king hid it well, but Bridei saw the irritation that seethed just beneath the surface.

Bridei inclined his head. "Lord Ecgfrith."

The Northumbrian king studied him for a moment, analyzing his face as if looking for a weakness to exploit. A heartbeat later he smiled, although the expression never reached his eyes. "This is an occasion indeed, to have you in Bebbanburg once more."

After you exiled me.

In truth, Ecgfrith had done him a great favor in banishing him from Northumbria. Bridei had traveled north, arriving at Dundurn to find his father, Beli, in ill-health. They had little time together before his father died, but Bridei was glad for the months they had shared. During that time, Beli had spoken of Bridei's mother, a Northumbrian noblewoman— daughter to King Edwin of Deira—and of the sudden sickness that had taken her away years earlier.

After his father's passing, Bridei set about learning how to become king of the north.

"A visit south was long overdue," Bridei replied. He had not knelt upon entering the Great Hall, nor had he addressed Ecgfrith as 'milord' or 'sire'. In his eyes, they were equals, although he knew Ecgfrith would not see it that way. He noted the way the Northumbrian king's eyes hardened after Bridei had spoken, but the king forced a smile.

"If you had sent word ahead, I would have organized a great feast to welcome you. However, if you and your men will join us for nón-mete, I will see our finest barrels of mead opened."

"I do not expect you to go to any trouble on our account," Bridei replied, "but I will take up your offer of a meal. If you would host us overnight as well, I would appreciate it."

Ecgfrith inclined his head. "You've traveled far just to remain here one night. Stay a few days at least, and enjoy my hall's hospitality. Your men are welcome to stable their horses with mine, and sleep in this hall."

Despite Ecgfrith's complaint that Bridei had not given him enough notice, the king's household put on an impressive noon meal that day.

Servants and slaves carried in wheels of cheese and legs of cured pork to sit amongst platters of braised onions, loaves of crusty bread, and tureens of hot bean stew. Long tables, arranged in a horseshoe around two of the four hearths, lined the hall. Daughters of the king's thegns circled the hall, pouring wine, ale, and mead for the feasters.

The rise and fall of voices, and the aroma of bean stew had greeted Bridei as he returned from the stables. He moved across the hall to the high seat, where Ecgfrith had invited him to join the king's table for the noon meal. Dogs skulked around the perimeters of the hall; lean and shaggy wolf hounds that eyed the food hungrily. A pall of smoke hung low over the tables, making Bridei's eyes water after the fresh air outdoors.

Bridei glanced back at Heolstor, who followed him across the floor. "Happy to be home?" He spoke to Heolstor in the tongue of the Picts, as he had done for years now.

The red-haired warrior snorted, answering in the same language. "Feels as foreign to me as it does to you."

"But you still have kin here. Your mother is still alive, is she not?"

Heolstor nodded. "She slapped my face when I approached her earlier— I don't think she was pleased to see me."

Bridei smirked. "You'll make peace with her before you go."

Heolstor's raised a ruddy eyebrow. "You don't want to hear the name she called me." He gave a shrug, although Bridei marked the hurt that flashed across his face. "I don't think I'll bother with her again."

The two men crossed the hall together and stepped up on the high seat. Bridei took a seat halfway down the long table, with Heolstor to his right, and turned his attention to the king—but Ecgfrith did not meet his eye. Instead his gaze flicked past him, resting upon a point beyond Bridei's left shoulder.

Curious, Bridei turned and saw that Ecgfrith was watching a woman cross the floor.

Bridei stared at her.

Chin raised, shoulders back, the young woman glided like a queen across the rushes. Her hair was unbound, signifying she was unwed—and what hair it was. Dark, springy, red curls cascaded over her shoulders, framing a pale face. She was small in stature, yet he could see the lush curves beneath the green woolen tunic she wore. The tunic was girded at the waist with a belt of plaited leather. Around her neck, she wore a heavy amulet, made of bronze and studded with garnets.

Bridei's stared. It was a seer's amulet.

As the young woman drew closer, her gaze met Bridei's, as if pulled by the weight of his own stare. She was striking rather than beautiful he realized, for her moss-green eyes were slightly too far apart and her mouth a little too full for her finely-boned face; yet she was mesmerizing, and Bridei could not take his eyes of her.

With a jolt, he realized he knew this woman.

She was Heahburh, daughter of Lewren.

May the Nameless one take him—he could not believe how she had changed.

The girl he remembered was thin and coltish with a frizzy mane of hair that was a garish shade of red. He remembered comparing her unfavorably to her comely mother, yet his memory of Lewren of Bebbanburg paled next to this wench.

Her cheeks flushed under his scrutiny, those full lips parting slightly before she shifted her gaze to the head of the table. She stopped before the high seat and curtsied.

"Sire." Her voice was low, slightly breathless, as if she had been running. "You summoned me."

"Aye," Ecgfrith replied. "We have guests from the north, Hea. I'd like you to join us for a feast."

She dipped her head. "Of course, milord."

Ecgfrith waved his hand casually in Bridei's direction, almost as an afterthought. "This is Bridei mac Beli. He fostered here years ago—do you remember him?"

Bridei watched Hea turn, her gaze meeting his once more. He saw from the look on her face that she did remember him.

"Aye, sire," she murmured. Her gaze shifted then, to the thegn sitting across the table—a broad-shouldered young warrior with yellow hair and a slightly flattened nose.

Bridei shifted his attention from Hea to where Rinan sat watching him. He had been so distracted by her, he had not even realized his old enemy sat just a few feet away. In truth, he had not even recognized him.

Bridei and Heolstor took their seats while Hea performed the task of pouring wine for the king's table. Bridei watched her as she moved from person to person, pouring sloe wine from a bronze ewer. She moved with fluid elegance; he could have easily gone on watching her forever if there had not been a wolf in sheep's clothing seated just a few feet away.

Ecgfrith could not be trusted.

The Northumbrian king had a mind like a newly-whetted blade. If he discovered a weakness he would exploit it; Bridei needed to keep his mind on the reason he had traveled south, not on the winsome fire-haired witch circuiting the table. When Hea leaned over his shoulder and filled his cup with wine, he did not look at her. He was aware that Ecgfrith was observing him over the rim of his own cup, a vulpine look on his face.

Even so, the scent of her—lavender mixed with the sweet musk of her skin—caused his pulse to quicken, his groin to harden.

Bridei inhaled deeply, fighting the urge to close his eyes.

Aye, she was distracting him terribly.

It was a relief when she moved on to Heolstor, exchanging a grin of welcome with him as she poured his wine.

After she had served the king's table, Hea took a seat at the king's right—a position which mystified Bridei. Such a seat was usually reserved for the warrior who commanded the king's men, not a young female of low birth.

Had the king claimed her as his lover?

Intrigued, Bridei looked over at the queen. Irmenburgh did not look pleased. Her mouth was pursed, her slender shoulders tense. As Bridei remembered, the queen wore a heavy wooden crucifix upon her breast. She was a pious, quiet woman who had never given the king a moment of trouble—yet Bridei suspected it was a passionless union.

For the king to flaunt his lover like this was a grave insult to his wife.

Bridei shifted his gaze back to Ecgfrith. The king had begun helping himself to food, signaling that the meal had started. Around them, men and women fell upon the spread before them, their voices echoing high in the stone tower.

Bridei took a mouthful of bean stew and washed it down with a sip of sloe wine. The food and drink here was as delicious as he remembered. The cooks in his own hall could learn a thing or two from those in Bebbanburg. He reached for some cured pork, and met Rinan's pale-blue gaze across the table.

The warrior stared at him, his expression aggressive, challenging. "Why have you come back?" he growled. "No one invited you."

Bridei grinned. "A flat nose suits you."

Laughter rumbled around the table, although it died away quickly when Rinan shot the warriors who were still chortling a filthy look.

Bridei glanced across at where Hea was taking a sip from her cup, and noted she was trying not to smile.

Chapter Seven

Ecgfrith's Game

HEA WATCHED BRIDEI out of the corner of her eye. Seeing him this close unnerved her. His presence was so strong it was almost impossible *not* to look at him, although she noted the lines of his face were harsher than she remembered. He was handsome, but there was an edge to his good looks and hardness in his dark brown eyes that had been absent eight and a half years earlier.

Yes, she remembered exactly how long had passed since the last time she had looked upon Bridei mac Beli. He had not recognized her at first when she had crossed to the high seat. Yet she had seen the naked male appraisal in his gaze before a flare of sudden recognition.

Hea glanced down at the spread of food before her. Bridei's unexpected arrival had robbed her of appetite; she could not think of food when the man who had once saved her from Rinan's unwanted attentions, whom she had dreamed of seeing again, was sitting just a few feet away.

She noticed Bridei kept stealing glances in her direction, trying to catch her eye. She could see he was used to not having to work for a woman's attention. Hea knew she should ignore him, focus on others at the table, but even so she felt her gaze drawn toward him.

A few feet away, Ecgfrith also watched his Pictish guest keenly. His expression was shuttered, unreadable.

For a while everyone at the table focused upon their meal. Conversation centered on the quality of the food, and the wine and mead. Eventually, it was Bridei who turned talk to other matters. He looked up from his platter, his gaze shifting to Ecgfrith.

"I thank you for your hospitality," he said, his voice low. The timbre of it gave Hea a shiver of pleasure. She imagined being in his arms, hearing that voice purr in her ear. "But I imagine you want to know why I'm here?"

The king glanced up. "I'm curious why you'd make such a long journey. You could have just sent a messenger, if you had news for me."

Bridei inclined his head slightly. "Some things need to be said face-to-face," he replied. "Surely you have heard what has gone on in the north."

The king held his gaze. "I've heard you've been busy of late, that you have been campaigning."

Bridei nodded. "After my father's passing there was much to be done. Many lands that had to be reclaimed."

"You've made quite a name for yourself." Ecgfrith raised his cup of mead to his lips and took a measured sip. "It seems you are now a warrior of some renown."

Bridei's mouth quirked. "I'm only putting things right. Too long have my people sat in the shadow of others. It's time for me to take back my birthright."

"Your birthright?" Ecgfrith gave a low chuckle. "You were never short on confidence, Bridei—even as a child."

Bridei gave the king a long, hard look. "Lord Ecgfrith, I wish to—"

The king lifted a hand, cutting his guest off mid-sentence. "Come now, Bridei. You've only just arrived here. Let us speak of more serious matters tomorrow, once you have rested."

Hea watched Bridei's gaze narrow and his expression darken. She glanced from one man to the next, realizing that Ecgfrith was playing a game—one of power, of dominance.

Bridei was not on his home soil; he would not dictate the terms here.

The noon feast finished mid-afternoon. Filled with rich food and too much mead, the warriors, Angle and Pict alike, got up from the table and slowly dispersed from the hall. Meanwhile, the rest of the folk who lived and worked in the Great Tower returned to their chores.

Bridei rose from the table, swaying slightly from all the sloe wine he had consumed. Yet he was irritated and barely able to keep his feelings from showing.

"Will you join me at a game of Cyningtaefl?" Ecgfrith asked. "Surely you still play?"

Bridei clenched his jaw and gave a brusque nod. "Later, if I may. I must see to my men and horses."

The Northumbrian king smiled back at him, an infuriating expression that Bridei remembered well.

"I hope they find their lodgings comfortable." His tone was low and polite, although the meaning behind it was not lost on Bridei. Ecgfrith barely tolerated his presence here; the tension between them was so taut now you could have sliced it with a blade. Bridei only wished to be out of this man's presence. He met Ecgfrith's eye once more. "Soon, we will need to exchange more than just pleasantries."

Ecgfrith smiled. "Perhaps, but it will be when I am ready—this eve, once you are rested from your journey perhaps." The king's gaze flicked to where Hea sat silently listening to their conversation. "I must take some advice first."

Next to him, Irmenburgh stiffened, although her gaze remained downcast. Bridei could see the tension in her slender shoulders.

Once again, Bridei wondered at this odd relationship. He had never heard of a king taking a lover to his high seat and treating her as an advisor—it made no sense to him. Nor did his use of a seer, flouting the old ways in a hall that was far more Christian than it was pagan.

Bridei cast a searching glance in Hea's direction, but her expression gave little away. The answers to his questions would have to wait. Without another word Bridei turned and stepped down from the high seat, making his way across the hall. Heolstor and his other warriors fell in behind him.

All of his men except Heolstor had feasted at the lower tables with Ecgfrith's warriors. Although none of the others spoke Englisc, the dominant tongue of Britannia, Bridei had seen them keeping a wary eye upon the conversation on the high seat, lest relations sour between the two leaders. Despite Ecgfrith's show of hospitality, Bridei and his men were not fooled.

The Picts were not welcome here.

When Bridei and most of the others upon the high seat had left, Hea struggled to gather her scattered wits.

I can't believe it ... he's actually here.

An odd excitement churned in the pit of her belly, a sensation that made it difficult for her to concentrate on anything else. Eventually she mastered her emotions and turned her attention back to the king. She noted the way he watched the Pict leader as he walked away, the assessing shrewd look on Ecgfrith's face.

What's he planning?

After a few moments Ecgfrith turned his attention back to her.

"I did not realize you and Bridei knew each other."

"We were friends when he lived here, sire," she replied. Hea flicked her gaze to Rinan, who still sat a few feet away, and wondered if Ecgfrith knew it was her whom Bridei had defended all those years ago. She wished Rinan had left the high seat with the other warriors as well. Ever since the day Bridei had broken his nose, Rinan had never bothered her again. Still, she was wary of him, and always would be. Nonetheless, Rinan had grown into a formidable warrior, and had earned his place at the king's side.

Sensing the tension between his seer and warrior, Ecgfrith waved Rinan away. "You can go—we'll speak later."

"Very well, sire," Rinan grumbled, before rising to his feet. He threw Hea a sour look and moved off.

"Come with me to my alcove," Ecgfrith bid Hea. "I need your advice."

Hea nodded and smiled, rising to her feet. "Of course, sire—but I must first fetch my seeing drum."

Ecgfrith nodded. "I will meet you in the alcove presently."

Hea left the hall, weaving her way through the throng of slaves and servants who were cleaning up after the feast. She did not want to keep Ecgfrith waiting. She knew he wished to ask her about Bridei, and of the reason for his arrival here.

Hea was crossing the stable yard outside, heading toward the high gate, when she spotted Bridei outside the stables. He was leaning against the doorframe, talking to Heolstor. The sight of him made her pulse race. She was aware of his presence keenly, even from many yards away. As she approached, Bridei looked up, said something to Heolstor, and then stepped out to intercept her.

"Greetings again, Hea."

She lifted her chin, tilting her face up so she could meet his gaze. His nearness made it difficult to concentrate, although she did her best to mask it with a light, teasing smile. "Hello, Bridei."

She was aware then that he had deliberately blocked her path; he would not be thwarted in speaking direct to her.

"You have grown up," he murmured, his voice low, intimate. "I barely recognized you."

Hea stiffened. He had meant it as a compliment but the reminder of the awkward girl he had left behind rankled. Her mother had been right; men were fickle creatures. "I knew you the moment you rode in through the low gate," she replied before her gaze flicked to Heolstor. "And I'd recognize your hair anywhere."

Heolstor laughed in response. "Says the woman with fire hair."

"Yours has darkened over the years," Bridei noted, his gaze still upon Hea. His voice had a soft, beguiling edge that made Hea's skin warm, made her breathing grow shallow. A man like this was dangerous.

"Just as well it has," she replied with a laugh. "I used to resemble a carrot."

Bridei smiled. "Much about you has changed. I remember a tiny scrap of a girl. Now I see a woman."

The intensity of his stare made her body flush. He spoke as if the two of them were alone, as if Heolstor was not standing there listening to every word.

Stepping back from him, she felt her breathing ease, for his very presence unbalanced her and made her feel lightheaded. She inhaled deeply and clutched her skirts, realizing as she did so that her palms were sweaty.

"I'd better go," she said, masking her discomfort with another smile. "The king needs me."

Bridei's brow furrowed. "So you're Ecgfrith's seer? That's an odd arrangement."

Hea's smile slipped. She did not like his tone. "What's so odd about that?"

"Seers are common amongst my people," Bridei replied. "But I thought Christians like Ecgfrith shunned the old ways."

"I thought your mother attended the king? Heolstor spoke up from behind them. "How is Lewren?"

Hea tore her gaze from Bridei's and shifted her attention upon Heolstor. "Mōder died a year ago today."

Both men tensed, their expressions growing serious.

"I'm sorry to hear that," Heolstor said quietly. "She was a good woman."

"Aye," Bridei added. "I'm sorry too, Hea."

The way he said her name made a shiver feather across Hea's skin. Bridei unnerved her. It had been years since she had seen him last, and in the past she had adored him, looking up at him as a figure of romance and protection—an image that had never been real.

Things were different now.

The man before her was no romantic figure she could admire from afar but a very real, virile man. A man used to getting what he wanted. It did not matter that his nearness caused all rational thought to flee her mind; she needed to be wary of him.

"I must go." Hea stepped around the men and nodded briskly at them. "I bid you both a good day."

Neither Bridei nor Heolstor spoke as she hurried away.

JAYNE CASTEL

Chapter Eight

The Shadow of War

THE KING WAS waiting for Hea when she entered the alcove. She sensed his presence the moment she pushed back the hanging and stepped inside, her bare feet crunching on fresh rushes underfoot.

Ecgfrith sat near a small window upon a wooden chair that was draped in a thick wolf's pelt. The wooden shutters were open, letting in the pale afternoon light. Beyond, the sky was colorless as the day grew chill. The king did not look at Hea, instead he gazed out the window, his expression introspective.

Hea clutched her small, leather drum to her breast and steadied her breathing. She had sprinted back here from home after retrieving the drum. "Apologies for the delay, milord," she gasped. "I came as quickly as I could."

Ecgfrith turned from the window and shrugged, before favoring her with a smile. "Worry not, the delay gave me time to think."

Hea smiled back, relieved that Bridei's arrival had not completely soured Ecgfrith's mood. However, she could see the king had been brooding and would be wanting answers. "Shall we begin?"

Ecgfrith nodded, and Hea made her way into the center of the alcove where a goatskin rug spread across the rushes. There, she sank to the ground and folded her legs neatly under her. The king rose from his chair and crossed to her, sinking down onto the rug opposite. It was a familiar ritual for them both.

Meeting her gaze, Ecgfrith smiled once more—this time the expression was warm, and oddly boyish. "I value your counsel, Hea. I'm glad you're here."

His words caught her off guard. "It's a privilege to serve you, sire."

He waved her polite words away. "Aye—but I hope you enjoy putting your gift to good use as well."

Hea dipped her head. "I do ... and I'll help you in any way I can."

She meant it too, although truthfully she was not in the mood for divining today. Her nerves were on edge, her thoughts in tatters. They kept turning to the arrogant Pictish lord. Bridei would not let her be.

Hea inhaled deeply, bracing herself. She would need to push her own thoughts about Bridei far from her mind, if she was to enter a dream state and seek answers for the king. She met Ecgfrith's steady hazel gaze. "What is it you wish to know, milord?"

His mouth twitched. "I remember Bridei mac Beli as little more than a cocksure upstart—yet now he returns to Bebbanburg like a conquering hero."

"His presence here bothers you, milord?"

Ecgfrith screwed his face up. "I raised that boy as my own, yet I fear he now sees me as his enemy ... I want to know why he has come, and what he's plotting."

Hea set her small drum between them and gathered her thoughts. In order to connect with the other side, she had to concentrate. The world she was about to enter did not like to be troubled by mortals. She would need to relax, to shut her mind off to all else.

"Give me your hand, sire."

Ecgfrith obeyed, reaching out his right hand. She took it, before placing her own hand upon his outstretched palm, her fingertips resting lightly upon his wrist. It was an intimate gesture, one that a lover or a mother might make. Initially, sitting this close to him and touching the king had made Hea uncomfortable; yet these days she was accustomed to it. As always, Ecgfrith's hand was cool and strong, his fingers long and finely molded; the hand of an intelligent man.

The king sat watching her steadily. He could have an unnerving calmness about him at times.

Hea closed her eyes and focused on clearing her mind; she blocked out the sunlight flowing into the alcove, the chatter of voices in the hall beyond. Everything receded into the shadow. Suddenly there was nothing but this still, dark place. She stood upon the threshold between two worlds.

With her free hand, she began to beat the drum. She started slowly, tapping in time with Ecgfrith's pulse, which she felt with her forefinger. Once again it was an intimate gesture between them. Yet doing so did not make Hea nervous.

Fortunately, the king had never shown any sexual interest in her.

Hea breathed deeply and slowly in time with the rhythmic beating of her drum. She relaxed further and the world around her receded. Suddenly there was nothing except for the dark, shimmering water of a great lake before her. A moment later she was no longer staring down at it, but swimming deep under the surface—only to find that it was not a lake but a dark void.

She had entered the land of shadow where her ancestors dwelt.

Over the past year Hea had often thought of going in search of her mother here, but Lewren had vehemently forbidden her from doing so, telling her that it was folly for a seer to go looking for dead relatives on the other side. It was a misuse of their gift, her mother had told her, and that to do so would only end in madness.

Hea drifted, weightless, through the darkness, remembering her mother's warning that the other side did not welcome the living; and that those who dwelt here only barely tolerated the presence of folk like her. Even so Hea was glad to be here. She enjoyed the peace, and the darkness and solitude that cocooned her. Around her the shadows swirled and gathered. She saw the outlines of figures— men and women—some of them still, others dancing and flitting in the shadows.

Out of the darkness she heard a chorus of voices; a few whispering, while some were more strident. They knew she was here, but did not seem to mind.

When she reached their midst, Hea halted and stretched out her hand. Silently, she called out to them, making her request on Ecgfrith's behalf.

A heartbeat passed, and she felt the air shift around her. Moments earlier it had been calm; the spirits had not been bothered by her presence. But now she felt them stir. The voices changed; muttering and hissing now filled her ears. Sometimes this happened when she delved deep and requested things on behalf of the king.

The spirit world rebelled against the arrogance of his requests. The living could not cheat death, and should not know what wyrd, fate, held in store. This time she felt the resistance keenly. Would Ecgfrith be satisfied with the answers she found here today?

Hea's eyes snapped open.

A few feet away, the king was watching her, his gaze keen. "You were away for a while," he noted. "I hope that bodes well?"

Hea blinked, her surroundings rushing back. It felt as if she had been gone for days rather than moments. Even though the alcove was dimly lit, her eyes smarted from the flickering candlelight and the last rays of sun that poured in from the open window.

"What did you discover?" the king pressed.

Hea closed her eyes, sorting through the fragments of detail she had learned while she had been on the other side. "They have a warning for you, milord," she said finally.

Ecgfrith's eyes widened. "Go on."

Hea released his hand, breaking the connection between them. "They say the shadow of war hangs over the north."

The king made a scoffing sound. "When hasn't it," he replied. "What else do the spirits say?"

Hea held his gaze and fought a wry smile. Ecgfrith did not really understand her gift of second sight. Hea certainly could not control the messages she received when she ventured into the world of the dead. "They say that a man must not underestimate his enemies," she replied. "Whether you instigate it or not, war is coming."

Ecgfrith leaned forward, eyes gleaming. "From whom? The south? The north. From across the sea? Is it Bridei I have to look out for or someone else?"

Hea shook her head. "They only say you must be ready, sire, for the days of peace are coming to an end."

Ecgfrith gave a huff of frustration. He then rose to his feet and brushed off his breeches. "Those spirits of yours ... why must they always speak in riddles?"

Hea watched him. Ecgfrith wore a long tunic girded at the waist with a heavy belt that had a gilded buckle. Dressed simply, he was not a physically imposing man. However, he had presence, and Hea could see how some women might find him attractive.

She climbed to her feet and picked up her drum. "The spirit world does not give away its secrets easily, milord," she replied. "You should be grateful for what you have learned today—few leaders get such a warning."

Ecgfrith's gaze widened at her tone. Few women would dare challenge him thus; yet over the past few months Hea had grown comfortable in his company. After a few moments he smiled. "You're right, Hea. I grow impatient that's all. I would like to know into the hearts and minds of men like Bridei mac Beli. I want to know whether he is here to slide a knife between my ribs, or whether he has some other subtler plan."

Hea answered with a smile of her own. "Then perhaps you need to speak plainly with him."

A chill, sunless afternoon was sliding into a grey dusk when Hea walked back toward home. Around her the daily life of Bebbanburg was drawing to its usual conclusion. The market before the low gate had packed up for the day and folk were returning to their homes. The smell of cook fires drifted through the cool air, and she inhaled the aroma of roasting mutton and the sulfurous odor of overcooked cabbage and turnip.

Hea passed the mead hall. It was a long, low-slung and windowless building with a thatched roof. The hall crouched between a byre and an armory; it was the only part of the fortress that was busy at this time of day, for many of the men residing here—warriors, merchants, tradesmen and farmers—came to the mead hall for company and conversation at the end of a long, hard day's work. A group of leather-clad warriors waited outside the entrance to the hall. They were Picts—their plaid cloaks and blue tattoos made them stand out amongst the other men inside the fort— although Bridei was not among them.

She felt the weight of the Picts' stares, their curiosity, as they gazed upon her red hair. One of them gave a low whistle as she passed, while his companions followed it up with laughter. Hea did not dignify them with a response, but kept walking, ignoring the catcalls of appreciation that followed her. She had learned over the years that the best response to men like this was no response at all—it just seemed to encourage them.

Hea continued on, following the Dragon's Back. She passed numerous timber dwellings, and heard the clank of iron pots as women prepared supper, along with the chorus and rumble of children's and men's voices from within.

A sense of well-being flowed over Hea. She felt safe here within the high wooden palisade; as if the rest of the world could never intrude. However, if her visions were true, the peace she had known since birth was rapidly drawing to a close. The messages she had received from the spirit world had been jumbled and difficult to decipher, as usual, but the threat of war had been clear.

Her belly clinched at the thought that everything she knew and loved might be at risk. Invaders, whether from the north or the south, might attack her home.

Hea's thoughts turned to Bridei then. Despite her warm memories of him, despite the fact that she had once worshipped him, she knew the Picts posed a very real threat to Northumbria. If the warnings from the other world were to be believed, Bridei mac Beli was a herald of dark tidings.

Turning right off the Dragon's Back, Hea made her way through the tangle of alleys toward her home. A sudden memory of that day years ago now, when Bridei had broken Rinan's nose, intruded. He had truly been her savior that day. Yet the man who had returned to Bebbanburg and now sought audience with Ecgfrith could very well turn out to be her enemy.

Chapter Nine

The King and the Steward

BRIDEI PICKED UP the figurine and eyed Ecgfrith across the board. "It seems you have me at a disadvantage."

The Northumbrian king meet his eye and gave a cool smile. "It was you who chose the weaker of the two armies," he pointed out.

The two men played Cyningtaefl—King's Table—a game where two unequal armies fought upon a checkered board. The black pieces, which gathered at the center of the board, represented the weaker force of the two, with the fewest pieces; whereas the white pieces that ringed the edge of the board made up the stronger.

It was true that Ecgfrith had let Bridei choose which army he would lead. It was also true that the Pict had deliberately chosen the black army. Bridei smiled back, showing his teeth this time. "I like taking the side of the underdog."

Ecgfrith threw his head back and laughed, a deep belly laugh that unlike his smile moments earlier was genuine. "I'd forgotten your pithy sense of humor," he remarked.

It was growing late. Most of the king's hall had retired to their alcoves or had laid out furs on the floor around the four fire pits. The embers in the hearths burned low, casting a red-hued light across the space. A few oil-filled cressets lined the pitted stone walls, illuminating the table upon the high seat where the two men sat playing Cyningtaefl.

Bridei completed his move, shifting the carven piece forward a square, toward one of Ecgfrith's spearmen. His opponent's mouth quirked. "A prudent though conservative move."

Bridei shrugged. "I'm not a man given to acting without thinking first."

Ecgfrith raised an eyebrow, observing Bridei coolly. "We're alone now," he replied. "I think it's time we both spoke our minds."

Bridei sat back and took a sip from his wooden cup of mead at his elbow. "I don't understand why you wouldn't do so earlier."

"I'd rather not have an audience. Some conversations are best kept private."

Bridei observed Ecgfrith. He did not trust this man, not for a moment. He knew the Northumbrian lord to be cunning, and if this was some new ploy he was already on his guard. "Very well ... I'm here to discuss the nature of our relationship," he replied.

Ecgfrith held his gaze. "It's clear: I am your overlord and you are my steward of the north."

Bridei inhaled deeply, gathering his thoughts. Even though he had been expecting this, Ecgfrith's response galled him. There it was—the thing that rankled him the most. This Northumbrian king, a man who had never set foot in Dundurn, sat here before him and calmly claimed rule over lands he had stolen.

"Unlike my father, I'm not a man who suffers an overlord," he countered. "Surely you've heard of my attack on Dunnottar, my campaign against Orcadia, and the war with Dàl Riata?"

Ecgfrith's expression did not change as he nodded. "I have—and I complimented you earlier today on your prowess as a warlord. Do you wish me to congratulate you again?"

Bridei forced back a smile. His dislike for Ecgfrith ran deep—but the man's dry wit amused him nonetheless. "I mention those campaigns again because they show what sort of man I am. I'm not your steward but a king in my own right—and I ask you to recognize me as such."

There it was—the reason for his visit had been laid between them.

He would no longer be ignored.

Ecgfrith picked up his king figurine. It was a beautiful piece, carved out of bone and yellowing with age. "So you see yourself as my equal?"

"I do."

"Your father bent the knee to me ... yet you will not?"

"I don't wish to be your enemy, Ecgfrith," Bridei replied, his tone unyielding. "I only wish to reclaim my lands."

The king stared down at the figurine, studying it, although Bridei could see that in reality Ecgfrith's mind was working, scheming—trying to turn this situation to his advantage.

"I don't wish to make an enemy of you either, Bridei," he said quietly. "However, if I give you independence, I will be seen as weak."

Bridei watched him carefully, on guard now. This was a new side to Ecgfrith, one he had never seen before. Yet he was sure it was a ruse. Ecgfrith was not a weak man and was certainly not a weak ruler. He cared little for how others perceived him.

As such, Bridei decided he would not soften. He would not try to negotiate with the Northumbrian ruler. That was what Ecgfrith wanted; to weave a net around Bridei with his words, to ensnare him and make him agree to something he did not want. Far better to speak plainly and avoid confusion.

"Recognize me as an independent ruler of the north, and we shall part as friends," he said.

Ecgfrith sighed heavily and placed the king figurine down with a gentle thud. His gaze met Bridei's once more. "I can't do that. The lands you oversee are mine—they are part of Northumbria."

Bridei shook his head, quelling the anger that rose within him. "My people and I will not suffer your yoke."

Ecgfrith picked up his cup and drained the dregs, waving Bridei away as if he were a moth that had just fluttered into his field of vision. "Come now, it is late—let us discuss this further tomorrow."

"There's nothing to discuss," Bridei ground out. "It's simple—give me what I want, and I will never bother you again. Deny me and you will wish you hadn't."

Ecgfrith rose to his feet. They had not finished the game, but since the conversation had taken a turn for the worse neither man was in the mood for it. "Words have power," Ecgfrith reproved him softly. "Don't make threats unless you intend to follow-through on them."

Bridei's gaze narrowed. "I don't talk merely to hear the sound of my own voice," he replied, his tone equally soft. "I meant every word."

The two men held gazes for a few moments more. Ecgfrith broke eye contact first, a sardonic smile curving his lips. "You were a conceited lordling when you lived here," he said finally, "and I can see your arrogance has only increased with age. It seems I must repeat myself: we will discuss this again tomorrow. Make sure you think hard on how you will approach me then."

Without another word, King Ecgfrith turned, stepped down from the high seat and made his way across the hall to toward his alcove.

It was a dark and moonless night as Bridei walked through Bebbanburg. Cool air, laced with the scent of wood smoke and the briny tang of the sea caught in the back of his throat. Muffled sounds of voices emerged from behind wattle doors and wooden shutters. Beyond that he heard the boom and hiss of surf on the shore below, accompanied by the roar of the wind.

The song of Bebbanburg, so different to Dundurn.

Sometimes within this wooden palisade it was easy to forget that they perched on the edge of the sea. Yet the rumble of the surf was a constant reminder when all other sounds ceased.

Bridei's men, including Heolstor, had all retired for the night, but after his conversation with the Ecgfrith, Bridei could not settle. Anger and bitter resentment churned in the pit of his belly. Years on, and Ecgfrith still knew exactly where to aim, what words would rile him the most.

Bridei had bested many men over the years and had subdued many a northern war chief. He had brought lands that his father had lost under his control. But the one territory he wanted was the one his fort of Dundurn stood upon. That was his land, and he would not share it with Ecgfrith of Northumbria.

Deep in thought, he walked down to the empty market square and looked around. Fires burned in the watch towers above, and he could see the outlines of men on the walls, their spears bristling against the night sky. Bebbanburg was both familiar and foreign; after so many years away it felt odd to return here.

As a boy this fort had seemed bigger, more imposing. As a man he realized that his memories had made the stronghold far greater than the reality. Ecgfrith was just a man, and a man could have his mind changed. He would have one more chance tomorrow to bend Ecgfrith to his will. Bridei was not afraid of war—he had waged many in the past five years— but he knew that the Northumbrian king could be a powerful ally, if kept onside.

I won't lose my temper, he promised himself. *Tomorrow I will make one last attempt at negotiations.*

Bridei found himself walking along the Dragon's Back; a street he had once spent many an afternoon on with Heolstor, as a lad. Once again, his memory of this street had been grander, the walls around him higher.

I was shorter then too, Bridei recalled with a rueful smile.

Without realizing, it his feet carried him toward the end of the Dragon's Back. Then he turned right down a narrow lane that led toward the fort's northern watch tower.

A short while later he found himself standing before a familiar hovel. It looked exactly as he remembered it. He could see the outline of the high, wooden fence behind which Lewren had grown her herbs and flowers. The news that Hea's mother had passed away still shocked him. Lewren had been a force of nature; he could not imagine her gone.

Hea lived here alone now.

The thought made Bridei frown—it was not safe for a young, attractive woman like Hea to live unprotected, even in Bebbanburg.

She must have the king's protection, he thought. *She's his seer, but what other services does she provide him.*

The thought made Bridei's frown deepen. The thought of the winsome Hea lying beneath Ecgfrith disturbed him—although truthfully, he had thought about her rarely over the years. When he had, Bridei had imagined her to be wedded with a brood of children by now. He had not expected her to follow her mother's path. As beautiful and fiery as Lewren had been, there had also been sadness in her that ran deep. A woman who chose an independent path made a difficult life for herself.

Bridei was not sure why he had come here, but now that he stood outside the seer's door he hesitated.

Seeing Hea again had been a pleasant surprise. Thoughts of her had distracted him all day ... but was it wise to take things any further? Bridei had lain with his share of women over the years, although he had not shared the furs with another since Mid-Winter Fire. Over the bitter months there had been much to take care of, including a number of skirmishes and uprisings to deal with. His body ached for release.

I shouldn't be here, he thought and took a step back. Whatever Ecgfrith's response, he would be leaving here soon. *I should let her be.*

Yet he did not move. Instead, he stared at the timber door before him. The temptation was too great—he had to see her.

Pushing his misgivings aside Bridei stepped forward once more and knocked on the door.

Chapter Ten

Honeyed Words

HEA WAS SITTING by the fire pit, enjoying a cup of damson wine and whittling a piece of rose wood when someone knocked. Surprised, she glanced up. Few people visited her after dark, and she preferred it that way.

The evening was her quiet time, and especially after the day she'd had, Hea felt in need of some solitude.

With a sigh, she got to her feet and crossed to the door.

"Who is it?" she called.

"Hea? It's me ... Bridei."

Hea went still. *What is he doing here?*

Long moments passed before she reluctantly reached out and lifted the heavy wooden bar that locked her inside; living alone, she could never be too careful.

She then opened the door and peered out into the dimly lit street beyond.

He was standing there, a few feet back from the door, watching her. Dressed simply, in plaid breeches and a leather vest which left his muscular arms bare, Bridei was as disarming as earlier. Shadows played across his handsome features as he observed her, giving her that same intense melting look that had flustered her so easily earlier in the day.

Hea met his gaze. She could not say she was pleased to see him, for she knew it was unwise for them to spend time alone together.

"Good eve, Hea," he said, smiling.

She held his stare. "Why are you here?"

He grinned. "That wasn't the sort of greeting I was expecting."

She frowned. "What did you expect?"

"A smile at least for an old friend." His smile was both sensual and infuriating; the swine knew the effect he had on her. He had known from the moment they had locked eyes inside the Great Hall.

"You shouldn't be here, Bridei," she said quietly.

His gaze widened. "Why? Are we forbidden to speak?"

"No, it's not that ... it's just this isn't a good idea."

"Why not?"

Hea huffed out a breath. He was deliberately being obtuse. He wanted her to speak plainly.

"You're a guest here," she said eventually, "and I am the king's seer—we shouldn't be spending time together."

Bridei snorted, making it clear that he cared not for her concerns. "Is it wrong for me to visit someone who was dear to me in the past?"

Hea exhaled sharply. While they tarried here in the doorway, someone was sure to walk past and spot them. It was clear that Bridei was not going away, so she decided it was best he came indoors.

Stepping back, she motioned for him to enter.

Bridei entered the dwelling, ducking his head to avoid hitting it on the lintel. Indoors, the hovel was much smaller than he remembered. However, he immediately felt welcome in here. Despite the slight fug of wood smoke, he caught the scent of lavender as his boots crunched over straw and scattered herbs. The dwelling was simply furnished, the wattle and daub walls unadorned. A small hearth dominated the center of the space and bunches of dried herbs hung from the low ceiling beams; a small wattle door led out into the enclosed garden beyond. Against the far wall he spied a pile of soft furs.

His gaze halted on the furs, his breath catching as he imagined lying naked with Hea upon them, their limbs entangled.

"Sit."

Hea's voice, edged with annoyance, pulled Bridei sharply out of his reverie. He realized she had seen the direction of his gaze and guessed at his thoughts. Unembarrassed, Bridei moved over to a low stool next to the hearth and lowered himself onto it. Seeing irritation flare in her eyes, he suppressed a smile.

He liked feisty women.

"Wine?" she asked with cool politeness.

"Aye, thank you."

He watched her move to a worktable near a tiny, shuttered window, and uncover an earthen jug. "It's damson," she said, reaching for a cup. "I hope that's to your liking ..."

"My favorite."

Hea glanced over her shoulder at him, another frown marring her smooth brow. "You've a honeyed tongue, Bridei mac Beli. Is there any woman alive you haven't charmed?"

He laughed, not remotely fazed by her directness. "Only one," he murmured, holding her gaze.

To his delight, her cheeks reddened slightly and she turned away, busying herself with pouring the wine. Her embarrassment pleased him, it meant that despite her frosty welcome, he affected her. He watched her pour the wine, his gaze sliding over her comely form.

He liked her green wealca, different from the long, plaid ankle-length skirts that Pictish women wore. The color suited her fiery hair and complemented her creamy skin, while the cloth hugged her curves.

Turning from the table, Hea crossed to the hearth and handed him a cup of wine. He took it, deliberately allowing their fingers to brush as he did so. A shiver of heat rippled up his arm, and he saw her eyes widen; she had felt that too.

Hea took a seat opposite him, on the other side of the fire, sitting primly while she picked up her own cup of wine and cradled it on her lap. He noted that she had lovely hands—small but with long, elegant fingers. His gaze then shifted to a piece of wood that she had set by the hearth with a whittling knife.

"Am I interrupting you?" he asked, quirking an eyebrow.

Hea saw the direction of his gaze and shook her head, her full mouth curving into a smile. "Not really, I was trying to carve my mother's likeness, but I lack talent I'm afraid."

"Can I take a look?"

Hea shrugged. "If you want." She leaned down, picked up the half-finished figure and passed it across to him. "But please don't laugh—I know it's crude."

Bridei took the piece of rose wood and studied it a moment. "You're too hard on yourself," he said after a few moments. "You need to spend a bit more time on her face and hair, but you're almost there."

"Now you're humoring me."

Bridei looked up, his gaze snaring hers. "No, I'm not." He passed the carving back to her. "Make sure you finish it."

She nodded, her face relaxing slightly. "I will, even if it doesn't look anything like her." He watched her gaze into the glowing embers of the hearth, sadness darkening her eyes. "It's only been a year—I still miss her so much."

Bridei did not reply. He had already lost both his parents, and knew what it felt like. Yet for him it had been different—he had not been as close to either his mother or father as Hea had been to Lewren.

"It must be hard continuing to live in here," he said finally, gesturing to the one-room dwelling in which they sat. "Surrounded by memories."

She nodded, and Bridei saw her eyes gleam with unshed tears. "Aye ... sometimes. She wanted a different life for me."

"What do you mean?"

Hea sighed and straightened up, brushing her wild, dark-red curls back off her shoulders. "She told me not to follow her path, to find a good man and have a family."

"But you didn't heed her ..."

Hea raised her cup of wine to her lips and took a sip. "She raised me to be free—I don't want to give that up."

Bridei watched her, intrigued. "But surely, life for you here is hard, without a man to provide for you."

She shrugged, and bestowed him with a tight smile. "It was ... until the king began asking for me."

Bridei took a draft from his cup, relaxing as the strong liquid burned down his throat and into his belly. The mention of Ecgfrith irritated him. "I don't understand the nature of your relationship," he said finally. "What does a Christian king need of a seer?"

Hea met his gaze steadily for a moment before she replied. "I wondered the same thing, but I know he'd asked my mother for guidance in the past. He's a complex man—and sometimes I feel as if he's torn between two worlds. You must remember Eanflaed, his mother?"

Bridei screwed up his face. "Aye—haughty old crone."

Hea laughed. "I think she forced the new ways down his throat ... and then he ended up wedding two incredibly pious women."

Bridei raised his eyebrows. "It sounds as if you feel sorry for him."

Hea pulled a face. "I don't ... I just realize that folk are the way they are for a reason."

"Irmenburgh isn't happy with your arrangement," Bridei replied. "I've seen the way she looks at you."

Hea sighed heavily. "I can't help that—I can't defy Ecgfrith because his wife disapproves."

"But ... is your skill as a seer the only service he requires of you?"

Bridei had not meant to ask the question. He had been thinking it, and then suddenly the words rushed out of him.

They fell like axe blows in the suddenly silent dwelling.

He watched Hea draw herself up, her face paling, her green eyes burning. Long moments passed before she responded. "Why would you ask that?"

Bridei held her gaze. The look on her face told him he had just made a mistake, yet to try and back out now would make him look like a fool. Now that he had stumbled out into dangerous territory, he had no choice but to keep blundering forward. Inwardly he kicked himself.

"It's a natural enough question," he replied slowly. "You're a comely woman, and he's a man still in his prime wedded to a wife he clearly doesn't desire. The whole fort must think you're lovers."

Hea's mouth drew in. "Well the lot of you are mistaken." She rose to her feet, her small frame stiff with indignation. "I think it's time you left."

Bridei set down his cup and got to his feet. "Hea, I—"

"Just go." She turned her back on him and stalked over to the table, slamming her cup down next to the earthen jug of wine.

Bridei ignored her command, instead following her over to where she still had her back to him. "I'm sorry, Hea," he began, contrite. "I really should—"

She whipped around to face him, tilting her face up so that their gazes met. "Have you got cloth in your ears? I told you to leave."

Irritation rose within him. She might have been comely, but she had a tongue like a seax-blade. "And I will, but not before I put things right. I didn't mean to offend you."

"Well you did."

"Will you forgive me?"

Her brow furrowed. "You really are used to women falling at your feet, aren't you?"

Bridei drew back slightly, surprised at her vehemence. He saw that he really had hurt her. Their gazes held for a few moments before he attempted a boyish, lopsided smile, one that usually melted even the angriest shrew. "There's only one woman I wish would soften toward me."

"You've just accused me of being the king's hōre," she countered. "Do you think a smile and a half-hearted apology will suffice?"

Bridei started to feel flustered. This was not going well. Instead of winning her over, he was just digging a bigger hole for himself. Her nearness was also unsettling him. He was aware of the heat of her body, the light musk of her skin, and the scent of lavender from her clothing. It suddenly felt too warm inside the tiny hovel.

"I don't—" he began, only to be cut off once more.

"Just get out."

"For the love of the gods, woman," he growled, his temper flaring. "Won't you at least let me explain myself?"

"I don't want to listen to your insincere excuses," she shot back. "You meant what you said, I don't need your lies."

Bridei cursed, frustrated beyond measure.

Then, without stopping to think for a moment about the consequences, he reached out and pulled her against him—kissing her fiercely.

Chapter Eleven

The Wild Night

IT HAPPENED SO suddenly that Hea did not have time to react.

One moment she had been glaring up at Bridei, her fists clenched by her sides as she resisted the urge to slap his face, the next she was in his arms.

Hea had never been kissed before. An overprotective mother, followed by an overbearing king had kept all would-be suitors at bay. She had seen couples kiss at the spring celebrations of Eōstre before some of them slipped away to spend the night together. Sometimes their embraces had seemed awkward, at other times she had sighed at the obvious passion between them.

But she had never expected this.

The feel of his arms about her, the firm, softness of his lips on hers, ignited a hunger deep within her belly that made the world spin.

She gasped, her lips parting, and his tongue delved into her mouth, dancing with her own.

The kindling fire in her belly burst into flame.

How could the act of fusing mouths with a man affect her like this? It was just skin against skin, yet it was as if a strong wind had gusted in and lifted her off her feet.

Her surroundings disappeared. No longer was she standing in the corner of her one-room hovel—instead she was flying, spinning out of control, pleasure thrumming through her body.

Her anger at him—which had been nothing more than hurt and shame—dissolved. She could think of nothing but how good he tasted, how warm and strong his body was, and how she melted against him like a pat of butter on a hot griddle.

The rasp of his chin, the warmth and the scent of his skin, and the possessive way he kissed her, caused all rational thought to scatter.

When Bridei finally pulled away from her, breathing hard as if he had been running, Hea nearly cried out in disappointment.

Releasing her, he took a step back, a rush of cool air flooding between them. He stared at her, his brown eyes almost black in the dim light of the hearth and the two oil-filled cressets burning on the walls. He looked shocked; his lips were slightly parted and gone was the teasing, arrogant expression he had worn since entering her home.

The kiss had knocked them both off guard.

Need twisted deep within Hea as she stared back at him. He had only given her a taste of what she craved; she could not let him take it away. She felt as if she would die if he did not kiss her again.

Moving on instinct, all rational thought now gone, she stepped forward and placed her palms upon his chest. Through the leather of his vest, she felt his heart pound. A thrill went through her—she was not the only one struggling to keep control.

Then, she went up on tip-toe and kissed him.

Bridei's low growl, at the back of his throat, unleashed a ravenous appetite within her. She flung her arms about his neck, her mouth opening under his.

Two steps brought them back, hard against the table. The edge of it dug into Hea's back, but she paid it no mind. All she cared about, all she wanted, was this man.

His hands dug into her hair as they kissed wildly, tongues tangling. Then his hands were tearing at her clothing. He unfastened the brooches which held up the straps to her wealca, and pushed the garment down, leaving her standing in the thin tunic she wore underneath. His hands left her hair and traveled down her body, cupping her bottom.

He lifted her onto the table, pulling up her tunic so that her legs were exposed.

Panting now, Hea spread her legs, wrapping them around his hips and pulling him against her as they kissed once more. She could feel his arousal, iron-hard, pressed against her belly, and excitement coursed through her.

She wanted to see him, touch him.

Frantically, she began clawing at his vest, at the laces on the sides. She had to feel his skin, taste it.

With a muttered curse, Bridei pulled away from her and yanked off his vest. The sight of his naked, muscular torso, the skin decorated with blue-inked swirls and circles down his left side, made Hea's mouth go dry.

Once again acting on instinct, she leaned forward and kissed the hollow of his neck, her lips trailing down his chest to the hard nubs of his nipples, while she traced the skin of his back with her finger nails.

She felt him shiver under her touch, heard him moan.

Hea looked up to find Bridei staring down at her, a look of feral need on his face.

Wild excitement soared within her, and a deep throbbing began between her thighs.

If she did not have him inside her, she would dissolve from wanting.

Holding her gaze, Bridei reached down and started to unlace his breeches. Hea watched him, forgetting to breathe—yet when she saw his shaft spring free, her breath rushed out of her.

He was beautiful.

Almost shyly now, she reached out and touched him, her fingertips tracing the soft skin, to the swollen head that glistened in the firelight. She then wrapped her fingers and around his girth, marveling at its size and hardness.

"For the love of the gods," he growled, his voice strangled. "Are you trying to kill me, woman?"

Hea glanced up at him, confused. "Kill you?"

His beautiful mouth twisted. Then he pushed her tunic high around her hips, so she was exposed to him and positioned himself between her thighs.

Hea felt the head of his shaft pressing against her, and her desire ebbed slightly.

Would this hurt?

Slowly, he slid into her—halting when he hit resistance. Bridei tensed. Hea clung to him, burying her face in the crook of his neck.

"Hea …" he began, hesitant, his voice husky. "I didn't realize … I'm sorry."

Hea barely registered his words, the throbbing ache at her core was almost unbearable. She did not see what he had to be sorry about; whether it hurt her or not she wanted him deep inside her.

"Please, Bridei," she whimpered.

Gripping her firmly against him, he thrust into her.

A sharp, stinging pain knifed through Hea, and she gasped. It did hurt— his flesh had invaded hers, driving to her core. She clung to him, eyes squeezed shut for a moment, her body tensing.

"Be still," Bridei murmured in her ear. "The worst should be over now."

Hea nodded, although she did not believe him. After a moment though she relaxed her body and became aware of the delicious, deep throbbing at the point where their bodies were joined, an odd, rippling pleasure that almost felt as if she was being tickled on the inside.

"Oh," she whispered. "What's that?"

He gave a soft laugh, withdrew slightly and slid with her once more. "What … this?"

Hea gasped before letting out a soft moan. "Bridei … I …"

But the time for speaking was over. He thrust into her again, and again—and she was lost. Hea arched back, her breasts, barely covered by her tunic thrusting up at him, her nipples like two hard berries. Bridei bowed his head and suckled one of her breasts through the thin material. Then, with a grunt of frustration, he grabbed the hem of the tunic and pulled it up over her head, exposing her nakedness to him.

Hea had never been naked in front of a man before, and under normal circumstances would have looked for something to cover herself up with— but not so now. She was lost; carried away on the crest of a wave. She wanted Bridei to see her nude body; she wanted him to touch it.

"Hea," he groaned her name like a prayer. "You're magnificent."

In a wordless response, she spread her legs further and wrapped them around his hips, pulling him hard against her. The rippling pleasure was building inside her, reaching for something she could not name.

Bridei lost control. He thrust into her again and again, all restraint gone. Moments later, she watched him throw back his head, his cry of release echoing through the dwelling.

They clung together in the aftermath, their ragged breathing and the gentle crack and pop of the hearth behind them, the only sound. After a short while, Bridei pulled back from Hea slightly, pushing a lock of sweat-damp hair out of his eyes. He stared down at her, his gaze devouring her flushed face, dark eyes, and bee-stung lips. Despite that he had just climaxed, he felt himself harden inside her once more.

Hea's gaze widened, and he responded with a rueful smile. "I meant for our coupling to last longer than that ... I forgot myself."

She gave him a dreamy smile in response. "It was wonderful."

"Yes ... but I wanted to give you more."

Confusion flitted across her face, and Bridei felt an uncharacteristic pang of self-recrimination. This woman was a force of nature—untamed and incredibly responsive—yet despite that she was still an innocent. Even though he had apologized to her about insinuating she was the king's whore, part of him had not believed that she was still a maid. How could such an attractive, earthy woman never have taken a lover? Yet their coupling had just proved it.

His comment just now had confused her; she had no idea what it could be like between a man and woman. She thought their frantic, wild coupling was the only experience to be had. A slow smile spread across Bridei's face—he would enjoy teaching her that there was so much more pleasure to be explored.

Hea noted his smile and frowned. "What?"

Bridei's smile widened. "I'm just reflecting on the fact that the night is still young, and there's much I want to show you."

She gazed up at him, her full lips parting slightly. He stared at them, hunger curling up from the pit of his belly once more. His shaft was now rock-hard inside her again. In wordless answer, her thighs tightened around him.

Their gazes locked, and desire pulsed between them.

Bridei's smile faded. He was done talking—he wanted to spend the rest of the night letting their bodies get to know each other. He picked Hea up, holding her hard against him, and carried her across to the furs.

Hea stirred, waking slowly. She lay on her belly and awoke to the feel of a man's leg slung over her back, pressing her into the warm nest of furs. Bridei slept next to her, his breathing slow and deep.

She remained there for a few moments, savoring an incredible sense of well-being. Never had she felt so relaxed; her limbs felt loose and weightless, her head clear—and the dull, pleasant-ache between her thighs was a reminder of what she had spent the night doing.

Hea sighed softly. She had not understood Bridei when he had told her there was more pleasure to be had. But he had shown her what he meant ... repeatedly.

Heat flushed over her at the memories of what they had done together, of how he had pleasured her ... of all the ways he had taken her.

The night had been magical, unforgettable—and Hea wished she could snap her fingers and stop time.

No moment could ever be as perfect as this one.

Life would never be the same.

Breathing deeply, she rolled over onto her side, dislodging Bridei's leg as she did so. Outside, the day was breaking. Pale streams of sunlight filtered into the dwelling from the top of the door and cracks in the shutters, and the muted sounds of voices reached her as Bebbanburg began another day.

Hea propped herself up on an elbow and stared down at Bridei's sleeping face.

Freya save me, a man shouldn't be this beautiful.

Awake, Bridei mac Beli's face was harder, his expression more often than not arrogant. Asleep, the noble lines of his face were impossible to ignore. Gently, Hea reached out and stroked his stubbled cheek.

Bridei stirred at her touch, his eyes opening—his dark gaze spearing hers.

Chapter Twelve

Mark My Threats

"MORNING," HE SAID, his voice gravelly with sleep, "my flame-haired temptress."

Hea smiled back. "And good morning to you too—my honey-tongued lord."

Bridei laughed softly, before stretching. Hea's gaze slid along the length of his body, admiring his long, muscular limbs and the thatch of dark hair at his groin. She would never tire of gazing upon him.

Bridei sat up, pushing his hair off his face. "It's late," he murmured before giving a jaw-cracking yawn. "I should go."

"Do you want to break your fast first?" Hea asked. "I have some bread dough rising—I can cook you some on the griddle."

"No need to go to any trouble." Bridei leaned forward and kissed her before he climbed off the furs. "I should join my men. Today is important— it's the day all will be decided."

Hea watched him reach for his clothes, admiring his tight backside as he did so. "It's no trouble," she murmured. "I was going to make bread for myself anyway."

Bridei glanced over his shoulder and favored her with a disarming smile. "I have to get back."

She watched him dress, her gaze tracking every moment. She did not want him to leave, for this magical encounter to end. Yet like a dream that fades with the dawning of the sun, she could feel him slipping out of her reach.

"What will be decided today?" she asked, forcing herself to focus on the present. "I still have no idea why you're here in Bebbanburg."

Bridei buckled his belt and glanced up at her. "I traveled south to claim my independence," he replied, "but it appears your king is intent on denying me."

"You want independence?"

Bridei nodded before reaching for his vest and shrugging it on. "The lands to the north have no ties to the Angles or the Saxons. It is the land of the Picts—Ecgfrith must give it back."

Uneasiness churned in Hea's belly, shattering her sense of well-being. "Have you spoken privately with Ecgfrith?"

Bridei nodded. "Last eve, before coming here. He refuses."

A chill feathered over Hea's naked skin, and she wrapped a fur around her. "What will you do?"

"Speak with him once more today."

"And if he insists you will remain his sub-king?"

Bridei met her gaze once more, his brown eyes glinting. "I will never accept it."

Hea swallowed, her mouth suddenly dry.

What have I done? Her breathing quickened and she started to feel queasy. *I've just lain with my people's enemy.*

"I received warning from the spirit world yesterday, Bridei," she said after a few long moments. "The shadow of war looms over this land."

Surprise flickered across his features before he frowned. "Between whom?"

"It wasn't made clear to me—however, with the demands you're making it now falls into place."

His frown deepened. "My *demands*? Do you disapprove, Hea?"

Her own gaze narrowed. "I'm an Angle—of course I do." She watched him lace up his vest, the movements deft. "This is my land; I don't want to see it threatened."

"And Fortriu is *my* land—I want to see it freed."

"No, it is part of the kingdom, Bridei. Your father swore fealty to Ecgfrith, whether you wish it or not."

Bridei had finished dressing. He now stood still, watching her—too still. Hea realized she had succeeded in angering him.

"My people will not suffer a southern ruler," he said coldly, "and neither will I. Ecgfrith has one last chance to change his mind—or there will be war between us."

Hea stared at him, her heart pounding, her belly clenched. A few moments earlier she had felt the happiest woman alive, and now she felt miserable. With just a few words, the pair of them were now on opposite sides.

"And where does that leave us?" she asked. Her throat constricted, but she fought down the urge to weep. She would not show Bridei mac Beli her tears.

That made him pause, uncertainty flickering across his handsome features. "What do you mean?"

"Last night ... is that it?"

His mouth compressed. "I didn't plan for it to happen, Hea."

She pulled the fur tighter around her, as if it were a shield. "Really? Why else did you come here? To offer your condolences for my mother?"

The sharpness in her voice made his brow furrow. "I don't know why I came here," he replied, his tone wary. "I just needed to see you. Some things you don't plan—but that doesn't mean either of us should regret last night. I certainly don't."

Hea's lip curled. Of course he did not. It was so much easier for men— they did not have to bear the consequences of such things.

Seeing her reaction, Bridei took a step toward her and flashed a charming smile. "You could always come north with me and live in Dundurn."

Hea stiffened. She had never met anyone who spoke so thoughtlessly as Bridei. "You can't just say that," she managed finally. "You don't know what you're asking."

He raised an eyebrow. "Don't I?"

"Bebbanburg is my home. I serve Ecgfrith—and believe it or not, I am loyal to him."

A shadow crossed Bridei's face. "So loyal you'd spread your legs for his northern enemy—a Pict."

A chill silence followed his words.

Hea drew herself up, a red haze obscuring her vision. "Get out."

Their gazes fused and held for a few long moments—and unlike the night before, Bridei did not try to make amends. The air was raw between them, full of things unsaid, yet to say any more would just worsen the situation. Perhaps Bridei knew that, for he nodded curtly, turned and strode toward the door.

Hea watched him leave, the door shutting behind him with a hollow thud.

She did not move for a long while afterward.

King Ecgfrith of Northumbria took a sip from his cup and watched his northern guest. Bridei did not look in good humor today. He sat, a few feet away at the table upon the high seat, and had hardly touched the trencher of food before him.

"Is the venison not to your liking, Lord Bridei?" Ecgfrith asked.

Bridei glanced up. "The meat is good," he replied curtly. "I've no appetite, that's all."

They had gathered for the noon meal—the last meal they would share together before the Pict leader and his band departed for the north. Ecgfrith had seen Bridei's men, including that red-haired traitor, Heolstor, getting their horses ready earlier that morning. No matter the outcome of their discussions, Bridei did not intend to stay on another night at Bebbanburg.

Ecgfrith took another sip of mead, hiding a smile. Bridei's black mood pleased him. However, as he looked around the table, he became aware that Bridei was not the only one who looked strained. Hea, whom he had summoned here for the noon meal as well, was staring down at her trencher, her expression pained.

"Ecgfrith."

His wife's soft voice reached him, drawing the king away from the study of his seer. He turned his attention to Irmenburgh, frowning. "What?"

For once she actually met his gaze, although her blue eyes were timid. He thought of the first time he had seen her, years ago now. He had been smarting over the disaster of his first marriage. His first wife had been a dark, fiery beauty, but her passion had been reserved for God, and she had refused to lie with him. He had hoped his second wife, Irmenburgh, would be cut of a different cloth. He had heard she was pious, but then a lot of Angle and Saxon princesses were raised that way; as his own sisters had been.

His heart had sunk the first time he set eyes on her. His new wife was a thin, mousy woman, who had all the sensuality of a turnip. She had been better behaved than his first one, for she had not refused him. Although bedding her had been like rutting a corpse. She gave nothing in return, and after a few passionless couplings, he had started taking this pleasure elsewhere, as he had done before her arrival.

These days, he and Irmenburgh conversed little, and she rarely offered an opinion on anything. As such her manner today surprised him.

"My Lord, Think well on how you treat Bridei," she murmured, her voice barely above a whisper. "He was once like a son to us."

Ecgfrith sneered. "For you perhaps. Since you're barren, a Pict fosterling was the best you could hope for."

His wife flinched. "Bridei meant something to you as well—that was why he could anger you so. He has grown into a powerful man. Be wary of making an enemy of him."

Ecgfrith went still. "I don't need a woman's advice," he growled.

She stared back at him, her face paling, yet she did not back down. "Really? You constantly ask for Hea's counsel."

Ecgfrith stared at Irmenburgh. If they had been alone, he would have struck her for being so bold. "She has skills you do not."

"But I am your wife."

"You know little of the world beyond these walls, and nothing of what it means to rule."

Irmenburgh held his gaze, and he was surprised to see anger flare in the depths of her eyes. "I'm a daughter of kings—I know just as much as you."

Ecgfrith's temper flared. He slammed his fist down on the table before him. "Hold your tongue, woman!"

Silence descended upon the table, and all eyes swiveled to where the king and queen sat together. Ecgfrith found Bridei mac Beli watching him.

"I grow impatient, Lord Ecgfrith," the Pict said, his voice carrying across the table. "Come ... tell me your answer."

Beside Bridei, the red-headed warrior, Heolstor, cast his leader a look of censure—but Bridei ignored him. His gaze did not waver from Ecgfrith.

"Why the urgency?" Ecgfrith asked, taking another sip from his cup and trying to settle the fury that still seethed in his belly. He would deal with Irmenburgh's insolence later.

"I wish to return north."

Ecgfrith forced a smile. Clearly Bridei knew he was beaten and wished to slink home like the cur he was. This visit, and his arrogant demands had all been a bluff—one that did not intimidate Ecgfrith in the slightest.

He put down his cup and steepled his hands before him, his smile turning apologetic. "Have you forgotten so quickly?"

Bridei shook his head. "I forget nothing of what passed between us, but the matter didn't end there. I give you one last chance, Ecgfrith, to recognize my birthright and acknowledge me as a sovereign in my own right: King of the North."

Ecgfrith threw back his head and laughed. "Once again, you speak of this 'birthright'. What's that exactly? A man should earn what he has. The blood that runs through your veins doesn't give you the right to claim a land for your own. That land is mine, and always will be."

A heavy silence fell upon the heah-setl. Further down the table, Ecgfrith saw Rinan grin, clearly delighted by his king's firm stand. Opposite the blond warrior, the seer's face was strained. Hea's gaze flicked between the two leaders. Her expression was almost pleading.

Ecgfrith turned back to Bridei. "That is my final word. You can leave Bebbanburg as soon as you are ready."

Bridei said nothing. Instead he pushed himself back from the table and stood up. Next to him, Heolstor did the same, his expression grim.

Bridei's dark gaze speared Ecgfrith. "Thank you for making your position clear." His voice was calm, although his tone was flat, belying the rage that simmered just beneath the surface. "However, your decision will have consequences. I won't let this matter lie. Ready your fyrd, Ecgfrith—and prepare for war."

Ecgfrith waved him away. "Enough … I tire of your threats. Be gone from my hall, before I have my warriors drag you out."

Bridei went still, his expression turning hard. "Mark my threats, for I don't make them idly. The next time you and I meet, it will be on the battlefield."

Chapter Thirteen

Opposite Sides

HEA STRODE DOWN the King's Way, her skirts flapping around her legs and hampering her stride. She was eager to be gone from the Great Tower of Bebbanburg, to return to her home where she could lock herself away.

Where she could pretend the last day had never happened.

Her temples throbbed and she felt slightly ill—she could not believe what she had witnessed in the king's hall: two stags roaring and posturing, neither willing to back down. Ecgfrith and Bridei hated each other—that much was evident—but they were willing to draw others into their dispute. Because of the stubbornness of both men, war would come to the north.

Their bull-headed behavior sickened her.

She had left the hall to see Bridei with his men in the stableyard, preparing their horses for departure. The lilting sound of their voices as they called to each other in the Pict tongue had reminded her of how different Bridei's world was. She had brushed by a sinewy warrior, covered in blue swirls—the same color as his keen eyes which had fixed upon her. Next to him, a heavy-set man with long, dark braided hair had also glanced in her direction; he wore a voluminous blue and grey plaid cloak that reminded her of a winter's sky.

Finding both men intimidating, Hea had virtually run through their midst, deliberately keeping her head down lest their leader look her way. Bridei called out to her but she had pretended not to hear.

She did not want to speak to him—she only wanted to be alone.

"Hea!"

She stiffened, slowing her stride as she inwardly cursed him. The man had followed her. Clenching her jaw, Hea turned, steeling herself to face him.

Bridei had stopped close behind her. She raised her chin, meeting his gaze, and felt her breath rush out of her. He still affected her as strongly as he had the night before. Her breathing grew shallow, and her heart started to pound against her rib cage.

"I called out to you before," he said, unsmiling. "Didn't you hear me?"

"I heard you," she replied, folding her arms across her breasts.

"Why didn't you stop?"

She held his gaze. "You know why."

"No," he stepped closer to her, ignoring the crowds of townsfolk that passed by on the busy thoroughfare. "I don't."

Once again he was being deliberately obtuse, forcing her to speak plainly with him.

Hea gritted her teeth. "You are a fool, Bridei mac Beli."

He raised his eyebrows. "Excuse me?"

She glared at him. "Is this a game to you? Do you enjoy playing with people's lives?"

"It's no game," he replied, not seeming remotely offended by her sharpness. "It's my right to demand my lands back."

"But you are going to launch this land into war."

Bridei shrugged. "War is a way of life, Hea. Peace is only ever fleeting. Borders constantly shift. Kings rise and fall. Although you'd like to believe it, Ecgfrith does not rule the world."

Hea stared up at him. His arrogance took her breath away. She felt mortified at how easily she had succumbed to him the night before. She had needed little encouragement to throw herself into his arms, and to give herself to him.

I should have realized that he came to Bebbanburg to warmonger, she berated herself. *I should have turfed him out of my home before he tried to kiss me.*

If she had not been so blinded by lust she would have.

"You're not the man I remember," she said finally. "To think mōder and I used to welcome you into our home. I wish you had never come back here."

Bridei frowned. "You don't mean that. I know how pleased you were to see me." His brow smoothed as he gave her a sultry look. "You showed me how much last night."

Hea went rigid. She had been waiting for this—she had known he would throw her poor judgement in her face. "Last night was a mistake."

That wiped the look of supreme male confidence off his face. "No it wasn't—don't lie to me, Hea."

"I'm not lying. Last night I made an error of judgement."

Bridei huffed. "It's too late now for regrets." He held her gaze as he lowered his head slightly toward her. "My offer still stands. Why don't you come with me? You would like the north. It would suit your character."

Hea's heart started to pound. The urge to laugh hysterically rose within her. He still did not understand. She realized he was never going to.

Hea took a few hasty steps back from him. "I'm not going anywhere." She turned then and fled down the King's Way.

This time, he did not follow her.

Bridei watched as Hea hurried out of sight. His first instinct had been to go after her. However, he quickly mastered that impulse.

The woman had grossly insulted him.

Hea disappeared, and Bridei let out a string of curses under his breath. He did not have time for this. His men were nearly ready to move out. Hea was a distraction he did not need. He had acted on impulse the night before, giving into his attraction for her, but he had regretted it the moment his eyes had opened that morning.

Last night had been unexpected ... he had never lost himself like that with a woman. Time had stood still for the night; the world had shrunk to the two of them. The taste of her, the feel of her skin, the softness of her hair, still lingered even in daylight.

Even so, when he had awoken by her side that morning, the enchantment that had ensnared him fell away. He was aware that he had lingered too long, that he should not have been there in the first place. Her offers of food only added fuel to the panic kindling within him—he had virtually run from her home.

He had not come to Bebbanburg for this—Hea was distracting him from his true purpose.

He turned on his heel and strode up the incline toward the high gate. Heolstor was waiting for him in front of the stables, his face stony. "Where have you been?"

Bridei shook his head, avoiding his friend's eye. "It doesn't matter."

Heolstor's gaze burned into him. "You should have let her be."

Bridei's head snapped up, and he frowned. "If you knew where I went, why did you ask?"

"I wanted to see what you'd say."

Bridei snorted. "It's none of your business."

"I've always liked Hea," Heolstor replied. "She deserves better."

Bridei stared at him, his gaze narrowing. He had not spoken of yesterday eve to his friend, yet Heolstor had guessed where he had spent the night—and after the words he had just exchanged with Hea, he had no desire to talk about it.

Wordlessly, he pushed past Heolstor and entered the stables to fetch his horse. His bay stallion awaited him, pawing restlessly at the straw in his stall. Croí Cróga—Braveheart—was a magnificent beast. The grey mare that Bridei had left Bebbanburg on all those years earlier, Léoma, was still alive, but he had gifted her to the wife of one of his warriors. These days, he rode a horse more befitting his role.

Bridei ground his jaw as he saddled Croí Cróga. For the first time since riding south, he regretted this journey. In truth, he had not expected Ecgfrith to hand him over power, and had eagerly anticipated meeting his nemesis on the battlefield. But this visit had left him with a sour taste in his mouth.

Bridei tightened the horse's girth, nudging the beast in the belly with his knee as the stallion tried holding his breath, before finishing the task. He led the horse from the stables to find his men amassed in the yard beyond, all mounted and ready to depart. The men were restless, their hands gripping the pommels of their swords and fighting knives, almost as if they expected Ecgfrith's men to surround them.

They were right to worry—the delay here could cost all of them dearly. They had to make haste before the Northumbrian king turned on them.

Bridei swung up onto the saddle and urged Croí Cróga forward, leading the way out of the yard. They passed under the stone arch of the high gate, the tall shadow of the Great Tower at their backs. Heolstor rode forward, drawing level with Bridei and the two of them led the company down the King's Way.

Crowds of local folk had gathered by the roadside to watch them leave. News of the discussions between Bridei and Ecgfrith had clearly reached them, for their gazes were not friendly. An elderly woman glared up at Bridei, hate in her eyes, mumbling curses under her breath. Next to her, a blond lad spat on the ground as the Pict band passed.

However, none were bold enough to shout insults, or to hurl stones. The heavily armed, grim-faced warriors warned them against such rash acts.

Despite himself, Bridei scanned the crowd for Hea amongst the sea of faces. He did not find her, and was irritated to realize this bothered him.

Forget her.

He and Heolstor led the way across the market square and through the low gate. He urged Croí Cróga into a trot down the incline beyond. A stiff breeze, laced with the salty tang of the sea, whipped Bridei's hair in his eyes. It was a bright autumn day, with silvery light. Soon the bitter season would be upon them, but for a short while yet the sun still had some warmth.

The moment Bridei rode beyond the walls of Bebbanburg, he felt a great weight lift from his shoulders. His return to this place had bothered him more than he had realized.

Pushing aside lingering thoughts of Hea, for there was little point dwelling on a woman he would likely never see again, Bridei shifted his focus to the future. He would return home to Dundurn and gather his army to him.

Excitement knotted in the pit of Bridei's belly. Soon he would bend the knee to no man.

Soon he would be King of the North.

Hea stood atop the wooden palisade next to the south-west guard tower, and watched the band of Picts ride away. The wind made her eyes tear but she paid it no mind. Instead, her gaze remained riveted on the company of horsemen below.

They had reached the bottom of the causeway and now skirted the base of the rocky outcrop on which the fort stood, heading toward the road that would take them north.

Watching them, Hea felt oddly hollow, almost as if the brisk wind blew through her. In just two short days Bridei mac Beli had re-entered her life like a tempest, and torn it apart.

It made her realize that for all her outward confidence, inside she was still that girl he had left behind all those years ago. Lost, lonely, and desperate for love.

Tears stung her hers, but she angrily blinked them away. *You're a dolt, Heahburh,* she chastised herself. That was what her mother would say if she were alive to witness this sorry scene.

She squeezed her eyes shut, blocking out the view for a moment as she struggled to hold back the tears welling within her.

Memories of the night before assailed her. She had never known such pleasure, such abandon, existed. Bridei had been a skillful lover; she had been with no other, but she had the wits to realize that. He knew exactly where to touch her, how to kiss her, to make her lose control. Despite everything, a fire in the pit of her belly kindled as she remembered how he had felt deep inside her.

For a brief period she had felt ridiculously happy, but her joy had been as fragile as an eggshell—crushed underfoot when he rushed off as soon as he awoke.

Hea opened her eyes, her gaze tracking the Pict band while they turned north. She could see Bridei out front, his dark hair flying in the wind.

Her chest constricted as a sudden thought struck her. *What if I'm with child?*

She had been so consumed with lust the night before, she had not given the consequences of their coupling a second thought. However, if she gave birth to a dark-haired whelp nine moons from now everyone, including the king, would know who had sired it.

She would be cast out of Bebbanburg.

Bridei had asked her to come with him, but the offer had been so flippantly made she could not believe it to be genuine. He had known she would refuse him. A man like Bridei would not want to be encumbered by a woman he had only spent a night with.

Instead, he was her people's enemy.

War is a way of life, Hea. The brash confidence in those words had made her want to knee him in the cods. He cared not that the folk here had lived in peace for the last few decades—that wives and children would soon see their menfolk depart for battle, some never to return. What would become of Bebbanburg if war came?

Hea could not bear for that to happen. Somehow she had to steer Ecgfrith away from conflict with the Picts. Her role as his seer gave her some standing in the fort—he would not cast aside her counsel lightly.

Tearing her gaze from the scene below, Hea turned and returned to the ladder that would take her back down off the walls.

Seven months later ...

Chapter Fourteen

Cuthbert's Counsel

Bebbanburg, Kingdom of Northumbria

Spring, 685 AD

"THE KING WISHES you to join him for nón-mete."

The messenger, a thin, pock-faced lad who worked in the Great Hall, stood in the street outside Hea's home. Dressed in a thin tunic and breeches, the boy shivered in the pelting rain that drove into the fort from the north. It was one of those sleety, spring showers, when winter seemed intent on returning. Hea could see the lad was soaked through.

"Very well." She gave a brisk nod and stepped back from the door, motioning for him to follow. "First come in out of the rain—I have some pottage on the fire that should warm you up."

The lad hesitated before shaking his head. "I can't ... I have to get back."

Not waiting for a response from Hea, the boy turned and fled back up the street. Hea watched him go, frowning. Was she imagining it, or were folk acting strangely around her these days. Her mother had always been respected in Bebbanburg, but of late Hea had sensed a change from folk inside the fort.

Only yesterday a group of lads had followed her along the Dragon's Back, calling her a wicce. A few days before that, the woman who sold her fowl at market had refused to serve her. Hea was used to some folk being uncomfortable around her, but this was different.

That boy had looked afraid of her, and it unsettled Hea. Fear and aggression were close cousins. She could not understand why people were avoiding her these days.

Frowning, she went back inside and took the cauldron of pottage off the fire. It was almost noon now. It was later than she had realized, and she would have to hurry, or she would be late. Hea took her fur mantle off a hook from behind the door, wrapped it around her shoulders and went out.

The rain hammered against the exposed skin of her face and hands in icy needles, the chill taking her breath away. It was hard to believe spring was upon them—in fact the meadows around the fort were bright with snowdrops, bluebells, and crocuses.

She had thought the foul weather would keep folk indoors, but industry greeted her as she turned onto the King's Way.

A company of warriors armed with spears passed her. Faces partially hidden under iron helms, they trudged through the mud, leather creaking. A few paces behind, two men hauled a cart piled high with limewood shields they had just collected from the armorer.

As she continued, Hea peered into Broga's forge and saw the huge blond smith bent over an anvil, hammering out a blade. A messy pile of freshly forged swords sat on a bench behind him. Usually Broga worked alone, but these days two brawny lads hammered blades at his side. The odor of hot iron wafted out onto the street.

Sensing someone watching him, Broga glanced up, his heavy brow furrowing. Hea hastily averted her face and hurried on.

Up ahead, the red bulk of the Great Tower of Bebbanburg loomed before her. Sheets of rain lashed across the street, driving against Hea—she would be soaked by the time she reached the King's Hall.

Splashing through puddles in the yard outside the tower, for there were too many to be avoided, Hea made her way to the stone steps leading into the hall.

The hall was already sitting down to nón-mete when Hea entered. She stopped just inside the entrance and removed her mantle, hanging it up against the wall at the end of a row of other dripping cloaks. Then, shaking rain from her hair and doing her best to tidy her bedraggled appearance, Hea made her way across the wide space. Her path to the high seat took her past huge glowing hearths. Long tables formed a square in the center of the hall, and Hea realized today must be a special occasion, for she breathed in the rich smell of venison stew—a dish the king only put on for visitors.

As she approached the high seat, she realized who the newcomer to the hall was.

A man sat at the table upon the wooden platform: his dark greying hair shaved into a tonsure, his handsome face composed. He wore a coarse brown habit, girded at the waist with a length of rope.

Cuthbert, Prior of Lindisfarena, cut an imposing figure. Two monks had accompanied the prior from the isle of Lindisfarena—the only inhabited island in the windswept archipelago that lay just off the coast.

Queen Irmenburgh was clearly pleased to have him here, a broad smile illuminating her pale face.

Bebbanburg's new priest, Oswald, sat to the queen's left. He had been in discussion with Cuthbert, but on seeing the prior's gaze shift as Hea approached, Oswald broke off, his full mouth thinning.

A slender man with black hair and bright blue eyes, Oswald had been in Bebbanburg since Yule. Although the king largely ignored him, Irmenburgh had welcomed the young man's company. These days, Hea rarely saw the queen without Oswald at her side.

At the head of the table, the king lounged back in his carven chair, his expression hooded.

Hea took a seat further down the table. She met Cuthbert's eye and smiled. "Good day, prior."

There was warmth in the prior's eyes as he greeted her. "Wes hāl, Heahburh. It's been years since I saw you last. How is your mother?"

Hea ducked her head, her smile fading. "She died, around a year and half ago, prior."

His face grew solemn. "I'm sorry to hear that, child. She was a good woman."

Hea nodded, her vision misting. Cuthbert's kindness made her feel tearful.

"Prior Cuthbert." Ecgfrith spoke up then. "As always, it is a pleasure to see you."

Hea watched the king, noting the way his tone and expression belied his words. He was not pleased to see Cuthbert at all.

Ignoring the king's coolness, Cuthbert turned to Ecgfrith. "News reached Lindisfarena that concerned me, milord."

"Really?" Ecgfrith took a sip from his cup of wine. "What news was that?"

"I heard that you have gathered your fyrd, the biggest army you've ever called to your side."

Ecgfrith nodded. "What of it?"

"So the rumors are true then? You are marching to war against the Picts?"

Ecgfrith held the prior's gaze, his own narrowing. "It would seem so, but surely you didn't make a special trip here just to ask me this?"

Cuthbert shook his head. His bow-shaped mouth pursed. "I came to counsel against such an act, milord," he replied quietly. "Few have gone against the northerners and won."

A chill silence settled across the table. The rumble of conversation died away upon the high seat. Hea glanced around, noting the different expressions on the faces of those present. Ecgfrith looked vexed, while his wife's eyes gleamed. She was staring at Cuthbert, nodding vigorously at his words. However, the king ignored her.

Further down the table, Rinan was frowning, his meaty hands clenched upon the table before him. The other thegns present shifted nervously in their seats. All of them sensed a battle of another kind looming.

Ecgfrith toyed with his cup, before his gaze settled upon Cuthbert once more. "I find your lack of faith in the Northumbrian army disturbing, prior."

Cuthbert gave a pained look. "It's not that, sire. I just question the worth of marching north to defend lands that have never truly been ours. The world north of here is savage. Even if you win a battle against Bridei mac Beli and his horde, you won't be able to hold back the tide against the Picts forever. The Romans tried and failed too, remember?"

Hea looked down at the trencher of stew before her. She agreed wholeheartedly with the prior. Over the past few months, she had tried repeatedly to turn Ecgfrith away from this path, but he would not be moved. For the king it had become a matter of pride. Bridei's father, Beli, had submitted to Ecgfrith, accepted him as his over-lord—why could not Bridei?

Ecgfrith's position was clear: the King of Northumbria ruled the north, and if Bridei could not accept that Ecgfrith had no choice but to go to war against him.

"The prior speaks wisely, sire," Oswald spoke up then, his voice low and sure. "War with the Picts should be a last resort."

"So you think he should stand back and let those savages defy him?" Rinan challenged from further down the table. The young priest flushed and opened his mouth to respond. However, the king forestalled him.

"Well said, Rinan." Ecgfrith raised his cup to his lips and took a sip. "Too long has Bridei flouted my rule. Since winter, news has reached me of numerous raiding parties into my lands. He is deliberately baiting me, goading me."

Cuthbert frowned. "And so, you shall give him what he wants?"

Ecgfrith shook his head. "I must defend our borders, as my father would have—as any man worthy of leading must. Would you have your king act as a coward? Would you have me offer up my arse for this Pict?"

Cuthbert tensed at the king's crudeness. But when he replied his tone was calm. "I merely ask you to think carefully before marching north to war. I feel it is folly."

The king lowered his cup to the table with a thump. "I have heard enough, prior. Let us speak of something else."

Cuthbert nodded, although his face was pained. He shared a glance with Oswald—one of weary resignation. Looking on, Hea felt desperation tug at her. Prior Cuthbert was highly respected, yet the king would not take his counsel. What hope was there that war could be avoided?

The meal resumed, as did the rise and fall of conversation in the hall around them. A woman, one of the thegn's wives, circuited the table with a ewer of wine and refilled their cups. She was heavily pregnant, her swollen belly thrusting before her as she moved from person to person. The sight of her reminded Hea of her own fears, just a few months earlier. She had been terrified that her one night with Bridei would leave her with child. Yet when her moon's flow came a few days later, her relief had been mixed with a little sadness.

Bridei was truly out of her life now—there was nothing of him left behind in Bebbanburg.

She glided like a wraith through the valley.

Steep, craggy hills studded with grey rock rose up either side, and the sky was a hard blue strip overhead. A carpet of bloodied and broken bodies covered the bottom of the ravine. The air reeked like a slaughter pen.

Hea's gorge rose and she stopped, her gaze sweeping over the grisly scene. There were Angles among the dead, but the Picts far outnumbered them. Dark haired men in their prime littered the valley floor, their bare limbs smeared with blue woad, eyes staring sightlessly up at the sky.

Shuddering, a warm wind in her face, she glanced up and saw a standard fluttering in the wind above the battlefield: a red and yellow flag.

Northumbria.

Hea's eyes flickered open.

Ecgfrith was sitting opposite, watching her intently. The moment their gazes met, he spoke. "What did you see?"

Hea drew in a shaky breath. Ecgfrith was so demanding. He always pounced on her too soon after she reemerged from a dream state. He did not seem to understand how much it exhausted her. Each time she ventured into the shadow world it cost her. Often, she would feel jaded and weary for days afterward. Even now, she felt as if she could lie down and sleep for days. However, the king had no patience for that. He wanted answers.

Hea inhaled, gathering her scattered thoughts and bringing herself back to the present. After what she had just seen she felt torn—and for the first time ever considered lying to the king. So much death ... so much pain. It was such needless bloodshed—on both sides. Yet after a few moments she forced herself to tell him the truth.

"I saw it, milord. I saw the battle ... and I saw Northumbria victorious."

His expression grew taut. "How do you know we were the victors?"

"I saw this kingdom's flag flying high above the battlefield. I saw the bodies of your enemy littering a bleak valley."

The words sounded so matter-of-fact, so cold. She did not go into details of just how harrowing that sight had been.

Meanwhile Ecgfrith was grinning. It was a savage expression. His hazel eyes gleamed. "This is good news indeed."

Directly after the feast with Cuthbert and his monks, Ecgfrith had demanded she retrieve her seeing drum and meet him in his alcove. Hea sensed that despite his brave face, Cuthbert's visit had sowed a seed of doubt. He wanted some assurance that he was taking the right path.

Unfortunately, Hea had just delivered him the news he had been hoping for.

War was looming, a great storm that not even God could hold back. The Northumbrian fyrd was mighty. Just the day before, she had ventured outside the walls of Bebbanburg and seen the huge encampment gathering at the base of the fort; it now spread out in a great, dark mantle across the meadows.

She could not imagine that Bridei had managed to draw such an immense army to him.

"And the location?" Ecgfrith leaned forward eagerly. "Did your vision give an indication of where we will meet?"

Hea closed her eyes, recalling once more the grim battlefield. This time she paid more attention to her surroundings. A few moments later, her eyes flickered open once more. "It is the north," she affirmed. "The landscape is mountainous and wild, the hillsides covered with heather and gorse. It was a steep valley, or a gorge of some kind. The light is bright; it appears to be early summer. I'm sorry, but there are no landmarks I can give you. It is desolate terrain, nowhere I recognize."

Ecgfrith nodded briskly. "Well done. You have given me much already. I will now send Cuthbert and his monks on their way."

Panic surged within Hea. She could not let this end here. "Sire ... you don't have to do this."

Ecgfrith rose to his feet, his expression dismissive. "Thank you, Hea—that'll be all."

"Milord, I—"

The king's gaze narrowed. "Do you doubt yourself? Are you not sure what you saw?"

Hea climbed to her feet, her pulse accelerating. "I saw your victory," she confirmed, "but—"

Ecgfrith turned away from her. "Then that's all I need to know. You may go now."

Chapter Fifteen

Warrior and Bride

Dundurn, The Kingdom of Fortriu

THE HANDFASTING TOOK place at noon.

It was a blustery day, full of the promise of spring, although the wind that blew across the hills had a bite to it. Bridei stood upon the banks of the burn beneath his fortress, and wrapped a length of plaid around the joined hands of the man and woman before him.

Heolstor and his bride Ciara both beamed at him, while Bridei attempted to keep his expression neutral—noble—as was befitting a king.

Heolstor had dressed for the occasion in his finest leather vest and plaid breeches. Swirling patterns of blue decorated his bare arms, adding to the blue tattoos that traced one side of his face. The color contrasted deeply with his bright red hair.

The warrior had grown over the years into a giant of a man. He was taller and broader than most of the Picts he lived amongst, and looked as different as a cuckoo in a nest of sparrows. Still, the folk had accepted him long ago as one of their own. Ciara, a comely lass with a mane of dark brown hair and sea-green eyes looked lovely today in a long, sleeveless plaid tunic, and with heather in her hair.

Ciara shifted her attention from the king to her husband-to-be, gazing at him with open adoration.

Bridei stifled a smile. It was just like Heolstor to capture the heart of the most winsome lass in Dundurn. Years earlier, Bridei had even considered pursuing Ciara himself. Seeing Heolstor and the girl together so happy now, so well matched, gladdened his heart.

The ceremony was coming to its conclusion. Heolstor and Ciara stood barefoot on the edge of Allt Ghoinean burn, where clear water trickled over stones and birds darted overhead. A crowd had gathered around the warrior and his bride. All that was needed was for Bridei to complete their handfasting.

Bridei finished tying the plaid and stepped back. "Heolstor, warrior of Fortriu, I join you to Ciara daughter of Arnor mac Durn," he began, his voice carrying over the crowd. "May The Mother light your way. May The Warrior protect you. May The Maiden grant you healthy children." He paused here, letting his words echo high above them before continuing. "And may The Hag bless you with long, healthy lives—and keep The Reaper from your door."

The wedding party feasted outdoors. A haunch of venison had been slowly roasting on a spit all morning, and the women had prepared breads and braised vegetables to serve with it. Long tables lined the edge of the burn, and the aroma of roast meat, accompanied by the pungent odor of peat, drifted across the hillside, carried by a brisk wind.

Bridei sat at the head of the longest table, his gaze surveying his surroundings. He loved this place—the great hill with the River Earn to one side and the Allt Ghoinean burn on the other.

His fort, Dundurn, reared above them, commanding a view for many furlongs in every direction. A very different structure to Bebbanburg, his fort was a great circular building: a broch. There was very little wood used here, instead even the huts surrounding the base of the fort were made of local stone, with turf or thatched roofs. Over the years, both Bridei and his father had added to the fort's outer defenses, and now stone walls eight-feet high ringed the base of the hill. A path, cut into the side of the hill, wound lazily up to the broch, in-between a patchwork of cultivated terraces and cottars huts.

To Bridei's left, one of his warriors—Fearghus—filled a drinking horn with mead and thrust it across the table at Heolstor. "Here, Fire Hair, down this!"

Heolstor grinned back at him before reaching across to claim the horn. "Aye, the first of many."

Bridei shook his head. It was not just a boast; he had never met a man who could drink like Heolstor. Most Angle warriors he had met had hollow legs.

Platters of venison, braised onions, mashed carrot with honey and butter, and boiled turnip arrived at the table then, and the feasters fell upon it. Bridei helped himself to some bread studded with walnuts and took a bite, chewing thoughtfully. Around him, his people laughed, joked and made merry, but he felt slightly apart from them.

His mood had been introspective of late.

He had no need for brooding. Everything was going well, yet an emptiness had taken up residence within him that he could not shake.

He had thought that today would cheer him up, for he had been looking forward to seeing Heolstor wed his sweetheart, but now that the ceremony was over, and the wedding feast was underway, a nagging sense of loss settled over him once more.

Curse her ... can she not leave me in peace?

He had believed thoughts of Hea would cease shortly after leaving Bebbanburg, that by the time he reached his stronghold she would be little more than a pleasant memory. He had never been more wrong. Instead, the opposite had occurred. He could not stop thinking about her; she had become an obsession.

Months had now passed, and still memories of her assailed him with every quiet moment. At first, he had done his best to distract himself. He had lain with another woman on his return to Dundurn—Una—a serving wench who had long drawn his eye. But his sense of loss, of emptiness had only increased afterward.

Annoyance surged through him. Hea, that witch, had ruined all other women for him.

Cursing her once more, Bridei took a long draft from his cup, his gaze travelling over the table to where Una was filling the feasters' cups. She carried a ewer of wine in one hand, a jug of mead in the other, and was laughing with one of the warriors.

Sensing someone's gaze upon her, Una glanced up and boldly met Bridei's eye. She then favored him with a slow, seductive smile.

Una was there for the taking, he knew that. Months had passed since Bridei had last lain with her, and his body cried out for a woman. Yet he knew the urge would only lead to disappointment ... for them both.

Una was comely, but he found himself comparing her unfavorably to Hea. Una was too tall, too thin, her skin sallow in comparison, and her walnut-color hair drab. In the furs, she was lifeless compared to his red-haired Angle temptress.

Bridei knew Una deserved better, and in fact she had appeared hurt when he did not invite her to his bed again. It was better that way though—there was little point bedding a woman he did not want.

It was like drinking a barrel of ale, when only one cup of wine was what he thirsted for.

I've a hand, he thought sourly. *I'll have to use that for the time being.*

Bridei looked away, to find Heolstor watching him. His friend had just downed his second horn of mead and was waiting for it to be refilled and passed back to him. Ciara was perched on his lap, and was nibbling a piece of venison.

"You look glum for such a day," Heolstor observed with a wicked grin. "What's wrong—did you want me for yourself?"

Bridei laughed, before raising his cup to them both. "I'd rather wed a goat. Ciara is welcome to you."

Still grinning, Heolstor raised his own cup to his lord. "So why the long face?"

Bridei shrugged. "Just the cares of a man who rules, nothing worth speaking of."

The mood changed at their end of the table. Heolstor's face grew serious and his bride's brow furrowed.

"When will you march south to face the Northumbrians?" Ciara asked.

"Soon," Bridei assured her.

"How will it start?" Heolstor asked. "Shall we name a time and place and meet, shield wall to shield wall?"

Bridei shook his head. "The shield wall is your way—in the north we prefer to lay an ambush for our enemies."

Heolstor's gaze grew intense. He took the drinking horn Fearghus passed him but did not yet drink from it. "Go on."

Bridei favored his friend with a sly smile. "I lived amongst the Angles long enough to know the types of warfare they excel at, and which they do not. Long have I lain awake at night deciding on the best way to confront Ecgfrith."

"And ....?"

Bridei's smile widened. "I think it's time we traveled south again and stirred up more trouble."

Heolstor raised an eyebrow. "Poke the adder with a stick?"

"Aye—I intend to rile him, so he has no choice but to come after me."

"What will you do then?" Ciara leaned forward, riveted by the men's discussion. "Turn and fight?"

Bridei leaned back in his seat and lifted his cup, saluting them both once more. "Only when I've got him where I want him."

Dusk settled over the hills of Fortriu, a rosy sunset that painted the sky in ribbons of mauve and pink. The feast had long since ended on the banks of the burn below, and folk had made their way back up to the fort—where the eating and drinking continued.

Soon after dark, the music and dancing began.

Two musicians, one playing a bone whistle, the other a harp, set themselves up on the wooden platform at one end of the circular space inside the great stone broch. Men and women pushed back the tables, so the area around the central hearth was clear, and began to dance.

Bridei, groggy and sated from a surfeit of rich food and mead, did not join them. Instead he took his seat upon the raised platform, at the other end from the musicians. He sat upon a carved oaken chair, decorated by a massive pair of stag antlers—his father's throne—and stretched his long legs out before him, crossing them at the ankles.

It had been a good day, but he was content to watch the revelry, rather than take part in it.

Una had been observing him all afternoon. She glanced up at him now, from where she danced in a circle with the other unwed men and women who lived within the fort, her gaze coy.

It was his fault; he should not have caught her eye earlier.

Pretending he had not seen her glance his way, Bridei leaned back in his chair and tapped his fingers on the armrests, in time with the music. After a few moments, he gave a great yawn, his jaw cracking.

He had been busy of late, rallying his men and training and arming them for battle. Most days he was awake before dawn and often the last to retire. However, it felt as if the long days had caught up with him. If he remained seated here, he would surely fall asleep like an old man, caught dozing after the noon meal—not a kingly sight.

Best he retired to his quarters instead.

Bridei rose to his feet, just as Una broke free of the dancers. She leaped nimbly upon the platform, blocking his exit.

"Lord Bridei," she greeted him, breathless. "Will you not join the dancing?"

"Not tonight, Una. I am weary."

Her pretty face creased in disappointment. "But surely, just one dance."

Bridei held her gaze and smiled. Then he slowly, and deliberately shook his head, stepping around her. "Good eve, Una—enjoy the revelry. There have been too few handfastings here over the last year."

He felt her gaze follow him as he stepped down from the platform. He skirted the edge of the hall, passing the curtained alcoves where his relatives and retainers slept. Bridei then crossed to the stone steps that led up to the second level of the broch, to where he slept. She would not follow him, not without an invitation.

It was a relief to climb the stairs and enter the solitude of his chamber. This space was his refuge. Thick furs covered the floor and tapestries hung from the damp stone walls, creating a welcoming feel. It was a masculine space; there was no woman's touch here.

Bridei heaved out a sigh and yanked off his boots before crossing the floor to his furs. He stretched out upon their softness and stared up at the rafters for a short while, listening to the laughter and music that drifted up from below. The celebrations would no doubt go on for much longer— although he had noted that Heolstor and Ciara had disappeared early into the night, to celebrate alone and in private.

Bridei envied them their happiness.

He lay there for a while longer, waiting for sleep to claim him—yet despite his weariness, it would not come. If anything the merriment beneath him had gotten louder. The sound of a man's drunken singing rose up, followed by shrieking and laughter.

The noise almost drowned out the sound of the wind, whistling against the exterior of the stone broch.

The wind song of Dundurn—how he had missed it all those years in Bebbanburg. Usually the lilting sound of it calmed him, but this evening it brought him little solace. Instead his thoughts shifted once more to Hea, and the angry words that had passed between them the last time he had seen her.

Months on, he wished he could take those things he had said back. Heolstor had been right, Hea deserved better.

Irritated at the direction his thoughts were taking—once again—Bridei rolled over. Muttering a curse, he covered his head with a fur, almost as if by doing so he could smother his thoughts. He needed to stop thinking about her. He needed to move on with his life. There would be other women ... he would forget Hea eventually.

Yet as the wind called to him across the hills, he wished he had behaved differently on that ill-fated visit to Bebbanburg.

Chapter Sixteen

Market Square

Bebbanburg

HEA ENTERED THE market square, bunches of spring flowers in her arms. Their sweet scent tickled her nose as she wandered amongst the crowd.

"Daffodils, jonquils, snowdrops, and bluebells," she called out, using the same sing-song voice her mother always had when she sold flowers. These days, thanks to the monthly sum of gold that Ecgfrith paid her, she had little need to make a living by selling flowers. However, she was wary of remaining dependent on the king. Although he appeared to be pleased with her of late, she knew him to be a fickle man. She had seen how he treated those who disappointed him, and realized that it would take little for him to treat her the same way.

Not only that, but the little garden behind her hovel was a riot of color this time of year; it seemed a pity not to share that beauty with others.

Unfortunately, few folk seemed interested this morning.

"Spring flowers," she called out. "All your favorites!"

Still nothing. A merchant brushed by Hea, his gaze looking through her. A few feet away, the woman who sold Hea cheese and butter every week avoided her eye.

Hea tensed. *Are they ignoring me?*

Her gaze traveled across the square, and she spied Oswald walking amongst the crowd. The priest was young, barely five winters older than her, and would have been considered attractive if not for that ridiculous tonsure. His bald pate gleamed in the spring sunlight.

Oswald had not seen her, so intent was he on greeting and conversing with the folk he passed. Hea watched him, frowning. People seemed to have time for the priest this morning, just not for her.

"Hea!" Fritha's voice hailed her from a few feet away. "I'd love some snowdrops, if you have any left?"

Grateful, Hea turned to her friend—the only person who had greeted her so far this morning—and smiled. "Of course."

She extracted a bunch of the delicate white bonnets on long green stems and handed them over.

"How much?" Fritha asked.

"For you, nothing."

"Nonsense, lass. How about one of my apple cakes, to take home for your supper later?"

Hea sighed. "Very well."

Fritha picked up one of the cakes and put it in a small cloth bag, before passing it to Hea. "What's wrong? Why the long face?"

"Nothing a little friendliness couldn't cure," Hea replied tightly. "I'm invisible today. No one will speak to me."

Fritha's ruddy face tightened at this news, and her gaze flicked to where Oswald was now laughing with a young couple. He then reached out and ruffled their son's hair. "It's that priest," Fritha said. "I heard him preach a few days ago. He rants on and on about the devil, about how those who practice the old ways must be shunned. How we must all avoid temptation. He's got folk all stirred up."

Hea spat an oath under her breath, still glaring at Oswald. "I wish he would leave us all in peace."

Fritha gave a humorless laugh. "There's not much likelihood of that. More men like him will come. Not all holy folk are like Prior Cuthbert."

Feeling the weight of the two women's stares, Oswald glanced up, his gaze meeting Hea's.

His expression grew serious, and his face turned pink. Gone was the genial smile and the easy banter with the good folk of Bebbanburg. He backed up—his conversation with the young couple forgotten—turned and hurried away, shoulders rounded.

"That's right, scurry off," Hea muttered, her gaze still tracking him through the crowd. "Like the rat you are."

Fritha gave a low whistle. "You don't like him much, lass, do you?"

Hea sighed. "Not if he's turning folk against me."

"Don't fret." Fritha put a motherly hand on her arm. "You will always have friends here, you know that."

Hea cast Fritha a look of gratitude. The woman had no idea what those words meant to her. To become an outcast here would make life intolerable. She then plastered on a brave smile and hoisted up her colorful bunches of spring flowers. "Well then, I'd better do another circuit of the square."

Fritha smiled back. "That's the spirit."

Hea set off once more, calling out to the crowd as she went. "Get your spring flowers here—daffodils, jonquils, bluebells, and snowdrops!"

A few yards on, a fisherwoman, who was selling smoked herrings by the gate, bought some daffodils, and shortly after a girl bought some bluebells for her mother. Clearly, now that the priest had disappeared from their midst, folk had relaxed somewhat.

She had almost completed her circuit of the market square, weaving out of the crowds of people haggling over produce, fish, meat and cheeses, when Hea spotted another familiar—if unwelcome—face.

Rinan.

Like Oswald earlier, the warrior had not seen her. Instead, his gaze was fixed upon a pretty young wench who was selling turnips, carrots, and onions. She was small, with hair the color of mead, and had a slender figure ... yet it was clear from her expression that she did not welcome Rinan's attentions.

Hea observed them as she walked slowly through the crowd. She had always enjoyed watching people interact; the things they said without meaning to by their gestures and expressions.

There was plenty being said now by both parties.

Rinan was keen. His ruddy face was beet-red and even at this distance, Hea could see he was sweating. He had combed out his unruly straw-colored hair and tied it back with a leather thong; he was also wearing what looked to be his best breeches and tunic, and sported a number of bronze and silver armrings on his bare, muscular arms—all tributes to his bravery on behalf of the king.

The girl was also flushed, although not for the same reason as Rinan. She did her best to avoid his intense stare, her gaze darting around like a hunted fawn. She backed off from him, picking up a turnip and clutching it to her breast, as if to ward off his attentions.

Undaunted, Rinan stepped closer, speaking passionately now, his hands gesticulating. The girl backed off further, shaking her head.

Watching them, Hea felt an uncharacteristic stab of pity for Rinan. She had never forgotten, nor forgiven, what he had done to her years earlier, but it seemed as if that day had cast a curse upon him. To her knowledge, he had never tried to force a woman to submit to his kiss again—but neither had any agreed to wed him. Watching him now, she realized he really was useless with women.

Hea guessed that the warrior had come here to propose to the farm girl—something she was not interested in pursuing.

Eventually, realizing that the object of his desire was on the verge of losing her patience and hurling the turnip she clutched at him, Rinan backed off.

Muttering what looked to be an embarrassed apology, he turned and loped away through the crowd.

Straight for Hea.

Their gazes met, and she realized he knew she had been watching his humiliation.

Rinan frowned. He marched across the few yards separating them and stopped before Hea, looming over her.

"Enjoyed that, did you?" he growled.

Hea stared back at him, refusing to be intimidated, and feigned innocence. "I don't know what you mean, Rinan," she said sweetly. "Perhaps you'd like to buy some flowers for your sweetheart?"

His expression darkened, and for a moment Hea worried that he might strike her. "I don't need your help," he snarled. "Have you put a curse on me, wicce?"

Hea glared back at him. "If only I could, I'd have turned you into a toad years ago."

His face twisted and he stepped back from her. "You'll not be so smug forever. One of these days, Ecgfrith is going to find another favorite. You won't be so quick with your insults then."

He stormed off, his huge frame rigid with outrage. Hea watched him go, and let out the breath she had been holding. Only then did she realize that she was shaking.

King Ecgfrith swung his wooden blade hard across the back of his opponent's legs, sending Rinan sprawling into the mud.

"Concentrate!" Ecgfrith barked. "What's wrong with you today?"

Rinan picked himself up, red-faced. "Sorry," he muttered. "Just distracted."

"There's no time for distraction in a shield wall," Ecgfrith snarled. "Do you want a Pict sword in your guts?"

Rinan's expression told him he did not. Ecgfrith pointed to the wooden practice sword that Rinan had dropped in the mud. "Pick that up and let's go again."

The warrior stooped to obey him, just as a man on horseback thundered into the yard, through the high gate.

Rinan momentarily forgotten, Ecgfrith turned to the newcomer. He did not recognize the young man who approached, his face flushed and sweaty. He looked as if he had ridden hard; mud splattered his cloak and boots.

"Lord Ecgfrith," he gasped, drawing his horse up at the edge of the ring of men who had gathered to watch the king spar. "I have ill-news from the north."

Ecgfrith wiped a forearm across his sweaty forehead and squinted at the man. "Who are you?" he demanded.

"My name is Theodred, sire. I'm son of Berht, Ealdorman of Ord." The man paused here, to gather his breath, before continuing. "Villages north of us, milord, they've been attacked."

Ecgfrith went still. "By whom?"

The young man held his gaze, unwavering, and Ecgfrith knew before he replied who was responsible. There was only one man who would have the nerve, who would dare raid Northumbrian lands.

Bridei mac Beli.

Chapter Seventeen

War is Upon Us

"WAR IS UPON us."

Ecgfrith's words fell like the blow of a heavy war axe, causing all upon the high seat to cease their evening meal. A tense silence settled.

Hea, who sat half-way down the table, put down the piece of bread she had just dipped in boar stew, her gaze shifting to the king. She had wondered why the king had bid her to join him for supper. She did not usually visit the Great Tower at this time of day. She had been at her work table, mashing herbs into a paste with a pestle and mortar—to make a healing tincture—when Ecgfrith had sent a slave to fetch her.

Hea had come quickly, bringing her seeing drum with her—for Ecgfrith did not like to be kept waiting these days. The lead up to war had made him irascible and sharp-tongued. This eve, his long face was stern. Irmenburgh sat beside him, eyes downcast, while beside her, Oswald lowered his cup. The priest's gaze was wary.

Ecgfrith met Hea's gaze across the table. "It comes sooner than expected … sooner than you foresaw."

Hea tensed. This was the first time he had ever openly criticized her. It probably would have been best not to answer him, but Hea's pride could not let his criticism go unanswered. "My visions do not give exact predictions, sire."

His expression hardened, making it clear her answer did not please him. Another brittle silence settled before Oswald eventually broke it. "What has happened, milord?"

Ecgfrith turned to the priest, his expression grim. "Bridei mac Beli has begun raiding deep into Northumbrian territory."

Hea's belly clenched at this news. He was right, she had not foreseen this. She had thought that the campaign was still some time off … high summer at the earliest. For the first time ever, she doubted her skills. Her mother had been so confident in her own abilities as a seer, but Hea sometimes felt as if she wielded her gift blindly.

"When will you leave for the north, milord?" Irmenburgh asked, her gaze flicking up to meet his.

"We march north in two days," he replied, "and we will hit the Picts with the full force of my fyrd." His attention then returned to the priest. "My army needs a man of God at their side—a man who can allay their fears and light the fire of righteousness in their bellies."

Oswald went ghostly white at this news. He glanced across at the queen but she was staring down at her trencher, avoiding his gaze. "Is that really necessary, milord," the priest asked, his voice faltering. "I would only get in the way."

Ecgfrith's mouth thinned. "You will be vital to keeping morale high—those blue-painted savages strike fear into the hearts of many men. You must remind them that we have Christ on our side."

Oswald swallowed, his throat bobbing, before he nodded.

Hea cleared her throat. "Lord Ecgfrith. I wish to join your campaign and travel north at your side."

A stunned hush settled over the table. Rinan, who had been listening to the conversation thus far, snorted into his cup of mead, while Oswald stared at her as if she had lost her wits.

Although she had little love for the priest, Hea agreed with him. The last thing she wanted was to ride to war—but if she remained here then the future she had glimpsed would surely come to pass. She had to find a way to change it ... if she did not, Bridei—and all his men—would die.

Ecgfrith watched her steadily, his face bemused. "Why would you wish that, Hea?"

"This battle is crucial for Northumbria," she replied. "Over the past few months, my guidance has been crucial to you, sire. I wish to continue my work. Not only that, but my healing skills will come in useful during the campaign."

"She'll only get in the way, milord." Rinan growled from further down the table. "Her presence will unsettle and distract the men."

Ecgfrith ignored his thegn. Instead, he watched Hea for a few moments more before a smile stretched across his face. "Your loyalty to your king pleases me," he murmured, picking up his cup and raising it to her in a toast. "Yes, Hea—you may ride north with us."

What have I done?

Hea walked from the Great Tower in a daze. Outside, the spring evening—which had felt balmy with the promise of summer earlier—now felt chill. Shivering, Hea rubbed her bare arms and wished she had brought a woolen shawl with her.

Deep in thought, she navigated the network of narrow lanes back to her hovel, her mind whirling.

What makes you think you can change anything?

She had never seen a battle, and had no wish to. She knew the king would not expect her to fight; instead, she would watch the battle from afar and then join the king once victory was assured. Even so, the thought of seeing death and carnage up close made her feel ill. She would have preferred to remain here in Bebbanburg, with her flowers, herbs, and remedies. Yet she had thrown herself into this situation.

Hea looked around her—taking in the low wooden dwellings with their thatch and sod roofs, the shadow of the outer palisade against an indigo sky. This was her home, and she could not bear to see it threatened. The folk here lived in peace. She had heard tales of wars in the years gone by, of all the women widowed, of all the children left fatherless. There had been times in the past when Bebbanburg had lost many of its menfolk to war.

Despite that Ecgfrith's trust in her appeared to be weakening, she had to keep trying to turn him away from violence.

Arriving home, she found Fritha waiting for her outside. Concerned, Hea quickened her pace down the narrow lane and approached her. "What is it?"

Fritha smiled. "Nothing to look so worried about, lass. Hengist has belly-ache again—and needs something to soothe it."

Relieved, Hea exhaled. "I'll make him up something now—come in."

She led the way inside the warm, smoky space, lit only by the glowing embers of the hearth. Deftly, she lit the cressets around the one-room dwelling, which cast a lambent light over her humble home, before she made her way over to her work table.

Hea worked quickly and confidently. This mixture was one she made for Fritha's husband often. It consisted of dandelion root, St. John's wort, lemon balm, calendula, and fennel.

"Tell Hengist he needs to stay away from rich food," Hea advised Fritha as she worked. "His belly will thank him for it."

"Aye, but his greed is stronger than his good sense," Fritha sighed.

Hea crushed the herbs together with a pestle and mortar, and added a little water before pouring the contents into a clay bottle. Inserting a stopper, she then passed it to Fritha. "Don't forget, he needs to take it before each meal."

Fritha nodded, smiling gratefully. Her gaze settled on Hea's face, before it narrowed slightly. "Is something amiss?"

Hea stifled a sigh; she could never hide anything from Fritha. "The king's army marches north in two days," she said after a few moments, "and I'm going with them."

Fritha's eyes went huge at this news, and she clutched at her chest, muttering an oath. "Has the king commanded you?"

Hea shook her head. "I asked to join him."

Fritha looked aghast. "Why ever would you do that?"

Hea's mouth twisted. She wanted to tell Fritha the full truth—that she had to do something to prevent Bridei's death—yet she held back from doing so. Hea trusted her friend, but knew she would not agree with her decision. "The king has come to depend on my guidance of late," she replied, avoiding Fritha's eye. "My herbal remedies will also be of use to the army. I want to do what I can to help."

Fritha's brow furrowed. "Ecgfrith's men can advise him, and there are other healers they can bring north. It's too dangerous for you, Hea."

Hea shrugged. "I shall be in the rearguard, with the supply wagons and servants. Worry not."

Fritha looked unconvinced, and so Hea placed an arm around her shoulders. "Stop fretting. I'll be careful."

Once Fritha had gone, Hea poured herself a cup of wine and sat down next to the hearth.

Fritha's cheerful presence had distracted her for a short while, but now that her friend had gone home, Hea was alone with her thoughts once more.

She took a large gulp of wine, sighing as it warmed the hollowness of her belly. This whole situation boded ill, she knew it in her bones.

Hea took another gulp of wine, willing it to be stronger so it would obliterate the anxiety that now curled like smoke within her. Hearing of Bridei's death many days afterward was one thing, but listening the roar of battle and knowing he would fall was another.

She had to do something to change the future. Bridei was supposed to be her enemy, but she could not bear to see him die.

Tears spilled over, the first she had wept for Bridei since the day of his departure months earlier. She had cried a lake of tears that day, wept till she felt hollowed out. After that she had forced herself to shove her grief into the recesses of her mind and get on with living. But her fortitude was a fragile thing.

It did not matter what lies she told herself, how outraged she felt at his presumption and arrogance—the fact remained that when Bridei rode away from Bebbanburg, he had taken a piece of her heart with him.

Hea hiccoughed, not bothering to wipe away the tears that now streamed down her cheeks. She wished she had not glimpsed a vision of the future. There were some things you were better off not knowing.

Chapter Eighteen

Pawns between Kings

THE NORTHUMBRIAN FYRD moved out on a warm, misty morning. A bank of cloud had settled over the sea to the east, its thick, milky tendrils drifting in and wreathing through the narrow streets and alleys of Bebbanburg.

Hea sat astride a small, shaggy bay gelding named Rowan, waiting while the army made final preparations before departure. Despite that the pony had long since shed his winter coat, he was still a hairy beast, with a spiky black mane that stuck out at odd angles. Rowan's furry ears flicked about inquisitively as he watched men and horses move around him.

Hea's gaze was elsewhere. She watched Ecgfrith emerge from the Great Tower and descend the stone steps toward the throng. His wife followed a few discreet steps behind.

If Irmenburgh was distressed about her husband's departure, she showed no sign. Her neat features were composed as usual into a serene expression, framed by a pale cream headrail.

At the foot of the steps, Ecgfrith turned to face her. Hea could not hear the words that passed between them then, although their body language spoke volumes. The king was a striking sight in leather, chainmail, and a wolf-pelt cloak that hung from his shoulders, making him look broader and stronger than he really was. His expression was cool as he met his wife's gaze and murmured a few words.

Irmenburgh looked up at him, and for a moment they stared at each other. It was the most intimate scene that Hea had ever witnessed between the pair; a moment of silent recognition. She had never thought their marriage close, or passionate, but in that look she saw affection—a wordless acknowledgement of the bond they shared.

Ecgfrith murmured something, and the queen nodded. Then, he turned and strode away, leaving her staring after him.

A massive chestnut stallion awaited the Northumbrian king. Rinan stood at its head, next to his own horse and held the beast while Ecgfrith swung up onto its back. The horse snorted and pawed the ground, the moment the king had mounted. It sensed the nervous tension in the air, and was eager to be off.

Ecgfrith's horse was not the only one excited to set out on this journey. Around them, male voices rose and fell, interspersed with laughter. The warrior nearest Hea—a rawboned man with long brown hair—cast her a wide grin. "We ride to victory eh, seer?"

Hea smiled back, although inside she felt sick with nerves. She was glad that news of her vision had boosted morale among Ecgfrith's men—yet their enthusiasm this morning also caused a heavy cloak of responsibility to settle over her shoulders.

They might be riding to victory, but Bridei was journeying to his doom.

Once the king had mounted, Rinan swung up onto the back of his bay gelding, a bigger, heavier version of the beast that Hea rode. The warrior then glanced over his shoulder at where the priest sat upon a stocky grey pony. Seeing the man's pallor and pinched face, Rinan grinned. "Ready for war, Oswald?"

The priest gave him a tight nod before forcing a sickly smile. "I will bring God's word north with us."

"Be sure you do," the king interjected, throwing Oswald a look of thinly veiled disgust. "You're to be of some use to me."

With that, Ecgfrith urged his stallion forward, cutting through the throng toward the high gate. Men and horses parted, before falling in behind him. Carried along with the tide, Hea rode out of the inner palisade and down the King's Way. Crowds of men, women, and children lined the thoroughfare, all gathered to see the king depart. Bannermen rode before the king, holding aloft the Northumbrian standards—eight yellow rectangles on a blood-red field.

Despite her own trepidation, Hea felt her skin prickle at the roar of the crowd and the pride on the faces of those she passed. A pretty young woman with curly brown hair approached the king as he rode by, adoration on her face. She rushed forward and passed him a posy of spring flowers.

"To Northumbria and your victory, milord!"

Ecgfrith smiled down at her, taking the flowers in his gloved hand. Around them, the folk of Bebbanburg shouted their approval, their voices echoing in the still morning. Looking on, Hea felt her chest tighten with pride.

However, her elation lasted only until they left the fort.

The moment she was riding north, over rolling farmland shrouded in sea mist, the nerves returned. She had barely been able to eat anything the past two days, for her stomach had closed and anxiety had robbed her of appetite.

She rode now, around half a furlong behind the king and his bannermen. Spears bristled against the horizon, piercing the mist, and the sound of heavy hoofbeats, the snorts of horses, the jangling of bridles, and the creak of leather filled the grey morning.

Rowan strode out, often breaking into a jolting trot in his eagerness to reach the front of the column. Hea had to keep a tight rein to hold him back. A few yards to her left rode Oswald. He was not a natural horsemen; one glance and she could see that. Although Hea had not ridden often over the years, she was enjoying it and bonded quickly to her mount. Yet with Oswald it was not so—grim-faced he clung to his pony's bushy mane, his jaw clenched tight. With every stride he lurched forward.

"Relax, priest." One of the warriors riding alongside Oswald called out to him. "Stop riding as if you have a spear up your arse—we've got a while yet before we meet the Picts."

Male laughter rang out around them and Oswald's shoulders hunched, before he cast the warrior who had spoken a quelling look. Still, he did his best to loosen his posture, much to the mirth of the men riding behind him.

Jedburgh burned. Smoke drifted up into the noon sky, staining it dark. The screams of village folk, as they ran from the flames and raiders, echoed over the soft green of the borderlands.

Bridei stood amongst the ruins of the village and surveyed the damage his men had wrought. His gaze narrowed as he watched the ealdorman's hall go up like a torch—wood, wattle and straw devoured by hungry flames. It was a pity to lay waste to Jedburgh—the hamlet had been one of the most prosperous of the borderlands—but it was necessary.

His men had killed any locals who opposed them, including the ealdorman himself, while letting the rest flee south.

Someone had to bring word to the Northumbrian king.

"This should put a wasp up Ecgfrith's arse." Fearghus had stepped up beside Bridei. The warrior was splattered with blood but unhurt; it had been a short but violent struggle to take Jedburgh, and they had lost three of their own men which was vexing.

Bridei nodded brusquely, his gaze still on the burning hall. "That's the intention," he replied.

Heolstor appeared at his side then, a burning torch in his hand. "That's all of the houses torched," he announced.

Bridei tore his gaze from the flames. "Did you make sure the homes were empty first?"

Heolstor nodded. "There was a child hiding under the table of one of the hovels, but I sent her away before I set fire to the dwelling."

"Good." Bridei's gaze slid around the market square in which they stood. Overturned carts and cabbages, parsnips, and bunches of kale littered the ground—the raid had interrupted the morning market. "Leave the food behind. As soon as we're gone, folk will come back to reclaim it ... I don't want them starving on our account."

Fearghus gave him an incredulous look. "You won't get any gratitude, Lord Bridei. They'll curse you anyway."

"I don't want their thanks," Bridei replied, resheathing the iron sword. "It's just unfortunate they're pawns between two kings."

"What now?" Heolstor asked. "Do you want to risk riding south, raiding another village?"

Bridei shook his head. "Ecgfrith will have mobilized his army by now—it's time we turned north."

Heolstor frowned. "We're retreating?"

Bridei grinned at him. Heolstor was a good friend, and a skilled fighter, but he lacked tactical skills and cunning. He slapped the Angle on the back. "No, we're going to leave a trail for him to follow."

Heolstor's deepening frown told him that the warrior still did not understand his meaning. Bridei gave a huff of frustration; he had already spoken of this campaign to Heolstor numerous times, but he still failed to grasp what Bridei had in mind. To him, such maneuvering was cowardly. He preferred to rush headlong into battle.

Bridei stepped back and gestured around him. "The lowlands will suit the Northumbrian fyrd—they are used to this land, and even though our numbers are likely to be evenly matched, they could easily beat us on this terrain. We need to lead the Northumbrians north, to the land of hills, gullies, and ravines. That's where we will make our stand."

"How far north are you planning?" Fearghus asked, his heavy brow furrowed.

"North of the River Forth," Bridei replied. "Let's make Ecgfrith sweat a bit first."

Both warriors laughed at that, although they looked surprised. The Forth was a number of days ride north—they had not expected Bridei to lead Ecgfrith on such a merry dance.

"He'll be livid," Heolstor warned Bridei. "By the time he catches up with us, Ecgfrith will be ready to strangle you with his bare hands."

Bridei grinned once more. "That's the idea."

Fearghus gave a low whistle. "You truly hate the man, don't you?"

"Aye." Bridei's grin faded. "I have many reasons to."

Memories that were best forgotten arose then.

The beating Ecgfrith had given him, one week after his arrival when he had referred to his father Beli, as 'Lord of the North'. Being made to sleep with the dogs for a month when he had insulted the king in Pictish. Ecgfrith's refusal to let him visit his dying mother. And then finally ... the whipping Bridei had been given for defending Hea from Rinan.

Every one of these slights stuck in Bridei's craw.

Aware that Fearghus and Heolstor were watching him, trying to read his face, Bridei shrugged. He was too old to carry around the slights of boyhood, and it irritated him that he still grew angry when he thought of Ecgfrith's mistreatment of him, and of his disdain for Bridei's people. Bridei did not want his men to pity him—for he was no sniveling weakling.

Even so, the need for vengeance burned like a torch within him. He had suffered the Northumbrian yoke for too long; it was time to cast it off forever.

"Ecgfrith knew this day was coming," he growled. "He has always known."

Chapter Nineteen

Into the North

HEA INHALED THE sweet scent of heather and looked out over a landscape of craggy, green hills. It was a warm afternoon. A humid wind blew in from the south-east, reminding Hea that they stood on the cusp of summer. It was Thrimilce—the Month of Three Milkings—her favorite time of the year.

Taking a bite of griddle bread, Hea chewed slowly and enjoyed the brief moment of rest. She perched atop a moss-encrusted stone, at the top of one of the rocky hills, enjoying a simple but very welcome noon meal.

The great Northumbrian fyrd—an army of around eight hundred spears and horsemen—spread around her like a great, bristling thicket. Men's voices drifted into the balmy spring air, and overhead two sparrows dived and fluttered against the pale blue sky.

Hea sighed. She had expected to find the lands north of her home desolate and depressing—and yet the farther they traveled, the more she liked it. The landscape had an untamed beauty that she appreciated.

However, not everyone shared her admiration. A few feet away, Oswald sat hunched over, his face pinched with discomfort as he nibbled at a piece of hard cheese. The past ten days had been a trial for the priest. He had suffered through every one of them. She had been observing him closely, curious to see how he would cope on the journey

Feeling her gaze upon him, Oswald glanced up and frowned. "Did you want something?" he demanded, his cheeks coloring. "You're always staring."

Hea snorted, while behind her some of the men laughed. "Watch out, Oswald," one of them shouted. "Or the wench will ensnare you with her beauty."

"Don't worry about that," another called out. "A priest wouldn't know what to do with a woman anyway."

Oswald went the color of a beetroot. He swung round and glared at his tormentors, his blue eyes narrowed—but this merely increased their mirth.

"That's enough," Hea interjected, swallowing a smile. She was not fond of the priest, but still did not want to see him humiliated. The warriors could be cruel at times.

Oswald cast her an odd look then—a blend of gratitude and resentment—before he turned his back on the men who, ignoring Hea's plea, continued to rib him.

Shifting her attention away from the priest, Hea looked down the hill, at where Ecgfrith was standing with a knot of his warriors, Rinan among them. They looked to be discussing the campaign—and although she could not make out their conversation, she could see from the king's facial expression that there was some disagreement going on.

Ecgfrith's mood had gradually darkened during the ride north.

Bridei's army had sacked many villages, including the prosperous settlement of Jedburgh. Ecgfrith had raged when he had seen the ealdorman's hall reduced to a pile of smoking cinders. They had also burned the wooden church to the ground, something which had horrified Oswald. Ignored by the king and his men, the priest had fallen to his knees and wept beside the charred ruins. Hea had surveyed the devastation, and felt a sense of foreboding prickle her skin. The Northumbrians were riding to victory, but they were likely to suffer losses all the same.

Bridei's actions had been deliberate, that much was certain. He had wanted to bait Ecgfrith—and seeing the fury on her king's face as he surveyed the remains of Jedburgh, she realized he had achieved his goal.

"That maggot will feel my blade," he had snarled, before turning away, his wolfskin cloak billowing behind him. "He will pay for this."

And yet they had not yet caught him.

The Pict army now cut north, leaving the ruins of border villages behind them. Ecgfrith's fyrd was in hot pursuit. However, last eve, Hea had overheard Ecgfrith arguing with his ealdormen and most trusted thegns. Some advised him against following Bridei so far north, warning the king he could be riding into a trap, but Ecgfrith cast aside their worries.

Perhaps they were having the same argument once more, for Ecgfrith's face had gone stony, and he was glaring at Rinan, whose own face had reddened. The warrior was one of the group who had questioned Ecgfrith's decision.

The Northumbrian king was not a man who liked to have his actions second-guessed.

Watching them, Hea felt frustration swell in her breast. For days now, she had tried to get close enough to the king to speak to him. But on the few occasions she had managed to get his attention at the end of the day, he had been too tired and preoccupied to talk to her.

"They're bickering again, aren't they?"

Oswald's voice behind her made Hea turn. Still pink in the face, his attention was now focused upon the king and his retainers below.

Hea nodded, watching the priest warily.

"The king should listen to them," he muttered. "We have no business traveling this far north."

"We're still on Northumbrian lands," Hea reminded him.

Oswald frowned. "They're ours in name only," he replied, keeping his voice low so that no one would overhear him. "Look around you—what real hold do you think Ecgfrith has over this place?"

Hea held his gaze for a moment, surprised by his candor. She wondered at his decision to confide in her. Yet after ten days of being shunned by most of the warriors he rode amongst, Hea was likely the nearest thing he had to a friend.

Although she would not voice it, she agreed with him. "So you think it's folly to follow him north?"

"Aye—only a fool would follow a wolf into its lair. Bridei mac Beli will know this land well, and he will be gathering more men to him as he travels north."

Oswald looked away then, breaking eye contact. His lean body tensed and he moved away from her, as if realizing that he had perhaps said too much.

Hea glanced back down at where Ecgfrith had just terminated his discussions and stormed off.

A horn blew across the hills; a long, lonely wail that never failed to make the hair on the back of Hea's neck prickle. The noon rest was over; they were moving on once more.

That night they camped on the hillside above a clear brook. As soon as the fyrd stopped for the day, Ecgfrith's men fell into the routine they had established on the first day out from Bebbanburg. Some rubbed down and watered and fed the horses, before tethering them, while others unrolled lengths of hide and fashioned low tents around four large fire pits.

There were few trees in this landscape, so most nights they burned peat on the fires; its pungent odor drifting over the encampment.

Hea did her share of the work alongside the men, helping with the horses before assisting with supper. Meals consisted of barley and vegetable pottage, roast rabbit or water-fowl, and hastily prepared griddle bread: simple but hearty fare that would keep an army on its feet.

Although she had left Bebbanburg with a knotted stomach, ten days on the road had made Hea's appetite return quickly. She was ravenous at the end of each day riding.

Her mouth watered now, as she roasted a row of rabbit carcasses on a spit over the fire. She had never appreciated food as much as she did on this journey.

A few feet away, Ecgfrith sat upon a stool by the largest of the firepits, a cup of ale in hand. His expression was introspective as he stared into the dancing flames. Hea wondered if the disagreements with his most trusted warriors were beginning to erode his confidence. Yet Rinan and the small group who agreed with him were the minority here.

Tonight, the mood in the camp was cheerful. A group of men were singing as they passed around a horn of mead; she could hear one of them boasting of his exploits in battle, while his companions heckled him. This game would likely last all night.

Feeling Hea's gaze upon him, the king glanced up. He blinked, as if he had not even realized she was present. After a moment, he favored her with a smile. "Enjoying the march north?"

Hea smiled back. "Well enough, milord."

"None of the men are giving you any trouble?"

"No, sire." For the most part, the men had welcomed her on this journey. Hea had predicted victory for this campaign; she sensed that having her with them reassured some of the warriors.

Ecgfrith nodded. "I require you this eve," he said, after a moment. "Can you come to my tent after supper?"

Hea inclined her head, pleased she would finally get the opportunity to speak with him alone. "Of course, milord."

A gentle dusk settled over the hills of Fortriu. Hea was making her way from her own small tent, across the clearing to the king's considerably larger one, when the sound of singing made her halt.

Somewhere in the camp, a man's deep voice rang out. A warrior seated around the fire sang a strident ballad. Clutching her seeing drum to her breast, excitement feathered across Hea's skin as she listened.

> *The warrior must fight*
> *The warrior must stand*
> *Behind the shield*
> *Before the wall*
> *For victory, for honor*

> *The warrior must slay*
> *The warrior must lay waste*
> *Destroy his enemy*
> *Defend his land*
> *For valor, for honor*

Hea stood there a while, listening to each verse, her breath catching. The man had a mesmerizing voice. Yet at the same time, the song unnerved her. It was a reminder of what was to come … of the slaughter in that bleak valley.

She forced herself to move on, and crossed the last few yards to Ecgfrith's tent.

Hea pushed aside the flap and ducked inside. Her boots sank into thick furs, and her gaze swept over the interior, taking in the intricately patterned tapestries hung from the ceiling, covering the hide walls. A brazier burned in the center of the space, throwing out a circle of warmth. The tent was cavernous compared to Hea's cramped lodgings, and a hanging made from rabbit pelts shielded the king's sleeping area at the back of it.

Ecgfrith himself sat upon a stool near the brazier. He was smiling as he listened to the final verse of the song.

"Morale is high amongst my men." His gaze shifted to Hea. "Thanks to you."

Hea smiled back, although nervousness fluttered in her belly. "I think you are the reason, milord," she replied. "Your men are loyal, they trust their king."

His shrewd hazel gaze met hers then. "And you know that for a fact do you?" he challenged. "Have you seen it in your visions?"

The sharpness in his tone made her draw back slightly. Was he still sore over the fact that some of his retainers disagreed with his relentless pursuit of the Picts north?

"No, milord," she replied, holding his gaze. "I do not need to consult the spirit world to know such things. I see it in their faces. They will fight for you, and they will die for you—without question."

The look on his face then surprised, and unsettled, her. He wore an odd expression: a blend of regret and longing.

"You are so like her," he murmured after a pause. "The same fire, the same courage."

Hea tensed. Whom was he speaking of … her mother?

His next sentence confirmed her suspicions. "Lewren was never afraid to speak her mind … even when it wasn't in her best interests to do so."

She stared back at him. A queasy feeling rose within her when a suspicion dawned.

"Were you lovers?" She had asked the question so quietly, breathed it, that for a moment she had thought he had not heard her. It was a bold thing to ask—something he was in his rights to punish her for, yet the words were out before she could stop them.

Ecgfrith's face tightened, and he held her gaze for a heartbeat longer before tearing his own away. He stared into the flames of the brazier, his expression unreadable. "Aye … for a time. Many years ago now."

Hea's heart started to pound against her ribs like a seeing drum.

Suddenly, it was as if a veil had pulled back. To her knowledge, her mother had only ever given herself to one man … Hea's father.

Chapter Twenty

The Bastard

A WAVE OF nausea swept over Hea. She stared at King Ecgfrith of Northumbria, as if truly seeing him for the first time.

Suddenly, the few details her mother had shared with her over the years fell into place. For the first time she understood why Lewren had been so vague about the man who had fathered Hea. Her tale of him riding away to war and never returning had been a deliberate lie to throw Hea off the scent.

To hide the identity of her real sire.

Hea swallowed with difficulty. "You're my father?"

Ecgfrith's face twisted. "You look horrified, Hea—did you really never suspect?"

Hea shook her head. Her tongue felt cloven to the roof of her mouth. She remembered her mother's final, bitter words on her deathbed—it all made sense now.

"Did you ever ask yourself why your mother and you both lived unmolested in my stronghold?" Ecgfrith asked.

Frankly, Hea had thought it was due to their positions as seer. However, the king's words felt as if someone had just dumped a bucket of cold sea-water over her head.

"Why ... why did she never tell me?" Hea finally managed. Her legs felt weak, and she stumbled over to a stool to the left of the brazier, where she seated herself without asking for the king's permission—something she would never have dared do ... until now.

"I warned her from doing so," Ecgfrith replied. "I had just been made king, and was awaiting the arrival of my betrothed from East Anglia—I could not have word reaching my new bride that I had sired a bastard."

Hea flinched at the word, but Ecgfrith did not seem to notice. Instead his gaze was upon the dancing flames of the brazier as he continued to speak.

"Not that it would have mattered if Aethelhild had learned of your existence—for she was a frigid bitch who refused to lie with me."

So you raped her handmaid instead ...

Bile rose in Hea's throat. She had heard the tale about the young, innocent Aelfwyn, and what the king had done to her.

This man is my father.

If Hea had been alone, she would have wept. "Did my mother lie with you ... willingly?" she finally choked out. She had to know the truth. Had Lewren loved this man?

Ecgfrith's eyes narrowed and Hea studied his face. She had spent little time gazing at her own reflection, just a few instances in a still pond over the years. Yet she knew that she bore no resemblance to him.

"Did I rape her, you mean?"

Hea's pulse accelerated, but she held firm and nodded. "Did you?"

A nerve feathered in Ecgfrith's jaw, and she saw anger flicker across his lean face. But she did not care if her boldness earned her a flogging, or if he sent her away. The shock of learning she was his bastard had made her cast aside all her cares.

She wanted the truth.

"I was young when I met Lewren," he growled finally. "Far younger than you are now, as was she. And when you have that age, you care not for the future. We had one summer together, and then her womb quickened. We could not continue to see each other, but Lewren took a while to accept that."

Hea choked down her own anger. She imagined her mother's hurt when her lover turned on her. Now she understood the bitterness that had festered within Lewren for years.

"A flower seller and a king." Ecgfrith ran a hand through his short sandy hair, and Hea was surprised to note that his hand trembled slightly. "What would my kingdom think of that? I'd have been reviled, a laughing stock. A king must wed to strengthen his political alliances, to secure his borders ... not for love."

Hea stared at him. "Did you love her?"

Ecgfrith snorted and rose to his feet, pacing the perimeter of the tent. "Women have such a simplistic view of the world," he muttered. "Your mother did too. What does love matter? What counts is power—the warrior and the sword are the only things of value in this world."

Watching him, Hea felt a pang of pity. What a hollow existence this man had led. He had forsaken human warmth and kindness for a cold, empty throne. Neither of his wives had produced an heir. If he survived the coming days, he would grow into a bitter old man.

"And yet you did care for her," Hea observed. "I see it on your face."

Ecgfrith stopped pacing and whirled round to face her. "It was all a long time ago." He bit out each word as if they cost him. "Another lifetime. It's all gone now—all dead and buried." His voice died away then, his gaze pinning her to the spot. "Except you ... my bastard daughter. My gifted daughter."

Hearing him claim her as his caused panic to grip Hea's ribcage in a vise. Confusion turned her mind to porridge and robbed her of her wits. She did not know what to say, or how to respond. There were no words that could convey how she felt at that moment.

As a child she had lain awake at night imagining what it would have been like to be reunited with her long-lost father. What if he had not died in battle, but returned victorious? She had imagined how happy she would be—how the three of them would become the family she had always craved.

Never in her wildest imaginings had she suspected this.

Alone in her tiny tent, Hea wept.

She had gone to the king, thinking he wanted her counsel. It would have been the perfect opportunity to caution him about his single-minded pursuit of Bridei's army north. She had wanted to advise him against being reckless and overconfident.

None of that seemed to matter now though ... not in the face of what she had just learned.

Hea's chest constricted as she attempted to muffle her sobs with her hands. Why now? Why reveal the truth about her parentage on the road to war?

Perhaps Ecgfrith had become aware of his own mortality of late—maybe he had wanted her to know the truth of her bloodline ... just in case the battle went ill. He was not a sentimental man, she knew that, and yet he was an inherently lonely one. It was his own doing—for he had made choices at a young age that had led to his current state.

Hea scrubbed at her burning eyes. She had come north hoping to make a difference, but hopelessness now consumed her.

My mother lay with that man.

The truth was that although she was loyal to Ecgfrith—for he was her king—she hated the thought of him being her father. He was a cold, calculating, and selfish individual. A chill went through her as she considered the truth.

His blood runs through my veins ... perhaps I am a little like him?

The rain pelted down, great sheets tearing across the land of green hills and shallow valleys. It was not cold, just unrelentingly wet—the rain had started shortly after dawn and as noon approached it showed no sign of ceasing.

The army moved steadily north, although the mood had changed this morning. There was a tension in the air that had not been there a day earlier; as if the men sensed battle was approaching. Even the horses seemed on edge, including Hea's pony, Rowan. She had to keep him on a short rein, as he jogged, tossed his head, and snorted.

Even so, Hea found it hard to pay attention to her surroundings as she traveled in the rear guard of Ecgfrith's mighty fyrd. Ever since the king's revelation the night before, she had been in a daze.

She had not seen Ecgfrith since their conversation—in fact she had made a point of avoiding him at sunrise. She still found it difficult to accept who he really was ... who she really was.

Up ahead, the line of horses drew to an abrupt halt. Jolted out of her brooding, Hea pulled Rowan up short and peered through the curtain of rain. "Why are we stopping?" she called out to Oswald. "Is it noon already?"

He glanced back at her over his shoulder, his face drawn with exhaustion. "Not yet."

"Something's happening up ahead," the warrior riding next to Oswald informed them. "Riders are approaching."

Hea tensed at this news, for she knew that Ecgfrith had sent out scouts ahead of his army. What news had they returned with?

It took a while for the word that had reached the fyrd's vanguard to filter down through the rest of the army—by which time Hea, Oswald, and the others around them had dismounted and were consuming a meal of dried meat and soggy bread.

"What news?" Oswald asked as the surrounding warriors muttered amongst themselves, ignoring him. "What word from the north?"

"War draws near, priest." One of the men cast Oswald an irritated look over his shoulder. "The Pict army has gathered on a plain around fifty furlongs north of here."

Oswald went still at this news, while Hea's heart fluttered. She looked around her, confused; for the first time that day she properly took in her surroundings. This was not the landscape she had seen in her vision—the hills were too low and rounded, the sky too large. She had seen a narrow valley with rock-studded sides rearing overhead. The news could not be right.

And yet, judging from the fierce looks on the men's faces, it was.

A horn blew one drawn-out, mournful note that seemed to go on forever—a call to arms.

The warrior who had spoken looked over at Hea and Oswald. "You two aren't much use in a shield wall. Stay behind the army where you'll not get underfoot."

Oswald's face tightened, and he drew himself up. "I should bless the warriors," he replied. "Give them words of courage before they go into battle."

"We've heard enough from you to last a life-time," another man—a heavy-set man with a mane of golden hair—called out. Hea cast a gaze over the warrior and noted that he wore Thunor's hammer proudly around his neck. The iron pendant glinted, even in the day's murk. Like many among the fyrd, he worshipped the old gods. "Get to the back," the man snarled, "and say your prayers where I don't need to hear them."

Hea took this as her cue to depart. She climbed up onto Rowan's back and guided him through the crowd of spearmen who were forming ranks, readying themselves for battle. Eventually, she reached the end of the column, where a collection of wagons bearing tents and supplies squelched over the waterlogged ground.

Falling in next to them, she noted that Oswald had followed her. However, he did not look pleased about it. The warriors had deliberately humiliated him, and spurned his assistance. Had the king been present, they would not have been so cruel; yet Ecgfrith was occupied farther ahead and there was no one to defend the priest.

Oswald knew when he was beaten.

"Heathens," he growled under his breath as he reined his pony in next to Hea.

Hea quirked an eyebrow. "I thought you were supposed to be praying for them?"

The priest huffed out a frustrated breath. "Cuthbert spoke the truth," he replied. "We should never have traveled to this godforsaken place."

Chapter Twenty-one

Retreat

THEY RODE FORWARD for a while; the creak of wooden wheels, the thump of heavy hooves and the hiss of rain accompanying them. Anticipation rippled through the army; Hea could taste it—even from this far back. Gone was the conversation, the easy banter between the men.

The army halted once more, and the wagons stayed where they were, protected by a tight circle of spearman, while the rest rode forward to engage the enemy.

Rowan snorted and jangled his bit, eager to follow the other horses. Hea leaned forward, stroking the pony's furry neck. "Best stay here, boy," she told him.

They had halted in a shallow vale, intersected by a burn. The rain had eased slightly; it was now falling in a heavy grey mist over the land, closing them in.

Hea looked north, peering through the mist at where the last of the men had disappeared. How far ahead were Bridei and his men?

Thinking upon Bridei made her stomach contract. For the first time in many months they were just a short distance apart, although he would not know that—and would likely not care either. She imagined him, tall and proud, his gaze hard as he watched Ecgfrith's army approach. A moment later, she pushed the image away, cursing herself for allowing her mind to stray.

Thoughts of Bridei were the last thing she needed right now.

It was a long, tense wait.

Hea and Oswald exchanged few words, their gazes trained north, their ears straining for the shouts of victory, or wails of defeat. The afternoon dragged, and the rain eventually stopped, yet the men did not return. Hea dismounted from Rowan and loosened his girth, letting him crop grass, for it appeared they would wait longer still.

It grew unnaturally quiet, and an odd stillness seemed to settle across the land—like an indrawn breath.

Hea grew increasingly nervous. Her vision had been so clear, but now she started to doubt herself. What if the spirit world had been playing tricks on her?

The shadows lengthened and the afternoon slid into evening. As the light started to fade, those left behind set up shelters in-between the wagons and eased their hunger with hunks of stale bread and cheese.

Eventually, as the last of the day drained from the western sky, Oswald spoke. He had spent most of the afternoon brooding, but now frustration appeared to get the better of him. "Where are they?"

"I don't know," Hea replied, her gaze riveted north, "but I don't like this silence. It bodes ill."

Oswald frowned, his slim face hardening. "Not so confident now, are we? It was your vision that sent Ecgfrith charging north. If things don't go as you predicted, you will have the blood of many on your hands."

Hea flinched as if he had struck her. "I know what I saw," she replied through gritted teeth. "The king trusts my word."

"Aye ... blindly."

Hea glared at him, although her heart had started to pound against her ribs. She hated Oswald for pointing this out, yet she knew he spoke the truth. Ecgfrith's belief in her vision was unshakable. He was blinkered.

"The king is a warrior," she said, struggling to keep her voice steady. "He knows how to conduct a campaign, how to fight his enemies. He will not do anything foolish."

Oswald opened his mouth, no doubt to disagree with her, when the thunder of horses' hooves reached them—approaching from the north.

Hea emerged from under the hide shelter and peered into the gloom. Suddenly, she felt exposed out here; for she carried no weapon save a small knife at her waist that she used for boning meat or filleting fish. Her argument with Oswald had unsettled her. What if she had misjudged everything? What if Ecgfrith had fallen and it was the Picts riding toward them?

Heart pounding, she fumbled at her waist and drew the knife.

"Wes hāl!"

Hea's breath gusted out of her as she recognized the language of her own people. They were Angles rather than Picts that rode toward them. Behind her, Oswald struggled out of the shelter and rushed forward toward the group of horsemen that emerged from the darkness.

"What news?" he asked. "How fares the king?"

"We met them five furlongs north of here," one of the warriors replied, gasping as he struggled to recover his breath, "and fought long. Their numbers are greater than we had expected, but we managed to push back against them, and they are now in retreat."

Retreat? This news shocked Hea. She could not imagine Bridei mac Beli retreating from Ecgfrith ... ever.

"Where is the king?" she asked.

"He and the bulk of the army have ridden north, tracking those Pict cowards," the warrior informed her. "We must ride north and join him, for at first light we will set after our quarry once more."

The sky had started to clear, and a waxing moon had risen high into the heavens, by the time the wagons and those who had waited behind with them reached the Northumbrian camp.

Yawning, for the stress of the day had exhausted her, Hea saw to her pony before making her way through the sea of weather-stained tents and smoldering fire pits, toward the center of the camp. The atmosphere was one of weariness but optimism. Men gathered around the fires, still in their battle armor.

Hea walked through their midst. She took note of the injured warriors she passed—for she would help them later—but first she had to see Ecgfrith. Oswald followed close at her heels. Like Hea, the priest was eager to see the king and hear of this afternoon's battle.

Ecgfrith's tent loomed before them in the center of the camp, the Northumbrian pennant fluttering from atop its peaked roof.

Hea entered Ecgfrith's tent, suddenly hesitant, for she had not been summoned. She found him seated inside, finishing a frugal supper of seedcake and cheese. He glanced up, smiling when he spied Hea. Then his gaze alighted upon Oswald who emerged at her shoulder, and his smile faded.

"I was wondering when you two would catch us up," he greeted them. "Sit down and pour yourselves a cup of mead. Tonight we have cause for celebration."

Cautious, Hea did as bid, pouring her and Oswald cups of mead from a clay jug on the low table.

"Is it not premature for celebration, milord?" Oswald asked, clasping the cup in his hands as he lowered himself to the ground. "The enemy has not yet been defeated."

The king waved away his words of caution and took a deep draft from his cup. Hea noted from the gleam in his eyes that Ecgfrith had already consumed a goodly quantity of mead before their arrival.

Although things had been tense between her and Oswald since their argument earlier, she agreed with the priest. It tempted wyrd—fate—to cite victory before you had achieved it.

"What happened, sire?" she asked. "How did you manage to push Bridei's fyrd back?"

Ecgfrith gave a tight smile. "We are the better army. My men are battle-hardened, and a Northumbrian shield wall is a force to be reckoned with. The warriors of Bebbanburg did me proud today—they fought like gods."

Hea felt Oswald shift next to her. He did not like Ecgfrith's reference, even though oblique, to the old ways. In his view there was only one God, and his name should not be taken in vain. Yet if Ecgfrith noticed the priest's disapproval, he showed no sign of caring.

"How many of our men fell?" Hea asked.

"Two dozen at most," Ecgfrith replied, his expression darkening. "But the Picts suffered greater losses before they turned tail and fled."

"Did you see their leader?" Oswald asked, frowning. "Is he among the fallen?"

The king's expression darkened further. "I saw no sign of that craven. No doubt he was hiding at the back of his army, sending his men forward to die upon our swords."

Hea tensed at these words, as she had earlier when the warrior had called the Picts cowards. This act made no sense—Bridei would not turn and run. Could no one see that such behavior was unusual?

She glanced over at Oswald then, and their gazes fused for a moment. In his blue eyes, she saw an unspoken challenge: *you have influence over the king, wield it.*

Inhaling deeply, she turned her attention back to Ecgfrith. "Bridei mac Beli is a warlord, sire," she reminded him gently. "Such a man does not retreat unless he has some other plan."

A chill settled over the interior of the tent. Hea watched, unease settling in the pit of her belly, as Ecgfrith's face hardened.

"You think we didn't beat them today then?" he asked, his voice deceptively soft. "That instead this is some clever deception, and I am a fool."

Hea's throat closed. She was aware that Oswald's gaze was flicking between her and the king, but she did not glance his way. He could not help her. "I do not think that, sire," she replied.

"You foresaw our victory, Hea ... did you lie to me?"

Hea held his gaze. For the first time, she realized why folk feared Ecgfrith. It did not matter that he was her father, that until now he had valued her opinion—at that moment she walked a knife-edge.

She swallowed, choosing her words carefully now. "I spoke the truth. I just ask you to look beyond what your eyes tell you. Bridei has earned his reputation for a reason. Maybe it is not wise to chase him into lands you do not know."

Ecgfrith stared at her for a moment longer before his face twisted. "Leave me." He reached for the jug of mead and refilled his cup. "Go to the healing tent and make yourself useful. I have no wish to listen to the prattle of a witless female who knows nothing of war."

"Milord ..." Hea begun, her heart in her throat. "Please listen to me. I only—"

"Go."

Hea rose to her feet, and cast a beseeching look at Oswald, who had gone pale and wide-eyed. Feeling sick, she turned away and moved toward the tent's exit. However, Ecgfrith's voice, cold and hard stopped her mid-step.

"You know a little too much about my enemy for my liking, Heahburh." The chill in his voice made her catch her breath and she froze, like a deer poised to flee before the hunter. "You may think your king is blind, but I know you made yourself his hōre when he visited Bebbanburg. I overlooked it for many reasons, but now I see where your true loyalties lie."

Hea did not move, did not breathe. The silence inside the tent was like being inside a cold barrow, the tomb of a long-dead king. Goose bumps rose on her skin, and for the first time in her life she felt as if she might faint.

Yet Ecgfrith's final words slammed into her, propelling Hea forward, out through the flap and into the night. "When Bridei falls tomorrow I will let you weep over his corpse."

"What's wrong with you, woman?" Rinan snarled. "Stop fumbling."

Hea cast the warrior a quelling look and picked up the bandage she had dropped. She then began to wrap it tightly around his right bicep. Rinan had received a deep gash during the battle, and she had done her best to clean it. Under usual circumstances, standing so close to this man would have put her on edge. Yet after the encounter she had just had with the king, Hea barely noted Rinan's presence.

They were inside the healing tent, and Rinan sat upon a leather pack while Hea knelt at his side, tending his wound. He was the fifth man she had seen to; she was exhausted but she welcomed the industry.

Best to keep busy. Best not think on Ecgfrith's words.

Even so, bile stung the back of her throat, making it difficult to focus on the task at hand. Mastering her inner turmoil, she attempted to distract herself by making conversation with Rinan.

"The king says the Pict army is weaker than ours," she said finally, avoiding Rinan's gaze as she worked, "that they ran from you today. Is he right?"

A heavy silence fell between them, and Hea was aware of Rinan watching her. Eventually, guessing that he would not answer her, Hea glanced up to find him frowning. "The king makes it sound like an easy victory," he muttered, his voice low as if he was taking care the others in the tent would not hear him. "But he didn't fight in the shield wall."

"But you will pursue the Picts?"

"Aye ... Ecgfrith will not rest till Bridei's dead."

Hea did not appreciate the glint in Rinan's eyes as he said those last words; although the warrior's hatred of the Pict leader was nothing new to her.

She finished wrapping the linen bandage and fastened it tightly. The cut had been deep and blood was already soaking through, but it would have to do for now.

"It's done," she said briskly, rising to her feet. "If you're still alive tomorrow eve, I'll change the bandages again."

Bridei stood by the firepit and watched the flames lick hungrily at the night. Moths fluttered around the fire, some dancing perilously close before being consumed by it. Around him, the rise and fall of men's voices drifted through the narrow vale where the Pict army had camped for the night.

He inhaled the odor of peat smoke, laced with the aroma of roast venison—for two of his men were spit-roasting a haunch over the glowing coals of a fire a few yards away. He ached all over and the graze to his right shoulder, where a Northumbrian axe had clipped him, was throbbing dully. Nonetheless, a grim sense of satisfaction filled Bridei. The day had been hard ... harder than expected, but everything was going to plan.

Heolstor appeared at his side then, his face smudged with dirt, his blue eyes hollowed with fatigue.

"How many dead?" Bridei greeted him softly, not taking his gaze from the fire. He had been awaiting Heolstor's return, and had not looked forward to the tidings the warrior would bring.

"Thirty-five dead, another twenty too badly injured to fight," Heolstor rasped.

Bridei frowned. The numbers were higher than he had expected. Those warriors had made a great sacrifice for their people, although he knew that would not bring the families of the fallen men much solace.

"And the others ... they're ready?" Heolstor asked.

Bridei heard the misgiving in his friend's voice. He glanced away from the dancing flames and met Heolstor's gaze. "Do you doubt them?"

Heolstor shrugged, although Bridei could see the skepticism in his eyes. "It was humiliating today, a loss of honor," he murmured. "To retreat in midst of battle ... we could have taken them. We could have won."

Bridei smiled. "Aye, but at great cost to ourselves."

Silence fell between the two men for a few moments before Heolstor spoke once more. "What if he doesn't take the bait?"

"He will."

"You sound so sure."

Bridei gave a soft laugh. "Ecgfrith won't let this go. He'd follow me over the edge of the world."

Heolstor's mouth thinned. "I hope you're right ... or he's about to make a fool of us all."

Chapter Twenty-two

The Valley of Death

THE NEXT MORNING dawned cool and bright. A seeking wind blew in from the northeast, but the sun warmed the backs of the Northumbrian fyrd as they rode.

Like the day before, Hea and Oswald traveled with the supply wagons at the back of the rearguard, while the rest of the army rode some distance ahead. As they rode, the landscape became gradually hillier, rocks jutting out from the deep-green of the hillsides.

Hea watched her surroundings, her breathing gradually becoming shallower; anxiety curled in the pit of her belly. Although she had never been so far north, this rugged land felt familiar somehow to her.

I've seen it before.

Yes she had ... in that vision. The one where she had also witnessed the slaughter of the Pict army. The sight disquieted her. Last night, unable to sleep, she had sat in her tent and beaten her seeing drum, in an attempt to cross to the other side. Yet the trance state that usually came so easily had eluded Hea. The spirit world did not reach out to her. It was the first time that had ever happened, and it unnerved her.

What if I have lost my gift?

The worry plagued her once more as Rowan picked his way up a stone-strewn hillside. They had just passed a still, dark mere and traveled toward higher ground.

This is my doing ...

Hea's stomach twisted. If she had not had that vision, Ecgfrith would not have been so confident in this campaign. She had seen his victory, but now she doubted everything. All her instincts screamed danger, but her attempts to dissuade the king had fallen upon deaf ears. And now he had turned on her.

King or not, Ecgfrith of Northumbria was someone she was starting to hate.

Her mother had thrown away her happiness for him. Lewren had once been young and beautiful, she could have chosen any man and yet she had fallen for one who could never love her in return.

You should have told me, mōder. I deserved to know.

Anger curled up through Hea. She felt betrayed ... by all of them. Her life, her identity, had been a lie. Suddenly she felt like running away, finding a cave or a hut deep in the forest and living alone, shunning the world and its disappointments.

Tears pricked at her eyelids, but she blinked them back. Weeping would not help.

The hillside led up into a gorge; a steep-sided valley that forced the wagons to slow. Emerging from her brooding, Hea took in her surroundings once more, panic gripping her chest when the sense of recognition grew stronger.

This was it ... the valley from her vision. The valley of death.

"Hea ... what's wrong?" Oswald's voice caused Hea to start. He was riding at her side, his gaze wary as he studied her face. "You look as if you're about to faint."

Hea wet her dry lips, unable to speak. She glanced ahead at the sea of warriors, their spears bristling against the green sides of the valley.

A moment later, shouts reached them. They were faint, from much farther up the valley, but Hea instinctively knew what they meant.

She reined Rowan around, her face panicked as she caught the priest's eye once more. "We must turn around," she gasped. "We need to ride ... before they—"

More shouts, this time from behind them, cut Hea off mid-sentence. Both she and Oswald craned their necks, their gazes traveling past the last of the wagons, to see a company of riders burst into the valley.

"God's Bones!" The panic in Oswald's voice mirrored her own.

Even from a distance, it was clear the approaching horsemen were not Angles. They were dark-haired men with blue swirls decorating their pale skin. Plaid cloaks billowed like wings behind them as they galloped toward the rear of the Northumbrian fyrd.

Hea glimpsed the glee on their faces, the triumph, and knew a moment of pure terror.

She had warned Ecgfrith, but he had not listened. The Picts had laid a trap for them ... and they had ridden straight into it.

The valley rang with the clank of iron and the grunts of men. The two armies fought in close combat. The cries of the injured and the dying as they fell—only to be trampled underfoot—echoed off the sides of the gorge.

Bridei urged Croí Cróga through the crowd, slashing his blade at the men who lunged for him. Likewise the stallion bit, and kicked, at any warrior that ventured too close to his massive feathered hooves.

Croí Cróga had been bred for battle, and yet Bridei was about to dismount—for it was safer in the confined space—when he spied a warrior on horseback coming for him.

Ecgfrith of Northumbria was not a big man, but dressed for battle upon the huge, chestnut warhorse he was a magnificent, terrifying sight. He carried a great, round, oaken shield with an iron boss upon it slung across his left arm, and a double-edged sword in his right hand. A heavy iron helmet, with a nose plate and eye-slits, obscured half his face. A fine wolf-pelt cloak billowed behind him as he rode. Sunlight glinted on the chain-mail that covered his chest.

Bridei saw Ecgfrith's face, twisted with wrath, his teeth bared, as he came for him.

Guiding his stallion with his knees, Bridei urged Croí Cróga forward and raised his square shield. The horse surged on, and Bridei braced his body for the shattering impact that would come.

The two men met in the midst of the valley. Warriors—Pict and Angle alike—dove out of their way.

Ecgfrith swung first, his blade slicing through the air. Bridei slammed his shield upward, his arm jarring as iron bit into wood. Ecgfrith snarled, drew his seax from his waist, and slashed at his opponent—the sharp blade cutting through the thick leather of Bridei's breeches, and biting into his thigh.

Bridei gritted his teeth against the pain and drove his own blade up under Ecgfrith's guard.

This blow was the deciding one, for it cut through Ecgfrith's chainmail vest and slammed home, up under his ribcage.

The two kings' gazes met, and Bridei watched Ecgfrith's hazel eyes widen.

It was a killing blow, they both knew it.

Ecgfrith was dead.

Bridei looked down at the Northumbrian king's corpse, surprised at how little he felt. He had expected jubilation; a fierce sense of vindication against the man who had once made his life a misery.

Yet he felt nothing.

Ecgfrith lay on his back, his eyes staring skyward. He wore a stunned look on his face, as if he had denied death even as it came for him.

Bridei clenched his jaw. Ecgfrith's end had been too swift, too painless. He had wanted to see fear in his foe's eyes before he finished him; he had wanted him to plead, to beg for his life. Yet the Northumbrian king had died a warrior's death, proving that despite Bridei's hatred for him, Ecgfrith was no coward. Like many of the kings ruling the southern lands of Britannia, Ecgfrith had been a battlelord.

Glancing up, Bridei took in his surroundings. The stench of blood and offal assaulted him on all sides, and a carpet of bodies now filled the gorge where the two armies had made their final stand.

Unbeknown to Ecgfrith, Bridei had a number of warriors in reserve waiting to the north—and when the Picts rode into this valley, their reinforcements joined them.

They had hit the Northumbrians with a hammer blow, a strike that the Angles had never recovered from. The Picts had held nothing back. This was their chance, the moment Bridei had been waiting for. He had deliberately baited Ecgfrith in the south, and then let him believe he had the stronger army. It had been galling to retreat, to let the Northumbrians believe victory lay within their grasp. But in the end his tactic had paid off.

Bridei, limping slightly from the cut Ecgfrith had given him to the leg, moved a few yards farther down the valley, to where Heolstor was sitting upon a boulder, recovering from the fight. A tangle of bloodied bodies spread around him; all men Heolstor had cut down at the bitter end of the battle.

Bridei met his friend's eye and grimaced. "Was it not hard to kill these men? They were once your brothers."

Heolstor snorted. "They ceased to be my brothers years ago. I'm a Pict now." He then favored Bridei with a fierce grin. "Well met, Lord. You were right, I should have had faith."

Bridei barked out a laugh but did not reply. He was too exhausted, too sore, and his leg hurt. Looking down the valley at a sea of bodies with broken standards and spears thrusting skyward, Bridei considered the path that had brought him to this moment.

My birthright.

He had done what his father had not—broken from the yoke of Northumbrian rule and freed his people. He was now the rightful king of the north—the Kingdom of Fortriu—and there was no one alive who would dare contest it.

Bridei's gaze swept back to where Ecgfrith lay, his wolf-skin cloak, stained dark with his own blood, spread out beneath him. And as Bridei watched, a raven landed on the Northumbrian king's forehead and plucked out his eye.

Dusk settled over the Pict camp, painting the sky blood-red. Bridei marked it as he strode toward the edge of the encampment, and allowed himself a rueful smile.

The Warrior—god of battle—saluted them.

"How many Northumbrian survivors?" he asked Fearghus.

"Twenty-five, although some of them won't last the night," the warrior, who walked to his right, replied.

Bridei nodded before he glanced to his left, at where Heolstor strode. "Fancy a Northumbrian slave?"

The warrior grinned back at him. "Only if he doesn't eat much."

The three of them walked to the edge of the camp, through a wide entrance to where a great low hearth burned. The Northumbrian captives clustered around it; a ragged, bloodied group of men. Bridei's warriors had constructed a wood and hide perimeter around the captives, hemming them in. Even so Heolstor had placed men outside, and they would stand guard all night. Just in case a desperate Northumbrian warrior decided to try and make a run for it.

A warrior should die in battle. That was an honorable death—while capture stripped a man of whatever honor he had once possessed.

Bridei stopped at the edge of the group, his gaze sweeping over the collection of weary faces. One of the men closest snarled at Bridei, before spitting on the ground. Next to him, a young warrior had gone the color of milk at the sight of the Pict leader, athough his eyes glittered with venom.

Bridei ignored their hate-filled stares, as he found himself looking for familiar faces. He had lived among the Northumbrians for so long, he had expected to recognize some of the men here. Yet they were all strangers to him.

All but a huge blond man who lay upon his side. The warrior's hair was a shade of yellow that Bridei had never seen on anyone but one man. The lump on the warrior's nose, caused by Bridei's own fist, confirmed the man's identity.

Rinan.

The warrior did not look in a good state: blood soaked his leather armor and even from this distance, Bridei could see a number of lacerations that marked his right flank and thigh. Rinan was too weak to sit up, yet his pale blue eyes were hard with an unspoken challenge.

Next to Rinan sat a slim, dark haired man. Dressed in a brown habit with his hair shaped into a tonsure, the man scowled at him. He was trying to brave, but it was a thin veneer. Bridei could smell the fear coming off him in waves.

Bridei gave a grim smile. Ecgfrith had brought a priest north with his fyrd, but it had not helped him.

Bridei was going to look away then, to issue an order to Fearghus, but instead he saw something that made him pause. His gaze strayed to a cloaked figure a couple of yards behind Rinan. Sitting hunched, his back leaning up against the perimeter fence, the man was much smaller than those surrounding him—and unlike the others, he wore a large hood, which hid his face from view.

Bridei frowned. Had they caught a lad?

"You," he called out, his voice carrying across the space. "The cloaked one. Lower your hood."

Silence fell around the fire. There had been little conversation, just low mutterings and the occasional groan from one of the injured, yet now they all grew tense, their gazes shifting to the cloaked figure in their midst.

"You heard the king," Heolstor called out. Besides Bridei, he was the only other man in the Pict army who spoke the tongue of the Angles. "Lower your hood, boy."

A few moments followed, before a pair of slender hands lifted and pushed back the hood, revealing a shock of unruly auburn hair, glittering green eyes, pale skin, and a full mouth.

Bridei's breath caught.

Chapter Twenty-three

Nechtansmere

ALONE IN THE tent, Hea sat upon a fur, hands clenched in her lap ... and waited for the King of the Picts.

The moment the Pict warriors had circled them, trapping them inside the valley, she had known it would come to this. Only now that the moment had arrived she felt sick. Defeat tasted like vinegar in her mouth. Not only that, but her vision had led Ecgfrith astray—resulting in his defeat and death.

Hea clenched her hands, her fingernails digging into her palms. Guilt swamped her. Oswald's prediction that she would end up with blood on her hands had come to pass. She would never forgive herself.

And now she was a prisoner in the enemy camp.

She was not sure why she had tried to hide her identity. They would have discovered her sooner or later. And yet she had been a coward; she had not wanted to face Bridei, and would take any measures to avoid it.

The look on his face, when she had lowered her hood, had almost been comical.

She had expected surprise—but the shock that rippled across his face, the way his mouth had dropped open—had disarmed her. Had she imagined it ... or had she seen joy flare in those dark eyes before he had quickly masked it?

Surely it had been wishful thinking, for the cool expression that replaced his unguarded surprise was the one she remembered him having all those months earlier, when they had parted in Bebbanburg.

He had turned to Heolstor, who still stood gaping at her, his voice low and clipped. "Bring her to my tent."

Those words had filled Hea will cold terror. And now, here she was a while later, still waiting for the executioner to arrive.

He was making her wait ... she knew it. The longer she waited, the more she would fret, and he wanted to make her suffer.

Hea inhaled deeply and twisted her shaking hands together.

Calm yourself. He's just a man, she counselled herself. *If this is to be your end, show some spine.*

The flap covering the entrance to the tent twitched then, alerting her to someone's arrival. A heartbeat later, Bridei entered the tent.

The tent was large, bigger than most dwellings, with a high domed roof that had a slit in the top to let out smoke. An iron brazier, in which a lump of peat smoldered, sat in the center of the space, and piles of soft furs lay around the edges of tent. Yet the moment Bridei entered, the tent felt tiny and airless. A cage.

His very presence sent Hea into crisis.

Half naked, save a pair of plaid breeches, Bridei padded barefoot across the fur and stopped before the brazier, his gaze settling upon Hea, pinning her to the spot.

Hea's breathing stopped, and a hot tide crept over her body.

Nithhogg take this man for being so virile.

His gaze stripped her bare. The past few months disappeared, and she remembered how it had felt to lie with him, taste him …

Stop it.

Hea blinked and tore her gaze from his, fixing it instead upon her clenched hands in her lap.

That night belonged to another life … it was gone, lost forever.

A long silence stretched out between them, before Bridei eventually broke it. "Why are you here, Hea?"

She glanced up, steeling herself as she met his gaze once more. "I asked to join Ecgfrith's fyrd … he needed my counsel."

Bridei stiffened. "And did you foresee this end?"

Hea's heart began to thud as she shook her head. She could not bring herself to tell him the truth. She swallowed, her throat suddenly tight, before she replied. "No … it seems my gift has deserted me."

"Really?"

"Aye—I was no help to Ecgfrith. He should have left me behind."

A beat of silence. "Yes, he should have."

Hea stared back at Bridei, for once wholeheartedly agreeing with him. The things she had seen today—the blood, the carnage—would haunt her dreams for the rest of her life.

She inhaled once more, steadying her nerves, as she lifted her chin slightly. "What will happen to us … those Northumbrians you have captured?"

Bridei crossed to a low, wooden table, where an earthen jug of wine and a stack of wooden cups sat. Hea's gaze followed him, marking the man's fluid, stalking gait. He mesmerized her; he always had. Hea clenched her jaw; she needed to fight this.

He poured two cups, before crossing to where Hea sat and passing her one.

"You're my slaves … to be executed, sold or traded at my discretion."

The words were cold, delivered in such a matter-of-fact manner that Hea flinched. She should not be surprised. Slaves were a part of their world; Ecgfrith had them, as did most of the kings of Britannia. Yet to know slaves existed was one thing … to be one was another.

Hea had always valued her freedom—more than most women. Her mother had been wild, and had brought up her daughter the same way.

Panic fluttered up under her rib-cage as the full weight of Bridei's words settled upon her. Still, she did her best not to show it, instead taking a sip of wine. It was blackberry: rich and spicy.

Bridei sat down a few feet away, settling to the ground with that loose-limbed ease she remembered. For the first time, she noted the blood stain on his left thigh. Seeing the direction of her gaze, Bridei gave a tight smile.

"A parting gift from your beloved Ecgfrith. Don't worry though—my gift to him caused more damage."

Hea watched him. "So *you* killed him?"

Bridei nodded.

"And how did it feel, to slay the man you've hated for so long?"

Bridei went still. He observed her a moment, studying her face. "It was the best moment of my life," he replied.

The flatness of his voice gave him away.

"Liar." Hea raised her cup to her lips and took a deep draft, welcoming the warmth that slid down her throat and pooled in her belly. "You're disappointed."

Bridei snorted. "You haven't changed a bit, Hea ... still far too sure of yourself for a woman."

She met his gaze, her spine stiffening. "And you haven't changed either. Still insufferably arrogant."

Bridei threw back his head and laughed, the deep sound echoing through the tent. To Hea's ire, his eyes were twinkling when their gazes met once more. "Gods, how I've missed that scald's tongue."

Bridei sipped his wine, watching Hea under lowered lids.

He had missed more than that. He had missed everything about her. The sound of her voice; the stubborn set of her jaw; the brightness of her green eyes; and those full, soft lips.

And that body, that lush, soft body hidden from view by the cloak she still wore. In the aftermath of battle, he longed to tear her clothes off her, throw her down on the furs and claim her as his.

Yet—as strong as his reaction to her was—he did not let it show on his face.

Truthfully, he was still in shock at finding her here ... and surprised by the strength of his reaction to seeing her again.

Joy—pure and undiluted. The first real moment of happiness in months.

Bridei reflected on this as he observed her. She sat, tense and nervous, a few feet away, clutching her cup of wine as if it were her salvation. He wondered at what was going through her mind. Had she missed him?

The attraction between them was still as powerful as it had been all those months ago in Bebbanburg. When their gazes had met outside, it had felt as if someone had punched him, just below the ribs.

But there was something different about Hea. Her face and eyes were not friendly, yet there was a brittleness to her, an edge, he had not seen before. Back in Bebbanburg she had been lighthearted, with a poise that was gone now. Out here, far to the north of the only world she had ever known, Hea appeared lost.

Bridei continued to watch her, noting that she had dropped her gaze to avoid his. He nursed his own cup of wine, drinking slowly and reflecting on the events that had led up to this moment.

Today should have been the happiest day of his life. He had accomplished his life's goal: Ecgfrith was dead, and he was now the undisputed king of the north. But Bridei felt strangely hollow. He had stood in that valley, listening to his warriors' roars of victory, and wondered why he did not feel jubilant.

Right now, the only thing that mattered was this woman sitting across from him.

Bridei did not share his thoughts with Hea. Now was not the time. After everything she had been through, she would not welcome—or trust—anything he said.

He would wait. Now that Hea was his captive there was no need to rush things.

Hea pulled her woolen cloak close and looked about her. After the sparkling sunshine of the last two days—for the battle had unfolded under a hard blue sky—the weather had turned gloomy to match her mood.

A thick, milky mist curled in from the still, dark mere the Pict army had camped beside: Nechtansmere, her people called it, although last night Bridei had named this place Dun Nechtáin. Nechtan Lake or Nechtan Hill, it did not matter to her. For Hea it would always be an evil place, full of dark memories.

Around her, Bridei's men readied themselves to ride west. The sea of hide tents heaved off the green hills as men rolled up the sheets of leather and slung them across the backs of their horses. Their mood was jubilant—although the day before the warriors had been somber as they prepared the bodies of their dead for the journey home, shrouding them in linen and leather, before placing their corpses upon tarpaulin-covered wagons.

Hea had heard that the Picts buried their dead in stone cairns, unlike her own people who burned theirs and let the wind scatter the ash. Bridei's men had cleared the valley of the fallen Northumbrian warriors the day before and burned them upon a great pyre as dusk fell. Oily smoke had stained the evening sky black, long before the last of the light faded.

This morning, the pall of grief had lifted. Hea watched the dark-haired Pict warriors, bodies still smeared with blue woad, laughing and ribbing each other while they packed up.

Hea's stomach cramped. The tight circle of Northumbrians she stood with had no reason for high spirits this morning.

Bridei stood a few feet away, next to a sturdy wooden cart drawn by a dun pony. Upon the cart lay a shrouded body … Ecgfrith.

"Priest." Bridei motioned to where Oswald cowered at the back of the group of Northumbrians. "Come forward."

Oswald did as bid, although he was trembling, his face ashen, his eyes hollowed. No doubt he expected this to be his end. The Picts were heathens, they would not suffer him in their midst. Pity lanced through Hea as she watched Oswald. They would never be friends, but she felt a kinship with him after all they had been through together. Would Bridei make a sacrifice of him, make an example of him in front of his men?

"Ecgfrith must have a king's burial," Bridei said curtly when the priest stood before him. "You will see it done."

Hea watched Oswald sag at this news, and for a moment she thought his legs might collapse under him.

Ignoring the priest's relief, Bridei continued. "Ecgfrith's half-brother, Flann Fína, lives upon the Isle of Iona. Take the king's body there, bury him, and inform Flann Fína that his time of exile has ended. Bebbanburg needs him."

Hea marked the looks of surprise among the Northumbrians, including Rinan's. The warrior could barely stand this morning, and did so only by leaning onto a crudely-made wooden crutch. He was glowering at Bridei, clearly not trusting him.

Hea knew what Bridei was up to. The Pict leader was no fool. She had forgotten how politically aware he was; of course he had grown up knowing of Ecgfrith's half-brother, sired by Oswiu, but whose mother had been an Irish princess. Flann Fína—or Aldfrith as he was known to the Angles—would make an ideal king in Bridei's view, for he was a man of peace who had voluntarily chosen to live a hermit's life.

It was a shrewd choice on Bridei's part … the last thing he wanted was another king like Ecgfrith challenging his rule.

"You will choose four warriors," Bridei continued, "those whose wounds will not slow your journey to the isle, and be on your way this morning."

Oswald nodded, seeming to have swallowed his tongue.

Bridei's gaze shifted from the priest then, seizing upon a young warrior who stood near the front of the Northumbrians. Barely out of boyhood, his chin covered with blond fluff rather than beard, the warrior met Bridei's eye boldly.

Bridei's mouth thinned. "You'll do … I need someone to ride south and bring word to Bebbanburg. Leave now, and when you return home tell them what happened here, what happens to those who try to enslave my people. Tell them that their new king will reach them shortly."

The warrior held his gaze before giving a curt nod. A wise response for, like Oswald, he had earned his freedom.

Satisfied, Bridei's dark gaze swept over the ragged group of Northumbrians that remained. "The rest of you are coming back to Dundurn with me," he said with a thin smile, "where your fate will be decided."

Hea pushed a lock of hair out of her eyes and approached the cart bearing Ecgfrith's body. Bridei had gone off to help his men get ready for their departure, leaving the ragged band of Northumbrians to say goodbye to their king.

Oswald climbed onboard the cart, while the four men he had chosen gathered near, ready to set out.

Standing at the edge of the cart, Hea looked down at the shrouded body. She was grateful that they had covered up his face. She did not want to see his wounds, his last expression before he died. She stood there for a few moments, and wondered if she was supposed to feel anything. This man was her father after all. Yet only numbness filled her.

"We will take our king to Iona, and give him the burial he deserves." Oswald's voice intruded, and Hea glanced up, her gaze meeting his. For the first time since they departed Bebbanburg, the priest appeared at ease. Bridei had given him a reprieve, and he intended to see out his task.

Hea nodded. He probably thought the solemn look on her face was grief at losing her king, but instead it was sadness. For Ecgfrith, for her ... for her mother ... for them all. She stepped back then, drawing her cloak tighter around her as a gust of wind tore across the exposed hillside. "I have no doubt you will," she murmured. "I wish you a safe journey, Oswald."

She saw something flit across his face, a shadow move in his eyes. Oswald's gaze flicked to where Rinan and the other Northumbrians stood a few feet back from Hea, and she realized he was wondering what would become of them. "May God protect you all," he said finally, crossing himself, "for whatever lies in your paths."

Chapter Twenty-four

Return to Dundurn

HEA SHIFTED ON the sack of grain, easing the cramp in her left thigh and the numbness in her backside. After long days of travel, she was beginning to loathe the rickety cart upon which she traveled.

Her faithful pony, Rowan, now belonged to one of the Pict warriors. She had trudged along behind the wagons for the first few days, until her feet grew sore, although now she regretted opting for the wagon.

It had been a relief initially, but days on she had never been so physically uncomfortable.

Rinan sat opposite her, back propped up against the slatted wooden side of the wagon. His eyes were closed, his face pinched in discomfort. However, he was one of the more fortunate among the injured—over the last few days they had lost six men, all of whom had died from their wounds. Rinan bore many lacerations down his right-side, but none had festered.

Rinan did not seem to care. His mood had turned morose, and he snarled at anyone who spoke to him. Not that Hea bothered with him—her own mood was bleak enough as it was without him darkening it.

Since their departure from Nechtansmere, she had barely seen Bridei, and had not spoken to him. Each evening, one of his men came to find her, and escorted her to his tent, where she found food and drink waiting for her. But Bridei never showed his face, clearly sleeping elsewhere.

The situation made Hea feel uneasy. At first, his absence in the tent had come as a relief, for things had been so awkward between them after the battle. But as the days wore on she found herself worrying over it. Their conversation in his tent that night had been tense, full of things unsaid ... perhaps Bridei was sore over it. Maybe he was playing with her.

He rode at the head of his army now, and Hea had only caught a glimpse of him at dawn that morning as he saddled his stallion—a massive, bay beast with hooves the size of iron griddles. Bridei had turned, catching her watching him, before favoring her with a cocky grin. Then he had turned away and resumed saddling his horse.

The frequency at which Hea's thoughts returned to him, made her angry at herself.

What does it matter to you? Best he leaves you be ... best you never speak again.

But she could not ignore the twist of grief deep within her as the last of her hopes frayed and snapped, casting her adrift in a sea of desolation. Deep inside she was still that pitiful waif of a girl who had followed Bridei around the streets of Bebbanburg. Even now, after everything she had been through, he still had a hold on her.

Loneliness cast its net over Hea when she considered her fate, turning the days dim and the wind cold. She was fast reaching the point where she did not care what happened to her. She only wished for the end to come swiftly.

The cart hit a pot-hole and jolted, dislodging Hea from her perch and launching her onto Rinan's lap.

Rudely awakened, the warrior gave a yelp as Hea scrambled off him.

"Devil's turds," he wheezed, his eyes watering with pain. "You kneed me in the cods."

Hea gritted her teeth and clambered back onto the sack. She could not bring herself to apologize, for she had not deliberately injured him. Plus ... he deserved it. "It's the road," she muttered. "It's badly rutted."

Rinan glowered at her a moment before pulling himself up so that he could survey their surroundings. They followed the tail-end of the vast Pict army, which snaked like a great crawling beast through a verdant valley. Wildflowers and heather bloomed on the hillsides, and the sky was robin's egg blue. The sun was hot on their faces, cooled by soft breeze that blew in from the south-east.

It was a beautiful early summer's day, yet the glory of it appeared lost upon Rinan. His scowl deepened. "Where are we?"

Hea shrugged. "I have no idea ... they tell me no more than you."

Rinan's pale-blue gaze shifted to her. "You expect me to believe that?"

Hea held his gaze, her irritation rising. "Believe what you want. I have nothing to tell you."

Rinan's mouth thinned. "Prickly today, wicce. What's wrong ... vexed your lover is ignoring you?"

Hea resisted the urge to throw herself at Rinan and rake her nails down his face. Was it so obvious? Was she that transparent that even a clod-headed dolt like Rinan could see it?

Like Ecgfrith, Rinan must also have known of her brief affair with Bridei during his stay in Bebbanburg. She should not have been surprised—the fort was small enough that few things went unnoticed. Even so, the smug look on Rinan's face caused her temper to flare.

"What happened between Bridei and me is over with," she replied, biting the words out. "He's now my enemy, as much as he is yours."

Rinan huffed out a laugh, wincing as the healing wounds on his chest hurt him. "If you say so ... although your words sound hollow to me."

Hea swallowed a bitter response. She wanted to rage at him, curse him. Only, such an outburst would draw attention to her ... would prove him right.

A sight on the southern horizon drew Hea's attention then—a welcome distraction from Rinan. Stiffening, she turned to look.

A vast hilltop fort hove into view. Five tiers cut into a green, domed hillside, ringed by grey stone. The Pict fort climbed the hillside, crowned at the top by a great stone building that resembled a beehive.

Seeing her attention shift, Rinan twisted round, his gaze travelling west to the fort. "So this is the fabled Dundurn." His words were bitter, but Hea caught the awe in his voice nonetheless. Like her, the grandeur of Bridei's stronghold surprised him.

"Aye," she whispered, her voice catching. "Our new home."

On the way in, Hea caught sight of rows of stone cairns carpeting a nearby hillside. The army did not stop at the burial mounds, instead making straight for the fort.

The procession snaked around the base of the hill, and along the banks of a glittering burn, before men and horses clattered across the bridge leading into the fort's lowest level. A deep ditch filled with iron spikes ringed the outer defenses, a sight which made Hea tense.

Bridei lived as a man under siege.

Clinging to the sides of the wagon, and gritting her teeth against each bone-shuddering jolt, Hea took in her surroundings.

Crowds of folk came out to welcome Bridei and his men home. Cries echoed out across the hillside. Hea watched, fascinated. The Picts were predominantly dark-haired. They were not as tall as her own folk, and many were of a lighter build. The men wore little, save plaid or leather breeches, and the women wore long, swishing plaid skirts and tightly laced leather tunics. Hea noticed some of the women wore nothing more than a strip of leather across their breasts, exposing their midriffs.

Hea knew she was staring but she did not care; likewise, the Picts stared back. She and Rinan were the enemy—but the sight of her bright, untamed mane, and his shock of straw-colored hair momentarily overrode any hostility the folk of Dundurn might feel toward them. Hea knew Heolstor lived among them, but few of them had seen a man with yellow hair before.

The children chattered and pointed before their mothers shushed them. They need not have bothered, for Hea did not understand a word. They spoke a lyrical, lilting language that was pleasing on the ear. It made Hea's own tongue sound guttural and grating in comparison.

Next to Hea, Rinan sank back down in the wagon, his expression morose. "Savages," he muttered. "The devil take them all."

Hea ignored him. Instead, she clung to the side of the wagon as it began its bumpy ascent up through the levels. The road wound its way up the hill, passing low stone houses with conical roofs of turf or thatch. The dwellings were so low to the ground that Hea realized they must be dug out of the earth—a wise choice for the winters would be bitter this far north. Other smaller buildings with conical roofs—most likely store houses—scattered the terraces, interspersed by wooden enclosures where goats bleated and fowl scratched for grain.

Up and up they went, each level filled with livestock, vegetable plots, and homes, until they rumbled up the final incline toward the fort itself.

Hea craned her neck, taking in the solid round-tower. It was windowless, although smoke drifted from two points in its roof. This close, Bridei's fortress appeared huge; bigger even than the Great Tower of Bebbanburg.

Crowds of folk waited for them here, and amongst the cries of joy at their return, Hea heard wails of grief—as some of the women discovered that their man had been among the fallen.

Hea's throat constricted at the mournful sound. That was the nature of war, for even victory was bittersweet.

A tall, stone wall loomed before them, the tallest of any they had encountered so far. Upon it, Hea spied the outlines of men, watching their approach. Her chest tightened, and she looked down. The journey west had seemed endless at times; long hard days of travel where she had spoken to no one. Guilt had consumed her for most of it, and she had cut herself off from her surroundings as she went over the events of the past few months.

How could my vision be so wrong?

To think she had agonized over Bridei's fate, when he had never been in any danger. All this time, it had been Ecgfrith who had been riding to his doom.

But now they had reached their destination, none of that mattered. Hea had her own future to worry about.

One way or another, her fate would soon be decided.

Bridei rode under the great arch, Croí Cróga's huge hooves clattering on the wooden bridge, and glanced up at his broch rising like a giant before him. A smile spread across Bridei's face.

It was good to be home.

He glanced across at where Heolstor rode next to him and saw his friend was also smiling, his blue eyes scanning the crowd that poured out of the broch to meet them.

Heolstor had good reason for his high spirits, for Ciara would be waiting for him.

The woman flew down the steps from the broch and launched herself across the yard toward her husband. Heolstor was ready for her. He swung down from his horse, caught her in his arms, and kissed her soundly. Hoots, lewd shouts, and whistles echoed around them, but the lovers paid them no heed.

Bridei grinned. Heolstor had a knack for the dramatic.

Turning away from the couple, Bridei dismounted Croí Cróga and led him toward the stable complex at the base of the broch. He felt bone-weary this afternoon and thirsted for a cool cup of ale before stretching out on the furs. It was as if all the tension of the past few weeks suddenly poured out of him.

He could have slept for a moon.

Bridei was rubbing down his stallion with a twist of straw when Heolstor finally entered the stables. The man looked insufferably pleased with himself.

Tying up his own mount next to Bridei's, he set to unsaddling it. A few companionable moments passed before Heolstor turned to Bridei and caught his eye. "So what are you going to do with Hea?"

Bridei shrugged, pretending he had not thought about it … when in reality he had thought of little else. "Not sure."

"Will you make her your bed slave?"

Bridei scowled, not appreciating the directness of Heolstor's question. "I don't know."

"Well if you don't, another warrior is bound to claim her."

Bridei's soft, warning growl made Heolstor grin. He held Bridei's gaze and gave a wry shake of his head. "I never thought I'd see the day."

"What?" Heolstor's smugness was starting to wear upon Bridei now. If he was not careful, Bridei would wipe that grin off his face.

"The great Bridei mac Beli … slayer of men, charmer of women. It seems you've finally come undone."

Bridei scowled. "You talk rot sometimes."

Heolstor threw back his head and laughed. "I see it now … why you were so evil-tempered after leaving Bebbanburg. Why you cast Una from your furs. All this time you've been pining for Hea."

Bridei snorted. "Cods. I've barely spoken to the woman in days."

Heolstor merely shrugged, still wearing that infuriating smile. "Aye, and I don't know whose benefit it's been for … but it hasn't been yours."

Bridei glowered at him. "She's been through a lot. I was only trying to give her some time."

"Time for what? To realize you're a dolt? To decide she really does hate you?"

"Enough," Bridei snarled. He knew Heolstor was only teasing him—and he usually enjoyed their banter—but he lacked a sense of humor where Hea was concerned. Heolstor's words cut too close to the bone. "Instead of baiting me, why don't you go and ride your wife."

Heolstor grinned back at him. "Aye, I intend to."

Chapter Twenty-five

Wise

"THE KING WANTS to see you."

Those were the words Hea had been dreading, yet the ones she knew would come.

She had been sitting inside the yard, upon a sack of grain, surrounded by the last of the Northumbrian captives—just twelve now after the deaths on the journey here. The emissary Bridei had chosen would have reached Bebbanburg by now. News of Ecgfrith's defeat would be ringing throughout the kingdoms of Britannia.

Heolstor had come for her. He watched her now, his gaze shuttered. "Come, Hea," he said softly. "There's no need to look so terrified."

Swallowing, Hea rose to her feet, ignoring the hard stares of the men around her. She had heard their whispers on the journey here; they thought her Bridei's whore. They thought her a traitor ... a liar.

Stiffly, she followed Heolstor across the yard and up the steps leading to the arched entrance into the fort.

"This tower," she murmured, noting the thickness of the walls and the sheer height of it above her. "I've never seen the like."

Heolstor grunted. "I thought the same as you, the first time I laid eyes on it. The Broch of Dundurn is a magnificent sight."

The warrior's reference to his past reminded Hea that like her he had once been a stranger here. "Heolstor," she murmured. "What will become of me?"

His expression softened. "There's no need to look so worried. Bridei means you no harm."

Although they had been meant kindly, Heolstor's words brought Hea no solace. He was wrong. Everything about Bridei mac Beli screamed danger. Heolstor had just led her into the wolf's den.

After the bright sunlight outdoors, Hea blinked at the dimness within, for there were no windows to let in the daylight. Even so, a number of flickering cressets illuminated the circular interior of the building. Hea's boots crunched over rushes, and she inhaled the fresh scent of heather that had been scattered amongst them.

Despite her jangling nerves and thudding heart, she found herself taking in her surroundings with interest. She crossed a vast, circular space dominated in the center by a wide square hearth lined by long wooden tables. A platform ran around the perimeter of the hall, and Hea spied a number of alcoves lining the walls, their entrances shrouded by fur hangings and tapestries. To the far right of the interior, a set of stone steps led up to another level.

Heolstor made his way toward the stairs, greeting folk as he went. Hea trailed after him. She had almost reached the steps when she felt the weight of someone's stare upon her. She glanced over her shoulder and saw a young woman observing her. Tall and slender with long walnut tresses, lightly tanned skin, and high cheekbones, the woman watched her with a narrowed gaze.

It was not a friendly stare. Although she had not encountered any enmity thus far, Hea imagined that this woman would not be the first hostile Pict she would meet here. Turning away, Hea followed Heolstor up the stairs.

Bridei was waiting for her above, in a wide, sparsely-decorated space illuminated by a handful of flickering cressets. He stood upon a fur rug that covered the floor, before a stone-ringed hearth, arms behind his back as he awaited her. Barefoot, Bridei was dressed in form-fitting leather breeches and a vest that showed off the sculpted muscle of his lithe body. Hea was relieved he wasn't bare-chested; she found the sight ... distracting. That night in the tent, after the battle, she had struggled not to let her gaze wander.

Heolstor gave a nod to Bridei before turning to Hea, favoring her with a conspirator's wink. "See you later, Hea."

She watched him leave, his boots scuffing on the stone steps, and fought the urge to follow him. She did not want to be alone with Bridei.

"Good eve, Hea." Bridei's voice, soft and tinged with amusement, made her turn toward him. "I hope you're not looking to Heolstor as your savior. These days, his loyalties lie with the Picts."

Hea stiffened, straightening her back as she met his eye. "I hadn't considered escape," she replied. "Something tells me I wouldn't get far."

His gaze narrowed. "You wouldn't."

Hea folded her arms across her chest, lifting her chin. "Good eve to you too, Bridei. I suppose you have a reason for calling me up here?"

The corners of his eyes crinkled as he grinned. "I thought you might be interested to learn of your fate."

Hea inhaled deeply. She was quickly tiring of this game, of men making decisions for her. She longed to be free as she once had been, living with her mother. They had been poor, for flowers and herbal potions did not earn much, but it had been a simple, happy life.

"Go on then," she replied crisply.

He frowned. "You're in a prickly mood this eve. What's wrong ... have I offended you in some way?"

"No ... to do that you'd actually have to speak to me."

He raised a dark eyebrow. "I was trying to be respectful—to give you time to adjust to the new way of things."

"What? The fact that I'm your slave? I don't think I'll ever get used to that."

Bridei crossed to an oaken table sitting against the wall and poured out two cups of wine. Unlike the wooden or clay cups Hea was used drinking from, these two were ornate: bronze and studded in garnets—kingly cups.

"You're not my slave, Hea," Bridei said quietly.

Her breathing stopped. "So if I wished to leave here I could?"

He shook his head, a rueful smile creasing his face. He then approached Hea, passing her a cup of wine. "You aren't a slave, but you *are* my subject. You won't be returning to Bebbanburg, but I give you leave to live in peace and safety here in Dundurn."

Hea watched him, her fingers fastening around the cup. His words were too smooth; she did not trust them. Her recent experience with Ecgfrith, and the way he had turned on her in the end, had made her wary of men. She had not told a soul of what he had admitted to her … that she was his bastard daughter.

She could barely admit it to herself.

"I imagine you want something in return," she said finally, "all men do."

He inclined his head, frowning. "So bitter … I don't remember you being like this in Bebbanburg."

Something twisted inside Hea as she held his eye. "I'm not the same person I was in Bebbanburg."

Bridei lifted his cup to his lips and took a sip, still watching her. "There are two things I'd ask of you," he said gently. "The first is that you put your skills with herbs and potions to use. We have a healer at Dundurn, but the woman skilled in herb lore died last winter. I would have you replace her."

Hea nodded, taking a drink from her cup to hide her surprise. She had always enjoyed working with herbs and healing folk, but had not thought she would get the chance to go back to her old profession. "And what's the second?"

Bridei gave her a slow, sensual smile that made Hea's toes curl inside her boots. Her heart started to pound, and she took another gulp of wine to calm her nerves. The predatory look in his dark eyes both alarmed and excited her.

"You will reside inside this broch … and will sleep up here."

Panic flowered in Hea's breast. "With you?"

Bridei stepped toward her, closing the gap between them. "I'd happily share my furs with you—if that's what you want—but until then we can sleep apart. There's plenty of space up here."

Hea glared at him. The man's arrogance was breathtaking. "*Until then?* You think yourself irresistible?"

"No." His voice dropped to a low, intimate purr as he reached out with his free hand and lightly stroked her cheek. "But *you* are … I lied earlier when I said I stayed away out of respect the past days. The truth is I can't think clearly when you're near."

Hea swallowed. His touch sent a trail of fire along her heated skin. "And yet you'd have me sleep up here." She choked out the words, forcing herself to concentrate. "Just a few feet away from you ... is that wise?"

He laughed, a low rumble in his chest. He was standing so close that she could smell him: the warm musk of his skin mingled with the smell of leather. "I tire of being wise. I wish to cast the rest of the world aside and lose myself in you, Hea."

Desire fluttered at the base of her belly, but she fought it.

Months ago in Bebbanburg she had longed for this ... would have thrown herself into a passionate affair without thinking twice. Yet now she saw the world differently.

She was indeed her mother's daughter.

Lewren had once let passion rule her, and it had broken her inside and turned her bitter. A selfish king had used her for his pleasure, and then cast her aside after her womb quickened.

The wheel had turned, and years on Lewren's daughter was following the same path. She walked a precipice, one there would be no returning from once she stepped over the edge. If she gave herself to this man she would be lost; and if he turned on her like Ecgfrith had with her mother her heart would never survive it.

Not only that, but Bridei did not know who she really was. He had loathed Ecgfrith—how would he look upon her if he discovered his enemy was her father?

"I would prefer to be wise," she murmured, stepping back from him. She saw disappointment flare in his peat-dark eyes. "I will sleep up here with you, if you command it, but I will not share your furs."

Silence stretched between them for a few moments. Bridei watched her, and she could see he was bemused by her coldness. But after a few moments he nodded. "I'd never force you, Hea ... surely you realize that?"

Hea nodded in reply, not trusting herself to speak. She took another step back from him and glanced about her, desperate to shift the focus from the attraction that shimmered between them.

"What about the others you've brought here?" she asked. "Will they also be freed?"

Bridei's expression grew serious, and he shook his head. "Rinan and the others will remain slaves ... and will serve me and my men till I decide otherwise."

Hea considered this a moment. The Northumbrians who awaited their fate in the yard below deserved better. Most of them now hated her, but they were warriors who had fought bravely ... and they were her people. She had failed them, and she did not want to see them suffer.

Watching her, Bridei's mouth twisted. "Don't look so horrified, Hea—it's the way of war. Any man unlucky enough to survive on the losing side of a battle faces a life of slavery. All of them knew it before they marched north to do Ecgfrith's bidding."

Chapter Twenty-six
The King of the North

DUNDURN HELD A great feast to welcome Bridei and his men back. The tables lining the fire pit inside the broch groaned under the weight of the spread—as women carried out never-ending platters of roast fowl, pork stuffed with walnuts and apples, and venison pies, all accompanied by boiled turnip and carrot mashed with butter, and huge loaves of bread.

Bridei sat at the center of the table upon the platform above the hearth, Heolstor flanking him to his right and Fearghus to his left, and watched as the last of the food was brought to the table. Then he rose to his feet and held a great drinking horn, filled to the brim with mead, aloft.

"Dun Nechtáin was a turning point for our people." Bridei's voice echoed across the cavernous space, quietening the hum of excitement within. "The day we reclaimed the north."

Cries of approval boomed off the smoke-blackened beams overhead.

"No longer will the Angles march on our lands." Bridei's skin prickled as he said the words. "No longer will they take gold from our villages and demand we kneel before them. From now on we are free."

Fearghus lurched to his feet then, face florid for he was already well into his cups. "From this day forth Bridei mac Beli kneels to no man. All hail the King of the North!"

"The King of the North!"

Bridei listened to their cries and witnessed the adoration on their faces, the fierce pride glittering in their eyes. Watching them, his people, the exhaustion sloughed off him and he realized that he had been born to rule. It was not an easy mantle to bear at times, and often the weight of responsibility could isolate a man—as it had his father—but at that moment Bridei had never been more proud of who he was and how far he had come.

He raised the drinking horn to his lips and took a deep draft.

Applause thundered through the broch, as all hailed their king.

Bridei sat down, signaling that the feast could begin, and the feasters fell upon the rich spread before them. He helped himself to a slice of roast pork, his gaze shifting to the stairwell leading upstairs.

A moment later, Heolstor spoke from beside him. "Is Hea not joining us?"

Heolstor never missed a thing. The warrior had seen the direction of Bridei's gaze and was now watching him.

Bridei scowled at him and shrugged. "You can't blame her. We're celebrating our victory—the defeat of Ecgfrith and his fyrd—it's best she remains upstairs."

"She's a striking lass," Ciara commented, brushing a lock of dark hair out of her sea-green eyes. She sat snuggled up next to her husband, while Heolstor slung a protective arm around her shoulders. "I can see why you're smitten."

Bridei gritted his teeth. After his conversation with Hea earlier, which had not gone the way he had envisaged, he did not want to speak about her. "You shouldn't listen to your man," he growled. "He's a teller of tall tales."

"Not this time," Heolstor replied, before taking a bite of venison pie.

Bridei bit back a sharp retort, knowing that it would merely encourage the pair of them, and focused on the pork. It was succulent, but as he ate, Bridei barely noticed its taste.

All he could think about was Hea.

Now that the excitement of speeches and toasting were over, he was starting to feel deflated. She had not reacted as he had expected. Contrary to her accusation, he had not thought she would throw herself into his arms, yet her coldness surprised him. That was not the Hea he remembered—not the lusty maid who had turned his head in Bebbanburg. He had been attracted to the wildness in her, but these days she took great pains to tame that side of her character, almost as if it scared her.

Was she bitter over his treatment of her?

Or perhaps it was less personal? Since she had been loyal to Ecgfrith, she was likely still coming to terms with Northumbria's defeat.

I handled that badly, he told himself, thinking of their conversation earlier. He had used the attraction between them as a lure, thinking she would not resist him. He had not told her what was in his heart. He had not told her he had missed her.

These thoughts were souring his mood, and so Bridei pushed them aside and held up his cup for Una to fill. The servant smiled at him, and did as bid, although her eyes were cool. The playful, coy invitation he had once seen there was gone. No doubt she had seen Hea go up to his quarters and remain there.

"Welcome home, Lord Bridei," she said demurely, ducking her head.

Perched above the revelry upon a nest of furs, Hea tried not to weep.

This whole situation was a mess; one she did not see a way out of. The boom of drunken voices and the rise and fall of singing and music made her flinch, causing her breathing to constrict. She was just moments away from letting panic completely seize her.

Calm yourself. She dug her fingers into the furs and gripped tightly, taking long deep breaths. *This isn't a death-sentence.*

It was not, but it still felt as if her life was over. Bebbanburg was lost to her; she would never return to that little hovel with its sheltered garden of flowers and herbs. Someone else would claim it, would clear out her stock of dried herbs, tinctures and potions. It would be as if she had never lived there.

Hea's vision blurred, and she felt a hot tear trickle down her cheek. She had not wept since Northumbria's defeat, not properly. Even on the journey here she had been clinging to some fool's hope that Bridei would decide to send her home.

Home. Besides a few loyal friends like Fritha, there would be no one who would miss her. Lewren had been an only child and had lost her parents early; there were no aunts and uncles, no cousins.

Never had Hea felt so alone.

Laughter reached her once more, echoing up from the vast circular hall below. She could hear the thumping of cups on the tables, as the revelers hooted and cheered. Hea ignored their levity, instead lying down upon the furs and curling up. She looked out across the space she would now share with Bridei, past the hearth which was not lit for it was a warm evening, to the pile of furs on the opposite side of the chamber. She had placed her own bed as far as possible from his, but it was a useless tactic for she would not be able to escape him.

She lay there awhile, lost in the fog of her own misery, the sounds of the feasting and celebrating below fading as she mulled over the series of decisions and acts that had led to this moment.

Was there anything she could have done to prevent it? She was not sure there was ... it was easy to be wise in hindsight.

Stop this brooding, she thought finally. *This is not the life you'd have chosen, but Bridei has given you some freedom at least.*

That was true—she would be able to go back to growing herbs and making healing balms and potions. Given time, she could find meaning in this new existence.

It was late when Bridei retired for the night. He walked, feline silent, across the skin-covered floor and crossed to his furs. Still awake, for her own thoughts would not let her rest, Hea watched him out of half-closed eyes. He had his back to her, and began to undress. Her breathing caught when she realized that, like most folk, he would be sleeping naked.

Hea's breathing quickened. She knew she should close her eyes, feign sleep, but she found she could not look away. Fortunately, he had his back to her. She watched him strip off his leather vest and let it fall carelessly to the floor, then he began to unlace his breeches. She watched them slide to the floor before he kicked them off ... and for a few moments she admired his long muscular legs; his tight buttocks; narrow hips and waist; and strong, broad back.

And then he turned around.

"Good evening, Hea."

Bridei was smiling as he met her gaze. Heat flushed through her as she realized he had known she was awake the whole time. He had put on a show for her benefit.

"Good evening," she muttered before rolling over so that she faced the wall, her back to him.

"Did the celebrations keep you awake?" She could hear the amusement in his voice and clenched her jaw.

"Not really," she replied, doing her best to keep her tone cool.

"Were you waiting for me then?"

Hea ground her teeth. "No."

A few long moments passed, and she heard him climb into the furs, before he spoke once more. "Having you here in Dundurn doesn't seem real. I never expected to see you again." Hea did not reply, keeping her gaze fixed squarely upon the rough stone wall. However, after another lengthy pause, he continued. "What I'm trying to say is that I'm not trying to hurt you, or humiliate you."

Hea flipped over and glared at him. Thankfully, Bridei had covered himself up with a fur, although she could still see far too much of his torso as he had propped himself up on one elbow and watched her. "If that's the case, why keep me here?" she demanded. "Send me home."

He held her gaze, the intensity of it making her catch her breath, before he shook his head. "This is your home now."

Anxiety churned in the pit of Hea's belly. "No, Bebbanburg is."

Bridei gave her a wry smile. "You never fitted in there," he replied. "You're too wild. They regarded you with suspicion, as they did your mother. An Angle likes his woman meek and biddable. Pict men prefer a woman with fire."

His words caused an odd sensation to feather across Hea's skin; a prickle of excitement just under her ribs which she swiftly repressed. "You talk as if you know me," she replied stiffly. "The reality is, you don't."

She watched a shadow flit across his gaze. "You're right, we're still strangers in many ways—but you also have made swift, hard judgements about me. What if I'm not the man you believe me to be?"

Hea lapsed into silence. His words made her uncomfortable. She preferred the man she had known in Bebbanburg: light-hearted, flirtatious, and passionate. This one, who looked at her with unnerving intensity, who asked her difficult questions, had the power to hurt her deeply.

She could fall in love with such a man.

"I'm a leader," he said finally, when she did not answer, "and that means I have to be ruthless. I've killed many men to reclaim my birthright, Pict as well as Angle, and I'd kill again to protect this kingdom. I'm proud and arrogant, I know that, but I'm not the lūtan you seem to think me."

Hea wet her lips. "I don't think you're a lout."

"Then why do you shrink back from me?"

She could not answer that—for to do so would mean revealing the truth about who she really was. Who her father really was. It would mean revealing her deepest fears—and her shame and guilt at failing Ecgfrith so badly. So, instead she gave him an easier answer. "You can't expect me to sit here smiling ... not after watching the Northumbrian fyrd fall, after watching their bodies burn. Those memories will stay with me forever."

His mouth twisted. "It's a wound ... but wounds heal."

"Perhaps ... but some of us bear the scars forever." With that, she turned over and faced the wall once more, signaling that their conversation had ended.

Chapter Twenty-seven

Slave and Savior

RINAN ENTERED THE broch, stooping to prevent himself from cracking his head on the low lintel. Like Heolstor, he stood nearly a hand span taller than many of the Pict warriors.

Hea watched him cross the floor, flanked by two of Bridei's men. Despite being dressed in the tattered remnants of his battle gear, his blond hair lank and greasy, Rinan still walked with the same swagger she remembered. However, his face was grim, his eyes guarded. He glanced around the interior of the broch, taking in his surroundings, as Hea had a day earlier. Then, his gaze swept over the inhabitants, resting on Hea—who sat at the foot of the high seat—before his attention shifted to Bridei who stood awaiting him.

Watching the two men's gazes meet, Hea thought on all that had passed between them over the years. They had always been rivals growing up.

Despite everything, Hea knew Rinan's childhood had not been easy—in many ways he had always been an outsider. He had later found his place at Ecgfrith's side, and proved himself as a fighter. Only on the journey north, Hea had witnessed the rift developing between Rinan and his king. The campaign had never sat easily with Rinan. Like Hea, he had suspected a trap, even when Ecgfrith had not.

Not that it mattered now ... for he was Bridei's theow—his slave.

Rinan halted at the foot of the wooden platform, ignoring Hea, his attention fully upon Bridei. The Pict king stared back at him. It was folly for a slave to eyeball a king in such a fashion—Hea had seen Ecgfrith beat theows for less—but Rinan refused to back down.

Still holding the slave's gaze, Bridei eventually gave a tight smile. "Not cowed yet, I see."

Rinan's lip curled. "If you think you can break me, go ahead."

The challenge made Heolstor, who stood behind Bridei, step forward. The red-haired warrior's face was hard. "It would be my pleasure," he growled.

Around them, the hall went silent. No one here besides the four of them knew what Rinan and Heolstor had just said, but their tone of voice betrayed that it had been a challenge. Fearghus scowled, while two older women behind him whispered among themselves. Hea noted the female servant who had glared at her the day before watched the scene unfold with interest.

Bridei flicked Heolstor a warning look. Then he glanced back at Rinan.

"I've no quarrel with you," he said gently, although there was iron just beneath. "Whatever dispute we had in the past matters not to me now. However, you know the rules of war. You know what becomes of captives."

Rinan nodded, his mouth thinning. "Aye—and I'd prefer you killed me."

Bridei shrugged, although his expression was not without sympathy. "It would be a waste, for we have need of your skills here. Rinan son of Broga, you now serve me. You will work under the instruction of my iron-smith Tolarggan, and will sleep at his hearth."

Silence followed Bridei's words. Hea watched Rinan's face and saw the man struggle. Rinan, who had apprenticed with his father, knew the craft of smithing well—yet the knowledge he would be making weapons for his enemy was difficult to accept.

Bridei saw Rinan's conflict and gave him a hard smile. "I'm not offering you a choice. This is your new life now, Rinan. Fight it at your peril."

Hea stepped outdoors and pulled a woolen shawl around her shoulders. It was a bright, breezy day, and despite that it was summer the wind had a slight bite to it. Even so, the sun felt good on her skin after nearly two days indoors, and Hea turned her face up to it.

A few steps ahead, Heolstor turned, beckoning to her. "Come on—this way."

She followed him across the wide yard, past where a girl was throwing grain for a cluster of clucking fowl, and through the thick wall rimming the base of the fort. The rumpled green landscape of Fortriu spread out around her. It was different to the rolling farmland surrounding Bebbanburg. The land this far north was a deeper shade of green; a jumble of valleys, dark woodland and tilled fields stretching out to a hazy southern horizon. Below, she saw the lazy flow of two rivers meet, their waters sparkling in the sunlight.

As much as she hated to admit it, this was a beautiful land.

Heolstor led her down through two levels of the hill fort. Hea was still getting used to her new attire. Gone was her old, green wealca and the tunic she wore underneath. She now wore a long, plaid skirt that swished around her legs as she walked, and a tight, sleeveless, leather vest laced down the front.

She and Heolstor drew many gazes on the way. Folk called out to Heolstor or waved, but with Hea they stared. She heard them chatter amongst themselves and tensed, glancing across at Heolstor. "What are they saying?"

"They're speculating whether you're my sister, since we've both got red hair."

Hea frowned. "Anyone can see we're not—yours is a much more garish shade."

Heolstor laughed. "That's what that woman over there just said."

Hea huffed. "I hate not knowing what folk are saying ... it makes me nervous."

He gave her a sidelong glance. "That's easily remedied. Ciara will teach you the Pictish tongue."

"She will?"

"Aye—she has suggested it."

Hea had met Ciara that earlier morning, a dark-haired beauty with eyes the color of the sea. The woman had seemed friendly, although vaguely amused by everything. The way she kept glancing between Bridei and Hea with a knowing smile as a group of them broke their fast together had irritated Hea. Of course folk would be gossiping about her; they probably all thought she was Bridei's bed slave ... and since she slept upstairs with him she did not blame them. Even so, Ciara's thinly veiled delight had stretched her already ragged nerves tight.

At the western edge of the tier, Heolstor led her to a low-slung stone house. A thin stream of smoke rose from a hole in the turf roof.

"This is where the healer, Modwen, lives," Heolstor told her.

As they approached the dwelling, a small woman of around forty winters emerged. Her face split into a grin when she spied Heolstor, an expression which lifted the years off her. She had a dark mane of hair, threaded with grey, braided in two long plaits, and large dark eyes. The woman's gaze shifted to Hea, and her smile faded. She glanced at Heolstor.

"Cò tha seo?"

"What did she say?" Hea whispered to Heolstor.

"She asked who you are," he replied before smiling back at the healer, answering her. He spoke the local tongue with ease and confidence.

The woman's face relaxed, before she asked Heolstor something else, in a rapid-fire succession of lilting words that made no sense to Hea.

Heolstor inclined his head to Hea. "She wants to know where you learned your herb lore."

"Mo mhàthair," Hea replied, using one of the only phrases she knew in their tongue—one she had learned from Bridei as a child. *My mother.*

Modwen nodded, considering her. The woman's gaze was so intense that Hea felt pinned to the spot.

After a few tense moments, Modwen glanced back at Heolstor and spat a few terse words. Then she turned and marched back inside her cottage. Hea watched her go, frowning. She looked over at Heolstor. "She doesn't look pleased to meet me. I thought she wanted help?"

Heolstor smiled. "She does ... don't mind her. Modwen's had a hard life—lost her husband and two sons in battle—but she's got a good heart. You two will get on fine."

"I don't know how that's possible, since we can't communicate."

Heolstor laughed and gave Hea a slap on the back, propelling her toward the stone cottage where Modwen disappeared. "Go on, she's asking for a demonstration of your talents."

The shadows were lengthening, a golden light bathing the darkly wooded hills and glens of Fortriu, when Hea finally emerged from Modwen's dwelling. Her back ached from bending over a workbench all afternoon, and she blinked owl-like in the sunlight after the dimness indoors. However, her mood felt considerably lighter than it had been this morning.

Working side-by-side with Modwen, she had almost forgotten her unhappiness. She had shown Modwen her mother's favorite remedies, including a paste for lacerations made from yarrow, or 'woundwort' as many folk knew it. She had also shown her a tincture made from nettles, which Lewren had sworn by for bladder or joint complaints, and a liver tonic made from mugwort.

Heolstor had remained for most of the day, patiently translating Modwen's stream of questions. Later, when it became clear that the healer had warmed to Hea, and that the newcomer could make herself understood by a series of clumsy hand-gestures, he had finally muttered an excuse and left.

Massaging a stiff muscle in her left shoulder, Hea made her way up the curving path that led back up to the broch. Like this morning, folk stared at her, but she found she minded it less. She had already picked up a scattering of new words during her afternoon with Modwen, and decided she would take up Ciara's offer to teach her. Life here would be very lonely indeed if she could not communicate.

Slightly out of breath, she reached the broch, passing under the great stone arch into the wide yard beyond.

A wide set of stone steps led up to the entrance to the round tower and the brown-haired servant girl was making her way down them, carrying an arm-load of rushes. Hea spied Rinan climbing up the steps toward her, his head bowed. For the first time Hea noted the glint of metal around his neck: Rinan now wore an iron slave collar.

As Hea watched him, noting the tense set of his shoulders, a scream echoed across the yard.

The young woman had been half way down the steps when she tripped. Rushes flew in all directions, and she toppled forward, plunging toward the sharp stone steps below.

An instant later, Rinan bounded forward and caught her.

Hea swallowed a cry of her own—for if Rinan had not been there the girl would have surely broken her neck—and rushed across the yard toward them.

"Be still, I have you," Rinan told the girl as he set her on her feet. "You're safe."

Not understanding a word he had just said, the servant gazed up at him, her eyes huge on her ashen face. She hung there a moment in Rinan's arms, and the pair of them stared at each other. Hea slowed her step, realizing that neither of them needed her assistance, and that she was intruding.

A heartbeat later, an older female servant bustled up the steps toward them. Like Hea, the woman had seen the incident unfold and rushed to the girl's aid.

"Una!" the woman clucked, collecting rushes as she approached. "Dè cho teann!"

Hea did not need to speak their tongue to know that the older woman was chiding the servant for dropping rushes everywhere.

Rinan released the quivering Una and stepped back from her.

"Tapadh leat," she murmured, still holding his gaze. Then, the older woman swept upon them, grasped Una by the arm, and hurried her away. Rinan watched them go, his expression stunned.

He was still standing there, looking up at the entrance to the broch where the servants had disappeared, when Hea reached him.

If Hea had not been wary of him, she might have laughed at the stunned look on his face. "Rinan ... are you well?"

He nodded, tearing his gaze away from the broch and scowling at her. "Aye—what's it to you?"

Hea smiled back. "In case you're wondering ... she said 'thank you'."

Chapter Twenty-eight

Who Needs a Man?

One month later ...

HEA WAS LEAVING the broch, a basket filled with gardening tools under one arm, when Ciara caught up with her.

"It's too beautiful a day to be indoors," the woman greeted her in Pictish before an impish smile creased her face. "Can I join you for some gardening?"

Hea smiled back. "Of course," she answered in the same tongue. Her proficiency in the Pict language had improved hugely over the past month. She still got lost when listening to fast-moving conversations, but could grasp most simple exchanges and could make herself understood. "I could do with some help ... come on."

The pair of them descended the steps and crossed the yard beyond. Hea glanced up at the sky, a smile curving her lips once more. Ciara was right, it was a gorgeous day. After a wet, misty start, the summer weather had settled into a stream of sunny days. It was perfect gardening weather, although the heat did mean she was forever watering the seedlings she had planted.

Walking in companionable silence, Ciara and Hea wound their way down two levels, and crossed the last stretch toward Modwen's cottage. A group of children, who should have been doing their chores, ran squealing across their path. A cluster of boys brandishing slimy toads were chasing two screeching girls.

Ciara watched them disappear with a wry smile. "Males," she scoffed. "They spend years either ignoring us or tormenting us—and then one day that all changes."

Hea huffed out a laugh. "Aye—although they then become pests of a different kind."

She saw Ciara's eyes widen at that, although her friend laughed. "Some of us like to be pestered ... why, don't you?"

Hea looked away. Ciara was cunning—Hea had come to realize that over the past few weeks—she never demanded answers from you directly, but rather preferred to trick them out of you.

Hea was not falling for it. "I prefer to be left alone," she replied, deliberately avoiding her companion's gaze.

It was the truth, not just bluster for Ciara's benefit. In the past month she had come to enjoy real freedom. Each morning she rose early, and broke her fast with Bridei and his retainers. Then she spent the rest of her day either helping Modwen make poultices, tinctures, and healing drafts; or cultivating herbs in the garden the healer had let her manage behind her dwelling. Her days were busy but satisfying.

Slowly, the mantle of guilt she had brought with her from Nechtansmere had begun to lift. She had told no one of the part she had played in Ecgfrith's ill-fated campaign, and some days she could almost fool herself into thinking it had never happened. Almost.

True to his word, Bridei had neither touched her, nor pressured her into sharing his furs. However, his wounded and disappointed looks of late—which she had caught when he thought she was not looking—told her that he was not pleased with the situation.

Their arrangement made her uncomfortable at times, although since she spent so much of the day outside the broch, it was easy to forget about the fact that she slept just a few feet away from a king every night. A young, virile king, who was used to getting his own way.

Let him suffer over it, she thought stubbornly. *I care not.*

She glanced back at Ciara, to find her watching her. The woman was far too sharp; like Heolstor, she missed nothing.

"I have my freedom, my herbs and friends like you," she said. "Who needs a man anyway?"

She had spoken the words merely to throw Ciara off the scent, but as they rolled off her tongue a sense of calm and wellbeing settled over her. She realized then that she meant them. All her life, she had followed her mother's lead. Although the two of them had lived independently—without a man's protection—Hea had grown up imagining the day her warrior father would ride back into Bebbanburg and take care of them once more. Then, she had developed an infatuation with Bridei; one that had lasted far beyond girlhood.

There had always been a man—at some point—ruling her life, whether it had been her absent father, Bridei, or King Ecgfrith himself.

Now ... finally ... she was not looking for a savior. In setting her free, Bridei had done her an unexpected favor. He had let her discover life for its own sake.

Ciara held her gaze for a moment, before a smile crept across her face. "You're right, Hea. We women flutter around our men like moths at times. We should remember that there are other parts of life that matter too."

They reached the herb garden, a small enclosure on the slope behind Modwen's cottage, and entered through a narrow wattle gate. Hea smiled at the sight of her garden—it was her refuge. Honey-suckle climbed one side of the wattle fence, its sweet scent drifting over the enclosure. Within, Hea had created circular beds, linked by rows of slate pavers, in an effort to make the most out of this small space.

Hea's gaze shifted from her garden to the smoke that rose from the healer's roof. She inhaled the aroma of baking, her smile widening.

"Morning, Modwen!" Hea called out.

A few moments later, the dark-haired woman entered the enclosure, her healing basket under one arm.

"Good morning," she greeted Hea with a smile, which widened further when she spied Ciara with her. "You have help this morning I see?"

"Aye," Ciara replied, glancing around the enclosure, at the riot of greenery and color surrounding her. "Sometimes it feels as if the walls of the broch are closing in on me."

Modwen nodded. "I'm just off to check on an old woman with a stomach complaint. I've got a few other folk to see after that so I'll be back later." Her gaze shifted back to Hea. "I've made some oat cakes—they're cooling on the griddle so help yourself if you get hungry."

"Aye, thank you—we will," Hea replied with a grin. Modwen made the best oat cakes she had ever eaten.

The healer went on her way, leaving Hea and Ciara to their work. Hea set down her basket and extracted an iron hook, which she passed to her friend. "Here, I use this for weeding. You can start over there next to the rosemary."

Ciara nodded, taking the hook and crossing to where an unruly clump of rosemary climbed the wattle fence of the enclosure. Thick grass had sprung up around its base, which would soon choke the herb if not pulled out.

Meanwhile, Hea set about tending the long bed of medicinal herbs she had been cultivating the past month: yarrow, sage, betony, chamomile, and comfrey. All of these had been staples for her mother's healing balms and potions. Many of the herbs here had a distinct smell. The woody scent of sage and the grassy aroma of chamomile greeted her as she knelt and extracted a wooden trowel from her basket.

The women worked in companionable silence, accompanied by the sounds of industry in the fort around them: the clang and hiss of the nearby forge, the cries and squeals of children, the lilting rise and fall of women's voices, the shouts of men sparring, and the bleating of livestock.

The sun beat down on the back of Hea's head as she worked, and soon she was sweating. Straightening up her aching back, she untied a skin of water from her belt and took a deep draft. Then she picked up her trowel once more and made her way over to where she was preparing a new bed for seedlings.

A few feet away, Ciara had gone red in the face and had taken shelter under the shadow cast by Modwen's dwelling. "I don't know how you manage out here all day," she grumbled. "This heat is making me wilt."

"Complaining already is she?"

A male voice drifted across the enclosure, and Hea turned to see Heolstor push open the gate and step inside. The tall warrior was naked to the waist, flushed, and sweating. He looked as if he had come straight from sword practice.

Hea laughed. "I think Ciara's wishing she was at her distaff right now."

Ciara climbed to her feet and scowled. "I am not, I was just taking a well earned rest."

Heolstor laughed. "Looks like you were slacking to me—letting Hea do all the work."

"Actually." Ciara sauntered across to him with a sly look on her face. "We were discussing earlier how useless men are ... how women would be much better off without them."

Hea flushed, panic flaring. "We were not," she spluttered. "That's not what I said."

Ciara waved her protest aside. She had a wicked gleam in her eye now as she stopped before her husband and gave him a challenging look, hands on hips. "What do you say to that?"

The amusement on Heolstor's face made Hea want to slap him. Actually, she felt like slapping them both and wished she had not spoken with Ciara so openly earlier.

"I'd say that was rot," he murmured, his blue eyes glinting. "As you well know, wife." With that, he pulled Ciara roughly into his arms and kissed her, not caring that Hea was standing just a few feet away.

The kiss went on and on. Ciara lifted her hands up, tangling them in Heolstor's red hair. She pressed her lithe body against his, while his hands slid down her back and cupped her bottom.

It was only when Hea finally cleared her throat that the couple eventually broke apart. They were both breathless, their cheeks flushed.

Heolstor glanced over at Hea, not appearing remotely embarrassed about the spectacle he and Ciara had just put on for her. "The healer, is she at home?" he asked.

"No," Hea replied. "She's out seeing patients."

Heolstor nodded before taking hold of Ciara's hand and leading her toward the gate. "We're going to make use of her home for a short while," he said, flicking Hea a grin. "Make sure Modwen doesn't burst in on us."

Hea stared at him, agape. Had she just heard correctly? Was he about to plow Ciara on Modwen's furs?

"I don't think Modwen ..." she began, but Heolstor and Ciara had disappeared. She heard the thump of the wattle door closing and the muffled sound of laughter, followed by a squeal of delight a few moments later.

Hea snorted in disbelief. If they thought she was going to remain here and listen to them, they were wrong. She was not their watchdog either. If Modwen came back early and caught the pair rutting it would serve them both right. They had a private alcove in the broch; could they not return there?

A man's deep groan filtered out of the hovel.

Hea flushed, threw down her wooden trowel and headed for the gate. Noon was approaching—she would return to the broch and leave them to it.

Chapter Twenty-nine
The Falls of Culloch

BRIDEI WATCHED HEA enter the broch. She did not look his way, did not even acknowledge his existence, but he watched her nonetheless. She knew he was looking in her direction; she was just pretending otherwise.

Life at Dundurn suited her, as he had known it would. The long plaid skirt and fitted leather bodice clung to her curves, accentuating the ripeness of those breasts, the dip of her waist, and the flare of her hips. Her auburn hair rippled in unruly waves over her shoulders, and her skin had tanned a little over the summer, bringing with it a smattering of freckles over her cheeks.

She was flushed, and Bridei wondered if she had caught the sun while working outdoors all morning.

He watched her greet one of the older women who resided in the broch. The speed with which Hea had learned their tongue did not surprise him; he had always known she was bright, and too inquisitive to allow a language barrier to defeat her.

Hea now spent most of her days outside the broch, working alongside Modwen. He had heard that Hea had extended the healer's garden, and now grew a variety of healing herbs. The weather had been warm, and it appeared she had a gift for cultivating plants.

Bridei watched Hea stop and exchange a few words with Una and Lora, who were mixing batter for honey oat cakes. He was pleased to see how quickly the other women here had accepted her. He had expected Una especially to shun her, but after the first few days in which Una watched Hea with suspicion, the woman had warmed toward her.

There was much industry inside the broch today, for the women were beginning preparations for Mid-Summer Fire. The aroma of baking wafted through the space. The longest day of the year was rapidly approaching. Mid-Summer Fire was a celebration where his people gathered in a nearby forest glen and celebrated around a large bonfire, eating and drinking late into the night.

Bridei lifted his cup to his lips and took a sip of mead, his gaze tracking Hea as she finished talking to the servants and crossed to the raised platform where he sat.

"Good day, Lord Bridei," she greeted him, moving toward the far end of the table where she usually sat.

"Greetings, Hea," he replied before motioning to the empty space beside him. "Come sit near me."

She frowned. "Doesn't Heolstor usually sit there?"

He smiled. "He does, but since he's late, you can take his place."

She obeyed, although he caught the wariness on her face. Disappointment swiftly followed by frustration flashed through him. How much longer would she keep this up? Had he not treated her well since her arrival here? True to his word, he had not laid a finger on her, even though some nights he had not been able to sleep for wanting her. She was civil to him but kept her distance with a cool politeness that he was starting to find offensive.

Masking his reaction, he picked up a jug next to him. "Mead?"

"Aye, thank you."

He poured her a cup and handed it to her. "I've seen little of you of late—how have things been going?"

"Well," she said with a polite smile that infuriated him. "Yesterday, Modwen and I traveled out of the fort and visited some villages that were in need of a healer. I hadn't realized this area was so populated."

Bridei smiled. "It's fertile land, folk live well here."

She met his gaze. "They speak well of you and your father ... you are much loved."

This news pleased him and his smile widened. "They were suspicious of me at first when I returned from Bebbanburg—I think some folk worried I was merely Ecgfrith's puppet. However, they soon learned differently."

Hea nodded, taking this in. Silence stretched between them for a few moments, before Bridei spoke once more. "You've worked hard of late. Tomorrow, you shall take a break—we'll go on a ride."

Hea put down her cup, tensing. "Really ... where?"

"There's a special place, around half a morning's ride from here, I'd like you to see."

"Modwen is busy at the moment ... she needs me tomorrow."

Bridei held her gaze. "She can spare you for one morning."

Hea nodded, her lips thinning. Bridei sensed her reluctance but ignored it. He did not know what she was punishing him for, but he'd had enough. Perhaps if they spent some time together ... alone ... she would warm to him once more.

The day dawned bright and sunny, the perfect weather for a ride. However, Hea had been hoping for rain.

Anything to avoid spending time with Bridei.

She had done well of over the past month, keeping relations between them polite but distant, but she sensed his frustration at the extent to which she managed to avoid him.

Her stomach fluttered as she mounted the shaggy chestnut pony he had chosen for her, while next to her Bridei swung up onto his bay stallion, Croí Cróga.

Braveheart—it was a good name for such a magnificent beast, she admitted.

Bridei gathered the reins and glanced over his shoulder at Hea, flashing her a smile that made the butterflies in her belly dance. "Ready?"

She nodded.

They rode out of the stable yard, through the great stone arch, and wound their way down the levels of Dundurn. It was the warmest day of the summer so far, and a sultry breeze feathered across Hea's bare arms. The sky was an unblemished canvas of blue from one horizon to another.

Her pony's furry ears flicked from side to side as it picked its way down the slope, for even at this early hour the fort bustled with activity. Children were out feeding fowl and bringing in goats for milking. Women worked outdoors, making the most of the balmy weather: bringing water up from the river below, hanging leather up to cure, and grinding grain for bread.

Unlike a month earlier, folk did not stare at her. Instead, some called out her name and waved. Despite the nerves churning on the inside, Hea forced a smile and waved back.

Bridei reined Croí Cróga back, so that Hea drew level with him. "You're popular," he noted with a grin. "Even Heolstor took longer to settle in here."

Hea's mouth quirked. She imagined the folk of Dundurn would not have known what to make of the hulking, flame-haired man from the south. Many would have been frightened of him. "I'm less intimidating than Heolstor," she pointed out. "Plus, I spend my days helping these people."

Bridei shrugged. "Even so, few newcomers here have been welcomed so quickly."

They rode out of the fort, past the company of men guarding the main entrance, and across the wooden bridge leading into the valley below. Once they reached the road that led east, Bridei urged his stallion into a brisk canter. Hea followed suit.

She had not wanted to come on this ride, yet now that she had Hea felt her mood brighten. A smile spread across her face as she followed Bridei east, through an unfolding landscape of emerald hills interspersed with dark-green pine woods. They rode along the northern bank of the River Earn. The crystalline waters glittered in the morning sun, and Hea inhaled the scent of grass and sun-warmed earth. It was too beautiful a morning not to smile.

They spoke little during the journey, mostly because Croí Cróga's longer gait made it difficult for them to ride side-by-side. Hea's pony made a valiant effort to keep up, but the stallion kept drawing ahead. After a while, the road veered south, crossed the burn and entered woodland. Dark pine grew next to thickets of lacy birch and the air was rich with the scent of pine resin. A short distance in, the road—which had narrowed to a forest path—forked. Bridei took the right fork, glancing back over his shoulder at Hea as he did so.

Their gazes met, and he flashed her a smile. "Not much longer."

Hea did not mind; she was enjoying being outside with the morning sun bathing her skin, the wind in her hair. As much as she enjoyed helping Modwen with her patients, Hea relished this morning's freedom. Not only that, but while they were riding, she and Bridei avoided conversation.

She followed him through the woods to the sound of bird song. The land grew hillier, and the path wound its way down into a valley and then up the other side, weaving between granite boulders that thrust out of the damp, peaty earth. As they climbed higher, the sound of rushing water greeted them—and a few moments later the pair rode out onto a wide ledge that commanded a view over the jade carpet of woodland below.

A waterfall welcomed the pair, a cascade thundering down the cliff-face and foaming into a deep blue pool at the base. The falls cast a veil of moisture around them, a light spindrift that settled over Hea's heated skin in a cooling mist.

Enchanted, Hea gazed around her. "What is this place?"

Bridei swung down from his stallion. "The Falls of Culloch. It's a sacred place for my people."

Hea dismounted, leading her pony over to where Bridei was tying up Croí Cróga on the far edge of the falls. "Why is it sacred?"

He smiled. "It's said the Fair Folk come here sometimes—that the pools are blessed."

Hea glanced around, taking in the tranquility of the spot. Since arriving in Dundurn, she had learned much about the Pict way of life. It reminded her of the old ways of her own people—back when Woden, Thunor, Freya and their kin were widely worshipped. Before the Christian god pushed them out. Hea had learned that the Picts had a god for each season of the year; summer belonged to The Warrior—god of battle, life, and growth. She had also discovered that they believed in the Fair Folk, a fairy people who were said to be both wondrous and dangerous.

A collection of large, flat rocks surrounded the wide pool, and Bridei climbed up onto one. He crossed his legs with loose-limbed grace. "This is where I come when I need to be alone, to think."

She climbed up next to him, upon the sun-warmed rock, and folded her legs up under her. "I can see why. It's magical."

They sat in companionable silence for a few moments, and for the first time in months Hea felt her limbs relax. The sun beat down upon the sheltered spot, and the roar of the falls had a lulling effect upon her. She could have lain down and fallen asleep.

However, as the silence stretched on, she became aware of Bridei's gaze upon her, devouring her.

Pulse quickening, she turned her head and met his eye. "Why are you staring at me?" she asked, hating the slight tremor in her voice that betrayed her nervousness.

Bridei's mouth curved. "Because you're beautiful … and because I wish to understand you."

Hea's breathing caught. She wished he would not look at her with those melting eyes, that expression of barely contained hunger. It made it difficult to draw breath, to concentrate on anything but the sensual curves of his mouth.

"There's nothing to understand," she breathed.

"There's a well of secrets within you, Hea … and I intend to discover them."

Panic reared up within her. He did not know what he was saying—some secrets were best kept buried. He would not look at her that way if he knew the truth.

"I can't give you what you seek," she whispered. "I can't—"

But then Bridei moved, reaching for her so fast that the words choked off midsentence. A heartbeat later she was crushed up against his chest, and his mouth was on hers.

Chapter Thirty

The Rest of the World

THIS KISS WAS different to any he had given her in Bebbanburg. Those had been passionate, heated and demanding—but this kiss claimed her.

Hea melted against him, her senses reeling as his mouth explored hers. She moaned, her tongue tangling with his, and then shivered with need when he gently bit her lower lip. Her heart thundered against her ribs, as if she had just run up the hillside to reach the pools. Her skin felt exquisitely sensitive; her clothing too tight, too restrictive.

Bridei pulled her hard against him and kissed her once again, his fingers delving into her hair and spanning the back of her skull. A whimper of pure need rose within her; she could not bear it. Who was she trying to fool? The past few weeks had been torture, seeing him every day, averting her gaze from him every night.

She had thought her coldness would put him off, make him look elsewhere—but it had not. He kissed her as if she was the only woman alive. The taste of him, the warm scent of his skin, and the heat of his body enveloped her, making their surroundings disappear. Her hands slid over his chest before linking around his neck, her fingers tangling in his hair. The movement thrust her breasts against the hard wall of his chest.

She heard his sharp intake of breath, before he pulled her onto his lap.

A dull ache throbbed deep within her as his mouth left hers and traveled down the column of her neck. Her breasts felt swollen and sensitive inside the tightly-laced leather vest. She longed for him to free them.

"Hea," he breathed. "I need you. Here … now."

His voice brought Hea back to the present. Somewhere in her lust-addled brain a shred of self-preservation struggled to the surface.

Breathing hard, she placed a hand on his chest and slowly pushed herself away. Bridei drew back, his gaze meeting hers. His peat-colored eyes were so dark they were almost black, his lips slightly parted. Something twisted deep within her when she realized that she would want no other man, love no other man than him. It had always been Bridei and it always would be.

And that was why this had to stop … now before she gave herself to him, before she threw herself over the brink.

Heart pounding, she pushed herself off his lap, and tried not to notice the considerable bulge in his breeches. Then she shifted away, so that at least three feet of sun-warmed rock lay between them, and watched him under lowered lids.

"This place," she said, her voice husky. "It makes you believe the rest of the world doesn't exist."

He watched her, his chest rising and falling fast as he struggled to master himself. In those dark eyes, she saw his confusion, his frustration. He was not used to being denied. No doubt he thought she was playing some game with him; yet he was the one with all the power. The tranquility of the past few weeks shattered. Suddenly she felt a fool for believing she could rebuild her life.

"The rest of the world has nothing to do with this moment," he replied, his gaze steady. "With us."

Hea shook her head and looked away, focusing her attention on the thundering column of water that crashed down the rock face at the other end of the ledge. "Yes, it does," she murmured.

Bridei was silent for a few moments before answering. "Do you really resent me so deeply, Hea?" She glanced back, to find him frowning. "Whatever I have done tell me, and I will make amends for it."

Her chest constricted. She wished he would not say such things; it made keeping him at arm's length all the harder. Was this how her mother had felt all those years ago? Had Ecgfrith looked at her as if she was the woman of his heart? Had he told her he would do whatever it took to win her?

Hea swallowed, blinking back the tears that loomed. Weeping would not help—it would only lower her defenses. She needed to be strong.

"The Falls of Culloch are lovely, and I'm glad I've seen them," she said. Keeping her voice steady was the hardest thing she had ever done in her life. "But I think I'd like to go back now."

Bridei reined Croí Cróga in, allowing Hea to ride ahead down the path away from the falls. He watched her back, her mane of dark red curls, and felt hurt twist inside him.

Perhaps he had misread her completely. Maybe she really had gone off him? Yet those kisses they had shared by the falls had not been imagined. She had responded to him with a hunger that had matched his own … only to push him away moments later.

He might have thought she was toying with him, deliberately making him suffer, if he had not seen the panic in her eyes. As much as she responded to him physically, she was also afraid of him, and he could not imagine why. He had never given her reason to fear him. He knew there were men who used force on women, who used fear to exert control, but surely Hea knew he was not one of them. Had he not saved her from Rinan all those years ago?

They rode away from the Falls of Culloch, away from a place that had always soothed his soul. There had been a handful of times over the years that he had sought solace here—after his father had died was one. It was somewhere he had wanted to share with Hea ... but now he wished he had not.

Initially he had been frustrated by her coldness toward him, yet now it was starting to worry him. Hea had become a stranger; one determined to protect herself from him.

They rode down into the dense carpet of woodland below, the thud of their horses' hooves and the jangling of bridles the only sound. Bridei let Hea continue to ride ahead, even if Croí Cróga chafed at the bit, for he did not like other horses to get ahead of him.

Bridei kept his gaze upon Hea, noting the tenseness of her posture. She was still upset, and appeared to be fighting a war within.

Bridei set his jaw. He was not beaten yet. Mid-Summer Fire was only a handful of days away—a time of feasting, festivity, and joy. By the summer's end he would win Heahburh of Bebbanburg over. Whatever the problem was, he would uncover it. He had never wanted anything more than to see her smile at him with warmth in her eyes, like she had all those months ago. He had not appreciated it then, but he did now. By the time the leaves turned, he would find a way to unlock her heart.

It was mid-afternoon when they returned to Dundurn. Hea rode alongside Bridei now, although she tried to avoid looking in his direction. They had spoken little on the ride back to the fort; after what had happened at the falls she did not feel like making light conversation.

Instead she felt sick, as if a heavy stone sat in her gut.

She should have been pleased, for she had shown considerable self-control in pushing Bridei away. She had been so close to letting herself go; for a few moments she had wanted nothing more than for him to lift her skirts and take her there on the rocks. She was not sure how she had managed to resist him, for where Bridei was concerned she had always been like a moth to a flame. But now that she had, she merely felt empty and sad.

She thought back to her conversation with Ciara the day before, her brave words about not needing a man. No doubt Ciara and Heolstor both thought her a goose—and after today's events, she was inclined to agree with them.

Outside the walls of the fort, folk were piling branches onto carts. There were a number of carts, a row of at least six, and for a moment Hea forgot her discomfort as her curiosity rose. She glanced at Bridei. "What are they doing?"

"Getting ready for Mid-Summer Fire," he replied. "All the folk in this area will gather in a forest glen—not far from The Falls of Culloch—and light a great fire."

Hea glanced back at the carts laden with boughs of pine and beech. Her people did not have this celebration. After Eōstre in the spring, there were no festivities until Hlaf-mas, a festival that took place in late summer to celebrate the first wheat harvest of the year. Her mother would often bake a special bread for the occasion, and they would go down to the fields below the fort together and watch games in the afternoon.

Pondering how different life was here in the north, she urged her pony across the bridge and into the fort. Had her stomach not been tied in knots, she would have looked forward to this coming festival.

They rode up the levels toward the broch. The great round tower loomed overhead, blocking out the sky as they approached. Hea had almost reached the high wall circling the broch itself when she caught sight of two figures sitting on a low wall to her right: Una and Rinan.

Neither had seen her and Bridei approach, as they were entirely focused on their conversation. The servant girl was explaining something, repeating the same phrase.

"Is mise Rinan. Tha mi ag obair le iarann."

My name is Rinan. I work with iron.

She watched as the blond man uttered the words, slowly and painfully, his face screwed up with concentration. Dressed in plain plaid breeches and a leather vest, his bare arms streaked with the grime of the forge, Rinan looked as if he had just finished work for the day.

Beside Hea, Bridei gave a snort. "Are my eyes deceiving me?"

Hea's mouth curved into a smile. "No, and neither are mine. She's teaching him your tongue."

"Why would she bother with Rinan?" he asked, his voice incredulous. "He has the charm of a boar."

Despite herself, Hea laughed. "Maybe she likes boars."

Bridei huffed out a breath. "Hardly likely—maybe I should warn him off. Tell him to leave Una alone."

Hea cast him a quelling look. "You'll do no such thing. Anyone can see she's there by her own will."

In response, Bridei raised an eyebrow, holding Hea's gaze for a long moment. In his eyes she saw the unspoken question. *But you are not?*

Deciding that it was best not to say anything more on the subject, Hea urged her pony forward and trotted under the arch into the yard beyond.

It was the quiet time of the evening. Supper had long since ended and many of the broch's inhabitants had retired to their alcoves, or stretched out on furs upon the floor.

Bridei sat alone at the table upon the high seat, nursing a warm cup of mead that he had no taste for. Hea had gone upstairs as soon as supper had ended, and Fearghus and Heolstor, seeing that their lord was in ill-humor this evening, had shifted to a table on the other side of the hall where they now played knucklebones. Ciara sat near the hearth, feet up on a settle as she wound wool onto a spindle.

Rising to his feet, Bridei crossed to the hearth, stepping over the prostrate bodies of men, women, and children who had already fallen asleep. Ciara looked up as he approached, favoring him with a knowing smile.

"I was wondering when you'd come talk to me, Lord Bridei."

Bridei scowled in an attempt to mask his sudden discomfort. "I don't know what you mean."

"I saw the look on both your and Hea's faces when you came back from your ride this afternoon. You're wanting a woman's perspective, aren't you?"

Bridei stiffened. "I can see you're busy. I'll leave you to your work."

He turned to leave, but Ciara's soft laugh stilled him. "It's not like you to be so prickly. Come … take a seat next to me. This task bores me, and once Heolstor gets into his games with Fearghus, he's no company at all."

Reluctantly, he turned and did as bid, seating himself upon a low stool next to her. Ciara continued to wind wool onto her distaff. It was a rhythmic, repetitive act that was hypnotic to watch. Bridei lapsed into silence, watching her work.

Eventually, it was Ciara who spoke. "She's not succumbed to your charms yet then?"

Bridei clenched his jaw. She was right, he lacked his sense of humor this evening. He did not usually mind Ciara's irreverent, teasing manner, but tonight it irritated him. She was making light of something that mattered to him.

Sensing his mood, her expression softened. "Has she told you why?"

Bridei shook his head, meeting her gaze. "I was wondering if she had said anything to you … I know women talk among themselves."

Ciara shook her head. "Nothing. Hea keeps her own counsel about such matters. She does seem troubled though."

"She won't speak to me of it," Bridei replied. "She just looks at me as if I'm a wulver about to carry her off to my cave."

Ciara watched him, her gaze introspective, for a few moments. "Have you told Hea how you feel about her?"

Bridei stiffened. "What?"

Ciara's mouth thinned. "Don't be dense, Bridei. Have you told her you're in love with her?"

Silence fell between them. Bridei shifted uncomfortably on the stool and looked away to escape Ciara's penetrating gaze. "No."

Ciara huffed out a breath. "Men."

Bridei frowned. "What is that supposed to mean?"

"You're clod-headed fools. You think telling a woman you want to plow her is enough? If she's reluctant then maybe it's because she thinks you'll just use her and cast her aside."

Bridei stared at Ciara, stunned, as if she had just struck him across the face. "Really, you think that's what's worrying her?"

Ciara gave a strangled sound, a mix of exasperation and irritation. "I don't know, but maybe you should try being honest to Hea. Her reaction might surprise you."

Chapter Thirty-one

Mid-Summer Fire

"DO YOU MISS Bebbanburg?"

Hea glanced across at where Ciara rode next to her. The question surprised her, but no more so than her answer. "I thought I would," she replied with a wistful smile, "but as time goes on I find I don't."

The woman gave her a piercing look. "But don't you have kin there?"

Hea shook her head—after their last intimate conversation, she was wary of being open with Ciara. Even so, her friend had not teased her again. "Not anymore." She thought about how Bridei had told her she had never really fitted in there; at the time she had disagreed with him but these days she was not so sure. "Folk never really accepted me," she admitted after a pause. "They found me ... strange, unsettling. Those who follow Christ distrust women like me. The priest at Bebbanburg was doing a fine job of turning them against me before we set off on the campaign to the north."

Ciara nodded, a wry smile curving her lips. "Heolstor told me of this God. He sounds dry and dour. I'm glad our ways are different."

Hea held her gaze before smiling back. "So am I."

The two women rode in the midst of a column headed toward the glen where the Mid-Summer Fire festivities awaited. It was the same route that Hea and Bridei had taken a few days earlier, although when they reached the fork in the path through the woods, the travelers from Dundurn headed left, not right which would take them to The Falls of Culloch.

Everyone had come from Dundurn—even the slaves and servants, who traveled on foot at the back of the group. Hea listened to the chatter of excited conversation around her; it appeared the folk of Dundurn had been looking forward to this night for a while.

The carts, laden with boughs of wood, bumped along behind them, while up ahead Bridei and Heolstor rode side-by-side. Hea watched them, laughing together over some shared joke. Those two had always been close, ever since childhood. She was glad Heolstor had followed Bridei here and made a new life for himself. He and Ciara appeared a good match too; although their happiness together was sometimes difficult for Hea to watch as it reminded her of what was lacking in her own life.

It was cool inside the woodland, a respite from the day's heat. The shadows were growing long. The night arrived very late this far north, and dusk still felt some way off. The light had turned golden, covering the world in a gilded veil. It was a lovely afternoon, and surrounded by laughter and merriment, Hea should have felt light-hearted. Yet she did not.

Ever since her trip to the falls with Bridei, she had been on edge. He had kept his distance over the past few days, which did not surprise her. The incident at the falls had cast a shadow over them both. Usually, he would chat to her in the evenings, as they lay on opposite sides of the hearth upstairs; but ever since that day, he had come to bed late and had said little. Once again, she did not blame him, and was grateful he seemed to finally understand.

The travelers from Dundurn reached the glen as the sun slid toward the western horizon, bringing another glorious summer's day to a close. Streaks of pink and gold stained the sky and the scent of pine filled the balmy air. Hea had never known such a warm summer—day after day of cloudless blue skies. Folk were saying that this year's harvest would be the best in a decade.

Crowds of people had already gathered in the glen, clustering around a great pyre of branches. It seemed everyone had brought fuel for the fire from their own village. Laughter filled the glen as men dragged the carts from Dundurn and threw their branches upon the already huge pile waiting.

Hea's gaze slid over the clearing, taking in the crowd. Picts seemed to wear less clothing than the folk she had grown up amongst, and the warm weather meant that most of the men were shirtless, while many women wore little more than a leather band covering their breasts, Ciara included. Hea was one of the few who were covered up, and she felt conspicuous. Most of the children here ran naked around the clearing.

Glancing down at her breasts, snug in the tightly-laced leather bodice, Hea wondered if she would ever be bold enough to walk around so scantily-dressed. In Bebbanburg a woman would be spat at and stoned for dressing so—but here folk were different.

Life was different.

The glen was a sheltered spot, with a burn trickling through its lowest point. Velvet-green grass covered the gently sloping ground where revelers spread out plaid and furs to sit upon. Everyone had brought food and drink with them, which they laid out ready for the feast to follow.

Hea swung down from her pony, and led it over to the edge of the trees, with the other horses. Bridei had just finished unsaddling his stallion, and he caught her eye. "It's the largest gathering in years," he said with a grin. "It should be a good night."

She found herself smiling back, for his enthusiasm was infectious.

After seeing to her pony, Hea followed Bridei through the crowd to where Ciara, Una, and the other women had laid out a spread ready for their king. Men called out to Bridei as he passed, their gazes gleaming and grins on their faces. Others barreled into him, crushing their king in a hug or slapping his back as he walked by. Bridei greeted them all, with the easy familiarity of a man completely at ease among his people.

He is a good king, Hea reflected. *His people love him.*

The scene contrasted with the times she had seen Ecgfrith engage with the folk of Bebbanburg. Rarely had he ever walked among them, and despite that the Northumbrians adored their king, they had always been a little in awe of him. Ecgfrith had never mingled with common-folk.

Hea clenched her jaw. *Except for my mother.* Even now, nearly two months after his death, the bitterness she felt toward Ecgfrith had not dimmed. She sometimes wondered if he would ever have told her the truth about her parentage, if the campaign had not lowered his defenses. He had never done anything unless he stood to benefit.

Pushing thoughts of Ecgfrith aside, for they cast a shadow over this joyous evening, Hea followed Bridei to a great fur spread out over the grass and sat down upon the edge, a few feet away from him.

Heolstor and Ciara joined them. Bridei filled his cup with mead and rose to his feet, while around them the crowd of revelers went silent, their faces turning toward their king.

"Welcome all." Bridei's voice rang out over the glen. "Let us all celebrate the shortest night, our victory over Northumbria, and the bounty of this summer." He raised his cup high. "To the Kingdom of Fortriu—may she last and prosper!"

Men and women rose to their feet and lifted their cups high. A roar went up amongst the glen, rising high into the sultry air.

Hea walked amongst the revelers, a cup of wine in hand. The light had almost faded, and they were getting ready to light the bonfire. A few feet away, two men were wrestling with shields while onlookers cheered them on. The first man to push his opponent to the ground using his shield would win. After the drinking and feasting, there had been a number of games to pass the time while everyone waited for night to fall. On the far side of the glen, a line of men were showing off their skills at wielding a hand axe, while a crowd of giggling girls looked on.

Smiling as the two shield wrestlers grunted and cursed at each other, Hea turned and nearly walked into a man who had stepped up behind her.

"Sorry," she murmured, pulling her cup to one side as wine sloshed over the brim. However, whatever else she was about to say stilled on her tongue when she realized whom she had nearly collided with.

Rinan looked down at her. Standing this close, he was intimidating, towering over her. His work in the smith's forge had bulked him out even more over the past month. Even all these years later, she was still wary of him. Apart from seeing him and Una together on that wall—she'd had no contact with him of late. Tolarggan the smith kept his new slave busy.

Hea forced a polite smile. "Evening, Rinan."

He held her gaze, and she waited for him to say something unpleasant, or to insult her as he had in the past. Yet he merely looked down at her, his expression serious. "Wes hāl, Hea," he replied in their tongue.

"Enjoying yourself?" she asked, keeping her tone light and resisting the urge to step back from him.

His mouth quirked in a half-smile. "The mead's not as good as home."

Hea smiled back. That was the first joke she had ever heard Rinan make. An awkward silence stretched between them after he had spoken. The intensity of Rinan's look was starting to put her on edge.

Hea stepped back. "The sloe wine is excellent though," she replied keeping her tone light. "You should try some. Good eve, Rinan."

She was about to move away, when he stopped her. "Hea ... wait." She met his gaze once more and was surprised to see that his cheeks had reddened. "There's something I need to say." She went still, while he held her gaze. "I'm sorry for what I did, all those years ago."

Hea stared at him. Was she hearing things? Was Rinan son of Broga actually apologizing? After a few moments she nodded. "Thank you ... although it's all in the past now."

"All the same I wanted you to know it."

She inclined her head, frowning. "Why?"

Rinan's face twisted before he glanced right, at where a group of women were laughing and chatting together—Una among them. The young woman looked like a wood-nymph this evening, dressed in a gauzy skirt with nothing but a wisp of leather covering her small, pert breasts. Her long hair flowed over her bare shoulders.

"I've never been good with women," he mumbled. "But I want to be."

As he spoke, Una glanced across at them. She and Rinan's gazes met, and Hea saw the girl's tanned cheeks flush.

Watching them, Hea smiled. For a moment she forgot the emptiness in her own heart. After years of being rejected by every woman he wooed, Rinan had found love in the last place he expected it.

Like Bridei, she was not sure what Una saw in him exactly, for Rinan would never be an easy man to warm to, but Hea was pleased for him nonetheless. Did not everyone deserve at least one chance at happiness?

Night fell and the bonfire whooshed into life, golden flames licking into the darkness, and throwing up sparks like fireflies. Mead, ale, and wine flowed, and some revelers danced around the fire while others played music upon a lyre and a calf-skin drum.

Heolstor and Ciara were among the dancers, their faces flushed as they flew around the fire. The lovers stared at each other, their gazes bright. The attraction between those two was so strong it made the fine hair on the back of Hea's arms prickle.

Hea was watching them, lost in her own thoughts, when Bridei approached her.

"Do you dance?"

She glanced across at him and winced. "Aye—but badly."

He snorted. "I don't believe that for a moment. I'd wager you dance like a Fair Folk maid."

Hea laughed. "I'm afraid not."

Their gazes met and her mirth faded. Bridei was looking at her quietly, a solemn look upon his handsome face. It was the first time he had looked at her this way since their trip to the falls, and she tensed.

Please ... not again.

"Come away from the fire for a short while, Hea," he murmured. "I would speak to you."

Hea's pulse quickened. She did not want to be alone with him. "Can't we talk here?" she replied. "No one will hear us."

He held her gaze for a heartbeat before shaking his head. "I wish to have some privacy ... and your full attention."

Chapter Thirty-two

Truth

HEA FOLLOWED BRIDEI to the edge of the woods, her heart pounding like the drums in the glen behind her. No one appeared to notice their departure. Whoops, shouts, and laughter rang over the wide clearing, and the music grew louder still.

Bridei did not lead her far, just out of sight into a thicket of pines. Out of the glow of the firelight, Hea noted that there was a waxing moon rising into the dark sky; it was not far off full now, for the month was almost at an end.

Turning to her, Bridei watched Hea approach. The silver light of the moon illuminated the chiseled plains of his face but cast his eyes into shadow. Hea stopped a couple of feet away from him and concentrated on steadying her breathing. Surely he could hear her thundering heart?

"What is it?"

He smiled, although the expression lacked his usual brash self-confidence. For the first time ever, Bridei mac Beli appeared unsure of himself. "I'm a coward," he murmured. "I should have spoken before now."

Hea tensed and folded her arms across her chest in an attempt to create a barrier between them. When she did not respond, Bridei continued.

"I was callous in Bebbanburg. I saw you, I wanted you, and I didn't care what the consequences were. I'll be honest; when I left you and set off north, I planned to put you behind me." He broke off here, the words having rushed out of him. "Only ... I couldn't."

Hea felt his gaze pin her to the spot, and wished she could see his eyes, to be able to read his expression better.

"Bridei," she began softly, injecting a note of warning into her voice. "I don't think—"

"Please let me finish."

Hea clenched her jaw, before reluctantly nodding. "Go on then."

He stepped forward, and in the coolness of the woods she felt the warmth of his body reach out to her. She inhaled the scent of him that had always been so exciting and yet comforting.

"I returned to Dundurn and readied myself for war ... but all I could think of was you. I set off south, to draw Ecgfrith and his men into a net, but at each still moment you were there." His words were quiet, powerful. Hea did not doubt the truth of them for a moment. Yet Bridei was not finished. "I could not forget you. You'd left a scar upon my soul."

Hea stared at him. The noise from the revelry in the glen, although only a few yards distant, felt as if it was a world away. These were the words she had once dreamed of hearing, yet now they felt like a blow to the belly. She wished for him to finish there, but Bridei was not yet done. Now that he had begun to open his heart, he could not stop.

"The day of the battle, after we won, I felt empty. There I was, having achieved my life's goal, but it was a hollow victory. When I saw you again shortly afterward, I have never known such joy. I realized then that there wouldn't be room for another woman in my heart ... that I love you and always will."

Hea's throat constricted. The urge to crumple to the ground and dissolve in tears crashed over her. The gods were cruel. What fun they must be having, sitting above watching her suffer.

She inhaled deeply, clenching her fists at her sides till her fingers bit painfully into her palms. "You would not say such things, if you knew the truth about me," she finally managed.

Bridei frowned. He had clearly not expected such a reaction, especially after pouring out his soul. "I wish to know all of you," he replied. "That's what love is."

Hysteria bubbled up within her. "Even if I told you that it was my fault Ecgfrith rode so recklessly into that valley?"

His gaze narrowed further. "How could it be? I set that trap for him."

"Aye—but a few months earlier, I had a vision ... and in it I saw your army defeated in that place. Many of Ecgfrith's men questioned his dogged pursuit of you north; yet he ignored their advice. Because of me."

Bridei folded his arms across his chest, his mouth quirking. "Then you have my thanks, Hea. I thought that victory was owing to my tactical skills. It seems I was wrong."

Anger surged within her at his flippant response. "What if I also told you that the woman you say you love is the daughter of the man you despise?" Bridei flinched back, as if she had just struck him, but Hea pressed on. "That's right, I'm Ecgfrith's bastard. He was the man my mother threw her life away for—the reason she died young of bitterness and a broken heart."

She stepped back from him, taking in the shock on his face. "I'm not so attractive now, am I?"

She turned and fled, making for the trees. However, she had only taken half a dozen strides when he caught her. Hea struggled as Bridei pulled her around to face him.

"How long have you known this?" he demanded.

She glared up at him, struggling in his iron grip. "Since just before the battle."

"So Lewren kept it from you all these years—you never suspected?"

Hea shook her head, clenching her jaw. "No ... now let me go."

He did so, although he remained standing close to her, ready to grab her again should she try to run. She felt him studying her face, trying to absorb the news. His shock was evident. It was as she had suspected—this did change how he thought about her.

All those tender, passionate words ... she had nearly believed him. Yet now that he knew she was Ecgfrith's bastard, he would forget he even said them.

"My mother loved a king once," she began, her voice low and angry, "and it brought her nothing but pain. I'll not make the same mistake."

He drew back, his face hardening. "I'm not Ecgfrith," he replied, each word flat and hard. "Do you really think so little of me?"

"You're a man—you take what you want, and use, while it serves you."

A chill silence settled between them. "I care not who your father is. I only want you," he replied, his voice barely above a whisper.

Her mouth twisted. "You say that now, but I saw your face before."

"I didn't expect it, that's all."

"Don't lie to me ... I saw your disgust."

He shook his head. "I would have loved you, have made you my queen ... yet you throw it all back in my face."

He stepped back from her, a chill draft breathing between them. "Very well ... I'll give you what you want. Go back to Bebbanburg, to your empty hovel and your new king. I'll send an escort of men with you tomorrow."

With that he turned and walked away, disappearing like a wraith into the trees.

Hea watched him go, her heart thundering. She had not wanted to hurt him, but had been so intent on protecting herself that she had done exactly that. The look on his face just a moment ago, would stay with her forever.

The strength went out of her legs, and she crumpled onto the bed of pine needles that covered the forest floor.

It's for the best, she told herself as tears scalded her cheeks. *I had to be blunt or he'd never understand.*

But if that was the case, why did she feel as if her world was coming to an end?

Hea stayed there awhile, trying to control the sobs that convulsed her. She had thought she would never know misery greater than that when her mother died—but this felt even worse. Lewren had been gradually getting sicker for some time, and in the end her suffering had been terrible. There had been relief mingled with grief when she eventually died.

But right now her soul ached with misery.

Eventually, Hea stumbled to her feet. She needed to pull herself together. She had to be strong. Spending the night curled up on the forest floor, weeping, would do her no good.

Scrubbing at her burning, swollen eyes, she walked back toward the glen—toward the sounds of gaiety and music, and the golden glow of firelight. She emerged, blinking, her gaze sweeping over the crowd that moved around the base of the roaring fire.

Taking it all in—the energy, the laughter, and the unabashed enjoyment of one of the four 'fire' festivals that marked the Pictish calendar—Hea felt grief tighten its grip within her. She could fight it all she liked, but the truth was that she had fallen in love with these people and their way of life. She should have been born a Pict—despite that she was a foreigner here, she was already more accepted than she had ever been in Northumbria.

And now Bridei was sending her back.

She could not blame him. After everything she had said, he must want rid of her immediately. But the thought of leaving Dundurn, and the new life she had built for herself there, made panic swell within her. It hurt, almost as much as the pain she felt at losing Bridei forever—even if it had been by her own hand.

This is your own fault, she chided herself. *You've already turned into a bitter shrew, without any man's help.*

She needed to talk to him, to convince him to let her stay.

Hea moved away from the trees, circling around the edge of the revelers. She imagined Bridei had returned and was somewhere among them. But she did not see him. It took a full circle of the glen before she admitted to herself that he had left the revelry ... and when she walked over to the line of horses and found Croí Cróga missing, she knew it to be true.

Hea glanced about, her throat constricting. *What have I done?*

She had acted out of fear, but in the end had pushed away the thing she wanted most. Not only that, but she had hurt the man she loved—the only man she would ever love.

It was then that she spotted the couple, seated a few yards away at the edge of the glen. Under the sheltering boughs of a birch sat Rinan and Una. He sat with his back against the trunk, while she perched upon his lap, her arms entwined about his neck. They kissed passionately.

Hea's vision blurred. Even Rinan had managed to forge a new life here. Unlike her, the warrior had shed the old hates and bitterness of the past, whereas she had carried them with her.

I care not who your father is. I only want you.

Panic swept over her. Bridei did not care that Ecgfrith had sired her ... he knew the truth and still wanted her. She had been blinded by her own fears, yet it was not too late—she had to find him and undo the mess she had made.

Hea stumbled over to her pony, where it was dozing under a tall beech. Hands trembling, she tightened the girth to the saddle and untied the pony from the tree. Then she led it away, around the edge of the glen, and onto the forest path that led north-west.

As soon as she was out of sight, Hea swung up onto the pony's back and urged it into a brisk trot. Fortunately it was a clear night and the hoary light of the moon illuminated her path.

Behind her, the sounds of the celebration soon dimmed and the quietness of the woodland surrounded her. As she rode, Hea attempted to marshal her thoughts. It took all her courage to go after Bridei, for he had truly been angry when they had parted earlier. However, the alternative was too lonely to contemplate.

If he rejected her, it would hurt—but to carry the responsibility for ruining both their lives would be worse.

Lost in thought, Hea hardly noticed the fork in the forest path approaching. It was only when she rode by the path heading south-west that she drew the pony to a halt. She had assumed that Bridei would ride back to Dundurn ... but had he?

Perhaps he had ridden to The Falls of Culloch instead?

She remembered his words, that day they had visited the falls. *This is where I come when I need to be alone, to think.*

Making a decision, Hea turned her mount onto the south-west fork, and urged it into a canter.

Chapter Thirty-three

You are Mine

IT HAD BEEN a mistake to come up here.

Alone with only the thundering falls for company, Bridei's thoughts spiraled. He glared into the darkness and raked a hand through his damp hair. He had been a fool, a love-sick dolt, and paid the price.

Humiliation.

He wished he had not taken Ciara's advice, had not borne his soul for Hea to rip to shreds. His whole life he had kept that part of him hidden from others—even those he trusted like Heolstor never saw his insecurities, his fears. A warrior did show his weaknesses, but he had been willing to let Hea see what was in his heart, to convince her his feelings were real.

She had thrown them back in his face.

The cool mist from the falls rose up around him in an enveloping shroud. Usually this place brought him solace, but tonight under the frosted light of the moon, he just felt lonely.

Why did you send her away?

The words had been out before he had realized what he was saying. The need to lash out at her, hurt her, had been too strong. He knew Hea loved living in Dundurn; he saw it on her face every day. Here she had a sense of belonging she had never found at Bebbanburg.

She did not want him, and that was bitter gall to swallow, but he did not want to punish her for that. Tomorrow, he would tell her so. Tomorrow he would try not to make a fool of himself once more.

Lost in thought, his knees drawn up under his chin, he stared at the glowing column of water a few yards away.

Hea really was his one weakness—but he would need to find a way to master it.

He did not hear the horse's approach at first; the roar of the falls obliterated most of the night's noises. It was only when he caught the sound of hooves upon gravel that he stiffened, his right hand going to the hilt of his sword.

Even out here, in this remote spot, it was unwise to let your guard down.

Bridei rose to his feet, and—hand still upon the hilt of his sword—stalked across the large flat rock to where a silhouette loomed out of the darkness.

A stocky pony with a small figure perched on its back appeared.

Bridei halted, his gaze narrowing. Even at this distance, he recognized her.

Hea.

He watched her dismount from her pony and walk up the slope toward him. She stepped up onto the flat rock on which he stood. The moonlight bathed her, making her look like a fairy maid as she approached. Her long, unbound hair spilled over her shoulders, and her hips swayed as she walked.

Bridei's mouth went dry. Even angry and humiliated, he still wanted her. Wanted her with a force that scared him. How would he ever get over this woman?

She halted a few feet away from him. Her face was solemn, although those expressive green eyes were cast into shadow. "I went looking for you," she greeted him softly. "I thought you might be here."

Bridei's mouth twisted. "And you were right ... congratulations." Her could hear the sarcasm in his voice, knew how bitter he sounded, but right now he did not care. "What do you want?"

A heartbeat of silence stretched between them, before she answered, her voice barely above a whisper. "You."

Bridei watched her, his gut clenching. "What's this? A new game now?"

She shook her head, taking a hesitant step toward him. "It's no game ... I want to apologize ... to explain."

He folded his arms across his chest, his frown deepening. "Go on."

He watched her nervously wet her lips. His chill welcome was unnerving her, yet he did not relent. He was not letting his shield down again—not without a good reason.

"I've loved you since I was a girl," she began softly. "I was devastated the day Ecgfrith banished you. Mōder told me to forget you, to find myself a local man and start a family, but instead I clung to your memory. When you returned to Bebbanburg I imagined it was a dream—but I soon realized we could never be together ... that one night was all we'd ever have."

She broke off there, her chest rising and falling as if she struggled to get the words out. "I told myself it was for the best ... but I couldn't forget you. And then when Ecgfrith told me that I was his daughter, I was furious—at him for treating my mother so callously, and at her for throwing her life away on such a selfish man."

Hea paused, watching him steadily. "I promised myself I'd never do that, and then when I saw you again, I convinced myself that I'd set out on the same path of self-destruction as my mother." She let out a shaky breath and raked a hand through her hair. "I've ruined things, Bridei, and I'm sorry."

Bridei watched her, not sure what to make of the tale she had just told him. "Your mind was playing tricks on you," he said after a pause. "You are not your mother, and I am not Ecgfrith. Had you removed that veil of prejudice from your eyes you would have seen that."

"I do now." The words were spoken softly, with much sadness. "I love you ... and not as I did as a girl. I love the man you've become: your strength, your sense of justice, your brave heart. I want you, body and soul. I'd do anything to undo the things I said ... but I understand if it's too late." Her voice faltered. "Is it?"

Bridei did not reply. He merely stared at her, his gaze shadowed.

What was he thinking? Was he still angry with her?

Silence stretched out, and despair settled over Hea. He did not need to say a word—she could see it was too late. She had wounded his pride too deeply.

Hea stepped back from him and attempted a brittle smile, although inside she was crumbling. "I shouldn't have come ... I'll leave you alone."

She turned and hurried toward the edge of the stone.

Bridei was on her before she had taken two paces. He moved so fast that she let out a cry of shock. One moment she had been struggling not to cry, the next he hauled her into his arms.

His mouth slanted across hers, hard and hungry. When he pulled back from the kiss, leaving Hea gasping for breath in his arms, the look on his face made her body dissolve against him. It was an expression of such desperate want that needed no further explanation.

"You're not leaving," he growled. "You are mine."

And with that, he kissed her again. Hea responded, giving herself up to the wild heat that pulsed up from the pit of her belly. Despair sloughed off her, replaced with a hunger that only he could sate.

Their clothes came off. Bridei, still only clad in leather breeches and boots, stripped naked in moments, whereas Hea's fingers fumbled with the laces of her vest, the buckle holding up her plaid skirt. He helped her, pushing down her skirt so that it billowed at her feet, and freeing her breasts from the leather bodice, so that he could feast on them.

Hea groaned, her legs going weak beneath her as she watched him cup her breasts, drawing each swollen nipple into his mouth. How she had missed this—how her body ached for more.

They sank down onto the rock. Despite that night had fallen, the stone was still warm against Hea's skin after a hot day. Bridei pinned her down upon the stone, spreading her limbs as he moved over her, his hot mouth leaving a trail of fire down her body.

Hea let out another moan and arched herself up toward him. She reached up, her fingers clutching for him, but he ducked just out of reach. "Soon," he murmured, "but let me touch you first."

Hea's eyes fluttered shut, and she gave herself up to sensation; the pleasure his fingers, lips and tongue brought her as he moved down her body. Finally, when she was a trembling wreck, he moved back over her, lowering his body against hers.

Their mouths fused once more, and Hea's fingers tangled in the softness of his hair, before trailing down the strong column of his back to his buttocks. When her hands journeyed to his shaft, Bridei inhaled sharply.

Hea smiled, enjoying the thrill of power while she stroked the long, hard length of him, her fingers circling the swollen, slick head.

He groaned, his body trembling from restraint as she continued to touch him in slow, deliberate strokes. Hea gave a soft laugh at his reaction, but it abruptly choked off when he took hold of her right leg, lifted it high and entered her in one deep, long thrust.

The sensation of him stretching her, filling her to the core made Hea gasp. But she had barely a moment to recover before he began to move inside her, taking her in slow, deliberate strokes.

Her cries echoed across the falls, mingling with the roar of the water. Exquisite ripples of pleasure pulsed out from her lower belly, steadily growing in intensity. This was even better than she remembered. Back in Bebbanburg, she had been a maid the first time Bridei had taken her. Lovemaking had been a delight but also a discovery. Months later, her body had now fully awakened.

The pleasure crested, so intense now that Hea could hardly bear it. She tried to push at the wall of his chest, tried to get him to stop a moment so she could regain her equilibrium, but Bridei was too far gone.

He plunged into her—and pushed Hea over the brink. She lost all sense of time and place, her body nothing more than a wet, pulsing core of pleasure. The world spun, and she was vaguely aware of Bridei's hoarse cry echoing through the night. Then, his body went rigid and he spent himself inside her.

The ragged sound of their breathing mingled with the hiss and rumble of the cascade behind them. The falls threw out a soft mist that caressed their heated, tangled limbs.

Still struggling to regain his breath, Bridei propped himself onto one elbow and gazed down at Hea. Never had she looked as lovely as at this moment: her soft pale limbs bathed in moonlight, her tangled hair fanned out across the stone. She stared up at him, her full lips slightly parted.

Bridei reached out—stroking her from the neck, down the valley between her lush breasts, to the pale curve of her belly. His gaze shifted to the nest of damp, auburn curls beneath, and he felt himself harden. He was not done sating himself with this woman ... he had only just begun.

Hea let out a sigh. He glanced back up and stilled, realizing that her cheeks were wet.

Bridei's chest constricted. "Why are you weeping?"

She favored him with a watery smile. "Because I'm a woman ... and because I'm happy."

His breathing stilled. "Is this real?" he asked, reaching up to brush away her tears. "Are you really mine?"

She nodded. "Yes ... I always have been."

He smiled. "Then we have some lost years to make up for, lovely Hea."

Chapter Thirty-four

Lovers and Dreams

DAWN PEEKED OVER the eastern edge of the cliffs surrounding The Falls of Culloch. The first rays of sun crept across the rock, filtering over the man and woman who lay sleeping upon one of the large flat stones near the waterfall.

Hea felt the sunlight kiss her naked skin, and her eyes flickered open.

A moment later, a sense of wellbeing, unlike any she had ever known, flowed over her. A smile spread across her face, and she sat up, gazing down at the man who still lay sleeping beside her.

Bridei mac Beli was a joy to gaze upon. In repose, his handsome face was beautiful, the sensual lines of his mouth relaxed. His long dark lashes rested like butterfly wings against his cheeks. Her gaze traveled down the long, muscular length of his body, taking in the blue-inked swirls and circles that decorated the left side of his body and arm. She would never tire of looking upon him.

Perhaps feeling the weight of her stare, Bridei's eyes opened. Their gazes met and held for a few moments, before that beautiful mouth of his spread into a smile.

"Sleep well?"

She smiled back. "Hardly at all—and you?"

He sat up, running a hand over his face. "We'll have all the time in the world to sleep when we return to Dundurn."

Hea snorted. "You do maybe. Modwen will have a list of jobs for me to help her with when we get back."

Bridei laughed, rising to his feet with fluid grace. "You can say no to her occasionally, you know. Modwen managed just fine for years without your help. Don't let her boss you around."

He reached down, took Hea's hand, and pulled her gently to her feet. Standing together, bathed in the soft dawn light, Bridei gazed down at her a moment. Then he reached out and brushed a curl that had fallen in her eyes. "If I could, I would stop time at this moment," he murmured. "Here at the falls—just you and me."

Hea smiled up at him. "What ... and give up Dundurn, your kingship?"

His expression was serious as he looked down at her. "Aye—without you it means nothing. I want you at my side, Hea. Will you be my queen?"

Hea's breath caught. She did not think it was possible to be any happier than this—any more so and her chest would explode. All her old fears dissolved like wood smoke on a windy day. She had misjudged Bridei all those months ago, or perhaps he had changed. Whatever the reason, he now wanted her to be his consort, his life's companion.

Hea reached up, her finger tracing the line of his stubbled jaw. "Aye, I will."

They rode back into the glen to find men fighting.

Hea's gaze swept the gently-sloping green expanse. She took in the still smoking remains of the great fire, and the crowds of people—many of whom were still breaking their fast with the remains of last night's feast—before her gaze came to rest upon a cluster of warriors on the southern side of the glen.

Rough, angry voices shattered the morning's peace. From a distance it looked as if two men were fighting off four others. Hea's breathing hitched when she caught sight of the two men who had been backed into a corner: one red-headed, the other blond.

Heolstor and Rinan.

Heolstor, face flushed, wore a murderous expression. Meanwhile, Rinan had a black-eye and was bleeding from the nose as he stared his aggressors down.

Ahead of Hea, Bridei urged Croí Cróga into a canter and rode toward the men. "What's happening here?" he shouted.

The men ignored their leader. Instead, they closed in on Heolstor and Rinan, fists raised.

"Lower your fists," Heolstor growled, "or I'll make you regret it."

One of them spat on the ground. "Angle dog!"

"The first moment you get the chance to side with your kind, you do ... even the likes of him," another added.

"You're drunk, Longus," Heolstor snarled back. "You're always an aggressive little shit when you've had too much mead."

The man he had just insulted, bellowed and lunged forward. Heolstor, who was bigger, stronger—and more sober—met him with a punch to the eye that sent him sprawling. However, the other men set upon Rinan, fists flying. The slave was ready for them, felling the first with a kick to the groin, and the second with a punch to the nose. Yet the third, a wiry, dark-haired man covered head-to-foot in blue tattoos, leaped upon Rinan's back and tried to gouge his eyes out.

"Gurid!" Bridei bellowed, swinging down from stallion's back and striding toward the brawl. "Get off him."

It was then they all realized their king had returned.

The felled warriors scrambled to their feet, cursing and cradling their injuries. Meanwhile, Bridei strode into their midst and pulled Gurid off Rinan by his scruff, shaking him like a dog. "What is the meaning of this?"

"It's that straw-haired letch," one of them mumbled, clutching his bleeding nose. "We caught him rutting Una, milord."

It was then that Hea, who had ridden up silently behind Bridei, caught sight of a tall, slender figure cowering a few feet behind Rinan.

Bridei's expression turned thunderous. "Una," he called. "Come here."

The young woman came forward, although she did not walk to Bridei's side but Rinan's. One slim hand reached out and disappeared into Rinan's much larger one.

Bridei's face hardened further. "Did he force you, Una?"

She shook her head, while Rinan merely glowered at Bridei, daring the king to challenge him.

"I went with him willingly," she said after a few moments, her voice surprisingly strong and firm. She cast a venomous look at the four warriors who encircled them. "I told these idiots that, but they wouldn't believe me."

"Slut," Gurid spat at her. "So you prefer an Angle rod to a Pict one, eh?"

Rinan, who had learned enough of their tongue to understand the insult, glared at the warrior, while Una drew herself up, her gaze hard. "Just as long as it isn't yours, Gurid."

"Enough." Bridei stepped forward. "If Una went with him willingly then that's her choice."

"But he's a slave," the warrior named Longus spoke up, his words slurring slightly. Anyone could see the man was so drunk he could barely stand. "He can't take one of our women."

Bridei hesitated and a tense silence settled over the group. Around them, the chatter of early morning conversation in the glen had died; all gazes were now riveted upon their king. Hea climbed down from her pony and approached the group. She knew Bridei faced a difficult decision.

The laws regarding slaves in Northumbria were strict: a slave could own nothing, claim nothing. He did not have the right to a woman; he did not even own the clothes on his back. She did not know if the same rules applied here, but if they did Rinan would lose Una.

She met Rinan's gaze as she approached, and saw from the look in his eyes that he was thinking the same as her. Rinan's attention then shifted to Bridei, and Hea watched a fatalistic expression settle over his face.

There was no friendship between these two men—Rinan expected the worst.

Stepping up beside Bridei, Hea met his gaze. She said nothing, for to intervene on Rinan's behalf would cause a loss of honor for both men. This was something Bridei had to decide. Her lover's face was difficult to read. He wore that cool, slightly distant expression she had seen at Dun Nechtáin.

Bridei's gaze held Rinan's for a few moments, before he shifted his attention to Una. The woman watched Bridei, her eyes glittering with tears. "Do you care for him?" he asked.

"Aye," she replied without hesitation.

"And would you willingly be his woman, if I allowed it?"

"I would."

Bridei's mouth curved, and then he looked back at Rinan. "Her taste is questionable," he said, shifting to Englisc for the first time since entering the glen. "But who am I to keep lovers apart?"

Rinan's pale-blue eyes widened. "You'll allow it?"

Bridei's face split into a grin. Reaching out he looped an arm around Hea's shoulders drawing her close. "Let's say you caught me in a benevolent mood this morning."

The folk of Dundurn returned to their fort in the late afternoon, as the shadows grew long and the sun sank toward the west. After the morning's excitement, the men, women, and children who flowed into the fort chattered excitedly amongst themselves.

The four warriors who had started the brawl that morning slunk at the back of the group, nursing their injuries, their faces sour. However, all of them knew better than to challenge Bridei's word. He was a fair ruler, but he would not be crossed.

Inside the broch, Hea helped the other women prepare a light supper of fowl broth and barley bread. As she kneaded the bread, Ciara gave Hea a conspirator's grin. "I see you and Bridei are getting along better."

Hea nodded, feeling her face grow warm as she did so. She cursed herself for being so transparent, for her blush made Ciara and the surrounding women grin. They were enjoying her embarrassment.

"Don't look so mortified lass," one of the women chortled. "A fine man like that, I'd be grinning like a ferret that got into the fowl coop too."

This set them all off laughing, and after a few moments Hea felt a smile curve her own lips. "I'm still getting used to the idea, that's all," she admitted. "It hardly seems real."

Ciara met her gaze. "Well believe it. A man like Bridei mac Beli doesn't do anything by halves."

The dream came upon her slowly, like spring mist creeping in from the sea. Hea left the nest of furs, where she was curled up against Bridei, and found herself walking up a hillside strewn with heather.

She recognized that this was not a usual dream, which were shadowy and fragmented. Instead, this was a seeing dream, like the visions she used to have. Everything was bright and sharp. She could smell the sweet scent of heather, the peaty aroma of sun-warmed earth, and feel the cool breeze on her face.

Hea crested the hill and stopped, catching her breath a moment. To the west she caught sight of the outline of Dundurn: a conical, tiered hill topped by a stone round tower. She stood on the edge of a wide valley, where a creek meandered its way through granite rocks. It was spring, for yellow, white and blue wildflowers carpeted the valley ... and walking amongst them she spied a tall, dark-haired man.

Bridei.

"Cinn ... Brei!" he called out, cupping his hands around his mouth so that his voice carried. "Where are you? Little buggers!"

Childish laughter erupted before two heads peeked out of the grass: one auburn the other dark. Two lads, both no older than four winters, leaped from their hiding places and rushed across to him.

"We've got you, da!" one of them called out, arms and legs windmilling.

Bridei let out a cry of mock-fear and sank to the ground, rolling onto his back as the boys leaped upon him. The sounds of their laughter lifted high into the air.

Hea walked down the hillside toward them, happiness flowering in her breast. This was a glimpse of her and Bridei's future ... their sons.

"Hea."

Bridei's voice reached her from afar.

"Hea!"

Her eyes flickered open, and she found herself looking up into Bridei's concerned face. The hearth had burned down low, casting a faint golden glow over them.

She gave him a sleepy smile, although she felt a sense of loss at being torn from that beautiful valley. "I was dreaming," she murmured. "Did I wake you?"

"You were thrashing about, mumbling ... I was worried."

Hea reached up and stroked his face. "There was no need to be ... it was a beautiful dream."

His expression softened. "Really, what was it about?"

"The future ... our future."

His gaze widened. "Your gift—has it returned?"

"I'm not sure," she replied, hesitant to admit such things now she had awoken. Recent experiences made her wary of trusting her visions again. The scene had been so real, so vivid that she wanted to believe it. "If it has, we have much to look forward to."

He grinned down at her. "So are you going to tell me of it?"

Hea shook her head, smiling. "I think the future is best let be," she replied, shifting her body under his so that her breasts rubbed up against his chest. "If what I dreamed comes to pass I shall tell you ... until then, let us focus on the present."

It was true. She did not want to reject her gift, only she was not defined by it these days. She was content to let the future unfurl as it should.

Bridei raised an eyebrow, his gaze darkening as her hand snaked down, under the furs to caress him. "Heahburh ... are you trying to distract me?"

"Aye, is it working?"

He gave a low groan, and rolled over onto his back, pulling her with him. A wicked smile crept over his face. "No—I believe you'll have to try harder."

Epilogue

The Miracle

Two years later ...

BRIDEI PACED THE floor in the broch, growing increasingly agitated with every circuit.

"Why's it taking so long? They've been up there all afternoon."

A few feet away, Heolstor huffed out a breath and filled a cup of mead. "For the love of The Mother, would you stop pacing? You're making me nervous." He thrust out the cup toward Bridei. "Here, have something to drink."

Bridei shook his head. He did not want to numb himself with mead, he wanted to know if Hea was well. He halted in the middle of the rush and heather-strewn floor and looked up at the ceiling. Hea had disappeared up there late that morning with Ciara and Modwen, and had not reappeared since. Even more worryingly, he had not heard any noise. He thought women screamed and groaned in childbirth, but Hea's silence unnerved him.

Was she too weak? Was she bleeding to death?

His stomach churned, sweat beading his skin. He had been less nervous before going into battle. Childbirth was dangerous—he knew many women did not survive it. Hea was strong and although her belly had grown extremely large in the last stages of the pregnancy, causing her to waddle like a goose, she had appeared healthy throughout the nine months. Not only that, but Modwen had fussed over her, and watched her carefully throughout. If the healer had been worried about Hea, she had hidden it well.

He swiveled on his heel, turning to face Heolstor. "I can't stand it—I'm going up there to check on her."

Heolstor rose to his feet, his face sympathetic. He and Ciara now had an infant daughter, Mila; he knew what Bridei was going through. Not only that, but Ciara's labor had been difficult, and it had taken her many long days afterward to recover. "I'll come with you."

They had just made their way to the foot of the stairs leading to the level above, when Ciara appeared at the top of them. Bridei's gaze went to her face—and relief crashed over him when he saw that although she was flushed, Ciara was smiling.

"I was just coming to get you." She beckoned them both upstairs. "It is over. You're a father, Bridei."

He rushed up the stairs, taking them two at a time. "And, Hea … is she well?"

"Aye, just exhausted. One birth is bad enough … but two."

Two.

Bridei entered the warm space, the air heavy with the metallic smell of blood. His gaze traveled to where Hea sat propped up against a pile of furs. Her face was pale and drawn, but she was smiling. Two tiny, red-faced babes suckled at her breasts.

Bridei stopped, awestruck. "Twins?"

Her mouth quirked. "You weren't expecting that, were you?"

Bridei shook his head, momentarily lost for words. That was why her belly had grown so large—Modwen had thought she was carrying a large babe, but instead she'd been carrying two small ones.

Modwen stood nearby, her face glowing with sweat as she grinned at him. "Two fine, healthy sons, milord."

Bridei smiled back at her before crossing to the furs. He then lowered himself so that he perched next to his wife. "You did well, my love." His gaze then shifted down to the two suckling babes. The sight of their scrunched up faces and tiny hands caused something inside him to melt; he had teased Heolstor at how he had cooed over his baby daughter, but now he understood. These were his sons, his flesh and blood. He and Hea had made them.

Bridei glanced up, his tears stinging his eyes, and met Hea's gaze. "I can't believe it," he said huskily. "They are a miracle."

She smiled back, her own moss-green eyes glittering. "They are, aren't they?"

"Can I touch them?"

"Of course."

Bridei reached out and ran a light finger over their downy heads, their tiny chubby arms. "Have you thought of names?" he asked.

"I thought I would let you choose," she replied. "Go on … do you have any preferences?"

Bridei thought for a moment, his gaze returning to his sons, before answering. "I had two uncles who died when I was young, before I was sent to foster at Bebbanburg, but I still remember them fondly," he said with a wistful smile. "I'd like to name our sons after them: Cinn and Brei."

He glanced up and saw an odd expression flit across Hea's face. Bridei frowned. "What's wrong? Don't you like the names?"

"They are warriors' names," Modwen said from behind him, pride in her voice.

"Perhaps one of them will wed our daughter," Heolstor piped up. He had stopped at the top of the stairs and leaned against the wall, an arm slung across Ciara's shoulders. His wife turned, giving him an arch look. "You're worse than a woman ... match-making already?"

Heolstor gave a shrug. "It pays to look ahead."

Bridei smiled at their banter, before he turned back to Hea. She was watching him with a soft gaze, a smile curving her full lips. To him, she had never looked so beautiful. He reached out, took her hand and raised it to his lips, kissing it. Even two years on, he did not take this woman for granted. There was always something new to discover about her; she stimulated his mind as much as his body.

"So the names will do?" he murmured.

Her smile widened. "Aye—they're perfect."

The End

Historical background for *Wind Song*

I usually put a lot of this information in the front of my novels ... but the background and historical notes are getting so lengthy these days I've decided to insert them at the end!

In the seventh century, England was not as we know it today. The Anglo-Saxon period lasted from the departure of the Romans, from around 430 AD, to the Norman invasion, in 1066 AD. My novels focus on the period in between the departure of the Romans, and the first Viking invasion in 793 AD—a 300-year period in which Anglo-Saxon culture flourished. The British Isles were named Britannia (a legacy of the Roman colonization) and split into rival kingdoms. For the purposes of this novel, we focus on Northumbria and the Pictish kingdom to the north: the Kingdom of Fortriu.

Many locations in Northumbria and Pictland (now Scotland) appear in this novel, although their names are somewhat different to modern-day England. Bebbanburg was the old name for Bamburgh, the seat of Northumbrian Kings for many centuries. At the time of our story, the castle would not have been built, however, there would have been a wooden fort at the top of the rocky outcrop, and, possibly, a Great Tower made of local stone. The nearby island of Lindisfarena is none other than Lindisfarne, also known today as Holy Island.

In the Kingdom of Fortriu, two locations are mentioned: Nechtansmere (in Old English)/Dun Nechtáin (in Gaelic) and Dundurn, Bridei's northern stronghold in Pictland. The fort was situated on a hill with the River Earn to one side and the Allt Ghoinean burn to another. This area later became known as the province of Strathearn, and today is part of Perth.

This novel centers around two real historical figures: Ecgfrith of Northumbria and Bridei mac Beli. Bridei was king of the Picts from 672 until 693 (I've altered the dates of his reign slightly for the purposes of this novel). He ruled the Kingdom of Fortriu, in Southern Pictland (today southern Scotland). His father was Beli, King of Alt Clut, and his mother was an Angle—possibly a daughter of King Edwin of Deira. Bridei spent most of his childhood living at Bebbanburg, under the charge of the Northumbrian king. He would have left Northumbria as a young man and returned to his father's lands, where he based himself at Dundurn, a hilltop fortress in southern Fortriu.

Bridei was an expansionary and active king—he led violent campaigns throughout Pictland, claiming new lands and taking back old ones for Fortriu. His relationship with King Ecgfrith of Northumbria was strained—Ecgfrith likely saw Bridei as a 'sub-king' rather than an independent ruler, and Bridei would have chafed under what he saw as the yoke of an Angle overlord. Their worsening relationship led to the famous Battle of Dun Nechtain in 685, in which the Anglo-Saxon army of Ecgfrith was annihilated.

The Battle of Dun Nechtain (or Battle of Nechtansmere as it was known in Old English) marked a turning-point between the Picts and the Anglo-Saxons. The battle ended with a decisive Pictish victory which severely weakened Northumbria's power in northern Britain. Before Ecgfrith set out on his campaign north, Prior Cuthbert of Lindisfarne was said to have tried to dissuade him—however Ecgfrith's mind was made up.

The battle took place on 20 May 685, during which, the Picts pretended to retreat and drew the Northumbrians into a bloody ambush at Dun Nechtain in a valley near the lake of Linn Garan. Ecgfrith was killed in battle, along with the greater part of his army. The Pictish victory marked their independence from Northumbria, who never regained their dominance in the north.

There are no records as to whether Bridei married, or had any children, so in my story I create a romance between him and a young Angle woman, Hea.

Background to Pict culture*

Gods and Goddesses

The Mother: Goddess of enlightenment and feminine energy—the bringer of change
The Warrior: God of battle, life and growth, of summer
The Maiden: Young goddess of nature and fertility
The Hag: Goddess of the dark—sleep, dreams, death, winter, and the earth
The Reaper: God of death.

Pict festivities

Earth Fire: Salute to new life and the first signs of spring (February 1)
Bealtunn: Spring Equinox
Mid-Summer Fire: Summer Equinox
Harvest Fire: Festival to salute the harvest (Aug 1)
Gateway: Passage from summer to winter (October 31/November 1)

Mid-Winter Fire: Winter Equinox

* Author's note: I have taken 'artistic license' when it comes to the names of the festivities and Pict gods and goddesses. The historical evidence is very scant, making it a challenge for me to get an accurate picture of these details. The Picts were an enigmatic people, and we only have their ruins and symbols to cast light on how they lived and whom they worshipped. To make my setting as authentic as possible, I have studied the rituals and religions of the Celtic peoples of Scotland, Ireland and Wales of a similar period and have created a culture I feel could have existed.

Glossary of Old English (in alphabetical order)

Cyningtaefl: "King's Table", an Anglo-Saxon form of chess
ealdorman: earl
Englisc: Old English
Ēōstre: Easter
fæder: father
fyrd: a king's army
handfasted: married
heah-setl: high seat (later called a "dais") for the king and queen
hlaf-mas: Lammas Day (an Anglo-Saxon festivity – takes place sometime from 1 Aug to 1 Sept to celebrate the first wheat harvest)
hōre: whore
Lindisfarena: Lindisfarne Island (Holy Island)
lūtan: lout
mōder: mother
Nithhogg: a fire-breathing dragon that lived in the underworld
nón-mete: midday meal (literally "noon-meat")
thegn: a king's retainer
Thrimilce: May (Old English – literally 'month of the three milkings')
thrymsas: Anglo-Saxon gold shillings
theow: slave
 "Wes hāl": "Greetings" in Old English
wicce: a witch or enchantress
wyrd: fate

Cast of characters (in alphabetical order)

Beli king of Alt Clut: Bridei's father
Bridei mac Beli: Pict prince who fostered at Bebbanburg, later becomes king of Fortriu
Broga: an ironsmith, Rinan's father
Ciara: Heolstor's wife
Croí Cróga: Bridei's stallion later in the story (Brave Heart in Scottish Gaelic)

Cuthbert: Prior of the Lindisfarena (Lindisfarne) monastery
Ecgfrith: King of Northumbria
Flann Fína mac Ossu: Ecgfrith's half-brother, currently lives on the island of Iona
Fritha: Hea's friend in Bebbanburg
Hea (Heahburh): seer and herbalist
Heolstor: An Angle warrior and Bridei's childhood friend
Irmenburgh: Ecgfrith's wife
Léoma: Bridei's first pony (Ray of Light in Old English)
Lewren: Hea's mother
Longus and Gurid: two Pict warriors
Modwen: healer at Dundurn
Oswald: priest at Bebbanburg
Rinan: Angle warrior
Rowan: Hea's pony on the campaign north
Tolarggan: smith at Dundurn
Una: servant at Dundurn

Acknowledgements

Thanks once again, to all my readers ... without you these novels would never have been written. I love hearing from you, and your feedback really helps me when planning out new stories. I'm always looking for ways to give you the emotion-filled stories you want!

I'm also grateful to Kindle Direct Publishing, who have given me a place to publish and promote my works ... and to the Kindle Unlimited program which has helped me reach even more readers!

And of course a HUGE thank you goes to Tim, who helps me at every step of the process. I couldn't do this without you, my love.

Lord
Of the
North Wind

BOOK THREE
THE KINGDOM
OF NORTHUMBRIA

Jayne Castel

WINTER MIST
PRESS

Maps

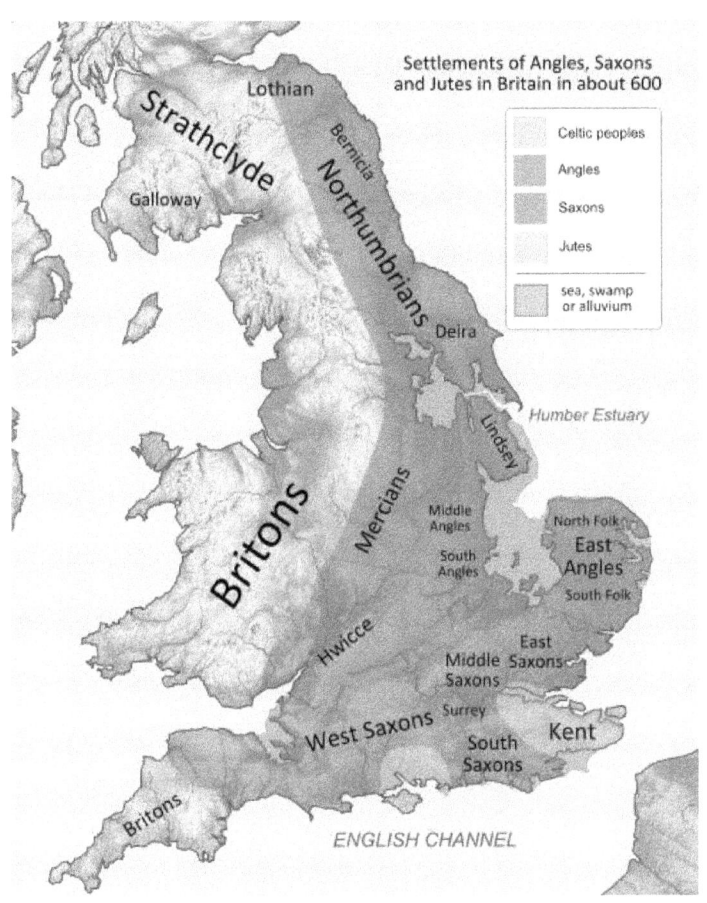

Settlements of Angles, Saxons and Jutes in Britain in about 600

Celtic peoples
Angles
Saxons
Jutes
sea, swamp or alluvium

Strathclyde
Lothian
Galloway
Bernicia
Northumbrians
Deira
Humber Estuary
Lindsey
Britons
Mercians
Middle Angles
South Angles
North Folk
East Angles
South Folk
Hwicce
East Saxons
Middle Saxons
Surrey
West Saxons
Kent
South Saxons
Britons
ENGLISH CHANNEL

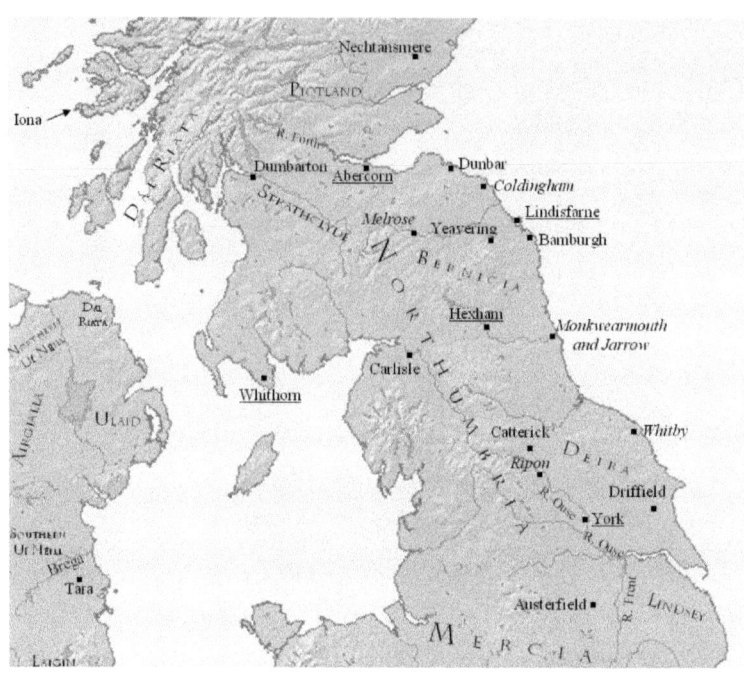

Better a warm blush than heated passions.
　　　　　—King Aldfrith of Northumbria

Prologue

The Angle's Bastard

Summer, 675 AD

Off the northern coast of Éirinn (Ireland)

FLANN WEPT FOR most of the journey.

Tears trickled down his face as he stared into the distance. Hunched at the bow of the long-boat, he watched the slate grey expanse of the sea before him. It merged into an overcast horizon. The whole world seemed drained of color this afternoon, a bleak cold place that mirrored his soul.

Behind him he was vaguely aware of the other men: the low rumble of their voices that the wind snatched away, the oarsmen's grunts, and the steady splash of the oars in the water that moved in time with his breathing.

Flann shivered and pulled his fur mantle close. However, it was not the cold that bit at him—for despite the grey day, it was summer—but grief and misery.

I will never feel warm again.

Flann glanced down at the dark waters rippling by. Shortly after they had left Éirinn, striking north toward Pictland, he had considered throwing himself overboard and letting the sea take him. He could not swim; he would sink like a boulder. But the thought had reminded him of his mother, of the sight of her bloated body floating in with the tide, her long tangled hair drifting around her like kelp. The memory had brought him up short. Then he had felt sick.

No, he did not have the stomach for such an end.

And so Flann remained where he was, a lone figure perched upon the bow, isolated in his misery. Around him the light started to fade. The wind buffeted the boat and seabirds cried overhead.

Flann paid none of it any notice; his thoughts had turned inwards. His drying tears now itched upon his cheeks.

"There it is, lad." A man's gruff voice sounded behind him. "Iona approaches."

Flann looked up from where he had been staring at the waves and spied a low rocky strip on the north-eastern horizon. The peaked outline of a church roof rose sharply against the darkening sky.

After a long pause, his uncle spoke once more. "Flann ... are you sure this is what you want?"

Flann swallowed. His throat ached, making it hard to speak. Rousing himself, he glanced over his shoulder. His uncle Daragh stared back at him. The wind whipped the older man's dark hair around a careworn face. His eyes, a penetrating dark-blue, were narrowed in concern. "A monk's life isn't for all men."

"Aye," Flann rasped. "I'm sure."

Daragh frowned. "I know it doesn't seem so now, but your heart will mend."

Flann glanced away, clenching his fists against his sides. His uncle was a good man, but he did not understand. "No," he ground out. "It won't."

"You only have eighteen winters," Daragh continued doggedly. "Too young to throw your life away over some vain wench."

Flann went still, and when he answered his voice was cold. "Don't speak of her."

Silence followed. The hiss of the waves hitting the rocky beach intruded upon their conversation. The isle had drawn closer as they spoke, a bare windswept rock that looked as bleak and barren as Flann now felt.

Good.

That was where he wished to be: in an empty, friendless place where there would not be any memory of her.

"You've got too much of your mother in you," Daragh said eventually, pain in his voice. "My sister was ruled by her passions, consumed by them. I'd hoped your cold Angle father would have tempered the fire in your blood, but you've taken after Fina. Love was her world ... and her ruin."

Flann did not reply. His uncle's words were all true, yet they changed nothing. He could not alter what had happened, or how he felt. He was not like Daragh: mild-tempered, steady Daragh who had a wife he adored and two young daughters who were his world. Flann was broken, clinging onto control by his fingertips. A new life on this rock was the only future he could contemplate.

The oarsmen navigated the long-boat into a shallow bay, grounding it upon a curving sandy beach. The last fingers of light were slipping from the eastern sky now, and the wind had whipped itself up into a fury.

Spots of rain hit Flann's face as he climbed out of the boat and followed his uncle's broad-shouldered figure up onto the shore. They were the same height, Daragh and him, yet Flann's body still held the lankiness of youth. He did not share his uncle's coloring though. Unlike most of the other folk upon Éirinn, Flann did not have dark hair. Instead, it was pale blond.

Another legacy of my cold Angle father, he reflected bitterly.

To his mother's people Flann would always be the Angle's bastard. Even those who loved him, like Daragh, must sometimes look upon his pale hair with distaste. It was a reminder of the man who had broken Fina's heart.

Daragh's men followed in a group behind Flann. They would all stay overnight in the monastery before, weather permitting, leaving with the dawn. They struggled up the shore, boots sinking into the pale sand. Flann kept his gaze up, searching for any sign of life.

A moment later he spied a group of figures, torches aloft, cresting the hill before them. Monks garbed in long dark robes, their hair shaved into tonsures, approached.

Flann's pulse quickened, and for the first time since leaving Éirinn, he doubted his decision.

Daragh had spoken true; he had decided in haste, in an attempt to run from pain.

Flann's panic was fleeting though, as the hurt that had driven him across the water slammed into him once more.

Suddenly it hurt to breathe.

No—this is the right decision. He needed to re-forge himself in this place, a harsh environment that would demand much of him. He would dedicate himself to a higher purpose. He would make himself strong; he would never let such pain in again.

Daragh glanced over his shoulder, eyes narrowed against the wind. His gaze met Flann's and held for a heartbeat. "Are you ready?"

Flann dragged in a deep breath, forcing down the nerves. "Aye."

"Very well ... let us go to greet them."

Daragh turned away and resumed his climb. Head bowed against the wind, Flann followed his uncle up the rise to meet the monks.

Ten years later ...

Chapter One

The Time Has Come

Summer, 685 AD

The Isle of Iona, Pictland (Scotland)

THE CLANG OF an iron bell echoed across the monastery. The noise jarred in the peace of the warm morning, carrying far over the surrounding sea.

Flann lowered his hammer and straightened up from where he had been bashing nails into a door. He glanced over his shoulder, watching the monks in the fields below down their hoes, rakes, and spades and make their way toward the church. The bell was calling them to None. It was a short service; soon they would all gather in the feasting hall for the noon meal.

Flann would join them too.

Glancing back at the door, he cast an eye over his work. A sense of satisfaction filtered over him—he had done a good job. The door had blown off its hinges in a storm a few days earlier. This store house held the monastery's most precious food: cheese and salted meats which they kept for special occasions. It was important to keep it properly sealed.

Flann wiped a forearm across his brow. He then slowly, sinuously, stretched his long body, enjoying the feel of warmth on his skin. He raked his fingers through his short blond hair, allowing a sea breeze to feather against his scalp.

It was a fine morning to be outside, and Flann was almost tempted not to retreat indoors after the noon meal. Instead, he could take a walk along the coast, past nesting puffins and seals basking on the sun-warmed rocks.

Only, Father Aiden had asked him to copy a manuscript this afternoon. He would feel as if he was shirking. A pity though for, even in summer, this isle was hit by prevailing winds that made days like this rare.

Collecting his tools, Flann walked down the path from where the cluster of store houses sat upon a rise and made his way toward the heart of the monastery. A sense of well-being settled upon Flann as he walked. His life here was a simple one, yet these days he found a quiet, steady contentment in it.

Flann walked past neatly tended beds where a riot of onions, kale, turnip, and carrots grew, and entered a long, windowless structure sitting behind the church. Indoors, a huge iron pot hung over a hearth at one end, where a thick turnip pottage simmered. Before going to None, the monks had laid the table ready, but—as was his usual habit—Flann finished off the preparations.

He retrieved a heavy loaf of coarse bread from the center of the table and cut it into slices: one for each monk. Then he set bowls of cheese curds, freshly made that morning with goat's milk, along the table—one bowl to be shared between four.

This was a typical noon meal here. Upon his arrival at Iona a decade earlier, Flann had struggled to adjust to the frugal diet and the lack of meat. He had spent his first few months constantly hungry. These days though, he was used to the fare.

Flann was collecting the earthen bowls for the pottage when the first of the monks entered the feasting hall, dipping his head as he entered.

"Good day, Brother Euan," Flann greeted him.

The monk grinned back. "And to you. Fine morning to be alive."

Flann dipped a ladle into the pottage and filled the first bowl, handing it to the monk. "Aye ... if only every summer was like this one."

The monks all agreed that this summer was the finest any had experienced upon the windy isle of Iona: day after day of sun.

More brown-robed monks entered the feasting hall then, Prior Aiden amongst them. He was an older man with heavy features and penetrating dark eyes. Once he had served the rest of the monks, Flann took a bowl of pottage for himself and sat down at the end of the long table. He tore a chunk off his slice of bread and dipped it into the thick vegetable stew.

"I'll start on that manuscript this afternoon, Father," he said, after he had swallowed his first mouthful. As usual the pottage was bland, overcooked, and in desperate need of salt. "Will you show me what you need copying?"

Prior Aiden nodded. "Thank you, Flann. Collect your writing tools and meet me in the scriptorium after we are finished here."

The scriptorium—a room built onto the far end of the church where monks wrote and copied documents—was one of Flann's favorite corners of the monastery. It had a large shuttered window looking out onto the herb garden. Flann was glad he would work there, for the hut where he lived on the edge of the monastery was windowless, forcing him to write by candlelight.

Flann reached out and helped himself to some cheese curd. He ladled it into his pottage, hoping it would improve the flavor. Taking another mouthful, he glanced up to see the prior watching him, a speculative look in his eyes.

Flann hesitated. "Father?"

Father Aiden smiled. "Ten summers you've been with us, Flann ... did you realize that?"

"Aye ... just this morning I was thinking how fast the years have passed."

The prior's smile faded a little. "You were lost when you arrived here ... I worried for you."

"You did?" The admission surprised Flann. He had not noticed at the time—he had not paid attention to much save his own misery. "Your worries were unfounded, Father," he replied with a smile. "I'm happy now."

Father Aiden's heavy brow furrowed slightly. "You understand why I didn't let you take your vows, don't you?"

Flann tensed. He did, and truthfully he had eventually grown used to being an outsider of a sort here. Yet he wished the prior had not asked him this when the others were sitting with them. He could feel the curiosity of the monks' gazes as they swiveled to him.

He knew many of them wondered why this scholar continued to live with them.

"It was for the best," he replied after a pause. "You told me a man shouldn't take refuge in God, that it must be a calling ... and you were right."

The prior continued to watch him. "You've changed much over the years, matured into a man of temperance and reason."

Flann's smile turned embarrassed. "Thank you, Father."

"The time has come for you to make a decision," the prior continued, reaching for a cup of watered-down wine. "If you wish to take your vows now, I shall allow it."

Surprised, Flann straightened up, his smile fading. The feasting hall went quiet around them, and he knew without glancing their way, that the monks were staring at him.

"Really, Father?"

"Aye ... I think you're ready."

Flann did not know what to say. If the prior had announced this during his first years here, he would have been overjoyed at the news. Yet, he was in his twenty-eighth summer now and had grown accustomed to the special role he held in the monastery.

Truthfully, he was not sure he wanted to become a monk.

He did not voice this opinion though, for the prior was watching him with a hopeful expression, while next to him, Brother Euan was nodding with obvious approval. "It's time, Flann," the monk added. "You've been with us long enough."

Flann smiled once more—forcing the expression this time—and hoped his lack of enthusiasm did not show on his face. "Thank you," he murmured. "You all honor me."

The noon meal finished quickly. The monks did not linger over meals, not even this one, which was the most substantial of the day. There were still many chores to get through before Vespers in the late afternoon.

Flann rose to his feet and helped clear away the bowls. It was his turn to help wash up, so he stood with Euan and two others scrubbing the wooden bowls, spoons, and platters, before he emerged from the dimly lit hall into the bright noon sun.

Squinting as his eyes adjusted to the light, Flann strode down the path toward the edge of the monastery. His hut, from where he would retrieve his writing tools, perched upon a rocky knoll, looking out to sea. It sat apart from the long dormitories where the monks dwelt.

If I become a monk, all this will change.

Flann enjoyed his privacy. He liked that although he spent his days working hard, he held a freedom the monks did not.

Do I really want to take my vows?

Ten years ago he had. He had wanted to lose himself in a monk's life. But the years had healed his pain; his uncle had been right about that. Sometimes of late, he had even caught himself feeling restless. Iona had started to feel restrictive. His thoughts often drifted to his kin in Éirinn. How was Daragh faring? His cousins would likely be wedded now and beginning families of their own. Sometimes he missed them.

Deep in thought, Flann made his way along the path, toward the low-slung wattle and daub hut. His gaze traveled the view he had seen every day over the past decade: a windswept, treeless landscape surrounded by a wide blue sea.

It was then he saw the boat.

The craft was crossing from the mainland to the south-east, a low, dark shape in the sparkling water.

Flann halted and watched it approach—a long-boat, propelled by oarsmen.

He frowned. As far as he was aware, the brothers here awaited no visitors.

Turning on his heel, he strode back down the path, returning to the monastery. The monks had gone back to their gardening. They bent over their tasks like brown storks, their bald pates gleaming. Behind them rose the thatched roof of the church, and beyond that the scattering of low buildings of the rest of the complex.

"Father!" Flann called out as he approached.

The prior looked up, a bunch of carrots in his dirt-encrusted hands. "Aye?"

"We've got visitors."

The change in the prior was instantaneous, as was that in the monks surrounding him. Iona was a lonely isle. They'd had problems with raiders in past years. The prior's face turned grim. He dropped the carrots into the wicker basket at his feet and dusted off his hands. "Let's see what they want."

Flann followed the group of monks down to the shore. The Brothers of Iona lived peacefully and went unarmed. However, Flann scooped up a hoe from the garden before he joined them. If these strangers had come with ill intent, someone needed to help defend the monastery.

Last autumn a boatload of raiders had alighted upon these shores. Flann had rallied the monks and forced some of them to fight, for the raiders had been intent on pillaging their store houses. The monks had been shocked by how Flann had handled himself: he had broken one raider's jaw and crushed the nose of another.

The approaching long-boat contained half a dozen men. Their leather vests, fur mantles, and gleaming armrings marked them as Angles from the south. His father's people. Reaching the shallows, four of the men jumped overboard and dragged the boat to shore.

Flann, who was taller than most of the monks, peered over the heads of his companions, his gaze settling on the dark-haired, robed figure sitting amidships. A priest. Behind him there appeared to be a large object shrouded in leather.

"There's a man of God with them at least," one of the brothers muttered. "They haven't come to rob us."

Flann did not answer—there was something about the intense way the priest was surveying them that put him on edge. The man's sharp blue eyes tracked over the group, moving from brother to brother.

He's looking for someone.

The newcomers pulled the boat out of the water onto the beach. Three of the warriors heaved the object they had brought up onto their shoulders and waded through the sand toward the waiting monks.

The priest led them, his face somber.

The prior stepped forward to meet them. "Good morning. I am Aiden, prior of this monastery. We welcome you to our isle."

The priest dipped his head. "And morning to you, Father. I am Oswald of Bebbanburg."

Now that the group stood close to them, the sweet odor of rotting flesh drifted over the shore. One of the younger brothers gagged, and Prior Aidan frowned. "What have you brought here?"

The priest Oswald's face tightened. "We bring the body of our noble king: Ecgfrith, ruler of Northumbria. We have carried him here for burial, and to see his half-brother, Aldfrith."

Aldfrith.

Flann tensed, the name slamming into him like a punch to the gut. He had not heard it in years. His mother had been the last person to call him by it; and even then it had been in anger as she ranted at him of his father's cruelty. That name was part of an identity he had always denied, one he wanted no part of.

A silence settled over the beach, and Oswald cleared his throat. "He goes by the name of Flann Fina. I must speak with him."

None of the brothers uttered a word; they all knew of Flann's identity but would let him be the one to reveal it.

Flann inhaled sharply. He had always worried that one day his heritage would catch up with him. He stepped forward, and the monks moved aside to let him pass. When he stood before the priest, he met his eye. "I'm Flann Fina."

Oswald's gaze widened, and Flann resisted a rueful smile. He imagined the priest had expected a different-looking man. His mother, Fina, had been a dark Irish beauty, but Flann had taken after his father. He looked like an Angle: tall and blond. The only physical trait he had taken from his mother was her midnight blue eyes.

"You're Aldfrith of Northumbria?" Oswald's gaze swept over him, taking in his homespun tunic, goatskin leggings, and bare feet. Flann knew he would be wondering why this half-brother to the king dressed like a peasant.

"Aye." Flann replied, his tone cool. "What do you want from me?"

Oswald took a step forward. "Your brother fought the Picts at Nechtansmere and fell. Northumbria no longer rules Pictland—King Bridei does. As Ecgfrith's brother, you are next in line to the throne." Oswald paused here. "I've come to bring you home."

A chill settled over Flann, dimming the warmth of the summer's day.

This peaceful isle was his home. Even if he was uncertain about taking his vows, he wished to be left here in solitude, alone with his chores, his studies, his writing, and his reflection. Here, he lived far from the noise, cruelty, and pettiness of the world.

"I *am* home," he replied after a few long moments, although deep in his gut he knew those words would not be enough. He should have known after his conversation with the prior during the noon meal that today would be a turning point in his life. Whatever happened from this moment on, things could not stay the same.

Oswald's answering smile was not without sympathy. "No ... my lord. Bebbanburg is where you belong."

Chapter Two

A Royal Handfasting

Bebbanburg, Kingdom of Northumbria
Britannia (England)

Three months later …

"I HEAR THE bride is a great beauty."

Osana inclined her head toward her husband and raised a delicate eyebrow. "Where did you hear that?"

Raedwulf, Ealdorman of Hagustaldes, favored his wife with an indulgent look. "Men talk in the mead hall, my sweeting. Some hail from Wessex and have seen Princess Cuthburh in the flesh. They say she's slender as a willow reed, with hair the color of sea foam and eyes the blue of a summer's morn."

Osana ground her jaw and feigned disinterest. "Men in their cups are known to exaggerate," she pointed out. "She may be plain and mousy for all you know."

Raedwulf chuckled. "We shall soon see for ourselves, wife." He gave Osana another patronizing look. "No need to be jealous. You're still a handsome woman … even if you're past your prime."

Osana dug her heels into the furry sides of her palfrey, sending it on ahead. Raedwulf's laughter rang out behind her, and she inhaled deeply to quell the ire rising within her.

They rode the last stretch toward Bebbanburg, the great northern stronghold bristling against the eastern horizon and a flat, blue-grey expanse of sea. The sight of its bulk—wooden palisades and four huge guard towers at each corner—filled Osana with relief. Finally, three days on the road with her husband had come to an end.

The road leading east cut through a patchwork of tilled fields, where cottars toiled under the late afternoon sun. It had been a hot summer, the warmest Osana could remember, and the sun had tanned the peasants' skin golden. A crisp, salt-laced breeze blew in from the sea, a welcome respite from the day's heat.

"Come now, no need to take offense, wife."

Raedwulf had ridden up alongside her once more. The grin on his handsome face only served to make her anger continue to simmer, reminding Osana why she rarely conversed with her husband these days. Perhaps she was over-sensitive, or maybe she imagined it, but it seemed as every word he spoke to her of late was a barely concealed barb at her failure as a wife.

Twenty-eight winters old ... and barren.

They had been wed twelve years now, but she had never given him a child.

Osana wanted to blame Raedwulf, but she knew he had sired at least three bastard children in Hagustaldes, all to local wenches. No—the fault lay with her.

What good was a wife if she could not bear a man sons?

"I'm not angry," Osana lied, before she met his eye, "or jealous. It's just that you make me feel old and useless at times."

The humor drained from Raedwulf's face. At thirty-five winters he was still a virile, comely man: big and broad-shouldered with a mane of golden hair and a short beard. She had been captivated when she had first seen him. He had been the ealdorman's eldest son, a brash, cocky warrior who had won her heart without even trying.

Perhaps she had been too easy to impress. Or maybe it was the fact that she had loved the aura of danger and unpredictability in him.

"I was only teasing," he said after a moment. "You are so prickly these days."

Osana inhaled deeply. He husband had all the subtlety and grace of a charging boar.

They had reached the foot of the causeway now, and the fort rose overhead blocking out the sky.

"It's my fault," Raedwulf continued, the good humor returning to his voice. "I've been away too often of late securing our borders. I've clearly been neglecting my wife." He flashed her a rakish grin. "Tonight, after the handfasting, I shall give you the humping you so obviously need."

Osana shot him a look of mute disbelief. How typical of him to think that a night in the furs would cure the tension between them. Her husband was a lusty man and a demanding lover. In the early years of their marriage, when she had still found him exciting, she had enjoyed their lovemaking. Yet these days when she lay under him, she felt numb. Afterward she was merely relieved it was over.

Unable to summon a response, she turned away from Raedwulf and urged her palfrey forward. They clattered up the final distance to the causeway, under the low gate, and into Bebbanburg.

"Are all the ealdormen here?"

"Aye, sire."

Aldfrith, King of Northumbria, turned to his personal guard, Cerdic. Tall and broad, with brown hair cropped close to his scalp, the warrior met his eye.

"I've heard their rumblings of discontent," Aldfrith continued. "Have a word with them before the ceremony ... reassure each man that I will be holding a council tomorrow morning. If they have any concerns about the security of Northumbria, they are to raise them then."

Cerdic nodded. The warrior said little but observed much, a useful trait in an advisor. Aldfrith had much to thank the man for, as over the past months Cerdic had provided invaluable guidance, especially when it came to dealing with the ealdormen. "Wise tactic, sire ... they are bound to cause trouble after the ceremony otherwise."

Aldfrith's mouth thinned. "Aye ... that was my concern too."

He had only been king a short while, but already his ealdormen—the men who oversaw tracts of his kingdom in his stead—had become demanding.

"Your betrothed awaits, sire." Bishop Wilfrid's strident voice interrupted Aldfrith and his captain. "Lord Aldfrith ... they are ready for you now."

The king tensed. *Aldfrith*. He still had trouble getting used to that name. It had wiped away his old life, his old identity. It did not belong to him. Aldfrith cast his gaze over his shoulder at where a tall angular man with a haughty face and intense dark eyes stood. Irritation flickered within him. Ever since his arrival at Bebbanburg, the bishop had become a persistent, and unwelcome, second shadow.

With a nod to the king, and to the bishop, Cerdic exited the alcove, leaving Aldfrith and Wilfrid alone.

Aldfrith grimaced. "I don't know why I couldn't meet her first, Father Wilfrid."

"There was no time," the bishop replied. "Now that the princess has arrived from Wessex, you must be wed."

"Aye." Aldfrith adjusted the wolfskin cloak about his shoulders that had once belonged to his father, and glanced down at the amber brooch fastening it. "But I'd have preferred to get to know her first."

Wilfrid favored him with a patronizing smile. "Cuthburh is a charming and beautiful young woman ... but better still she comes from nobility and is exceedingly pious. She will make an excellent wife for you, milord. She will be a good influence."

Aldfrith did not miss the sting in those last words. He knew the bishop disapproved of the new king's upbringing in the north, his time spent with the monks on Iona. Only a day earlier, he had given the priest Oswald a tongue-lashing for the wording of the prayer he had spoken before supper. They worshipped the same God as he did, but Wilfrid looked down his nose at the manner in which those of the north followed Christianity.

"Very well." Aldfrith brushed past the bishop and made for the heavy hanging that sheltered him from the rest of the hall. Beyond he could hear the rise and fall of excited voices—folk from all over Northumbria had traveled here for his handfasting. He was about to be at the center of a public spectacle. "Let's get this over with."

"There he is!" The woman beside Osana hissed in her ear. "The new king ... isn't he handsome?"

Osana gave the woman, whose breath smelled of onion, a polite smile and glanced over at where the king had just stopped before the heah-setl—the high seat.

Her gaze settled upon him. She had to admit the woman was right. She had not expected Aldfrith of Northumbria to be handsome—for both his half-brother, Ecgfrith, and his father, Oswiu, had been too sharp-featured and sly-faced to be named so.

Yet the new king was taller than both of his dead kin, and better looking than either of them, with short, ash-blond hair and sensitively drawn features. Folk were calling him 'the philosopher king', for before coming here, he had lived a hermit's life upon some distant isle.

Osana's gaze lingered upon the new king. She had expected a pale, weedy man of middling years, yet the man before her was no older than her and held himself with unconscious masculine grace as he stood awaiting his bride.

Aware she was staring, but not caring as everyone here was observing the king keenly, she took in his rich dress: the deep-blue of his tunic that matched his eyes, and the fine gold edging. He wore a magnificent wolfskin cloak about his broad shoulders, and doeskin breeches clad long, athletic legs. Osana could not envisage this man bent over a table, scribbling upon vellum.

"He doesn't look like a scholar." The onion-breathed woman was back, echoing Osana's own thoughts. "He's so tall and strong. I wonder if the rumors are true though ... that he's never had a woman."

That got Osana's attention. She swiveled around, eyes wide. "Really?"

Delighted the ealdorman of Hagustaldes's wife was finally giving her some attention, the woman—presumably the wife of one of the king's thegns—grinned. "Aye—I'd like to be the one to show him the way of the furs ... a fine-looking man like that. Wouldn't you?"

Feeling her face warm, Osana turned back to see a slender figure sheathed in rose and gold glide across the floor toward the king.

Cuthburh of Wessex had arrived.

Raedwulf, damn him, had been right—she really was a beauty. Pale skinned and delicate-featured, Princess Cuthburh looked radiant with her white-blonde hair spilling over her slender shoulders.

Osana's thoughts shifted back then to the question posed by the woman beside her. Truthfully, her answer was no—she had no wish to show Aldfrith how to bed a woman. As attractive as the new king was, she could not think of anything she would like less. She had a husband with the sexual drive of a ram, and did not welcome the thought of any man touching her these days. Sometimes she wished Raedwulf would never lay a hand on her again.

Her husband met her eye now and grinned. "I told you so," he mouthed before winking at her.

Osana cast him an exasperated look and shifted her attention back to where the princess had just stopped at Aldfrith's side. Their gazes met, and the king smiled.

Osana's chest constricted then, as she remembered her own handfasting.

How nervous she had been and how handsome Raedwulf. The feasting and revelry had lasted late into the night, before Raedwulf had carried her off to the furs and claimed her as his. It had hurt, as her mother had warned her it would, but she had found that first night wondrous, exciting. How she wished she still felt that way.

Osana's vision blurred as she continued to watch the couple.

They stood surrounded by the grandeur of the Great Hall of Bebbanburg: walls of red stone, a high ceiling, and flickering oil-filled cressets. Shields, axes, and swords hung from the pitted walls, all trophies from past victories and campaigns.

A tall, spare man with hawkish features and a receding hairline, dressed in fine purple robes, an iron cross around his neck, stood before Aldfrith and Cuthburh.

This must be Bishop Wilfrid, newly returned from exile, Osana reflected. She had heard tales about this man. The stories went that King Ecgfrith had banished him from Northumbria after the bishop had helped Ecgfrith's first wife run away to a convent. However, with Ecgfrith's death a few months earlier, Wilfrid had returned to the north, where he had taken up residence at Inhrypum, a town to the south of Bebbanburg.

The bishop's voice droned on while he began the ceremony, outlining the responsibilities of man and wife. He wrapped a ribbon around the couple's joined hands as he spoke.

Osana blinked rapidly. She was far too sentimental at these gatherings; she always got weepy at handfastings. Ridiculous really, when her own marriage had not turned out as she had hoped.

Yet her reaction surprised her, for it showed that there was still a tiny part of her remaining that believed in love. She believed there could be a happy union between man and wife, only that belief was not for her, but for others.

Chapter Three

The Feast

"A QUAIL EGG?"

Aldfrith held up a platter and smiled at his bride. The bishop had not lied, she was indeed comely. Although now he was seated next to her, the girl seemed incredibly young.

Cuthburh daintily took the egg. "Thank you, milord."

"Please call me Aldfrith," he replied. "Or you can call me Flann, if you like … for that was the name my mother gave me."

A startled expression flitted across those blue eyes, and her smile tightened. "As you wish, milord."

Aldfrith's smile slipped. She was hiding it well, but he sensed the unhappiness that bubbled just beneath the surface. Just that one brief exchange told him that she did not welcome this match.

Picking up his golden cup studded with garnets, Aldfrith took a sip of sloe wine. Around him voices thundered off the stone walls. The king and his chief retainers feasted at a long table upon the high seat, while the other folk within the hall sat at tables that formed squares around the tower's four massive hearths.

He and Cuthburh sat at the head of the king's table, upon carven chairs. Bishop Wilfrid sat to the queen's right, his stern gaze surveying all. Oswald, the priest who had accompanied Aldfrith from Iona, had taken his place next to the bishop. The young man did not look entirely happy with the seating arrangement; the priest seemed to visibly wilt every time the bishop swung his gaze in his direction.

Aldfrith's mouth curved in a half-smile. He had gotten to know Oswald quite well on the journey home, and had learned a little about his half-brother Ecgfrith during that journey too. It seemed that Ecgfrith had sired a bastard daughter, a woman who had once been his seer but now lived with the Picts.

Oswald had been nervous of revealing too much about Ecgfrith's reign at first. Yet the journey from Iona to Bebbanburg had taken a few days, and by the time they spied the fort on the horizon, Aldfrith felt he knew enough about the politics of this place to be able to hold his own here.

Sometimes though—like this evening—he wondered just how well he was actually managing. Kingship was already revealing itself to be a heavy responsibility.

Aldfrith's gaze shifted then to Cerdic, sitting to his left. This evening, as usual, his captain wore an inscrutable expression. Feeling the king's gaze upon him, Cerdic glanced up from his trencher of venison stew. "Sire?"

Aldfrith met his eye. "Were you at the Battle of Nechtansmere, Cerdic?"

Cerdic shook his head. "Lord Ecgfrith bid me to remain here, to watch over Bebbanburg's garrison."

Silence fell while Aldfrith digested this information. When he spoke once more, his voice was low, thoughtful. "Do you think Ecgfrith was a good king?"

Cerdic's brows knotted together. "He was *my* king, sire. I trusted him."

Aldfrith took another sip of wine. "Aye ... but did you approve of the way he ruled?"

Cerdic watched him, his expression wary.

Aldfrith inclined his head. "I'm not trying to trick you," he assured the warrior. "I'm just trying to get a sense of the kind of leader my brother was."

Cerdic snorted, although his gaze was still watchful. "Ecgfrith ruled wisely for the most part, sire. He was a warrior and a natural leader, although he had a prickly temper ... quick to anger. On some things he could be stubborn, blinded."

Aldfrith nodded, taking this in. He had never met his half-brother, and did not even remember his own father, for Oswiu had left when Aldfrith was an infant. Yet he was curious about the man he had replaced. Although Oswald had told him a bit about his predecessor, he still felt as if there were many gaps in his knowledge.

"I wonder what folk will make of me," he murmured, speaking almost more to himself than to anyone else. "I'm a scholar ... not a warrior king."

Cerdic smiled at that—an unexpected expression that softened his face and made him appear younger. Aldfrith realized then that the warrior was around his own age; his severity had made him appear older.

"Folk of this kingdom have seen much blood over the years, milord," he said after a pause. "They'll thank you for a bit of peace."

Aldfrith watched him before nodding. Their conversation reminded him of why he liked Cerdic. The man was gruff, but there was an honesty to his words.

The king's gaze shifted from his captain and swept over the table. He took in the faces of the others seated upon the heah-setl. His ealdormen sat nearby. These men governed Northumbria's biggest settlements: Hagustaldes, Gefrin, Catraeth, Eoforwic, and Inhrypum.

The ealdorman of Hagustaldes sat nearest Aldfrith. He was a big, blond man named Raedwulf, a warrior with a wide smile and a booming laugh. Raedwulf's wife sat next to him. Unlike her garrulous husband, Osana of Hagustaldes appeared a softly-spoken woman.

Aldfrith's gaze settled upon her for a moment.

The ealdorman's wife was quite lovely. Not in the girlish way his bride was, but with an earthier beauty. She had walnut-colored hair that she wore coiled into braids around her head—as only unwed women wore their hair unbound. He silently admired her creamy skin, expressive hazel eyes, neat features, and delicately drawn mouth. She wore a becoming green sleeveless tunic, the bronze ring upon her right arm her only adornment.

Realizing he was staring, Aldfrith tore his gaze from the ealdorman's wife and looked down at his cup. *What's wrong with me? Staring at another man's wife when I have just taken one of my own.*

This wedding had unsettled him. He was used to solitude and peace, to spending his days in male company. Having women around him again after so long was distracting, and Aldfrith did not like the feeling. He missed the serenity and isolation of Iona—he had chosen that life for a reason.

Raedwulf of Hugustaldes had not appeared to notice the direction of Aldfrith's gaze. He was too busy exchanging boasts with Edwin, the ealdorman of Gefrin, farther down the table. Edwin was Aldfrith's cousin; a blond, florid-faced warrior who was around five years the king's elder. Aldfrith had met him for the first time two days earlier and was not sure he liked him. His cousin was brash with a vaguely patronizing manner.

"I killed ten men in my first battle—and I was just a lad of fourteen winters," Raedwulf boomed. "Could you better that?"

"Ten?" Edwin scoffed. "That's the number you've slain in your entire life. I'm sure I can better that!"

Harsh male laughter echoed over the table, although Aldfrith did not join in. He felt at sea here, surrounded by warriors—men who could wield a sword before their voice broke, before the first whiskers grew on their chin. They were another breed, a class of man he did not understand or like much if he was honest.

His father had been one such man. He remembered his mother telling him so, her blue eyes filled with pain and grief. *Your father is a ruler of men, a warrior. He was not meant to remain in exile with us.*

"Cousin!" Edwin's booming voice roused Aldfrith from his thoughts. "So you've finally joined the rest of us. A wedded man at last. Better late than never, I say!"

The ealdorman of Gefrin's comment brought a rumble of laughter from the other ealdormen, although Raedwulf of Hugustaldes merely smirked. Next to Aldfrith, Cerdic frowned.

"Aye," Aldfrith replied, raising his cup to Edwin, who had just downed a horn of mead. The man's cheeks were ruddy with drink, and yet there was a belligerent look in his eyes that made Aldfrith wary. "It was time."

Secretly he would rather have remained unwed, yet he did not share his thoughts with these men. Some opinions would only be mocked.

"Make sure you get her with child soon, sire," Wulfred, the ealdorman of Catraeth, spoke up. He was a short, barrel-chested man with thick dark hair and a wild beard to match. "Your predecessor failed to produce an heir. You don't want Oswiu's line to die out."

"It won't," Edwin cut in, gaze narrowed. "I'm Oswiu's nephew, and I have three sons."

Wulfred favored his fellow ealdorman with a sly look. "Aye, but Aldfrith is Oswiu's *son*."

His bastard son.

The words hung unspoken in the air. Aldfrith knew none would have the nerve to speak those words, but they would all be thinking it.

"Now you are wed, you will be able to focus on other matters, sire," Raedwulf of Hagustaldes interjected, his jovial tone shattering the tension that had settled upon the table. "Ecgfrith left us quite a mess."

"Aye, he did," Edwin growled, holding out his empty horn of mead to a woman—one of the thegn's wives—to fill. "Thanks to him, Northumbria has no fyrd ... most of our best fighting men died in the north."

Aldfrith heaved in a deep breath and cast a questioning look in Cerdic's direction. Had his captain not spoken with the ealdormen as he had asked? Cerdic did not look his way. Instead, he was glaring at Edwin, his jaw clenched.

The king turned his attention back to his cousin and favored him with a cool smile. He was aware of the state of the kingdom. Oswald, Cerdic, and the bishop had all given him their opinions on what needed to be done. He planned to sit down with his ealdormen soon and discuss their territory and army—just not today. "We will talk of this tomorrow," he replied, meeting his cousin's gaze and holding it. "When our bellies aren't full of food and our minds blurred with drink."

The comment was a direct jibe at Edwin, who had already consumed enough mead to have him swaying in his seat.

Many around the table chuckled or smirked at this, knowing whom the king was referring to. Yet the ealdorman of Gefrin merely scowled. Aldfrith tensed, knowing that his cousin was not finished trying to assert his dominance.

I've got a fight on my hands with him.

Aldfrith held up his cup to be filled, as a woman appeared with a jug at his elbow. He did not usually drink much, but a little more wine would not hurt. Tonight he was a king surrounded by strangers and men like Edwin who probably wished he had stayed on Iona.

Not only that, but tonight he was a husband and would be expected to bed his bride—a young woman who could hardly bring herself to meet his eye.

Aldfrith turned his attention back to Cuthburh. Although timid, she was lovely. Things would be easier between them later if he managed to thaw the wall of ice between them. "Do you have any brothers or sisters, milady?" he asked.

She glanced up, meeting his gaze for an instant before hurriedly looking away.

"Two younger sisters, sire," she replied. Her voice was breathy and sweet, yet he found himself irritated by it. The tone sounded affected, as if she had been tutored in the art of meekness.

"And are they still in Wessex?"

"No ... they are both brides of Christ, sire." Her gaze darted up again, and this time he saw heat light in those pale blue eyes.

Now he understood.

"You wished for that life too," he murmured, holding her gaze. "Didn't you?"

Her jaw tensed, and she stared at him for a long moment. Then she nodded.

"But your brother had other plans for you," he added. "I understand how you feel, Cuthburh. I too had little choice in the path laid before me."

She looked away then, staring down at the platter of food they shared, which she had barely touched. Her slender shoulders had gone taut, as if one word more would have her bolting from the table. As such, Aldfrith held his tongue.

Instead, he leaned back in his chair and drank from his cup. Voices boomed around him, almost drowning out the strains of the lute from the musicians playing on a platform next to the high seat. Drunken laughter lifted high into the rafters. The faces of his ealdormen were slack with drink, and the revelers feasted like ravenous dogs.

Suddenly, Aldfrith had no appetite for the rich food or for the merriment. He felt an odd hollowness inside, a feeling he had not experienced in a long while—not since the bleak days of his childhood. He was not sure where he belonged, or even if Iona was really the home he had longed for, but it certainly was not here.

He felt someone's gaze upon him then. It was a pleasant sensation, like a soft feather trailing over his skin. It was a welcome distraction from his thoughts, and Aldfrith looked up.

With a jolt, he saw that Osana of Hagustaldes was silently watching him.

Chapter Four

A Wife's Duty

ALDFRITH FOLLOWED CUTHBURH into the alcove and drew the heavy tapestry closed behind him. Over the past two moons this warm, comfortable space had become his refuge, the place he had found peace in the turmoil of his new life.

Now he would have to share it with another.

Hooting and cat calls followed them. His ealdormen, now well into their cups, had wanted to carry the newlyweds into the alcove and dump them onto the waiting bed of furs. Aldfrith had forbidden them.

His bride was frightened enough—such roughness would traumatize her.

The alcove had been prepared for them. Sprays of meadow flowers lay scattered across the plush furs covering the floor. Tallow candles burned either side of the pile of furs dominating one end of the space, illuminating the alcove in pale gold.

Aldfrith took two strides inside and stopped, watching his bride make her way over to the furs. She had a regal walk, with a straight spine and shoulders back; only the tension that rippled off her in waves gave her fear away.

She stopped, her back to him, and looked at the far wall, as if hoping a door would appear there through which she could flee.

"I can't remove my gown without your help, milord." Her voice trembled.

Aldfrith unclipped the brooch fastening the wolfskin cloak to his shoulders and shrugged the mantle off. Then he crossed to where Cuthburh stood silently waiting and began to unlace the back of her gown. It was a beautiful, intricately sewn garment that would have taken a number of women many moons to make.

All for one special day.

He finished unlacing her gown and stepped back. He supposed he should slip it off her shoulders, take advantage of the moment to force intimacy, yet he did not. She was lovely though, and the smoothness of her skin made his breath catch.

After a moment she removed the gown, stepping out of it. Underneath, Cuthburh wore a thin gauzy tunic that revealed the slender length of her body, the curve of her buttocks, and the coltish length of her legs.

Aldfrith felt the stirrings of desire. It had been years since he had been this physically close to a girl, and it was hard not to be aroused by the sight of a beautiful half-naked woman standing before him.

Perhaps this union would not be such a burden after all.

"Turn around, Cuthburh," he commanded softly.

Slowly, reluctantly, she complied.

From the front she was even lovelier. High peaked breasts showed through the thin fabric, and he could see the shadow of the blonde triangle of her sex.

"You are beautiful," he breathed, meaning it.

He had no feelings for his bride, he barely knew her, and yet he did in that moment want her.

Her face went rigid, and she looked down, appearing fascinated with the furs beneath her feet.

It's just nervousness, he told himself. *She isn't as horrified as she looks.*

Aldfrith unlaced the heavy tunic he wore and shrugged it off. Then he began to unfasten his breeches. However, when he saw his bride was now trembling like a reed in the wind, he stopped.

"Cuthburh ..."

Her head bowed, a curtain of white-blonde hair obscuring her face, she did not answer him.

"There's no need to be afraid," he said after a long moment. "I will be gentle with you."

She remained silent; if anything, her trembling increased.

Aldfrith inhaled deeply. He could not bed his wife while she was in this state. She needed to be calmed, soothed. He would show her that love play could be gentle, unthreatening.

He refastened his breeches before bending down to remove his boots. Then he stepped close to her, placing a hand upon her shoulder.

"Let us lie down upon the furs, Cuthburh."

She nodded and wordlessly turned, padding across to where the pile of furs awaited. There she lay down, rolling over from him to face the wall.

Aldfrith stretched out next to her. They were close, barely a hand span apart. After a long moment, Aldfrith reached out and stroked her shoulder. Her skin was as smooth as it looked. His groin hardened in response, and he suddenly became aware of the heat and nearness of her body.

"Do you know what happens?" he asked for a moment, continuing to caress her. "Between a man and his wife ... have the other women told you?"

"Aye." Her voice was choked. "It sounds vile."

Taken aback, Aldfrith stilled his caresses. "It doesn't have to be," he replied finally. "It can give pleasure. We must lie together as man and wife ... if we are to have children."

"I don't want them." Cuthburh answered, speaking the words in short panicked gasps. "I was to be a nun ... I don't want to be a wife or a mother."

And I don't want to be a king ... but sometimes we don't get a choice in matters.

"Cuthburh." He reached out once more and placed a hand on her upper arm. "We were given a duty, you and I, to unite Northumbria and Wessex in marriage. We must fulfill it."

She turned to him then, so swiftly that they nearly collided. Her face shocked Aldfrith. Gone was the meek, blushing bride. An enraged young woman with cold eyes glared at him instead.

"Don't touch me," she snarled. "The devil take duty. I will not lie with you."

Osana was sitting upon a stool, brushing her hair, when Raedwulf stumbled into their alcove.

Disappointment flooded through her at the sight of his florid face and glazed eyes. She had hoped, even whispered a prayer, that he would drink himself into a stupor with the other men and fall asleep at the table. However, God had not answered her.

"Good eve, wife," Raedwulf greeted her with a grin. "I have not forgotten my promise to you, see?" His gaze raked over the long tunic she wore. "Take that off."

Osana put down her hair brush. "I'm tired, Raedwulf ... can't we just go to sleep?"

Raedwulf shrugged off his tunic and started unlacing his breeches. He was a strongly built man. Crisp blond hair covered a muscular chest. The bronze and silver arm rings he wore gleamed in the light of the cressets burning on the alcove wall. Yet Osama was not inflamed by the sight of his half-naked body.

Her stomach clenched. *Just leave me alone.*

He finished unlacing his breeches and freed his manhood. Red and swollen, it thrust up at her, eager and hungry.

"I'm not ready to sleep yet. Take off your tunic, wife," he growled, impatient now, "and get down on your hands and knees."

Osana recognized the warning edge in his voice. If she hesitated any longer he would rip her tunic off her and take her roughly. She tensed, hating him at that moment. However, she knew that if she did as bid it would be over soon enough.

Rising to her feet, Osana pulled the tunic over her head and lowered herself on all fours onto the furs. Then she closed her eyes and prepared to be serviced.

Chapter Five

Solitude

THE DAY AFTER the handfasting dawned grey and chill. After long moons of mild weather, summer seemed to finally have given way to autumn.

Stepping outside the Great Tower of Bebbanburg, Osana heaved in a lungful of fresh, cold air.

The interior of the tower was cloying, smoky, and full of unpleasant odors that morning. The smell of mead and stale food had made Osana feel queasy as she had helped herself to a heel of bread and a cup of broth. She had left Raedwulf asleep in their alcove. After the amount he had drunk the night before, he would sleep till noon.

A salt-laced breeze gusted across the yard before the tower, sending straw and dust flying. Osana pulled the fur mantle she wore about her shoulders close and descended the steps.

There was a market in front of the low gate most mornings, and she wanted to visit it, to wander amongst the stalls and pretend she was another woman—with a different life.

She passed through the high gate and walked out onto the King's Way, a wide swathe that led down to the market square. Unlike those in the slumbering tower, the rest of Bebbanburg—the folk who kept this fort alive—were already up and about.

The clang of iron rang out into the street, carried from a row of forges. As Osana approached the market, she heard the cry of hawkers, mingling with the shriek of gulls circling above.

Osana entered the busy market square, weaving her way through the crowds of local women, shopping baskets under their arms. This was a special market today, for merchants and farmers had come from afar to help celebrate the handfasting. Despite the lack of sun and warmth this morning, Osana saw that most of the folk she passed were smiling. A butcher selling blood sausage and haunches of salted pork was sharing a story with the man he served, his loud, deep laugh booming across the square.

Everyone loved a handfasting, especially a royal one.

Osana wished she shared their merriment. Not that she wished the king and his young wife ill—only that these days she found it hard to dredge up any feelings of happiness at all.

Melancholy had settled over her in a heavy shroud.

She circuited the market square, declining the offers of a handful of vendors, before turning to retrace her steps. It was then she spotted the small wooden church at the corner of the square.

Osana was not ready to return to the fetid, smoky Great Hall, to sit amongst the other wives and pretend to be interested in their prattle.

She wanted peace—solitude.

Osana pushed open the oaken door and entered the church, leaving the noise of the market behind her as she pulled the door shut.

A simple timbered space greeted her. The floor was beautiful though: a sea of grey tiles that whispered underfoot as she made her way to the altar. Above stretched a ribcage of wooden beams. The air carried the odor of tallow from the bank of candles burning behind the altar. A row of tiny windows along each length of the building let in streams of pale grey light.

Osana reached the altar, where a cross carved from dark wood rose up before her. Silently she knelt, clasping her hands in front of her.

The small church in Hagustaldes was also a refuge for her, a place she withdrew to when life in the ealdorman's hall became insufferable. She loved the quiet, to be left alone with her own thoughts.

Lord forgive me, she thought, bowing her head. *I do not wish to be a wife.*

They were dark traitorous thoughts, ones she dared not utter aloud.

My husband is not a bad man. She clenched her fingers hard together. *But sometimes when I look upon his sleeping face I wish him dead … just so that I wouldn't have to suffer his touch ever again.*

"It is a heart-warming sight, to see a woman so pious at this time of day."

The rumble of a male voice forced Osana out of her reverie. She straightened up and twisted round to see a tall, rangy man with hawkish features and a receding hairline approach. He wore dark robes, his sandaled feet scuffing upon the tiled floor. Beside him walked a small, slight, dark-haired man with bright blue eyes wearing priest's robes.

Osana recognized the taller of the two figures as Bishop Wilfrid, but although she had seen the priest at the handfasting feast, she did not know his name.

"Wes þu hal, Bishop Wilfrid," she greeted him.

The bishop halted and inclined his head, his keen gaze sweeping over her. "Have we met?"

"No … I am Osana of Hagustaldes," she replied, rising to her feet.

The priest stepped forward. "My name is Oswald. I'm the priest here." He favored her with a smile then. "I saw you yesterday at the feast. Your husband is the ealdorman of Hagustaldes?"

Osana nodded.

"Did you enjoy the handfasting?" the priest asked.

"I did."

Beside Oswald, the bishop allowed himself a small smile. "A splendid match is it not?"

She dipped her head. "Aye ... it seems so." She did not speak what was in her thoughts, that the king and his bride had seemed ill at ease with each other the evening before—that Aldfrith of Northumbria had the loneliest eyes she had ever seen.

Bishop Wilfrid watched her a moment; he had a piercing look that made her uncomfortable. Then he stepped back, motioning to the altar, his sleeve whispering in the cavernous space.

"We have interrupted your prayer ... please continue."

Osana dipped her head and moved away from the altar. "You didn't interrupt me," she replied. "I was finished anyway." She stepped around the two men and headed toward the door. "Good day."

Osana stepped back into the sunless morning and heaved a deep breath. All she wanted was a moment of solitude, a space where she could lower the mask she wore day-in-day-out. However, it sometimes felt as if the world conspired against her.

Peace was rare these days.

She made her way back up to the high gate and passed into the courtyard beyond. The Great Tower of Bebbanburg, made of the same red rock as the outcrop this fort stood upon, cast a deep shadow over the yard.

Osana did not want to return inside—not yet.

Instead, she cut left and walked into an orchard. Apple and pear trees, their branches laden with ripe fruit, covered this private space. There was a well at the end nearest the tower, but the orchard itself appeared deserted.

Osana wandered amongst the trees. The scent of apple tempted her, and she plucked a fruit from a low-hanging branch, biting into it as she walked.

Finally—alone.

A wave of melancholy hit her then, and she blinked back tears. Even the sweet, crisp flavor of the apple could not keep her sadness at bay. Life at times seemed such hard work. Her coupling with Raedwulf last night had darkened her mood. She wished she had remained in Hagustaldes and let him come to the handfasting alone. Then she would have at least have had a few days' peace from him.

The sound of music intruded then—the lilting, gentle strum of a harp. It was a sad, soft song that matched her mood.

Osana followed the music to the back of the orchard, and there, seated upon a low bench in profile, sat King Aldfrith. He played a small wooden harp, his long fingers dancing across the strings. However, his gaze appeared distant.

Frozen to the spot for an instant, Osana listened to the song. It was haunting in its beauty, and she could have stayed to listen all morning.

Yet she knew she was intruding. Like her, the king had sought out solitude; he would not welcome company.

Slowly releasing the breath she had been holding, Osana took a step back—hoping to edge away unseen—but a twig snapped underneath her foot, and she froze. The king looked up, the music halting as his fingers stilled.

His gaze swiveled to her.

Chapter Six

A Meeting in the Orchard

"I'M SORRY, MILORD." Osana took another hasty step backwards. "I was taking a walk. I didn't mean to intrude."

His dark blue gaze remained upon her for a long moment, before his mouth quirked. "You aren't intruding."

Osana gave a hurried curtsey and backed off farther. "I bid you good morning, sire."

She turned to flee, still clutching the half-eaten apple. His voice, faintly tinged with amusement, stilled her. "It's Osana, isn't it?"

She turned back, her face warming under his scrutiny. "Aye … Raedwulf of Hagustaldes is my husband."

He nodded. "I noticed you at the feast last night."

He said those words without the slightest flirtation, yet Osana's cheeks grew hotter still at that. What was wrong with her? She never blushed. He had caught her watching him at the feast. She had been observing him, thinking his attention was elsewhere, when his gaze had snapped up, ensnaring hers. She felt mortified now, as she had at the time.

One did not stare at the king—he would think her common and far too bold.

But when she forced herself to meet his eye, she saw that the king did not appear offended or disdainful.

Instead, he was watching her with cool interest. A moment later his gaze dropped to the apple she still clutched. "I didn't think they were ripe enough yet. Was it a good apple?"

Now he'll think me a thief.

Osana swallowed, mortified. "Yes sire … I'm sorry … I shouldn't have taken one."

He shrugged, giving her a slow smile that made Osana draw a sharp breath. He was disconcertingly handsome when he smiled, although his face was so solemn when he did not.

"I don't mind," he assured her. "I'm new here too. I don't feel like I 'own' any of this. I certainly don't care if you help yourself to an apple."

Osana watched him, suddenly feeling foolish. She stood there, wanting to flee, but now that the king had engaged her in conversation, she could not.

"You play the harp well, sire," she murmured finally. "I've never heard that song before."

His smile turned melancholy, and he glanced down at the instrument upon his lap. He was dressed simply this morning, in a long woolen tunic, leather vest, and doeskin breeches. It was very different attire to last evening's. He wore no crown this morning, nor arm rings or gilded amber brooch.

"It's a song my mother used to play to me," he replied after a pause. "An Eriu lament."

Osana quirked an eyebrow. "A lament, sire. It seems an odd choice of music on the morning after your handfasting?"

He went still at that.

Osana cursed her loose tongue. What had come over her? Only a goose of a woman asked such a question. She tensed, bracing herself for anger—for that was usually Raedwulf's response when her tongue ran away with her.

However, he merely watched her—a shadow moving in his eyes. "The music suits my mood," he said finally. "This wasn't a union of my choosing ... or of my bride's. I doubt it will be a happy one."

The look of fatality on his face, the dead sound in his voice, touched Osana. Despair was a close friend of hers these days; she recognized it instantly in others. "Your marriage has just begun," she replied softly. "You and Lady Cuthburh have a lifetime to grow accustomed to each other ... to forge a bond."

He watched her, a flicker of hope lighting in his eyes. "How long have you been married, Osana?"

The way he said her name caused a feather-light shiver to caress her skin. However, that question made her grow wary. She did not want to speak of her marriage. "Twelve years," she murmured.

"And was it arranged?"

Osana nodded. "I knew Raedwulf before, but my father organized the match."

"And were you willing?"

Osana stiffened, deeply uncomfortable now. "Aye," she said softly, sadness and regret welling within her. "I was."

She could have wept then, for the memory of the girl she had once been. How easily she had been taken in by Raedwulf's blond good looks, his ready smile. No—it had not been a forced marriage. She had happily left her father's hall, had eagerly thrown herself into her new life. It made disappointment all the bitterer now.

She was aware that the king was still watching her. There was an unnerving intelligence to that gaze, and she had the intuition that he could read her silence and the emotions she was trying to smother.

Osana found it impossible to meet his eye now. Instead, she stared down at his hands.

"You're not happy then?" he asked gently.

She shook her head, still avoiding his gaze. She wanted to lie, to pretend, as she always did whenever she was in company. Yet her emotions felt rubbed raw this morning.

Raedwulf had rutted her like a hound the night before; he had been rough, and there had been no pleasure for her—only discomfort and a simmering rage that he dare use her so.

The truth of her life had become clear in the cold grey light of the morning—and when confronted by a simple question, she found she could not pretend.

"I am sorry to hear that."

She glanced up, meeting his eye then. "Don't be ... take hope from my story, sire. Even those of us who go willingly to our handfasting are not guaranteed a happy end. Perhaps you and the queen are the fortunate ones ... maybe it's better to begin without illusions."

His gaze narrowed, and she saw a nerve flicker in his cheek. "My wife despises me," he replied. He had not raised his voice, yet there was now an edge to it that had been missing before. "She wished to enter a nunnery, but her brother forbade it. The idea of being a wife repulses her ... in every sense."

Osana did not look away from the directness of his gaze. She felt sorry for him, although she did not voice that sentiment. No man liked being the object of pity. "She may warm to you eventually," Osana offered. "Once she accepts that this is her life now."

Aldfrith gave a humorless laugh. "Aye."

Drawing in a deep breath, Osana took a step back. This was a dangerous conversation and an improper one. If one of the servants heard them, there would be gossip circulating the Great Hall by nón-mete.

She had never spoken to a man in this fashion before—not even Raedwulf. Her husband was too obtuse. He never looked at her as this man did now.

"Milord," she said finally, wetting her lips as nervousness assailed her. "I heard you were schooled to become a monk. If you had followed that path, you would have been spared this responsibility."

He leaned back on the bench and dragged a hand through his short blond hair, leaving it spiky and tousled. It gave him a boyish, vulnerable look.

"I wasn't ready when I first arrived upon Iona," he replied, an edge to his voice. "I was frustrated about that at first, but then with the passing of the years, I decided I liked a scholar's life better. I could live in quiet contemplation without the harsh demands of a monk's life. Ironically, the day they came to collect me, the prior at Iona had told me I was ready to take my vows if I was willing."

Silence followed his words. Osana felt at a loss to know how to respond. Her own spirits were at a low ebb this morning—yet seeing the bleak look that flitted across the king's handsome features, she realized she was not alone in her melancholy.

"Listen to me," the king scoffed, rising to his feet to face her. "I'm weary of hearing the self-pity in my own voice and apologize for burdening you with this."

Osana smiled, bobbing into a quick curtsy. Something about this man disarmed her. The rueful look on his face told her that he was not usually given to such a bleak mood. "It was no burden," she said. Their gazes met and held for a long heartbeat. "But I fear I should return to the Great Hall. My husband will be awake by now."

"Of course," he replied, a light smile curving his lips, although she could still see a shadow in those blue eyes. "Good day, Osana ... it was a pleasure to share a few moments with you."

King Aldfrith watched Lady Osana of Hagustaldes walk away through the orchard, between the columns of apple trees.

She was a small woman, yet she walked tall and proud. Her thick brown hair was braided and wrapped around her crown in a severe style that did not detract from her comeliness. Instead, it revealed the pale curve of her neck.

Dolt.

What had made him say all those things?

She had looked at him with those soulful eyes, and he had felt compelled to open his heart. He had told her things he had not even realized he felt—and as she walked away a wave of loss crashed over him.

He had come out into the orchard to find a little peace and play his harp. The music soothed him, softening the sharp edges of the previous night—blunting his memory of Cuthburh's face as she rejected him.

His conversation with the winsome ealdorman's wife had brought it all back.

Osana disappeared from view, and Aldfrith sat down heavily upon the bench.

He had never met a woman like her. She was fair to look upon, but her appeal lay far beyond that. There was a quiet purpose to Osana, an ageless wisdom and kindness in those eyes.

A strong desire to seek Osana out and speak with her again reared up within him.

Enough.

Aldfrith silenced his thoughts with an iron will he had spent a lifetime developing.

Such thoughts will only lead you down a dark path.

With that, Aldfrith cast lingering thoughts of Osana aside and began to play his harp once more. However, this time the music did not soothe him.

Chapter Seven

For the Best

"YOUR HUSBAND IS a handsome fellow—you are a fortunate woman."

Osana glanced up from where she was winding wool onto her distaff. A basket lay at her feet, and she sat with a wooden spindle, teasing out the sticky fiber before winding it onto her distaff. She never went anywhere without her distaff. Ever since she was a girl, it had been like an additional limb.

Eldflaed, the woman who had spoken, grinned across at her. The group of wives sat before one of the fire pits, sewing, spinning, and mending as they discussed the events of the last day. Eldflaed, the wife of one of the king's thegns, was the loudest of the group. The onion-breathed woman of the day before now had a name.

"I suppose he is comely," Osana forced a smile. "Only that, after years of marriage a wife ceases to notice such details."

As she had hoped, this comment caused laughter to echo around the fireside.

"I wish my man was so fine," another of the wives said with a sigh. She was the ealdorman of Catraeth's wife. "I swear with each passing year Wulfred grows more and more in the likeness of a boar."

Laughter erupted once more, and even Osana raised a smile. Wulfred of Catraeth was the hairiest man she had ever seen—with dark hair tufting from his nostrils and ears.

The conversation resumed, and Osana shifted her attention back to her distaff. It grew late in the afternoon, and the air inside the Great Hall was heavy with the odor of simmering pottage. At the fire pit opposite, servants were starting to cook great wheels of bread upon a griddle. After the indulgence of the night before, this supper would be a simple one.

The rumble of men's voices filtered across the hall, and Osana glanced up to see the king enter the space.

Aldfrith walked in long, confident strides, Bishop Wilfrid at his side. Wilfrid was talking to the king, his voice low, his expression fierce. In contrast, the king's face was solemn, his eyes stern as he listened to him.

A group of ealdormen—Raedwulf among them—followed Aldrfrith and the bishop, laughing and teasing each other as they entered the tower.

Osana's gaze tracked the king across the rushes. She knew she should not gawk so, yet she could not help herself.

She had been in an odd mood ever since their conversation that morning. She kept thinking of the words that had passed between them—the man's disarming candor. At the time she had been happy to flee, for she had been embarrassed by the intimacy. But as the day progressed, she found herself longing for a chance to talk to him again.

Osana dropped her gaze to her spindle, a heaviness descending upon her. That conversation had been an unexpected, stolen, moment. The king was usually surrounded by retainers, and she and Raedwulf were to depart the following morning.

Osana would not get the chance to speak with Aldfrith again.

It's just as well, she consoled herself, teasing a piece of lamb's wool with her fingers. *It was improper anyway.*

And yet part of her did not care. She had been brought up in a pious, conservative household. Manners had mattered a lot to her parents, as had proper behavior. Her father was an ambitious thegn and her mother an ealdorman's daughter. Osana had always felt smothered by them. The eldest of three daughters, she had been relieved to marry and escape their constant judgement. Even though they were both dead, she felt she was defying them now, by wishing for another private conversation with the king.

"Cuthburh!" Eldflaed's strident voice interrupted Osana's reverie once again. "Come sit with us, milady."

Osana lifted her gaze to see a slender figure glide across the rushes toward them.

Like the other women, Osana automatically rose to her feet before dipping into a curtsy. However, as she did so, she noted the dramatic change in the girl.

Cuthburh's flowing flaxen hair, which had cascaded down her back the day before, was now hidden by a white headrail—only a glimpse of the end of a braid was visible under the hem of the veil. Unlike the form-fitting gown, the queen now wore a loose-fitting tunic made of cream linen, girded around her narrow waist. Her face, framed by the headrail, was still lovely, although the queen's appearance this afternoon was austere and cold. Her expression was shuttered as she took a seat next to the hearth and picked up a delicate piece of embroidery.

"Good day, all." Her voice was low and sweet, although Osana heard the guarded edge to it. Cuthburh did not trust them.

"That is a lovely tunic, milady." One of the ealdorman's wives commented. "Such fine weave—and a lovely color."

Cuthburh's rosebud mouth pursed. "It is too gaudy for my liking, but my brother refused to let me bring my usual clothes. Tomorrow I will see about having plainer garments made."

The queen's comment caused a ripple of surprise to go through the knot of women. Cuthburh was queen—she was expected to wear fine clothes. Osana watched the queen bow her head and begin work on her embroidery, her slim, nimble fingers working with expert speed. She thought back to what Aldfrith had told her and realized he had not exaggerated Cuthburh's wish for a different life to this one.

Osana stifled a sigh.

Don't we all?

"Osana!"

She glanced up to see Raedwulf hailing her. He was seated upon the high seat, holding up a bronze cup. "Come, wife—get some wine and fill our cups!"

Osana heard a few of the women giggle at Raedwulf's command. No doubt they thought him manly and authoritative.

Osana just found him boorish.

Putting down her spindle, she left the women, murmured an apology, and crossed to the high seat. A servant girl had filled a ewer of sloe wine, which she passed to Osana. Silently, ever the obedient wife, Osana circuited the table, pouring wine into each man's cup.

Now that he had hailed her to his side, Raedwulf ignored Osana. He was deep in conversation with the ealdorman of Gefrin, discussing perimeter defenses, and did not even look his wife's way as she passed.

Osana was grateful.

Reaching the head of the table, Osana filled the king's cup. She was drawing back—about to move on to the bishop—when Aldfrith looked up.

Eyes the color of the summer sky just before sunset met hers. And just for a moment Osana paused, ensnared.

"Thank you," the king said quietly.

Heart hammering, Osana dipped her head and moved on to Bishop Wilfrid. However, as she did so, she realized that it was not only the king who had noticed her. The bishop had too.

Wilfrid watched her under hooded lids, his gaunt face stern. Osana met his gaze, and her heart slammed painfully against her ribs. One look at the bishop's narrowed stare, his thinned lips, and she felt stripped bare. They had done nothing wrong, but she felt as if the bishop had caught the pair of them cavorting naked.

A flush spread up from her chest at the thought, and Osana hastily moved on to continue pouring the wine.

They left Bebbanburg with the dawn. Raedwulf rose before Osana, leaving her to pack their belongings while he went out to ready the horses. They had brought a small party with them—just four of Raedwulf's most trusted men but no servants. Osana would serve and tend to their needs during the journey home.

Osana readied the leather trunk in their alcove and called two of her husband's men to carry it out to the wagon. Then she made her way out into the hall.

Women were shouting at servants, children wailed, and men hauled leather bags and trunks across the space, kicking dogs out of the way as they went. Raedwulf and Osana were not the only ones to be leaving.

There was no sign of the king—or queen—this morning.

Disappointment settled over Osana that she would not see Aldfrith again, but she quickly shrugged it off.

Goose. Pull yourself together.

Osana crossed the hall and left the tower through an arched entrance way. A grey, misty morning and the smell of wood smoke greeted her. She huffed out a breath. Summer, it seemed, was over. The scent of autumn lay heavy in the air.

Pulling her thick fur mantle close, she descended the steps to the yard below, spotting her husband leading their horses from the stables. A wagon filled with their baggage sat waiting surrounded by Raedwulf's men—who were mounted and ready to go.

"Always the last to arrive, wife," Raedwulf grumbled, handing over the horse's reins.

Osana favored him with an arch look. "And rightly so, husband. Someone has to ensure you didn't leave something behind."

He grinned at that. Raedwulf had always enjoyed her spirit—unlike some men who might have beaten it out of her. There had only been a couple of occasions when he had taken a hand to her: when she had dared to contradict him in front of his brother and retainers. After that, Osana had taken care to save their arguments for their alcove.

"Gossiping with other wives more like," he said before turning to his horse and swinging up onto the saddle. "I know how women like to prattle."

Osana rolled her eyes, knowing he had his back to her.

You know nothing about women.

Gathering her skirts, Osana mounted her palfrey. She bowed her head as a chill wind gusted through her layers of clothing. Osana shivered, pulling up her fur lined hood. The journey from Hagustaldes had been a pleasant one—but with the turn of the weather, the return would not be such an enjoyable ride.

Raedwulf urged his horse forward, and Osana followed, the wagon rumbling behind them as the driver flicked the reins and the stocky pony drawing it moved off. The wagon had been laden with wedding gifts: a fur-lined cloak for the queen, two beautifully crafted seaxes with amber-studded hilts, and a bounty of cheeses and cured meats for the king's stores. It was far lighter for the return journey.

Against her will, Osana found her gaze drawn back toward the Great Tower of Bebbanburg. She glanced over her shoulder, half expecting to see a tall blond man standing on the steps watching them go. However, no-one was there to see them off—just the ealdorman of Catraeth, who was bickering with his wife as he lumbered down the steps to the yard.

It's best I didn't see Aldfrith this morning. Osana dragged her gaze away and urged her mare under the high gate. The expanse of the King's Way loomed before her. *Best I return to reality.*

That conversation, those stolen moments in the orchard, had been a dream; that scene seemed as if it had belonged to someone else's life. For a few brief moments she had forgotten that she was Osana: barren and lonely. For a short spell she had merely been a woman in the company of a man who had made her feel alive.

But that man was king and as untouchable as a star. And she was wedded, bonded for life to another. It would do her no good to think on Aldfrith of Northumbria—for it would only make her melancholy grow. She glanced right at where Raedwulf rode, his thick blond hair tumbling over his shoulders, his profile ruggedly handsome as always. Raedwulf of Hagustaldes was her life. It would be better for her to forget she had ever spoken to the king.

Chapter Eight

A Promise for Life

Bebbanburg, Kingdom of Northumbria

Two years later

"YOU ARE LEAVING then?"

"Aye ... it's time, Aldfrith."

He stiffened at the use of his name. In the two years of their union, Cuthburh had rarely used it—usually addressing him as 'sire' or 'milord'. However, there was no warmth in her voice now, and his name sounded clipped and cold on her lips.

They faced each other—man and wife—inside the alcove they shared. Aldfrith had returned from hawking to find Cuthburh standing amongst trunks and bags, servants scurrying around her. At the arrival of the king, they had dipped their heads and backed out of the alcove, leaving the king and queen alone.

"We made a promise at our handfasting," Aldfrith said, his voice flat and toneless to his hearing. "It was a promise for life."

Cuthburh drew herself up at that, her mouth thinning. "The only promise worth anything to me is the one I made to God years ago. I will be wedded to no one but him."

That was it then—the way of things.

Aldfrith observed his wife, taking in her haughty face and cold eyes. She was barely more than twenty winters now, yet to him she appeared much older. As always, she wore heavy woolen robes that shrouded her figure, and an enveloping headrail. Her face—which he had once found so pretty—now just seemed austere.

The attraction he had once felt for her had eventually died.

He had tried to consummate their marriage again on several occasions, for only a weak fool would give up so easily, yet she had rejected him each time. On his final attempt they had been alone together in their alcove, undressing to retire for the night. He had told her she was beautiful and reached out to stroke her hair. Cuthburh had then shrieked as if scalded before beginning to sob.

Aldfrith never bothered again after that.

"So you are set on going to Berecingas?" he asked.

Cuthburh responded with a brisk nod. "I have sent word to Abbess Hildelith—she has space for me at her nunnery."

Aldfrith's gaze dropped to the luggage at her feet. "Have you organized an escort?"

"Aye ... the bishop has organized a party of four horsemen to accompany me south."

Aldfrith's jaw clenched at the mention of the bishop.

It seems I'm the last to know.

"Berecingas is a long ride," he said, forcing down his irritation. "Four men aren't enough. I will have another four warriors accompany you."

Her blue eyes widened at that, and for a moment her ice-queen façade cracked. She almost looked ... guilty.

Cuthburh dropped her gaze, her fingers twisting around the end of the rope she used to gird her waist. "You're a good man, Aldfrith ... better than I deserve."

He frowned, his irritation rising further. Not only was his wife about to humiliate him, but she made him feel like a cuckold. Other men would not have tolerated her behavior. Other men would have taken her whether she wanted it or not.

Suddenly, he just wished to be rid of her, to have this ice-cold wraith out of his life.

Aldfrith stepped back, schooling his face into an impassive mask and smoothing his frown. He motioned to her luggage before turning away. "I shall leave you to your packing."

Aldfrith stood upon the palisade to the right of the low gate and watched his wife leave.

A chill breeze whispered in from the sea. The water was a leaden expanse that stretched east, and the sky in that direction looked ominous, warning of bad weather on its way.

However, Aldfrith paid the storm clouds no mind. Instead, his gaze tracked the slender figure atop a bay palfrey who rode—spine straight—down the causeway to the road below. Two of his men led the way, the Northumbrian banner fluttering in the wind between them, while the rest of the party rode behind the queen.

Watching her go, Aldfrith felt nothing.

Not a shred of sadness, not a glimmer of regret, or even a flicker of anger.

Nothing.

This was how his life was meant to be—he had known it from childhood. He had been alone for so long it felt like his natural state. Actually, he preferred it. There was a simplicity in being alone.

He was king, ruled a vast tract of land, and had thousands of men to command, yet he felt utterly alone. He had felt less lonely living a hermit's life upon Iona than he did now in a busy hall. The Great Tower of Bebbanburg only ever grew quiet in that short space after the last warrior stretched out upon his cloak, and when the first servant rose at dawn to stoke the embers of the fire pits.

Aldfrith watched Cuthburh kick her palfrey into a fast canter, as if she was in a panic to leave, as if he would change his mind and come after her.

He would do no such thing.

Aldfrith inhaled deeply before letting the breath escape—and with it the tension of the past two years.

"So you couldn't convince her to stay?"

A deep voice interrupted Aldfrith, and he turned to see Bishop Wilfrid standing next to him, his dark robes fluttering in the wind.

Aldfrith frowned. The bishop was not a welcome sight. "Did you encourage Cuthburh?"

Wilfrid's heavy lidded eyes narrowed in response. "Excuse me?"

Aldfrith held his gaze. His mood this morning made him reckless, made him speak plainer than he usually did with the bishop. "The tale of how you helped Queen Aethelthryth flee from my brother is now legend."

Wilfrid held his gaze, before his mouth twisted in a rare smile. "That was different. Ecgfrith had abased himself by raping the queen's hand-maid. Aethelthryth was left with little choice. She could not stay with such a black-hearted sinner."

The bishop's gaze glinted at this, revealing the depths of his hatred for Ecgfrith. Aldfrith's half-brother had exiled the bishop from his lands after his wife's disappearance. Wilfrid had been waiting for many years to return to the north. The bishop had settled now into his new life in Inhrypum, which lay to the south of Bebbanburg, yet it did not stop him from making regular trips to the fort. Aldfrith had the feeling he was being checked up on.

Aldfrith watched the bishop for a long moment, not believing him, before he spoke once more. "So it was true ... she refused to lie with Ecgfrith?"

The bishop shrugged. "That is what she told me."

"And you think it's right—that a wife should shun her husband's affections?"

Wilfrid's features tightened. "If she truly feels Christ's calling ... yes."

Anger surged within Aldfrith although he tamped it down "But you encouraged me to wed Cuthburh?"

"Aye, she was a good match. I did not know the depths of her piety though." Wilfrid broke off here and glanced south, at where the party were now specks in the distance. A trundling wagon laden with Cuthburh's belongings and gifts for the nunnery followed the group. "You did well to let her go. We shall find another wife for you. One who will bear you sons."

Aldfrith clenched his jaw. "I shall not marry again, Father."

The bishop's dark gaze snapped back to him. "It's your duty as king, sire. Look what happened to your brother ... dying without an heir."

Aldfrith shook his head, the shield he usually wore before the bishop slipping slightly to reveal his true feelings. "I gave this kingdom the king they wanted," he ground out, "—but I will not give them my soul." Aldfrith inhaled deeply before continuing. "I did my duty, but my union with Cuthburh didn't endure. I'll not repeat it."

The bishop's lips compressed. "You speak out of bitterness, sire. With time, you will see sense."

Aldfrith shook his head, turning swiftly from the bishop. He hated the way Wilfrid talked to him, as if he were some wise uncle and Aldfrith a young fool who had yet to grow a beard. He would not suffer Wilfrid's company any longer. Not today.

"I see sense now," he bit out the words, heading for the ladder leading down from the wall. "Time will make no difference."

Aldfrith returned to the Great Tower, but he did not go inside. Instead, he entered a low annex that had recently been built on its western side. He had commissioned its construction a year and a half earlier, after the lack of solitude and reflection had gotten to him.

Three stone steps led up to an arched doorway and a heavy oaken door. Sanctuary lay behind.

Aldfrith pushed his way inside, the door closing after him with a thud that rattled the stone walls.

Argus, who had been asleep in his basket, raised his shaggy head at his master's entrance. The wolfhound gave a soft whine in greeting, his heavy tail thumping. And despite his dark mood, Aldfrith's mouth curved into a smile.

"Lazy dog," he muttered. "So that's where you've been all morning. How did you get in here?"

Argus's tail increased its tempo, and he lowered his head guiltily.

"It was Cerdic, wasn't it?" Aldfrith knew the warrior was fond of the dog. Gruff with everyone else, Argus was the only creature who roused a smile in the man.

Aldfrith sat down upon a stool before his desk and reached down to pat the wolfhound's head. As he did so, his gaze took in his surroundings. His 'sanctuary', as he named it, was starting to look dusty and cluttered. Cuthburh had never set foot in here, and Aldfrith did not let servants clean it. The last thing he wanted was one of them to spill ink over the costly vellum he used to write on, or to accidentally damage one of the leather-bound volumes sitting upon the shelving.

It was a small, monkish space, certainly not kingly like his lodgings within the tower—yet he much preferred it here. The shuttered windows were slightly open, letting in pale sunlight over his table and illuminating his disorder.

With a sigh, Aldfrith rose to his feet and opened the shutters wide. The rise and fall of voices and the clucking of fowl intruded, but he did not mind. He would light the bank of tallow candles and close the shutters later. For now the watery sunlight and the sounds of life calmed him.

He glanced down at the piece of vellum before him. The day before—struck by inspiration—he had scribbled a few lines. He read them again now.

Foolishness results in crudity
Repression results in greater repression
Hatred engenders reproach
Abandonment results in slander

Aldfrith paused, gazing down at the words.
Abandonment.
It was almost as if he had known this was coming. Of course, he must have. He and Cuthburh had been strangers to each other for a while now.

Aldfrith was still looking down at his writing, frowning, when a sharp knock sounded at the door.

He glanced up. "Aye ... come in."

The door opened, and Cerdic stepped across the threshold, his broad muscular frame filling the doorway. "Morning, sire."

Aldfrith clenched his jaw. Usually the thegn's presence did not bother him. However, this morning he wished for solitude. "What is it?" he snapped.

Cerdic's face, unreadable as always, did not alter at the cool welcome. He merely dipped his head respectfully. "Sorry for intruding, milord, but a messenger has just arrived from Hagustaldes."

Something in his captain's voice made Aldfrith pay attention, his ill-temper momentarily forgotten. "What is it?"

"It seems the ealdorman of Hagustaldes, Raedwulf, was gored by a boar while out hunting a few days ago," Cerdic informed him. "He is dead."

Chapter Nine

Go in Peace

FOLK ALWAYS SAID that the dead looked as if they were sleeping, but Raedwulf did not.

Osana stood inside the alcove where she had helped prepare her husband's body for burial, and stared down at Raedwulf's face.

Raedwulf looked grimmer than he had in life, his features still bearing the grimace of agony he had worn in his final moments. His skin was waxy and bloodless, his unruly mane of blond hair combed neatly over his shoulders.

He looked like what he was—dead.

Osana drew in a deep breath and cast a glance across at where her sister-by-marriage, Edlyn, sat at the back of the alcove. The woman was weeping again, her green eyes glistening, her small mouth pursed in grief.

Osana watched Edlyn a long moment, studying her. The woman's upset at Raedwulf's death surprised her. Edlyn was usually so cold and aloof.

Was she in love with Raedwulf?

The thought came, unwanted and unbidden.

Osana's chest tightened. She had no proof, yet her female instinct stirred. She remembered Edlyn favoring Raedwulf with a coy smile at Yule and dancing with him once during midsummer festivities. But for the rest of the time, she had kept her distance, playing the part of doting and submissive wife to Raedwulf's younger brother, Deogol.

Osana had no proof, but suddenly she knew with a surety that shocked her.

How long?

Did it matter? Was she even jealous? Jealous no—made a fool of, yes.

Seized by the urge to fly across the annex, grab a fistful of that thick auburn hair, and slam Edlyn's head against the wall, Osana looked away. Struggling to control herself, she heaved in a deep breath.

It was the last in a long line of insults she had suffered over the years. Osana was not sure she could bear it.

The wail of a horn reached them then, muffled by the thick wooden walls of the ealdorman's hall.

Osana straightened her spine and smoothed out the skirts of her long dark gown.

"The king has arrived," she said breaking the long silence between the two women. "It's time."

Edlyn glanced up, her features tightening. It was almost as if she had forgotten that Osana was there. Not bothering to answer, she nodded and rose to her feet.

Raedwulf's men had built him a pyre upon a long-boat. It sat on the muddy banks of the Tyne, awaiting the ceremony that would begin Raedwulf's journey to the afterlife.

A light rain fell as the crowd of mourners gathered on the riverbank. It was a still afternoon and the light was dimming, warning them all that winter was coming. The days had started to shorten. The harvest was now behind them, and there was a nip to the air which had not been present days earlier.

Osana pulled up her hood, drawing it forward so it obscured as much of her face as possible.

She had not wept since Raedwulf's death, and although she wore a strained expression, she knew it would not be enough. The folk of Hagustaldes expected to see the ealdorman's widow grieve.

Eyes downcast, Osana blinked furiously, wishing she could summon tears to appease them all. She did not hate her husband, and she had not wished him dead—yet it was impossible to cry when she felt nothing but emptiness inside her.

A procession of warriors approached the long-boat, crossing the water meadow from the town's walls. The leaders carried a bier where Raedwulf lay, dressed in his finest doeskin breeches, a long tunic hemmed with gold, and a fur mantle. His hands were clasped over his broad chest, holding his sword in place. The armrings he had earned over the years glinted in the watery afternoon light.

The terrible wound to his belly—which had taken days to kill him—had been bound and covered.

The procession arrived at the water's edge, and the men lifted the bier onto the long-boat before fanning out around it.

At the back of the group, Osana spied the king.

Two years had passed since she had last seen him, and he looked different. He still wore his blond hair shorter than most men, and was clean-shaven, but his face was sterner than she remembered. It made him look older, more of a king and less of a philosopher.

She had forgotten how tall he was. He stood almost a foot taller than some of the men surrounding him and even taller than the lanky, dark-robed figure that followed two steps behind him. Bishop Wilfrid had accompanied the king's party from Bebbanburg even though Hagustaldes had its own bishop. Bishop Godwin was a small, fey-looking fellow who now hovered on the edge of the mourners and who, Osana had assumed, would lead the funeral ceremony.

However, Osana's gaze did not linger upon Bishop Wilfrid. Like two years earlier, she found her attention drawn back to Aldfrith. His presence—different from the loud, arrogant warriors she had grown up with—had a magnetic quality, an aura of calm strength that captivated her.

Careful.

Osana snapped her gaze away and glanced right to find Edlyn watching her under hooded lids. Her sister by marriage wore a thoughtful expression, her green eyes sharp.

Heart pounding, Osana dropped her gaze once more. Why did she feel so guilty? She had done nothing wrong. Edlyn did not know that Osana had thought often about Aldfrith upon her return to Hagustaldes, that he had intruded on her thoughts far too often for a long while afterward.

Still, this was not the place to stare like a besotted maid—not when her husband lay dead just a few yards away.

Bishop Wilfrid left the king's side and made his way up to the water's edge. His sharp-featured face was screwed up in a scowl, and Osana wondered if the bishop disapproved of this style of funeral.

It was too close to the old ways—to the funeral pyres of their elders when folk worshipped Woden, Thunor, Freya and their kin. Amongst the high born those ways were no longer followed, although common folk still paid tribute to the old gods at festivals and at the four solstices during the year.

Raedwulf had been baptized, yet he had never been a good Christian—worshipping in name only. Unlike Osana, who had been brought up in a pious household, Raedwulf's father had been proudly pagan. In the agony-filled days before his death, Raedwulf had insisted he would burn upon a long-boat, as his father had.

Godwin ventured forward, his head bowed, and approached Bishop Wilfrid. They spoke together on the water's edge, a brief exchange in low voices that did not carry. Bishop Godwin appeared cowed by the older man's presence, although his thin face flushed as he spoke to Wilfrid.

Surprised, Osana realized they were arguing.

Wilfrid barked something sharp at Godwin, and the younger man moved back, hunching his shoulders. Then, an affronted look upon his face, Godwin shuffled off to rejoin the crowd of mourners.

Osana frowned. She did not know what exactly had passed between the two bishops, yet Wilfrid was out of line. It seemed that he had *insisted* on carrying out the ceremony.

Osana glanced across at the king, wondering if he would step in. Yet although Aldfrith wore a displeased expression, he did not.

Standing before the long-boat, Bishop Wilfrid stooped down, his fingers scooping up a handful of mud. Then he spoke, his deep, gravelly voice echoing through the stillness.

"Here lies Raedwulf, son of Eorpwald, Ealdorman of Hagustaldes. Strong in life and proud in death—God watches over you." The bishop paused here, letting his words settle, before he resumed his prayer. "The Lord is our Light and our salvation ... our strength. Our hearts shall not fear death, for there is a time to be born and a time to die."

The bishop let the mud drop from his fingers, his gaze fixed upon Raedwulf's corpse.

"And so we commit this warrior's body to the water, the earth, so it may be cleansed by fire. Earth to earth, ashes to ashes, dust to dust."

Osana listened, her chest constricting. She had to admit that Wilfrid was a far better speaker than poor Godwin. His voice was powerful, full of conviction.

Wilfrid stepped back then, turned, and nodded to the king. Aldfrith left the edge of the crowd and approached the riverbank. Then he removed a jeweled seax from his belt and placed the ornate fighting dagger upon the bier, next to Raedwulf. He then murmured something and bowed his head.

A few moments later Aldfrith turned, his heavy fur mantle billowing, and strode back toward the crowd, toward where Osana stood a few feet in front of the other mourners.

For an instant their gazes met, and then he nodded. It was now Osana's turn to pay her last respects. Feeling the weight of the crowd's stares upon her, she walked down to the long-boat. Standing before it, she reached up and removed the single bronze armring she wore upon her left arm.

It had been Raedwulf's morgen gifu—morning gift—all those years ago. She remembered him giving it to her, as she stirred in the furs on the morning after their handfasting. She had felt queasy, for she had consumed far more mead than she was used to the night before. Yet her gaze had misted when her handsome young husband had knelt before her and handed her the armring.

It symbolized the bond between them, but it would go with Raedwulf to his watery grave.

Osana placed the armring upon the bier, her gaze resting one last time upon her dead husband's face.

She felt nothing but a yawning chasm of emptiness.

"Go in peace, Raedwulf," she whispered before stepping back from the boat.

A heartbeat later her husband's men, his brother Deogol among them, brushed past her and waded into the water, pulling the long-boat away from the banks. They heaved the craft into the current of the Tyne before returning to the shore.

Then Deogol took up his long bow and lit the end from a brazier that burned upon the shore. Her brother-by-marriage was a skilled bowman, the best in Hagustaldes. It was fitting that he would send Raedwulf off.

Silence settled upon the riverbank, the rain falling in a fine mist around them. Deogol drew his bow string back, his brow furrowing in concentration as he marked his target. The long-boat was drifting lazily out toward where the current flowed more swiftly.

The fiery arrow flew, arching high into the air and dropping onto the pile of dry straw encircling Raedwulf's body. A long pause followed, and then the dry tinder ignited with a whoosh.

Osana watched it. She was vaguely aware that the king stood near her, as did Deogol, but she paid neither of them any mind. Instead, her gaze remained upon the flames that now roared high into the misty air.

Fourteen years she had been wedded to that man, and now she was a widow. Osana had been lonely through most of her marriage. She never felt understood by her husband. His liking for other women had driven a wedge between them, as had her barren womb, but he had been her rock in a hostile world.

Without him, she was truly alone.

Chapter Ten

Choices

ALDFRITH WATCHED THE ealdorman's wife.

The cowled cloak she wore hid most of her face from view and cast a shadow over her eyes, yet there was a quiet dignity in her presence, in the way she held herself.

He had not forgotten their conversation in the orchard that morning two years earlier. She and her husband had left Bebbanburg the following day, and so he had been unable to talk to her again. But that brief conversation had stayed with him.

She had understood how he felt, and had revealed the loneliness in her own marriage.

He wondered what she was feeling now. There were no tears on her cheeks, although the air of melancholy shrouding her did not seem feigned.

A dozen yards away, Raedwulf's pyre burned upon the river, a dark plume of smoke now lifting into the sky.

The mourners gathered along the river bank, and Aldfrith noted one or two of the women weeping. One woman in particular, a comely female with thick auburn hair tied back in messy coils from her face, looked beside herself.

She stood next to a tall blond warrior who bore a striking resemblance to the dead ealdorman. This must be Deogol, Raedwulf's brother, and the new ealdorman of Hagustaldes. The weeping woman must have been his wife.

There was another woman crying nearby, a slender blonde girl who looked no older than eighteen winters. A fair haired boy clung to her skirts as she sobbed.

Aldfrith took in the scene with interest before his attention shifted back to the widow.

He realized now why she did not weep.

Raedwulf's household put on a great feast after his funeral, to honor his memory.

Deogol sat at his usual place at the table, having given the ealdorman's seat to the king, and held up a drinking horn filled with mead.

"To my brother!" he boomed. "May he find feasting, wenches, and plenty of mead in the afterlife!"

This toast brought roars of approval from many of the warriors seated at the long tables that formed a square around the fire pit. However, Bishop Wilfrid—who sat opposite Deogol—glowered at the warrior when he sat down. It was no Christian afterlife that Deogol spoke of. Farther down the table, Bishop Godwin's face was expressionless.

Watching Hagustaldes' bishop, Aldfrith felt a pang of regret. He should have stepped in when Wilfrid had bullied the man earlier, yet it had not been the place for a scene. Even so, he would need to have a word with Wilfrid when they were next alone. He could not have him upsetting the other bishops like this.

Aldfrith swallowed a sigh at the thought. Wilfrid was fast becoming a thorn in his arse; the man's arrogance and bullish approach to the other men of the cloth in the kingdom was fast making him unpopular. It appeared there was only one right way to follow God—and that was Wilfrid's way.

Osana, who had been given her usual spot at the head of the table one last time, took a sip of mead from her cup, welcoming its sweet pungency.

She was glad of Deogol's toast though. Raedwulf would have enjoyed that.

Beside Deogol, Edlyn sat, red eyed and wan faced. The sight of her made Osana's anger rise in a slow heat that caused her to tighten her grip on her cup. The woman did not even try to hide her grief, not even before her husband.

Is Deogol blind?

Maybe he was. Deogol was the same breed of man as his dead brother: brave, strong, and utterly oblivious to the feelings of others. He completely ignored his wife as he offered the king some roast boar.

"This is the beast that ended my brother, sire," he informed Aldfrith. "He asked us to roast it for his funeral feast."

Osana took a larger—more fortifying—gulp of mead.

Of course he did.

"The creature might as well be put to good use," Aldfrith replied with a half-smile, taking a slice of meat. He passed the platter to Osana. "Some boar?"

Osana took the dish and gave herself a tiny slice before passing it on. "Thank you," she murmured.

The feasting began, accompanied by numerous toasts and even more mead. A lad sat near the hearth playing a bone whistle, the music almost drowned out by the roar of conversation.

"Are you well, Osana?"

The question, spoken in a low voice, caught her off-guard. Osana had been staring at the platter before her, forcing down each mouthful of food, before she washed it down with mead. She did not usually drink so much and was starting to feel quite light-headed.

She glanced up, to find Aldfrith watching her.

"Aye," she replied. "I've little appetite this eve, that's all."

He nodded. "I can understand that."

"More mead?" Edlyn appeared at Osana's shoulder then. She had been given the task of filling the feasters' cups. However, the woman wore a pinched expression.

"Aye, thank you." Osana held out her cup.

Edlyn sloshed mead into it, so violently that it splashed over the rim and onto the bust of Osana's mourning tunic: a dark, high necked garment made of wool.

"Sorry, Osana." Edlyn chimed, a gleam in her eyes. She moved on then to the king.

"Some mead, milord?" she asked sweetly.

Aldfrith shook his head, and Osana's sister-by-marriage moved on.

Drawing in a deep breath, Osana glanced down at the dark patch covering the front of her tunic. The garment was dark anyway, so it did not really matter. What mattered was that the balance of power had already shifted within the hall.

Raedwulf's ashes were still warm, but already Edlyn was assuming her role as lady of the house. A sinking sensation made Osana reach for her cup of mead once more.

Life was about to get difficult. She could sense it.

Osana raised her eyes once more, to see the king's gaze still upon her. The concern on his face made the sinking sensation grow. He was a stranger to this hall, and had only just met Deogol and his wife—and yet he knew.

"And how are you faring, milord," she said, after a moment.

He favored her with a tired smile. "Well enough."

"And your queen? How is Cuthburh?"

She was surprised the queen had not accompanied him here.

He stiffened at that, his gaze narrowing. Osana immediately regretted the question.

"Cuthburh is well ... I believe," he began, his voice low as he glanced down at the knife he was toying with. "However, I cannot know for sure. She has left me ... has gone to Berecingas to take her vows."

Osana stared at him, surprise rendering her mute. When she eventually found her tongue, her face grew warm with mortification. "I'm sorry, sire ... I didn't realize ..."

He waved her feeble apology away. "You didn't know—few do. It happened just a few days ago."

Osana watched him, searching his face for signs of grief. But he wore an unreadable expression. Only his eyes gave him away, and they bore a look of resignation rather than sadness.

"So things never improved?" she asked softly.

He shook his head. "She suffered through every day of our marriage. She's happier now ... I suppose we both are."

He did not look happy, Osana observed. Her gaze dropped then to where he continued to toy with the blade of his knife, a nervous gesture and the only sign that this conversation put him on edge.

Like that day in the orchard, which seemed so long ago now, she observed the beauty of his hands: strong, with long fingers, and yet sensitive. So different from Raedwulf's heavy, blunt hands.

What would it feel like to have him touch her? What would his fingertips feel like trailing across her naked skin?

God's bones—what am I doing?

Osana jerked her gaze away.

It must be the shock of losing Raedwulf, the emotional-wrench of the funeral, and her anxiety at her new status in this hall. Otherwise, why else would she entertain such thoughts?

"Will you wed again?" she asked lightly, shifting her gaze to the barely touched platter before her. Osana's stomach clenched in a knot.

"The bishop would have me wed another—possibly a princess of Mercia or the East Angles—to strengthen our alliances in the south. However, I'd prefer not to."

Osana nodded. "I can understand that." She paused then, glancing up and meeting his eye once more. "It's easier for men. You can choose never to wed again and folk will accept that. However, a widow is useless ... an embarrassment."

He frowned. "Is that what you think you are?"

She clenched her jaw and paused before responding. "I know it to be true. I can weave, cook, and sew, but there is little other purpose for me here now that Raedwulf is gone." She broke off here, aware just how bitter she sounded. Yet now that she had started to reveal what lay in her heart, she could not stop. "Deogol and Edlyn will wish I'd thrown myself upon the bier and burned along with Raedwulf. A truly devoted wife might have."

The look of empathy on Aldfrith's face made her want to weep.

"You have choices, Osana," he replied. "You don't have to stay here."

She huffed out a breath. "Aye ... I could enter a nunnery or wed again. Yet I fear a nun's life would wear me down, and no man will have me."

He made a scoffing sound. "Nonsense."

Osana shook her head. "I cannot bear children," she said softly, her voice barely above a whisper. "No man wants a barren wife."

Her vision swam then, and she glanced down, blinking furiously. Curse her for drinking so much mead. It had made her imprudent.

A long silence drew out between them, while the hall roared with drunken laughter, cheering, and music. It was as if they sat upon an island, apart from it all.

Aldfrith spoke first. "You have another choice too, Osana."

She glanced up, forcing herself to look at him. He must think her hysterical and indiscreet. Yet she saw no scorn on his face, only compassion.

"If you decide you cannot remain here in Hagustaldes, Bebbanburg will welcome you," he continued. "You will always have a home in my hall, and will live under my protection if you need it. I promise you that."

Chapter Eleven

Slight Dignity

A GREY MANTLE settled across the land as the king and his men headed out of Hagustaldes—bound east for Bebbanburg.

The light levels were low, and the heavens heavy with the promise of rain.

Aldfrith squinted up at the grey sky, wondering how long the rain would hold off. One thing was certain—at some point during their two-day journey home, they would all get soaked.

He rode alongside the bishop this morning—not his choice of travel companion. However, Wilfrid seemed to have assigned himself as Aldfrith's personal escort and counsellor. He sat now, perched upon his dun gelding like an ill-tempered crow. Wilfrid had been in a sour mood since their arrival in Hagustaldes, and the day they had spent there had done little to lighten his spirits.

The bishop crossed himself and muttered a prayer under his breath as they left the last of the scattered wattle and daub hovels around the town behind, and entered a road through dense woodland.

Aldfrith's mouth curved in a wry smile. "Pleased to see the back of Hagustaldes?"

Wilfrid grunted. "Aye ... full of heathens."

Aldfrith raised an eyebrow. "Most of them are Christian folk, all baptized."

Wilfrid cast him a long suffering look. "They worship God, aye ... but in the manner of many folk in the north. Their pagan ways lie just beneath the surface." He broke off here, his craggy features darkening. "That funeral ceremony was an offence to God."

Aldfrith shrugged. "Folk have their traditions; we should respect them. You conducted the ceremony ... although you should have let Bishop Godwin do it."

Wilfrid scowled at the reprimand. "The man's a weak fool. I needed to set the folk of Hagustaldes a firm example."

"But they like Godwin ... he's a pious man."

"He should have never allowed them to organize such a ceremony. If I was bishop, things would change." Wilfrid's intense gaze settled upon Aldfrith. "Get rid of Godwin, sire. Let me have Hagustaldes under my influence."

Aldfrith frowned. He should not be surprised that Wilfrid was making such an audacious demand, and yet he was. "No, Father. Inhrypum is under your care, not this land. Bishop Godwin will stay where he is."

"But the fool prays in his church while the folk of Hagustaldes practice the old ways." Wilfrid's voice rose as his ire grew. "Soon they'll be sacrificing animals to the pagan gods for Blood Month and hailing Woden at Yule, while girls dance barefoot around fires with flowers in their hair at Eostre."

There's no harm in it," Aldfrith replied, deliberately not rising to the bishop's heckling tone. "A change of faith takes time."

Wilfrid glared at him. "That's what those monks upon Iona told you?" The scorn in the bishop's voice made Aldfrith tense.

Aldfrith let out a long sigh. He was not getting into this discussion again. Wilfrid took offense at the manner in which those of northern Britannia worshipped Christ. He missed no opportunity to criticize. However, his sniping had little effect on Aldfrith. He had his own faith, a steadying constant in his life, and did not care if the bishop thought it was a lesser one.

The bishop's views spoke of a vanity, of a need to feel superior to those around him. Wilfrid had not taken those years of exile well.

"No, they are my own views," Aldfrith replied, a warning note in his voice. "Ones I stand firm on."

With that, he nudged his grey stallion into a canter and left the bishop's side.

He had no desire to spend the day listening to Wilfrid's criticisms. Instead, he urged his stallion along the column of riders to where Cerdic rode just behind his bannermen.

"Good morning," Aldfirth greeted him.

The warrior blinked, coming out of a reverie. "Morning, sire." A half-smile curved Cerdic's lips then. "Had enough of the bishop already?"

Aldfrith snorted. "How did you know?"

Cerdic favored him with a wry look.

"I've seen the way the man shadows your steps. Does he ever spend any time in Inhrypum? He follows you around like a hound."

Aldfrith laughed. "Only he's far worse company than Argus."

The pair of them rode in companionable silence for a distance, their horses passing through mist-wreathed trees. The leaves were turning, the canopy a riot of gold and red. Aldfrith breathed in the scent of rich earth, moss, and damp vegetation.

His thoughts turned inward as he rode, traveling back to the funeral feast the night before—and to Osana.

Even pale with grief, and anxious about the future, she was lovely. After his experiences as a younger man, he now deliberately ignored the flirtatious smiles and limpid gazes of women, but there was something about Osana that made him unable to concentrate on anything else.

When she was near, he turned into a gawking fool.

He should not have made that offer—to invite her to live at Bebbanburg had been foolish. But the words had escaped before he had time to check them, and he could not take them back.

The last thing he needed was to be distracted by the comely widow. After Cuthburh, he vowed to have nothing to do with women. And yet when he looked at Osana, he forgot that promise.

She had looked so alone the night before, he'd wanted to help her.

Aldfrith exhaled sharply. *Enough.* He needed to turn his mind to other matters. Glancing right, his gaze alighted upon Cerdic's serious profile. His expression was grim, and Aldfrith wondered why.

He realized then that he knew very little about the warrior who had served him so loyally over the past two years.

"Why the frown, Cerdic?" he asked.

The warrior glanced across at him, surprised. Recovering, he grimaced. "I'm from Hagustaldes, sire," he said after a moment. "This visit brought back unwelcome memories."

Aldfrith watched him. "How so?"

He saw the discomfort on the man's face and immediately regretted the question. But a moment later Cerdic answered. "It reminds me of my wife … She died five summers ago, giving birth to our child. Both she and the babe died."

The raw pain in Cerdic's eyes as he said those last words was visceral. Even years on, the memory was an open wound. Suddenly, Aldfrith saw Cerdic with fresh eyes. The man's aloofness now made sense.

"I did not know of this loss," Aldfrith replied. "I'm sorry to hear it."

The warrior shrugged, the impenetrable mask he usually wore sliding back into place. "It's in the past now," he said, his tone making it clear that he wished to change the subject. "This visit just dredged up old memories … that's all."

Looking at his face, at the lines that formed deep grooves either side of his mouth and furrowed his brow, Aldfrith knew Cerdic was lying. He hid it well, but Aldfrith could see the warrior carried his grief with him every day.

It occurred to Aldfrith then that they were not really that different. He too carried scars from his past. He liked to think of himself as healed of them, yet his reaction to the ealdorman's widow revealed that, despite the passing of the years, they still pained him.

"Where shall I put these, Osana?" the servant asked. The woman—Lora—stood outside the space Osana and Raedwulf had once shared, her arms full of furs.

"Take them to my new alcove please," Osana replied. "This way."

Her own arms filled with clothing, Osana led the way around the rim of the hall to the alcove nearest the doors. It was the smallest of any of the sleeping spaces and the draftiest too—but at least she was not to sleep out on the main floor with the others.

At least they had left her some dignity.

Osana looked around the space, at the ceiling so low that she could not stand at her full height without knocking her head. Her mouth compressed.

A slight dignity.

"This isn't right." Lora's voice, low and angry, made Osana turn. The servant had deposited the furs but was now standing at the entrance to the alcove, hands on hips.

For the first time, Osana took proper notice of Lora. Small and curvaceous with curly blonde hair, a pert face, and bright blue eyes, Lora was roughly the same age as Osana. She had not been a servant in the ealdorman's hall for a long time—a handful of moons at most—and during that time Osana had been too immersed in her own unhappiness to take heed of her.

But she did now. Lora was genuinely outraged on her behalf, and Osana found that quizzical.

"You're Raedwulf's widow," Lora continued, her voice quiet yet brimming with indignation, "and this is the best they can give you. I've seen bigger store rooms. What about the alcove to the left of Deogol's?"

"Edlyn has kept that for her sister. She is moving in tomorrow."

Lora's face pinched at that. "Aye ... of course she is."

The servant's protectiveness of her made Osana smile. She had often felt so alone here; she had not realized she had a friend. With a sigh she glanced away, looking over at the trunks stacked in one corner—all her belongings from fourteen years of marriage.

"I'd hoped for a little more space," she admitted, "although if I'm honest, the farther I am from Deogol and Edlyn the better. I'll sleep easier in here."

She turned to find Lora watching her. The outrage had faded from her pretty face and was replaced by pity. Osana stiffened. The last thing she wanted was for Lora to feel sorry for her: the sad widow whose husband had humiliated her, and whom her brother and sister-by-marriage barely suffered.

"I know why Edlyn hates you," Lora said softly. "I saw her and Raedwulf together once ... when I was out blackberrying."

Osana flinched. Her gut had told her that Edlyn and Raedwulf had been lovers. But Lora had just confirmed it.

Osana's shoulders sagged. "Maybe I should go."

"Do you have relatives who would take you in?"

Osana shook her head. Both her parents were dead, and her sisters would not welcome her into their homes—not that there would be space in any of them for her. "I have an aunt in Jedworth," she said finally. "My mother's sister … although I haven't seen her in years." Osana broke off here, dismissing the idea. "She was always a bit shrewish."

I could go to Bebbanburg.

The thought came unbidden, and Osana shoved it aside. She was not sure why the king had made such an offer, yet it was not one she could ever take up. Tongues would wag; everyone would think she was his mistress.

Osana felt a blush rise up her neck at the thought.

"Well then," Lora huffed out a breath and gave Osana a determined look. "We'll have to make the best of this situation."

Osana laughed. "*We?* Don't trouble yourself, Lora. I'll survive … I always have."

Lora grinned back. "I don't doubt that. I just want you to know you're not alone here, that's all. Both of us could do with a friend in this place."

Osana held her gaze, a rush of gratitude bringing tears to her eyes. She was more starved of kindness than she thought.

"Thank you, she whispered. That means a lot to me."

Chapter Twelve

The Shamed Widow

"THAT BITCH HIT me. She must go!"

Edlyn's voice, shrill with rage, echoed through the hall.

"Calm yourself. You've the voice of a fishwife when riled." Deogol's patronizing rumble followed shortly after.

Inside her alcove, Osana allowed herself a tight smile. It sounded like Edlyn was not getting the sympathy she had hoped for. Reaching up, Osana touched her cheek. It still stung from the vicious slap Edlyn had delivered.

Osana had been helping chop vegetables at one of the worktables, chatting to Lora as she worked, when Edlyn had stalked up to her. She had thrust a pair of badly-mended breeches in her face. Osana had denied being the one to mend them, and Edlyn had struck her.

Osana was not given to violence; she had an even temper, and although she had been tried sorely of late, did not usually respond to Edlyn's attacks.

Yet until now they had only been verbal. Edlyn had never struck her before.

Osana's reaction had been instant, instinctive. She had punched Edlyn in the eye.

"Did you hear me, husband?" Edlyn's voice rose higher. "That woman, that *nithing,* dared strike me."

"I heard that you hit her first," Deogol replied. His tone sounded bored, as if he could hardly be bothered with this pettiness between women. Like his brother, he preferred to speak with men about hunting, fighting, and defending their borders.

"I did it because she is slovenly and must be punished," came Edlyn's reply. I am the ealdorman's wife. She must accept my punishment."

"Clearly, she does not."

"Have her whipped then."

Osana sucked in a breath at this. She had not considered how her behavior might be punished. She had not stopped to consider the consequences at all.

She glanced down at her right hand, still fisted. Her knuckles stung. She felt exhausted.

Six months of belittlement.

Six months of being treated like a dog, lower than the lowest servant.

Osana clenched her fist. *Let them whip me—I couldn't take any more.*

"She is my brother's widow," Deogol replied. "I'll not have her humiliated over nothing."

"Nothing?" Edlyn snorted, her voice raw now. "She struck me, and I will not tolerate it. She must go, Deogol. I don't care where. I won't have her under my roof for one more day!"

A chill silence fell, and even through the heavy tapestry that hung between Osana's alcove and the hall, she could feel the tension. She hoped Deogol would reprimand his wife for being so shrewish—Raedwulf would have done in his place—and yet the silence stretched on.

"Osana," the ealdorman called her name, raising his voice only slightly. As if he knew she would be listening—waiting. "Come here."

"Are you sure you want to come with me?" Osana glanced over her shoulder, from where she was tightening her palfrey's girth, and met Lora's eye. "It's not right that you should be banished too."

Lora snorted before busying herself with tying on the last of the packs behind the saddle of her horse. "Deogol did me a favor. I've tired of having Edlyn for a mistress. You can't travel alone anyway."

Osana huffed out a breath. Deogol had offered to provide them with an escort, yet Osana had refused. She knew two women traveling alone was not safe, although they had horses at least, but she did not want his assistance. Despite that she had no idea where she would go, a part of her thrilled at the thought of leaving Hagustaldes. She had felt muzzled, suffocated, by this place for so long that all she could see was a grim, colorless future. Now, the path ahead had promise.

Saddled and packed, the two women led their horses out of the stable into the yard beyond. It was a chill, windy morning; gusts blew straw and dirt across the hard packed earth. It was the second moon cycle after Yuletide, and it had been a strangely dry winter. At least they would not have to contend with mud on their journey.

Osana swung up onto the saddle and adjusted her skirts. Under her tunic, which had splits each side, she wore goat-skin leggings and high fur lined boots—this attire was more practical for riding and would keep her warmer too. She had ensured Lora was dressed the same way, although the woman did not look at ease, seated upon her palfrey.

A few yards away, Osana caught a flutter of movement out of her eye. The ealdorman and his wife had emerged from their hall to see her off. Tall and blond, his shoulders broad in the fur cloak he wore, Deogol's face was expressionless. Beside him, her right eye purpled, Edlyn was smiling. Their servants clustered around them, necks straining, as they watched the shamed widow take her leave.

Osana felt like spitting at them.

For years those men and women had smiled at her face and pretended to care about her—yet it had all been a lie. The relationship between them had only ever been that of master and servant. They had only seen her as a means of survival, and she could not blame them for that. Only, seeing the naked curiosity on their faces, she felt betrayed.

Osana glanced right at Lora. Her friend was trying to get comfortable in the saddle, her face creased in worry. Friends were rare, and yet over the past six months Lora had shown herself to be worthy of trust. They had worked side-by-side, cooking, cleaning, weaving, and sewing, becoming as close as sisters.

She sensed Lora's nervousness this morning but knew she would not leave her side.

"Are you ready?" Osana asked.

Lora glanced up and nodded.

Osana turned her palfrey, glancing back over her shoulder as she did so.

Deogol alone lifted a hand to bid her goodbye. No one else moved. Edlyn watched her, eyes bright with victory.

Aye, you might have won, Osana thought, *but I have no wish for your life. You are welcome to it.*

With that, she urged her palfrey into a trot and headed for the east gate out of Hagustaldes.

She could not leave this place soon enough.

Lora drew level with her as they passed through the gate and clattered over a wooden bridge. The road beyond led through the midst of fields filled with winter crops: kale, cabbage, garlic, and onions. Skeleton trees rose like supplicating hands into a pale sky.

"So you know where we're headed?" Lora asked, her blonde curls bouncing, cheeks flushed with cold.

Osana exhaled sharply, meeting her gaze.

"The only kin who'd have me lives to the north ... an aunt in Jedworth."

Lora's blue eyes narrowed. "You have no one else?"

Osana shook her head. "My sisters would all turn me away if I went to them."

Lora's frown deepened. "God's bones—why?"

"I'm the eldest of four girls ... there was a lot of competition between us growing up ... something our parents encouraged. None of my sisters could wed until I did, and they resented me for marrying so well. The rest of them wed thegns, but I ensnared an ealdorman." Osana did not bother to temper the irony in her voice.

"But surely they won't still resent you?"

Osana sighed. "None of them came to Raedwulf's funeral. None sent word to me afterward. No ... I will not darken any of their doors."

"And you're sure your aunt will welcome you? Jedworth is a long way to travel if you aren't sure ..."

Silence fell between them then, broken only by the rhythmic clump of their horses' hooves and the caw of a raven sitting in a nearby yew tree.

You will always be welcome at Bebbanburg.

Aldfrith's voice taunted her. How many times had she thought over his offer in the past months? How often had she dismissed it?

Osana swallowed, wetting her lips. "At Raedwulf's funeral the king ... made me an offer."

Lora's eyes went as big as moons. "What kind of offer?"

The naked suspicion in her friend's voice made Osana smile. "It's not like that. Or I don't think he meant it that way ... he saw how isolated I would be in Hagustaldes without Raedwulf. He took pity on me and said that if I wished to reside at Bebbanburg, he would offer me his protection."

Lora stared at her, stunned. "And you've waited till now to tell me?"

Osana sighed. "I've not truly contemplated his offer ... not till today." She broke off here, pushing aside a lock of hair that had escaped her braid and kept blowing into her eyes. "What do you think, Lora? Should we make new lives for ourselves in Bebbanburg?"

Lora watched her a moment longer before her cheek dimpled in a smile. "I think you'll receive a warmer welcome there than in Jedworth."

Dusk settled early that evening, windy and cold. The two women made camp a furlong from the road, in a hazel thicket.

Lora, who had brought flint and tinder with her, lit a fire in a narrow clearing while Osana went in search of wood. She returned, her arms full, to see that Lora had seen to the horses and was getting their supper ready. Osana squatted next to the fire and fed the tender flames some twigs. The fire was a beacon of warmth in the grey gloaming. The thicket protected them a little from the biting wind, but they would spend the night wrapped in their fur cloaks.

"Edlyn wasn't generous with her stores, but we've enough food to last us the journey to Bebbanburg," Lora announced, handing Osana a slab of bread with a peeled hard-boiled egg and a wedge of cheese.

Osana favored her with a wry smile in response. "Given how she feels about me, we're lucky she let us take any food."

Lora raised a sandy eyebrow. "I'll not miss that woman. Even before Raedwulf died, she made life difficult."

Osana swallowed a mouthful of bread. Over the past months, she had learned that Lora too was widowed, although her marriage had been a much happier one than Osana's. "It must have been hard for you, to go from being a wife to a servant?"

Lora shrugged, but Osana saw the tension on her face.

"I had a good life with Broga. He was a big man with an even bigger heart. We had a hut by the river, and when he was not out fighting for the king, he would fish for eels and trout, and help me tend our garden."

Lora paused, her gaze turning unfocused, for she was staring back into a past only she could see. "I knew when he marched north with King Ecgfrith that I'd never see him again."

Osana frowned. "How?"

Lora's gaze unclouded, and she met Osana's eye once more. "On the morning he left, I was helping him lace his leather armor and his bracers when I knew ... I just knew with a chilling certainty that he would never return home to me."

Osana lowered her bread to her lap. "He fell at Nechtansmere?"

Lora nodded.

"And did you say anything to him before he left ... try to warn him?"

Lora gave a soft laugh and shook her head. "He'd have thought me a goose. I had no proof, only a woman's intuition." She sighed then, as the memories washed over her. "No, I held my tongue and watched my man ride away."

Osana's eyes misted at Lora's words. "You should have not lost him so soon," she said gently, her voice catching, "but until you did, you were happy and in love. Nothing can take those memories from you." Osana's gaze shifted to the hungry flames that licked at the gathering darkness. She wished she had such memories to bring her solace on nights such as these.

Chapter Thirteen

A Wrong Decision

IT WAS COLD inside Aldfrith's annex. A low hearth flickered in one corner, but it barely seemed to throw out any heat. Argus huddled next to it, his whiskery muzzle resting on the river stones lining the hearth. A few feet away, Aldfrith sat, a heavy fur mantle about his shoulders. His breath steamed before him, and his fingers that held the quill ached with cold.

He barely noticed the chill, such was his concentration. The quill flew across the sheet of vellum as he wrote.

A low whine from his hound eventually roused him. Aldfrith raised his gaze, glancing over at where Argus was now watching him with pleading eyes. It was late morning, and the dog had not yet gone out for his walk.

Aldfrith smiled. "I haven't forgotten you, lad. Got lost in my work, that's all."

Argus thumped his tail, disturbing the thin layer of ash that lay around the hearth. Aldfrith frowned. This room was really getting filthy; he needed to let a servant in here to clean.

Leaning back, he flexed his numb hands before stretching his cramped back. The chill in here bit at him then, and his belly growled, reminding him he had retired to his annex without even breaking his fast that morning.

The door behind him was open, and grey, cold light filtered in. The lilt of servants' voices as they worked in the yard beyond reached him.

Aldfrith turned his attention back to Argus. "So, do you want to hear it?"

The wolfhound gave a soft whine and dropped his chin to the ground, his tail stilling.

Aldfrith snorted. "Your lack of enthusiasm stings ... yet I will read it to you all the same." He looked down at the page he had filled with slanted letters. Pleasure filtered through him, making the cold fade into the background once more. It was ridiculous really, the joy that writing gave him. He had awoken before dawn that morning, full of ideas that demanded to be given a voice.

Clearing his throat, he began to read, his voice low and steady in the quiet room.

"Learning is a beneficial occupation.

It makes a king of a poor person.
It makes an accomplished person of a landless one.
It makes an exalted family of a lowly one.
It makes a wise person of a fool.
Its commencement is good.
Its end is better.
It is respected in this world.
It is precious in the next."

"Well done, sire ... although I fear the wisdom of your words is lost on Argus."

The voice behind him made Aldfrith whirl toward the doorway. Cerdic stood there, leaning against the doorframe, muscular arms folded across his chest.

"How long have you been listening?" Aldfrith attempted to mask his embarrassment with a frown. He never read his work aloud to others.

Cerdic's mouth quirked. "Long enough ... folk will start calling you the 'mad king' if you keep talking to your hound like that."

Aldfrith huffed, his mortification fading. He was glad Cerdic had interrupted him and not someone else. Bishop Wilfrid was visiting from Inhrypum at the moment, and he had a habit of sneaking up on Aldfrith. The bishop had started visiting this annex, and the king had been careful to shield his writing from him.

"Let them." He rose to his feet and stretched the kinks out of his back. "They're probably right anyway."

Cerdic raised an eyebrow. "You're the sanest man I've ever met, sire."

Aldfrith smiled back, warming under the unexpected compliment. "Have you come to drag me into the hall for the noon meal?" he asked. It was not uncommon for folk to come looking for him in his annex; when he got engrossed in his work, time ceased to hold any meaning. The sun could rise and set without him even taking note.

Cerdic shook his head. "It's not yet time. You've visitors from Hagustaldes, sire. They await you indoors."

Osana shifted nervously upon the rushes and fought the urge to wring her hands together. Her decision to ride to Bebbanburg had felt like the right one on that first night out from Hagustaldes. She had not wanted to face her stern aunt, and the memory of the king's invitation had beckoned like a roaring fire.

At Bebbanburg she would have a real chance to start again. It was worth a try.

Only, with each passing furlong east, her resolve had started to crumble. And by the time the imposing outline of the fort appeared upon the horizon, she had been ready to turn her palfrey and try her luck with her aunt.

Lora had been the one to steady her nerves. "You said the king is a good man, a fair one. You should at least see if his offer still stands."

Lora gave her a reassuring smile now, her cheeks pink with cold. The weather, although still dry, had turned bitterly cold, promising snow. It was wonderful to be indoors out of the wind, warmed by the heat of the roaring hearths inside the Great Hall.

"He's here," Lora whispered, her blue eyes widening dramatically. "Woden's cods, the man's comely."

Osana cast Lora a quelling look, but had no time to shush her. Instead, she took a deep breath and turned to meet the tall blond man who strode across the rushes toward her.

Aldfrith looked imposing this morning; the fur mantle he wore made his shoulders look broader than she remembered. A few steps behind him followed the leather-clad, muscular warrior who had met them upon their arrival. That man had short brown hair, an intimidating face, and a scowl that made her feel nervous.

To make matters worse, Bishop Wilfrid was sitting upon the high seat, playing Cyningtaefl—King's Table—with a warrior. He was watching her with a look of thinly veiled suspicion. In fact, there had been few smiles from anyone since she had stepped inside The Great Tower of Bebbanburg, just curious stares. Two women traveling alone and seeking an audience with the king would have tongues flapping all over the fort by mid-afternoon.

Perhaps I misheard the king all those months ago.

"Lady Osana," Aldfrith stopped before her, his midnight-blue gaze meeting hers. His face was serious, giving nothing of his mood away. "This is unexpected."

Panic surged through Osana. *I shouldn't have come here.*

She could feel Lora's gaze burning into her and wondered if she thought her a liar. Swallowing, Osana took a nervous step toward the king and curtsied. "Good morning, milord. I'm sorry to disturb you ... but I recall our conversation last year." Her voice faltered, as his expression did not change. "In Hagustaldes ... you said that if I should ever need it, I would have your protection." Her face was burning now, and it felt as if every pair of eyes in the hall was now riveted upon her.

They'll think me a wickedly bold woman.

Osana dropped her gaze to the rushes, her heart hammering now. Never had she wished for the ground to open up and swallow her whole, yet she did now. Desperation had turned her into a fool. "I apologize, sire," she said softly. "I must have misheard you."

"No ... you did not," the answer came, almost as soft as her own, and she glanced up to see he was watching her, a rueful look upon his face. "I did promise you my protection ... should you ever need it." He inclined his head slightly, the intensity in his eyes unnerving. "What happened?"

Osana heaved in a deep breath. She felt exposed standing here with everyone gawking at her, yet she had no choice but to answer him. "Life in Hagustaldes became impossible, sire ... the ealdorman's wife will not suffer my presence under her roof. Deogol sent me away."

Aldfrith's gaze flicked to where Lora stood behind her. "You traveled with no escort?"

Osana shook her head. "Just my handmaid, sire. Deogol offered an escort but I refused."

The king's mouth thinned. His eyes darkened as his blond brows drew together. Osana wondered if he thought her foolish.

"Surely you have relatives, woman?" Bishop Wilfrid called down from the high seat. "You have no need to throw yourself at the king's feet."

Osana dropped her gaze to the rushes once more and fought a cringe. It took all her will to remain standing where she was. She wanted to bolt, to run from Bebbanburg and never return.

"That's enough, Father," the king's voice was clipped when he spoke. "I shall ask the questions here."

Surprised by the commanding edge to his tone, Osana glanced up to find the king still observing her.

"I made you a promise, and I shall keep it," he said.

Osana held his gaze for a moment, wilting under its force. He still had not smiled. He was clearly regretting his offer. "Sire," she spoke up. "I will not hold you to it, for I see now I was rash to come here. I will go now ... sorry for disturbing you."

She hurriedly dipped into a curtsey before casting a glance over her shoulder at where Lora stared at her, her face flushed with embarrassment. "Come, Lora."

Osana stepped around the king with the intention of bolting across the rushes toward the doors, but he caught her by the arm, pulling her up short.

The physical contact shocked her, and her head snapped round. Their gazes met and held for a heartbeat.

"You aren't disturbing me," he said. His voice was as gentle as his grip was firm. Heat flooded through Osana, only this time it was not embarrassment but something else—a sensation she had not felt in a long while.

Pure, undiluted desire.

"I'm sorry for the cool welcome," he continued, "but your arrival was a surprise."

Osana wet her lips, aware that his gaze had now lowered to her mouth. "I had no time to send word," she replied.

Aldfrith blinked and released her, stepping back. A gulf of cold air rushed in-between them, and a strange disappointment swept over Osana. Mastering it, she watched as a smile curved his mouth.

"You will stay here, Lady Osana. I will have an alcove prepared for you and your handmaid."

His tone brooked no argument. Although softly spoken, there was a power to this man's voice that checked her.

"We will earn our keep, milord," she replied, wretched. It was still there, even after all this time—this heat between them that made her senses come alive. For that reason alone she should have stayed away from Bebbanburg. He knew it too; she could see it in his eyes. That was why his welcome was cool. He had made that offer at an unguarded moment and now regretted it. "My handmaid and I can cook, weave, and sew. We can—"

"I'm sure of it," he cut her off, still smiling. He took another step back from her and gestured toward the high seat. "The noon meal is almost upon us. Please join me, and take a cup of mead to celebrate your arrival."

The words were cordial, but forced. With a sinking heart, and a beseeching look at Lora, Osana followed him across the hall.

Chapter Fourteen

Out of Sight

ALDFRITH SETTLED INTO his carven chair, his gaze returning to the pale-faced woman who now took a seat to his left. Osana's face was taut, her hazel eyes startled, and her shoulders tense.

The widow looked different to the last time he had seen her: gone were the mourning clothes and head-rail that had framed her face in Hagustaldes. Instead, she wore a high-necked, woolen tunic that fitted her curvaceous form snugly, girded at the waist with a narrow leather belt. Her hair—the color of richly polished oak—fell in a thick braid over one shoulder.

Opposite Osana, Bishop Wilfrid helped himself to another cup of mead, studying her with a jaundiced eye. "You are a bold woman," the bishop commented. "To walk into your king's hall and demand he take you in. Have you no shame?"

Osana visibly blanched at the reprimand. However, she did not look away from the bishop. Her chin rose as she answered him. "The king invited me here, Father."

"I did, so let us dispense with the accusations," Aldfrith swiftly added. "Let us eat in peace."

"Aye," Cerdic piped up from where he sat next to the bishop. "You've a scowl that could curdle milk, Father."

Osana's handmaid, who was circling the table with a jug of mead, grinned at Cerdic's comment. She was blonde with a pretty smile and bright blue eyes.

Aldfrith too fought a smile; Cerdic said little, but when he did speak, his words were known to hit the mark.

Wilfrid's scowl deepened, and he cast the warrior an icy look. Yet Cerdic just ignored him and held up his cup to be filled. As he did so, the warrior saw Osana's handmaid was still smiling and favored her with a wink.

The woman inclined her head in answer.

Watching them, Aldfrith noted it was the first time he had seen Cerdic interact with a woman in such a light-hearted manner. The arrival of this bright-eyed woman had drawn his eye.

Cerdic was not the only one distracted.

Aldfrith found it difficult to focus on the trencher of mutton stew and braised onions that a servant placed before him. Osana—even pale and tense as she was—made his hunger disappear.

It had been a shock to see her.

He had regretted making that offer after her husband's funeral, had thought upon his rash words all the way back to Bebbanburg. But with the passing of the months he had relaxed, confident she had dismissed his offer as folly.

Bishop Wilfrid, despite his blunt way of putting things, was right. It was not seemly for an attractive widow to walk into his hall, unescorted, and remind him of his promise. He had seen the panic on her face though when they had locked eyes earlier; she had regretted coming here, had wanted to flee.

Even now, she looked poised to run. If the bishop continued to sting her, she would, for she was a proud woman with an independent spirit.

Aldfrith drew in a deep breath and started on his meal.

Fool.

He should have kept his mouth shut. But she had looked so lonely sitting there after the funeral—a show of brittle strength—that the words had been out before he could stop them.

The truth was that he did not want her here.

Life had been simpler after Cuthburh's departure. For the first time since leaving the peace of Iona, he had begun to enjoy life again. He no longer had to suffer stony silences at every meal time, or lie watching his wife's back night after night. These days he shared his alcove only with his hound, and Argus was far more pleasant company.

He had fallen into a comfortable routine at Bebbanburg now; his time was divided between ruling, writing, and hawking. He enjoyed his contact with the people he ruled and had grown comfortable with making the decisions that went with his role. The folk of Northumbria seemed to have accepted him as their king too.

Aldfrith glanced up, his gaze settling once more upon Osana. She was picking at her meal, eyes downcast. The light of the cressets behind her illuminated her smooth, milky skin and long eyelashes.

The truth was that this woman had fascinated him from the first moment he had set eyes upon her. She made him feel restless, she took away his peace. If she was to remain in Bebbanburg, he would need to keep her at arm's length.

Aldfrith had fought hard to regain his equilibrium, to find his place in the world. He liked his life as it was—safe, predictable, and measured.

"We should leave." Osana folded up a tunic and placed it upon a narrow wooden shelf. "I can't live here."

"Hwaet?" Lora's incredulous response made Osana glance over her shoulder. Her friend wore an exasperated expression. "After everything you put yourself through today? For that alone you deserve to stay."

Osana huffed out a breath. "You saw the king's face. He was mortified. I embarrassed him by coming here."

"Aye, but he recovered swiftly enough." Lora's expression grew sly then. "He couldn't take his eyes off you."

Osana's chest constricted. This was not welcome news. "Even more reason to leave," she replied, turning away so Lora would not see her embarrassment. "The bishop spoke true. I've been overly bold."

Lora snorted. "That old crow."

Osana pulled out another tunic from her pack and folded it. Despite her tense mood, a smile tugged at her mouth. Lora's irreverence was comforting. She had even made the king's captain soften his expression.

"He wasn't the only one who glared at me," Osana said after a long pause. "Did see the way those women weaving looked at me after the noon meal."

"No worse than how Edlyn used to glare. At least none of them carries a personal grievance against you."

Osana sighed and looked around the alcove. It was easily three times the size of the space she had occupied in Deogol's hall. A large pile of furs for her dominated one corner, with another bed for Lora opposite. The scent of crushed lavender, for the herb had been scattered over the rushes underfoot, filled the alcove, and a single cresset burned on the walls. Beyond the heavy tapestry that shielded them from view, she could hear the murmur of voices as folk readied themselves to retire for the evening, the clang of pots as servants cleaned up, and the groan of the wind buffeting the tower walls.

"Do you want to stay here, Lora?" she asked, glancing over at her.

Lora met her gaze, her expression turning serious. "I'll happily go wherever you do, Osana."

"That doesn't answer my question."

Lora shrugged. "Aye, I'd be happy to remain here, but if you'd truly prefer to travel to Jedworth then so be it ... only you should give Bebbanburg a chance. At least wait the winter out. By spring you might see things differently."

Snow fell the first night of Osana's arrival in Bebbanburg. She awoke the following morning to find a blanket of white covering the world. The chill seeped into the tower through the damp stone. Away from the four roaring fire pits, the cold drilled into her joints and numbed her fingers. Swathed in furs, Osana broke her fast with bread and broth, before she and Lora joined the group of women who spent their days spinning and weaving.

Osana picked up her distaff and a basket of wool, preparing to start work.

The women—thegns' wives—did not give Osana a warm welcome. Even Eldflaed, the woman who had been so chatty with Osana during her last visit to the fort, ignored her. The morning stretched out, and Osana started to enjoy being left in peace. As Lora had pointed out, there was no strong ill-feeling toward her, only a watchful distrust.

If she worked hard and minded her manners, Osana would be accepted in time.

Across the hall, she spotted the king emerging from his alcove and cross to the high seat, where he broke his fast with his men. She watched them talking, glad that Aldfrith had not seen her. It was best she remained a shadow here: out of sight, beneath notice.

The king did not linger at the table long. After a short discussion with his companions, he rose from the high seat and strode from the hall, a grey wolfhound loping at his side. His men followed him.

The morning passed slowly, and after a long spell winding wool onto a distaff, Osana put her spindle aside and went outdoors while Lora went to help the other servants prepare the noon meal.

The sting of the icy air hit Osana across the face as she gingerly made her way down the slippery steps to the yard below. The wind had died, and it had started to snow again, gentle fluttering flakes that drifted down from an ashen sky.

She turned her face up to it, enjoying the feel of the snowflakes kissing her skin. A moment later a group of horses rode under the high gate into the yard.

The king led them. Snow frosted his mantle and blond hair. His hound followed close behind, tongue lolling. Aldfrith carried a quiver of arrows and a long bow over one shoulder, as did many of his men. A boar carcass was slung over the back of one of the horses.

Standing there in the midst of the yard, Osana felt dangerously exposed. She looked around for somewhere to hide, but it was too late. Aldfrith had already seen her.

He pulled up his horse just a couple of yards away from Osana and swung down off its back, his boots sinking into a foot of snow.

"Good day, Lady Osana," he greeted her.

"A chill morning for a hunt, milord," she replied.

He smiled at that before gesturing to the boar that dripped crimson blood onto the milk-white snow. "It's easier to spot prey in the snow." He reached down and patted his hound's head, for the beast had sat down at his feet. "However, Argus nearly got himself gored."

Osana pulled her fur mantle close, casting an eye over the dog. "I've never heard a hound called by that name before."

"It's a name from my mother's people," he replied. "Argus is a mythical creature with a hundred eyes. A good name for a sight hound, I think."

"Aye, the beast has his uses," the king's captain, who had entered the stable yard behind Aldfrith, added. He dismounted from his horse and nudged the dog with his foot. "But for the most part he just takes up space before the fire ... and farts."

Osana laughed, the sound echoing out across the still morning. Shocked at the loud sound of her mirth, she clapped her hand across her mouth. Yet when she glanced over at Aldfrith, she saw he was smiling.

Their gazes locked and held for a long, drawn-out heartbeat.

Lora trudged through the snow, her fur-lined boots sinking through the pristine crust. The air was so cold outdoors that it stung her face. In one hand she carried a wooden bucket, while with the other she did her best to pull her fur mantle close.

"Thunor's balls," she muttered. It was one of her favorite curses—one that her father had taught her. "Any colder and my breath will freeze."

She walked toward the stone well that sat on the edge of the stable yard, just beyond the orchard. She and Osana needed some fresh water for their alcove, for washing.

Crossing the yard, she saw men leading out horses from the stables while the stalls were mucked out. One of the warriors—the man who had winked at her the day prior—was checking the horses' hooves.

He had been the first person to greet them upon their arrival at the Great Tower. She could not recall his name, but there was something about him that fascinated her. He wore an intimidating expression most of the time, and yet she had seen yesterday that he had a dry sense of humor. It had been a while since a man had made her laugh—not since Broga.

Lora's gaze slid over the warrior, taking in the breadth of his leather-clad shoulders and chest, and the strength in his arms that gleamed with armrings. Not since Broga had a man even drawn her eye, yet this one did.

So intent was she on staring that Lora failed to notice the patch of ice that spread out around the well, where the snow had frozen solid. The moment her booted foot stepped upon it, her legs flew out from under her.

With a scream, Lora fell onto her back, the bucket flying from her hand.

"Cods," she muttered as she struggled to right herself. She had sunk into the snow and was now cast like a sheep. Her face flamed; she hoped none of the warriors outside the stables had seen her tumble. She needed to get to her feet before one of them did.

Too late.

A shadow fell over her, and a deep male voice intruded. "Are you hurt?"

Lora looked up into laughing male eyes, heat rising up her neck when she realized it was the warrior she had just been staring at.

"No," she replied, embarrassment making her snappish.

"Here." Grinning now, he held out a hand. "You look like you could do with some help."

Lora reached out, grasping his hand. The warmth and strength of it felt good, and she tightened her grip on him before pulling herself up. He lifted her easily, as if she were no more than a child.

A moment later they were standing close. Lora let go of him and made a fuss of brushing snow off herself, flustered now. "Thank you," she murmured. She was not usually this coy, did not usually have problems meeting a man's eye. Yet she suddenly felt shy.

"You're welcome," he replied, his voice warm, the laughter now gone. "We weren't introduced yesterday. I'm Cerdic."

She glanced up, her gaze meeting dark brown eyes. His expression was warm, a slight smile tugging at his mouth. Warmth spread through her then, and she felt her own lips curving in response. "My name is Lora."

Chapter Fifteen

I am my own man

A VISITOR ARRIVED at the Great Tower of Bebbanburg five days after Osana's arrival.

The last of the snow had melted, leaving a sea of mud in its wake. Men kept tracking it into the hall, only to earn a scolding from the women who tried in vain to keep the rushes clean. Mid-morning, as Osana sat mending a tunic, humming a tune under her breath to help ease the monotony, the doors to the Great Hall swung open, and a slender figure swathed in voluminous, brown robes entered.

The newcomer wore a solemn expression. He had a gaunt, bearded face, and a neatly shaved tonsure. His dark eyes swept around the interior of the hall with interest. Two monks in simple brown habits flanked him.

Osana continued to sew, observing the man with interest. He was so frail that it was impossible to discern his age. He walked stiffly, yet carried an air of authority with him.

"It's Cuthbert, Prior of Lindisfarena," one of the women next to Osana whispered. "We've not seen him here in years." Her name was Mildryth, and she was one of the few of the gaggle of wives who bothered with Osana, for Eldflaed and her friends still paid Osana scant attention.

Osana's fascination increased. News of Cuthbert had spread far and wide across the north over the years. Tales of his miracles and his unshakable faith had first reached Osana when she was a child. Folk spoke of his extraordinary powers: healing the sick and freeing those who were possessed by demons.

"He looks much older than I expected," she mused aloud.

Mildryth made a clucking sound. "Aye, years of fasting and praying are taking their toll."

"I heard he healed a man of leprosy," Lora whispered, her gaze fascinated as she tracked Cuthbert across the floor. "Folk say the fisherman was covered in sores when he traveled to Lindisfarena, and that he returned home healthy."

Mildryth nodded, her long face serious. "Aye, there are many such tales."

A draft of cold air rushed into the hall, and Osana tore her gaze from the newcomer to see the king stride indoors. She had not yet seen him today. Mildryth had told her that he often spent mornings writing and studying in the stone annex adjoining the tower. Osana had passed the annex the day before, after returning from Bebbanburg's market. The door was open, and she had been tempted to go inside. Fortunately, she had curbed her curiosity.

The priest Oswald entered a few paces behind the king, his robes fluttering in his haste.

Aldfrith's face was alive with joy as he approached Cuthbert. The interior of the Great Hall fell silent, all gazes riveted upon the king and the hermit. Aldfrith dropped to one knee before Cuthbert then, bowing his head. He took the frail hand that the prior offered and kissed it.

"Father Cuthbert ... it's an unexpected pleasure to see you here again. I'd heard you were unwell?"

Cuthbert grimaced. "Aye, my health worsens I'm afraid."

"Welcome to Bebbanburg, Father." Oswald bowed low, his face flushed. "May God grant you a speedy recovery."

The Prior of Lindisfarne favored Oswald with a wry smile. "If only he could ... alas, I fear there's little anyone—even Our Lord—can do."

A subdued mood fell over the interior of the Great Hall then, dimming the excitement of the prior's arrival.

Aldfrith rose to his feet. Standing next to the prior—tall and strong, and in the prime of life—Aldfrith made Cuthbert look even more fragile. Reaching out, the king placed a hand on the prior's shoulder. "I'm pleased you have managed a visit here, Father. Will you stay a night or two?"

Cuthbert nodded, smiling. "Aye, a warm fire and a good meal would ease these old bones."

Osana carried the ewer of wine to the high seat, stepped up onto the raised dais, and began a slow circuit of the table. The rich aroma of boar stew filled the tower, mixed with the scent of freshly baked griddle bread. Her mouth filled with saliva as she watched the stew being served from a huge tureen. The cold had given her a voracious appetite of late.

She could not take her seat at one of the low tables yet though; this evening she had been given the task of serving the king and his retainers wine. This role usually fell to the womenfolk of the household, but since the king had no wife, and she was an ealdorman's widow, the task had fallen to her.

Osana stopped at Aldfrith's elbow, waiting until he had finished speaking to Cuthbert, before she drew his attention. "Wine, sire?"

Aldfrith looked up, and their gazes met. The impact of it unnerved her, as it had that day in the snow. She had avoided looking at him directly ever since, for she was sure she had looked flustered that day—as she most likely did now.

"Aye, thank you, Osana."

She leaned forward and poured the wine, acutely aware of his nearness, of the scent of leather and the male musk of his skin. Osana swallowed, her belly fluttering.

What was wrong with her? Merely standing next to the king turned her into a giddy maid. Ever since arriving here, she had found her gaze drawn to him whenever he was in the hall. A few times she had caught herself staring, only to admonish herself afterward. She knew enough about the world, and of men, not to let herself become infatuated.

She had been infatuated with Raedwulf once, before they had wed. The disappointment that had come later had been almost too much to bear.

"Osana ... that is a fair name." Prior Cuthbert's voice drew Osana's attention. Grateful for the distraction, she glanced over at him and smiled. "Thank you, Father."

Up close, his face was even gaunter: his cheeks hollowed, his eyes sunken. However, there was a clarity, an understanding in those dark eyes, that made her instinctively trust him.

"You are a newcomer to this hall, are you not?" he asked.

"Aye, Father. I'm the widow of Raedwulf of Hagustaldes."

Cuthbert's gaze widened, before he glanced over at the king. "Why does an ealdorman's widow live here?"

"I've granted Osana my protection," Aldfrith replied, his face giving nothing away. "She is my ward."

Cuthbert pursed his lips. Watching him, Osana was glad that Bishop Wilfrid was not here. The bishop had returned to Inhrypum three days before, and it was just as well. He would have enjoyed this. Finally, someone to vindicate his opinion, and the Prior of Lindisfarena nonetheless.

"I heard that Queen Cuthburh left," the prior said after a lengthy pause.

"Aye, she took the veil at Berecingas," Aldfrith replied. Did Osana imagine it, or was there a warning note in his voice. She glanced back at him, trying to read his features. Aldfrith of Northumbria was an enigma. There were times he appeared gentle and distracted, as if his thoughts were far from here, but when challenged she saw him shift. Folk mistook his gentle manner for weakness at their peril.

Cuthbert was no fool either. He inclined his head, observing the king for a moment before offering his cup to Osana.

"Just a drop please ... with my water."

Osana nodded, poured the prior's wine, and moved on. As she did so, Cuthbert spoke again. "So you intend to remain unwed?"

"Aye." Aldfrith's response was clipped.

"What of an heir to the throne?"

"I have a cousin who would be happy to be my successor."

"But surely you want a son?"

A hush fell. Osana continued her way up the table, filling cups as she went. She deliberately did not look the king or the prior's way, although she could almost taste the tension that had settled upon the high seat.

Was this what had brought the prior—ill and frail as he was—to Bebbanburg? A plea for the king to remarry?

Eventually, Aldfrith spoke. "As Oswiu's son, I've always known I might be called upon to rule," he said quietly. "I've accepted that responsibility, but it ends there. For the rest I am my own man. I will not wed again; I will not father a son."

The finality of his words, the barely masked bitterness behind them, surprised Osana. She finished pouring the priest's wine and straightened up, her gaze traveling back to the king. He sat back in his carven chair, apparently relaxed; only the clenched fingers that curved around his cup gave his mood away. His eyes were narrowed.

What happened to you? She thought sadly. Had his experience with Cuthburh scarred him so deeply that he would not consider marriage ever again? No—it had to be something else, something from his past. For all his apparent serenity, Aldfrith bore deeper wounds that he took great pains to hide.

"That is sad news indeed," Cuthbert replied. The prior's voice was subdued in his response. "You are a worthy king, milord, and would bear worthy sons."

Osana could not sleep.

Cuthbert and his monks occupied Osana and Lora's alcove tonight, and the women slept in the hall, stretched out upon furs. Osana did not mind her new lodgings much, although Lora complained that the men's snoring would keep her awake.

Cerdic slept near them, to ensure the women were not bothered by some of the younger men who slept around the hearths. Osana could not help but notice that the warrior's presence appeared to put Lora on edge. She was usually light-hearted and chatty in the evenings, but as soon as he lay down his fur cloak and stretched out upon it, Osana's maid went quiet. However, she could not seem to keep her eyes off Cerdic, her gaze darting to him whenever he looked elsewhere. Osana observed her with interest, noting that Cerdic too had taken to looking Lora's way when her gaze was averted.

A dance, as old as time itself.

Osana wondered where it would lead. Although Lora had lost her husband, she had such an infectious joy for life that Osana could not imagine her alone forever. Yet Cerdic appeared so aloof. In fact, his expression only softened when he looked Lora's way.

Lora stretched out onto her furs without any of her usual observations about the day they had just spent, bid Osana good night, and pulled a fur over her head.

Lying on her back in the dimly lit hall, staring up at the shadowed rafters far above, Osana listened to the sounds of the slumbering hall around her. Neither Cerdic nor Lora stirred, although nearby a babe was whimpering. A moment later, a woman's soft voice soothed it.

Osana lay there a while longer, willing sleep to come. Yet she felt wide-awake tonight, her mind far too active.

Cuthbert's visit had set her thinking. The prior's presence had unsettled the daily routine of the hall, and although he had not brought up the subject of Aldfrith taking a wife again, there was a tension between them.

Time stretched on, the hall quietened further, but slumber still eluded her. Eventually, with a huff of annoyance, she sat up. Perhaps a walk in the yard and some fresh night air would bring tiredness upon her.

She pulled on her boots and rose to her feet. Then she scooped up the fur cloak she had been sleeping on, cast it over her shoulders, and picked her way out of the hall.

Twin braziers burned beneath the tower outside, casting the pitted stone in a red-gold hue. The air was damp and chill, and the sky overcast. A waxing moon played hide-and-seek with the clouds overhead. Two guards flanked the doors, their spears glinting in the light of the braziers.

Clasping her cloak close, Osana greeted them. She then took a torch off a bracket beside the doors, lit it from one of the braziers, and made her way across the yard to the orchard. It was deserted tonight, the naked limbs of the branches spidery against the sky. There was no sound save the rumble of the surf on the shore below the fort.

Osana walked slowly, deep in thought. The quiet and solitude calmed her active mind, as they always did. After days in the busy tower, she sometimes felt overwhelmed. Raedwulf's hall had been crowded, yet the Great Hall of Bebbanburg was never still. Only at the darkest hour of the night, or in the grey light of early dusk, did it lie silent.

Can I stay here?

Cuthbert's visit had put her on edge. She had just begun to relax, to hope she might find a new life in Bebbanburg, when the prior had drawn attention to her again.

Perhaps I should go to my aunt in the spring. The thought did not thrill Osana, but at least in Jedworth she would not be an embarrassment to anyone. How many times would Aldfrith have to defend his decision to let her live here before he tired of it?

Circling back to the tower, Osana slowed her step further. She was loath to return to her place by the fire. If it had not been so cold, she would have remained out here all night.

She was approaching the steps when a faint glow to her right drew her eye. *Firelight.* The door to the king's annex was ajar, and a fire still burned bright in the hearth within.

Osana paused, surprised. It seemed she was not the only one who could not sleep this evening.

Chapter Sixteen

Cast Her Out

OSANA TOOK TWO steps toward the stairs leading back to the Great Tower and stopped.

I shouldn't disturb him.

A wiser woman would go back to her place by the hearth and attempt to sleep, yet Osana did not feel like being wise tonight. She had barely exchanged more than a handful of words with the king since her arrival at Bebbanburg, and longed to speak with him. Frustration boiled up within her. She would get no better chance than now.

Inhaling deeply, she retraced her steps and walked toward the annex. She stopped before the door and knocked softly.

A dog's growl sounded from within, a low warning.

"King Aldfrith," Osana said, forcing herself to speak, before her nerve failed her. "It's Osana. Can I enter?"

A long silence followed before a low male voice replied. "Aye."

Osana pushed open the door. The wolfhound, which had been lying down near the hearth, rose to his feet, hackles raised, growling.

"Be still, Argus," Aldfrith commanded, getting up from where he had been sitting at a wide table strewn with sheets of vellum. At the sight of Osana, he inclined his head. "It's late to be awake?"

Osana smiled, hoping the expression would mask her nervousness. "I couldn't sleep and thought a walk in the orchard might soothe me. Then I saw I wasn't the only one still up."

Aldfrith stretched, a rueful smile creeping across his face. "I sometimes have trouble sleeping."

"So, it's not Prior Cuthbert's visit?"

His gaze widened at her directness, and Osana resisted the urge to bite her lip. Raedwulf had always chastised her for speaking boldly. She had not wanted to anger the king; she was just curious to understand the man who wore the crown. In just her short time at Bebbanburg, he had become a fascination to her. He seemed both wise and insecure, resolute and lost.

"Aye," he huffed out his response after a pause. "Cuthbert was only giving me wise counsel, but he doesn't understand me. I'm not my father ... or my brother."

Osana raised an eyebrow. "I think he'll be grateful you're not." News had reached Hagustaldes of how Cuthbert had begged Ecgfrith not to go to war against the Pictish warlord Bridei mac Beli. The king had ignored him at his peril. "Yours is a peaceful reign ... is that not better for the kingdom?"

Aldfrith raked a hand through his short blond hair. "I don't have the right character to rule. I'm a scholar ... that's all I ever wanted from life."

Osana moved over to the hearth and warmed her chilled fingers over the dancing flames. She was aware of Aldfrith's gaze tracking her. He was still standing by his desk.

"I like this room," she murmured, glancing around at the pitted stone walls, where two clay cressets burned. A wooden shelf above the king's writing table held two leather-bound volumes. Osana's gaze widened. "Are those *books*?"

Aldfrith's mouth quirked. "Aye ... a parting gift from the monks on Iona. Would you like to see one?"

Osana nodded. She had heard that monks knew their letters and spent long days creating beautifully illustrated pages.

Aldfrith retrieved one of the volumes and handed it to her. It was heavy, and she opened it with trepidation, careful not to damage the spine. Her breath caught as she slowly leafed through the vellum sheets: intricate drawings of the lives of saints, accompanied by columns of beautiful calligraphy.

"How I wish I could read," she whispered.

"I can teach you."

Osana's head snapped up. Only monks, scholars, and a handful of nuns could actually read. "You would?"

He gave her a slow smile, one that made her belly flutter. "Aye ... how about tomorrow afternoon for your first lesson."

Cuthbert did not look well at all the following morning.

His face was pale, his eyes watery, as he nursed a cup of weak broth. He would touch no food, not even a piece of dry bread.

"Shall I send for a healer, Father?" Oswald asked. He had been watching the prior with an anxious gaze ever since Cuthbert had shuffled from his alcove.

Cuthbert shook his head. "There's no need. No healer can help me now."

At the head of the table, Aldfrith stiffened. The desolate look in the prior's eyes alarmed him. Cuthbert spoke as a doomed man.

Seeing his expression, Cuthbert's small pursed mouth curved. "Don't look so horrified, Lord Aldfrith," he said quietly. "From the day we're born, we're all dying ... some of us just know our time is near."

The admission made Oswald suck in his breath and caused the two monks who had accompanied Cuthbert to exchange nervous glances.

Aldfrith leaned toward the prior, frowning. "Maybe you should remain at Bebbanburg until the weather warms. You'd be more comfortable here."

Cuthbert shook his head, resolute. "The Farne Isles are where my heart belongs, and where I wish to die. I will return to Lindisfarena and end my days there."

There was no fear in the man's voice, no self-pity, just a gentle acceptance and a dignity that moved Aldfrith. He hoped when his own end neared, he could show such strength. "I'm sorry about yesterday, Father," he said after a pause, suddenly regretting he had been so harsh with a dying man. "I know your counsel was well-meant."

Cuthbert's gaze held his. "Aye ... but that doesn't mean you will take it."

Aldfrith responded with a wry smile. "My mother once said I've the stubbornness of an ox."

The prior's smile widened. "A trait you no doubt inherited from your father. Do you remember Oswiu?"

Aldfrith's smile faded. "He left when I was a babe. I have no memory of him at all."

"You have his presence, his quiet strength," Cuthbert observed. "He too was a man who knew his own mind. Yet you are different to him in many ways."

"He was a warrior, I'm a scholar," Aldfrith replied, surprised that bitterness rose within him as he spoke. "We are as different as the sun and the moon."

Cuthbert shook his head and raised his cup of broth to his lips. Aldfrith noted that his hands were trembling. "There is more to being king than being able to wield a sword, Aldfrith."

Despite Aldfrith's insistence that he stay on longer in Bebbanburg, Cuthbert took his leave mid-morning. Leaning heavily on a cane, he shuffled from the hall, flanked by his escorts. Aldfrith and his men followed close behind. In the yard outside the tower, the prior climbed upon a small cart, and they rumbled out of the inner perimeter, following the King's Way to the low gate.

Folk lined the thoroughfare to greet Cuthbert as he passed, craning forward to catch a glimpse of the man who had become legend across Britannia. They called out to the king too, their faces alight with smiles. Aldfrith smiled back, acknowledging the folk of Bebbanburg with a wave.

They had nearly reached the low gate when they met a group of travelers entering the fort. Aldfrith's heart sank when he recognized the tall, rawboned figure perched atop a horse, a cluster of servants riding behind him.

Wilfrid.

The bishop rode toward them before swinging down from his horse. He then moved over to where the prior had stopped, and knelt before him.

"Father ... I heard you were here and came as soon as I could."

Cuthbert favored the bishop with a tired smile. "There was really no need, Father Wilfrid. As you can see, my visit was too brief to warrant you traveling all this way."

Wilfrid's heavy features creased in concern as he rose to his feet. "You're unwell?"

Cuthbert nodded. "Aye, and returning home to rest."

The bishop gestured to his servants, indicating that they should continue up to the Great Tower without him. "Then I will accompany you, Father."

Watching the deference with which the bishop spoke to Cuthbert, Aldfrith gritted his teeth. Wilfrid rarely spoke to him using such a gentle tone.

A damp wind blew in from the sea as the small procession made its way down the sloping causeway and along a path through the dunes to the beach. The tide was in, and a small boat awaited on the shore. Seabirds wheeled overhead, their cries mixing with the roar of the surf.

Cerdic and three other warriors pushed the boat onto the edge of the waves, while Aldfrith, Oswald, and the bishop helped Cuthbert and his companions climb in.

"God speed, father." Wilfrid grasped hold of Cuthbert's hand and squeezed. The bishop's dark gaze gleamed, and he looked on the verge of tears.

"Farewell, Wilfrid," Cuthbert replied, his voice raspy from the effort it had taken him to climb off the cart and into the boat. The prior's gaze then shifted to Aldfrith. "I wish you well, milord. God bless you ... and your reign."

Aldfrith nodded, suddenly choked up. There was something about Cuthbert's gaze when it fixed upon you that made you feel as if the man were looking into your soul, flaying it bare. It felt as if Cuthbert had seen him, even the things he took such great pains to hide. He saw, and understood.

"Farewell, Father," he answered. "Thank you for granting us this one, last, visit."

They pushed the boat out into the waves, wading in deep, before guiding it through the surf. The water was freezing, its chill penetrating layers of leather and fur in an instant. Aldfrith and the others were gasping from the cold as they waded back to shore.

Squelching up onto the sandy beach, Aldfrith turned, his gaze following the small craft that bobbed in the surf as one of the monks picked up the oars and steered it left. The isle of Lindisfarena was but a short journey, just beyond the headland to the north. At low tide travelers could skirt the coast north before walking out across the sandflats to the isle. However, the prior was too weak to make the journey on foot.

The group of men upon the beach stood and watched till Cuthbert and the monks were out of sight. Then they turned and made their way back to the fort. Bebbanburg rose above them upon a great rocky outcrop, its palisades bristling against the pale sky.

"The prior is not long for this world," Bishop Wilfrid announced, falling in step next to Aldfrith. "Someone will need to take his place at the monastery. The monks will need a new leader ... someone with a deep piety ... someone who understands Cuthbert's work."

Aldfrith cast him a sharp glance. "The prior isn't dead yet, Father."

The bishop's mouth thinned. The grief he had shown when bidding the prior goodbye had gone. The Wilfrid that Aldfrith had come to know well had returned. "I'm aware of that, sire. I'm just acknowledging the fact that Lindisfarena will soon need a new leader."

And that would be you?

Aldfrith did not voice the question out loud. Yet they both knew that was what Wilfrid was implying. Aldfrith's gaze narrowed. "Cuthbert worships God in the manner of the north ... does that not bother you?"

Wilfrid's nostrils flared. "Not overly ... but that is why the monastery at Lindisfarena could do with my influence."

Aldfrith clenched his jaw, forcing himself not to reply. If Wilfrid wanted to become prior of Lindisfarena, he would need the king's permission. And as things stood, Wilfrid would be the last man he would choose.

Perhaps sensing his king's mood, the bishop fell silent. It was only when they were climbing the causeway to the low gate that Wilfrid spoke once more. "Did Cuthbert speak to you about that widow's presence in your hall?" he asked quietly, as if he was wary of Aldfrith's men overhearing them.

Aldfrith tensed, realization dawning. "You sent word to him about Lady Osana?"

Wilfrid nodded, not remotely cowed by the king's glare. "She is a corrupting influence, milord. You should send her away."

"Lady Osana is a good woman," Aldfrith replied. "I see no corruption in her. She only wishes to be useful, to find her place in the world."

Bishop Wilfrid favored him with a pained look. "Has she cast the wool over your eyes so easily, sire? The woman watches you; she meets your eye too boldly. She is a temptress who covets a place at your side. She wishes to become your consort and control you with lust and wiles. Cast her out of Bebbanburg, and find yourself a gentle virgin to wed."

"Enough," Aldfrith snapped, his patience finally giving out. "You forget your place. The widow Osana has done nothing to merit such accusations. Do not speak to me of this again."

With that, Aldfrith strode forward, leaving the bishop behind. Fury boiled up within him; he clenched his fists at his sides. Wilfrid's words were outrageous, ridiculous. And yet they also bothered him.

Temptress. Consort. Lust and wiles.

I shouldn't have offered to teach her to read ... what was I thinking?

The wistfulness on her face the night before, the light in her eyes as she had pored over the page of that book, had made him speak without thinking. It was something he was getting into the habit of doing when it came to Osana. He gazed into her eyes and lost his wits. The loss of control concerned him; it reminded him of a past he had spent many years trying to forget.

Wilfrid was wrong, Osana was not the problem. He was. He could not spend time alone with her, could not risk opening his heart to her.

I shall have to cancel that lesson.

Chapter Seventeen

Learning Letters

OSANA GRIPPED THE quill tightly and moved it across the sheet of vellum:

O S A N A

Leaning back, she surveyed her work, her gaze roaming over the spidery script.

"Is that really my name?"

"Aye."

She glanced up, her attention shifting to where Aldfrith sat beside her at the table. He had remained silent while she laboriously copied the letters he had written out for her. His expression was solemn; in fact, he had been in an odd, distracted mood since she had arrived at his annex for her lesson.

He had not smiled once and avoided her gaze.

"But they're just marks on vellum. Do they really have meaning?"

The corner of his mouth twitched then, the beginning of a smile. "Each letter has a sound. Look at the word you've just written … let's sound out each letter." He reached out, the sleeve of his tunic brushing her hand as he did so, his finger resting under the first letter of her name. "Repeat after me."

Osana did as bid, sounding out each letter. When she had done so a handful of times, Aldfrith sat back, nodding in satisfaction. "Now run each of those letters together … what do you get?"

Osana frowned, looking back at the sheet of vellum. "Ooosaanaa."

His mouth quirked once more. "Well done. Once you learn the sound of each letter of the alphabet, and what they sound like when grouped together in words, you can read anything."

Osana traced her name with a fingertip, pride thrumming through her. "It's like magic," she murmured.

"No, it's much easier to understand than that. One day many folk will be able to read and write." Aldfrith gestured to his two precious leather-bound volumes on the shelf above them. "And there will be many books filled with histories."

Osana's gaze traveled from the shelf down to the desk once more, her gaze alighting upon a messily stacked pile of vellum full of Aldfrith's slanted writing. She then glanced back at him. "Are you writing a book?"

He actually did smile then, the expression illuminating his face. "Those are just scribbles ... ideas ... thoughts. I don't think anyone besides me would be interested in them."

Osana huffed. "I would ... can you read something to me?"

Aldfrith went still, his smile fading. "I'm sure you wouldn't find it interesting."

"How do you know that?" Osana reached out and plucked the first sheet of vellum off the pile. "I'd very much like to know what you write."

Aldfrith took the sheet, although his expression was now guarded. "Very well, although I hope you don't find it too dry." He looked down at the piece of paper, his gaze narrowing. "These are just my musings on life."

Osana did not reply, instead waiting for him to begin. She wondered at his reluctance to read to her; was he really that insecure?

Eventually, after a long pause, Aldfrith began to read.

"Generosity engenders wealth.
Willingness creates one who gives.
Good sense results in fair form.
Lechery leads to disgrace.
Foolishness results in crudity.
Repression results in greater repression.
Hatred engenders reproach.
Abandonment results in slander,
Reluctance leads to reliance on conjecture.
Love begets words.
Humility wins good favor."

He had a beautiful voice, its low timbre sliding over the words like a caress. Osana listened quietly, and when Aldfrith finished, she smiled. "Love begets words ... I like that."

Aldfrith replaced the sheet with the others. Was she imagining it, or did a slight blush stain his cheeks. "Thank you."

"So these are maxims for life?"

"As I see them, aye."

Osana paused, biting at her lower lip before speaking once more. "You must be very sure of your beliefs, of the nature of folk, to write so confidently."

He inclined his head. "What do you mean?"

"Is life really that easy to summarize? Surely things are more complex than that. For example, not all generous men become wealthy. Not all letches end up disgraced."

Aldfrith stiffened. "You think I've over simplified?"

"No," Osana replied quickly, regretting her candor now that she could see she had offended him. "I just think the older I get, the harder it is to make such statements about life. It seems that when I think I understand something, the world makes a mockery of me."

She saw him straighten up further, and with a sinking feeling realized she was just digging herself into a great hole. She was beginning to wish she had not spoken so frankly.

"Man should seek truths about life," he replied coolly. "It gives us something to aspire to."

"I'm aware of that," she answered, sharpness now entering her voice. She did not enjoy being patronized. Raedwulf used to do so if ever she voiced an opinion that did not relate to the running of the household. "All I was saying is that we should be wary of reducing our existence to a list of maxims. They could easily become a cage."

A heavy silence followed her words, the easy companionship during the lesson now forgotten. Disappointment flooded through Osana; she had so enjoyed this afternoon. She was sorry she had offended the king, but even sorrier that he was so easily wounded.

"I should go," she murmured, pushing back her stool. "Lora will need help with her chores."

She rose to her feet, with the intention of stepping around Argus's sleeping form, but instead, her skirt caught on the stool, and she stumbled. Osana reached out for something to steady her but missed the edge of the desk with her hand.

A heartbeat later she tumbled onto Aldfrith's lap.

The shock of Osana's warm, soft body landing on him jolted Aldfrith out of the anger that had rendered him speechless. In just a few words this woman, who until today had not been able to spell her name, had made him feel like a fool. He had been ready to send her away when she arrived at his annex earlier; he had been telling himself all day that he must. Yet one glance at her hopeful face, and his resolve had scattered like leaves in the wind.

There had been no malice in her observations, just curiosity and plain-speech. Unwittingly, she had just destroyed the one thing he was most proud of: his wisdom, his ideas.

Yet when she fell onto his lap, he forgot his upset.

The scent of lavender and the sweet smell of a woman's skin enveloped him. He was much taller than her, and when standing, Osana had to look up to meet his eye. Their gazes were level now though. He looked into those hazel eyes flecked with green, and saw the shocked look on her lovely face. His attention shifted to those lush, slightly parted lips, and lust hit him with the force of a battering ram.

"Sorry, milord," she gasped, her eyes glittering with mortification. "I'm clumsy, I—"

Instinct took over. Aldfrith reached out, his hand cupping the back of her neck. Then he drew her close, his mouth covering hers.

The feel of her lips against his, the flutter of her pulse under his fingertips, drove the last of his good sense away. With a strangled groan, Aldfrith ran his free hand up her back, exploring the firmness of the flesh beneath her fitted tunic. Then his tongue parted her lips, and he kissed her deeply.

Osana's response was primal. Her soft whimper of pleasure, the way she melted into him like molten wax, awoke something deep within him Aldfrith had thought dead forever.

The Lord save his soul, but he wanted Osana. Her taste was like honey, like rich wine. The feel of her body against his brought him alive. The ache in his loins was almost unbearable.

She kissed him back, her hunger matching his. Her breasts pressed up against the wall of his chest, and he slid a hand from her back to cup their fullness. He wanted to see her breasts naked, to suckle them. He needed to tear away the layers of clothing separating them, to take her here and now on the desk. He wanted to lose himself inside her.

Everything he knew about the world ceased to matter. His existence narrowed to this moment, this woman.

Thud. Thud.

"Lord Aldfrith."

The moment shattered.

Aldfrith and Osana sprang apart as if doused with a bucket of icy sea-water.

Fortunately, the door was closed. A cold wind had sprung up in the afternoon, and Osana had closed the door upon entering to avoid putting out the fire with a draft. It was that which had saved someone from walking in on them.

"Aye," Aldfrith said roughly, rising to his feet, while Osana sank down—trembling—onto her stool.

The door opened, and Cerdic appeared. His gaze swept over them both, his expression impassive. However, Aldfrith was sure guilt was written over his and Osana's faces.

"Yes, Cerdic?" Aldfrith said shortly. "We're in the midst of a lesson."

The slight raise of one of Cerdic's eyebrows was the only sign that he knew what he had just walked in on. "Apologies for the interruption, sire. However, the ealdorman of Gefrin is here. He wishes to discuss rebuilding Northumbria's armies. He claims the conversation is long overdue."

That man is like a dog with a bone. Aldfrith raked a hand through his hair. This was the last thing he needed. After that kiss he could barely think straight. Thankfully, the tunic he wore over his leggings reached mid-thigh, concealing his arousal. He had to gather his wits before returning to the Great Hall to meet his cousin.

Edwin had become troublesome of late. He imagined the King of Mercia, or the Pict King Bridei, were plotting against them and planning an attack on Northumbria. As far as Aldfrith was concerned, his cousin's worries were entirely unfounded. They had never enjoyed such peaceful relations with their neighbors as they did now.

"Thank you, Cerdic. Tell Edwin to enjoy a cup of ale in the hall. I will be with him shortly."

The warrior nodded, his gaze darting once more to Osana, before he turned on his heel and strode from the annex.

When he was gone, Aldfrith heaved in a deep breath and turned to Osana.

She sat, stiff-backed, upon the stool looking as if she would flee at any moment. Her lips were swollen from his kisses, her cheeks slightly flushed. Aldfrith inwardly cringed; Cerdic was no fool. He would know what they had been doing. They were just lucky that it was Cerdic and not the bishop who had interrupted them.

Thinking upon Bishop Wilfrid sent a chill through Aldfrith, dousing the last of the lust that had driven away all rational thought.

Temptress.

Aye she was, but Osana was not to blame for what had just happened. He was. All his resolve, his decision to keep away from the alluring widow, and he had fallen upon Osana like a ravenous wolf.

Lechery leads to disgrace.

His own words returned to mock him. Osana was right. He locked himself away in this room, pondering life from afar, like an eagle perched upon a rocky eyrie. Yet the first moment he had been tested his resolve had crumbled.

"Go back to the hall, Osana," he said quietly, turning from her as self-disgust settled upon him. "I think it's best if we don't have any more lessons."

Chapter Eighteen

Beyond My Grasp

HER LEGS WOULD not work properly.

Osana stumbled back into the Great Hall, leaving Aldfrith behind in his annex. She barely paid notice to her surroundings. After that kiss her wits were still scattered. She was still reeling, still trying to make sense of it. She had not expected him to kiss her. And she certainly had not imagined Aldfrith could kiss like that.

She had never experienced an embrace of its like, had never lost herself in a kiss so completely. It had been a wrench to pull herself away, even if the knock on the door had made it necessary.

What would have happened if Cerdic hadn't interrupted us?

Osana flushed hot at the thought.

She crossed the floor of the Great Hall, her legs like jelly, making her way over to where Lora stood kneading bread at a long table.

Lora's brow furrowed when her gaze alighted upon Osana. "You're flushed ... are you unwell?"

Osana shook her head, flashing Lora a quick smile. "I'm fine. It's just hot in here compared to outdoors. Do you need help with that?"

Lora gave her a searching look. The woman was sharper than most folk realized, and she had an uncanny ability to read your mood. Yet Lora held her tongue and nodded. "There's dough in that bowl that needs working."

Grateful to have a task to occupy her, Osana rolled up her sleeves and got to work. She sprinkled a dusting of coarse flour on the wooden work surface and poured out the bouncy lump of dough. Then she began to knead it.

A gust of chill air blew across the floor as the doors opened, and Osana glanced up to see the king enter.

The sight of him made her breathing catch. Just a short while earlier she had been perched upon his lap while he ravaged her mouth and ran those strong sensitive hands over her body, setting her on fire.

He looked stern now though; not even the ghost of the earlier passion that had smoldered in those dark blue eyes was visible.

Osana's chest constricted. Once the kiss had ended, she had seen the change in him, the invisible door that had slammed shut between them. His gaze was shuttered now, riveted upon the heavy-set blond warrior who sat upon the high seat, cup of ale in hand, waiting for him.

Aldfrith did not glance her way, even though she knew he would have seen her upon entering the hall.

He was determined not to make eye contact with her.

Osana dropped her own gaze to the dough she was pummeling, her vision blurring.

Stop it, she chided herself. *Why would you weep over such a thing? Of course Aldfrith isn't going to look at you. Not now.*

And yet she could not hide from the disappointment that settled over her in a heavy blanket. The attraction between them had been there from the first, simmering during every meeting over the last two and a half years. It was only natural that spending time together alone would ignite it.

I think it's best if we don't have any more lessons.

Aldfrith realized his mistake in tutoring her. She would not learn to read or to practice writing her name and other letters. A vise gripped Osana's chest at the thought, squeezing tight. How she had loved that lesson: the smell of the ink, the scratch of the quill across the vellum, and the magic of seeing her name written there. She thirsted to learn more and felt cheated that one lesson would be all she would receive.

Arrogant woman. Osana punched hard at the dough. *Raedwulf always said it. No wonder I've never been happy ... I've always wanted what's beyond my grasp.*

Aldfrith approached the high seat, deliberately keeping his gaze focused upon the blond man waiting for him there, and away from the dark-haired woman standing at one of the work tables.

Even so, it took a monumental effort to focus his thoughts and not allow memories of that passionate kiss to distract him.

Her soft lips. Her sweet taste.

Enough. Concentrate.

Seeing the mutinous look upon his cousin's face, Aldfrith knew he had to keep his wits about him. Edwin of Gefrin was a sharp, blunt-tongued man who knew how to manipulate others.

He stepped up onto the high seat, and the ealdorman gracelessly heaved himself to his feet and bowed. The gesture was rushed, bordering on disrespectful. However, Aldfrith let it pass; he did not care much for formalities, although in Edwin the slight grated.

"Wes hāl, Edwin." He nodded at the ealdorman and sank into his chair at the head of the table. "What brings you to Bebbanburg?"

A servant appeared at his elbow with a jug of mead and poured him a cup. Wordlessly, Edwin thrust out his own to be refilled before turning his gaze upon the king.

"Concerns, sire ... grave ones."

Aldfrith frowned. "What's wrong?"

"Northumbria still has no army. Where is our fyrd?"

Aldfrith let out a long breath. He could not believe Edwin had again traveled all this way to berate him about his army. It seemed the only thing his cousin thought about. Every time they met, he repeated the same complaint. "I don't need to gather a fyrd, Edwin," he replied, his voice flat. "Northumbria isn't at war."

"Aethelred of Mercia is strengthening his garrisons to the north of his kingdom," Edwin growled.

"And?"

Edwin gave him a withering look. "He's clearly planning something."

Aldfrith clenched his jaw. He was not in the mood for this. "I'm on good terms with King Aethelred. There's no trouble between our kingdoms."

The ealdorman's mouth drew up. "You can't trust a Mercian. Thousands of our warriors have died upon their blades over the years."

"As have thousands of theirs."

Edwin scowled at him, his gaze narrowing. He was clearly unconvinced; this was an argument between them that would not easily be resolved. And yet Aldfrith sensed this complaint was merely a shield. The man's resentment toward him hung over them like a fug of smoke.

It is not an army you want but the crown. If Aldfrith had not been alive to succeed Ecgfrith, Edwin would have taken the throne.

It must gall him terribly.

He was not without sympathy for Edwin or his frustrations. Edwin was an ambitious man who had been thwarted. Yet his cousin's belligerence put Aldfrith on edge. The man seemed to think the king should follow his counsel unquestioningly. He did not like being obstructed.

I must be wary of him.

Lora knew Cerdic was headed her way. The determined set of his shoulders, and the way his gaze bored into her, made his destination clear.

Putting down the washing board and cake of lye she was using, Lora rose to her feet to greet him. He was a tall man, and she did not want him looming over her.

Cerdic was a distraction; he made her feel an odd restlessness. After losing Broga, she had felt sad and empty for a long while. Was she even ready to give her heart to another? She liked Cerdic, but she barely knew him. Perhaps it was better to keep him at arm's length.

The grim look on his face now unsettled her.

Lora dried her hands on her apron as she watched him cover the last handful of yards to the well where she stood. A basket of her and Osana's tunics sat at her feet. She was halfway through washing them.

"Good afternoon," she greeted the warrior when he drew up before her.

"Wes hāl," he rumbled, dipping his chin in greeting.

They stood on the edge of the yard, near where Lora had slipped in the snow. The snow had gone now, leaving mud in its wake. It was a sunny but chill afternoon. Lora could feel the kiss of the sun on her back. In another moon its touch would have more heat.

"Why the serious expression?" she asked, injecting a light-hearted tone into her voice. "You look the bearer of ill-tidings."

He scowled. "Aye, I am."

Lora stiffened. "What's wrong?"

Cerdic cast a glance around them, to ensure they were not being overheard. "Aldfrith and your mistress grow close."

Lora stared at him, confused. "Sorry?"

Cerdic huffed out a breath. "Earlier, when Edwin of Gefrin arrived, I went looking for the king in his annex. I found them there ... together. I think I interrupted something."

Lora cocked an eyebrow. "And how to you know that?"

"I may look a dolt," he growled, folding his muscular arms over his chest, "but I know the look of a man and woman who've just leaped from each other's arms."

"Are you sure?"

"Aye. I've never seen such two guilty faces."

Lora sighed, pushing a strand of hair that had escaped her braid out of her eyes. This news concerned her, for Osana was putting both their futures at Bebbanburg at risk. However, she would not share her fears with Cerdic. Instead, she decided to take the opposite approach with him. "Should either of us be worried? Aren't they both free to do as they wish?"

He favored her with an incredulous look that made Lora wilt slightly. "I took you for a clever woman," he growled. "Surely you realize that a widow like Osana can't consort with the king without ruining herself. Likewise, he has a responsibility to take a highborn wife to strengthen this kingdom's position in Britannia."

Anger spiked within Lora. It annoyed her that Cerdic thought her a goose, and she wished she had spoken her mind to him rather than trying to diminish the situation. However, she was stubborn and would not back down now. "Surely Lord Aldfrith can consort with whomever he wishes?" she replied tartly. "He is king after all. Likewise, Osana knows what she's doing. We shouldn't meddle."

His gaze bored into her with such intensity that Lora felt her breathing quicken. This man's nearness distracted her. "Speak to her, Lora." The sound of her name on his lips made her pulse quicken. "Warn her of the situation she risks putting herself in."

Lora held his gaze before wetting her lips nervously. She instantly regretted the act when she saw his eyes drop to her mouth. "What situation is that?"

"Aldfrith can't take her as his consort openly. If she lies with him, she will always live in the shadows. Folk will treat her as his hōre." Lora flinched at the baldness of his words, but Cerdic had not yet finished. "And you too will be tainted by association." They stared at each other for a long moment, before Cerdic's mouth softened. For an instant the severity of his face eased, and Lora caught a glimpse of the man beneath. "I would spare you that."

"Cerdic came to speak to me today."

Lora's words, quietly spoken, made Osana glance up from where she was unlacing the front of her woolen dress. They stood inside their alcove, readying themselves to retire to their furs for the night. Osana was in a tense, distracted mood, and was glad to be able to hide from the rest of the hall, to be able to crawl into her furs and be alone with her thoughts.

"Did he?" Osana replied with a smile. "It seems that warrior has his eye on you."

Lora huffed. "He spoke to me of you ... and Aldfrith," she replied, ignoring Osana's comment. "He's concerned."

Osana stiffened. Of course—Cerdic had known exactly what he had stumbled upon earlier that day. "I hope he hasn't gone around the hall sharing his concerns," she said tightly. "I didn't take him for a man with a loose tongue."

Lora shook her head. "No ... I think he has only spoken to me." Her blue eyes were pleading as they met Osana's. "He believes you are putting your life here at risk ... and I agree with him."

The words fell like heavy axe blows between them. Osana went still. Her first reaction was anger. She hated the thought of Lora and Cerdic discussing her. A moment later panic swelled within her breast. Life here would become unbearable if rumors started circulating about her. It would be easier for Aldfrith; he was a man and could take lovers without ruining his reputation. She, on the other hand, had a tenuous position in the Great Tower at best.

"We only kissed," she said after a long pause, her voice barely above a whisper. "Neither of us planned for it to happen."

The look of sympathy on Lora's face made her want to weep. "It cannot go any further than that," Lora replied softly, coming forward and placing a comforting hand on Osana's arm. "Or you put both of us at risk."

Osana's mouth twisted. "You don't fancy living with my shrewish aunt in Jedworth then?"

Lora shook her head. "Not particularly."

Osana sighed heavily and sat down upon the furs. The strength had gone out of her suddenly; she felt weary beyond her years. "You don't need to worry, Lora," she said, trying and failing to keep the bitterness out of her voice. "Aldfrith realized he'd made a mistake the moment the kiss ended. We won't be spending any more time alone together."

Lora nodded, and Osana saw the relief in her friend's eyes. Self-recrimination stabbed at her. Upon coming here to live, she had only focused on herself. She had not stopped to consider what Lora wanted.

That would have to change.

Chapter Nineteen

Earthly Cares

THE WINTER PASSED quickly, and Sōlmōnath slid into Hrēðmonath—the third moon cycle of the year. The first spring bulbs started to appear on the meadows below Bebbanburg: snowdrops with their delicate white bonnets, and tiny crocuses and jonquils.

The days lengthened, and warmth returned to the sun. Osana found herself spending more and more time outdoors. She would often take her distaff or sewing outside, and sit working alone in the orchard. The bare branches of the fruit trees were developing buds now, promising a sea of delicate cream and white blossom to come. It gave Osana hope to see them; she always felt as if she was reborn in spring. The long bitter season weighed heavily upon her, and this year had been harder than most.

After that one lesson, and the stolen kiss, Osana had avoided Aldfrith. She tried not to think about that incident—or of him—but it was difficult when she caught glimpses of the king most days.

They were nearing the end of Hrēðmonath when news arrived from Lindisfarena that Cuthbert was dead.

It came as a shock, yet Osana remembered how frail and weary the prior have looked upon his visit. Even so, the tidings sent waves of upset through the Great Hall. There were few in Bebbanburg now that followed the old gods. Most, Osana herself included, worshipped Christ. Cuthbert, and all the miracles attributed to him over the years, had become a local legend. The folk here had been proud to have such a holy man live so close. They had been proud of Lindisfarena and the work Cuthbert had done. The prior was one-of-a-kind; no other could replace him.

The heavy iron bell of Oswald's church, just off the market square, rang for an entire morning after word arrived, its mournful song echoing out over the thatched rooftops of the fort.

Osana, who was picking up some items at the market, noted the despair on the faces around her. Two older women wept before the steps of the church, their sobs forming a discordant music with the ringing bell. Even the vendors were distracted this morning, some muttering under their breath and fingering the wooden crucifixes they wore about their necks. A heavyset woman, selling bread and cakes where Osana had stopped to buy some treats to share with Lora, looked troubled.

"It will bode ill for Northumbria, this death."

Osana frowned. "What do you mean?"

The woman's gaze met hers. "Many of us believe that Cuthbert laid a charm over this place. In the war against the Picts, no fighting or bloodshed reached Bebbanburg. He protected us."

Osana held her gaze a moment, but did not reply. She believed in Cuthbert's work, and in the good he had done, yet she could not bring herself to believe he was the protector of this land. Even so, the melancholy in the air this morning affected her.

Buying two buns crammed full of dried plums—to share with Lora later—Osana placed them in her basket and began the walk up the King's Way toward the high gate. It had become a morning ritual that every few days either she or Lora would provide a treat to share together in the evening while they sat mending clothes.

Osana entered the Great Hall to find an excited crowd was gathering around the high seat. Lora, her blond curls bouncing as she bobbed up and down trying to catch the conversation in the midst, was at the back of the group. Upon the dais a few yards away, the king and the bishop were discussing something intently.

Bishop Wilfrid had timed his latest visit to Bebbanburg well, for he had arrived from Inhrypum the night before—just in time to receive the news of Cuthbert's passing.

At this distance Osana thought it looked as if the conversation between the king and the bishop teetered on the verge of descending into an argument.

"What is it?" Osana reached Lora's side, nudging her with her basket.

Lora glanced back, smiling when she saw Osana had returned. "It appears that the monks on Lindisfarena plan to bury Cuthbert today. The bishop wants him and Aldfrith to go alone to the burial, but the king has decided to organize a mourning party to travel to the isle to pay their respects."

"Do you wish to go?" Osana asked, incredulous. As far as she was aware, her friend, although not vocal about it, was still a follower of the old ways. She had seen the amulet of Freya that Lora kept by her furs, and the small carven figure of Woden that had once belonged to her husband.

Lora shook her head. "No ... but I'm curious to see who they will let go." Lora paused a moment, her gaze narrowing. "Will you join them?"

Osana shrugged. "I suppose I would ... if they permitted women."

Truthfully, she did want to go. She had always wanted to visit that rocky, windswept isle, to see where the great Cuthbert had lived and prayed.

Lora huffed a moment. "Why should women be excluded? You worship the same God as men." A wicked light illuminated in her friend's blue eyes. "Well then ... make sure you get to the front and put your hand up." With that, Lora placed her hand between Osana's shoulder blades and shoved. Osana stumbled forward into the crowd, almost tripping. Righting herself, she then steered herself forward using her basket as a battering ram. One or two folk cast dark looks over their shoulders at her, but still moved aside to let her through.

A moment later Osana was standing at the foot of the high seat.

Still clutching her basket grimly, Osana silently cursed Lora.

Wicked vixen. This wasn't what I had in mind.

Of course, after such an entrance, the king noticed her. He glanced up from where he had been talking with Wilfrid, his eyes narrowing.

"Lady Osana," he greeted her formally. Those had been his first words to her in many days. They were little more than strangers to each other now. Osana could almost believe that their earlier friendship had never happened, that it belonged to another life.

"Lord Aldfrith," she replied, dipping her head and curtseying. "I hear you are organizing a group to go to Lindisfarena ... I'd like to join you."

Her own boldness shocked her.

Aldfrith's gaze widened a moment before he nodded. "Aye ... I don't see why not."

"Sire," Wilfrid choked. "When you suggested a group of mourners follow us, I did not think you meant *her*."

The derision in his voice made Osana's spine stiffen. She squared her shoulders and met the bishop's eye. "Why not? My faith is as real as yours." She shifted her attention to Aldfrith who was watching her, a quizzical expression on his face. "I would not be any trouble, sire."

"The woman has a forked tongue," Wilfrid cut in. "She should stay behind."

Aldfrith ignored the bishop, his attention remaining upon Osana. "The Lady has as much right as the rest of us to pay her last respects to Cuthbert," he replied. His gaze then swept across the waiting, breathless crowd. "As does anyone here who wishes to join us. Go and gather your cloaks—we leave now."

The tide was out, leaving behind an expanse of glistening sand. The group from Bebbanburg did not take boats across to the isle, like Cuthbert had during the winter. Instead, they walked.

A narrow path, The Pilgrim's Way, was the only safe path during low tide to the island. The travelers walked two or three abreast, following the king; the bishop; the priest; and the king's men, who rode on horseback. The rest of the group were on foot.

The red and gold of the Northumbrian pennants fluttered in the breeze as they crossed.

Osana walked at the back of the group, next to Mildryth.

Inhaling the cold, salty air, Osana gazed around her as she traveled, marveling at the openness of the surrounding landscape. It felt magical to walk out across a stretch of sand that was usually covered by water: strangely exciting and frightening at the same time.

Once they arrived upon the isle, they would have to wait for the next low tide—which would come that evening—before they could return home. It would give them plenty of time upon Lindisfarena. The monks would host them, give them a tour of the monastery after the burial, and feed them before they took their leave.

Ahead, Osana spied the low profile of Lindisfarena draw ever closer. It really was a barren spot. There were few trees, and what vegetation there was had a stunted look, sculpted by the prevailing winds. There were few signs of spring here, unlike on the mainland. Upon the Farne Isles, winter still resided. Lindisfarena was the largest of the group of islands. Until his health failed him, Cuthbert had lived as a hermit upon one of the smaller isles. Osana had heard that some of the islands were completely covered by puffins and other seabirds.

As they approached the shore, Osana's gaze shifted south to where a complex of low wooden buildings, including one with a high pitched roof, rose against the windy sky. The faint peels of an iron bell reached them, calling the mourners to Cuthbert's burial.

Osana glanced over at Mildryth then. The woman had been uncharacteristically silent during the walk. Her long face was solemn, her large eyes watery and red-rimmed. She had wept noisily upon hearing that Cuthbert had passed away, but had been insistent that she would join the group to farewell him.

"Are you well, Mildryth?" Osana asked gently.

"Aye ... it's just ... this is such a sad day," the woman sniffed.

It was, although sadness was an emotion that dogged Osana's step *most* days. She had become part of life in the Great Hall, yet melancholy cast a shadow over everything. She felt lonely, especially after Aldfrith's dismissal of her, but she knew she was lucky to have a roof over her head, to have a warm, dry place to sleep at night, and to have food in her belly.

She was grateful for a great many things, yet at unguarded moments sadness would still creep up on her like a thief.

Not for the first time that morning, she cursed Lora for pushing her forward. Life was easier at Bebbanburg when she was invisible. She was a woman with too much to say for herself; her tongue only got her into trouble. Not only that, but the other women in the hall had finally started to accept her; they would cease being friendly if she made a spectacle of herself.

Osana's boots crunched upon pebbles as she followed the procession of mourners onto the shore. Here, they turned south, following a narrow path up to the highest point of the island, where the monastery stood.

"It looks shabbier than I expected," Mildryth observed, disappointment in her voice.

Osana cast her a wry look. "I too expected something grander. Maybe this is better though ... Cuthbert was not a man for earthly possessions. Gleaming walls and towers would not suit him."

"I suppose you're right," Mildryth replied, although she sounded unconvinced.

The two women said no more as they approached the monastery.

Aldfrith stood before the bier and gazed down at the corpse upon it.

Cuthbert lay there dressed in a simple brown robe trimmed with a fur collar. His thinness shocked Aldfrith; he was painfully emaciated, his head nothing more than a skull with parchment skin pulled over it. His hollowed, sunken eyes were closed, his claw-like hands placed across his chest, where they clutched a small wooden crucifix.

"He looks at peace."

Aldfrith glanced right, at where Wilfrid stood next to him. For once, he did not disagree with the bishop. They rarely saw eye-to-eye on anything these days. Beside Wilfrid, Oswald was silently weeping. The priest's mouth trembled with grief as he stared down at the prior's corpse.

Aldfrith glanced over at the cluster of monks opposite, their heads bowed, their bald pates gleaming in the morning sun. "How did it end?" he asked.

One of them, a slender man of around forty winters with graying blond hair, answered. "He was very weak of late, sire. Cuthbert eventually fell into a deep sleep and did not awake from it."

"Good," Aldfrith said, glancing back at the prior's body. "He went gently then."

They stood behind the church of Lindisfarena. The prior's body had been laid out upon the wooden bier ready for burial. Behind him the monks had dug a deep grave. Unlike the heathens of the past, this would not be a fiery burial. The prior's body would be interred so that one day he could be resurrected.

Wilfrid, his austere face composed, began the burial rite for Cuthbert.

Aldfrith had heard the words before, and yet they carried more weight today. Despite the fact he was not fond of Wilfrid, he had to admit the bishop was a powerful speaker.

Wilfrid spoke of Cuthbert's kindness and patience. He spoke at length of all the miracles attributed to him, near and far: children who had been healed of deathly fevers, lepers whose skin had cleared of boils, barren women who had miraculously conceived. After that Wilfrid spoke of what the prior had done to make Lindisfarena a place of pilgrimage.

Soft sobs accompanied Wilfrid's words. Oswald had covered his face with his hands now, his slender shoulders shaking. Most of the monks were weeping, and many in the surrounding crowd were struggling to keep their composure.

The bishop's voice rang out loud and clear, his own cheeks wet with tears. "Fly free from the earthly cares of this world, Cuthbert. We will never forget you."

Aldfrith listened to the bishop's words, closing his eyes a moment as the wind pushed at him. It was a sad day, and yet his thoughts felt scattered. He found it difficult to focus on the burial, or on the rite.

Instead, he was acutely aware of the dark-haired woman, dressed in a fur-lined mantle, who stood at the edge of the crowd to his right.

Osana.

He glanced her way now, taking in her solemn expression as she listened to the bishop. Her gaze, like that of many others in the crowd, was focused upon Wilfrid. The past months had been torture. How often had he yearned to seek her out, to speak to her? He had often caught glimpses of her in the hall, but he always had to be careful lest she, or someone else, catch him looking her way.

Everyone's attention lay elsewhere now though, and so his gaze drank her in, committing every inch of that lovely face to memory. Long moments passed, before Aldfrith forced himself to look away, focusing instead upon Cuthbert.

An ache of loss that had nothing to do with the prior's death fisted in the center of his chest, squeezing hard.

Chapter Twenty

Meeting in the Scriptorium

OSANA STOOD AT the edge of the mourners. Hands clasped before her, she listened to the rise and fall of Bishop Wilfrid's voice. The king stood next to the bishop, his gaze upon Cuthbert's corpse.

Osana took in the king's profile. He looked deep in concentration.

She would never tire of looking at him. His blond hair had grown a little longer over the past couple of months, and it ruffled slightly in the sea breeze. He had turned his fur collar up against the chill, its silvery tones highlighting Aldfrith's pale skin and dark blue eyes.

Aye, she still wanted him. It hurt to look at him, but she could not stop herself.

A hollow sensation settled in the pit of her belly. She missed Aldfrith; each encounter with him made her feel alive. Even a brief exchange of words with him made her feel understood. It felt unnatural to live under the same roof as him and not spend time talking together, sharing ideas and beliefs.

Perhaps I offended him deeply that day.

She had been blunt with her opinion of his writing, but she had not meant to give offense. She had only wanted to know what he thought.

Osana dropped her gaze, closing her eyes to shut out the world for a moment. Spring was coming; soon she would have to make a decision about her future. Her aunt would take her in, even if she did so in ill-grace. However, the thought of living with Hagona, her sister's spinster sister, did not fill Osana with joy.

The only true joy she had known of late had been in Aldfrith's arms, and that experience would not be repeated.

Bishop Wilfrid's voice died away, bringing the burial rite to a close, and Osana opened her eyes once more. The monks lifted the bier and carried it the few feet to the open grave. Then, using ropes, they lowered the prior's body into the ground.

A few of them were weeping, the muffled sound of sobs blending with the sigh of the wind. The shroud of grief lay so heavy upon the mourners that Osana could almost taste it.

Once Cuthbert's body had been settled in the grave, the monks placed a layer of fresh rushes over him, before shoveling a few feet of dirt on top. Then, they started to lay rocks. Aldfrith and his men helped at this stage, before the blond monk stepped forward and placed a wooden crucifix on top.

The crowd drew back, leaving the lonely cairn of stones upon the windswept slope. It was done: Cuthbert of Lindisfarena, the holiest man who had ever lived in this corner of the world, was buried.

Bishop Wilfrid strode back to the priory, bringing Oswald and a flock of other mourners with him. The tide had now come in, and they would not be returning to the mainland until much later in the day. The bishop and the mourners would pray for Cuthbert's soul.

Aldfrith went with them. He did not glance Osana's way; it was as if she was invisible.

A handful of monks remained outside and took those who had not followed the bishop on a tour of the island and the monastery. "You're welcome to explore our home," one of the monks told the group that Osana now stood at the back of. "No doors are closed to you on this day."

The monks led them into the monastery and began the tour at enclosures where goats lay chewing the cud and fowl pecked for grain in the dirt. They then led them to gardens, protected from the elements by high stone walls, where rows of neatly-tended cabbages, kale, onions, and turnips grew.

The monks started to explain their growing practices at length, and after a while Osana wandered off. She felt the need to be alone now, to discover Lindisfarena at her own pace.

She walked through the deserted complex: past a network of low-slung thatched dormitories where the monks presumably slept, between a scattering of storage huts, and out through a narrow gate at the highest point of the promontory.

Standing upon the edge, Osana's gaze traveled south to where Bebbanburg's bulk shadowed the sky, smoke from the cook-fires rising high. On the rocks below her, she spied a cluster of puffins. A smile curved her lips as she admired their fat bodies, large red feet, and waddling gait. They looked such happy birds.

The wind gusted here, and so Osana did not linger. Wrapping her fur cloak about her, she turned and re-entered the monastery, circuiting round to the largest buildings in the heart of it.

She entered a large feasting hall, which was empty at this time of day, although the sulfurous odor of cooking cabbage, onion, and turnip drifted in from where a pottage was most likely simmering over the fire. It would be a simple noon meal, even today.

Osana wandered out of the feasting hall and crossed the courtyard, stopping before a heavy wooden door. An annex came off the side of the church, and she wondered what lay inside.

The monk had said no doors were closed to them today; yet even so, Osana hesitated. She did not want to intrude. However, curiosity got the better of her, and she pushed the door open and went inside.

Closing the door gently behind her, she entered a long, windowless chamber illuminated by a row of cressets burning along the stone and mud wall. The air smelled of pitch and something else—a scent that Osana did not recognize.

Below the row of cressets ran a long bench with many low stools under it. And there, spread out like the wings of multi-colored butterflies, were sheets of the most beautiful illustrations Osana had ever seen.

She realized then that she had stumbled upon the monastery's scriptorium.

Her breath hitched as she moved forward to the end nearest and took a closer look. She had admired Aldfrith's flowing handwriting, and had marveled at the book he had shown her, but the illustrations here made that volume look crudely drawn.

Osana could not believe that a man had crafted these: the colors were even deeper than in nature, the calligraphy exquisite. She recognized a few of the letters, for she had not forgotten her one lesson with Aldfrith. She had practiced writing her name in the dirt in the orchard outside the Great Tower when she was alone. It frustrated her that she could not read the stories upon these sheets of vellum.

She recognized a few of the illustrations, for she knew the story of Christ's birth, life, death, and resurrection. Yet some of the drawings mystified her.

Captivated, Osana slowly moved down the bench, drinking the pages in. She was so enraptured that she did not hear the gentle swish of the door opening behind her. It was the draft on the back of her neck that made her glance over her shoulder.

Aldfrith stood in the doorway.

Slowly, he closed the door behind him. "The scriptorium is a private place, Osana," he greeted her. "You shouldn't be in here."

"Apologies, sire," she replied. "The monk giving us the tour said we could go where we wished. I didn't know this room was forbidden."

"The items in here are precious … irreplaceable."

"I know." She glanced back at the page she had just been studying. It showed a man, swathed in wine-red robes, sitting upon a stool with a blue cushion. A halo around his head marked him as a saint, and a golden winged lion leaped over him. "I've never seen the like. How do they produce such colors?"

"Minerals and vegetable extracts, I believe."

He moved across the room toward her, stopping at her side. "That's the evangelist, Mark. He was represented as a lion, symbolizing the Resurrection of Christ."

"He almost looks alive," Osana breathed. She resisted the urge to reach out and trace the picture with her finger tip. "How does one learn to draw like this?"

"The monks here dedicate their life to it ... and many will go to their grave still learning the craft."

Osana was suddenly aware how close he was standing next to her. She could feel the heat of his body, smell the scent of leather, and the warm spice of his skin. Osana's breathing constricted. She wanted to drown in that scent. Tamping down her reaction to him, for it could lead nowhere good, she glanced up, meeting Aldfrith's eye.

"I was rude to you a moment ago," he said, his expression achingly serious. "Sorry about that."

"Don't apologize." Osana forced a brightness into her tone she did not feel. "I should have asked before entering the scriptorium. I've always been too curious. My father once told me it was an ill-trait in a woman."

Aldfrith smiled then, an expression that lit up the dim space. "He was wrong ... it's a sign of a sharp mind. A good thing in a woman."

Osana huffed. "My husband would have disagreed with you there. He said I'd have been happier if I'd been born dull-witted."

"Well, he was wrong too." Their gazes held, and Aldfrith's smile faded. "It's a long while since we last spoke."

Osana heaved in a deep breath, summoning her courage. "Did I do something to offend you, sire?" She knew the question was bold, but they never had the chance to speak privately, and she would get few opportunities to get the truth out of him.

"You did nothing wrong," he replied. "I've kept my distance for my own reasons. My hall is full of sharp eyes, flapping ears, and wagging tongues. I wanted to protect you."

Osana arched an eyebrow. "Really? Was it me you were trying to protect ... or yourself? You don't seem the type to care what other people think."

His mouth curved into a wry smile, although there was no humor in his eyes. "You see through me, Osana. You've always been able to do that."

Flustered, she looked away. "I don't know what you mean."

"Aye, you do ... you don't let me lie to you. When I talk to you, I feel things I'd rather not. Life is easier without you. I can immerse myself in my writing, my philosophy ... in the role of king. But you shatter my shield."

Osana's head jerked up, her belly clenching. "Then I should go ... I should leave Bebbanburg."

Aldfrith stepped closer and raised his hand, lightly tracing his fingers down her cheek. His touch made her legs tremble. It suddenly felt airless inside the scriptorium. His gaze ensnared hers; she literally could not look away. A shadow moved in his eyes, revealing the war raging within him. "Aye ... I think that would be best," he murmured.

Chapter Twenty-one
What have we done?

HIS GAZE WOULD not let her go. Time froze as they stood there, staring at each other.

Osana's pulse fluttered in the base of her throat.

He wants me to go.

Part of her had been expecting it would come to this, but to hear him say the words hurt like a seax-blade to the gut. There had been another part of her—a secret yearning part—that had hoped to hear the opposite.

Why can't life be like the songs?

Osana swallowed. "I will go then. As soon as we return to the fort, I will begin my preparations."

He said nothing, just watched her with a hunger in his eyes that made her soul ache.

"Don't look at me like that," she whispered, her voice breaking. "I can't bear it."

A low growl escaped him—a mix of anger and frustration—and the next moment he reached out and pulled her into his arms. Osana melted into him, any thought of resistance fluttering from her mind. Like when she had accidentally tumbled onto his lap after their lesson, his nearness completely disarmed her.

Aldfrith's mouth claimed hers: fierce, almost angry. Osana uttered a soft cry, parting her lips for him. She had yearned for this moment ever since their first kiss; she had lain awake in her furs reliving those brief instants in his arms over and over till her body burned with need.

Yet that first kiss had been a surprise, and it had taken her a few moments to relax in his arms.

This time, she ignited like dry tinder under a naked flame. She raised her arms and reached up, burying her fingers in his tousled blond hair. She had dreamed of doing so for months now.

Aldfrith swung her away from the bench, his hands sliding down the column of her back. Still kissing her, he walked them both across the narrow space to the far wall. There, he pressed himself up against her, his mouth ravaging hers.

Osana's head spun, her pulse pounding like a drum in her ears. Even her fevered imagination had not come up with the sensations that now coursed through her. She trembled under his touch; her core pulsed with a deep ache that demanded to be satisfied. She would go mad if he stopped kissing her now.

She felt him reach up and unpin her hair. She wore her long brown tresses braided and wrapped around her head, as many wedded or widowed women did. The heavy braid fell onto her shoulder, and his hand slid down to its tufted end, removing the band of leather keeping it tied. Then, in slow, sensual movements, he began to unbraid it, tangling his fingers into the thick coil.

Osana moaned against his mouth before gently biting his lower lip. He murmured a soft curse in response before claiming her mouth once more—his kiss achingly gentle, his tongue's exploration making sweat bead across her skin.

Who taught him to kiss like this?

The thought was fleeting, dissipating like wood smoke. Who cared—she just wanted more of those kisses; she was greedy for them.

Their bodies were entwined, but layers of heavy clothing separated them. Osana was frustrated; she longed to tear away the heavy woolen tunic she wore so those magician's hands could explore her nakedness. The thought of him doing so on the dirt floor of the scriptorium made heat pulse between her thighs.

Her hand slid down his leather vest to the breeches beneath, her fingertips tracing the hard bulge that strained toward her.

Breathing heavily, Aldfrith drew back from kissing her. His gaze ensnared hers once more. They continued staring at each other, before Osana reached down with her other hand and began to unlace his breeches.

He sprang free: a hot, hard rod in her eager hands. Still holding his gaze, Osana let out a whimper; it was an animal sound, and one that needed no further explanation.

Aldfrith knew what she wanted—what they both craved.

He reached down and pushed up her skirts: the heavy woolen tunic she wore and the linen one underneath it. The air was cold inside the scriptorium, but the sensation of the cool feathering across her naked thighs just heightened Osana's excitement.

With her skirts about her hips, he slid his hands under her naked buttocks, kneed her trembling thighs apart, and thrust deep into her.

Osana took him in easily, to the root. She was ready for him, and the sensation of his shaft filling her, stretching her, sent waves of pleasure rippling out from her core. She cried out, her body shaking from the force of it, arching up against him.

Aldfrith muttered another curse—one the monks here would blanch at—and ground himself against her.

Osana let out a low moan and bent her head back, letting the exquisite sensations sweep her up and carry her away. Coupling had never been like this for her, even in those heady first days with Raedwulf. She did not know her body was capable of such pleasure.

Aldfrith continued to move his hips against hers, bending his head down so that his lips branded her neck.

Osana shuddered and moaned as he moved up the column of her throat to the shell of her ear—and when he kissed and licked her there, she gave a choked cry, her pleasure cresting once more.

Holding her tight, he began to move inside her in slow, deep thrusts. The pleasure was almost unbearable now. Osana tipped her head forward, gasping his name. She was about to ask him to slow down, so she could regain control, but his mouth claimed hers once more.

This time the kiss was savage, bruising. Osana responded in kind, her tongue tangling with his. He thrust deep and hard into her, pinning her against the wall. A moment later Osana screamed into his mouth as he pushed her over the brink, and she spiraled into a vortex of pure sensation.

She felt him reach his climax too, his muffled cry against her mouth. And then his body went rigid as he spilled his seed within her, the muscles cording in the arms she now gripped.

They sagged against the wall together, the raw sound of their ragged breathing filling the scriptorium. Aldfrith buried his face in the crook of her neck, breathing Osana in as he recovered, while she buried her own face in the tousled crown of his head.

"You're finished, I take it?"

Osana and Aldfrith both froze, their breathing stilling.

A chill stole over Osana's skin, and she shivered, noting for the first time just how cold the room was. Reluctantly, she raised her face and looked over to the doorway. Framed there, the pale afternoon sunlight silhouetting his tall, spare figure, stood Bishop Wilfrid.

The look on his face made her blood run cold. Mortification flooded through Osana. How long had he been standing there ... watching?

Aldfrith raised his head, his own gaze traveling to the bishop. "No," he rasped. "We're not ... get out, Wilfrid."

The bishop's gaze narrowed and he clenched the hands that hung at his sides. "You have defiled a holy place," he hissed.

"Get. Out."

The chill in Aldfrith's voice made Wilfrid pause, and a nerve ticked in his cheek. His gaze, full of outrage, slid from Aldfrith's face to Osana's. He then spat upon the ground. "Hōre."

Wilfrid stepped back, drawing the door shut after him with a dull thud.

Osana swallowed the bile that stung the back of her throat. She felt as if she was going to be sick.

Gently, Aldfrith shifted away from her, and she felt his shaft slide free. A pang of acute emptiness followed. She did not want him to leave her. His gaze was shuttered as he refastened his breeches; however, his attention remained upon her.

589

"I don't care that Wilfrid found us," he said quietly. "But I *am* sorry that I lost control ... I shouldn't have done that."

Osana stared at him. "Aldfrith," she whispered. "I—"

He reached up and placed a cautionary finger on her lips. "Don't," he warned, his blue eyes full of pain. "There are no words that can change this. We need to rejoin the others now."

"But ... we need to talk. We won't get another chance to be alone."

He shook his head and took another step back from her. His eyes gleamed now and his throat bobbed. He wore a panicked look, as if talking with her was the last thing he wanted. "That's for the best." He finished readjusting his clothing and moved toward the door. "I shall see you at the noon meal."

A short while later, Osana walked into the feasting hall. She was in a daze, vaguely aware of her surroundings. The meal had already begun: trenchers of coarse bread filled with steaming pottage. The clatter of wooden spoons and the rumble of conversation calmed Osana, and she slipped into the hall as discreetly as possible.

A dull throb between her legs reminded her of what she and Aldfrith had just done. Unlike him, she could not bring herself to regret it. Her blood still sang in the aftermath. The world looked different, as if draped in a soft, golden veil.

Aldfrith sat with the bishop, Oswald, and the senior monks at a table at one end of the hall, near the great hearth. Osana took a seat as far away as possible, at a long bench, next to Mildryth.

However, the woman was staring at her as if Osana had just sprouted a third eye in the center of her forehead.

Mildryth was not the only one. Many of the folk were gawking at her, mouths rudely open, before one or two of them nudged each other with their elbows. One of the men gave Osana a lewd look, and she went cold.

God's bones ... no.

"You and the king made quite a noise," Mildryth hissed in her ear. "I doubt there was anyone in the monastery who didn't hear your cries."

This was ill news indeed.

Mortified, Osana dropped her gaze to her trencher. The sight of food made her bile rise once more. She would not be able to stomach a mouthful.

What have we done?

She had not cared at the time, and neither had he. But she did so now. How would she ever face the folk of the Great Hall again? News of this would spread like the plague, likely racing ahead of her arrival back in Bebbanburg. Life there would become unbearable.

Aldfrith had warned her of this. So had Lora. But she had barely listened to the warnings. She had wanted Aldfrith so badly, still wanted him with an ache that made it painful to breathe. Yet she wanted the impossible; the look on Wilfrid's face had confirmed it.

"Hōre."

The whispered insult from Elflaed, the thegn's wife seated across from her, made Osana flinch. Aye, that was how they would all see her now.

Chapter Twenty-two

A Different Path

THE RETURN TO Bebbanburg was cold and miserable. A light rain had started to fall, and an icy wind gusted in from the north. Osana walked at the back of the group, head bowed.

What had been the most magical experience of her life had quickly spiraled into her most humiliating. Aldfrith had not looked at her at all throughout the meal. He had not been able to shield his unhappiness from the world though; his face had been pale and tense, his gaze haunted.

Reaching the shore, Osana followed the party of mourners south toward the stronghold. She deliberately lagged behind, letting the others draw ahead. None of them glanced over their shoulders to make sure she was still following. She could have turned away and disappeared into the hills and none of them would have seen.

Osana was tempted to do just that. However, she carried no food on her, no thrymsas. She would leave Bebbanburg, as the king had said, but it would have to be with the dawn. They had both agreed she would leave— only that was before the kiss.

Osana's thoughts raced ahead at what she must do when they arrived back at Bebbanburg. She would need to tell Lora that she was leaving, and that she would do so alone. Lora would not be happy about that, but Osana's mind was already made up. She would not take her friend with her. After that she would have to pack swiftly, so that she could leave at first light.

Osana would not show her face in the hall.

She was already an outcast here. The group of mourners now shunned her; even Mildryth had left her side. The king had not acknowledged her either, although she was relieved about that.

It would only make matters worse.

What had happened between them had not been planned. She was not his betrothed, or his wife. He did not owe her anything, and the same went for her.

It was getting dark when they reached the causeway that led up to the low gate. Despite that she had been walking, Osana felt chilled to the bone. She wrapped her mantle close about her, shivering. Her mind was a whirl.

She blamed herself for the mess she had gotten into. She had always been too instinctual, too driven by her emotions. Her attraction to Raedwulf all those years ago had catapulted her into an ill-suited marriage. But she had been so young and full of girlish passion; at least she had an excuse then.

She had known for a while now that she wanted Aldfrith. The desire in her blood had gradually heated over the past months till it had become unbearable. Nothing could have cooled it; being so close to him, being able to talk to him, had just increased her longing.

No wonder she had not sought the life of a nun after Raedwulf's death. Passion ruled her, and it was now proving to be her ruin.

Aldfrith strode into the Great Hall, his mind set upon an evening of solitude and a cup of strong wine. He would call for the iron tub in the corner of his alcove to be filled with steaming water, and bathe. He would see no one, speak to no one, and gather his thoughts.

However, upon entering the hall, his plans dissolved like wood smoke carried away by a strong wind.

He had visitors.

Aldfrith's gaze swept to the high seat, where two leather-clad warriors, their bare arms gleaming with bronze and silver rings, and a small solemn-faced girl with dark hair, sat waiting for him.

Shucking off his cloak, Aldfrith handed it to a waiting servant. "Who's that?" he asked the young man.

"Lady Eldrida, sire ... the King of Mercia's niece. She and her escort arrived just after the noon meal."

Aldfrith frowned. "Why are they here?"

He glanced over at Cerdic, who shrugged. "I didn't know they were coming, milord."

Someone cleared their throat behind them, and Aldfrith glanced over his shoulder to see Bishop Wilfrid. Unlike during the walk back from Lindisfarena, when the bishop had worn a look of scorn and outraged dignity, he appeared sheepish now.

"Lord Aldfrith." He dipped his head. "I invited them."

Aldfrith held his gaze. "Why would you do that?"

Bishop Wilfrid drew himself up, inhaling deeply. "You need a good wife, sire."

Aldfrith closed his eyes for a moment and reined in his temper. This day was certainly one he would never forget. He reopened his eyes, fixing his attention on Wilfrid once more. "But I didn't ask you to invite this woman here. I told you that I have no wish for a wife."

Silence fell. Aldfrith was not the only one looking at the bishop. Oswald was wide-eyed, his gaze flicking between the king and the bishop, while Cerdic was glaring at Wilfrid, looking like he wanted to reach out and throttle him.

Aldfrith shared the feeling. He was naturally slow to anger, having seen what uncontrollable emotion did to people. Yet he was furious now. He felt as if he had no free will. Everything he did was under scrutiny. He could not even look at a woman without folk like Wilfrid making a judgment. He had not planned on making love to Osana at the monastery, but the fact that the bishop had knowingly walked in on them, in order to humiliate them both, made cold rage kindle in the pit of his belly.

However, seeing that the bishop had gone behind his back to arrange a marriage was even worse.

Wilfrid squirmed slightly under the scrutiny. Two high spots of color rose on his gaunt cheeks. "It's for your own good, milord," he said, after a long silence. Aldfrith had to admit that the man had balls. "Lady Eldrida is a pious maid, fresh from the nunnery. You will be her first and last. Surely after today you see why you must wed. The widow has done her wicked work. You need a wife to keep such women at bay." His voice rose as he ended his last sentence, and everyone surrounding them grew still. Aldfrith realized then that they were not looking at the bishop but at a point behind him, where the last of the returning group from Lindisfarena were entering the hall.

Aldfrith turned to see Osana in the doorway.

Her face, framed by fur, was ashen, her hazel-green eyes huge. She had heard every word.

Osana had not thought that this day could get any worse—but she was wrong.

Upon stepping inside the hall, she had heard the bishop slander her to everyone. Humiliation made her stomach tighten into a hard ball. Even so, she had noticed there was a party waiting for Aldfrith upon the high seat. She had also heard the tail-end of the argument between the king and the bishop. She knew what Wilfrid had done. And she did not blame Aldfrith for being angry with him over it.

The king loomed over Wilfrid, his face hard, his eyes blazing. The bishop was not a small man, but he seemed to shrink now under the force of Aldfrith's simmering rage.

Osana just wished the ground would open and swallow her into its maw. Drawing in a deep breath, she inched past the king and the bishop. Her alcove was to the right, just a handful of yards away. Never had a destination held so much appeal.

Across the hall Lora was stirring a pot of stew. Her friend's face was tense with concern as she observed the unfolding scene in front of the entrance.

Was there anyone here who had not witnessed her humiliation?

Osana's throat closed, her vision blurring. She'd had enough. The sooner she fled this place the better. However, she was halfway to her alcove when the bark of Aldfrith's voice stopped her in her tracks.

"Osana ... wait."

Heart pounding, she turned back and stood there, eyes downcast, waiting for his command. She could not bring herself to meet his gaze, could not speak.

"I would speak with you briefly," he said after a pause. "Go to my alcove, and wait for me ... please."

Osana hesitated, torn between doing as bid and disobeying him. She could not be alone with him—not after what had happened at the monastery.

"Sire ... you shouldn't converse with that woman. Send her away now, before she corrupts you further."

"Enough, bishop." Aldfrith's command was harsh. "Another word, and it will be you I shall cast out."

A mutinous silence followed. Osana dared raise her gaze to see that Wilfrid stood, hands clenched at his sides, his face red. However, he wisely held his tongue.

"Osana," Aldfrith repeated her name, his voice softening slightly. "Please go to my alcove."

Defeated, she turned and walked across the hall, under the weight of curious stares. It felt like the longest stretch she had ever traveled. Humiliation bit deep with every step. Reaching the northern edge of the hall, she stepped up onto the platform that ran around the perimeter. She then pushed aside the heavy tapestry that shielded the king's alcove from sight and went inside.

Osana had never been inside Aldfrith's private quarters. She had often wondered what it would be like. Yet this was not the day to find out—today it was the last place she wanted to be.

Letting the hanging fall behind her, she gazed around, taking in the expanse of furs covering the floor and the huge tapestry that covered the wall. There was a single shuttered window, and three cressets burned low. A hearth glowed in the center of the space, throwing out long shadows.

Osana's gaze shifted to the large pile of furs in one corner, and her breathing caught.

God's bones ... don't look there.

She hurriedly glanced away, instead focusing on the small table and stool that sat under the window. They were the only items in the room that spoke of the character of the man occupying it.

Hands clasped before her, Osana moved toward the glow of the fire pit. Her heart fluttered like a caged bird as she waited for Aldfrith to arrive.

Beyond the alcove, she heard the rumble of conversation and the clang and rattle of supper being prepared. She caught raised voices then—one of them clearly the bishop's—and winced.

No doubt he was saying more foul things about her.

Osana closed her eyes. *I wish I could leave here tonight.*

A moment later she felt a draft behind her. Her eyes snapped open, and she turned to see Aldfrith stride into the alcove.

The look on his face cowed her. His eyes had darkened almost to black, and his skin had drawn tight across his cheek bones. His hands clenched in fists at his sides.

Osana swallowed. She had never feared the king before, but having once been married to a man who had raised his hand to her on occasion, she suddenly felt a tremor of fear.

The emotion must have shown on her face, for Aldfrith stopped short. "You look at me with dread in your eyes," he rasped. "Do you really think I'd harm you?"

Their gazes held for a long moment, before Osana shook her head.

Aldfrith took a step toward her before raking a hand through his hair. "Satan's bones, Osana ... I've made a mess of things. I'm sorry ... I—"

"Is this why you wanted to see me?" Osana finally found her voice as her anger rose. "To apologize?"

He stared at her, his gaze pleading. "Aye ... you don't deserve to be treated this way."

Osana watched him, her fury simmering. She was tired of his apologies, tired of being made a fool of. "I will go at dawn," she growled. "I never wanted to cause trouble here."

His face twisted. "This is my doing. I knew what would happen if we were alone together. I knew, and I sought you out anyway. I saw you go into scriptorium—and I followed you."

Osana frowned. "I don't understand ... why should we be ashamed of what happened between us? All we did was succumb to something as natural as breathing."

The king flinched. It was as if she had loosed an arrow and scored a direct hit.

"I don't want this." The words tore out of him. "Love has always been madness for me, and I will have no part of it. Long ago I chose the path of reason. I can't have you near me."

Osana stared at him, her anger ebbing as confusion rose within her. Why would someone make such a choice? When she spoke, her voice shook. "Not everything can be reasoned, Aldfrith. Some things must be guided by your heart."

He shook his head, vehement. "I will not live that way."

Osana clenched her jaw. "Then you have chosen a lonely life."

His expression tightened, and Osana watched a shield rise between them. Despite the hearth behind her, it suddenly felt cold in the alcove. When Aldfrith spoke his voice was devoid of emotion. "Aye, but that is my decision to make."

Chapter Twenty-three

No Place For Me Here

"WHAT HAPPENED AT Lindisfarena?"

It was the question that Osana had been dreading, although she knew Lora would ask it eventually. She glanced up from where she was stuffing clothes into a pack. "Surely you've heard the news." The bitter edge to her voice made her wince. Anger turned her waspish.

Lora's mouth thinned. "The thegns' wives have been in a huddle since they returned from the burial, but they don't share their gossip with the likes of me. If something befell you there, I'd prefer to hear the news from you."

Osana frowned. "I'd rather not speak of it."

"Why?"

"Because it's ... humiliating."

"Better I hear it from you then. Once those women are finished embellishing their tales, it will have no bearing on reality."

Osana sat down heavily upon her furs, her fingers digging into them as if to anchor herself. "I was exploring the monastery alone," she began, her voice low and flat, "and ventured into the scriptorium. Aldfrith found me there. We talked and then ..."

"You coupled?"

Osana clenched her jaw. "Aye, that's right ... we *coupled*. And after it was done, Bishop Wilfrid walked in on us."

Lora's face blanched. "Woden's chariot! That's unfortunate."

Osana ran a tired hand over her face and tried to ignore the anger that still simmered in the pit of her belly. She longed to take a rod to the bishop for his deliberate humiliation of her, both upon Lindisfarena and when they returned to the fort, but instead she was the one who was to be punished. "That's why I'm leaving at first light tomorrow."

"Has the king ordered you to leave?"

Osana nodded, not trusting herself to speak. Her throat now ached from the emotions she was suppressing.

Lora's expression clouded. "I was afraid this would happen. The way he looks at you ... he was never going to leave you alone forever."

Osana rose to her feet and resumed her packing. Her movements were jerky and rough as her anger spilled over. Beyond their alcove, the excited chatter that had erupted after their arrival home from the burial had died down. However, tales of today would circulate for many days to come.

"Do you think he'll wed that whey-faced maid of Mercia?" Lora asked.

"He should. He's better suited to an arranged marriage than wedding for love. Aldfrith reviles emotional attachment."

"Why?"

Osana shrugged, resisting the urge to reach up and massage her temples. A dull throb had taken up residence inside her skull. It hurt to think. "Something in his past scars him. He wouldn't speak of it."

Sympathy flitted across Lora's open face. Yet Osana was not in the mood for anyone to feel sorry for her, any more than she wanted another apology. A lifetime's worth of fury surged up within her.

Not once in her life had she been allowed to simply be herself. Her parents had forced her into a role she had never wanted, as had her sisters. Then Raedwulf had tried to shape her into his idea of the dutiful wife. Every time she had ever spoken up for herself, or expressed her needs, there had always been someone there to tell her how she had to behave.

She had thought Aldfrith different, yet he was just like all the rest.

"I'm leaving at first light tomorrow," Osana said finally, her voice flat, "alone."

Lora's face froze. "No, you're not. I'm coming with you."

"No, Lora. You must stay here."

Lora placed her hands on her hips. However, despite her aggressive stance, her friend's eyes glittered with tears. "The king won't let you travel unescorted ... it's dangerous."

"He's sparing four warriors." Osana's reply tasted sour as she spoke. "I'll not come to any harm on the road to Jedworth."

"You don't want me with you." The hurt in Lora's voice penetrated the veil of anger around Osana. She put down the tunic she had been about to pack and crossed the space between them. She then put her arms around Lora, hugging her tightly.

"I'll miss you," she replied, and she meant it too. Lora had become closer to her than any of her sisters ever had. She would miss her easy banter, her laugh, and her mischievous sense of humor. "But this is where our paths must split. You belong here in Bebbanburg."

Lora disentangled herself, scrubbing away tears. "Why do you say that? I have no more bond with this place than you do."

Osana shook her head, smiling. "You have Cerdic."

Lora snorted. "Why do you keep bringing him up? He's not my man."

"No ... but he could be."

Lora snorted, brushing at the tears that now trickled down her cheeks. "You make it sound like the man has been throwing himself at my feet. He hasn't."

Osana forced a smile. "Give Cerdic time. Maybe you need to offer him some encouragement."

Lora sniffed and favored her with a watery smile of her own. "Why don't you try that with Aldfrith?"

Osana shook her head, her smile fading. "He wants to live in a world he can control ... there is no place for me here."

The first fingers of dawn were lightening the eastern sky, turning the sea to molten gold, when Osana saddled her palfrey and readied herself to leave.

Four of the king's men waited impatiently for her in the stable yard. Jedworth was a little over a day's ride inland from Bebbanburg, and they were keen to arrive there as soon as possible.

Cerdic led the escort. Osana was relieved that Aldfrith had asked his most trusted warrior to accompany her. Cerdic said little, yet she had not lied when she had told Lora she thought him a good man. She was relieved he was with her today.

She led her palfrey out of its stall and into the yard beyond. A breeze tugged at her cloak as she mounted. Although the morning was chill, the sky above had a limpid quality that promised a beautiful day.

Osana adjusted her stirrups and glanced up at where the Great Tower of Bebbanburg loomed above her. Gilded by the dawn light, it was a breathtaking sight. This place had been her home for the past few months, and despite everything, she had been the happiest here of anywhere since childhood.

Disappointment filtered in, dimming the anger that still clenched her belly. She had dared hope to settle in this place, but now realized that that hope had been a foolish one. She should not have put her fate in the hands of others.

Osana drew in a deep breath and looked away from the tower. There was no sign of the king. He would not come out to see her off.

From this day forth things would change. From now on she would be her own mistress. Happiness would come from small pleasures, in carving a simple life for herself. She had never been to Jedworth, and had not seen her aunt Hagona in nearly a decade, but she would make her new life work.

She had no other choice.

Even so, the decision did not make Osana feel any better. A dull ache had taken up residence under her ribs. She wished to weep, to rage against the world, to beat at it with her fists—but she would hold on to her tears for a while yet.

I'll weep when I'm far from here.

"Osana." Cerdic's gruff voice reached her. She turned to find him watching her, sympathy in his dark eyes. "Are you ready?"

Osana nodded, before gathering the reins and urging her palfrey forward. Without uttering a word, she rode out under the high gate, and did not look back.

Aldfrith crossed the hall, his wolfhound at his heels.

Lady Eldrida was waiting for him upon the high seat. This morning the girl looked impossibly young, around sixteen years his junior. Pity stirred within Aldfrith at the sight of her: small and elfin, her tiny frame swamped in the pale tunic she wore.

Poor child.

They had brought her here like a breeding sow, offering her up to him with no thought to her feelings on the matter.

All the same, he had noted the evening prior that Eldrida was not like his previous wife, Cuthburh. This maid seemed keen to wed him. She had appeared crestfallen when he had exchanged sharp words with the bishop the night before, her mouth trembling as if she might weep.

Eldrida looked brighter this morning though. She smiled at Aldfrith as he approached. However, the faces of the men flanking her were less welcoming. They barely restrained their glowers as he stepped up onto the high seat.

He knew they all hoped he had reflected upon his decision overnight, that he had revised it. The look on Eldrida's face warned him that she had not lost hope.

Aldfrith was about to disappoint her.

"Good morning, Lady Eldrida," he greeted her, taking his seat at the head of the table. Argus flopped down at his feet in the hope that a stray crust might find him. A servant appeared at the king's elbow, placing a plate of fresh bread and a cup of milk before him. Pots of freshly churned butter and honey dotted the table.

Yet Aldfrith had no appetite this morning. His stomach churned.

Not touching the food before him, he met the eye of Thorin, the warrior who led the Mercian party. The man stared back, his expression challenging.

Aldfrith shifted his gaze to Lady Eldrida then. "I'm sorry, but you have had a wasted trip," he began. He had intended to approach the subject softly, but suddenly found that he had no patience for it. "The bishop called for you without speaking to me first. I have no wish for a wife."

Beside her, the Mercian warrior snorted. "You don't mince your words, milord."

Aldfrith's mouth twisted. "I don't see the point in doing so," he admitted, bitterness edging his voice. "Although it seems that even when I speak plainly, folk willfully misunderstand me."

"My uncle will be angry." Eldrida spoke up then. Tears welled in her large, dark eyes. Her small mouth pursed as she struggled to contain her disappointment. The hope he had seen moments earlier drained from her face. "He will think you sent me away because you find me ugly. He will punish me."

Aldfrith paused, struggling between guilt and irritation. Yet he was not about to be manipulated. "I shall write the king a letter," he replied firmly. "I will explain my reasons. Do not worry—you will not be blamed."

His answer did not please her. The girl's pursed mouth flattened into a thin line.

It was as Aldfrith suspected. She had made a desperate attempt to change his mind. She had no fear of her uncle.

Irritation surged through Aldfrith. This was what he hated most about being king. Ever since he had worn the crown, folk did not see him as a man. He was an authority figure; folk came to him wanting something. They wanted a pardon, lands, weregild, or justice.

How he missed his days upon the isle of Iona, spent in the company of the monks. They had not wanted anything from him but his companionship. They talked to him because they liked him, not because they wanted a favor.

Aldfrith sat back in his chair, pushing aside the plate of bread. On the floor below him, Argus gave a soft whine, reminding him of his presence. With a sigh, Aldfrith stretched out his hand for a piece of bread and handed it down to his hound.

"You've all traveled far to reach us," he said after a moment. "Please accept our hospitality, and stay a few days longer."

"I think not, milord." Thorin's voice was wintry. "If you will not take Lady Eldrida as your wife, we will not remain at Bebbanburg. Prepare your letter in haste, for we depart at dawn tomorrow."

Aldfrith nodded, secretly relieved. He wanted rid of these Mercians as much as they wished to leave him. The sooner the better.

All he wished for right now, was to be alone. He was aware of the prying eyes of his retainers and their wives, who surrounded him as he sat on the high seat. Their gazes tracked him, studying his face.

News of what had happened between him and Osana would have traveled quickly from one end of the fort to the other. Fortunately for her, Osana would be many furlongs distant by now—she would not have to suffer their whispers, sneers, and stares.

At the thought of her, Aldfrith's throat constricted.

It was a mistake to dwell on Osana, for the feelings those thoughts roused made a sickening sense of desperation well within him.

He could not be near her, he could not speak to her, without a strong need consuming him. Aldfrith had nearly lost control again the evening before when they had spoken alone inside his alcove. He had felt himself weakening, for the sight of her standing near the hearth, the naked vulnerability in her eyes, had almost unraveled him.

But then she had asked him of his past.

After that it had been easy to shut himself off from her. His past belonged to another life, another person. How hard he had tried to put it all behind him. Osana had risked reopening a wound that had taken years to fully heal.

Time rolled back, and he remembered the wreck he had been that day he had arrived upon Iona: young and full of desperation and hurt. That island, and the kind monks who lived there, had healed him. Living there had helped him wash the past away—yet it appeared that the walls he had built around his heart could not withstand this new life as king.

Ever since moving to Bebbanburg, they had slowly been crumbling. Now that Osana had left, he would have to painstakingly rebuild them.

Chapter Twenty-four

Alone

JEDWORTH WAS SMALLER than Osana had expected.

The burg, surrounded by a wooden palisade, had a new, fresh look, as if the town had recently been built. They rode in upon a bright, windy spring morning. The scent of spring bulbs laced the air and birdsong surrounded them.

A narrow river, named the Jed Water, cut its path through the town. Osana spied men fishing on the banks. They turned, their faces curious, watching the party trot in through the gates.

Osana tensed at the sight of them before forcing herself to relax.

No one knows me here, she reminded herself. *I left my shame behind me in Bebbanburg.*

She glanced over at where Cerdic rode next to her. "I thought Jedworth was older than this," she admitted. "It looks as if folk just settled here."

"Much of Jedworth was burned to the ground by the Picts," Cerdic explained. "The warlord Bridei and his men were trying to provoke King Ecgfrith into war by raiding deep into his territory."

Osana shook her head. "Well they succeeded. I heard the king even went against Cuthbert's advice."

Cerdic snorted a laugh. "Aye ... Ecgfrith couldn't see straight where Bridei was concerned. The Pict fostered at Bebbanburg as a lad, and there was bad blood between them. Ecgfrith wanted vengeance at all costs; in the end it was his undoing."

Osana gazed around her, surprised at the news that the Picts had been so bold as to raid this far south. No wonder the king had been enraged. Although Jedworth sat in the heart of the borderlands between the two kingdoms, it was clearly an Angle settlement.

The party of riders made their way up an unpaved street to a large open space, flanked on one side by the ealdorman's hall. This too had been recently rebuilt; the hall boasted a pristine thatched roof and a golden timber frame that had not yet been darkened by the seasons.

A circle of stalls ringed the wide space. Vendors filled it, hawking spring greens, fresh meat, and bread. Women wandered amongst the stalls, wicker baskets under their arms. Many of them were smiling as they chatted to the stall-owners.

Osana watched them, envy rising within her. These women appeared to have simple lives, the kind of life she had always wanted. However, as the wives of cottars, merchants, and craftsmen, their lives would likely not be easy. They would work hard and bear many children. Still, Osana envied them all the same.

"Do you know where your aunt lives?" Cerdic asked her.

Osana shook her head. "I never visited her here."

The warrior pulled up his horse and dismounted. "I'll be back shortly."

Osana watched him stride over to one of the stalls, where a florid-faced man sold live geese, ducks, and fowl. The honking, quacking, and clucking coming from the pen next to him was deafening. Cerdic spoke briefly with the vendor, before nodding briskly and returning to his horse.

"Did you find out where she lives?" Osana asked.

"Aye," he replied with a wry smile. "It appears your aunt is well known in Jedworth ... by all accounts she is a woman with a strong character."

Osana frowned at this news, apprehension fluttering in her belly. The last time she had seen Hagona, she had found her acerbic. Her aunt had never wedded. Even as a young woman, she had been a force to be reckoned with. And now that Osana was about to be reunited with her, she wondered at the wisdom of coming here.

I had no choice. It was either here ... or a nunnery.

They left the market square and rode to the northern edge of town, to where a low timber building sat just a few feet from the palisade that ringed the town. A carefully tended garden surrounded the dwelling, as did a scattering of outbuildings. Fowl scratched in the dirt, and a goat, tethered outside one of the sheds, bleated as they approached.

Osana's gaze alighted upon the small figure kneeling in the center of the vegetable plot. The woman worked deftly, pulling out weeds from around onions.

The woman glanced up, upon hearing the thud of approaching hooves. It had been a while since Osana had seen Hagona. She was her mother's eldest sister, and in her youth was said to have been a beauty. Yet the years had not been kind to her. She looked like a sinewy old fowl. Her face was gaunt, her mouth bitter. Her once thick brown hair was now completely grey.

Hagona watched the party of riders and her gaze narrowed. "Wes hāl," she greeted them, although there was no warmth in her voice, only suspicion.

Cerdic drew up his horse. "Good morning ... are you Hagona?"

The woman nodded curtly. "Who wants to know?"

Osana spoke up then. There was little point in letting Cerdic speak on her behalf. "Good day, aunt. Do you remember me?"

Hagona went still. Those hazel eyes—so similar to Osana's mother's—shifted to her. "Osana?"

"Aye ... it's been a long while, has it not?"

The woman nodded. "What brings you here, girl? Where's that brute you married?"

Osana heard snorts behind her, as the men escorting her choked back laughter. Only Cerdic did not look amused.

Osana had forgotten how much her aunt disliked Raedwulf. The pair of them had only met twice, and on both occasions Raedwulf had named her a scold. "No wonder no man would have her," he had grumbled. "Her shrew's tongue would have sent them all running."

"Raedwulf died," she answered after a brief pause. "Over a year ago now."

Hagona watched her. She did not say she was sorry, and Osana was grateful for that. Her aunt was not one to say things she did not mean. She would not pretend to grieve over the death of a man she had never liked. A long pause drew out between them then. It became clear that Hagona was not going to be the one to speak next.

Inhaling deeply, Osana gathered her nerve. "I'm no longer welcome in Hagustaldes," she said quietly. "Raedwulf's brother is ealdorman now, and his wife hates me."

Hagona straightened up, brushing soil off her hands. Her thin face had hardened, as the reason for Osana's arrival dawned on her. "So you thought you'd be welcome here?" Her voice was clipped. "You thought your old spinster aunt would look after you."

The words stung. Osana clenched her jaw. She hated prostrating herself like this. Yet she could not lose her temper, for the alternative was to take the veil.

"I will earn my place under your roof," she replied evenly. "I would not ask this of you if there was any other choice. My parents are dead, and my sisters all live in cramped homes with barely enough room for them and their families. Please, aunt … you are my only hope."

Lora descended the steps into the yard outside the Great Tower, a load of dusty furs in her arms. A balmy spring morning greeted her. The sun kissed her face, and she noted that blossom had now appeared on the branches of the apple and pear trees in the neighboring orchard.

Osana would have liked to see that, she thought with a pang. *She spent a lot of time in the orchard.*

Just over two days had passed since Osana's departure, and Lora already missed her terribly. She missed sharing an alcove with her and chatting together at night in the darkness. It had been wonderful to have a space that she only had to share with one other. With Osana gone, Lora had been forced to give up her alcove. She now slept upon the rushes in the Great Hall.

She did not sleep well out there. The night before, one of the warriors lying next to her had tried to grope her. She had slapped him before wriggling away, yet the incident had unnerved her. She would sleep in a different place tonight, but how long till another man tried his luck?

Frowning at the thought, Lora strode over to a long railing near the stable complex and hung up the furs. She then picked up a long wooden paddle. Now that the weather had started to warm, it was time to clean out the alcoves. During the long, cold months furs became the home of mites and rodents. Now these unwelcome guests needed to be turfed out.

Whack. Lora hit the furs with her paddle, sending a cloud of dust into the air.

I should have made Osana take me with her.

Whack.

I don't belong here either.

Whack.

Anger rose within Lora as she beat the furs, her movements growing increasingly savage.

Osana's all I have left, and now she's gone too.

Tears pricked Lora's eyes as she continued to beat the furs. Never had she felt so lonely.

"You keep beating that fur like that, and you'll rip it to pieces."

A male voice, edged with wry amusement, intruded.

Lora halted, panting from exhaustion, and straightened up, pushing a stray blond curl out of her eyes.

Cerdic stood behind her, next to his horse. The small group of warriors who had accompanied Osana west were dismounting behind him.

"You're back," she said before cursing herself for being a goose. Clearly he was back—here he was standing before her.

Cerdic raised an eyebrow, observing her. "Aye."

"Osana ... how is she?"

"Well enough. We left her in the company of her aunt."

Lora frowned. There was something in his tone that put her on edge. "Is something amiss?"

"No ... I just pity Osana, that's all. Hagona of Jedworth has a tongue that could cut stone."

Silence fell between them then. Lora glanced across at the fur. Indeed, she had given it a good thrashing. She should take it back inside and get another.

"Lora." The way he said her name made her tense. She glanced up to find that Cerdic had stepped closer. "I didn't have the chance to talk to you before I left ... are you well?"

She held his gaze and deliberated whether she should lie to him—tell him she was as happy as a newborn lamb on this fine spring day. Yet she could not bring herself to say the words.

Cerdic looked at her in such a way, she felt only the truth would do.

"I miss her," she said quietly. "And I wonder what my place here is now."

"The same as it was. You know you're welcome in the king's hall."

Lora huffed. "Am I?"

"Do you still have your alcove?"

She shook her head. "A servant doesn't get to have such a space to herself. One of the king's thegns and his wife took it."

She looked into his rugged face and saw a softness settle in his eyes. It was unexpected, and it made a strange warmth rise within her. It was not pity she saw, but something deeper, stronger.

He was the only one here who really noticed Lora. Ever since Osana's departure, the other women hardly bothered with her

"I feel so alone," she said finally, her voice barely above a whisper. "I was wed once, but when my husband died, I lost my purpose. I don't know who I am anymore."

He stepped closer to her still, their bodies so near they were almost touching.

"I lost my wife a few years back," he rumbled. She stared up at him, feeling the tension that now emanated from his big body. "Since then I've served my king and done my duty ... only it doesn't fill the emptiness."

Lora's eyes pricked with tears at this news. "I'm sorry," she breathed. "I didn't know."

Cerdic raised a hand then, cupping her cheek gently, his thumb tracing the swell of her lower lip.

Desire arched up within Lora, a sensation she had never thought to feel again. She inhaled sharply.

"You brought sunshine into this tower the moment you stepped into it," he said softly, uncaring that they stood on the edge of a busy yard, surrounded by curious eyes and sharp ears. "Before meeting you, I'd forgotten what it was like to smile."

Chapter Twenty-five

Impossible

Two months later ...

OSANA SAT MILKING the goat. Snowdrop was its name, a creature that Hagona doted on like a child. Osana could understand why: Snowdrop had a sweet, inquisitive temperament and was undemanding company. The rhythmic squirts of milk in the pail, and the first rays of morning sun on her back, relaxed Osana as she worked.

With the pail full of frothy milk, Osana carefully lifted it from under the goat, patted Snowdrop on the flank, and straightened up.

Her vision dimmed as she did so, a wave of dizziness sweeping over her. Osana swayed and reached out with her free hand, catching the edge of the pen where Snowdrop spent her nights.

She had been feeling out of sorts the past couple of days, with the odd dizzy-spell and mild bouts of nausea.

She hoped she was not sickening from something.

Osana made her way up the path, in-between growths of rosemary, thyme, and sage, to the front door of Hagona's home. Knocking gently, she then went inside. She did not sleep under the same roof as her aunt; Hagona had given her the old fowl house, an annex that joined the back of this building. Initially Osana had despaired, but once she had cleaned the space thoroughly and made it into a comfortable, albeit cramped home, she was glad she lived apart from her aunt.

Hagona was not easy company.

"There you are." A sharp voice greeted her as she entered the dwelling. Hagona stood next to the hearth that dominated her home, cooking a wheel of bread over a griddle. "I swear you get slower at milking that goat with each passing day."

"It's spring ... Snowdrop is giving a lot of milk at the moment," Osana replied. "Look. She filled the bucket to the brim."

Hagona gave a snort. "Well, pour us a cup each then. The bread's ready."

Osana carried the pail over to the scrubbed wooden table that stretched down the western wall of the dwelling. There, she took a ladle and two wooden cups before filling them. Meanwhile, Hagona had torn the freshly baked bread in two and was sitting by the hearth, a wooden platter on her knee. She was slathering the bread with butter and honey.

Osana's mouth quirked. Her aunt was a tiny woman without an ounce of fat on her, yet she ate like a famished hound. Granted though, Hagona worked hard too. Osana rarely saw her rest during the day.

Joining her aunt, Osana passed her a cup of milk and took a seat opposite. But when she lifted the cup to her lips, she stopped. The warm rich scent of milk made her gorge rise.

Swallowing, Osana lowered the cup.

Hagona glanced up, her mouth full of bread. "What's wrong?"

"Nothing."

Her aunt's brow furrowed. "The milk doesn't taste bad, does it? The goat hasn't been eating buttercup again I hope."

Osana shook her head. "It's fine, aunt."

"So why don't you drink it?"

Osana lifted the cup to her lips once more and forced herself to sip. This time, nausea hit her in a wave. She gagged, slapping a hand over her mouth to prevent herself from being sick.

Across the hearth, Hagona went still.

"God's bones, girl … anyone would think you were with child."

A chill settled over Osana.

That's impossible. She was barren—the healer in Hagustaldes had told her so. In all her years with Raedwulf, her womb had never quickened, while he had sired a number of bastards in the surrounding village.

She had now missed two moon flows, although since her cycle had never been regular, she had not thought much of it.

She did now.

"It can't be Raedwulf's," her aunt said, her thin face turning thoughtful before her eyes widened. "That's why you came to live here, isn't it? You were running from someone."

"No," Osana replied quickly, although the sharpness of her tone and the speed of her answer merely confirmed her aunt's theory.

Hagona's mouth compressed. "Who is he?"

"It doesn't matter."

"He's wedded then."

Osana shook her head. "Please leave it be, aunt."

Hagona drew herself up. "You're a guest under my roof. You'll have no secrets from me."

Osana set aside her cup and untouched platter of bread, and rose to her feet. Nausea warred with confusion and panic now. She could not bear her aunt's nagging. "Some things are best not spoken of," she replied firmly as she tried to gather her scattered wits. "Please … I'll tell you when I'm ready."

Her aunt's mouth thinned. Hagona was not so easily put off. "We'll see about that," she muttered.

Jedworth's healer confirmed what Osana already knew in her bones to be true. The elderly woman had run her hands over Osana's abdomen and asked her a few questions before giving a brisk nod.

"Aye, lass ... you're with child."

Shortly after, Osana stumbled from the woman's hovel, which was located near Jedworth's south gate, her mind whirling, her stomach churning. Panicked sweat beaded her skin. She could never tell Hagona who the father of the child was; she could speak of it to no one here.

Aldfrith can never know.

She walked up the dirt street, her thoughts turning inward. Overhead, the sky had clouded over, dimming the day—yet Osana barely noticed it. All she could think about was the fact that soon her belly would start to swell. In a few months' time, folk would start to notice.

They would stare and whisper behind her back. What would she do then?

Osana swallowed as her throat constricted. Would Hagona allow her to remain with her? As sharp-tongued as her aunt could be, she was not a pitiless woman. Surely she would not cast a pregnant woman out?

Despite that she had told herself she would not weep, Osana's vision misted. She blinked rapidly, fighting the tears that threatened to well. She could cry later when she was alone in her annex, not here in the middle of town where folk would see. Her arrival had set tongues wagging as it was.

Wait till they realize I'm bearing a child ... they'll have fodder for gossip for years.

Despite that the day was not cold, Osana drew the woolen shawl she wore around her shoulders tighter. She felt shivery and light-headed. Inhaling deeply, she fought against the panic that now cramped her bowels. She needed to calm down, to think clearly.

The news had felt like a condemnation, yet she knew that once the shock passed she would learn to live with it. She needed to plan for the future and decide how she would keep her aunt's prying at bay.

What would she tell the child about its father?

Stop it. She was getting ahead of herself. Many women lost their babes during the early period of pregnancy. There was a chance she might lose hers. She would deal with what to tell the child later, after this first hurdle had been scaled.

Osana made her way across town, passing through the market square where the ealdorman's hall loomed over the busy cluster of stalls and shoppers. The sight of the hall made her remember her old life in Hagustaldes, her daily unhappiness as Raedwulf's wife.

The memory calmed her.

As upset as she was this morning, she was no longer that woman. Penniless and pregnant she might be, but she no longer lived under Raedwulf's thumb. She no longer felt like a failure as a wife—as a woman. Strangely, despite her hurt and lingering anger toward Aldfrith, he had somehow freed her. And Hagona, although bossy, did not treat her like property. She was happier in her fowl coop than she had ever been in the ealdorman's hall.

She walked on, and presently found herself passing Jedworth's church. A sturdy building made of timber, with a steep pitched roof crested by an iron cross, the sight of the church made Osana pause.

The church in Hagustaldes had been her refuge. Before Raedwulf's death she had taken to visiting regularly, for it was one of the few places where she could sit alone with her thoughts. She had not visited the church in Bebbanburg so often. The priest, Oswald, was not an offensive man, and left her alone to pray, yet Bishop Wilfrid was such a frequent visitor at the fort that Osana often worried he would corner her there.

Jedworth was different. The bishop did not live here, and Osana was reluctant to return home to Hagona's interrogation.

Instead, she climbed the stone steps before the church and went inside. She entered a quiet space where the scuff of her shoes on the stone pavers seemed suddenly loud, as did her breathing.

Grey light filtered in through the high windows, illuminating floating dust motes, and Osana breathed in the fatty odor of tallow and the scent of incense. The local priest—a portly fellow named Torht—did not appear to be in residence.

The realization relieved Osana. She wanted to be alone for a while so she could sort through her thoughts.

Low wooden benches filled the church, and Osana walked up the aisle between them. Before her loomed a high altar, where a crucifix gleamed in the morning light. It was an arresting sight, and Osana kept her gaze upon it as she sat down upon one of the benches near the front.

Seated there, she clasped her hands together and raised them before her.

She did not pray. Instead, she closed her eyes a moment, letting the peace of this place settle upon her.

Osana was hesitant to pray. It had been a while, and where did she start? She had never used church as a place to divest herself of sin and salve her conscience, and she did not want to start now. Instead, it was a place where she could just 'be', without being questioned or judged.

And so she remained there, still and silent, looking for answers she knew she would never find.

Chapter Twenty-six

Only One Cure

ALDFRITH STARED DOWN at the sheet of vellum before him. He had spent all morning on these lines, had concentrated so much over them that the muscles on the back of his neck felt stiff and sore, and a head-ache formed in his temples.

A few months earlier, he would have looked upon the words with pride, yet now they irritated him. Frowning, he read the first paragraph aloud:

> "Abandonment results in slander.
> Humility wins good favor.
> Stinginess is disparaged.
> Humility engenders gentleness.
> Familiarity fuels strife.
> Arrogance produces disfavor."

Aldfrith finished reading. Hollow. Those words he had labored over now seemed meaningless. Osana's words returned to him then. Months ago she had sat next to him in this annex and questioned him.

You must be very sure of your beliefs, of the nature of folk, to write so confidently.

He had once been very sure, but these days he was less so. He had always liked the idea of having ideals to live by; it had made the messiness of life easier to deal with. It created order out of chaos.

The Philosopher King. He had thought himself so wise, yet now he felt a fool.

Without those ideals who was he? A man with an empty heart and a barren soul, who sat upon a lonely throne.

Aldfrith cursed and pushed himself back from his desk. "Damn you, Osana," he muttered. "This is your doing."

Next to him Argus stirred and rose to his feet, shaking himself off after a nap. The wolfhound moved forward, pressing against his master's leg for some affection. With a sigh, Aldfrith reached down and stroked the dog's ears. He was fortunate in Argus. The hound's love was simple, uncomplicated.

"Come on," he muttered. "Let's take a walk in the orchard. I need some fresh air."

They left the annex, Aldfrith crossing the yard in front of the Great Tower in long strides with his hound trotting at his heels. Lora, the companion Osana had brought with her from Hagustaldes, was kneeling by the well, scrubbing linen tunics on a wooden washing board, a cake of lye in hand.

"Good morning, sire," she called out with a wide smile as he passed.

Aldfrith acknowledged her with a nod. The woman had looked miserable for the first days after Osana's departure, yet two moons on she appeared to have recovered her spirits. Whenever Aldfrith saw her of late, she was smiling.

Aldfrith continued on to the orchard. The blossom had come and gone on the apple and pear trees here, and the branches were bright with tender new leaves. They were nearing the end of spring now, and soon the first tiny fruits would start to appear.

The orchard was Aldfrith's favorite spot in Bebbanburg. Hidden away inside the inner palisade of the fort, it was a private space that only those who lived in the Great Tower had access to. Even so, the king often had the space to himself.

He wandered down the avenue between two rows of apple trees and breathed deeply, enjoying the heat of the sun on his back. Despite that it was peaceful in here, the sounds of daily life in the fort intruded: the clang of iron from the forges on the King's Way, the shouts of vendors in the market square, and a burst of laughter from one of his warriors in the training yard behind the tower.

The sounds of life.

Today Aldfrith felt apart from it all. He did not like feeling so alone. In the past he had sought solitude, reveled in it. Upon Iona there had been days in the winter, especially, when he would not see anyone; yet it had not mattered then. He had been lost with his reading and writing, his musing.

His thoughts no longer brought him solace. Instead, they had begun to torture him.

Reaching the far side of the orchard, he stopped before a low wooden bench. Aldfrith's gaze settled upon it. It had been a mistake coming here, for this spot reminded him of Osana and the first time they had spoken.

He remembered how guilty she had looked, for she had been eating an apple when she stumbled upon him playing his harp. The conversation that had followed between them had been the most revealing of his life.

Osana had a way of challenging him that excited him, body and soul. Life with her would never be dull.

Enough ... stop thinking of her.

Aldfrith turned away from the bench and walked back the way he had come. Argus trotted off and lifted his leg against a tree, oblivious to his master's despair.

And despair it was.

It was an illness he could not shake. He had thought her absence would heal him, cleanse him, that life would go back to the way it was. Instead, with each passing day he felt the lack of Osana in his life ever more keenly. He ached to see her, to hear the softness of her voice, to touch her soft skin.

Aldfrith swallowed a groan of frustration. *Why do I torture myself so?*

It seemed the more he tried to push her from his thoughts, the more Osana intruded.

I just need more time, he told himself as he lengthened his stride. *I need to weather this.*

A scene greeted him when he emerged from the trees.

Cerdic and Lora stood together near the well. She was giggling and flicking sudsy water at him, while he grinned and tried to catch her.

Aldfrith's step faltered; he was intruding.

But they had not seen him. The couple had eyes only for each other. Lora squealed and tried to dodge past Cerdic as he made another grab for her. He caught her around the waist and pulled her into his arms, kissing her deeply.

Aldfrith halted. Of course. *I must be the last person in the tower to realize.* His thoughts had turned inward of late; he had barely noticed the warming of the weather or the turning of the season. And all the while Cerdic and Lora had been falling in love.

No wonder Cerdic smiled more of late. No wonder Lora's eyes shone.

Aldfrith watched them, noted the way Lora melted against the warrior, how he placed a possessive hand in the small of her back.

He knew Cerdic's story, of the loss he had suffered. The warrior had dedicated himself to serving the king afterward, had shunned any emotional attachment. But meeting Lora had changed him.

He's a braver man than me.

And yet a sliver of jealousy wormed its way into Aldfrith's heart. If there was hope for Cerdic, could there not be hope for him too?

Aldfrith clenched his jaw and walked across the yard, giving the couple a wide berth. No, he would not relent.

"Sire, I would speak to you a moment."

Aldfrith glanced up from where he was playing his harp, his fingers stilling. The sound of the lament he had been playing cut off.

Bishop Wilfrid, seated to his left, was watching him with an expectant expression. Aldfrith forced himself not to frown. Wilfrid had taken to visiting Bebbanburg so regularly these days that he spent far more time at the fort than at his home in Inhrypum, where his bishopric was based.

He was a trying presence in the Great Tower, for he brought a huge retinue with him on each visit and required four alcoves for himself and his servants.

Wilfrid was still not content with his lot, and wished to extend his land farther afield. Aldfrith sensed this was what the bishop was about to raise with him now. It was all he talked of these days.

"What is it, Father?"

Wilfrid frowned, perhaps catching the sharpness in the king's tone. "Cuthbert's passing has left a gulf that needs to be filled, sire. Is there any word on who will be appointed the new prior?"

Aldfrith reached for his cup of wine and took a sip, letting the bishop wait before he answered. "A monk named Eadberht has come to my attention. I'm considering him for the position."

Wilfrid's mouth puckered. "Eadberht of Dùn Bàrr?"

"Aye, that is the man."

"But he is a northerner, sire."

Aldfrith favored him with a tight smile. "Aye, as am I."

The bishop clasped his bony hands before him, his dark brows knitting together. "Milord ... I have overseen Lindisfarena over these past months."

"So I've heard."

Wilfrid's frown deepened at this, but he continued nonetheless. "I have ensured their northern habits have been tempered with my influence—of Roman ways. They were hesitant at first, but they will accept the new order soon enough."

Aldfrith reached for a cup of wine, took a large gulp, and swallowed. "Lindisfarena is a holy place, and I will not have everything Cuthbert worked for tampered with," he replied coldly. "A man like Eadberht will respect it."

Wilfrid drew himself up. "And you think I won't?"

"I think you're best to focus on Inhrypum. Another will become prior of Lindisfarena."

A chill silence settled between them. When Wilfrid eventually spoke, a muscle ticked in his jaw. "Ever since I returned to the north, you've made my life here a trial ... sire." The words were ground out, the title at the end uttered almost as a curse.

Aldfrith cocked his head. He was not in the mood to be criticized by the likes of Wilfrid. "All I've done is look after the interests of this kingdom," he replied, "and if that means tempering your ambitions then so be it."

"You need a man like me here," Wilfrid shot back, undeterred. "A man who has lived in Rome, who has studied under the Pope himself. Instead, you have obstructed me at every turn. You denied me Hagustaldes, and now Lindisfarena. The Pope shall hear of this."

Aldfrith went still. "I have been generous and lenient with you, Father Wilfrid," he said, his voice chill, "overly so."

The bishop stared back at him, determined not to back down. "The Pope shall hear differently. He shall hear the truth."

Aldfrith leaned toward him, holding his gaze. "I care not what you have to say to the Pope. He's in Rome, and we are a world away. This is Northumbria, and here, I rule."

The bishop blanched. "That is blasphemy."

Aldfrith set down his cup with a thump. "My patience with you is at an end. I suggest you gather your servants and depart for Inhrypum this afternoon."

Wilfrid gaped at him, his outrage faltering. "You're sending me away?"

"Aye ... and if you test me again, I'll send you much farther than Inhrypum. I now understand why my brother was so keen to send you into exile. You push too hard, Wilfrid. Learn your place, or someone will teach it to you."

Aldfrith rose from the table, signaling that the conversation had come to an end. Around them, the others who had been enjoying a cup of ale after the noon meal had all gone silent, their gazes watchful. Cerdic was among them, his expression hooded.

Not acknowledging any of them, Aldfrith turned his focus back to the bishop once more. "Be gone from Bebbanburg by dusk," he said, his voice flat and cold. "Or I'll have you chased out."

Cerdic caught up with Aldfrith as he crossed the stable yard. "You've vexed the bishop. The man's just taken a rod to one of his servants for packing his trunk too slowly."

"Just as long as he's gone from here before dusk," Aldfrith growled back. "He tries my patience."

"For what it's worth, you should have done that months ago, sire."

Aldfrith halted, his gaze sweeping to Cerdic.

The warrior grinned at him, not remotely cowed by the king's wintry expression. "It's rare to see you so riled, sire. Has Wilfrid really gotten under your skin so?"

Aldfrith loosed a breath. "The bishop has been a thorn in my arse ever since I arrived at Bebbanburg ... but you're right ... it's not just him."

Cerdic's gaze widened. "Sire?"

"It's life," Aldfrith replied shortly. "Sometimes it feels as if I wear a millstone around my neck." He turned then and continued on his way to the stables. He needed to be free of this fortress for a while. He would saddle his horse and go for a ride along the beach; perhaps the sea air would sweeten his mood. Cerdic was right, anger burned within him this afternoon, and it took little for the flames to kindle.

He entered the stables, a low-slung building with two rows of stalls and a wide aisle between them. His stallion was stabled at the far end. Aldfrith had almost reached his destination when he realized that Cerdic was right behind him.

"I'm ill company today," he said, not looking over at the warrior. "Best you leave me."

"Do you wish for your old life, sire?" Cerdic asked. "Would you go back to Iona if you could?"

Aldfrith halted and turned. Cerdic had stopped a few feet back and was watching him, his expression shadowed, for it was dimly lit inside the stables.

"No," Aldfrith answered, surprising himself when he realized it was the truth. "I was a different man ... and I can't go back to that life."

"What then?"

Aldfrith frowned. "Cerdic ... you're trying my patience."

"What would it take then," Cerdic pressed, ignoring the warning, "for you to find peace?"

Aldfrith tensed, irritation surging. "I don't know. I don't have the answers for anything anymore."

Cerdic gave a wry smile, folding his arms across his chest. "I was wondering when you'd realize that."

Aldfrith clenched his jaw. Anger smoldered in the pit of his belly. Cerdic was coming perilously close to receiving a black eye. "I'm happy to oblige. You can go now, Cerdic."

Only, the warrior did not leave. He stood, legs apart, staring Aldfrith down with a look that only served to make the king's mood darken further. "I didn't mean that as an insult, sire. Only that I'm pleased to see you've flown down from your eyrie to join the rest of us."

Aldfrith gaped at him, momentarily lost for words. But Cerdic had not yet finished. "Admit it, you've not been right since Osana left," Cerdic continued, his tone softening.

Aldfrith flinched. He did not want to hear this. "I thought you once shared Wilfrid's view of her?" he growled.

Cerdic's expression tightened. "Aye ... I once saw things more like the bishop—that a king needs to wed a woman of equal rank, a high born woman who will serve to weave peace or extend territories. But I see things differently now."

Silence fell between them.

Aldfrith inhaled sharply. He did not want to hear this. "You're not helping," he said finally. "I need to forget Osana, not pine for her."

Cerdic snorted. "In my experience, once a woman gets under your skin, you can't forget her ... and the harder you try, the worse it'll get."

Aldfrith cursed under his breath. "There must be a cure for this ... something I can do." Truthfully, he was so miserable these days he was ready to try almost anything. All his ideals, everything he had once believed, no longer mattered to him. The wall he had so painstakingly built around his heart could not be rebuilt.

Watching him, Cerdic favored Aldfrith with a rueful smile. "There's only one cure sire ... you know what you must do."

Chapter Twenty-seven

Why Are You Here?

AT THE SIGHT of the wooden perimeter around Jedworth, Aldfrith tensed. Sensing the change in its rider's mood, his horse shifted under him. The stallion side-stepped, tossing its head.

Aldfrith inhaled deeply, breathing in the scents of warm earth, grass, and horse, before glancing right at Cerdic. "Remind me why this is wise?"

The warrior smiled. "No one said this was wise, sire."

"Then why am I here?"

Cerdic's smile widened in reply, yet he did not answer.

They both knew the answer to that. It was not wise—it was necessary.

Aldfrith loosed the breath he had been holding and urged his stallion forward, leading the way in through Jedworth's south gate. He had brought a small group of men with him, just his most trusted warriors, and he traveled without banners or fanfare. To most onlookers he appeared a well-dressed thegn traveling north. Aldfrith hoped to avoid the ealdorman of Jedworth on this trip.

Aldfrith did not want distractions. He needed to focus on the purpose that had driven him west from Bebbanburg.

His stomach knotted when he thought on what lay ahead. He recalled the last time he had seen Osana, the cold fury on her face that she would not voice.

"What if she doesn't want to see me?" He voiced the question aloud, without meaning to.

They rode along a dirt street now, beside a river that sparkled in the noon sun.

"That's a possibility," Cerdic agreed.

Aldfrith frowned at him.

Ahead, the northern perimeter of the town loomed, and there—as Cerdic had described—was a long, squat building with a thatched roof, surrounded by a garden and huts. A woman was walking down the path, carrying a basket.

Aldfrith's heart leaped at the sight of her, but as he drew closer his pulse slowed. It was not Osana. The woman before him had grey hair and a hard face. Yet there was a family resemblance in her stance, her wide hazel eyes.

The woman eyeballed him as he drew up outside her gate. Then her gaze flicked over to Cerdic beside him and recognition flared. Her mouth pursed, and when she spoke, her voice was as unwelcome as her expression. "What are you doing back here?"

"Niece ... there's someone here to see you!"

Hagona's voice reached Osana as she knelt amongst the garlic patch, pulling weeds. This part of the garden lay behind her aunt's hall, almost in the shadow of the wooden palisade that ringed the town.

"Osana!"

The edge of outrage in Hagona's voice made Osana scramble to her feet. She could not imagine who was paying her a visit. She kept to herself here in Jedworth, and apart from her visits to the market, she had little to do with folk. She hoped none of the men in town had taken a liking to her from afar and decided to woo her. She did not have the patience for it.

Why can't Hagona just send them away?

"I'm coming," she called. Osana left the garlic patch, dusting soil off her hands as she went. A butterfly fluttered past, its red and black wings catching the sunlight. It was a balmy early summer afternoon, the kind that made it hard to believe winter existed. The sun warmed Osana's back as she made her way round the side of the hall and up the path, past her annex, to the gate.

A group of men on horseback had drawn up on the dirt road outside. Clad in mail and leather, they sat upon heavy horses. One of their number, a man astride a magnificent grey stallion, stood apart from the rest. A thick wolf-pelt cloak hung from broad shoulders. His blond hair glinted in the sunlight.

Osana's step faltered, and she came to an abrupt halt. *Mother Mary ... no.*

Sensing movement in the garden behind Hagona, the man's gaze swiveled and came to rest upon Osana.

Heart pounding, she stared back. The devil take him, Aldfrith of Northumbria could still make her feel exposed, like she was standing naked in front of a village of people. Just one look and her knees wobbled beneath her. Those dark blue eyes remained on her as he swung from the saddle. Behind him Cerdic took the reins of the king's mount.

Aldfrith moved toward the gate, a hand reaching out to open it.

"Wait there." Hagona's voice cracked between them. "I didn't give you leave to enter my property."

Aldfrith stopped short, his gaze swiveling to Hagona. The woman stared back, hands on hips, not remotely intimidated.

"I'd rather talk to Osana in private," he replied.

"You can speak to her here."

"Hagona," Osana spoke up, finding her tongue. Clearly her aunt had no idea whom she was addressing. She risked getting herself in trouble if she was allowed to continue. "It's alright ... I can—"

"I'm not inviting him in," Hagona shot back. "He can say his piece at the gate."

Aldfrith's gaze narrowed, while behind him his men shared dark looks. Cerdic placed a hand upon the hilt of the sword at his side. "Would you deny your king?" the warrior demanded.

Hagona stiffened, her thin face draining of color. When she spoke, her voice came out in a low rasp, as she gazed at the blond stranger before her. "Lord Aldfrith?"

The king nodded, stepping forward and letting himself inside. "Aye ... although I'd prefer you kept the news to yourself. The ealdorman doesn't know I'm here."

Hagona nodded, suddenly struck mute. Her gaze swiveled from Aldfrith then and shifted to her niece.

Osana saw realization dawn in her aunt's eyes. Panic flooded through her, making Osana break out in a cold sweat.

Keep a leash on your tongue, she silently begged. *He doesn't know.*

Aldfrith entered the garden and strode up the path toward her, ignoring Hagona now. His attention was focused entirely upon Osana. He stopped four feet away, his gaze fixed upon her. "Shall we go inside?"

Osana nodded curtly, not trusting herself to speak, and turned, leading him back down the path to her annex. Stiff backed, she walked past a small herb garden she had recently planted, opened the door, and ducked inside. The smell of pottage greeted them, reminding Osana that she had put her noon meal on to cook before going out into the garden.

"Mind your head," she instructed, her voice coming out colder and steadier than she had anticipated. Inside, her belly was churning; her heart felt ready to burst from her rib cage, but her voice gave none of that away.

Good. Hold onto your anger. He deserves it.

Aldfrith followed her into the annex, straightened up, and looked around. The space, although neat and clean, was cramped, and she saw the shock in his eyes. "You live in here?"

Osana nodded.

"Why doesn't your aunt let you stay in her hall?"

"She likes her privacy ... and in truth I prefer these lodgings. As you've seen, she has the tongue of an adder."

His gaze roamed over her face. "Osana," he said softly. "How have you been?"

She stared back at him. In the light of the hearth that burned low between them, his features looked drawn, tired. Yet it just added an edge to his attractiveness, another layer to the face she had missed sorely over the past two moons.

She had missed him. There was no point in denying it. Only, she was also furious with him and that mattered more.

"Why are you here, Aldfrith?" she asked, ignoring his question. "Wasn't it enough to send me away ... you had to come and see for yourself what I've been reduced to?"

His eyes shadowed. "I'm sorry."

She stiffened. "For what? For sending me away, or for coming here?"

"For all of it ... for hurting you."

Osana clenched her jaw so hard it hurt. Folding her arms across her chest, she took a step back from him. She needed distance; this space was too confined and airless. Yet it was the only place where they could have privacy.

"It's too late for apologies," she ground out eventually. "It's all done with anyway."

He shook his head. "It's never too late to tell someone you've wronged that you're sorry for it," he replied. "I mistreated you, Osana. You brought light into my life, yet I cast you away. I will go to my grave being sorry for that."

She stared at him. Aldfrith had a way with words. Even so, there was a rawness to his voice that almost ensnared her, almost made her believe him.

Almost.

Hold onto your anger. It's the only thing that will get you through this.

"What's changed?" she demanded, bitterness turning her voice sharp. "You were only too pleased to see the back of me a few months ago. You didn't care what happened to me then."

He took a step toward her, but she backed off. He stopped then and raised his hands, as if placating a nervous animal. The pain on his face halted her breathing. "I've given up, Osana," he said softly. "That's what's changed.

He dropped his hands, and the pair of them stared at each other.

"I don't understand," she whispered back. "What does that mean?"

"No one in Northumbria knows about my past, about the demons I've tried to outrun," he replied, his mouth twisting. "The man you met in Bebbanburg was a fraud. The *Philosopher King* is an identity I carved for myself years ago. It's a lie."

Osana frowned. Her gaze slid over his face, noting how he struggled. She felt the inner battle raging within him even from across the room. "Why don't you start at the beginning then," she replied after a pause. "Tell me who you really are."

He heaved in a deep breath before reaching up and dragging a hand over his face. "Sometimes I feel as if I'm a hundred winters old." His gaze met hers once more then. "To understand my demons you'd have to go back thirty years to Éirinn—back to when Oswiu sired me. Aldfrith is my Angle name. For most of my life I was known as Flann Fina mac Oswiu: Flann, son of Fina and Oswiu. He met my mother during his exile, and their love was said to have been a tempest. But when Oswiu heard that his birthright was waiting for him back in Bebbanburg, he left Fina behind without a moment's hesitation. He broke her heart."

Aldfrith paused there, his handsome face taut as the memories from his past assailed him.

"My mother dealt with it by trying to find another man's love … yet one by one they disappointed her. One day she could bear it no longer. She walked into the sea and drowned." Aldfrith looked away, his gaze focusing upon the hearth where the iron pot of pottage bubbled. "It was I who found her the following morning … I would have been around eight."

Silence fell between them. Osana did not try to break it. She knew better than to try and fill emptiness with words. Sometimes silence was what was needed.

"I was cast in the same mold as my mother," he said finally, his voice bleak. "From the moment I left boyhood behind, my passions ran high … and when I was seventeen, I met a maid named Clodagh. She was wild and beautiful, and I was young and rash. I gave her my heart without hesitation. In return she made a fool out of me." Aldfrith's mouth curved into a bitter smile, his gaze desolate. "We were to be handfasted, but three nights before the ceremony, I returned early from a hunting trip with my uncle and found her in the furs with someone else. She mocked my tears and told me there had been others … that everyone knew and laughed behind my back. For a short time afterward I wanted to kill her … and then I wanted to take my own life."

Osana's chest constricted as she listened. She tried to imagine a young Aldfrith weeping as his lover spurned him, yet could not. She had always seen him as self-contained, a man in control of his emotions. Still, there had been glimpses of the passionate man underneath.

"And that's why I sought isolation in Iona," he concluded, his voice flat and dull. "I wanted to become a monk, but the prior said I lacked faith. So instead I became the hermit scholar and chose reason over passion. Life was easier that way."

Osana watched him, understanding settling over her. She knew now why he had been so torn, why he had reacted so badly when they had kissed in his alcove—and when they had coupled in the monastery. It was a path he could not take for fear of losing control. Now, finally, the missing pieces of the puzzle that was 'Aldfrith of Northumbria' fell into place.

"You should have told me before," she said finally. "It would have made things easier to bear."

He shrugged, his gaze shadowed. "I'm a coward. There are some things I have trouble admitting to myself, let alone others."

Osana inhaled deeply. "Thank you for telling me. You don't need to worry … I don't hate you. Return to Bebbanburg with your conscience lightened."

His eyes widened. "You think that's why I'm here?"

"Isn't it?"

He shook his head. "You need to know about my past … but I didn't come here to burden you with it so I'd feel better. Is your opinion of me really that low?"

"Why then?" Despite everything, anger still simmered deep within Osana. She had not realized till then just how deeply she had been hurt. "There isn't anything left to say."

He moved toward her then, closing the gap between them so that they stood barely two feet apart. "Is it not obvious?" he murmured, his gaze snaring hers. "I'm here because I'm in love with you."

Chapter Twenty-eight

Mine

OSANA STARED UP at Aldfrith, and he watched her features tighten, her gaze narrow.

"You aren't," she whispered. "You can't be."

Heart hammering, Aldfrith forced a smile. "I am ... I have been for a while now."

Her nostrils flared, and she drew back from him. "And you think that changes things?" Her voice rose, and he caught the edge of panic in it. "You're still king, and I'm still the shamed widow. Do you wish to make me your consort, is that it? Come to me in secret so the likes of Bishop Wilfrid don't damn your soul?" She looked ill as she spat out those last words, yet she did not back away from him.

Aldfrith went cold. The years rolled back, and he was standing in front of Clodagh while she jeered at him. He remembered how it felt, to open your heart to a woman only to have her revile you.

Only, Osana was not making fun of him. She was angry, hurt. She was a wounded animal lashing out.

"I don't want any of that," he replied, forcing down his fear of being spurned. "I just want you ... will you be my wife, Osana?"

There he had said it.

The words, the offer, was out there in the world. He could not take it back. He had ripped those words from his throat. It had taken every shred of courage to ask, yet he felt a great weight lift from his shoulders now it was done.

Whatever happened next, she would know how he truly felt.

Osana gaped at him, her lips parting in wordless shock. When she finally spoke, her voice trembled slightly. "Have you lost your wits? The King of Northumbria can't wed the likes of me."

Aldfrith smiled again, and this time the expression was not forced. "The king can wed whomever he pleases."

"But the ealdormen, they'll protest ... the bishop will—"

"Let them," he replied, cutting her off. "It'll be too late anyway. By the time they hear, we'll already be wed."

"But what if folk don't accept me?"

"They will in time."

"But ... I'm a widow."

"I care not." Aldfrith stepped close to her and reached out. He was afraid to touch her, afraid that she would slap his hand away or shrink back from him. Yet she did not. His fingers traced the curve of her cheek. "I've missed you," he whispered. "I can't breathe without you. Please be my wife."

Her throat bobbed as she swallowed. He could see the conflict in her eyes; her mind was still whirling, trying to find further reasons why she could not wed him.

"Aldfrith," she whispered his name and lifted her hand, her own fingertips tracing the line of his jaw. "There's something you must know ... I'm with child."

He stared at her a moment, before the words sank in. A heartbeat later, a joy unlike any he had ever known flooded through him. His vision blurred. "You are?"

She nodded, her gaze dropping. "I don't know how it happened," she murmured. "Raedwulf and I tried for years. I thought I was barren." She paused here, her body tensing. "You're not angry, are you?"

Aldfrith huffed out a breath. "Of course not." He hooked a finger under her chin and gently lifted it so that their eyes met once more. "But I do worry that you would never have told me. You're as proud as I am bullheaded."

She drew in a shaky breath. "What could I do? Turn up at the Great Tower and tell you the news. How did I know you would not have me run out of Bebbanburg?"

"I'd never do that." He moved closer to her; their faces were only inches apart now. He inhaled the sweet musk of her skin, the scent of rosemary in her hair. Hunger, the same sensation that had taken him prisoner upon Lindisfarena, reared up. His breathing quickened, and his belly knotted. He reached up with his free hand and brushed away a tear on her cheek with his thumb. "I'd stand against an army to keep you. Will you be mine?"

She nodded, her eyes glittering. "Aye ... I am already."

He pulled her into his arms, his mouth slanting over hers. He had not planned to kiss her, yet the relief her answer had given him could not be expressed in words. He needed his body to show her what she meant to him.

And as before, whenever they kissed, the floodgates loosed a moment later. The taste of her, the feel of her softness pressed against him, made Aldfrith forget who he was. He forgot that his men and the cantankerous aunt were waiting outside, that the ealdorman of Jedworth had probably heard he was here by now and would expect a visit. He forgot everything in the world except Osana.

His tongue parted her lips, and she moaned, melting against him. His hands moved up, reaching for the heavy braid down her back. He unfastened it, as he had done that day in the monastery, and tangled his fingers in the heavy tresses. A low groan rose in his throat.

He wanted to see her naked with her hair spilling over her body. He wanted her to drag her hair over his own naked skin.

Osana kissed him back with a hunger equal to his own, leaving him in no doubt of her desire. This energy between them was like a summer storm, like flames devouring dry wood. Its intensity was violent, overwhelming.

Suddenly, the layers of clothing separating them felt suffocating. He had to see Osana naked.

As if reading his mind, she drew back from him, her breathing coming in gasps. Then she heeled off her boots, unbuckled the heavy belt around her waist, and reached down, grasping the hem of the long linen tunic she wore with a woolen overdress covering it.

In one movement she drew the garments over her head, exposing the long, naked length of her body and her full, pink-tipped breasts. Then she tossed the clothing aside and stood there, her chest rising and falling sharply. Even in the dim light of the hearth, Aldfrith could see her cheeks were flushed, her eyes dark pools of want.

His pulse thundered in his ears as he stripped off his own clothes. Her gaze devoured him as he did so, unabashed. Her lips parted, and he watched her attention travel down the length of his naked body to where his shaft now strained toward her.

One step brought them together, and then Aldfrith's hands were everywhere. Her naked skin felt better than he could have possibly imagined: smooth as cream, firm and soft in all the right places. He fell to his knees before her, his mouth hungrily fastening upon her breasts. He suckled one hard, his teeth gently nipping her pebbled nipple.

Osana let out a high keening cry and dug her fingers into his hair, pulling him harder toward her. Aldfrith released her nipple and focused his attention on its twin, suckling her until she sagged against him, her moans filling the small room. His hands roamed over her body, over the smooth curve of her belly—where his child now grew—to the firm globes of her buttocks.

"Aldfrith," Osana gasped. "Please ... I can't wait ... *now*!"

The desperation in her voice roused him. He released her swollen nipple and sank down onto the low stool behind him. It sat just two feet from the glowing hearth where Osana's noon meal still bubbled, forgotten. He pulled her with him, drawing her down so that she sat astride his lap. Osana gazed down at him a moment, before she leaned down and kissed him, recklessly, wildly. Her arms entwined around his neck, her breasts pressing against his chest.

Heaven preserve him, she addled his senses faster than strong wine. When she gently bit at his lower lip, her fingernails raking down his back, he felt the last shred of his self-restraint snap.

Aldfrith slid his hands down her back and cupped her buttocks, lifting her up to straddle his shaft. She reached down between them then and stroked the swollen length of him, before positioning his shaft at the entrance to her womb.

Tight velvet heat engulfed him as she lowered herself onto him in one long, achingly slow, movement—not stopping until he was buried deep within her. Aldfrith threw back his head and groaned, letting the sensation carry him away. If his heart stopped right now, he would die a happy man. Nothing had ever felt so good.

"Osana," he gasped. "You slay me."

She let out a soft, throaty laugh. "I hope not, milord."

He opened his eyes and dipped his chin to meet her gaze once more. They sat entwined, breathlessly still. The heat of her enveloping him made it difficult for him to think straight. Wordlessly, he caught hold of her hips and rocked her against him. Osana's eyes widened, and she let out a soft cry. Aldfrith repeated the action, this time raising his hips to grind against her.

Osana's cry turned into a keen, and her body shuddered against his. He felt the walls of her womb contract against him, felt a rush of heat that nearly pushed him over the edge.

How long had he fought against this? Denying himself of Osana had nearly killed him.

Her mouth claimed his, kissing him deeply—and then she began to ride him. He steadied her hips as she moved, sliding up and down the length of him, slow at first, before tremors convulsed her body once more. Osana cried out against his mouth, her fingernails digging into his shoulders.

Aldfrith took control then. He held her hips tight and slammed her down hard onto him, again and again. He let go of control, let go of any rational thought, taking Osana until his cries joined hers— and he too flew over the edge of the abyss.

Osana recovered her breath and pushed herself up from where she had collapsed upon Aldfrith's shoulder. Her body felt weak and boneless in the aftermath. He was still buried inside her. His body was slick with sweat, his chest still heaving from his explosive climax.

"Woman," he murmured against her neck. "You are delicious." His tongue snaked out, tracing her throat. Osana shivered, heat pooling in her lower belly. Would there ever come a time when this man could not melt her with merely a touch? Even his look made her pulse quicken.

She sighed, leaning against him once more and letting him work his way up her neck to the shell of her ear. "You are mine," he whispered when he reached it. "Now and forever. The moment we return to Bebbanburg, I shall call for the priest."

His words filled her with warmth. When she had seen him standing by the gate earlier, she had expected the worst: that he had come to slake his lust before he left her. Their last meeting in Bebbanburg had left a scar. She had felt betrayed, used, humiliated. He had turned the most beautiful experience of her life into something to be ashamed of.

But none of that mattered now. He had come to her, opened his heart, and revealed his past. She knew he loved her—and the depth of what she felt for him scared her.

Osana straightened up, her gaze meeting Aldfrith's. "I had no idea you were called by another name. It must have seemed odd to hear folk calling you 'Aldfrith'?"

His mouth curved. "Aye. I gave up asking folk at Bebbanburg to use my real name. To them I will always be Aldfrith, son of Oswiu."

"I shall call you 'Flann'," she replied, smiling, "when we're alone ... if you'd like?"

He gazed up at her, his eyes soft and dark in the firelight. "Aye, I'd like that."

Chapter Twenty-nine

The Return

"THE KING?" HAGONA'S face was pale in the firelight as she wrapped up some bread and boiled eggs for Osana to take with her on her journey. "No wonder you didn't tell me."

Osana smiled. "Aye, some secrets are best kept."

Her aunt straightened up, observing her niece keenly. "Does he know … that you're carrying his child?"

Osana nodded.

"And he'll take you back with him, wed you … make you his queen?" Hagona's expression turned incredulous. Osana did not blame her. She had difficulty believing this was actually happening herself. She had woken this morning a different person to who she was now. *Then* she had been resigned to a future where she would give birth to the king's bastard and raise it in a tiny annex behind her aunt's hall; a future where folk would whisper about her, stare, and point. A future where she would gradually grow as bitter and hard as her aunt.

"Aye … he says he will."

Something moved in Hagona's eyes then, a shadow that almost looked like grief. "That's the test of a man," she said softly, "… how he treats you when you have nothing to give him but your body, your heart."

Silence fell between them. Shocked by her aunt's words, which were so unlike her, Osana frowned. "What happened, Hagona … how did you end up living here alone? Why did you never wed?"

Her aunt heaved in a deep breath and turned back to wrapping the food. Aldfrith and his men waited outside; the women did not have much more time together. "I gave my heart to the wrong man … long ago," she replied, her voice barely above a whisper, "and I never recovered from it."

Osana watched her aunt, wondering who the man had been. Osana's mother had never mentioned Hagona's past. For as long as Osana had known, Hagona had merely been the sharp-tongued aunt you did not want to visit.

"I'm sorry," she said softly, for she knew what it was to be hurt and to live without hope. She did not ask anything further; she had the feeling Hagona would refuse anyway. Her aunt was prickly at the best of times, and Osana could see by the tense line of her jaw that she was not prepared to reveal anything else about her past.

Hagona straightened up and passed Osana the neatly wrapped package of food. "That's why I know the value of a good man," she said with a smile that did not quite reach her eyes. "For I have plenty of experience with a bad one. The king loves you and will go against tradition to wed you. Wyrd shines upon you, niece."

Osana huffed, smiling once more as she took the food. She rarely heard folk speak of 'wyrd' these days. It was part of the old ways, the old gods—when folk believed that fortune ruled your fate. These days most people believed that it was God's will that charted the course of your life.

Osana was not sure she believed in either. Some things you could not control—yet the past year had taught her that you always had choices in life. The difference was whether you had the courage to act upon them.

Osana leaned back against the hard wall of Aldfrith's body. The strength and safety of his encircling arms, reaching forward to hold the reins, gave her a sense of peace she had never known before.

They rode across wide rolling hills, the sky a swathe of cloudless blue above. The sun was warm on their faces. Cerdic and another warrior rode up front while Aldfrith and Osana followed just behind. The remainder of their party brought up the rear.

They had left Jedworth without delay, departing through the north gate so that they would not have to pass through the town and risk the ealdorman or his men spotting them.

They had lingered just long enough for Osana to thank her aunt and wish her goodbye. It seemed an irony to give Hagona thanks after her cool welcome, yet she had allowed Osana to live with her when many would not have.

Osana had even felt choked up as she rode away. She glanced back over her shoulder, her gaze settling upon the solitary figure standing in the midst of her garden. Hagona was not one to reveal much about herself, yet that brief conversation had told Osana much.

It made her own happiness now even more precious, for she knew how harsh life could be, how not everyone received a happy ending.

Warmth suffused her, and she closed her eyes a moment, absorbing the feel of Aldfrith's body against hers. She breathed in the rich scent of earth and grass surrounding them.

She loved him, and yet she had not told him so. There was a part of her, the part that sought to preserve her from harm, that made her hold back. They were still far from Bebbanburg, and she was not yet Aldfrith's wife.

I will tell him soon, she promised herself silently. *When we are alone and I feel safe.*

There was still part of her that wondered if this was real; she half-expected Aldfrith's men to start laughing at how foolish this woman was. But they did not.

"You're quiet," Aldfrith spoke up. They were pressed so close he did not have to raise his voice to be heard. His breath feathered her ear, causing a shiver of delight to arrow through her. "Although I can hear your mind working from here."

Osana gave a soft laugh. "Aye ... not that my thoughts do me any credit. They keep telling me this is all a dream. That any moment I'm going to wake up in my fowl coop to the sound of Hagona berating me because I'm late milking the goat."

Aldfrith huffed out a laugh. "No, you're not dreaming," he assured her. "This is real, and very soon you will be my wife."

His words filled Osana with a warmth that had nothing to do with the friendly face of the sun.

A moment later Aldfrith passed the reins to his left hand, and with his right gently cupped Osana's belly. "Will the babe be a boy or a girl?"

Osana was glad he had whispered the question. It was still early on, and she did not wish for anyone besides the two of them to know about this for the moment. Folk at Bebbanburg would make her life difficult as it was.

"Which would you prefer?" she asked.

"Either ... although a girl with her mother's eyes and smile would please me very much."

A smile curved Osana's lips. "What if it's a son with your character and eyes the color of the sky just after dusk?"

Aldfrith snorted. "I wouldn't wish that upon him."

"Why not?" Osana replied. "You've the best character of anyone I've ever met. Your only mistake was not trusting your own instincts. Passion doesn't have to rule you, Flann ... but it can guide your heart."

Aldfrith's hand stroked her belly. "Thank you, I shall remember that."

They reached Bebbanburg the next morning after setting off early, as soon as the first blush of dawn lightened the eastern sky. The party had camped in the midst of a stand of holm oaks, and since the weather was fine, they had not bothered to erect tents. Instead, they had sat around a crackling fire, the warriors taking turns at watch.

Despite that she had lain upon the hard ground festooned with tree roots, Osana had slept surprisingly well. She had awoken rested to find Aldfrith seated beside her, ready with a cup of hot broth.

The smile he had given her made it the most beautiful awakening ever.

Now they rode the last stretch toward the fort, the walls of Bebbanburg rising high above. It was the same path that Osana and Raedwulf had ridden nearly three years earlier on their way to the king's handfasting.

Much had changed since then—Osana had indeed changed much. For the first time since girlhood, she truly felt happy.

Yet as they clattered up the causeway toward the low gate, her stomach knotted and her throat closed. Happiness was a fragile thing; she was still afraid to re-enter the Great Tower of Bebbanburg. How would folk there treat her?

"Please tell me that Bishop Wilfrid isn't in residence at the moment?" she asked, voicing the worst of her worries.

"The bishop and I haven't gotten on well of late," Aldfrith replied. "A few days ago I sent him away, back to Inhrypum. He won't be making any visits to Bebbanburg for a while."

Relief crashed over Osana at this news. She realized that most of her worries stemmed from that man. The memory of Wilfrid's face the day he had walked in on them on Lindisfarena would haunt her forever: his hard, haughty expression, and the judgment in his dark eyes.

Osana let out the breath she had been holding. "That's welcome news indeed."

Aldfrith cantered his horse in through the high gate and drew it up in front of the stables. He swung down from his stallion's back and helped Osana dismount.

"Cerdic!" A woman's voice carried across the stable yard.

Osana glanced up to see Lora, her blonde curls fluttering, bound down the steps from the tower and hurry across the stable yard toward them. Joy flowered within Osana at the sight of her friend. She was a welcome sight indeed.

Ignoring his companions, even his king, Cerdic strode forward to meet her. Reaching Lora, he gathered her up in his arms and kissed her. She responded in kind, winding her arms around his neck, and standing on her tip-toes to reach him. They were both oblivious to the fact they had an audience.

Osana turned to Aldfrith, a smile curving her lips. "You didn't tell me this news."

He returned the smile. "It wasn't mine to tell," he replied. "I'm sure Lora will wish to tell you in her own words."

Eventually, Lora and Cerdic broke apart, and the woman peeked around him to see who accompanied the warrior.

Lora let out a squeal. "Osana!"

Osana huffed, pretending to be affronted. "I wondered when you'd notice me."

Her friend left Cerdic, who was now grinning, and rushed to Osana. The women hugged, and when Osana pulled back, her eyes were smarting. "I missed you," she muttered. "You've got no idea what an acerbic tongue my aunt has."

Lora smiled, her blue eyes gleaming. "And I have missed *you* ... more than you can possibly imagine."

Osana raised an eyebrow before flicking a look in Cerdic's direction. "Much has changed I see?"

Lora responded with a sly look. "Aye ... for us both."

"Cerdic," Aldfrith called out. "Go fetch Oswald. He will come to the Great Hall and wed us at noon."

The warrior nodded, still smiling, and turned on his heel to do the king's bidding.

Lora met Osana's eye, her gaze wide. "You're having your handfasting *today*?"

Osana nodded, her belly fluttering with a mixture of nerves and excitement. This was really happening. "It seems so."

"But you don't have a dress ... and what about the feast?"

"Don't worry about that, Lora," Aldfrith cut in. "Take some of the other women out with you into the fields below the fort and gather flowers for the hall. We'll have whatever's already planned for supper for our feast—I'm sure there are some cheeses and cured meats we can bring out of the stores."

"Aye, sire." Lora dropped into a neat curtsey, her face taking on a look of determination. "You will have guests for the handfasting too ... forgive me, I forgot to tell you before."

Osana watched the smile fade from Aldfrith's face. Likewise, Osana's buoyant mood dimmed. Neither of them wanted guests at the fort today.

"Who is it?" Aldfrith asked, after a pause.

Lora's gaze flicked from the king's face to Osana's, her own smile dimming. "The ealdormen of Catraeth and Gefrin are here to see you, milord."

Chapter Thirty

Unwelcome Guests

WHY NOW? IT sometimes seemed as if the world conspired against him.

The last thing Aldfrith wanted was a visit from Edwin of Gefrin and Wulfred of Catraeth. The ealdormen—these two especially—were not supposed to know of his wedding until after the fact. He did not want their interference.

"Aldfrith?" Osana's voice intruded. He glanced down to see her watching him, her brow furrowed. "Is something wrong?"

He shook his head and forced a smile. "Nothing ... I just wish the ealdormen would give me some peace. Not a month goes by without one of them riding here to complain about some inconsequential." He linked his arm through hers and feigned a lightness of tone. "Come, love. Let me escort you into the Great Hall. I shall have an alcove cleared for you, so that you can prepare for the ceremony."

Osana flashed him a grateful smile, and Aldfrith's chest constricted. He would not have anyone ruin this day. He had already put Osana through too much. He would not make her suffer again.

Yet as they entered the tower, and his gaze settled upon the two heavy-set figures awaiting him upon the high seat, Aldfrith's pulse quickened. He knew Edwin and Wulfred would make their opinions of this handfasting clear.

Aldfrith clenched his jaw. *Let them have their say ... it won't change anything. By the time the sun starts its path toward the western horizon, Osana and I shall be wed.*

The ealdorman of Catraeth spotted him first. Hirsute and broad, his girth even wider than the last time Aldfrith had seen him, Wulfred heaved himself to his feet. However, the greeting he had just been about to boom died on his lips when he spied Osana at the king's side, her arm linked through Aldfrith's.

Beside him the ealdorman of Gefrin rose to his feet. Edwin's gaze flitted past Aldfrith before spearing Osana. His mouth thinned. Aldfrith felt Osana's step falter at his side. He squeezed her arm. "Don't let them bother you," he murmured. "Remember, it is *I* who rule here."

And yet from the way these two men, both warriors past their prime yet fighting men nonetheless, stood upon the high seat, you would have thought either of them was the lord of this land and not Aldfrith.

"Lord Aldfrith," Edwin drawled as the king drew close. "We heard you were away hunting ... is this your catch?"

"Good day, Edwin," Aldfrith replied, keeping his voice as flat and emotionless as he could manage. There was no point in dancing around the subject with the ealdormen, better to have the truth out in the open. "I went to retrieve Osana from Jedworth, where she has been staying with her aunt. I plan to make her my wife shortly. Will you stay for the ceremony?"

That shocked them.

Aldfrith almost smiled at the way Wulfred's mouth gaped and at Edwin's slack-jawed stare.

Wulfred was the first to recover. "Sire ... you cannot wed *her*."

Aldfrith quirked an eyebrow, stepping up onto the high seat with Osana at his side. She clung to his arm, her fingers digging into his flesh. "I *can*, and as soon as the priest arrives, I *will*."

"Do the other ealdormen know of this?" Edwin growled.

Aldfrith met his gaze unflinchingly. Anger was starting to curl up from the pit of his belly. He was tired of these men treating him as if he was their lesser. "They don't need to know," he replied. Now that he stood upon the high seat he was at an advantage. He was nearly half a foot taller than either of the ealdormen; both of them had to raise their chins to eyeball him.

His cousin locked gazes with him. It was a dominant, challenging stare that made Aldfrith's hackles rise.

"I take it there's a reason you are both in Bebbanburg?" Aldfrith asked. "Let us speak of that."

Edwin of Gefrin folded his heavily muscled arms across his chest. "Aye ... we're here to see what you've done about rebuilding this kingdom's army."

Aldfrith watched him, feigning calm when inside he was beginning to seethe. Would Edwin ever let this subject rest? "Are we at war?"

His cousin sneered. "This period of peace will not last ... it never does."

"Edwin has spoken to me of his concerns, and I agree with him," Wulfred added, "You need to start gathering a fyrd: a king's army. Spears and horsemen who will ride against our enemies with only a few days' notice."

"A king only needs to call upon a fyrd in desperate times," Aldfrith countered. "I'd prefer to let the men of this land tend to their fields, their families."

"A king needs to think of his kingdom," Edwin interrupted, his face reddening. "And that's why you don't wed who you want. You wed to make Northumbria strong."

Aldfrith clenched his jaw; his cousin had slyly managed to bring the argument full-circle—back to his impending handfasting to Osana.

"Northumbria is already strong," he replied. "The kings who have gone before me have seen to that. We have no quarrel with our neighbors, and I have no need to wed in order to weave peace. The East Angles and the Mercians leave us alone these days."

Wulfred of Catraeth snorted. "Complacency is the first step to defeat. Next you'll be giving what land still rests to us in the north to Bridei mac Beli."

Aldfrith stepped forward, releasing Osana's arm as he did so. "Enough, Wulfred." His glare swept over both men. "I never met my half-brother, Ecgfrith, but I do know he wed twice in the best interests of his kingdom and died a bitter angry man as a result." His voice carried across the hall. "You forget, I already wed a princess of Wessex and learned just how empty a loveless union can be. It rots a man's soul. Do you think Ecgfrith might not have rushed headlong into war if he had not been so bitter and full of rancor at the world?"

Silence followed his words, and so Aldfrith filled it. His blood was up, his hands clenched by his sides. He would not be caged, nor dictated to. He would break the jaw of the next man to question him. "Listen to me well, for I shall not repeat myself," he growled. "*I* shall decide whom I wed ... and no one else."

Aldfrith glanced over at Osana then, noting how pale and strained her face was. "Don't worry," he murmured, managing a smile. "The priest will be here soon."

At that moment the doors to the Great Hall opened, and Cerdic strode in. However, the priest was not following him. Aldfrith watched him approach; his stomach clenched at the serious look on the warrior's face.

"Oswald's away," Cerdic informed him.

Aldfrith's belly dropped. "Where?"

"He's gone to visit Bishop Wilfrid in Inhrypum."

Aldfrith swallowed a vicious curse. It suddenly felt as if all the gods—the old and the new—had turned against him. "Take some men and ride fast to Inhrypum," he ordered. "Get Oswald but tell the bishop nothing."

Cerdic stared back at him a moment before nodding. He then turned on his heel and strode out of the Great Hall, the doors booming shut behind him.

Wulfred of Catraeth broke the heavy silence that followed. "So the bishop's not to know?"

Aldfrith glanced his way and frowned. He did not like the sly look in the man's eyes. "No," he replied. "This handfasting is none of his business." His frown deepened as he gave up all pretense at civility. "Nor is it yours."

"What do you think?"

Osana glanced up to see that Lora was holding up a green gown. It was a simple dress, with long bell-like sleeves and a hem embroidered with gold thread. "This belonged to the Lady Cuthburh," Lora continued. "She was as thin as a reed with no bosom, so I have let the dress out at the bust and adjusted the seams slightly; it should fit you perfectly now."

Osana nodded and forced a smile. In truth she had a lump in her throat, and it felt as if a boulder had lodged itself in the pit of her belly.

Lora's hopeful smile faded. "Do you not like it?"

"It's lovely," Osana replied. "I'm just preoccupied ... that's all. Aldfrith and I should be wed by now. I'm starting to think it'll never happen."

Lora snorted. "Nonsense. The king wants you, and he'll have you. Don't worry about those scheming men. Long have they wanted to exert control over the king. But you saw Aldfrith earlier; he will not have it."

Osana had, and that worried her too. "What if he ruins his relationship with the ealdormen over me?"

"And what relationship would that be?" Lora replied, her gaze narrowing. "As I see it, there's no relationship to be salvaged. It's up to Aldfrith to forge a new one. Don't let their disapproval ruin your joy." Lora's brow smoothed then. "Plus there's nothing wrong with having to wait a little ... it's given me time to ready a dress for you. The other women are out there decorating the hall, and the cook's baking a huge hare pie for the feast. I know you want to wed immediately, but what difference does one day make?"

"Little, I hope," Osana replied. The churning in her belly had now ceased; Lora's practicality never failed to make her feel better. Her friend had spoken true. It was the king's word that mattered here, not that of his ealdormen. He had done right to respond harshly.

Even so, she would be happy when the wait was over.

The two women sat on low stools inside an alcove. This space, which had until earlier today been occupied by a thegn and his wife, lay just a few feet from the king's quarters. Osana would spend tonight in here, and then after she and Aldfrith wed, this alcove would go to Lora and Cerdic.

Osana watched Lora for a long moment. Her friend was examining the hem of the dress, in the light of the cresset that burned on the stone wall beside her. Curiosity rose within Osana. Ever since she had returned, her head had been filled with thoughts of her own handfasting; she had not had time to speak to Lora about what had happened in her life during Osana's absence.

"It warms my heart to see you happy with Cerdic," she said eventually. "When I left I feared you had closed your heart to him."

Lora glanced up and smiled. "I almost had. I know I sometimes act as if I don't have a care in the world ... but that isn't the truth. Of late I've grown mistrustful of others. I was angry with you for leaving and not taking me with you. I felt abandoned here. All I saw before me was a life of drudgery, and having to fight off the advances of men every night until I was too old and wrinkled to warrant their attention." Lora broke off here, plucking at a loose thread on the gown. A blush suddenly stained her cheeks. "But upon his return from Jedworth, Cerdic came to me."

Osana smiled. "I'm glad he did. Will you be wed?"

Lora glanced up. "Our handfasting is planned for just before Winterfylleth. It's a good time of year to be wed."

Osana rose from her stool and crossed to where her friend sat. She then knelt down so that their gazes were level. Reaching out, she took hold of Lora's hand. "True friends are rare," she said softly. "I'm sorry I left you here, although now I see it was for the best. You would have hated my aunt anyway ... Hagona has a good heart, but she's as prickly as a hedgehog."

Lora chuckled. "Aye, and Cerdic might not have worked up the courage to approach me otherwise." She placed her free hand over Osana's and squeezed tightly. "Now, enough of this talk ... you'll have me weeping in a moment. We have a mountain of things to organize before your handfasting. I've picked a selection of flowers from the meadows. They're sitting in jugs of water so they don't wilt. You need to choose which ones you'll wear in your hair."

Chapter Thirty-one

My Bride Awaits

CERDIC RETURNED FROM Inhrypum in the early afternoon the following day. He cantered into the inner palisade upon a lathered horse, the priest Oswald perched behind him. The other members of Cerdic's party thundered in moments later.

Oswald's face was pinched and tired. He looked as if Cerdic had made him ride through the night, which he probably had in order to get to Inhrypum and back in this time.

Aldfrith stood at the top of the steps before the Great Tower and waited for the priest to dismount. Oswald did so, wincing as his sandaled feet hit the ground. Straightening up and brushing off his dark robes, Oswald's gaze traveled to where the king stood watching him.

The priest's brow furrowed.

Not bothering to say a word to Cerdic, Oswald picked up the hem of his robes and hurried across the yard, head bowed, before mounting the steps. Cerdic tossed his reins to one of the other men and strode after him.

"Milord." Oswald stopped a few feet below where the king stood and gave a hurried bow. Aldfrith could see he was bristling, indignant.

"Good day, Oswald," Aldfrith replied with a smile. "I take it that Cerdic has told you why you've been summoned back to Bebbanburg so urgently."

Oswald nodded, his throat bobbing. It was clear he held a strong opinion about this, which he was wisely keeping to himself.

The priest was no fool. Over the past years he had skulked in Wilfrid's shadow whenever the bishop visited the fort, often appearing his disciple. But without his mentor at his side he was less brave. He knew his place, and Aldfrith was grateful for it; he was tired of being constantly challenged.

Relations with the ealdormen Wulfred and Edwin had been frosty ever since his return. They had both tried to heckle him over his lack of interest in rebuilding Northumbria's army during supper the night before. His calmness and accompanying stubbornness had riled them both. However, he knew it would not be the end of the matter.

It seemed his ealdormen were only too eager to warmonger, but Aldfrith would have no part in it.

Before the king, Oswald bowed his head, his shoulders rounding. He was not a happy man, yet he was ready to do the king's bidding.

"Come, Oswald," Aldfrith ordered gently. "My bride awaits."

Osana stood upon the high seat and faced the King of Northumbria. Dressed simply, yet richly, Aldfrith was distractingly handsome today. A black leather vest studded in gold and iron covered his chest, leaving his finely muscled arms bare. His father's fine grey wolfskin cloak hung from his shoulders, clasped by a gleaming amber brooch. He wore doeskin breeches and long dark boots.

Aldfrith looked down at her, his expression soft, his eyes tender.

Finally, they were about to be wed.

There had been moments, as she lay awake in her alcove listening to the soft sound of Lora's breathing, when she had worried it would never happen. And yet here she was, dressed in a soft green gown that fitted her curves snugly, with meadow daisies woven through her hair.

The aroma of roasting meat drifted through the hall as the final preparations were made for the feast that would follow the handfasting. A murmur of voices surrounded them as the folk of Bebbanburg—both those who resided within the inner palisade, and many of those who lived in the tightly packed streets beyond—pushed into the Great Hall.

Osana breathed in the excitement surrounding her. Despite her fears, the mood was joyous. There would be a handful of folk among the crowd, Mildryth and Eldflaed among them, who watched her with hard eyes, but most people who jostled for position on the floor below the high seat seemed in high spirits. There were few who did not like a handfasting.

Lora and Cerdic stood nearby, with the king's most loyal retainers. Lora and Osana shared a look, before her friend grinned. Beside Lora, Cerdic was smiling, his arm draped protectively around her shoulders.

Osana shifted her attention back to Aldfrith. He gave her a melting look in return that made her breathing hitch. Tonight they would lie together as husband and wife.

They stood before Oswald, who hunched between them like a trapped hare. The priest's face was solemn, his gaze pained. He cleared his throat and stepped forward, a length of linen in his hands.

The hum of voices around them died. Expectation charged the air.

"The union of man and wife is a union of two souls," Oswald began, holding the ribbon aloft. "This cord is not permanent but perishable. It is a reminder that all things of the material eventually return to the earth, unlike the bond and the connection that is love, which is eternal." The priest's voice, although low, carried over the now silent hall. Oswald's gaze darted up to Aldfrith and then Osana. "Please join your right hands."

They did as bid. Osana's breathing quickened as Aldfrith wove his fingers through hers and squeezed. Then Oswald stepped close to them and started to wind the ribbon around their joined hands. And as he wrapped the ribbon, he spoke the words that would bind them.

"With this cloth I bind your souls
May you know nothing but happiness from this day forward.

May the road rise to meet you
May the wind be always at your back
May the warm rays of sun fall upon your home
And may the hand of a friend always be near.
May green be the grass you walk on,
May blue be the skies above you,
May pure be the joys that surround you,
May true be the hearts that love you."

Oswald finished speaking, and a deep hush fell in the hall. The priest, who had now lost his cowed expression, straightened his spine, his gaze returning to Aldfrith and Osana. "I now—"

"Wait! This handfasting is a farce—it must not take place!"

A harsh voice carried across the hall.

Unfortunately, it was a voice that Osana had come to know well. She tore her gaze from Aldfrith's and let it travel across the sea of heads between them and the heavy doors that led out into the entrance hall.

There, framed in the doorway, was a tall robed figure.

Bishop Wilfrid's face was the color of liver, his gaze livid. Even at this distance, Osana could feel the weight of his rage.

"This ceremony must stop," he roared, spittle flying. "I name the bride a 'wicce'. She has ensnared the king, but now this evil business will end."

The vehemence in those words caused ice to wash over Osana, dousing her excitement and joy in an instant. Such hate. Yet as she watched him, she realized that Wilfrid's wrath was not aimed at her but at Aldfrith. His gaze speared the king, dislike carved into his gaunt face.

Realization dawned. This was revenge for every imagined slight against him over the past years, every time the king had thwarted his plans. After Aldfrith had so effectively curtailed the bishop's power, Wilfrid would not see the king happy. Like the ealdormen, he wanted Aldfrith as his puppet. If he would not do his bidding, then he would be punished.

During the interruption, Aldfrith had not spoken a word.

Tearing her gaze from the bishop, Osana glanced across at the man who had just been moments away from becoming her husband—her breathing stilling when she saw his face.

His skin was bloodless and pulled tight over his cheekbones. He wore an expression she had never yet seen, chilling in its fury. He looked dangerous—angry enough to kill.

Aldfrith had been watching the bishop, but now he shifted his attention to the foot of the high seat where two leather-clad figures stood: Edwin of Gefrin and Wulfred of Catraeth. Osana followed Aldfrith's gaze, her belly clenching when she observed the men's faces.

Both had worn sour expressions before the ceremony, yet their mood had altered now. Wulfred smirked, his mouth twitching as if he was swallowing a laugh. Next to him Edwin did not even attempt to hide his glee. A broad smile twisted his face, and his eyes gleamed.

"Cousin Edwin," Aldfrith growled. "Please tell me you're not behind this?"

Edwin's broad smile widened further. "I cannot lie, sire." The victory in the ealdorman's voice made Osana wince. "I had one of my men follow yours south to Inhrypum. Someone had to tell the bishop."

"You slippery bastard." Cerdic had left Lora's side and now stepped forward, hands clenched, his face a mask of fury. "You had no place to have me followed."

"But it was just as well he did." Wilfrid was now elbowing his way through the crowd.

"And as for you, bishop," Cerdic growled. "Someone should teach you how to speak to a king."

"Cerdic." Aldfrith's voice held a sharp warning. "Step down. I will deal with this."

The warrior frowned. "But sire—"

"You heard me."

Cerdic's frown deepened to a scowl, yet he did as bid.

Meanwhile, the bishop had nearly reached the front of the crowd. "Oswald you fool—what are you doing?"

"Father ..." The priest blanched, shuffling back slightly. "I had to—"

"Faithless craven," Wilfrid spat. "I shall deal with you later. For now, untie the ribbon. Let this travesty end."

Oswald did not move. "Father, I don't think—"

"Do it!"

Still, the priest did not move.

"Untie the ribbon, Oswald." It was Aldfrith who made the command this time, his voice low and cold. The king did not look Oswald's way as he spoke; instead his gaze remained fixed upon the bishop, who bore down upon him like an enraged crow.

Wilfrid had drawn a wooden crucifix out from under his robes. He now held it out before him as he approached, as if he was warding off Satan himself. "I shun the witch's evil eye!"

Around him, the crowd shuffled back from the high seat to let the bishop through. His comment brought mutterings, and many folk crossed themselves, sharing nervous glances.

Osana's heart started to pound. Wilfrid was clever; he was playing on the mob's superstitions. If he had his way, she would be stoned out of Bebbanburg and drowned in the sea.

Meanwhile, Oswald had done as Aldfrith had bid and deftly unwrapped the ribbon binding Osana and the king's right hands.

As soon as he was free, Aldfrith moved.

It happened so swiftly, in barely a heartbeat, that Osana had no chance to reach out for Aldfrith, to forestall him.

One instant he had been standing at her side, the next he stepped down off the high seat and struck out with his right fist.

The crunch of the blow echoed through the hall. Wilfrid, who had just opened his mouth to spew forth another volley of vitriol, staggered, his head snapping back under the force of the punch.

A moment later the bishop went down like a sack of millet on the rush covered floor.

Chapter Thirty-two

Not Worthy of the Crown

SILENCE REVERBERATED AROUND the hall.

Edwin of Gefrin was the first to recover from the shock of seeing Bishop Wilfrid laid out for all to see. He stepped away from Wulfred's side, his face a mask of self-righteous anger. "Witness all. Your king has struck down a man of God!"

Aldfrith turned, fists still clenched, to face the ealdorman. "Still your tongue, Edwin." The warning was spoken softly, cold rage inflected in every word.

But Edwin would not be silenced. Watching from atop the high seat, frozen to the spot as if her feet had grown roots, Osana felt a sickly realization wash over her. She felt as if this whole scene had been orchestrated, as if all of them—Wilfrid included—had merely been playing a part.

It was this man, Aldfrith's cousin Edwin, who was manipulating them all. And now he stepped forward to perform the last part of his carefully planned act.

"A king who would strike down a bishop is not worthy of the crown." A groan followed his words as, on the rushes a few feet away, Wilfrid stirred. However, Edwin was not looking at the bishop. His attention was upon Aldfrith, whom he now stalked toward with the predatory stealth of a wolf.

A warning screamed in the back of Osana's skull, a moment before she saw Edwin stoop down and retrieve something from his boot. Iron gleamed in the firelight.

A seax.

Weapons were forbidden inside the Great Hall: to carry one was an insult to the king. Yet Edwin wielded a blade now, and Osana knew what he planned to do.

Edwin wanted the crown.

"Aldfrith," she gasped, lunging toward the men. Oswald grabbed hold of her, hauling her back. "Wait, Lady Osana," he grunted. "It's too dangerous."

But Aldfrith had also seen the blade—as had the folk clustered closest to the foot of the high seat. Many of their faces blanched, their eyes growing wide with fear.

"It's time a warrior fit to rule took his rightful place in this hall," Edwin said, flashing Aldfrith a vicious grin. "Not a craven scholar."

And with that Edwin lunged.

A scream split the air. It was Lora, for Cerdic—casting aside the king's earlier command—leaped forward to intercept his attacker.

But before Cerdic reached Edwin, Wulfred of Catraeth tackled the warrior, bringing him down. The ealdorman of Catraeth was not going to let Edwin be thwarted. Grunts ensued as the two men fought on the floor.

Edwin kept moving, the blade of the fighting dagger flashing as he swung it toward the king.

Helpless, unable to do anything but watch the scene unfold, Osana stared at that blade. Grief ripped into her chest, making it impossible to breathe. The man she loved was about to die.

Aldfrith did not panic, did not cry out. He watched Edwin lunge for him, and then did the last thing Osana expected.

He moved toward him, sidestepping the blade, and grabbed hold of the ealdorman's thick wrist.

Edwin had been moving so fast that the momentum carried him straight into the king. Aldfrith brought his leg up sharply and kneed his attacker in the cods before felling him with a sharp blow to the side of his neck.

Edwin of Gefrin was a big man, his body a coiled mass of muscle built over a lifetime of fighting, but Aldfrith's blow easily felled him nonetheless. Edwin roared as he fell, clutching his injured cods with one hand, his blade still gripped in the other.

Aldfrith stepped forward and slammed his foot down on the ealdorman's wrist, grinding it into the ground until the man released his hold on the seax.

Then, the king reached down and retrieved it. When he spoke, his voice carried over the hall. "Aye, I'm a scholar, Edwin ... but that doesn't mean I don't know how to defend myself." His voice was chill. "My uncle Daragh taught me well it seems."

"Your mother was an Ériu hōre," Edwin grunted, still defiant. "Just because Oswiu sired you doesn't give you the right to be king. I'm of pure Angle blood, Oswiu's nephew ... it should have been me."

"It takes more than blood to make a king," Aldfrith replied, "and you've just proved you're not worthy of the crown."

Edwin spat out a series of expletives that caused the crowd around him to gasp. Aldfrith remained unmoved.

A few feet away, Cerdic got to his feet, blood streaming from his nose. Wulfred of Catraeth did not rise. He lay curled up, hands cupping a bloodied mouth.

Aldfrith turned to his captain. "Cerdic, see to it that these two men are stripped naked, tied over the back of their horses, and driven out of Bebbanburg. Send word to Gefrin and Catraeth that they are in need of new ealdormen, for these two men no longer hold that rank."

Cerdic nodded, pinching his bleeding nose. "I will see it done, sire," he replied, his voice muffled.

Osana felt the priest's grip on her arm release. Like her, he realized the danger had passed; Aldfrith had taken control of the situation. A respectful silence now filled the hall.

Cerdic and his men closed in on the two former ealdormen, hauling them to their feet. Around them the crowd opened, creating a passageway to the doors. Pallid and wild-eyed, Wulfred and Edwin struggled against their captors, their howls of rage and curses echoing for a long while after their departure.

Aldfrith turned to his remaining warriors, who had now formed a protective horseshoe around the king. "Get the bishop to his feet."

Wilfrid groaned as two men hauled him upright. A purple welt now showed on his jaw where Aldfrith had struck him, and his gaze was glazed.

"You're an ambitious fool, Father," Aldfrith said after a long pause, regret shadowing the coolness in his voice. "Edwin played you like a lyre, used you as his weapon, and you never saw it."

The bishop sagged in the warriors' arms, and seeing the desolation on his face, Osana almost felt sorry for him. A moment later she remembered how he had treated her, how he would have had her killed if it had served his purpose, and her pity faded.

"Forgive me, sire," he rasped.

"I will, in time," Aldfrith replied. "But that does not mean I will suffer your presence in my kingdom any longer. Bishop Wilfrid, you are exiled. Take your leave of this hall, and be gone from Northumbria, never to return."

Wilfrid blanched, his eyes bulging. "Milord, I—"

"That is all," Aldfrith cut him off, his voice sharp. "Another word, and you shall suffer the same fate as the ealdormen."

Wilfrid's mouth worked, yet no sound came out this time. Silently, he allowed the warriors to lead him from the hall.

A shocked hush followed in his wake. All gazes swiveled back to the king once the bishop had departed. Osana watched their faces, her own shock mirroring theirs. She too had never seen this side to Aldfrith. It both impressed and frightened her.

Did she know the man she was to wed at all?

Aldfrith turned from the crowd and stepped back up onto the high seat, sheathing the seax in his belt as he did so. His gaze, when it met hers, was of the man she had come to know and love. The cold fury of earlier had gone.

"Aldfrith," she whispered. "I …" Her voice trailed off. She was not sure what to say.

His mouth quirked, and his eyes shadowed. "I'm sorry you had to see that, my love," he replied, regret edging his voice. "It seems I have far more of my father in me than I thought."

"And we are glad of it, sire." Oswald spoke up nervously. "The bishop went too far … and Edwin had to be stopped."

"Aye," Aldfrith replied, his gaze never leaving Osana's face. "But I see the fear in my bride's eyes." He stepped closer to her, and, reaching out, took Osana's hand. "Your skin is so cold." His gaze narrowed. "Are you well?"

Osana wet her lips before nodding. "I'm in shock ... that's all."

He gazed into her eyes and gently squeezed her hand. "After all you've just witnessed, do you still want me?"

The question was asked with a light tone, yet she saw the aching tenderness, the concern in his gaze. He really was worried she would no longer want to wed him.

Osana raised an eyebrow. "Do you believe me to be so fickle?" She paused then, searching for the right words before continuing. "You forget ... I was wed to a warrior for many years. I know what men are capable of ... what they have to do to survive. Edwin forced your hand. You had to fight or die." They watched each other a long moment, before Osana smiled. "They all underestimated you though ... a mistake no one will make again."

Aldfrith huffed. "Is that respect I hear in your voice? It seems I should have used my fists to settle quarrels years ago."

Osana's smile widened. She did not want to admit it, but there was something magnetic about the way he had handled himself. "You make me sound shallow," she admonished him softly. "I already respected you. I love you, Aldfrith."

Aldfrith smiled then, an intimate, beguiling smile that made Osana's belly flutter.

A few feet away, the priest cleared his throat. "Sorry for the interruption, sire ... but you are not yet man and wife. I didn't get the chance to complete the ceremony."

Aldfrith glanced Oswald's way, his smile fading. "Very well ... let us pick up where we left off." He shifted his attention back to Osana. "If the lady is willing?"

Osana squeezed the hand that still held hers. "Aye, I am."

An excited hum built around them as Oswald retied the ribbon around their joined hands. Osana did not have to glance over at the watching crowd to know that folk were smiling; she could sense their approval, for it bathed her like a warm bath at the end of a cold winter's day.

The bishop and the ealdormen had unwittingly transformed her and Aldfrith before the folk of Bebbanburg. Stories would be told about this day around the fire pit for many years to come.

"May true be the hearts that love you," Oswald said when he had finished binding the ribbon. "I now pronounce you man and wife." He paused here, his cheeks reddening as an embarrassed smile creased his face. "You may kiss your bride, milord."

The hall thundered with applause as Aldfrith did just that. He drew Osana into his arms, his mouth slanting across hers in a deep kiss.

Epilogue

From Your Heart

Two months later ...

THE WIND WHIPPED Osana's cloak about her. She tilted her face up, her gaze narrowing as it fixed upon the dark clouds rolling in from the sea. A moment later a raindrop splashed onto her upturned face.

Argus trotted next to her, tail wagging and tongue lolling. The hound had refused to remain behind when she had left the fort. Osana drew her cloak close and hurried her step, her attention shifting to the tall figure clad in a long wine-red tunic who stood at the water's edge farther along the shore. Her husband seemed to be oblivious to the coming rain. He stood watching out to sea, his expression distant.

"Flann!" she called out. "The weather's turning."

Next to her the wolfhound let out a loud bark and rushed forward to greet his master.

Aldfrith, King of Northumbria, turned, blinking as he came out of his reverie. "Osana." A smile spread across his face. He bent down to ruffle Argus's ears. "You came looking for me?"

Osana gave a frustrated huff. "Aye ... I was beginning to think the tide had swallowed my husband up."

My husband ... how she loved to think of him so. Even two moons since their handfasting, she still felt a thrill of happiness to think that they were wed.

"I like to walk on the shore," he replied, linking his arm through hers and pulling her close. "It quietens my mind."

Fat drops of rain hit Osana's face. She glanced back up at the sky. "We're going to get soaked."

"It's just a summer rain squall," Aldfrith replied. "When we get back to our quarters, I shall just use it as an excuse to peel your wet clothes off you."

Osana laughed, although heat pooled in the base of her belly at the suggestion. She looked forward to the time they spent alone together in that warm, comfortable alcove. As king, Aldfrith had a lot of demands put on his time during the day. Yet at night, he was all hers.

She favored him with a sidelong glance. "So … what were you doing, gazing out into the waves so intently?" she asked. "You seemed in another world."

"I was thinking of the poem I've been working on," he replied with an embarrassed smile.

"You're writing again?" The news pleased Osana. It had been a while since he had spent time in the annex adjoining the tower. She was glad he had taken up his study once more; it was an important part of who he was, a part of him she loved.

"Aye, although only Argus has heard the poem so far."

The hound in question bounded on ahead, barking as he spied a seagull swooping low.

"And did he appreciate it?"

Aldfrith shrugged. "He made no comment either way."

Osana smiled. "Would you like to recite it to me?"

He tilted his head. "Are you sure you want to hear it? Last time I read something to you … you didn't enjoy it much."

"Nonsense. I loved it … I just questioned you about it that's all. I was fascinated how a man could hold such unwavering beliefs in such a changing world."

Aldfrith's mouth curved. "I reread those lines the other day … what a pompous braying ass I must have appeared."

Osana laughed, the sound snatched away by the wind. The rain was falling hard now, pattering onto the sand and wetting their cloaks. "I've never seen you that way … now what of this poem. Please, Flann. I'd like to hear it."

She liked calling him Flann when they were alone, and saw from the tenderness in his eyes that he felt the same way.

"Very well," he said with a sigh, "although if you mock me, woman, I'll not read another one ever again."

"I would never mock you," she said, all mirth fading. "And I am listening."

They stopped then, oblivious to the rain that slanted across the beach, turning the world grey. The solid bulk of Bebbanburg fort loomed above them, yet they only had eyes for each other.

Aldfrith held her gaze and began to speak.

"You lie upon my heart like a song
Wise like the earth

Like the ageless moon
You are branded on my soul

We are bound, you and I
There is no choice in it

You shadow my thoughts

Every waking breath

You are my dawn
My noon
My twilight."

Silence followed Aldfrith's words. The pair clung together, the rain sluicing across them, plastering their hair to their scalps. The pause drew out, and Aldfrith gave a pained expression. "I knew it ... you think it's awful, don't you? Sentimental drivel."

Osana hitched in a breath, blinking back tears. "I think no such thing. It's beautiful. It comes from your heart, and I love it."

Relief suffused his face. "Truly?"

"Aye, truly." She held his gaze. "I love you, Aldfrith. I will cherish those lines for the rest of my days."

He leaned in, kissing her deeply. Osana clung to him, the driving rain forgotten as his mouth moved over hers. She melted against him and placed her right hand over his heart. The thunder of it against her palm was all the proof she needed that he had meant every word of that poem.

The love they shared had an intensity that sometimes felt as if she was drowning in it, and yet she would gladly do so. There could be no sweeter end.

Finally drawing back, his face slick with rain, Aldfrith favored her with a smile that made Osana's knees tremble beneath her. Then he reached down and placed a hand over her belly; it had just started to swell now. The midwife had told her the babe would be due at Yuletide.

Aldfrith linked his arm through hers once more, and they turned west, walking toward the dunes and the causeway that would take them back to Bebbanburg's low gate. "Come, wife," he said, his smile turning wicked. "Let's get out of the rain. I promised to divest you of your clothing, did I not?"

The End.

Historical background for *Lord of the North Wind*

Seventh Century Anglo-Saxon Britannia was quite different to what we know as 'England' today. The Anglo-Saxon period lasted from the departure of the Romans, from around 430 AD, to the Norman invasion, in 1066 AD.

My novels focus on the period in between the departure of the Romans, and the first Viking invasion in 793 AD—a 300-year period in which Anglo-Saxon culture flourished. The British Isles were named Britannia (a legacy of the Roman colonization) and split into rival kingdoms. For the purposes of this novel, we focus on Northumbria with a brief visit to the Pictland (now Scotland) island of Iona. I also make mention of Éirinn, which was the ancient name for Ireland.

Many locations in Northumbria appear in this novel, although their names are somewhat different to modern-day England. Bebbanburg was the old name for Bamburgh, the seat of Northumbrian Kings for many centuries. At the time of our story, the castle would not have been built, however, there would have been a wooden fort at the top of the rocky outcrop, and, possibly, a Great Tower made of local stone. The nearby island of Lindisfarena is none other than Lindisfarne, also known today as Holy Island.

I mention a number of other places in Northumbria. These include:

Catraeth: Catterick
Gefrin: Yeavering
Eoforwic: York
Inhrypum: Ripon
Hagustaldes: Hexham
Jedworth (Jedworð): Jedburgh

In case you hadn't already realized, this novel centered on a real historical figure: Aldfrith of Northumbria. He ruled Northumbria from 685–704/705 AD, and was known as 'The Philosopher King'.

Aldfrith (whose Irish name was Flann Fína mac Oswiu) was Ecgfrith of Northumbria's half-brother and King Oswiu's bastard son. As a young man, Oswiu was exiled to Ireland, where he was said to have fallen in love with an Irish princess. However, when things settled down at home, he left her to return to Northumbria and take up the crown, and he presently remarried ... twice.

Aldfrith lived a hermit's life upon the island of Iona until, with Ecgfrith's death at the Battle of Dun Nechtain in 685 AD, he was called back to rule. His was supposed to have been a peaceful reign, marred only by a tempestuous relationship with Bishop Wilfrid. He did indeed marry Cuthburh of Wessex, and she did leave him to take up the veil. Aldfrith also had contact with Prior Cuthbert of Lindisfarne. Cuthbert is a minor character in all three books of my Kingdom of Northumbria series. He played a pivotal role in Northumbria's history, having tried to dissuade Aldfrith's brother Ecgfrith from going to war against the Picts. Cuthbert, who became one England's most famous saints after his death in 687 AD, lived upon the Farne Islands as a hermit. Many miracles were attributed to him.

Aldfrith was not just a king but a poet. He wrote a number of maxims (many of which I quote in this novel).

However, there are many gaps in history, and so I have let my imagination fill them in! Historians don't know who he actually remarried, although there are records of children. As such, I introduced him to Osana—his perfect match. History is also similarly foggy about what caused him to fall out with Bishop Wilfrid in the end and exile him to Mercia. There were rumors that Wilfrid's constant attempts to expand his interests and his disdain for the northern style of Christianity may have caused a rift between them. I took that one step further!

Aldfrith is a little different to my other heroes. He's not a warrior but a philosopher—although others learn that they underestimate him at their peril. I saw him as a complex, passionate man who had spent far too long hiding from his true nature. Enter Osana—a woman of quiet indomitable strength.

Glossary of Old English (in alphabetical order)

Cyningtaefl: "King's Table", an Anglo-Saxon form of chess
ealdorman: earl
Ēōstre: Easter
fyrd: a king's army
handfasted: married
heah-setl: high seat (later called a "dais") for the king and queen
hōre: whore
Lindisfarena: Lindisfarne Island (Holy Island)
nón-mete: midday meal (literally "noon-meat")
thegn: a king's retainer
thrymsas: Anglo-Saxon gold shillings
"Wes hāl": "Greetings" in Old English
wicce: a witch or enchantress

Winterfylleth: Anglo-Saxon Halloween
wyrd: fate

Cast of characters (in alphabetical order)

Aldfrith (Flann Fína mac Oswiu): bastard son of King Oswiu, King of Northumbria
Bishop Wilfrid: bishop of Inhrypum (Ripon)
Cerdic: captain of Aldfrith's guard
Cuthbert: Prior of the Lindisfarena (Lindisfarne) monastery
Cuthburh of Wessex: Aldfrith's wife
Deogol: Osana's brother-by-marriage
Ecgfrith: King of Northumbria
Edlyn: Osana's sister-by-marriage
Edwin: Aldfrith's cousin, ealdorman of Gefrin
Eldflaed: thegn's wife at Bebbanburg
Hagona: Osana's aunt who lives in Jedworth
Lady Eldrida of Mercia: a Mercian princess
Lora: Osana's friend and hand-maid
Mildryth: thegn's wife at Bebbanburg
Osana: wife/widow of Raedwulf of Hagustaldes
Oswald: priest at Bebbanburg
Raedwulf: ealdorman of Hagustaldes
Wulfred: ealdorman of Catraeth

Acknowledgements

Thanks once again, to all my readers ... your support and feedback has been amazing!
Over the years I've learned that the stories you love best seem to be the really emotional ones—so I hope this one had you reaching for your hankies ... it certainly had me tearing up!

Thanks too to my fellow author friends at RWNZ. The conference every August gives me inspiration and ideas without fail, and it reminds me why this is the best job in the world.

And as always I'm eternally grateful to my husband Tim. His support is amazing, and something I never take for granted.

ABOUT THE AUTHOR

Award-winning author Jayne Castel writes Historical Romance set in Dark Ages Britain and Scotland, and Epic Fantasy Romance. Her vibrant characters, richly researched historical settings and action-packed adventure romance transport readers to forgotten times and imaginary worlds.

Jayne lives in New Zealand's South Island, although you can frequently find her in Europe and the UK researching her books! When she's not writing, Jayne is reading (and re-reading) her favorite authors, learning French, cooking Italian, and taking her dog, Juno, for walks.

Jayne won the 2017 RWNZ Koru Award (Short, Sexy Category) for her novel, ITALIAN UNDERCOVER AFFAIR.

Get Jayne's FREE prequel novella to her first series, THE KINGDOM OF THE EAST ANGLES: http://www.jaynecastel.com/home/sign-up

Connect with Jayne online:
www.jaynecastel.com
Email: contact@jaynecastel.com

www.ingramcontent.com/pod-product-compliance
Ingram Content Group UK Ltd.
Pitfield, Milton Keynes, MK11 3LW, UK
UKHW031307070225
4494UKWH00034B/621